Source

ALSO BY SYLVIA KELSO

Amberlight
Riversend

Source

SYLVIA KELSO

WILDSIDE PRESS

For Helen Merrick,
with thanks for much long-term encouragement,
and for old times' sake.

Acknowledgements
With warmest thanks to Paula Guran and
Carla Coupe, two superlative editors.

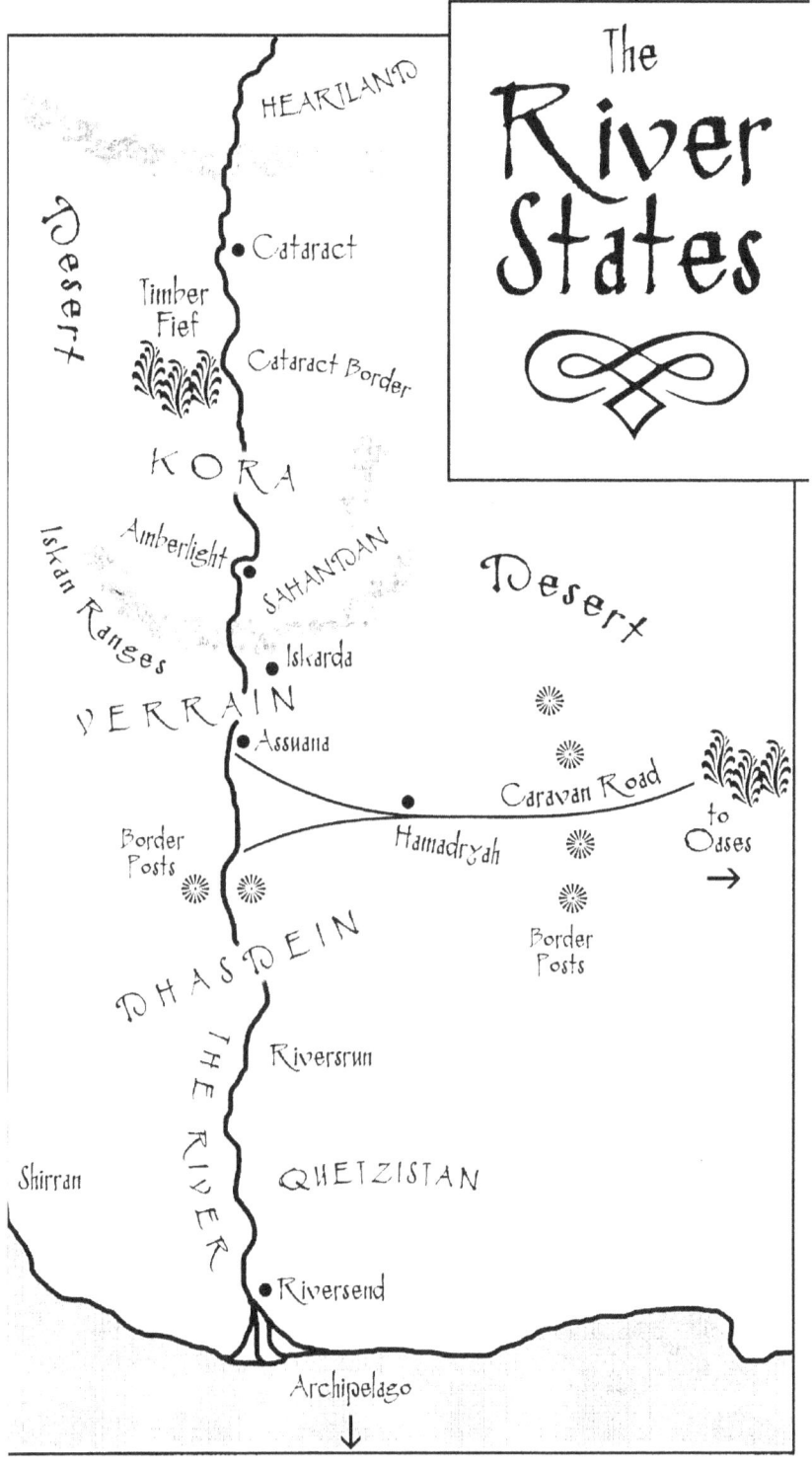

DRAMATIS PERSONAE

ISKARDA-AMBERLIGHT

Tellurith	Head of Telluir House, leader of Telluir emigrants to Iskarda
Sarth	Born Hafas tower, husband to Tellurith
Tez	Daughter of Sarth and Khira, ex-Navy, marble-factor for Iskarda and Telluir's Heir
Alkhes	Outland, husband to Tellurith
Iatha	House-steward
Roskeran	Husband to Iatha
Hanni	Head's secretary
Esrafal	Sister to Hanni, musician, member of the Quest
Shia	Head's cook
Zuri	Troublecrew Head, member of the Quest
Azo	Troublecrew, partner with Verrith, member of the Quest
Verrith	Troublecrew, partner with Azo, acting Trouble-head, Iskarda
Herar	Husband to Azo, member of the Quest
Ahio	Shaper, member of the Quest
Fira	Ahio's second daughter
Charras	Power-shop senior – building planner in Iskarda
Hayras	Cutter's Head ex officio
Huis	Husband to Hayras
Quetho	Power-shop head ex officio
Zariah	Cutter – Iskardan house-head
Asaskian	Zariah's second daughter, house-steward in Amberlight
Dhanissa	Telluir house, Assembly leader in revolution Amberlight
Caitha	House physician
Fetha	Zariah's house, assistant cook
Desis	Troublecrew

Ferrias	Assembly leader, Dhanissa's cousin and partner, revolution leader in Amberlight
Juiza	ex-troublecrew, Uphill Amberlight Assembly delegate
Tesra	Amberlight assembly male stevedores' delegate
Qualla	Amberlight assembly female stevedores' delegate
Eizo	ex-Shaper, Amberlight assembly delegate
Dheya	ex-Amberlight Steward, steward of Tanekhet's Verraini embassy
Hathris	Amberlight Downhill man, Tanekhet's embassy secretary
Kheizo	Amberlight, Tanekhet's embassy troublecrew
Darthis	Village-Head, Iskarda
Eria	Darthis' eldest daughter
Keraz	Darthis' second daughter, member of the Quest
Quiran	Keraz' betrothed, physician to the Quest
Zdana	Seer, Iskarda
Krestyr	Zdana's son, bonded to Eria, Darthis' daughter
Sunya	Waterwoman from Marbleport, member of the Quest
Gearth	Sunya's husband, member of the Quest
Deor	Waterwoman from Marbleport, member of the Quest
Chenath	Deor's husband, member of the Quest
Damas	Jerish House head, old and new Amberlight
Quizo	Jerish House Trouble-head, new Amberlight
Ciruil	Terraqa House head, old and new Amberligh
Eutharie	Prathax House head, old and new Amberlight
Sfina	Head-Shaper, Amberlight, wife to Sarth
Khira	Navy captain, Amberlight, wife to Sarth
Phatha	Telluir sub-clan head, Amberlight, wife to Sarth
Averion	Keranshah House-head, de facto general in siege of Amberlight
Amanazar	legendary founder of Hafas House and Amberlight

THE RIVER

Shuya	President of Verrain
Keshaq	Quetzistani by birth, ex-slave, Tanekhet's partner
Nathyx	Leader of Council in Verrain
Rihasso	Cook in Tanekhet's embassy
Antastes	Emperor of Dhasdein
The Empress	Quetzistani born, married to Antastes, then ruler herself
Therkon	Dhasdeini Crown Prince, army commander
Tanekhet	Dhasdein noble, Riversrun Suzerain, court eminence gris
Saarieq	Tanekhet's first love and first wife
Tarriz	Dhasdein army field commander
Queziar	Dhasdeini torturer
Dinda	Ex-tyrant of Cataract
Wonsa	New tyrant of Cataract
Jirba	Heartland, father of Wonsa
Varris	Heartland, sister of Wonsa, member of the Quest
Haturi	Tribal leader in Cataract
Tibari	Lieutenant of Wonsa's faction in Cataract
"The Hazi"	Leader of Forest-Landing, Heartlands
Ihar	Woman of Thilliansar
Errissal	Woman of Thilliansar, border scout
Atha	Woman of Thilliansar, hunter, cousin-kin of Errissal
Pryax	Priestess of Thilliansar

CHAPTER I

Iskarda
14th Day, 2nd Spring Moon

R ~~uand~~
~~Tellurith~~
~~My lady Tellurith~~
This is most embarrassing.

With my former—in my former position, the correct mode of address was always at my fingertips: "His Imperial Majesty, Antastes son of Thearkos, Overlord of Shirran, Riversrun, Mel'eth and Quetzistan, High King of the Sealands and Archipelagoes, Emperor of Dhasdein." For feastday rituals, proclamations, dispatches announcing the successful closure of a campaign. "The Emperor Antastes": for Court memoranda, official communiqués.

"Sire."

Face to face, in audience chamber or presence room. With the exact shade of gratitude, pleasure, protest, outright anger, conveyed by the turn of voice and mouth and eyelids. As I chose.

How does one address the Head of Telluir House?

A—woman. Neither my sovereign nor my overlord, without titles, without fixed precedence. Whose folk accost her to her face as, "Tellurith," or, at best, "Ruand." Or, the River-lord marvel, as unceremoniously as, "'Rith" or, "Tel." And in the open passageway.

"'Rith" is Iatha's sole prerogative. Her Steward, Head's right-hand. Oldest comrade. More than friend.

As for "'Tel . . .'" A lover's, a beloved's impudence. That one cannot imagine suffered from any but the man who invented it.

* * *

Since this is clearly to be a draft, in which my pen has already run away with me, since I cannot conceive of—my ruler—reading such stuff, had I the face to inflict it on her, I may as well go on.

Very well, for the nonce—Tellurith:

I am supposed to report, from the House, for the House, on the state of affairs along the River and at home.

Here. In Iskarda.

Small. That is the most surprising thing. Oh yes, I was supposed to know that. Coming from Riversend, the Dhasdeini Court, the height of empire, the River's greatest nation, I was supposed to find it so. But when the mules finally clambered round that last road-bend, and the light caught on the ribboned tools and festival clothes and waiting faces—and beyond them the cup of the range-front held the houses, sixty, seventy at most, high gables, weathered timber, faded paint, raw new blocks of rough-cut stone, the huddle of outhouses and stock-byres, the mud in the single uncobbled street . . .

Well. There is a view. Walk out the front-door and the hill falls to it like a hawk's plummet: fifty, a hundred miles of tawny ploughland, gray-blue timber-clots, the opulent green of newly risen grain. And the great band of the River, laid like a zone of argent and silver through the midst. If I have lost a world, I have prospect of another in exchange.

And the houses are sound. If the walls lack tapestries, and they are still struggling for any sort of running water, it is warm. There is food enough, if it has cost me a month of stomach gripes. Of all my renunciations, I never thought a decently milled poppyseed roll would be the worst loss of Dhasdein.

Work there is naturally in plenty. One confronts life's staples bare: carry the water you wash with, chop and carry wood to heat you, cook the flour you ground, or the beast you have slain. Of that I was warned, at length, with relish stretching to the gruesome. I think they wanted to revel in it: the image of me with an axe in my hands—or my shins, no doubt—my fingernails broken and my back bent—or "pneumonia from chopping our firewood in the rain."

In truth it took longer to settle quarters for an unmarried, unrelated man, than it did to fathom my use. A single day found me in Zuri's disemboweling clutches, the one thing I truly expected. What else, from the House's chief intelligencer, with a man who had been in every secret council of Dhasdein?

Her lieutenant still turns to me at any River signal, demanding, "What's behind this?"

And I have done my best for her: it is what earns me the water to wash, the blankets I sleep in—if there is one other thing I miss, it is linen sheets!—even the food I eat. But to fill the balance, the Craft-heads have ruled that I should not be wasted—perhaps, entrusted?—with shovel or bucket or axe. Instead I am—

In Dhasdein's terms, I suppose, I am a scribe.

Not a word current in Iskarda. Hanni, the only other whose value is in such skill, is the Head's—aide? secretary? At all events, a place she has held since Amberlight. I, on the contrary, am no-one's adjunct. Instead, Iatha and Charras and the rest have decreed I am to go where there is writing and figuring's need. Which has meant three days of four up at the quarry, working out tallies and weights. Whence I am fit to die of boredom, since in three days I could do it in my sleep.

Bless the days, then, when River news comes in. Couriered up on muleback, flashed by the signal towers, from up or down the River.

And most of it comes through Marbleport.

Also essential, also shrewdest good sense. There is a very good road, the way they have always packed the marble out, fifty miles of it from quarry to port, leading downstream. The way to the richest market, the quarter of greatest threat. Dhasdein.

So naturally, they have a factor to run the export business, and in their case, again only to be expected, the intelligence net. When Telluir was one of the Thirteen Houses who ruled Amberlight, the one thing they never scanted was intelligence.

Amberlight. Here, in the mountains, three years after the city's fall, it looms above us like—an emperor. They talk about it continually, in nostalgia, in exasperation, when lack or longing overflow. "In Amberlight we had hot running water. And carpets. And coffee. And ivory, and ebony, and all the gold of the Riversrun." And none of it is exaggeration. Amberlight was the River's queen.

Because Amberlight had the qherrique.

* * *

I have touched that. With my own hands, a man's hands, and was probably lucky to suffer no more than fingers knocked numb for five minutes or so. Everybody knows the stories, from legend to the yarns of siege-survivors. Qherrique. Pearl-rock. Used to rule the River. Used to power ships, and light-guns, and horseless vehicles, used to light and warm whole Houses. Used by rulers to sway nations. Mined, shaped, tuned, sold, and worked by women alone.

That past I find wholly unimaginable. Amberlight: the city where women ruled. Where the whores are still men, and lower quarter men and women work together, and Uphill clans aspired to follow their bloodlines to the splendor of a House. Where they exposed three out of four boy babies, and married the men to four and five women together. And kept the survivors in the towers.

The Tower. When Sarth says it, you can hear the capital. But I can imagine what losing their child must mean to him. Because I know that, while he gave his other wife four daughters, he gave Tellurith three sons.

And all of them are dead.

A pity, in so many ways. A great pity. If I were to remember Court habits, I would speculate about the child they lost down-river, and whose paternity it showed. Alkhes, whose hair and eyes are blacker than Heartland ebony, slight and lithe and deadly as a Heartland tigersnake? Sarth, tall and splendid as a River-god's statue, with eyes as bronze as his waist-long hair?

Probably it had the brandy-colored eyes and sharp nose and high cheekbones that are pure Tellurith. Pure Amberlight.

Pure—

Is there a demon in me, that I have ended here again?

Enough. I have a report to write. If this is a draft, let it function so.

* * *

Tellurith:
 The House has commissioned me to report on matters in Iskarda and on the River. And firstly, I must say that the advice I gave you was good.

Word of the qherrique's rediscovery has indeed run from here to Riversend. You, then, might confidently predict that here we have already had a plague's worth of intelligencers. You will be pleased to know that your acting Trouble-head is a fine teacher. Hiring the work gangs, Charras and Quetho can sniff one out now, twenty paces away.

A somewhat messy transition, there. Yet it is how most of them have come: in the flood of workers, from the Kora, the River, Amberlight itself, who have answered the call for spring employment in Iskarda.

If your House has all my secrets, I must confess, my lady Tellurith, I find it somewhat churlish that none of you breathed a word of yours to me. Cataract silver, I presume, and obviously brought here after the siege, though I—even I—still have no idea of where or how much there is. No wonder, though, that you have a plethora of workmen, when you pay in minted silver. And such workmen are a perfect screen for intelligencers.

So far we have unearthed two from Amberlight—one, Verrith considers, from Jerish House—four from Cataract, three from Verrain, and seven from Dhasdein.

Naturally enough, Antastes is anxious. As I would be, if, with the kindest of partings, I had exiled him. You will be—you may be relieved, as I certainly was—to hear that my monies have been allowed through.

You will probably be amused by Verrith's treatment of the intelligencers. I must admit, when I was forbidden to question them, if with my own hands, in something like an efficient Dhasdeini manner, I was distinctly piqued.

Verrith's method is to escort them through the establishment, from your work-room to the village altar, to point out the spot where Zariah used her cutter to behead another intelligencer, to let them watch the cutters working on a quarry block. Assure them that Tellurith really did find a qherrique seed—with my pledge to vouch for it—and that River-word is correct about what she has done with it, and send them to enquire further down at Marbleport.

The Nine-armed Adversary avoid me. I have ended there again.

You, my lady, will doubtless be most interested in what the gangs are working on. Or would it be the River? Pest take it. The River first.

To the best of—our—knowledge, then, Dhasdein has honored the treaty. The intelligencers are no more than anyone would expect. But apart from my funds, the—we—have had three notable orders from downRiver: a temple facade in Shirran, a colonnade repaired at Deyiko, something in Riversend itself. You may, with some justice, detect the personal hand of the emperor. The quarry is working to capacity; in truth, your cutter is sorely missed.

You will undoubtedly be delighted to hear that Antastes has made good his understanding with the Empress. I recognized one of her people among the Dhasdeini intelligencers—doubtless some sort of advantage, though I have trouble deciding to whom. What the Crown Prince will make of it . . . Well, Therkon knows how the ledger lies. He has stayed a perfect cipher for most of his life. I see no reason for him to alter yet.

Verrain, to move upRiver, is as deceptively uproarious and as actually stagnant as before. The Forty have made censure motions, and there is talk of a Ruler's election, but nothing will come of it. The cause is that Shuya lost a rich Hamadryah gold convoy to "bandits," in the first spring moon. The rumor is that they were from Quetzistan.

Therefore, my lady Tellurith, I have advised Iskarda to keep particularly sharp watch, and if something does arise toward us, to develop a counter-initiative. Quetzistani are notorious robbers, especially in such a poor season as the last. It will need *very* careful management, but it would be possible to embroil Verrain and Dhasdein, to our advantage, without unseating the Empress.

You will, by now, know the state of Amberlight for yourself.

Of Cataract I have very little word. These men were underlings, and their intelligencers are notoriously tough nuts. If I thought this would reach you in time, I would counsel the greatest care in passing Cataract. They have not yet even begun to quarrel about the downRiver border with Amberlight. I must suppose them salving their losses, straightening their affairs, and digesting Alkhes' gift of the timber-fief. But the new tyrant can hardly be settled, and the losses at Amberlight will be niggling his purse. I could wish that I was with you—

Just as well this is a draft. How am I to suppose my—ruler—and her husbands, one bred and schooled to River-intrigue, the other steeped in the bitterer stew of Tower-politics, not to mention a Trouble-head used to fencing with all Amberlight, would take a mere—dangle—and a Dhasdeini, actually a noble dangle—saying they could not manage without him?

Nevertheless, it concerns me most of all, Tellurith. Granted a patrol-boat, cutters, fifteen skilled and subtle folk bred in Amberlight, granted the—putative—assistance of the qherrique. What will that be, against the armed, habitual, roused malignance of a city like Cataract?

I am aware it was a gods' stick-fork. There was nowhere to take the qherrique, except out of Iskarda. Out of Iskarda, there was nowhere to go except upRiver. Given that, only one goal was legendary enough to justify the expedition.

The Source.

And given that choice, there is no choice but to pass Cataract.

To put your precious burden, the hope of Iskarda, and you three, who are the hope of my new world, the dream for which I renounced the glories of Riversend—down to my fourteen tailors and my perfumier, as she will never let me forget—into its most potent enemies' hands.

Just as well this is a draft. To what sniveling have I sunk?

I am particularly sensible that this news is of less than use, where you most could use such help. Tender Zuri my especial apologies.

* * *

So much for the River. As for Iskarda . . .

The gangs are mostly occupied with the pipeline. Still. As you know, the reservoir was delved by the beginning of last winter, and they had Alkhes' pictures for the valve, the pivotal point which will bear the massive pressure needed to drive water over the reservoir rim. Charras' reports are horrendously technical. I am bidden tell Alkhes that she actually sent to have it forged in the workshop of one Kestishiar, the—smith? engineer? he recommended, in Riversend. It arrived this second spring moon, on one of my ships, and Charras says it seems workable.

There, of course, is the rub. Charras is *not* a Dhasdeini army engineer commander, accustomed to every sort of hydraulic work, up—or down—to mounting siege catapults. Any more than the rest of—us—are used to surveying and calculating flows, gradients, water pressures . . . The River-lord aid me, I have commanded campaigns, but as a Viceroy. I did not construct such marvels. I said, "Do thus." And they were done.

We need Alkhes. Just as we need you, Tellurith. As we needed you in that Riversend audience hall, when you plucked me, with the purest thunderbolt of inspiration, out of Antastes' hands.

Do you know exactly how much you matter, Tellurith? I can see the dreams you limn. They can all see them, once they are shown. They cannot produce them. Above all, none of them, even I, even under the spur of panic, can produce those leaps of—of—well, I know what you would call them, even now.

Answers. Vision. The dower of the qherrique.

Would it surprise you, I wonder, to know that, so far as I can see, that gift is wholly, entirely, within you?

* * *

So.

I have fenced round and round it, and every turn brings me to the center I am trying to avoid.

I know that your next question about Iskarda will be—about me. I am quite aware that I am part of your—construction: a stage, an experiment, a change you probably foresee as inevitable, if not a necessity. I am the first man expected to make his way in this new world, without the shields of blood-kin or marriage-tie, with nothing but his self and his native wits.

Just so I am a test for the folk of Iskarda. From me they must learn to cope with men in the new way: as neither satellite nor chattel, but as another member of the House.

I have done my best, Tellurith. I have been quiet, and modest, and inconspicuous to the best of my ability . . .

I can see you laugh at that. I am acquainted, intimately as a lover, with the way your lips twitch, then your eyes slit, your brows fly upward—and it bursts out of you, that rill-spring laughter, impetuous as a girl's, fleet as any passing bird. I can see it as you picture me, Tanekhet, Warden of the Crown Prince, Suzerain of Riversrun, and so on and so on, less notorious for his private amusements than for the extravagance of his raiment, the Court's scandal and lasting cynosure—

Trying to be modest and inconspicuous, in Iskarda.

I *have* tried. I have kept quiet, except when I am questioned. I have been obliged to attend the councils—why am I here, except for the value of my knowledge as they try to ride the River's rapids and keep Iskarda afloat? I have been *obliged* to speak out, to intervene, to argue . . .

Very well, to outrightly circumvent. Especially your cursed village Head-woman. Darthis.

Sooner try to argue round Antastes with a flea in his ear. I swear that woman sets her opinions in harbor-mole cement. She is deaf to pleas and impregnable to flattery. Reason? Better a mallet and sculptor's chisel. The only sure way I can outflank her is to subvert the entire meeting under her.

Hayras and Quetho, on the other hand, have been all I could ask. Attentive, reasonable, intelligent. Susceptible to flattery—

Just as well this is a draft.

At any rate, Ruand, your Craft-heads will usually come round to me. Especially if I can convince Iatha, and Verrith.

Iatha's armor-flaw I fathomed early. When Darthis has overrun all else, I can always get Iatha to apply the Steward's veto. I need only ask, "How will this affect the Quest?"

They call it that now. A name out of legend, like the Source itself. But for Iatha, all fifteen of you, I suspect the qherrique as well, boils down to a single person.

You, my lady Tellurith.

Be that as it may, Iatha is my best ally, after your temporary Trouble-head, Verrith. Her pragmatic intelligencer's sense is worth its weight in gold for military matters. Policies are a little beyond her, yet. That has always been Zuri's field. And even now . . .

There is Tez.

* * *

Well. I have written it down, at last. But if you wish the full report of my fortunes in Iskarda, my lady Tellurith, I must speak of another woman first.

The River-lord succor me. I can picture your expression. I can predict your answer, down to the last barb and snort. "Rot and gangrene you, lord Tanekhet," nobody else can make that honorific cut to the bone, "I pulled you out of Riversend because you cried about the trouble your cock made for you. Do you tell me you've let it ravage among the women—the women!—of Iskarda?"

Allow some defense. *I* am not the one responsible. *I* am not the aggressor. I swear, I have truly tried to be as modest and decent and—and—inconspicuous—as a Kasterian anchorite!

If you consider that sounds injured, it is. If you consider it to be—embarrassed—and—harassed—and—well, if you wish it, at my downright wits' end—it is.

At first it appeared a welcome diversion. A fortnight—a half-moon, as they say here—after your departure, when I was already bored to yawning by quarry-work, when I had settled matters with the men—there is no problem there, I do assure you. Apart from Roskeran, who shares my suppers with Iatha, I hardly cross another man's path. There are none in the quarry, and none, of course, among the Craft-heads, where my counsel is most often sought. And if I am moved to share the kitchen of an evening—my room, saving your gracious hospitality, is somewhat dank—none of them presumes to address a word to me. If I talk, it is to—

Those with power.

I had not thought that through before. My living-place has always been among those with power.

Even, as you know now, when I was a child: a child pursued, courted, harassed, by Dhasdein's own emperor. As much for my bloodline as my—personal felicities.

But at first, it seemed a welcome diversion, when Zariah paused by the tally-shelter, hefting her cutter, wiping her big gloves across her muddy, chip-scarred face. She gave me one of those neutral nods that your Craft- and House-heads gauge so beautifully, and while I was expecting some complaint about a misjudged block-weight, she said, "There's something you could do for us."

"Ma'am," I said. Naturally I had already got off the tallyman's stool . . .

Tally-*woman's*. I beg your pardon, my lady Tellurith. I have let this—distress—take me back to the past.

I bowed, then. Ironic, how the nicety of a Dhasdeini courtier's courtesies is wasted here. If one of those minions saw me, Tanekhet, offering her, Zariah, the courtesy of a landlord to a wealthy tenant, what looks!

Well. I bowed, at any rate, and she nodded again, and said, "We've a heap of written stuff in the house there. Came with us." Meaning, in the exodus. It is the one context where none of them will say the name Amberlight. "It's cluttering up the steward's room. We need someone to go through it. See what's fit to keep."

If the Court jackals could conceive of *that*. Their eminence reduced by boredom to leaping at a chance to sort a pile of muddled, muddy, out-dated Amberlight ledgers, like the lowest of merchant scribes.

"I'll ask Charras to find a tally-marker, then." Give them this, my lady Tellurith, your folk can read answers in the turn of an eye. "Go down to the house tomorrow. See Asaskian."

* * *

Because you know she is Zariah's house-steward. As well as her daughter.

Just seventeen years old.

With looks, as I need not tell you, that would haunt an emperor's sleep. The handsomeness of Amberlight folk is proverbial the River's length, and she—

Is one of the most beautiful women I have ever seen.

Slim and tall and elegant, grace in every move, with the Amberlight coloring brought to exquisiteness: the tawny skin, the fine-cut features, the great amber eyes, the bronze-copper cloud of breathing, floating hair.

Small wonder she has already been one man's death.

Saarieq was that age, my lady Tellurith. Seventeen years old, the day before we wed. I recall that she complained how the splendor of the nuptials swamped her birthday feast.

Small and brown-complexioned, with no more figure than a winter-robin. Never showing to less vantage than in the full Court garb of an Earl's heiress. Which she wore the night when, to repay the usual scurrilous debt over some province-broking—it was the Gray Island governorship, as I recall—the family propelled me to make her reputation at her inauguration ball.

For which her mother, who never enjoyed the brains god gave a sparrow, had dressed her in the season's most fashionable style and color, saccharine pink satin ruffled wide as a balloon. The River-lord aid us. As well put Saari in a horse-blanket and be done.

She knew it, naturally. When I walked up to request the first couples' dance, the moment that can make or break a Court maiden, she caught my eye. Bowing over her hand, I felt her spluttering till her laces must have sprung. Straightening up, I fell right athwart her glance, and that look—

That we shared through eight years' childhood, when she had run us into mischief, and sworn, cajoled, outright lied us out again, and she would glance behind the nurses' backs, under a snapped bough or a broken window, across a mud-mired pony, and—

And yet again send me within a hairsbreadth of ruining everything, because it was run or laugh or burst.

No doubt it amazes you, my lady Tellurith. Indeed, the black eminence of Dhasdein had a happy childhood. From Riversend to my mother's estate every summer, and from there, half a mile across the stud-paddocks to the little irrigation chute, and a scurry through the sugar-field to the Earl of Assuana's summer residence. And Saarieq.

She could ride anything on hooves. Her ponies, my mother's racing stock. The estate bullock-teams. When we both tried to ride the Earl's majestically humped white stud-bull, it was I who fell off first. It was a crying injustice, she used to say, that she was born the Earl's daughter and not his jockey-boy, because she would be far richer and more famous if she could do it for herself.

I was eighteen then. I had not seen her for six years. Instead I had seen Court. The emperor. My mother's—death. My father's death. And I was two years toward my own emperorship, so when I smiled at them, half the people in that ballroom already cringed.

I made her name, naturally. I made a sensation of her. I made myself a scandal over her. I gave a great many persons who had been feeling the chill breath of personal danger an enormous relief. Look, rumor cried, I was no peril, I was a love-sot after all. Only see what I companied with!

Saari knew that too. I had to explain to her. Had to put aside the—the carapace, that I was already building, the armor of Lord Tanekhet, and tell her—swear to her—beg her not to make me company with some exquisitely brainless suitable female for my reputation's sake. Not when all that remained of joy, childhood, the unattainable past, was standing between my two hands.

I had to go into a decline, in the end. Spread rumors that I had given up amusements along with machinations, declined invitations, refused food, and taken to my bed, where I would do nothing but lie with the blinds drawn and weep.

She could never resist the entirely ridiculous. She flounced into the town-mansion's master-bedroom, took one look at me languishing amid the bouquets and tonic bottles, and could not control her face.

So I had the best of her, after all.

* * *

No wonder so few great lords write reminiscences. It has a way, this writing, of running upon truths that crack the heart. "The best of her." Oh, indeed I had the best. Eight years childhood. Six months courtship. Twelve months marriage—

I wonder, my lady Tellurith, what I might be, if that had been twelve years? Twenty years? Perhaps I would have declined into the innocuous. I might never have come here. You and I, my lady Tellurith, might never have met.

Had I not taken her hunting, one blowing gray Delta day when she was four months pregnant and plagued me out of good sense because she swore she would die of another day inside the house, and if we had not had Antastes himself as progress-guest, so I was too busy being noble among the entourage to stop the grooms' fall to her blandishments, so we were in the estate woods, waiting for the first covert's draw, before I noticed she was up on her new and utterly witless however magnificent chestnut colt—and if the wind had not gusted that cretin's hat up behind the windrow of fallen trunks—

Haemorrhage. The Court physician told me that. When we— Afterwards.

And Gods be thanked that I made him explain it all, because it was the last link I had with her, and it was something to blot out that afterwards: to keep my mind off the funeral, and the sound of the pyre, and what I should do now until I died myself.

So it was there, that knowledge, when you needed it. And if you lost the child, my lady Tellurith—

I did save you.

* * *

Dhe's eyes, to steal Saari's oath. This is morbidity turning maudlin, and as useful as on that other morning, when I donned my second-best shirt and wended decorously among the water-carriers to Zariah's house.

They—we—call them houses, and technically, I suppose they are. At least, they are not *the* House—with a capital—which in Amberlight meant both the web of kin and marriage and working ties, and the single building, and which now seems to mean all Iskarda. Rather, they are dwelling-places: a most wonderful hodgepodge of suites and private space and kitchen common-rooms, cobbled from Iskardan family houses or workmen's barracks, studded through the village domiciles, above or below the street.

Which latter level was once reserved for stock-byres and itinerants. So having crossed the road, I descended a newly cobbled path to the men's entrance, through the back-door and washing bay, which in Zariah's house gives on a long passage of cubby-rooms marking the original barrack structure. With the Steward's office, as a passing sweeper told me, at the extreme quarry end.

Here they orient by their own compass-points. Uphill, down-hill. Track-end, quarry-end. Turning off the original veranda, I tapped at the open door and murmured, "My lady Asaskian?"

Some dislike the title. I will admit, it gives me sword and buckler, as once, you will remember, I could use a drinking cup. It allows me to set up a barrier. To be decorous

The one thing I never dreamt. That in Iskarda, I would need such armor, all over again.

She turned about from a pile of tally-sticks. Too young and delicate for labor, you would imagine, let alone authority. Give me this, I did not crumble the moment I looked in those amber eyes. Thirty-five years in Riversend: I have seen, been courted, by the most beautiful women of the Empire, if the manners did not always match the face. So I bowed quite calmly and said, "You have some papers you wish me to sort?"

They occupied an entire precious cupboard. They had clearly suffered stuffing in a mulepack and possibly sousing in a creek. More than half were ledger-pages. The River-lord knows which conscientious tally-keeper had hauled them from the city's ruin. "Most of it," she explained as I wrestled the heap up on her accounting desk, "can go straight out. But . . ."

But among the tally columns were sheets of word-work. Old sheets, in different hands, on different paper-widths, their series broken, their numbering lost. But cyphers it is impossible to mistake.

"Lady," I said, and took my hands out of the pile, "I think you need Verrith."

"They're old." The scent washed across me as she shook her head. Chamomile and rosemary, and a spider-gossamer flick of floating hairs against my cheek. "And I think—they may not be about Telluir House."

I do recall that I turned around and stared.

She touched the pile with one elegant but unpolished finger-tip. "Mama thinks this was Archive stuff. But Slianna died in the camp."

Verrith mentioned Slianna once. Retired troublecrew. Living, the reference inferred, in the central block of Telluir House.

It needs no sage to recognize secrets whose key lay in a living brain. She was probably the intelligence archivist. They wanted more than grandma's diaries sorted: they wanted decryption, and probably defusing of some dangerous old snares, by an outlander who would not recognize the triggers he undid.

Or they were risking that chance. And testing where my loyalties lay.

It was in her eyes when I looked back to them. Cool eyes, far too old for a beautiful seventeen year old girl.

"Ma'am," I said. "Where will I be out of your way?"

* * *

Be easy, my lady Tellurith. The stuff is Trouble-head records of the House-wars in Amberlight, from your mother's time, by the few House-heads given proper names. Archive work, no doubt of it, and encrypted by chance as much as intent. I was a fortnight teasing the handwritings apart, in a cubby-hole off the Steward's office. They gave me a stool, a pair of planks between shelves for desk, a lamp, the old ledger-sheets for scribble paper. Once started, the cyphers were easy enough. One need only claw out a single intelligible reference point. The rest is patience. One sheet in clear that mentioned Keranshah House was enough.

The first morning, she left me quite alone. By mid-afternoon, the ledger-pages were separated. House-stewards live on the wing. When she flitted through her office I tapped the connecting door and asked what she wanted done with them.

"Oh," she said, and smiled at me. "That was quick."

Meaning, efficient. A compliment. A reward?

I bowed. I did not feel my face heat, though I have watched it happen with Iskardan men up to grandsires' age. I do not think she is innocent of the effect. On the other hand, I think she employs it as a good leader would. For its worth, not its own sake.

We riffled through the heap, with me explaining their provenance. "Iatha can settle it," she said, and gathered them up. "Thank you—Tanekhet."

Mostly it is the elder women who hesitate over that possible preface. Those who know what I have been. But I was tired, and my eyes ached, so I took it as the same cause, and asked leave to finish for the day.

* * *

She dropped in next morning. Watched at my shoulder a while. Made a suggestion or two. Someone called her out, I thought nothing except a good overseer's check. At midday the kitchen boy set both our food on the Steward's record table, she gestured me to her second stool and said, "Tell me about Riversend."

The River-lord witness my fatuity. I saw all the simpering provincial misses who have begged me to detail the glories of the capital. The River-lord forgive me, I think I actually preened.

She listened a sight more shrewdly than a provincial miss. With my wits about me, I might have properly decoded that intentness, have understood those rare questions' real bent. But being cocooned in my—noble? Dhasdeini? male? stupidity, I burbled away her meal-break. And when she called through the doorway at mid-afternoon, asking if I wished to share her tea-spell, what did I do but agree?

The River-lord have patience. I, who have flown half the snares of the Imperial Court, who never yet let a woman lead me into dalliance against my will. Who—

I suppose I may be honest, if only with myself.

I who, before my latest—pastimes—had the blackest reputation as a trifler in the width of Riversend.

That came after Diathan.

My second wife was everything Saarieq should have been. Beautiful, well-bred, royal blood two generations back, all too schooled in noble marriage-politics as well as a Court lady's wiles, and utterly willing, whatever her charades of modesty, to entrust her maidenly virtue to me. When at twenty-five, with seven years as marriage-prey behind me, I was growing vicious in my play. If they wished to pursue me so mercenarily, so lovelessly, what better revenge, I was coming to think, than to give them what they sought?

It was a most splendid wedding. Everything Saari and I—

It was a Court spectacle. Managed, with consummate timing, a month before the yet more amazing spectacle of Antastes' ceremony with his empress.

The crown of my own emperorship. I who advised her choice, I who oversaw the secret marriage negotiations, I who—shall we say, presided over? the consequent stir in Quetzistan, which saw the older, and inveterately hostile leading clan all but stamped out, and the Empress's Jhuir folk established in the ascendancy, where they have remained ever since. For a twenty-five-year-old Court journeyman, even one raised dodging the Emperor's bedside, quite a master-work.

As was Diathan. Shirran blood, exquisitely trained and groomed to match her birth-born shape, lustrous black hair that went up as superbly under coronets as with artless garlands of fresh flowers. Exquisitely mannered and restrained. Even in bed.

A great noble and his wife can make their excuses. Can, if they choose, live their lives apart in the same house, through the same calendar of Court attendance, summer estate-visits, entertainments, frivolities. With proper discretion, great nobles and their wives can have entirely separate love-lives the length of those same years. So long as any children bear an approximate paternal stamp, who will care?

Saaris bore that stamp. Diathan's hair, if not my eyes; an approximate copy of my chin, if not her lusciously full mouth: something near our closely similar heights.

It is possible she actually was mine. Although *I* know where I was that year, and it was not—often—in Diathan's bed.

It was what she made pretext for the divorce.

Common Court knowledge. Common Court behavior. Given discretion, who would care?

Given any feelings of—anything like what I felt for Saarieq, I would have seen her murdered first.

But I had nothing such, and she had given me a daughter, to be raised in my house, when Diathan took off her magnificent muniment to become a Court star in her own right. One of Therkon's earliest enthrallments, among others. Quite the love-goddess, Diathan.

Varya . . . That was more deliberate. My last essay at family duty: Saaris was a daughter, the maternal uncles had beleaguered me those six years over the necessity for a proper heir. What wholly uncovenanted pleasure, when the midwife held up a girl instead!

It truly broke Varya's heart. Dynastically obsessed, marrying me, with what was then a thoroughly putrid reputation, solely for the Dhasdeini noblewoman's single justification, as a son-breeder, sure she could succeed where Diathan and—Saari—failed. I took her to bed on the wedding night, which she had set to match her fertile time. The next night, I was in the stews, and the night after . . .

Was the first time I took a—man—into my rooms.

Neither you nor I, my lady Tellurith, needs the details here. You know—I know you know what things I did. My life, my loyalty to you, my presence here, is only because, when Antastes broke that ambush over me, you looked him in the eye, and let him see you not only knew, but understood.

Both of us, no doubt, could rationalize the causes. The Court's true emperor, ten years enthroned, challenged as little as I am now by writing tally-marks: disillusioned, from the end of childhood onward, with the Court, the jackals around him, the masquerade of his life. Turned to cruelty, to torture and perversion. By boredom, and power, and jaded appetite.

The perversion is not that they were men, my lady Tellurith. It was in what I did with them.

Well. It appears this is not merely to be a memoir, but a confessional. The Nine-Armed Adversary avoid me, why drag myself through this again?

* * *

Again? I hear you say. And no doubt you will upbraid me for this, my lady Tellurith. I assure you, it was more than somewhat out of my control. It was all out of my control by then. Which was in the third week of the job, when I broke your long-dead Trouble-head's worst cypher, and was foolish enough to exclaim aloud.

She—Asaskian was in her room. She came quickly into mine, asking, "What is it?" And what must I do but smile at her, and crow, "Got it!" like the silliest boy.

An Iskardan phrase, in this case both true and merited.

I saw her blink. I actually noticed that. Before she came to my shoulder, saying, "Let me see."

The minutes of some old Head's meeting with Hafas House, their purpose an intrigue against Diaman and Keranshah. She leant closer. So close I felt her body-warmth. And I—cretinous, imbecile, vainglorious—was still focused on the cypher when she put a hand on the back of my neck.

And ran her fingers, slowly, sensuously, down my fastened hair.

Why did I not cut it as the Iskardan young men do? Why am I stupid enough to value my vanity—lacking fourteen valets and a perfumier—and keep it washed? Even, Gods defend me, pleasant to touch?

It was a mutual misunderstanding. I see that now. Coming to Iskarda, entoiled by your vision, my lady Tellurith, of a world where women and men might live as equals, in amity, in trust . . . Knowing these women were from Amberlight, with what I understood by that . . .

I imagined, on the one hand, that all of them would share your future-sight, so they would treat me without calculation, cupiscence, or scorn: and on the other that, coming from Amberlight, they would think me beneath noticing.

While—she—Asaskian thought that I, coming from Dhasdein, a great nobleman, would pick up, would have read all her messages. Even as, coming from Amberlight, she took my lack of response for a modest man's interest, and thought her own part as initiator was understood.

"Tanekhet," she said. "You have such pretty hair."

Court reflexes got me off the stool. Found a bow. Gulped out, "Ma'am."

She frowned.

"Lady," I amended, "Asaskian."

Another frown. Softly but quite definitely, she said, "Asaski-an."

I have fine eyes and well-cut features and a figure that, by the gods' grace, has not softened with age. My valets have proclaimed the one flaw since I was twelve. My hair is plain brown and must be cut by a master to look like anything. It was that, as much as the—advance—as much as the far worse implications, that graveled me.

She waved a hand and murmured, "I interrupted you. Please, sit down."

I had been misled again, I know now, by her youth, her looks, that I translated as Dhasdeini girlhood, innocent, virginal—the River-lord knows, my own intelligencers have left her no innocent, and she may not be virgin either, given your festivals. If I sat down, I could see all too clearly what might result.

Some god saved me: a tap on the outer door, an apologetic woman's voice, "What happened about the gutter pipes—are you there, Asaskian?"

She frowned, gestured me to be seated, elegantly as a queen, and was gone.

* * *

My lady Tellurith, what was I to do? Run screeching to the custodians of modesty? If I could have found one, as modesty is understood in Iskarda. Let alone my ignominy, what would it have done to your dreams? To Iskarda itself?

I doubt her mother would chastise her for harassing servant-boys. If Zariah did not consider *me* a scandal near *her*, she would probably call it an honor to me. Asaskian is unmarried, but not for want of trying, by women or men. Half the boys in Telluir House dangle after her. Half the women have plagued her to carry the blood on, from Darthis and Iatha down. I can—could—feel sympathy.

I confess I ran that afternoon like a virgin myself, and sweated half the night over any escape. An extra stool in Hanni's workroom, a pretext of more light, advice—

She was waiting when I went back. I got through the story with more address than I expected. But when I mentioned advice, her brows straightened in a frown.

"That may not be safe," she said.

"Ma'am?"

"Asaskian."

And she held my eyes, hers saying clearly, Accept it, or stop here.

I am Tanekhet. I have stared down Emperors. I did manage, "Could you explain—Asaskian?"

"Those are Archives." How can a flower-like seventeen-year-old flirt and play Trouble-head all at once? "Out of code, there are people in Tellurith's cluster who may understand."

I daresay I looked like a hunted deer. She stepped back, gravely gesturing me past her Steward's table. "But," she said, "if you feel you cannot go on . . ."

How can looks offer such damnable falsehoods? She should not have known what a cypher was, let alone security. She should have blushed if I looked at her—and there she was, coolly, ruthlessly asking: Is your modesty worth admitting yourself worthless to Iskarda?

I burned my bridges: I brought myself here. I have, implicitly, agreed to accept whatever that choice brings. I did not expect this.

She has been mannerly enough, at least in comparison with the old emperor. She has not tried to trap me in her bedchamber, or fondle me indecently. Corner me in the store-room, yes: lean on my shoulder, touch my cheek, stroke my hair. Keep me, when she chooses, in conversation, by the simple stratagem of standing in the door, when she knows I will not come within reach willingly. She has merely spoken—looked—

How can such a face convey such sensuousness, such—experience—so shamelessly?

I miscall her. It is not shameless. At least, not in the Dhasdeini sense. In the good sense, she is truly without shame. She merely desires me, and has been raised where a woman can frankly, openly—no doubt, she would say, decorously—express her desire.

May the River-lord's Nine-Armed Adversary fly away with me, lady Tellurith, if I know what I should do.

CHAPTER II

My lord Tanekhet,
It will probably gall you that I retain the title, but this may never reach your eyes at all. It is simply that—there are things I cannot put in the House report, things for which my journal is not enough. I need to set them out, however provisionally, for another's eyes; and I can find no better eyes to imagine reading them than yours.

That is not a reflection on Alkhes; far less on Sarth. The Mother knows, Alkhes understood me in the truest way of all; he has staked his life on understanding me. And the questions my other husband has begun to ask are as far beyond my ken as, once, they would have been beyond his.

It is simply, I think, that of all those around me, those who follow me, who trust me, as wife and lover, fellow-crafter, Head, you alone have shared the vision's birth. You alone have paralleled my conception; my gropings toward what you, coming from such an old one, described to me, who had not yet truly envisaged it, as a "new world."

I wonder how you progress, back in Iskarda. Have they yet given you pneumonia, however unintentionally, from chopping our firewood in the rain? How do you go on with Iatha, with my Craft-heads and House-folk, and their compatriots in Iskarda?

I must admit, I have whiled myself to sleep not a few nights, picturing your encounters with Darthis.

Hopefully there will be letters, somewhere upRiver; after all this delay, your freighters should overtake us comfortably. Most likely our letters will cross, and I shall not hear your reaction to the news for months ahead. What I would give to watch you read; to see your face.

* * *

The House report has all the sober news, prices, weather, River gossip; leaving Marbleport, we have sailed comfortably upRiver with your freighter for pretext and company, and not a few merry shared moorings on the way. The spring winds have been good. The crew is shaking down, even such arrant lubbers as Quiran and Keraz. I must admit, that Darthis let us reeve her second daughter, and betroth her to a boy just founded as a medical apprentice, is still almost more than I can believe.

I must also admit that the rest of us are hardly better on the water, even the troublecrew, Azo and Zuri herself. Or Ahio, who has spent her life in a shaper's shop, or Esrafal, a musician from birth, or young Dhanissa, nearly as feckless as Keraz. As well that Tez did gift us Sunya and Deor, and their men, who are as water-wise as they. But even I, now, can tell a sheet from a halyard five times of seven.

I had to stop and laugh there. I can picture you, reading this blithe tale of nautical bumbling, your world's core hazarded like a bale of Verrain cotton and you unable so much as to interfere. You will raise your brows, fine-plucked and elegantly arched as Sarth's own, and cast those forest-light eyes to heaven, and with hardly a motion the rest of those exquisitely cut lord's features will convey the most martyred disgust.

But we have managed our way past the Iskan shallows, and two—no, three weeks ago, on a hazy spring mid-morning, with the Sahandan rice dense emerald green and the Kora grass silver with seed on the opposite bank, the languid breeze bore us round the last bend where we used to watch the ships disappear; and there it was.

Amberlight.

* * *

I could not make reports convey that moment; oh, I have told them everything looks different. The skyline, where Arcis fell, now sinks like a navel rather than rising to a nipple at the city's heart, and the slopes are empty on High and Dragon Spurs; not that I ever knew, from downstream, how they looked. It is the most disconcerting thing about coming back, that in truth, I am seeing my city for the very first time.

But not my House. Because Telluir is gone.

All the Houses are gone. Between High and Dragon Spurs, there is nothing left above Hillfoot road but one tumbled, riven, rock and rubble mess. Above that the whole hill is gone, not simply the spurs where Hafas blew itself away, or the ridge-back that supported Jerish and Khuss. As Diaman is gone, and Keranshah, and Vannish, whose Head was too proud to fall into the enemy's hands. Averion did the same with Keranshah. My lovely general, throwing herself and her folk headlong upon the Mother's grace.

I had to stop there a while. One can blot a journal with easy or not so easy tears, but this is for another's eyes.

Below Hillfoot, the business and River quarters are in better order than you would expect; to be sure, there are patched roofs and broken unbuilt spaces, but there is trade, and traffic, and the sign of healthy human habitation, a goodly cloud of smoke.

And the one thing they have retained, would you believe, is Amberlight's excise rights.

Backed, in the old days, with Navy muscle, one or another of our little qherrique-powered stingers idling behind the customs craft as they bustled officiously out, flying the Customs pennant and the River signal for, "Heave to." Exacting tolls before the ship could so much as dock.

Apparently the charges now include clean water and store supply, as well as market fee for any trade you take ashore. Certainly they are officious. If any of my House-officials had so addressed shippers, I would have kicked them off the Hill. Admittedly, it did make our part easier; at least, in some ways.

Because the cutter was barely alongside, with the bustle of setting sails precisely to counter the River's thrust, and tossing lines and fenders, and noises about a jump-board, if you please; the customs officer, I suppose you have to call her, had barely touched our deck when she reared back and squeaked, "Ruand!"

"Kamya," I said. The Mother's chance that I remember her. A ship-Second in the old days; I have no idea of her manners then, but I knew she was Jerish House.

"Ruand—you've come back!"

A talent for the obvious. But what better way to break the news? Customs crews used to sell it once, right off the quays.

"Not back, actually. Just passing through." And while her eyes were still popping, "We're escorting her," I can remember a Head's lordliness, I discover, in small gestures, "to Cataract."

Her eyes followed my hand. Give her this, she knows her trade. She recognized your freighter at a glance.

"But Ruand! That's a Dhasdeini ship! That's—!"

Then she saw the men behind me, and I thought her eyes really would fall clean out.

Evidently Amberlight, or for Amberlight read Prathax and Jerish and Terraqa, the three Houses left intact, have heard but not credited the scandal from Iskarda. When Kamya regained her wits, the first thing she asked was Customs' reflex, if not Customs' right.

"Ruand? Your purpose in Cataract?"

If they have four cutters for a trade that once busied ten ships day-long, they retain the caution; whatever goes to Cataract may recoil straightly on Amberlight. And when I answered, "Trade," I saw the next move in her eyes.

A House-head, a renegade House-head, whose dissension, perhaps her assent, had led in Amberlight's ruin. Who had certainly apostatized, to scuttle off with her men to Iskarda. I cannot say I blame her. Had I been running Customs, and one of my underlings let such a prodigy through unreported, I, like Damas, would have had her head.

"Ah—Ruand—I'm sure you'll pardon me—but the House . . ."

Given a snip of Uphill manners she would have found some courtly way to say it. I was lucky, or it is due to my reputation, that she made an apology first; what she meant, of course, was that I would have to explain us. To the authorities.

Which came down to Eutharie and Damas.

"This wind's not for wasting," I said. "If I come ashore, I trust the Head can see me at once."

I had them in an eye-corner; all my trouble crew's faces, Zuri, Azo, Alkhes, Sarth. All wearing the same expression; a mouthful of vinegar and a bad belly cramp.

Oh, I can see your face too, Tanekhet. But what choice had the Mother left? Send Zuri, and risk the mother-lode of our defense? There was no one else who would not affront Damas. And at the least, if she did play the fool, I had some hope that troublecrew could get me out.

And no, I did not act the complete idiot, and yes, I did anticipate the worst. Which was why, before we ever came on deck to await the view of Amberlight, I had told my husband in what passes for our cabin, "Ask Quiran to come here."

As foolish to trust it to my own men as to carry it myself. If they did not know our goal, they would know about Alkhes using my cutter. If he was sib to my blade, then he could carry my treasure; and if any word had spread about Iskarda, they would know the dreams had come to us all.

I have no idea what thing, if anything, might damage it. In panels, cutters, light-guns, the question never seemed to arise. In anything else, you worried about it damaging you. But to do otherwise seems blasphemous, so I carry it now in wrapped in silk in a soft inner pouch. When Quiran stuck his head round the curtain, I thought he would drop in his tracks at the sight.

Pass over the splutterings and stutterings. No doubt from centuries of inbreeding, Quiran, short, stocky, darker than most men in Amberlight, has the broad face and the slightly hooked nose that say, unmistakably, Iskarda. And then, inevitably; Darthis.

The Mother knows what *she* would say. You can imagine my own men's faces; although by the time we were on deck, Sarth, at least, had begun to understand.

So those were the expressions I carried with me over the side. Zuri, glowering like a Verrain tomb monument, and Sarth in full tower inscrutability, and Alkhes ready to confront a firing squad. And the rest, thank the Mother, had work to keep them somewhere else.

I recall thinking, as the cutter cast off, that I should have told my husbands my thought. That if it wanted us to succeed, in the final pinch, the qherrique will have to look out for itself.

I have been requited, at least, for that.

* * *

To be candid, Tanekhet, I expected going ashore to be much worse. It was my city, after all; and I had helped destroy it, and had last seen it firsthand in the shambles of military defeat, before the qherrique turned a shambles to a charnel house.

It was a wrench, I will freely confess it, to work our way up through River Quarter, amid the meanness that follows a losing war. I never realized before, that, even in a slum, a city shows its wealth. The candles and the silver votives were gone from the little phallus shrines, the shutters were cracking out of their paint, the gutters held refuse instead of wilting flowers. And the gangs' graffiti have vanished from the walls in business quarter. Nowadays, there is so little up there to raid.

That made it hardly less strange to follow the escort between the decrepit coffee houses and out across the buckled flagstones of Exchange Square, to look back where the Downhill money-workers still take their morning coffee, under the umbrellas, in the clear light of a late spring day. Before we passed under the somewhat battered facade into Engravers' House.

Damas always did do well for herself. Apparently the three House-heads are the Council now, and their home, divided into House wings, is Engravers' House.

So sad, to think that there will never again be an Engravers' Guild; if the qherrique ever does make some sort of bond with us, there will never be such honor, such opulence, ever again.

Damas is relatively unchanged. Still solid as a House wall, iron-and-tawny hair, flood-brown eyes under those bristling bars of brow. Still that damnable air of consequence that announces, *I am the Head of Jerish House*. Still, unfortunately, that astuteness that is less wits than razor-edged self-interest. And I knew, oh, yes, I knew the first thing she would say.

"Tellurith! Is it true?"

The qherrique; no stopping that word, it would have flown up from Marbleport faster than anything on wings. So I also knew that she would pitchfork me in at the one point I wanted least to be.

I said, "It's true."

She sat back in her chair with one of those long, soundless Damas sighs that seem to deflate her like a luffed sail. A big chair, behind a desk that tried hard to be a table where the Thirteen might have met. But I will give Damas this: whatever her pretensions, she had sound intelligencers.

"We've heard the most damnable tales!"

Waving me to the visitor's chair, comfortable, leather-seated, a Head's condescension to underline a Head's resources, a Head's rank. How many folk in River Quarter are sitting on leather seats? The room, too, reflected good scavenging. Solid public furniture, however meager after Riversend extravagance, tapestries, a sideboard with wine and silver cups. Proclaiming, this is still Amberlight.

"I can imagine." I sat down, and waited to see her hospitality's scope.

"And it's true?"

The eyes devouring me. Oh, Tanekhet . . . but maybe you can imagine, you who spent a lifetime fencing with emperors, what it is to dance a bout with an opponent you have contested all your life. To know, just as you read that quick V-shaped knit of brows over her nose which means she will hide her bluff, that she too is reading every nuance of your mouth, the clothes you wear, the very way you choose to sit.

"As the Mother sees me, there's so much to say!"

She got up then; found the jug, set the wine cups out. I rose too. Standing by the window, we toasted each other, with the mended breadth of Exchange Square outside, the new spring leaves dancing in a gust of River wind, to remind us that the city too might live afresh.

And she was going to take the affable tack. Always an effort, for Damas.

"Eutharie and Ciruil will be beside themselves. We never thought to see you again."

Harder still, to avoid mention of those hill-folk perversions, that gossip, so utterly sensational. I beamed and lifted my cup.

"I can't wait to hear what you've been doing here, first-hand."

At the last, we were Thirteen, both of us. Who should tread the double-tongued innuendoes' dance better than we?

"Ah, it has been difficult." She tossed back half the cup in a swig. But there is nothing of the wine-sop about her eyes. "But we're on the River. We pick up tolls. And there's the Kora. Always a rice-market in Verrain."

Do you need my deciphering, Tanekhet? *We know you have kept your holdings in the Kora, that you draw on them for grain. And you have not offered us a share of the marble from Iskarda. But we are doing quite well downRiver ourselves.*

"Of course." I took a good swallow, too. If it was no Wave Island red, it was probably something out of Shirran; those little bony hills can surprise you with their flavor sometimes.

"You'll stay to dinner? We've given up most of the festivals, but the first cedar raft should be through in the next couple of days."

"I would imagine so." She was pushing the affability, I had to respond. "All the same, Damas, I don't think we'll wait that long. There's some cargo to off-load, and we'll provision, yes, but this wind is too good to waste."

"You're going on?"

The sharpness, the speed, said more than enough. They knew the Marbleport talk, yes, about the qherrique's return. They knew the next story as well, whether from Iskarda or not.

I took another good swallow and tilted the cup foot up. "Oh," I said coolly, "I think, yes."

We know each other, ploy and riposte, tactic and stratagem, down to the bone. My lifted chin would have told her, Yes, it is true, and yes, however incredible it may seem, it's happening. I have qherrique, and I'm taking it upRiver with me. Into legend. Into lunacy. Out of the remnants of your little world.

And her eyes' slitting answered, clear as that indrawn breath: Tellurith, this is madness. You've been handed the foundations for a new Amberlight. You can't, for the sake of some dangle-hugging imbecility, throw it away.

I put the cup down. Once I know the odds, I have never been one to wait.

"I'll be delighted to have dinner with you all. First-watch tonight? The usual time? Meanwhile, it's only a patrol boat, but there's certainly business I should see to today."

She let me bow to her, the old Moon-meet courtesy, given only between Heads, palms joined on my breast. She let me nod, a personal extra, and turn away. She let me get my fingers on the door-handle, and I have no doubt she did that deliberately, before she pursed her lips. I had no need to see that she pursed her lips; her voice carried easily, affably across the room.

"Tellurith, the city's not precisely safe."

I let the door-latch go, without trying anything so unmannerly as a lunge out into the foyer and a brawl with her troublecrew, who would certainly have been poised for any bandit escape. I turned about and answered as easily, "Really? I don't think I've forgotten that much."

While we disembarked she had probably been apprised of my personnel; I certainly would have sent messengers ahead, and Kamya had to pass our destination to the Customs' post. Damas knew Zuri's worth. She knew I was testing hers. She picked up the bluff.

"To be quite truthful, Tellurith, I could not in all conscience let you risk yourself out there—not in River Quarter, certainly—alone."

* * *

So detainment, yes, with the best softening available. A room of my own, on the upper floors of the House. Under triune guard. She made quite clear that she was loyal to her Council-mates; it was share and share alike. I had flowers on the table, a bath-room, attendants at call, and troublecrew discreetly out of sight. Damas' own Steward offered to shop for me; clothes, anything I fancied, the city would see to it. I was the city's guest.

I did wonder if Damas would take solidarity so far as having me to eat with Eutharie and Ciruil, who would have far less chance of maintaining aplomb, and retaining indirection, than she herself. I need not lie to say, I awaited dinner with interest that night.

And I did work hard, damnably hard, not to think what would be happening out on the River; not to imagine their waiting, and their comprehension, and what would come next. I prayed to the Mother with my entire heart that Zuri and her cohorts had not flown to panic-stations already and were planning a raid, premature, inevitably scanted of intelligence, thinking that the only strategy was to preempt the risk and get me out.

Damas was thinking that too, naturally. And if she began on the affable tack, she scored me shrewdly enough. No Eutharie or Ciruil that night. Ciruil had a quinsy throat, some "civil upsets Downhill," had kept Eutharie late to exhaustion point. A perfect underline of Amberlight's risk.

We ate in the Head's private dining room in the Jerish block; good food without the grace-notes Shia would have added once. We chatted about the season, the River, the latest word from Cataract, and the wonders emanating from Dhasdein. Which led us, sure as a well-launched ship, to you, Tanekhet.

"So the Suzerain of Riversend really did run off to clean Iskarda's pots?" she asked it lightly enough, a passable imitation of urbanity for Damas. "You'll excuse me if I say, that took some crediting, Tellurith."

I did not betray you, Tanekhet; I will say this here, for it will be mentioned nowhere else. I did not laugh and make some hoary Amberlight jest about male flibbertigibbets whose loyalties spun like weathercocks; I did not re-accept complicity in that old, that cruelly comfortable woman's fellowship. I looked across the table and answered levelly, "I have never, yet, refused an honest suppliant."

So I did not betray you the other way either. I did not unveil the dream that brought you, or the key that you used to open my door. In that, I suppose, I kept faith with us both.

But having invoked sanctuary and supplication, the Mother's holiest claim, I had cut Damas' probings off at the hilt. So it is no wonder she made me pay in my own right.

"Oh," she said, lazing back, half on an elbow, lifting her cup. However travestied, the gesture of appeasement to the Mother's will. "I daresay it repaid you, after all."

I do not know why I had not expected it. But I felt my muscles seize, as Alkhes' would, back in those days when he had not regained his memory, and my probes came too near the quick.

"We heard this story," Damas gazed into her cup. "I'm not sure if it wasn't the most incredible of them all. That in Dhasdein—you were carrying again. And that you lost it—in the wreck."

We were still dancing Thirteen style; the brutal style, when affability comes off and you cut to bare the bone. She knew the tale of my lost children and the daughters Sarth gave someone else, she dragged the blade clear across what she knew were the most precious of hopes. But I have danced my life's length that way too.

"It's true, the Mother did touch me with both hands that day. I lost the child . . . it was a little difficult to tell just whose it was. But Tanekhet was the only one who knew what to do when I hemorrhaged. So he did save my life."

You too know how it feels to make a sword-blade of your tenderest flesh. I think the tone cut me to every finger's quick. I know I felt the words come, in blood all the way from my heart.

Nor was it mercy that made Damas turn her winecup and murmur, "Ah."

I sipped from my own. There was a momentary insurgence of noise from the distant streets and I said, "Is there a festival after all?"

Her head had to turn, to identify it, before she spoke. "Nothing unusual. It's restless Downhill, nowadays. Especially at night."

The room she sat in fronted Engravers' Square, the business quarter's heart. How far Uphill is that?

"Restless? I would have called a Clan patrol." Meaning that it sounded like full-scale riot. Aspersion on her government, a most grateful tangent; but she did not let me follow up.

"Tellurith, answer me this." And it had all gone, steel and affability both. "On the Mother's name—was the rest truth?"

She was looking full at me. A woman with whom I had shared a lifetime of governance. A woman with whom I had shared Headship. A woman who, like me, had heard the qherrique.

I said, "Yes."

She set the cup down; her muscles undid, as after a heart-bursting fight. She leant forward and said it rapidly, urgently, no longer maneuvering but a plea.

"You know what it means, then. You're its emissary. It chose you, it came back to you. How can you mistake that? You've got the whole thing, the city, the future, everything, right there in your hands."

I lifted my hands and looked at them. I had worn the Head's ring, for occasion and rank. It quivered like living pearl in the light, and Damas actually put her own hand on my wrist.

"Do what it wants, Tellurith. Take it up and plant it here. Wherever you choose, I—we don't care, you can claim the first outcrop for Telluir, you can head the Council, it doesn't matter. Just bring it back."

I looked at her in that too revealing candlelight, and I saw clear to the bottom of her soul, Tanekhet; and there was greed in it, and calculation, and ingrained, irreducible stupidity, that had never understood what we did with the qherrique, or how it might have been wrong, or why it caused the City's fall, and there was desperate determination to have that ascendancy again, and herself in her old place. And of the future I—we see—of the future that waits, unimaginably, in the visions of the qherrique, there was no inkling at all.

But there was longing; there was hunger, close to ravening. Hunger I knew as well as I know Sarth's heartbeat, because it was my own.

"Damas," I said. "If I could, believe me, I would."

I tried to tell her then; the Mother help me, I told her everything about the wreck and going home, all our questions and our hurt. For an hour, Tanekhet, I belabored her with all the reasoning of politics, that we *could* not keep the qherrique, not in Iskarda and far less in Amberlight, I beat the River's dangers over her ears until they should have rung from the cuffs. I even told her about the dreams.

The questions, she heard. She too has wondered a long time, I think, exactly how we stood with it. Were we puppets, or servants, or confederates, or friends? We knew what we had from it, but what, all those years, did it have from us? Her mind too has opened in the City's fall. But, may the Mother help her, it has not opened far enough.

Because when I finished—when I had told her that vision of the River-source, the day-fount, the impossible, inconceivable target of our quest—she looked at me sadly, and spoke as to a ranting girl.

"You'll never get there, Tellurith."

She rehearsed the dangers then; all the stuff that you have heard before, Cataract, *the* cataracts, the Heartland, the absolute impossibility of it all, and not least the presence of the men. "It's lunacy, Tellurith. It's absolute, unutterable lunacy. Men have *nothing* to do with qherrique."

I understood then. Not only did she want the city back, she wanted the city back entire. With women in the seats of power, and men back in the River Quarter; or the Craftless tasks.

Or the towers.

I picked up my cup and drained it and said, "I've no wish to be unmannerly, Jerish. But it's been a long day, and I'm beginning to need my bed."

Her eyes narrowed. Signal too clear from too many skirmishes. I knew now how she could touch me; I confess, my guts cringed.

But her mannerliness was more frightening than a strike. She said, "Yes, of course. I trust you sleep well, Tellurith."

* * *

As she knew very well when she launched that poisoned wish, I did not. Not least from trying to guess the logistics of an immediate escape, pre-empting even my troublecrew, with no oracle at all to say if the onus of initiative should be on me. Would she ever listen? How far would she take persuasion? How far could I resist? Which hazard would be the worse?

In the end I decided an immediate break was far too danger-ous. If I did reach the wharf, I had no idea where to find a boat-man, to hail our folk would be as crazy as to carry money on the chance of finding a bribable rogue. I would only help the River Quarter cut my throat.

And who, then, would head the Quest?

I am not an idiot, Tanekhet; I know quite well it is I who holds this crew together, as it is I who holds the House. I am the one who could hear Alkhes in Amberlight. I am the one who could envision Iskarda, the one to whom your entreaty spoke. I am—at whatever the price—the chosen of the qherrique. I am the rod where the Mother's fire strikes.

So I was waiting in the morning for Damas to come back. Or to be conducted to the Council's chamber instead.

They chose the Council. Compress the general arguments and pleas, Ciruil quavering in what has suddenly become old age, Eu-tharie whining about gratitude and fellowship, Damas scowling like a brewed thunderhead. Until I rose and said politely, "I think we've spent enough time here. Ruands, I wish to return to my ship."

No harm, after all, in trying.

Damas moved then. Smiled; it must have hurt her mouth. Said, "Of course, Telluir. You're free to go. As soon as you give us the qherrique."

When I looked at her, she brought out all the spurious claims; they were the Houses, they were Amberlight, it was the qherrique's place. I had travestied the City at Iskarda, no-one could doubt the qherrique wanted to be back where it belonged, no doubt that was why I had lost the child. "The Mother," oh, so sanctimoniously! "sets her own balance-weights."

I did not try to rip out her eyes. I did, somehow, keep quiet, and mannerly, and say, "Is that all, Ruands?"

Damas looked at the door, then. At the waiting troublecrew. And said, "Tellurith, you bring this on yourself."

I let them search me. In earnest, in ways your intelligencers have never imagined, as Tez told me once, gruffly amused. When they gave me my clothes back, I put them on. Then I looked at Damas and said, "Do you think it can't shield its own?"

Eutharie blenched; she was always superstitious to squeaking point. I felt the troublecrew's hands falter. Ciruil bleated some-thing. But Damas' jaw went really hard, and when she spoke it was through her teeth.

"Quizo. Search the rooms."

And when the troublecrew came back, Damas turned from Quizo's one brief headshake, and the thunder burst.

"You didn't," she said.

I raised my brows.

"Mother's eyes," she said. Gurgled. I was never more surprised; Damas, whom I thought wholly pragmatic, was rabid. Incoherent with righteous wrath.

"You gave qherrique to one of *them!*"

It was nearly time to embroil the others. I raised my brows again and said, "Really, Damas."

She came within a hairsbreadth of throwing the gavel at me. I thought she might have a seizure, before she recovered aplomb and threat at once.

"I could have you tried for heresy."

"Really, Damas!" I did not have to counterfeit that. "Look outside that window, will you? Just who, do you imagine, would countenance such a farce?"

She nearly lost it all then; I really did look to have my throat cut on the spot. But she was one of the Thirteen, after all. She got her breath, and looked away to the other two, and said, "Telluir House has gone beyond scandal. Its Head has entrusted the qherrique—the new qherrique, the City's hope—to a man."

"This," Damas proclaimed through the yammerings, "is blasphemy. If we do not remedy such abomination the Mother will blast us as well."

I said, "That boat is a registered escort from Marbleport. The Mother *may* blast you. The River assuredly will."

Ciruil wavered. Damas waved it away with something about religion outweighing any politics. I said, "They'll cut the anchor rope the minute you put out."

Damas laughed aloud at me; she had lost that much composure. "And leave *you* here! Their," pass over the words she used about my sexual habits. "You've got the lot of them by the balls!"

"I," I said, "am not the qherrique."

That did give them pause. Including Damas.

"Give it over," I said, "Ruands. If you have a grain of sense about the River, you know anything else is suicide. If you claim piety, accept that this is from the Mother, and honor Her will. If you ever truly loved the qherrique—then give us a chance, this one and only chance—that somehow, it will come back."

It silenced them all; in the pause, I heard the street rumor, far too prominent. Loud enough to carry through the Council chamber's walls.

I said, "The City hears."

It was what, following the qherrique, we would always say. And it bit Damas like a stinging fly.

"Shick the City! And shick you, Tellurith!"

She stopped then; and still, she got control of herself.

"Ruands, excuse me. It's Jerish's quarter for street patrol, and there is, undoubtedly, work to do outside. I vote that this—person—who has defied the council, and upset the City, and profaned the Mother, should be herewith detained. Quizo, escort her upstairs. Ciruil, lend me those people of yours. And Quizo, put a guard on the door!"

Their hands shut on me. I did manage one last shaft.

"You can take the boat apart, and seize the crew, and torture every one of them, Damas! The qherrique will be in the River first, and nothing will bring it back!"

* * *

I do not think there was a harder time than those next few hours in that elegant little prison, with nothing to do but dismantle azalea flowers, and pace, and stare out the window—Uphill—and sweat. Waiting to see if Damas would dare my final bluff. Praying that now, even now, Zuri and Alkhes would wait; would not try the wildest, most frantically urgent foolishness and come to break me out.

Just after noon Damas came back. She stalked in without heraldry, glowered at the shredded azalea petals; glared at me and said rigidly, "You can't go to Cataract."

I had control enough, through the beating of my heart, to be polite.

"Is there some reason why not?"

I got the budget emptied then. Whatever the dangers in Amberlight, Cataract would never let us pass. We would be captured, tortured, murdered, and calamity of calamities, the qherrique would be in Wonsa's hands.

The new tyrant, bloodier than any for years past. All perfectly reasonable, perfectly justifiable. Arguments I would have made myself.

And all I could say in return was, "Damas—there's nothing else we can do."

She swelled as if to burst; then she said quite quietly, "A lot of those ships come through here."

Your ships. We both knew what she meant.

"I hear he's gifted you his revenues."

The blood? The lifeblood of Iskarda.

"It's quite dangerous, upstream."

She did not have to touch the patrol boat. Or me. Or any of us. Or even contravene River-law. She need only turn back your ships, Tanekhet, and watch Iskarda strangle in my stubbornness.

She turned to the door. "I understand your arguments, Tellurith," she said. "But you see ours too. I'm sure there is no need for bloodshed, on either side. But the Council—the Houses of Amberlight—feel it would be both pointless, and dangerous, for you to continue your journey at present. For us both."

You understand, yes. Castle-block. The Mother knows, playing castles on the River, you brought me to it often enough. They would not touch my men, and they would not let me loose. But they would quarantine the ships; and that meant no stores, and no shore contact, and that meant no intelligence. And without that, Zuri would never mount a successful raid, and if she tried, her blood would be on my head. And the blood of my men as well.

But if, by some unimaginable chance that Alkhes and Zuri just might manage, they lifted me and we ran, Damas would take her vengeance for it.

On Iskarda.

* * *

You may imagine that I did not sleep, and that I did my brains' best to find any ridiculous, cloud-leaper's chance of a way out. But I was in the keeping of Jerish troublecrew, old House, forewarned. Even with some ruse like a midnight seizure or a feverbout, physical mastery was beyond me.

I could try to suborn someone, but I knew Damas. Narrowminded and self-interested, but never less than criminally astute.

I could throw something from the window or try to chip myself out. Except that the window looked into the upper courtyard of the Engravers' House, and the bars had been designed, I should think, for something like a treasury.

Or I could pray, with all my heart and mind and soul, for some chance to intervene, for my troublecrew to pick up intelligence, for something to happen in Amberlight, for the Mother to look on me.

Or the qherrique.

Damas came with the breakfast tray. Asked how I slept. Established what I knew would be a ritual, asking, "Have you changed your mind?"

When I shook my head, knowing she wanted me to ask what she had done, what had happened to my folk, she went quietly away.

I passed the day listening; to the House around me, for the trails of workers and guards, to the court outside, with the window open and maledictions on the fine upRiver wind that skirled about its jambs, for the sound of the streets beyond. At the last, for the feet that would bring my tray.

But it was troublecrew, her stance and motion unmistakable. No hope at all of suborning that.

So I had to take the next step. When Damas came next morning, I said, "I want a meeting. With the Ruands."

Standing in the council chamber, I harangued the three of them. But though my eyes moved among them equally, it was to Ciruil, and above all, to Eutharie I spoke.

About the qherrique's message, and its tie to the Mother's will, and the blasphemy of hindering the Mother's messengers, and the certainty that the Mother would take care for them, however imbecilic Her commands might appear. About the curse that such profanation would bring on the City, whose turbulence already presaged it; and the weight of condemnation, if that curse fell, that would lie upon their heads.

I knew that stroke about the City was good when I saw Ciruil flinch. River Quarter might have been stunned, at first, into docility, but it was three years since the fall, and the bonds would be wearing thin. If only, I thought, I could get some word outside.

So I spoke loudly, in the further hope that some troublecrew might listen, just might waver, just might seek counsel or consolation and pass the whisper, gossip, rumor on.

When they sent me back to my room, despite all Eutharie's mumbling and rolling her eyes at Damas, it was the sole hope that remained.

That was the fourth day of my imprisonment, and I will freely tell you that hope was dying fast. My one plan was to sit them out somehow, convince Damas, somehow, that I was obdurate, and look, however fatuously, for a change of heart. The hopes of my crew? There I was less sanguine.

And what terrified me most was that each passing day brought closer the moment when Zuri would decide they could no longer wait.

* * *

But it was Damas who walked in that afternoon and told me quite conversationally, "You have the night to consider, Tellurith. But if you haven't seen reason by morning, the Houses will impound that boat." She paused, and gave me a look like a dagger point. "At whatever cost."

Impound; meaning challenge, and fence in, and board, and I knew what would be the end of that.

I sat looking at the wall. Seeing women's faces, familiar women's faces, seeing men's, my beloveds' faces, laid out on a burning deck, with their bodies smashed, their throats cut, lying in their blood.

And there I was, alone with half a chicken and a wine-glass in the closed end of evening; the last aery rose fading from a tall cumulus above the House wall, the rumor of the city dwindling into the lull before night. With a pair of troublecrew inside my door, the lamp set very firmly between them. And if I had broken the wineglass, or smashed a bottle of unguent in the bathroom, what help would Zuri find in that?

I will make you a confession, Tanekhet, that I do not think I could make even to Sarth. I quail, writing it; but his mind, I am nearly sure, has delved into such questionings as make the Mother's reality almost irrelevant. He thinks I, on the other hand, am solid in my faith. And I think, in the wildernesses he must traverse now, that the idea comforts him.

But you, though you swear by the River-god and his Adversary, and even that shadowy old Mother-goddess of Verrain, for I heard you, that night by the River; somehow, I think you have entered the fastnesses of extremity when you know, in your inmost soul, that whatever deity you call upon, they will not heed.

I can say to you, then, that I did not behave like a true daughter of Amberlight that evening. Because when I had washed and changed into the charmingly embroidered night-shift, I knelt down by the bed, right under their approving or uncaring eyes, I did not care which, and prayed as if I was a child again.

But it was not to the Mother I prayed.

Address the qherrique, yes; that I have done so often, oftener than I woke it in gun or cutter-panel or mother-face or in the shaper's shop, working the new-cut block. But that was always with the substance of it under my fingers, or in my consciousness, or threaded round me through the supporting earth. In that room, there was nothing of substance at all. I was throwing my words into emptiness, a spider spinning vainly at the heart of an unanchored web.

And though I knelt there till my bones ached, for all I could tell, it behaved like a true god. For it did not reply.

* * *

I do not expect, without evidence, that you would credit this. *I* did not credit it. But as the Mother sees me, I ought to have . . . not known, perhaps, not even expected, but at the least, had in mind the possibility. Because after all, it had happened before.

But in that case I would not have been posted, so futilely and stupidly, behind the door with the azalea vase when Damas and her substitute troublecrew tramped in behind the collector of the breakfast tray. And I would not have almost broken my wrist in that very undignified struggle with Quizo's second that left her with a scratched nose and Damas with a faceful of vase. Before they disarmed and pinioned me; and panting in their grasp and my degradingly, fatally lost control, I saw through a tangle of plait the expression on Damas' face.

She set the vase away. I had expected anger, or gloating, or complacent triumph. But she never even remarked on the assault. Just looked at me, so solemnly, with such dazed, such aweful disbelief. As if she were, in all truth, the messenger of a god.

"Tellurith," she said.

And stopped. Waved the troublecrew away.

I had taken in that much already; when they released my wrists I stood there, the witness to a revelation, and waited for her to go on.

"Tellurith," she said again. And then, "I had a dream."

You will have heard by now, I do not doubt; this word will run the River faster than the wind. You will be past the stage of capering and hallooing and probably of offering thanksgivings, and if you do not know firsthand what she tried to convey to me, the mind-leveling conviction and more appalling urgency, you have heard them described often enough not to mistake.

It was quite a short dream; the last, as so often with us, of the night. It had lifted her out of the bed, running and stumbling with its impetus, and the image was branded clearer than the most violent real-life memory on her brain.

The patrol boat on the River, Amberlight in the background, me with my crew on the deck. Waving, smiling, sailing Upstream. For Cataract.

You may not believe this either, but in the core of the shared vision, Damas and I actually embraced. Not at the solution, nor in reconciliation over defeat and victory; no, it was elation, it was a madness of grievous longing lost.

Because our hope still existed, and now we both had proof of it. The City had fallen, but the heart of the City had returned. No matter if it was a seed in a man's hand out on the River, being taken from debate into peril's heart. No matter that both of us might be losing it forever. We had heard the words of the true, the only oracle. And now neither of us doubted the way to take.

* * *

They broke the quarantine that morning and brought the crew ashore. All the crew. I was waiting at the House door as they were escorted up. At sight of Zuri's face, as she processed amid a howling cavorting squall of River Quarter raff, with beggar brats tugging her trouser pockets and whores importuning her and business clerks packing garlands chin-deep round her neck, I would have had ado, had my heart been made entirely of lead, not to burst out in a laugh.

Oh, Tanekhet, you cannot conceive how they feted us! They danced and feasted and toured us round the city, they even took the men off—if you could have seen Alkhes! For some kind of thanks-offering down at the main shrine of the Phallus god. Yes, if you can believe it, in the heart's quarter of the whores. But that joy, that freely given assent, that was the most delirious of all.

Not that Damas did not do her best; in between trying to load us with stores to the gunwales, she harangued me an hour together about the perils of Cataract. She told me every grandpa's tale about the rapids and the Jump-up cliffs and lamented because I would not take a hundred fathoms of extra rope. She tried to argue that simply because she had dreamt us sailing upstream did not mean we had to go right *to* Cataract, made me swear that if there was no hope of passing we would come back, would seek Amberlight's help.

Meanwhile she tried to give the men light-guns and she did load Zuri with the best contrivances Amberlight troublecrew retained. Quizo gifted us all her latest Cataract intelligence. And the city treated us like heroes going out to certain death, offering us all they had, everything that was Amberlight's best.

I should have known that in their benevolence also, gods extract a price.

Gods? The Mother? The qherrique?

That, above all, I do not know, Tanekhet. There are so many questions that lie unanswered, from that birth-death on the Riverbank to the nature of the qherrique itself. No words, no categories we use will fit around it. Mineral, animal, vegetable, alive, conscious, sentient? None of them works, any more than the divisions that Antastes' earth-scribes tried to push on me. Was it rock or pearl? Was it growing or made? Did it conduct lightning or store it? Did it conduct lightning or light? Or was it heat? And did I really imagine it could influence minds?

To which my only answer, then as now, has been, Your questions are irrelevant. The words you give me do not work, do not work, do not work.

But the mechanisms of gift and recompense, those I have understood all my life.

So it was shock, and unbelief, but not unthinkable, when Dhanissa found me under the garlanded pergola they had erected in the centre of the old Main Quay, the day the entire City assembled to see us off.

I was about to assume my chair among my flower-laden crew, to hear the first speeches, before the great choir came out, to sing the hymn to Water's Rise and ceremonially wish us farewell. I remember, under the choker of spring flowers and a most unbecoming diadem, I had on Damas' gift of a double-wool gold-brocaded festival coat, untimely warm on that balmy spring day. And I recall how the garlands bit, when Dhanissa flew up to me, face wreathed in smiles, towing the other, a pair of wood-nymphs running, at the length of her arm.

"Ruand!" she cried. "This is Ferrias!"

As if the world explained itself in that one name.

I must have said something. I assume this, because she beamed, and both of them made me a bow.

Ferrias was Dhanissa's age, with the same brandy-brown eyes, crinkly hair, the face and features of Amberlight. Heavier-built than Dhanissa, who even before her sickness two winters past had been built like a summer waterfly, but armored in the same star-struck, impregnable delight.

"Ferrias is my cousin's kin, I thought they were all dead; but I've a cousin and her husband and a partner and two other children and a guild-circle and they've rebuilt quarters behind the wood-carver's shop, just over there," gesturing with a queen's lordliness to the fringes of River Quarter. "And Ferrias . . .!"

Their hands told the rest, louder than their faces, with that dazzle beyond the things of earth. The fingers twined, tighter than the tendrils of the climbing vine whose little cerise blossoms laced their wrists together, the blossom they still call Maiden's Blush.

That Amberlight women have used, time out of mind, to plight their troth.

* * *

They were still waving when we had climbed up out of the Customs' cutter, and shed our floral carapaces, and begun to make sail on the boat. Past the freighter, with the brisk sound of the flute as they settled the capstan bars, I could see the quayside, a great bar of variegated color, faces, festival clothes, brandished flowers. I could hear the choir singing as at some great City event.

I could almost make out, for I remembered the spot, the smile, visionary, ecstatic, on Dhanissa's face.

It was midday by the time we won past Dead Dyke's northern mouth, making the great round of the city as the River turns about its foot. The wind was with us again then; we shook out the lateen-rigged mainsail and forged ahead of the freighter, with Ahio calling insults past Sunya at the tiller-bar. And presently somebody joined me at the rail.

Sarth took the last garland before it frayed apart. Clematis and sweetflower, that men preparing for night used to twine into their hair. He nursed it in his hands, leaning beside me, the dear, familiar weight and warmth of him filling the wind's turbulent space.

On my other side, Zuri stared back southward, and all but inaudibly growled.

"I couldn't have kept her," I said.

Zuri's only reply was a snort.

"Whatever luck it meant."

Zuri's growl had words in it somewhere. I caught, "broken . . . numbers . . . fellowship."

"We were all chosen. If that wasn't chosen; shouldn't we have had word?"

Zuri grumbled again. But Sarth put his arm around me; and as his forearm touched the bulge of the silken pouch under my ribs, he said very softly, "Isn't it supposed to be—a seed?"

Seed, said my mind, restoring the image of it, small as a pearl in my palm, the texture, silken but not silk, pearl and yet not pearl, warm, always warm, as I have never thought before, whether or not it has lain against human flesh. Seed, said my mind again, recalling what we had left on that River bank, the wreckage of hopes, my hopes, his hopes, in the blood and ruin of a dying birth.

I said, "Uh—"

He gave me that mountain king profile, with the wind walking ruffles down the bronze cable of his hair. I have never understood how someone who looks so much like a temple statue can have such a mind beneath.

"Seed?" grunted Zuri, a dozen shiplengths behind.

"Seed," I said. Staring out across the River too, where the Kora hayfields were silver-beige with grass nearing the cut.

He looked from one to the other of us. Then he said, at last sounding hesitant, "Aren't seeds—meant to sow?"

I put out my hand. A finger-length of thistledown swirled into it, the flying seeds of spider-grass, that rides the wind to some far random earth.

"Yes," I said. "You have to sow them. You have to throw them away, before they'll shoot."

CHAPTER III

Iskarda
24th Day, 2nd Spring Moon

My lady Tellurith:
     We have, as yet, no letter from you. I am certain that by this time, you are past Amberlight. I trust the voyage goes well. The weather here is fine. After considerable trouble, they have settled on limestone, from that third hill northward, for the pipeline bastions. There would have been worse trouble with the building, but some masons have turned up from downstream. Most likely Riversrun men. I am quite sure at least one is an intelligencer.

Oh, Tellurith. I cannot sustain it: I do not give a Quetzistani horse-peddler's curse for anything else in Iskarda. I need your ear, your help, your counsel—Gods, I need you here for my own sake. Not a message, not a projection or an imagining. In the flesh.

Pitiful. A grown man, a lord of Riversend, squalling like a forsaken brat.

Well. I can lay it out, and find what counsel may be within myself.

You may or may not remember that last letter, where I told about Asaskian—hunting me. The quandary I found for myself. But I did think I understood what *she* would come at next.

Ha. I never thought—never dreamed—of coming home to encounter Roskeran, with the news that I was moving quarters. That night.

"It's too dank in that cellar room, so early in the spring." Roskeran is a good enough fellow. Amberlight looks, a certain amount of authority, or at any rate, officiousness, reflected from his wife. "There's a room free over at Zariah's—"

I must have changed color. I, who have kept my aplomb before emperors. Lascivious emperors. I heard Roskeran spluttering about, All right? Rest a moment, Not so strong as you imagine, Asaskian was right . . .

My lady Tellurith, what could I have done? Appeal to Iatha? Bleat out before the House assembled that the eminence of Riversend was in open rout before a seventeen-year-old girl?

Perhaps it is a flaw, that I still have too much pride.

The new room *is* better. Drier, lighter, nearer the house's centre: one of the cubbies off the old veranda, that I passed the first day.

Not three down from the Steward's office step.

Can you imagine Antastes' face, could he see his puissant renegade, cowering like the silliest bird in cover, lest the feet on the veranda after lights-out should stop at his own door?

I will confess my ignominy. The first night, I actually locked down the latch, wedging the clothes chest under it. I should have expected better. Of course she was not so crass, let be so dishonorable.

She waited a week, for a day that I left early, pleading headache. The River-lord knows, some of those scripts would blind a genuine scribe. So I had taken refuge, in the only refuge I had, when she tapped on the door.

I knew who it was. I knew to pretend sleep would only give her entry pretext. I got off the bed—there is no other place to sit—and called, "Come in."

"I brought you a pain-easer." She set a cup on the clothes-chest. "Caitha swears by it."

Correct, open, legal. Requested from the House physician. How could I claim it had any other role?

I made proper noises. She listened, watching—holding me—in those great eyes. When I did not move to the cup, she took the two steps across the room.

"You work too hard," she said, "Tanekhet."

Could I have offered to take days off, requested other duties? Ha. If she had not found some way to—re-invest me—how could I so quickly admit defeat? Confess myself worsted, even without catching pneumonia in the rain?

She reached to adjust my shirt collar. Gods, I have felt less—cornered—by the old emperor.

I said, "It's just a touch of eyestrain. Don't let me waste the house-steward's time."

She looked up at me, full face, eighteen inches away. "Not wasted," she said.

I could have found a riposte: pretended to faint, produced some pretext to leave, something should have occurred to me. Had that look not—

Because despite it all, she is a beautiful, a very desirable woman. Bending all her attention, expending all her effort, concealing nothing of her attempt to conquer me.

So her fingers closed on one collar lapel, and she slid her free hand up my other shoulder and only brutal evasions were left.

I pulled her hands down and said, "If you knew what I am, you would spit in my face."

Her eyes got bigger. Liquid topaz, amber lakes. She said, "What are you?"

So you see there was cause, and defense, for my indiscretion. For the way I stood there, barefaced, and told her—told her—

I did look away. I could not have watched the cesspool pour into those unsullied, undefended eyes. I looked at the floor, or the chest, or the pane of the half-boarded window, and recited it all, from the Emperor's first advance to—

How I treated Alkhes.

Her timing is always immaculate. She never spoke a word until I finished. I had sat down, at some stage. And put my head in my hands. She put her own hand on my shoulder and said with purest compassion, "Oh, my dear. If only you'd been born in Amberlight."

I did look up. I think my jaw dropped. Those lovely eyes were abrim. Sorrow and pity, ready to overflow.

"In a Tower," she said, "you would have been safe."

That may be how one feels a mortal stab: the heart-stop, the sinking in the belly, the spreading ice inside your chest.

She slid her palm down my cheek. Affection. Protectiveness. Cherishing.

"No man," she said, "should have to suffer that."

You know why I felt—what I felt. You should praise my address, because I managed to ask, quite temperately "You don't approve of—Iskarda?"

She dropped her hand then, praise the River-lord. Instead she looked at me. I hope no seventeen-year-old ever gives me another look like that.

I stood up. The River-lord be my witness. When I said, "This is between us," I meant what I said.

She assayed the truth of that. For a small eternity, before she spoke.

"I know there were injustices. The River Quarter. The qherrique. But in Amberlight, men were safe. They had rules, they were protected. They didn't run mad, fighting, killing, torturing—" She looked up then, and her eyes were hot. "What we have now is only one step from Dhasdein."

My face must have answered for me, as it has not since I was a boy. She said, "Would you have found an emperor in Amberlight?"

I opened my mouth. She said, "Or an Alkhes?"

No, in Amberlight I would have been a gang-runner, or a dock-slave, or a whore. Or locked up for a woman's plaything—if I had survived at all. It flew to the tip of my tongue and I bit it down so hard the blood-taste filled my mouth.

She has your women's wits. She read it from my eyes, my face. She gave a tiny shrug, and began to turn away.

"Wait!" Marvel, Tellurith, at my revolutionary fidelity. I could have let her go, and known myself—my person—safe again. But it shot out like a very catapult bolt.

"Don't you see this is neither Dhasdein nor Amberlight? Don't you understand what Tellurith—that Tellurith is trying to make somewhere we can all be free—"

She turned right round and looked at me, full face. When she spoke, its very quiet was a dagger-point.

"Lord Tanekhet, I only wanted to be safe."

* * *

Her case, her wishes—they are too understandable. She was House born. She has seen the fall of Amberlight. The end of a world where she and her sex were indeed safe. Secured, honored, as they can be—nowhere else.

And it was my own intelligencers who committed the second betrayal. Here. In the new world. Against Asaskian herself.

What if it is explicable, if men given unexpected freedom after long tyranny fell to outland poison: to repeating, Women are weaker than we are, they ruled us illegitimately, in the freedom they gifted us, why should we not take the license we want? What if the one still bears the tattooed "R" on his cheekbone? What if Zariah gave the other the dustiest answer of all? What if you, Tellurith, wept and blamed and punished yourself, because a key-stone you had raised fell on innocents you never thought to ward? Because, in trying to end oppression, you were betrayed by the oppressed?

What is that to Asaskian, who bears that betrayal, and its aftermath, in her own mind and flesh?

What is it to her, then, that you—that I—that we, who have tried to bring a new world beyond dream, should find our own betrayal—not among the men, but among the women, the young women we must trust to carry the torch-flame on?

* * *

The day after Asaskian's—disclosure—I pleaded sick in earnest. Not cowardice. I needed time to—recover. To use, however belatedly, what little I retain of wits.

The first questions were those of a Court intriguer, an intelligencer. Is Asaskian one case, or the tip of a faction's iceberg? How far has this gone?

Intelligencer's cautions came next: what ruse, what subtleties would gain my answers? And if unmasked by a counter-intelligencer, given the evidence of those old cyphers, how long would I live?

Twenty years as Head of Dhasdein's intelligence have taught me the lethal properties of women in Amberlight. I see no change in Iskarda. And one must ask, if Asaskian is not alone, then who has joined her cause? What is their intent?

How long would I live, if such a faction included women like Darthis?

The River-lord was kind. A packet came from Marbleport, a Dhasdein report, so I could totter from sick-bed to council-chamber. And when the discussion ended, luck left me with Verrith. Acting Trouble-head. Bereft now of Azo, her long-time partner, gone with you, Tellurith. But so far as anything I recalled, Verrith was utterly, unquestioningly loyal, to both you and the House.

So when we finished with Antastes' punitive border-patrol in Quetzistan, and Verrith grumbled something about, "Never had this fuss in Amberlight," I had the perfect opening to murmur, "So many of you must wish it back."

Bless Verrith's stout heart. She sat bolt upright and stared. And said straight out—the River-lord bless her bluntness too— "Huh! And where 'ud you be then?"

I have learned some things from watching Sarth. With Verrith I can play the Amberlight man. I dropped my eyes and bent my head.

There was a pause. When she leant over to tap my hand's back, her tone had utterly changed.

"Water, walls, Navy. Qherrique. Ha. All the walls in Riverslength wouldn't get me back in there."

I looked up. She snorted, word-shy troublecrew, and looked away in turn, but I have no doubt. If there is faction in Iskarda, Verrith is no part of it. And the troublecrew does not know.

* * *

With Darthis, such a gambit would have been suicide. I did see Iatha, and share concerns about the report, and fret over the need for a full council to soothe their foolish outland male.

Iatha is armed and armored in her troth to you. Reverse the world, put men as overlords and women their slaves. So long as you decreed it, my lady Tellurith, Iatha would shout and howl and protest. And then do as you asked.

Darthis I cannot read: a humbling admission, for one whose life has hung on reading power. I know, from my own intelligencers, that her vassalage has been unswerving as Iatha's own. I did waylay her as the meeting broke up. I did murmur, with manly modesty, of a matter where I sorely needed advice.

She shot me a look under her brows. Gray-haired, massive, somnolent as a bear. She reminds me of my own father, at times.

"Mmf," she said. "Private, huh?"

With a jerk of the chin that ordered, Accompany me.

We climbed the hill toward the women's sacred retreat. More alarming than the way Darthis puffed on the ascent. At the boulders' edge I did manage to mumble, "Should I be here—" and she speared me with a look across her shoulder point.

"Isn't it what you want?"

She speaks in layers deeper than any courtier: men in a woman's place, men there by right, the new world I was seeking, was I not its viceroy, what hypocrisy was it to deny my right here now?

I took breath and walked, softly as possible, into the brilliant chartreuse shade of new hellien leaves, among the trouser-polished boulders, with the Riverworld laid out, a map of cloisonné and crystal, at our feet.

When we settled, I told her about Asaskian.

I have watched Iskardan men too. I can do the modest demeanor, the broken sentences, the silences, as well as her husband himself. What came out, if I do say so, was the picture of a reformed sinner abashed by his unworthiness of a unstained maiden's pursuit. I did not even ask, as I would have given my right hand to do some evenings, my lady Tellurith: What am I to do?

She sat silent for so long I actually started to sweat. And after the birds had come to disregard us, she said, "That might not be—so bad."

I replied with utmost elegance. "Huh?"

She stared out onto the Riverworld, her massive chin in her more massive fist. I had the address to wait.

Until she turned about and scrutinized me from head to foot. Shook her head, as at a mystery of the gods, and said, "It's probably what Tellurith wants."

I jumped up. Though I did manage not to gabble, her eye held a certain glint.

"She must," she said, "mean you for something more than making tally-marks."

I know they talk about opening the blood between Telluir and Iskarda, Tellurith. But is that all you intended? Am I here to build a new world, merely as a man buys a stallion, for his breeding stock?

Darthis read my face as easily as Asaskian, and shrugged. "She's Head."

Hence her schemes are inscrutable, irresistible. Who would doubt, deny, dispute?

"It must distress you," I said, "at times. All of you."

Her eyes narrowed. I find no shame in confessing, my lady Tellurith, that my heart beat up in my throat.

She said, quite flatly, "Yes."

The wind had dropped. The birds had paused. I could have supposed some damnably officious god was underlining the moment's significance.

"But you wish—you want—this new way."

There is no telling what happened behind her face. Something did happen: because it seemed forever, before she turned and gazed out over the Riverworld again. And I heard vision, and vision's disbelief, and the touch of that vision on a mind that knows it could never conceive of it, but is wooed and enthralled till it can only follow, wondering, in vision's wake. When she answered, the note went deeper than surprise.

"Yes."

So, my lady Tellurith. There is no faction of traditionalists— no faction broad enough to be dangerous—in Telluir House.

* * *

I was grateful then, twice grateful, for your festival. "Your" festival in good truth, I understand. Spring Thanksgiving. Founded in thanks for more than the return of spring. And for the third time running, I am told, it was a fine clear day, with a young moon and an exquisitely lucid night. I will say this for Iskarda: nothing in Riversend—in all Dhasdein—can rival the purity of its air, or the beauty of its nights. Starlight, moonlight, unadulterated by human illumination, unstained by city smoke.

You may be astonished, but I appreciated the festival too. Certainly, it is no great spectacle, and set at the bridge-point of spring and winter, its provender is as motley as the celebrants' festival gear. Assuredly, folk-dancing to a village consort is a far cry from entertainment by the foremost artists of Riversend. Nevertheless—

It is truly merrymaking: a gaiety, a sparkle, that I—have rarely seen. And if I did not brew beer or help make barrel-butt festival cakes, they let me haul cups to the village square, and Roskeran gave me a cloth to wield, down among your kitchen-folk. And when the dancing began . . .

Tellurith, this is past embarrassing. Am I, the cynosure and bored spectator of the Empire's adulation, to confess myself charmed by a sufficiency of partners at a village festival?

But it was the first time I have felt . . . welcome. The first time I felt, however remotely, as if I might belong.

Was it relief or panic then, when the hand out-held to draw me into my fourth dance became Asaskian's?

Luckily it was a circle dance, both simple and fast, with energetic partner changes. Except that its finale deposits you, inexorably, by the partner you started with.

Whereupon—I swear, by her foreknowledge—the musicians announced a break, and as we emptied the dancing floor, her hand slid under my arm. "Fetha's made savory pancakes," she said, demure at my elbow. "If you don't try them, after spending all that time in Shia's kitchen, he'll be devastated."

And—I could laugh, my lady Tellurith, at how expertly she echoes my own machinations—it was she who ate them with me, propped on the fountain rim at the top of the square, looking out over the torch-painted crowd.

Spring festival is not, I gather, the license of Midsummer, of which the men's hints and passing words have told me more than enough. But there were sufficient couples sliding into the darkness, sufficiently close at her back, to make a diversion pressing necessity.

"So," I said, leaping inelegantly headlong, "you want to go back to Amberlight."

She chewed her mouthful, waving to a friend, catching a worshipful boy's eye with a fleeting smile. Set the plate on her knee. Said, "I don't want impossibilities."

"You would wish—would like—to rebuild Amberlight here?"

She turned a little. The melting look had gone along with the sway against my arm. This was a House-steward's stare worthy of Iatha herself.

"Are you calling me a traitor?"

"Gods forbid!" She had ambushed me that time. "Why should you think—"

"To go back—now—would be to go against the Ruand. Against the House."

With an inflection that said clearer than any avowal, my House is my folk. My folk are me. We cannot exist apart.

"I beg your pardon." It was truth: to the marrow of my bones. "I have been too long in the empire, I think. And in power. To see any sort of—reluctance—disaffection—is to—"

"To set you hunting traitors and expecting factions to overthrow the emperor?" Now the irony was open. "Was that why you talked to Darthis?"

She set the plate aside. She had not moved, but the space between us was rivers wide.

"After your folk," she said it without inflection, "destroyed our city, we all had a choice. We all knew, when we pledged ourselves to follow the Ruand, that we would be giving up the qherrique. And everything the qherrique stood for. Including—peace. Safety. The towers."

She stood up. The torchlight caught her profile as she stared down at me, fine and clear-cut as the edge of a blade.

"But we made the choice. And whatever we may feel about it—there's no going back."

* * *

Iskarda
3rd Day, 3rd Spring Moon

My dearest lady Tellurith . . .
    I must confess myself entirely bemused. I understood you a House-head, which means ruler as well as diplomat. I did not think you sowed revolution broadcast in your wake—

I am babbling like an idiot. Ruand, House-head, my lady Tellurith, I am babbling because the word has just come up from Marbleport, Iskarda has flown to council and out again, and the entire—House—is still reeling where it sits.

Since Tez's message informed us that this morning they spoke a convoy out of Amberlight. Bearing the three House-heads, Damas, Eutharie and Ciruil, with some of their folk and a good deal of dunnage, over the border to Verrain.

Tellurith—*what* in the name of the River's gods assembled, have you done?

* * *

Well. The rest of the tale has flown in now, this time from Amberlight itself. One of Verrith's conceits, to establish a signal-site along what they all call, "that bloody-minded cart-track," which leads north across the Kora. The signal-catcher rode the rest, in a pelter I can more than understand.

They are calling it the Lovers' Revolution, Tellurith. Do you know that?

And I know the names: or one of the names.

Let me at least attempt to get this orderly. Tellurith, we have had no direct word from you, but news of your doings at Amberlight had already come up from Marbleport. Garbled gossip, Tez's gloss remarked, though electrifying enough. Apparently there was—confusion—or some sort of parley when you first arrived. And then the chief House-head, I understand that is—was—Jerish House—received some portent: the entire city turned out to welcome you, and nine days later you set sail. With a full-scale departure ceremony, and the blessing of the City and the Mother and anyone or everyone else.

However garbled, I will admit I found this something of a relief. Verrith and Iatha have looked like gargoyles for weeks, but I never expected trouble at Amberlight. A few days negotiations, at most. It is pleasing to be proven right. And some solace to my hounded self-esteem, when they glower at my face, which doubtless says with some complacence, I told you so.

As for the rest . . .

It began, the Kora message says, in a wood-carver's shop, in River Quarter, just off Main Quay. Where the House's tax-collectors called as usual, and some of the folk disputed both their tallies and their rights. And dispute swelled to a considerable affray. During which the tax-people called for troublecrew: whereupon the Quarter section rose up with wood-carvers' tools and frying pans and paving stones and beat the lot of them from the field, if not to a pulp.

The pulp is rumor, says the signaler. The names of the ringleaders are beyond all doubt.

Dhanissa, a girl from a Telluir Uphill clan, and her cousin-kin and partner, one Ferrias.

Who did not merely claim that the toll was unjust, and then that it was unwarranted, but refused to pay it, and summoned help to see the refusal made good. After which, at the enemy's rout, the entire Quarter went up in flames.

The signaler says it was flames more than once, in very earnest truth, when they came to hands among the business quarter shops. She supplies as background that Amberlight has been like a hive ready to swarm this year and more, that unrest has grown furiously over the winter, when the slum folk went short, and worse with every punitive stoppering of discontent practiced by the heads of House.

And anger at their harshness has been fuelled for months by whispers that they are not only unjust, they no longer have any right. That the Houses and their supremacy were founded on the qherrique. And the qherrique is gone.

A tureen well and truly simmering. But what did you throw in, Tellurith?

Dhanissa, I don't even remember her. Young, Iatha says, and Verrith adds that she ran the signal-station down on the Marble-port road: sent there in sickness from Ahio's house. So far as I can tell, less than seventeen years old.

How did she raise and lead an entire city quarter, a whole city in a day's length, how did she know what to do, where to go, what to say? What vision guided her, what dream, what, what—

Was—is *this* the doing of the qherrique?

If that is so, then indeed, Tellurith, I glimpse a new world I never dreamed of. And I tell you without equivocation that I am afraid.

* * *

One presumes one's wit sufficiently recovered to assemble the rest. That the "rising" moved out and up from River Quarter, and before the House knew it, the young avengers were in their court-yard, waving myrtle boughs and calling for an end to tyranny. For change, and revolution, and "a people's government."

Grant your House-heads this: they could set a sail when the wind changed. Although the signaler claims half their troublec-rew had already deserted them. She has some astonishing tale of portents and omens in the House itself, connected to you in person. Evidently half the Uphill folk were, like River Quarter, already falling away.

However it came, I had imagined any change would have to be enforced, pebble by pebble, in blood. But the pre-eminent Head—is it Damas? abdicated, if that is the word, that very night. They bargained for goods and chattels and income and those who wanted to leave with them, and your young visionary—your gods' messenger—let them go. They loaded the ships next morning. So now, if you can credit it, there is a people's commune, drawn from the city's every Quarter, ruling Amberlight.

And with the women, men.

Six hundred years of House-rule. Five hundred years of matriarchy. Overthrown.

You must forgive me if I am still rubbing my eyes and walking about blinking at things. We do not make revolutions so easily in Dhasdein.

I wish passionately that I could go to Amberlight. No intelligencer, even with a pact of amity, can ask the things I want to ask. How did she do it? How did she imagine it? How did she know which way to go?

Was she—was she hearing it, the way you have said you could? Tellurith—has it come back?

As well ask answers of the passing wind. She is there, burning like a lighthouse torch, a beacon of liberty in Amberlight. You are somewhere on the River: the gods know if you have actually heard what you left in your wake. Or have time to consider it. In some ways, I pray you will not have time to consider it.

Because that will mean the news is behind you still when you reach Cataract.

And what Cataract might do, confronted with word of a neighboring regime's overthrow, with the instigators of that revolution in their own anchorage, I cannot bring myself to think.

* * *

Any other River news is worthless until we can read the backwash from this boulder in their midst. Of Iskarda itself . . .

Of I myself . . .

After such upheaval, you may credit I was more than ready to swarm out of my own danger-zone. But when I announced to Hanni this morning, "I think I could handle a quarry-shift tomorrow," she asked, "Have you finished the cypher work?"

"The cyphers are broken. It would be better if the rest were done by someone—ah—less outland—"

She looked up from the tally-column and said without hesitation, "No."

Picture me then, my lady Tellurith, slinking and scrying for time to reach my cubby-hole with the Steward away. Picture me, like a fox with every bolthole shut, hunting frantically for some other lair. Regard me snared by Iatha with an armful of cypher sheets in the office-door and all but hurled back inside. "Take them out of here? Are you losing your mind!"

And, yes, my first visitor was Asaskian.

Who stood in the doorway till mere manners forced up my head. Held my eyes, with that flower-innocent, lake-deep stare. And said, "I'm sorry, Tanekhet."

I did have some defenses left. I murmured, as with an empress, "It was a misunderstanding. No person of courtesy would mention it again."

She smiled. A sunrise crammed in a moment: a rainbow's lifespan across her face. And came straight up to lay her arm across me, hand caressing my neck, voice a whisper of happiness.

"Oh," she said, "then it's all right."

What was I to do? Leap out of reach like an unbroken horse? Squirm and splutter, "Lady Asaskian—please—"

She let go. She was smiling, all the way to those eyes' depths. "I'm sorry." Sorry? She was radiant. She tapped a finger on the cypher pages. "I can wait."

After that, the bed-clothes were my only retreat.

The stratagem worked with Saari. It worked with the old emperor. Asaskian gave me one day's grace. One mid-morning visit was abbreviated, thank the River-lord, by her own work. When she swooped in that afternoon and settled with every sign of loving intent on the bedside, I found a sudden necessity to throw up.

It was a good excuse to miss supper. And breakfast. Next morning, it fetched Caitha herself.

Unlike the physician who gulled Saari, I do not give her a living. Nor is she the emperor's healer, to feel pity above any bribe. "Hmm," she said, shaking her head. "Unless it's some lie-low plague from Riversend—so far as I can tell, lord Tanekhet, you're in perfect health."

Asaskian was standing behind her. With such concern in those eyes, such transparent love and trust—

At least I did not have to watch the understanding come, and then the contempt. At least I could manage to mutter, "No-one's ever found anything. I have a day or two of dizziness—feeling sick—then it goes."

So there will be no hiding in a sick-room here.

You may well ask, Why demur at all? A young woman, beautiful, desirable, masterful enough to court me: enamored enough to ignore my outland blood, my age, my past, a young woman other men have literally died for, begging to share my bed. Dhe's eyes, what courtier would think twice?

At the most inglorious level, there are the consequences in Iskarda. Darthis might raise an eyebrow and talk about bloodlines, but Zariah? More reputably, what if this did blow the House apart?

And there is Sarth.

Who was ready to kill for her, after that attempt at rape. Who loves her like a daughter—more than a daughter, perhaps. Who has tolerated my attachment to Tellurith, my foisting myself into his house, my treatment of Alkhes.

Whom he loves for himself, as much as for Tellurith.

Who would without a moment's thought have put a knife in my ribs or seen me over-side before he let me near Iskarda, were it not for his marriage-partners' decisions: their choices.

If I put a hand on Asaskian, in or out of wedlock, with or without her consent, once Sarth learned of it—how long would I live?

Besides—

* * *

Which god requited me that cowardice, with such malice, such speed, so opportunely immediate—so—

Dhe. I am fluttering and squawking like a half-beheaded fowl.

Dhe help me. I think—I think, my lady Tellurith, I have done worse than half-behead myself. I think I have—

Broken my heart.

Ludicrous, that such banality hides physical truth. The stopped breath, the rending, as if bone or sinew tore inside you, the broken rib, that pangs every time you think, somewhere between memory and flesh—as if humans carried a china Shirran vase between the lungs, and it is cracked to bits.

Pathetic. Ludicrous. Ridiculous.

The truth.

Well. I will have to tell you some time. Some—formal—notification. It may, perhaps, search the wound, however cruelly, if I write it down here first.

* * *

Asaskian—came into my room. My work-room, the malicious god had so much mercy. Mid-afternoon, the worst time. Mornings, she is mostly outside. I had contrived evasions for midday: consult Hanni, discuss things with Iatha. Mid-afternoon, though, Heads and counsel folk are busy or absent, I am tired, open to temptation. And I have to do the work sometime, I must finish these thrice-blasphemed cyphers before something worse—

No. There can be nothing worse.

So then. Mid-afternoon, and myself stupidly attentive to a tricky passage, so she was there before I realized. Her hand on my neck, her warmth against my shoulder, her murmured, "Are you feeling tired?"

And I was tired. With concentration and—apprehension—my back was aching. And I was so tired of running, and—

I put the pen down, and leant back on my stool. And when she set both hands on my shoulders, and began to work her fingers into the neck muscles, I thought: what can it matter, just this once? So I let my head lie against her, and shut my eyes . . .

And the outer door resounded to a brusque rap: a quick stride crossed the office and a crisp voice demanded, "Tanekhet?"

It is branded on my memory deeper than a lightning strike. Asaskian and I, in a pose worse than coupling itself: a pose that spoke affection, closeness, the trust of a long-term connection, the kindnesses of very marriage—and the door open under her hand, the bristling half-grown hair and sharp nose and slitted Amber-light eyes and upright Navy carriage—

Tez.

I have retrieved myriad Court disasters. I could only sit. Feeling the blade disembowel me, as her face changed—as she—

As she turned on her heel and walked away.

Now at last I have to confess. The real centre I have fenced around and fenced around, the real reason I have withstood Asaskian, the real cause you have to flay me for the trouble my prick has caused, my lady Tellurith. Dhe's eyes, if my past is to be revenged on me, could there be a prettier way than this?

That I, who have tortured men and broken women's hearts, from my wives to the most temporary flirt, should now—should now—

I ought to have known. To have realized, from the way my flesh clings to her darts. *Fourteen tailors and a perfumier. Catch pneumonia chopping our firewood in the rain.* Alkhes cut me twice as deep and twice as often, and I do not recall a word he said.

And from the way the images persist. Tez on that filthy sampan, hefting a frying pan, pale and crop-headed from her own prison-cell, but those eyes dagger-points, ready to stab what menaced her Ruand, and die. Tez slashing at me across the jewel-heap, the morning you let me plead my case. Tez on the freighter deck, sniffing weather, her slim, sinewy figure tense. Tez in the mud and blood that last dreadful morning: a half-naked white-faced scarecrow with her eyes full of tears, beating Alkhes with a broken branch.

Tez in the council-room, those two or three times she has come up from Marbleport. The cut of those copper eyes, the inflection of that Navy officer's voice, the bristle of corkscrew-curly bronze hair. The angle of cheek as she reads a line again, the hand, scarred and muscled almost like a man's, planted on the dispatch. Dhe's eyes, I who have passed thirty years of Court beauties unscathed, I who have Asaskian's beauty available at a word, I who—

I did not realize, when I began this dream, my lady Tellurith. Did not understand that new worlds are not spun from air. They are built, with grief and pain and wholesale demolition, from the rubble of the old. Down to the builder's self.

This is another foundation I never plumbed before: that I was not proof against beauties from my own integrity—such as may be left of that. I was proof because—

Because the great and disdainful Lord Tanekhet's weakness, then and now, is those who are not beautiful at all.

In this abyss of demolishment, that must be the unkindest cut.

* * *

I cannot credit that I have sat here, in the depths of misery, and written that.

And had to laugh.

At my indignation, my pomposity, my—arrogance—that can count my choice of women a shame—because it lacks in taste.

Gods, what further indignity will You wreak on me, before this ends?

* * *

Well. I am aware of your position, my lady Tellurith. I can predict your reaction without the slightest doubt. Tez is ex-Navy, the old guard of Amberlight. Tez is your intelligence head and marble factor, a vital part of the House.

Tez is your daughter. By marriage tie, the dearest marriage tie, Sarth's child. And your daughter in good earnest now. The House-head's proclaimed heir.

I am Outland, a House irrelevance, probably twice her age, with a past to shock Kasterian martyrs. You know it all.

And she snaps every time I call her, "Lady," she despises me as an Outland fribble who might at best be dangerously treacherous: even yesterday she would never have considered—

Why do I not go now and slit my throat?

* * *

Oh, gods, if this is from the gods—is my undoing to be not a tragedy but a farce?

So. As you see, my lady Tellurith, I did not act the tragedy hero. I did not even manage a seemly fit of the vapors, or a manly pose of silence shuttering a nobly broken heart. No. I was still sitting in that, that thrice-be-blasted room, with my jaw on my chest and my life in shards around me, when Asaskian took me by the shoulders and turned me about.

And said, "My dear, I am so sorry. Let me make it up."

I think I simply stared.

She took a deep breath. "I've destroyed your reputation. We—" a wave of her hands that said it all: what Tez thought, how I had compromised her, the reaction of the House—

No. I have it wrong again. *She* thought she had compromised *me*.

And I could not—Tellurith, I could not say to her, "It's not my reputation"—Gods, *my* reputation!—"that you've lost."

I dropped my eyes and mumbled: probably some Court commonplace. But I felt her fingers stiffen. I heard her take in her breath.

"Tanekhet." She sounded like Alkhes commanding a death charge. "Will you marry me?"

Is this the gods' revenge on me, who at the worst extremities of Court, parents' deaths, imperial harassment, three marriages, was never entirely confounded before?

"Our clan is a very good line. We are cousin-crossed to the old Head, Tellurith's mother. Our children would be among the best-founded in the House. There's not a line here that wouldn't—that isn't looking to join with us."

She meant, with her. She had begun with her advantages, not as boast, I understand now, but because it is the Amberlight dower-promise. Marriage's solid base.

She touched my cheek.

"And—if we were married, I'd look after you. You'd have a good room, decent clothes. I'd make sure you didn't wear yourself out over these stupid—I'd see people *respected* you!"

Passion, compassion, love and partisanship. Everything an aging villain could dream of: all he had no right to claim. I will freely confess, my lady Tellurith, I was gagged by tears.

"Poor love."

She put her arms around me. To be gifted with all that, unreservedly, undeservedly. Oh, Gods. Indeed, I have my own again.

I must have said something: some platitude, passing for manly modesty. Because she did let go. And it must have been some intelligible version of, "I am too much honored, give me time to think." Because she put her hand under my chin, and looked deep in my eyes, and smiled. And kissed me, lighter than a butterfly's breath, and said, "Of course. I don't want to rush you. That wouldn't be right either. Take as long," with those eyes waking to radiance, "as you like."

May all the gods help me, my lady Tellurith. If only there were some way I could truly ask you.

What am I to do?

CHAPTER IV

Summer
Cataract

It appears this letter has become conflated with my journal; partly since the writing is so perilous, and the materials so precious, that I cannot afford letter and journal both; partly because I *will* write, if only for sheer contrariness. And partly that I am all too sure this, at least, will never reach your eyes, Tanekhet.

I had your first, your only letter, no more than a quarter-moon from Amberlight. Still in our old farming country of the northern Kora, where the River runs languidly between those elegant copses of creamy-trunked plains hellien, while the desert retreats beyond wide but meager grasslands that stretch, so I am told, clear to the Jump-up Cliffs. Pretty country. Rich country; more than enough to feed Amberlight, despite the timber fief's return to Cataract.

Where we had hove to for the night when the Customs cutter came racing round a jink in that great right-handed swing of the River, with shouts of delight and cries of, "Dispatches! Ruand, dispatches from Amberlight!"

Let me dwell on that awhile, however precious the paper, however great the risk. The truly miraculous harvest, vindication of our loss. Zuri herself has to admit that revolution, and an end of Houses, and a people's government, with men among them, comes cheap at the price.

I think of that often nowadays. Taking it out to dandle in my mind as I dare not take the seed itself in my hand, a jewel to outweigh all the rest. That we have freed our city, whatever comes to us.

If this were a letter, I doubt such stuff would interest you. I can see you, it feels now a world away, running your great lord's eye down this page fast as a huntsman's skinning knife. I can see the curl of lip and tweak of brows when you find nothing but complacent maunderings. Nothing for yourself.

What can I say, Tanekhet? If you did get this letter, it would be worse than useless, being wholly out of date. If we are to take an ideal solution, if I could speak to you only once . .

Then I would have to offer the hardest counsel. Asaskian is Iskardan, and a grown woman. If she fixes her choice on you, you will have to say, Yes, or, No, for yourself.

I will admit there might be worse outcomes; I will say here, where you will not read it, that I had hoped for something else. We have married men enough. But if your enterprise, and your experience, and to be honest, your vanity, cannot preserve your independence, then it probably cannot be done.

* * *

But first, let me recall that evening just once more; with the fish cooked, the news traded, all three crews round the fire on the little pebbly beach while the moon rose, whetting down her blade in her third quarter, so the stars came with her, clear in that pure sky that made me yearn for Spring Thanks in Iskarda. When Sarth and Alkhes and I had rolled out our blankets in a bay of sweet-scented shiver-bush, where the slightest touch will bring a rain of little white flowers. The Mother knows, I could accept the necessity of the patrol-boat, and live amiably with thirteen others' elbows in my ear; but even if Alkhes could have faced making love behind a cabin curtain, it would have been impossible on those bunks.

So we luxuriated in solitude no less than in the opulence of lying side by side and touch for touch. Shadow and silver tapestry of branches and moonlight on our bodies, on the labyrinthine smoke of Sarth's hair; my head on his breast, the light-drinking black of Alkhes' head on mine. The dear, familiar warmth and shapes of them, the dwindling interchanges that, as in Iskarda, would see us into sleep. Alkhes tucking an arm closer round me, so his hand splayed possessively on Sarth's breast. Murmuring round the final sigh. "Never do that again, Tel. Thought I'd go crazy. So damn *long* . . ."

And I felt the rise of Sarth's answering breath. Knowing clearly as he did, that it was not the River and love's rationing, but the prison-time in Amberlight that Alkhes meant. Hearing as easily the inflexible note of the answering murmur that vibrated up to me through his flesh.

"Never again, Tellurith."

How too like an omen that looks, written down. Let it stand. Because it was that resolution, so damnably calm as all Sarth's notions, that would have undone any caution you could give me about Cataract. In the Mother's name! As if I, and Zuri, and Sarth if not Zuri, and Alkhes before any of them, did not know the danger before the start.

At any rate, we sailed peaceably enough through the timber fief, where the River runs blue-shadowed under the cedars' immensities. Every nation's ship-womb, long-standing bone of contention and greatest prize Cataract ever ceded Amberlight. The wisest thing Alkhes ever did was to gift it back as soon as the city fell.

Because so far as I can tell now, Tanekhet, that is Cataract's only resource. Oh, they have the Heartland exotics, the wild beasts and hides and gold and ebony, but those come down in exotic quantities; little enough for a family in Verrain, let alone a whole hungry turbulent convocation like Cataract.

The silver? There is that pathetic mine where Dinda used to send his enemies, but silver was the tyrant's prerogative, and it went wholly on making war. Which is Cataract's chief, almost its only trade. Except for one.

I think now that the Heartlands must be poorer yet; only dire impoverishment will make a nation trade in men, and that is what they trade. Warriors, young landless men who stream downRiver to sell their spears to Cataract. Or others, boarded at the way station under the Jump-up falls, wearing chains rather than shields.

As Telluir House-head I found Cataract economics of peripheral interest. So we kept the tyrant's fingers off our lands and scalped him for his statuettes, what did we care what went on beyond? But I think now that the Heartlands are less a nation than a faction of clans and tribes within a race, all at each other's throats. So they export their own young men, and raid or intrigue away the neighbors', to sell them off as well.

It is a black stain on the River, and Amberlight's one saving grace that we would never dabble in slaves. As Zhee said flatly, the one time I remember it raised, it was far too dangerous. A truth Cataract knows to the bone; how long have the tyrants balanced one foot on their scanty resources and the other on the flesh-trade, draining off the price of statuettes to control mercenaries whose attention they kept on wars in the Heartlands or grasslands, if not down the River itself? How much of Dinda's last assault on Amberlight was flat necessity?

That scrambling danger speaks from every line of Cataract. There is a sort of anchorage, in the back eddy behind a long spit, every scallop of shoreline daubed in black upRiver mud; a wasps' nest of anchored freighters and the low-slung menace of city galleys at their buoy-lines, a stewpot of Heartland trade and local fishing canoes, all glaring and dazzling in the harsh upRiver light. Strange how it hardens, beyond the timber fief. There is a sort of citadel, no equal to the hill of Amberlight, with wooden palisades and a plethora of catapult heads lowering over the city walls that are, as Alkhes once recalled, new-split side-piled logs. And between them lies a low, dun-gray, windowless stew of uncobbled marketplaces and rat-run alleyways. A city that is all River Quarter. Whose danger comes off it, palpable as the miasma of the slave and army barracks and the mendicant bivouacs, with every passing breeze.

* * *

We had hoped to slip into anchorage with your freighter, whose captain would claim us as protection for downRiver. He had already coached us in Cataract shipping ways. No Customs, however bumptious. Instead you blow a conch-horn and lie to in mid-stream, until whoever has toll-right that season sends a boat to negotiate the bribe. Only then will a fly-cloud of officials allot you mooring and water and victualing privileges, all at an outrageous price. As the Mother sees me, how you have made a living here is beyond me.

We, however, had hardly seen the envoy board when signals began to fly above the city's, for want of a better word, water gate. At least, there was a waving of pennanted lance-heads and a great many halloos, and then another boat shot from the beach, a double-handed paddler that fairly flew across to us.

Its crew hung bawling on the freighter-side. We all understood. We were waiting, when the captain reached the stern-rail to speak.

"Lady Tellurith." He is a good, competent ship's captain, nothing more, nothing less. Now his sober Dhasdeini trader's brows were somewhere near his hair. "The—ah—Ruler wants to speak with you."

I daresay the first word upRiver outstripped even the spring fresh. I will freely confess that my stomach squirmed when I called back, "On whose authority?"

That brought us a half a glass's grace, while the canoe-boys skated away for stronger backing. Which had to come, judging from the fuss, clear from the citadel; a high official, or at any rate high army officer, in parade gear to his silver plumed helmet, who requested the honor of escorting the City's guests.

For all his obvious Heartland blood, he spoke clearly enough. And the blighted summons was just broad enough for Sarth to say with justification atop that note of soft-voiced danger, "That means all of us."

I did argue, Tanekhet. At least, I raised my voice once or twice. It was not the foreign audience, or the stance on Zuri, or the way Sunya and Deor had already gathered their shore-harness, or Quiran's pallor, or that copy of her mother's worst obduracy on Keraz' face, that silenced me. It was Sarth, watching from the rail. Quiet, and decorous as ever, and bland as porridge without salt.

And I knew that he would disable guards, and get out of any restraint, and swim ashore behind me if I said anything but, Yes.

I did almost manage a schism belowdecks, when we retired to don suitable gear; and I asked Zuri, "What about the guns?"

Even on Zuri's face, dismay was eloquent. She and Azo had genuine light-guns, Ahio her shaper; Alkhes had annexed my cutter. No doubt at all the Cataract high command would know light-guns, at least, at a glance. A good chance the envoy himself had been at Amberlight.

Zuri talked in a glance to Azo, and Alkhes, whose jaw-set matched hers, and Sarth as well. Before she grunted, "Get the blades."

Broad-bladed, slashing-hooked Amberlight belt-weapons, that every Navy deckhand once wore by right. Half of them with gold-blazoned hilts, gifted us in Amberlight.

A choice that, again, was no sort of choice; if they wore other weapons openly, the light-guns still would not survive a proper search. But no doubt, by Zuri's hard reasoning, if it came to the worst scenario, they would be armed for a brawl; and at the very worst, the weapons would be ashore with us if we lost.

And there was the small consolation that they would work for nobody else.

They charged up and disappeared the light-guns as trouble-crew know how. I did not ask. But I did wish a better time for taking them all into the fire. A musician, a shaper, a quartet of Amberlight men, a pair of junior Navy officers, a Ruand's daughter and a medical apprentice; what sort of war-team is that?

A series of little paddler-boats landed us. An escort waited on the glacis, under the stare of a pair of big unmanned catapults. The gate proper was a pair of huge cedar trunks with steel-shod slabs of timber hung between, to lock with enormous swinging bars of iron. The gate guard were every color from midnight black to near-Dhasdeini white, with weapons from Dhasdein infantry short swords to the long stabbing spears of the Heartland itself, and gear ranging from loin-cloths and bull-hide shields to the back-and-breast corselet of the officer. Nor did they show any sort of military discipline, even when a group peeled off to escort us.

The messenger, as by right, walked with me at the front. Zuri set the infants next, then Ahio and Esrafal, then the Navy women, and then all the men, with Sarth and Alkhes next to her and Azo at the back. I caught a single scuffle, but after that, the procession was decorous.

That tramp to the citadel was, I confess, all I saw of Cataract; not that it was not noisome enough, with the stench of offal and excrement and undried mud in the alleyways, and market yammer in the open spaces, you would not call them squares, that we passed. The clothes seemed a River's cast-offs; the people scuttled like rats. Most of the architecture looks as lasting as this year's rains; mud-brick and occasional dingy plaster, blank outer walls and measly little entrances, with never a tree or a flowering vine in sight. I could reckon my way out again, I daresay, blindstabbing by the stars or sun, but otherwise, I know far more of Riversend.

And I may not get the chance.

The citadel gate did at least have a portcullis, if of wood, and a ramshackle sentry-coop, above the equally ramshackle fighting walk that matched the rampart logs. Upright, deep-planted, solid cedar trees, the Mother knows how old. The one place the tyrants have been profligate with their resource.

Inside was another medley of mud-brick, hardly grander than the streets, with a couple of stone buildings that resemble Dhasdeini work; the armory and treasury, I suspect. I wish I had taken more note of your upRiver intelligence, Tanekhet. And the tyrant's hall atop the crest.

Doubtless Cataract has administrators and scribes, and does not conduct its affairs entirely like an Oasis chief. I know they wrote decent letters to us. You would never think it from the hall, barely two stories high and thatched, if you can believe it; slab walls and plaster stuffed into the chinks; and inside, a positive beehive of idle military and waving weaponry, with the tyrant sprawled like a drunken dekarch on a throne at the farther end.

The great chair of Heartland mahogany is overlaid with a sunburst of leopard hides: the fiercest hunter the Heartlands know. It appeared to be the hall's only furniture, beyond the ceremonial fire-irons beside the great rectangular central hearth.

We entered to an uproar that may or may not have been a ceremonial greeting, but sounded more like a feeding shout. There must have been two hundred men inside, most armed with Heartland shields and stabbing spears. But their security was good enough. On the threshold another military peacock halted us, hand upheld, subordinates bristling at his back. They wanted the weaponry.

Zuri glanced at me. I lifted my shoulders; public charade of troublecrew doubt, leader's assent. She unbuckled her belt. Following suit, Deor squared her burly waterwoman's shoulders, glowered at the taker and growled, "Watch what you do with that."

They propped the lot against the wall. Then they marched us down to the space between the tyrant's honor guard and the hearth, where the messenger brought us to a halt. Smote sword-hilt to breast, and abandoned us.

The new tyrant, Wonsa, is almost certainly pure Heartland blood; if any blood is not Heartland, in Cataract. Darker than Dhasdeini or Amberlight bronze, but no trace of the true Verrain black. No brute to look at; fine open eyes and carven mouth and eagle's beak of nose, limber and young enough to fulfill the promise of well-shaped legs and defined arm muscle, that was showing aplenty as he sprawled in sleeveless corselet and crimson kilt. Gold on his forearms and throat, flaunted in the manner of a high military officer, in guards rather than ornament. Waving a lordly hand, weighted with the glitter of a seal-ring, and that an emerald.

"Ssso," he said. "Ruand."

The "s" is often drawled in Upriver speech. Not so deliberately, so insolently, as that. Inclining my head, I heard Alkhes smother a snort at my back.

Wonsa is a tyrant of Cataract; given that, his ploy was still more than forthright. He straightened by half an elbow and stretched out a regally peremptory hand and said, "Give me the qherrique."

I did control my face; I was trained in Amberlight. But I shaped manners to circumstance. I simply shook my head.

The fine brows arched together like a falcon's strike. There can be few times Wonsa was gainsaid, even at his mother's breast.

"It's not yours," I said.

I could wish to imagine your laughter, Tanekhet. But what would imperial manners have done for me?

He shut his mouth up short. Such flat refusal evidently took some thinking on.

"You are in my power," he said.

I shrugged.

"You want to keep it from me! You think—!"

But he is tyrant of Cataract; brains as well as bloodthirst are inevitable. The tirade snapped off like a breaking hilt.

"Why not?"

"You can't use it."

He smiled then. Brief and perfunctory as his other sketches of courtesy. "Then neither will anyone else."

Inevitable as the rest.

I said, "You know why we are here."

He waved the other hand. Stupid stories of a Quest and the River Source, women's gabble. Irrelevant.

"Do you know what happened to Amberlight?"

The brows arched.

"They tried to stop us too."

A pause; and I will admit, a laudably short pause, while he fathomed that; all that. From the fact that we were here, to the assumptions I had left, to the question he would have to ask.

Then he smiled, as economically and emptily as everything else he did. A gesture for an audience, and it was not us.

The hand waved. "You will change your mind."

Behind me came a, shush! and a short thick thunk and I whipped about to see Sunya's man Gearth drop in his tracks.

To a grunt and an animal scream as Azo whipped the light-gun from her sleeve and fired on the draw and the slinger behind the spear-fringe watched his throwing hand hit the floor, whap! while he clutched his cauterized stump of wrist.

The sling landed too, a scrickle of tangling leather, drum-loud in the hush. Then the spearmen bellowed like wounded lions and jumped.

Azo cut the right-hand leaders off at the knees. Zuri leveled the men behind the fireplace, Alkhes swept the cutter over it like a scythe. Ahio was not behindhand. She too had fought at Amberlight. The sound and stink breached heaven; burnt flesh, warcries and hideous screams, agony's urine and excrement. The more hideous sight of thirty men writhing amid amputated legs where Azo's first slash had swept below the shields, a dozen others screaming like half-beheaded chickens from Zuri's slice across their eyes, going down like foundered drunkards, dying . . .

I cannot finish it; I could not finish it then. As the Cataract recoil swirled into backlash I screeched, "Stop!" in chorus with Wonsa's, "Halt!"

As I whipped about my limbs shook, my heart pounded like a bolting horse. He glared back at me, a leopard half out of his lair, bloody massacre teetering on a finger-tip. Then the snarl twisted and he gestured, pure obscenity, as if ushering me through a door.

Look past your casualties, that gesture said. Consider their maddened survivors, the multitude beyond, the limited charge in those four guns, the absolute unlimitedness of my will. *I* will cheerfully waste them all. Will you?

And if you do fight your way out, what lies beyond? A boat that could never outstrip galleys, if there were somewhere to sail? A foot-race upRiver, to be trapped against the Jump-up cliffs by hounds like these?

A backlash upon Amberlight?

And Iskarda?

In one spring Wonsa hurled himself clear over the throne back. A fire-slash bisected the chair back with slashed leopard-skins curling and stinking in its wake and I screamed, "No!"

Sarth got Alkhes' other arm. He fought the pair of us, the cutter-beam slashing perilously and perhaps vitally; because it checked the honor guard just long enough for me to shriek at him, "Iskarda!"

Even in that extremity, his wits worked. He had struck at Wonsa to have a leaderless enemy if all else failed; now he too remembered the rancor, the eternal memory with which the state of Cataract will hold a killing grudge.

I slapped his fist; the cutter died. I spun back to the throne and bawled, "*I* respect guest-truce!"

Wonsa charged round the throne with shield and throwing spear, and he as much as Damas could subdue wish to wits. Because he stopped—he posed, in his stride. Drew himself up. Roared at his men, whose wounded were still screaming, howling, thrashing around us.

"Take them away!"

My grip had bitten Alkhes' wrist to the bone; he had never flinched and I did not dare let go. We stood heaving, panting, the sweat slick under my fingers, until Sarth's hand closed over mine.

Wonsa too was panting like a bellows, glaring like a gargoyle. He had broken truce first, and he knew it. And it had cost a bitter price.

"Throw them down!"

The light-guns. Elaborately, I scanned the hall.

"Have all your slingers gone?"

He looked murder at me. Gestured with the spear. The honor-guard hissed; the survivors backed off, rumbling and glaring over their shields.

"Throw them down!"

I gestured at Zuri, then at Ahio. The beams died. I said, "Who will pick them up?"

His face contorted. I heard Alkhes wrestle Sarth.

"Give me the qherrique!"

"All of it?"

"All of it!"

The shambles had subsided behind me. I waved Zuri back, and looked once at Gearth's slight, tall, slumped body, with Quiran kneeling over him. The diagnosis was in the bend of his head.

I slid the pouch out of my shirt, took the seed in my hand, and turned to Wonsa.

"Catch," I said.

He had a soldier's eye. The spear fell, he grabbed automatically as the tiny white comet arced over the guards' heads, his fingers shut, he had time for half a savage grin. Before he screamed like another wounded lion and hurled.

The qherrique landed halfway down the hall, between Zuri and the enemy's margin, a white flash on bloodied stone. Wonsa wrung his right hand and bellowed filth at me like the veriest backstreet whore.

When he sucked in breath I too spoke as a Head.

"My lord Wonsa, you requested this meeting. You demanded what is not yours. Then you broke guest-truce. You have killed one of my folk. An innocent man," I could not quite control my voice there, "who had taken no weapon against you. Is the god's message still not clear?"

He was breathing like a winded runner and his mouth-corners wore a rim of foam. It was no time to let face-saving drive him to a true holocaust.

"I will accept truce," I said.

He spat at me. Then he cursed, an incomprehensible gout of malice, and then he yelled. "Pick it up! Put the rest in there!"

The wood-container by the fireplace, an immense bucket-shaped brass bowl. Empty now, at summer's dawn.

I picked up the qherrique; for some reason the blood had not clung to it. But blood clung to my fingers, and to my shoes as I walked back, leaving a line of red, red tracks.

Face distorted, Wonsa pointed again.

Alkhes' hand bit my arm. I understood all too well. Relinquish the guns, be left weaponless; Wonsa need only order a massacre, and the Quest was over. What could we do? What could even the qherrique do?

I cupped it in my palm and looked up at him, rolling it to and fro. Then I held it out to Sarth.

Who took it, face inscrutable. Wonsa's eyes, following my hand, said it all.

"It will come to no-one but the chosen," I said. "If you destroy the chosen, it will only find more."

In Cataract. He turned gray, then, at last.

Before he got his bravado back and trumpeted at me. "Put the weapons down. Or I finish the lot of you here and now!"

The warriors surged. He bawled, they hung on the leash like rabid dogs. He pointed at the bucket and roared, and I knew we had reached the end of bluff.

I gestured to Zuri. Her face was always like granite. It was Alkhes' that spoke.

Ahio glanced at me; that look too spoke volumes in a single question, and laid an intolerable load on my shoulders. Of faith, of broken bonds. Of unredeemed trust.

I bent my head.

Her hard, scarred face set. Gently, she laid her shaper down; carefully, with the stance of a mother leaving her child's funeral, straightened up.

Wonsa let his breath out. No longer gray, or livid now, but as wild-eyed and shaky, however he tried to hide it, as the rest of us.

"You do not go." He had to wave to signify it. Out of here. UpRiver. "You stay here. They stay here." The guns. "Until you change your mind. Until you *make* it come to me."

I did not say, When the River runs back to Cataract. I let him see it, in my eye, the line of my shoulders, before I began to turn away.

He did not notice; his eyes had gone past me, whipped by a struggle's whirl, and then fixing with a glow of unholy joy.

Quite softly, but very clearly, he said, "Assandar."

Sarth let go then. Alkhes turned, slowly, carefully, knowing all too well what he had done. Fatal, too fatal conspicuousness, that had not only drawn attention, but shown Wonsa a lethal flaw.

To intervene would only affirm the breach's mortality. So I had to stand there, while Wonsa set down his shield, the insolence of a very leopard now, and stretched, his eyes never moving, and the murder clear in that unnatural smile.

Then he said, all but in a whisper, "The gods are truly kind."

I did not look; I did not want to look. I did not need to see Alkhes' face.

"What a splendid—coincidence." The sweat was drying on his cheeks, he was as brutally cool as when we arrived. "What a splendid chance." Dhasdein caricatured in every vowel. "After all those days, weeks, months, dancing to your tune, fussing with your fidgets, paying for your whims—*General*." He spat it like blood. "Watching you squander our troops, and waste our time, and betray the City's leader, the great Ruler, the god's child," he had slid from Dhasdeini manners to Cataract leader in a stride. "And now—here you are."

Alkhes said nothing. What could anyone say?

Wonsa stretched his arms wide; spreading the whole insolent width of muscle and chest and corselet, knowing that, now, he was perfectly safe.

"Charming." He kissed his fingers, and it became a true tiger's grin. "Be sure, 'general', that I will be seeing *you*."

He waved again. The troops moved, the stabbing spears came down, the way opened, beside the firepit, down the left side of the hall. The unlucky, the doomed, prisoners' side. There was a delay, as Quiran and Herar gathered up our fallen, on a makeshift litter of gripped hands. Wonsa leaned on his throne, a leopard's regained grace against the ruined leopard skins, to watch us led away.

* * *

They must be hardened to slaughter in Cataract; even among their own. The guard shoved us and hustled us, but with nothing like the retribution we would have exacted for such a—an obscenity.

I am not hardened, Tanekhet; I am in a muck sweat, just writing it. Even after Amberlight. It is printed on my eyelids, that cauterized wrist, the amputees, the others dying, eyes, brains burnt out . . . Sweet Work-mother, how can such things be done?

And done with qherrique?

I was shivering then too, as they herded us into the prison-halls, which are dug down in the hill, their entrance just behind the tyrants' own quarters; they like to oversee their prey. The mayhem did begin then. The first in a series of truly villainous jailers grabbed Keraz' breast and got his face scratched to blood just before Zuri all but kicked his belly out his mouth.

She must have intended to make it spectacular, for I have seen Zuri kill with much less fuss. But the great ox fell down as if poleaxed, and Zuri looked at the rest over him. Unlike Wonsa, she did not bother to smile.

The jailcrew are probably damaged soldiers; not a woman among them, mostly huge, fat to grossness, with a truly hideous array of false limbs and villainous scars. If they are Wonsa's own choice, then the man knows how to parody his role. Beyond the dirt and the stench, they carry the air of petty, uncontrolled power; no doubt most prisoners suffer all too bitterly.

After that, they were wary with us. I know I could not have taken too much more; I feared worse for the rest. I ought to have remembered that all except Quiran and Keraz had chosen to come to Iskarda; they had been through the fall of Amberlight. And even Quiran and Keraz had grown up in the hills, aware of worse predators than men. Sunya herself bore the gropings and obscenities with a face of hewn stone.

That, of course, was not the worst. Nor were the petty galls of confiscated personal possessions, not just Quiran's few instruments but the merest keepsakes, anything we might treasure, anything that took their eye. Nor the battle I had, working off my own backlash in Headly ferocity to stop them throwing Gearth's body on the midden under the wall.

After which they made us take the corpse ourselves.

That, I think, was the cruelest part; that, and the way, when they lined us up to have the chains hammered on, I had Alkhes next to me, to feel how he was shaking, and see his face in the grimy torchglow, bloodless white.

I shut my hands on his, saying silently, You were only a pretext. It was not your fault. And felt Sarth press close too, slipping both arms round him as he stood just behind.

Zuri had usurped first place; the jackals understand that in prison or not, leaders have some rights. Under the hammer noise I pressed back into Alkhes and said in his ear, "We're here. It's all right."

He could not speak. He tried three times. It was Sarth who leant down to us and said in that lion's purr, "He was at Amberlight. A junior officer. He gave you trouble before."

Alkhes did manage to nod.

Sarth's face said the rest, still so implacably polite. With the knowledge that goes beyond every imaginable sort of corruption in those topaz eyes.

I understood too. Wonsa had been more than a military rebel. He had been one of those Alkhes fears worse than death itself.

One like you, Tanekhet.

It is not my husband's fault, any more than his choice, that he draws some men's desire. Even if it has all but ruined his life.

Sarth's arm tightened, for I felt it. And I saw the look with which he said, quiet as ever, "Don't worry, Aglis."

I do not know what Sarth could do if he were pushed to it; remembering that look, I know I do not want to find out. But I felt Alkhes catch a breath, and the shuddering tension eased, if only for that instant. Before he exhaled again and looked past me at the jailers trying to get Azo into manacles, and said quite quietly, "I won't."

And I said, loud enough for the others to hear us, "The qher-rique got us into this. It will get us out."

* * *

It could be worse. We are on the lowest floor, three cellars down, the River's level, so paved in all but liquid mud, and open right along one side on a lattice of bars. Which means no privacy, even at night. The walls re-grow the vilest mildew within a day, how-ever we scrub, with what little we have, and the stench . . .

But we buried Gearth in one corner, with the shovels I made them bring us. And we have two slop buckets, if we have to dig them into the other corner once a day, and a water bucket changed every two days. And we wear chains, but not fastened to the wall as they do with slaves, which was my blackest fear. And they give us food, if only the filthiest soup and a couple of porridge pots. And the one compensation for the way they stand to watch us through the bars whenever we have to relieve ourselves, is that we are all together; if all but in the dark.

I daresay I shall come out looking pale as winter-wasted grass.

* * *

False bravery. We have been here twelve days.

I am in the nearest corner to what passes for light; they have to keep a torch down here, to maintain their guard. Irrita-tions, more like. I am sitting on the shelf, the one place we can sleep, along with the precious, precious papyrus roll that Esrafal used to pad her drum on the boat, and the soot and water mixed in Ahio's perfume vial that passes for ink, and the whittled reed Quiran had, for some reason, in the pouch that once held his in-struments. And I have this lull, between the midday guard change and the time they grow bored and begin baiting us, to say to you what no-one else can hear me speak.

The very first thing I did that very first night when we had finally settled down, so far as anyone could, on this miserable crowded shelf, with torchlight glaring and jackals tramping and hallooing beyond the bars and sleep impossible . . .

Was to invoke the qherrique.

As near as possible I tried to imitate the way I prayed in Damas' cell at Amberlight. I shut out the foulness along with ev-erything else, drew into myself as if to approach the face, and I threw the filaments of thought and demand as I had that night, out into unresponsive space. This time I was not deterred when it did not reply.

"It will send me a dream," I said to the others as we crowded the breakfast bucket. "Or it will send one somewhere else."

Only it has not.

* * *

We have waited eleven days, Tanekhet. In this dank pit where they will not so much as let us talk together without shouts, and orders, and then punitive charges inside. After Herar was beaten senseless and Azo all but raped, just because they wanted to hug each other, husband and wife, we have not spoken much. They will not even let Esrafal tap a rhythm on the shelf, so either she or we can sing aloud.

The sole exception was when Deor's cycle began.

Naturally none of us has a proper moss-pack that you can use once and throw away. None of us had brought ashore a cup or sponge, although we should have had the wits. We have had to use pads torn off our clothes, and wash them in the hoarded drinking water, turn and turn about; and every second of it before our own men's eyes.

But not the jackals'. Ha! The seven of us had hardly gathered around Deor, who was biting her lips after she muttered the news in my ear, even her Navy composure sorely tried, when they started howling and roaring, and when we ignored them the arch-oaf headed a posse for the door.

Where Zuri met them, looking down her nose, with the ice only a Trouble-head can achieve, to announce, "She's bleeding. Do you want to search for that?"

I never thought, in this pit, that I could want to laugh.

Because they do search us women, at the slightest provocation, my moments of greatest terror, for Sarth rather than myself. But this time the minions recoiled, and the leader brought up in his tracks.

Zuri examined them, a regard to make matricides blush; I thought it was time to back her up. So I strolled across and said, "Don't worry. It's only magic in Amberlight."

And that frightened them clear up the stairs. Amberlight's witchcraft, it seems, extends from qherrique to ruling a women's courses as well as causing abortions and ruining a man's potency or actually, dread thought, making his little weapon drop off.

So we women, if only for a scatter of moments, can talk.

I cannot answer them, Tanekhet. Because it has not spoken; there have been no dreams, for me or anyone else. Not in here, and surely, not outside. If Wonsa had dreamed like that, Cataract would be upside down.

It has not heard us. It is not listening.

I know already what this is doing to Sarth. I see the way he looks at me, each morning; or at least, when they rouse us to take the porridge through the bars. I know what happens behind those eyes of his, so redoubtably inscrutable, I make no doubt, to anyone else. I know the questions he asks. I know what he asked, after that morning on the Riverside. For him, this journey is as much an interrogation as a Quest.

And it is the qherrique, and the Mother Herself, and the way the world is made, and the foundations of his own soul that are on trial.

It is easier for me. Oh, Mother, it is far easier for me than for either of them, Alkhes who must be awaiting Wonsa's personal attention, a torture that increases every day. And Sarth, whose world, or whatever he staked on the qherrique, is crumbling under his feet.

The Mother aid us, Tanekhet. Why will it not help us? *Why?*

* * *

For this question the Mother may not be enough. Sarth did it; this morning, as we brushed past on the way to the bars. Bending his head, so briefly the jackals never noticed, as he breathed in my ear, "Is this a test?"

May your own Mother goddess sustain me, Tanekhet.

Because if he is right; if it has heard me, which it did before, and it has not answered, not because it cannot help, simply because it wants to see if we are, if we have whatever such a test could prove, our courage, our tenacity—our wits?

Then I have chased a will-o-the-wisp, and wasted, on a thing that does not merit a copper fiel to a beggar brat, not only blood but my comrades' suffering, and a decent man's, a quiet, harmless, kindly human's life.

* * *

It is getting worse, Tanekhet.

Ordered or not, the jailcrew have moved from tormenting to outright provoking us. Especially the men. I am terrified they will get what they want from Alkhes, even before Sarth. Sarth does have the better control, if he is as bloodily unreasonable about seeing his women struck, groped, pushed . . . all the petty indignities they can inflict on us, and always, always before the men's eyes.

I think they take Quiran, or Herar, or Deor's gentle Chenath to be the same as Alkhes or Sarth; outland masculine, all war-skilled, all troublecrew, and used to requiting such insults in blood.

When it is the women that they really ought to watch.

And if they are not careful, I will have to stop Zuri myself.

Sweet Work-mother, does it not realize that Wonsa may come for Alkhes any day? Does it expect us to break out of here alone? Are we supposed to die as martyrs and let some other take up the load? Did I speak in too sober truth? If that is so, why doesn't it tell me, then? Why doesn't it *answer* us?

I have made a decision. This cannot continue. We must act, before it is too—

CHAPTER V

Iskarda
4th Day, First Summer Moon

Tellurith—
My hand is shaking too much

* * *

Evidently even cider can be a restorative. If Fetha does think me an irreclaimable lunatic, to raid the kitchen in the first hour of the day.

Tellurith—I cannot think how to begin this. What am I—how am I to—

I had a dream.

* * *

I know what you will say. Would say, if you ever set eyes on this, and the chance thins every day. Did you get any of my letters, Tellurith? Do you know what quagmires I founder in, while you sail upRiver on your stainless Quest?

Let us assume that you have read them both. And can remember what I said to you, that day a moon ago, when Tez had cracked my world and Asaskian—offered to carry away the bits.

Well. It is easy enough to live with a cracked world: especially once you have the way of it, and I learnt the way long ago. And it is easier yet to dance the delaying waltz, I was schooled in that at thirteen years old.

It pains me cruelly to admit she has been more patient and more loving, and the gods cover me, more constant, than any man I ever watched in such a case. And I have kept putting her off, and hoping against hope that news would come. That a letter would come. That by some god's grace you would have received my distress signals, and written me some clean way out.

The news has not helped. Oh, nothing serious here in Iskarda. The worst trials have been another cutter's collapse, with a full order for the Dhasdein temple facade in progress, and the thrice-damnable waterpipes. You know—yes, you would remember they meant to cast the pipes on a long-spindled wheel? That is easy enough: what is not easy is to cast pipes, three or five feet long, whose mouths will mate exactly. When you are throwing them by hand.

And from two different potters' shops, since Dhera, the other whose cutter died, has set up to help the Iskardans. Charras tells me she has a very good hand, thanks to working with the qherrique.

Outside Iskarda? The shock of Amberlight's—revolution—still reverberates the River's length: there has been a flood of intelligencers, Tez reports, from Dhasdein and Verrain both. Meanwhile, neither Antastes nor Shuya have hurried to recognize the new "commonwealth."

And there is trouble in Amberlight itself.

Ah, Tellurith, you know you could have predicted it. Do we—humans—and gods be kind to us, in especial, human men—can we learn *anything*?

Because they are causing faction in the commune: what else would you expect, after your own lesson in Iskarda? There has been contumely, bad blood. Spiteful opposition, claims for more than their just desserts: if not yet outright battery and rape.

After all, there never was a matriarchy in River Quarter, just an armistice the Houses enforced. And the qherrique. And there are no Uphill men now. None with the vision of Sarth, let be the courage and patience to practice equity in a new world.

So your little visionary contends with outright threats in her assembly-room, while out on the streets women who worked as stevedores are rumbling that they are no weak-limbed Uphill virgins. They can beat the lesson of equality into male malcontents' heads for themselves.

You need no more telling than I do, that the intelligencers will stir whichever pot promises advantage to Dhasdein or Verrain.

So far, so much as I can tell, they have not seen greater vantage in bringing the government down.

* * *

I have talked myself composed: have had time to wash and breakfast, and immure myself here in the workroom before needing to confront it again.

The dream.

Very well, I will confess I was piqued and I was exasperated with her fidelity, and hating myself for the exasperation and aching to be free to—make myself a fool elsewhere. So I lay in my cubby last night and straightly made it a dare. Here I am, I said: where, presumably you wanted me. Or if not, I am a part of Tellurith's plan. And Tellurith's plan is yours, mystery. So if you want your plan to work, answer me now. Prove yourself a presence or a sentience or a divinity. Reach out, openly, palpably, and tell me what to do.

And it did.

I understand what you mean now: that message is indeed unmistakable. Terrifying as a god's voice in truth.

For all that mine was so simple, of such brevity. A snatch of heartbeats in those guest rooms of mine in Riversend, an ice-crisp winter morning: and you, Tellurith. With Sarth, and Tez, and open consternation at a council's end. You are turning from Sarth, with that look that says you have just leapt again where only visionaries can go. As you say, obviously answering his question, "Maybe, it's time the House had men who were there in their own right."

I know the flowers on the table, the chair Tez stands beside, Sarth's elegantly understated indoor coat. Terracotta wool, bought and tailored somewhere in Riversend. I know the leggings you wear, dun with honorable discredit from that sampan of yours, under that ancient gray and green checked shirt. You are fully five months on, yet the pregnancy hardly shows.

It is all completely familiar. Except I know—I know! that I never heard those words with mortal ears.

An omen, then. As this, here on the page, is my own inner oracle. Telling me that now I have an ally, an ally whose weight is indubitable. Certifiable truth.

* * *

Dhe's eyes, why do I persist in inciting calamity with such arrogance?

No doubt you will have seen ahead and be laughing already. Or tearing your hair over your outland experiment's imbecility. I admit that, surely.

Which I did *not* do when I paraded up the hill to Darthis' house, and requested an interview. In her—parlor, I suppose. Certainly a guest room, from the immaculate neglect and ponderous furniture. Where she gave me all the other marks of a ranking woman's visit, I understand now, down to sitting across the table where one of the men had set out wine. So, after a sip, I drew myself up and announced, with all the pride of my fatuity, "Ruand, I have had a dream. From the qherrique."

Did you ever see Darthis leap clean out of a chair?

May the River-lord help me, that was the least of it. She called a council on the spot. Whirled me down into your old council room, actually gripped my shoulder as she announced in their astounded faces, "He has had a dream. From the qherrique."

Picture your Craft-heads, your Steward, dancing up and down, over-shouting each other, quarrelling outright, while Darthis and her cohorts contended through the wrack. Pass over the disbelief and outrage and the demands to be told, How? Pass over the speculations, from some sort of blood-affinity to the unthinkable of a man with a cutter's ear. I suppose I should thank the gods for Alkhes, who bore the first reaction to a man having anything at all to do with qherrique.

They had shouted that out, and got past schemes to notify you, Tellurith, and plans to test the other House-men. And postulations about my use, from Quetho's idea that I could take shifts with a cutter to Charras' arguing that I could dream a way to fix the pipes: when Zdana rose at Darthis' elbow and used what, I am told, was the Mother's Voice.

"We should speak this," she said, "in the Mother's Ear."

The Telluir folk gave me one look and shut up. I did not know what she meant: but I have instincts, after all.

Charras opened her mouth. Zdana stared at her. "It's no more," she said, "than we asked of the Stheir."

When Hayras spluttered Zdana gave her a glare for herself. "Whose Word do we need more? What better, surer way to know we have it in all truth?"

Iatha split a look between Zdana and Darthis: the tuck of her mouth told me I did not want any more of Zdana's plan, and the colder knowledge that Darthis would not protest. Then she turned her Steward's scrutiny and overspoke them all.

"What," she asked me, "did you dream?"

I daresay you can credit, amid the hullabaloo, that none of them had thought to ask.

Afterwards there was silence in earnest: and that trading of eye-talk that drives me crazy because I still cannot read the code. Before Darthis looked at Iatha, and raised her brows, and Iatha cocked hers in turn, and Darthis inclined her head: all of which I translated as an exchange over precedence, before Iatha spoke.

To Darthis, as if I did not exist. Saying, "That would be an excellent reason, after all."

I was—I will freely admit, my lady Tellurith, I was myself somewhat out of balance. Which is reason, if not exculpation, for the way I snapped, "Reason for *what*?"

They all looked at me then. With some astonishment, which I ought to take as compliment, that I had not followed from the start. Before Iatha said, "A House-woman has offered you troth."

I took in my breath. "Madam, I am somewhat obtuse today. Surely the qherrique's answer is clear enough?"

Iatha passed that to Darthis. Who studied me, gravely as a Court judge pronouncing sentence of death.

"The message is clear," she said, in that boulder-roll of a voice. "The Mother has gifted us another Ear for the qherrique. It is not a gift we should waste."

I thought myself skilled and steeped in intrigue, in politics. I understood, I thought, marriage ties: after all, I managed them three times myself. But I do not, I will freely confess it, begin to imagine the premises from which your women work. I only thought she meant Zdana's plan: and that, may the River-lord see me, promised badly enough.

I said, "The Mother's Ear?"

Iatha gave a snort. Zdana was scandalized. Iatha took pity on me—my voice must have cried I was beleaguered enough—and said it aloud.

"The Mother's Ear hears Her words. For the questions the Mother will not answer, her Chosen asks. Not the priestess. The—Chosen for the year."

I must have looked blanker than ever. She finished explosively, "He's a man."

"You want me to be Chosen?"

I might have assaulted Antastes. It was Verrith who leant past the nearest Iskardan to slap me hard on the arm, as much warning as solidarity: before she snapped, "He has no idea what it means!" And to me, "No, man, no. She just wants you to Ask."

I could hear the capital. My spine crept. "Ah—Ruands—"

"No," said Darthis flatly. "That may come. But it is not what the message means."

"Then. . .?" I have seldom played an Iskardan man in truth.

It was Iatha who met my eye and supplied brusquely, "What Iskarda's Ruand means is that we have a man who can hear qherrique. And a House-woman seeking his troth. And it's not a blood to waste."

Do you know what it is, Tellurith, to think you have found a sure refuge from all besetments, and discover it a trap?

I think I said, "But—" staring and spluttering like the most callow intriguer ever snared. "But the message was, No!"

Iatha looked past me. I could not meet the hunger in Zdana's eyes. Charras and Quetho and Hayras squirmed and Verrith dodged my gaze. Darthis held it. Solidly and blankly as that boulder on which they sacrifice.

"You asked me," she said, "for advice."

With an emphasis on "me" that told me plainly, And a greater has answered you.

"But the dream—the qherrique—Tellurith herself said, Men in their own right!"

"It will," Darthis responded, "be in your own right."

Because I had dreamed. Because I might transmit the capacity. Message clear enough for insult at any other time: that they would have married me into their House for nothing less.

"Ruands—!"

I ought to have been able to manage more. If I had not been so shaken by the dream itself. And then so thankful for what I thought a refuge beyond test, and then so—so confounded by the way they meant to twist the thing—still, I suppose I should have been able to fight back. And yet—

And yet I kept remembering Darthis that day on the mountainside, saying, "She must mean you for more than making tallymarks."

For once Amberlight training was on my side. Charras took one look at me and stood up, saying firmly, "This has been a shock to all of us. Let the man take a rest and think it through."

So now I have to face it for myself. Alone. The question of all questions that I need to ask of you, Tellurith.

Is this what you wanted? Is this all you needed? Solely the virtues of my seed?

And if it is not your plan—then is it the qherrique's? Have I been betrayed, even by that dream?

Even by what may be—in good truth—a god?

Or have they—have we betrayed the god instead?

* * *

Amberlight
24th Day, First Summer Moon

I must admit, Tellurith, that I am now in confusion so complete not even gods could get me out.

You see the direction of this. Yes, all—well, two of my desires have been fulfilled. I am clear of Asaskian, and I am in Amberlight.

I imagine you knitting your brows at the thought. As I did, for all of thirty seconds, as I weighed the possibility of drawing Antastes' attention: of appearing too forward in state matters, and affrighting the empire with the specter of Riversrun's Suzerain resurrected, on the other side. To be sure, Tellurith, I did consider it. But—

But beyond my own concerns, that letter bore a summons I could not deny.

She asked for me especially, Tellurith. "From the Commune of Amberlight to the folk of Telluir House. The Commune urgently requests that the House temporarily second Tanekhet, their adviser on River affairs, to Amberlight. Signed, the Commune-leaders for First Summer Moon, Dhanissa and Ferrias. Representatives for the River Quarter of Amberlight."

I may be more than breeding stock, after all.

Though I must be honest here if nowhere else. If you are breeding for intelligence, Tellurith, you had best discard me now.

Because I did not have the wit the River-lord gave a sparrow, to say, "Send me across the Kora, it may be rough and slow but it's most direct." I let them—Dhe scourge me, I egged them on to send me to Marbleport, because it would be easier on my fragile health—I, who have caught an hour's sleep between orgy and council for half my life! Conceding it would be easier to ride fifty miles muleback on a good road, and then sail upRiver, when—

When all I really wanted was a pretext to encounter Tez. To explain that day in the work-room: to have my heart, if not salved, at least free of debt.

How did I manage an empire, and achieve such blunders as this?

I saw her, yes. She came to meet the mule-train, as you would expect. The muleteers deployed their beasts for sheer-legs to heave the blocks straight on the ship that she had waiting, perfect efficiency. And I scrambled off that sawback saddle trying to find something that resembled courtly command of my legs, wondering if my hair resembled a mud-lark's nest, with a very good view.

Of Tez's back.

I would have known it across the River's width. Brown worker's leggings, nondescript shirt, straw Korite hat. The carriage, the gestures, the shape that is scribed on me bone-marrow deep. Dhe help me, Tellurith. You have seizin of both your men. How long since you knew that sensation, the molten dart that goes clean through you at the sight, the recognition of one beloved?

But not possessed.

I ought to have known better. I ought to have read that back the way any woman of Iskarda would, the way it was so carefully meant. But like any blundering male, I dropped the reins and went to position myself at Hassa the train-leader's elbow. Looking full at Tez.

She did not break her sentence, let alone stutter: far be it from blush. She heard the reply, and disposed of the topic. Before she turned her eyes and enquired, "Yes?"

I have been snubbed by emperors. Lacking that armor, I would still have answered, "I need to see you a moment, Ruand, before I leave."

She has fleshed out since we came back, Tellurith. The circles have filled in under her eyes: her hair is almost long enough to plait, the ends lightened, so in sunlight it glitters almost bronze. And crowsfeet frame her eyes' golden-brown in patterns of brown and brown, like the brocade of a pheasant's breast. I can imagine now the quick-moving, compact, lithely balanced Navy-officer on her own ship's deck.

It was how she led me crossways through the dockside mess, into the shack with bills of lading and the rest of it spiked to the dusty walls, and the sun laying grids across the tangled desk. Where she turned about, armored in her position as in that sun-glare, repeating, "Yes?"

I said, "It was not what you think."

"I beg your pardon?"

"The day in my work-room. It was not what you think, lady Tez—"

She made one brutal gesture, a hand-sweep, almost a fist. "I've told you not to call me that!"

"I beg your pardon—Tez. But I must tell you—"

"Is this about Amberlight?"

"No—Tez, this is about—"

"I have work to do, *lord* Tanekhet."

I was between her and the doorway, and that voice, that face, armored in indifference harder than contempt, drove me clear out of my wits. I did what I have never done to a woman in my life. I caught her by the wrist.

Her reaction was Navy-trained and Navy fast. A wrench forward with that arm and the other palm chopping across my wrist. A handful of shirt with a jerk whose ferocity I never knew a woman possessed and a tiger's snarl right in my face.

"Don't you *dare!*"

I should think I probably yelped.

She threw me off. With all the pent up rage of Iskarda, and Amberlight, and Dhasdein, I make no doubt, of imprisonment, and war, and being left wounded in enemy hands, and having to fettle stupid men's independence ever since. And probably some of it for Asaskian, in one way or another. After all, she knew about the rape.

"Get away from me." By then she was almost whispering. "Away," came out long drawn and low as the rasp of an unsheathed knife. "Get out of my office. Get on that ship. Do what you're wanted for. Get out!"

Here, in the privacy of this—letter, memoir, confession, whatever on earth it is—with time to over skin the wounds, I can admit the truth: I deserved it. I bungled the thing completely. I lost my courtier's poise and lacked the barest wits to mention Amberlight first. I will not—as I have heard so many men—claim it was her attitude, her disgust with any man, she is probably a woman-lover, it was all her fault. For all I know, she may love women. It happened, in Amberlight's Navy, often enough. Does that change this—this thrall, this spell, this impossible unbreakable enamourment?

Ah, Tellurith. I hope, I hope and pray things go well upRiver. I would not wish this heart-load on anyone else.

* * *

No doubt I should report on Amberlight.
  Firstly, then, would you believe that when the Quarter and the City ignited round them that day, your revolutionary had no god's voice to follow? Do you know what she used instead?

She told me, that first evening we talked together, new lines smoothing out into the sheen, the vision's light, as she set down her winecup and laughed across the lamplight at me. "Listen to the qherrique? Know what to say next? Mother, no! I just pretended I was Tellurith!"

My lady world-founder. You seed visions, in most earnest truth.

It does cheer me to report that we can work together. That if she has no awe of me—and I must seem old as god to her—she has no resentment or suspicion either. I am yours. I am from Iskarda. It is voucher enough.

And I have been of use: I bought my place with the commune the first morning, over a newly snared creature of the Empress's. Whom I counseled they send back downstream with a solid flea in his ear, and a warning in my own words to have more respect for what they were dealing with.

If the Empress does not hear, I am very sure Antastes will.

Thence I have expanded to political adviser. They want a constitution, and none of them, from the cobbler who heads Main Quay section to the Diaman clanswoman who stands for Uphill, has the faintest idea of legal affairs. So I have been conscripted to pen and ink again, and endless hours in the assembly chambers— a warehouse just below Exchange Square—where they quarrel over political terminology. There, indeed, I have earned my keep, using skills honed these thirty years: to ease the meeting, to clarify the clumsy and anticipate the trouble-makers, and work always to the hidden purpose's will.

Have no fear, Tellurith. If it is your vision I shape, believe me, it is with your eyes, or at least Dhanissa's eyes, that I try to see.

I have already suggested stratagems for her trouble-makers in the full assembly. I know all the ways to rig a council-meet: why not use them? It gives me a twisted pleasure, I must admit, to use them against the men. Have I become a traitor, not only to my nation, but to my kind?

It is not inconceivable—it would not be inconceivable, if I stayed, that they would give me an assembly-seat. I have been slumming with Dhanissa in River Quarter, and I can hit the right note, it may surprise you to learn, with rice-diggers and stevedores. Especially at the moment, when I carry the mantle of your passing, atop the mythical air of Iskarda.

And there has been no word from Upriver. Your first letter, yes, with the cutter that overtook you on the way to Cataract. Nothing else. Including my freighter, that should have been back half a moon ago.

* * *

Well. The River-game has opened, Tellurith. They showed me the letter in the unofficial council-chamber, between dusty barrel-stands and deep-stained watermarks on the old paven floor. All properly rolled, stamped and sealed with the big red rams' horns that I know so well: an official communiqué. From the President of the Families, conveying the will of Verrain.

Which is to protest previous illegal annexation, and reclaim the lands and town of Marbleport.

To be sure, nothing you would not expect. I was able to convey that, at least.

"So," I said, and pushed the scroll delicately away amid the draft-scraps and half-trimmed pens. "How very—usual."

The cobbler's eyes bugged. But Ferrias—a most disrespectful infant, Ferrias—I am almost sure Ferrias smothered a laugh under that sneeze.

While Dhanissa—the River-lord aid me, Dhanissa looked at me as if I truly were the River-lord, and demanded, "What's usual?"

"Verrain has declared against us." I made it sound everyday. The wretched children have troubles enough. "It may be the House-heads' influence. More likely Shuya finally hopes to recoup from Riversrun. That was," nor do they have any idea of history, "the bad war they had downRiver. When they lost half a province to Dhasdein. And Verrain's first concern is always territory."

Juiza, the Uphill delegate, was also troublecrew. "So they think we're weaker," she said.

"Madam, Amberlight itself was never stronger than Dhasdein. But in a word—they have watched events, and decided you are vulnerable: and chosen to open their initiative—officially."

Dhanissa has the Amberlight eyes. When they open like that, they are uncannily reminiscent of Asaskian.

"Officially?"

"On the diplomatic level. Notes, demands, embassies. They may be prepared to negotiate. Or merely to proceed with caution. You are still an unknown quantity. And . . . there is Iskarda."

Dhanissa's pupils dilated. Now she understood.

"Iskarda can't do without Marbleport!"

"No," I said.

They all broke out then. You may supply the most yourself: they were free of women's rule, they were the new Amberlight, what did Marbleport matter to them? They had neither debt nor obligation to Iskarda. Combated, the cobbler and his two Downhill cronies grew abusive. Ferrias and the Far Quay women bawled back at them, Dhanissa, as is her custom, watched and waited. Juiza rattled her fingers on the table. Watching me.

She has a good eye for body-talk. Just as I drew breath she bawled into the riot, "Shaddup!"

They stopped in sheer shock. I inclined my head to her—a gracious ally—and said, "Your ties to Iskarda are irrelevant."

The cobbler started to bay. I stared at him.

"What matters," I said, when he looked down, "is that Verrain sent the note to you."

Dhanissa said, "You mean *they* think we're connected?"

"I mean they are asking: will you back your allies? Can you hold this territory? Are you a River power or not?"

And as they gaped, I finished in the voice I would use to silence Antastes.

"If the answer to any of those is, No, then they will walk over you."

It was Dhanissa who stirred first. Looking round the silenced faces—the cobbler was swallowing—before she said formally, "Envoy, advise us. What should we do next?"

What would you have had me say, Tellurith? Omens, dreams, guidance we may have, but without light-guns and ships we are a toothless wolf. Yet we cannot let Shuya think she has carried her bluff.

Any more than we can cede her the dispute's rudder, and the choice of mode: whether by diplomatic note, or open warfare, or less—officially.

I requested a night's thinking time. Superfluous. I can, I have threaded such dances in my sleep. But there is a protocol here as for everything, and we could not send the envoy back at once. One cannot, as you well know, appear browbeaten outright. I will admit I wanted another consultation as well.

Perhaps I was too sure, too confident. Perhaps there are factors I know nothing about. Perhaps it only answers when you ask from personal need.

In which case I do not understand this, Tellurith. The River-lord knows, my need is desperate enough: my own hopes are committed to Iskarda. And clearly, now, Verrain reads Iskarda as part of Amberlight. It has answered before. It *did* answer. Why, this time, will it not favor me?

It is not as if, given another choice, I would still take the path I understand, the only path, without that choice, that is open to me. The Gods know, it is dirty and perilous. I understand that. Given another choice I would take that willingly, thankfully.

But I do not have another choice.

Has this happened to you, Tellurith? Do you know the impact of that double betrayal? I only hope you have not to bear heart's hurt as well.

* * *

When we met next morning, I gave the unofficial assembly the rest of my plan.

"We send an official reply. Official notice of reception. Official puzzlement. The President's scribe appears to have used some confusing vocabulary. The President's message is disordered. We are unsure what Verrain means."

Dhanissa stared. Ferrias did burst out laughing. Juiza's eyes narrowed. She said, "Why are we making time?"

"Because," I answered, "if we go to war with Verrain, we will lose."

Even the cobbler found that clear enough.

You know its truth, Tellurith. No trained troops, let alone Navy folk, and what sort of resources? And if Shuya calls on them, the House-heads will be a goldmine of internal intelligence. If it comes to military contest, Amberlight is dead.

So why does Shuya simply not take Marbleport?

I wish to all the gods I could discuss this with you. You know the old fox as well if not better than I. She is canny, she can be ruthless, she knows the Forty like the lines in her own hand. Is she unsure what you may have left in Iskarda? Or what new prodigy might surface in Amberlight? The gods know, that might give pause to anyone. Is there disaffection in Assuana, or does she fear we might incite some? Or is something building in Dhasdein?

I never felt such want for intelligencers. This is worse than dancing a sword-ring blind.

Or is she waiting to see what comes downRiver from Cataract? To know that you are captive, the Quest ended, and she can take Amberlight in the pincers with Cataract and quarrel over the kill, dismissing Iskarda?

Or is her main quarry really Iskarda? Is Amberlight the stalking horse, and she means to cut Iskarda's wind at a stroke, and like Damas, quietly strangle us?

Is Amberlight's resistance, then, and intervention, and inveigling into an unwinnable war, the side-dish rather than the banquet-plate?

Or, perhaps—

This is something you *could* tell me: Adversary take the chance that leaves you beyond hearing this last, this all-resolving question—

How old is Shuya's statuette?

* * *

I did learn the answer to that. There are women here who were shapers in old Amberlight, and Juiza found me someone who worked on Shuya's piece.

It will wane sometime at the closure of this year.

Not that this reverses the military odds, but it does illuminate Shuya's strategy. She is pushing while she can, but not moving outright, lest something new arise here, and the backlash catch Assuana at her most vulnerable. Had she declared war, and moved troops upRiver at once, still she could hardly hope to have swallowed Amberlight before the year's end.

Let alone Iskarda.

Especially with the Riversrun Suzerain ensconced in the councils of both.

I wish I could explain this to you, Tellurith. I have warned Dhanissa what will be said. I have sent a coded dispatch to Verrith, and told her to explain to Iskarda. I will go myself, as soon as possible. I need to make the clearest affirmation in the clearest way I can, face to face.

They must believe it is a ruse. That my loyalty is unshaken, no matter what threatens, even—

Even marriage to Asaskian.

I have told Dhanissa everything. In truth, at length. There are two blades to this dagger, as all good Archipelago arena fighters understand.

First is what I counseled Iatha, through Verrith.

The River-lord give them schooling to manage it, and intelligence to accept the need, for He knows, it is ramshackle enough. Round up a half-dozen of Iskarda's best intelligencers, or whatever else she has, and send them down with what silver they can spare, to Marbleport. To meet whatever handy women Juiza can find for me, and slip downRiver to the border with Quetzistan.

It is the plan I had in mind, originally, against Dhasdein. But Quetzistani are perpetually restless and rapacious. So it is worth their while, what do they care who asks them to raid the Oasis caravans?

I can instruct Juiza's folk. Given the women you used to send against us, there should be no problem, my lady Tellurith. A careless raider who drops a few gold fenn, a Dhasdeini belt or dagger-hilt left beside a looted caravan, a loose-tongued gossip in some Oasis rendezvous. The word will fly to Shuya with all the haste of her own lash. Because Verrain, and Shuya's eminence with it, rests on the safety of those caravans.

The other blade . . .

I have to rattle Shuya, Tellurith. The raids will shake her, but they might as easily decide her to make a counterbalance out of Amberlight. There must be more weight in the scale.

And that, too, is easy, far too easy: I need only make pretext to address a known Dhasdeini in the street. Ask the way to a tavern would do. They are all on a hair-trigger. A breath awry and Shuya's and Antastes' men would cut each others' throats.

But if Shuya thinks I have a connection with Antastes . . .

Then, how much will she dare, with the empire enlisted, perhaps already working undercover at her back?

I wish, I desperately wish I knew this letter would reach you. And that it does so before the River brings the news some other way. Because it will run, this news. I have to let it run, or the plan will fail.

And I confess freely, Tellurith, I fear less what Antastes will make of it, than what it may mean to you.

Pointless, here, to swear my faith thrice over. Pointless, it seems, to ask an omen from the qherrique. You were there, that day outside the palace in Riversend. You know—you cannot help but know—my loyalty is yours as long as I live.

Well. We have a long passage yet in the diplomatic minuet. Let be the time to send envoys to and from Assuana, there are the ripostes and feints: Marbleport is none of Amberlight's business. It belongs to Iskarda. Refer your messages there. If that happens, I will go back, naturally. Whatever the—the personal price.

And with that diversion accepted, we can raise Dhasdein's shield in truth: Iskarda is an Imperial ally, any threat to Iskarda's lands will be referred to Riversend, any damage will be answered by Dhasdein. And Antastes will have to save his own face by making good the pledge.

In any case, there is any amount of obfuscation to make first, here or in Iskarda. By what right does Verrain claim land legally ceded to Amberlight, and as legally ceded by Amberlight to Telluir House, which is now the polity of Iskarda? The entanglements will feed a flock of lawyers for months. And again, if the matter goes beyond diplomacy, we can invoke Dhasdein.

If it is using a tiger to expel a wolf, at that point, we will have little choice.

But I would give my eye-teeth, now, this moment, to know what has happened in Cataract.

CHAPTER VI

Summer
Upriver

Tanekhet . . .
       Where do I start?

Crying; laughing; blinking at blots on this pen-killing excuse for paper that has more ruts than a Kora road. If I could tell you, if I can halfway manage to convey this to you . . .

* * *

This is ridiculous; I shall start where I ended. In the prison, that day after a quarter's worth of waiting; when I had just decided we must act.

And been pre-empted in mid-scratch as the usual brangle of mid-afternoon jackal-baitings that I had ignored in my self-absorption became a howl and thud and awful masculine grunt.

I remember now, I threw the whole writing apparatus in the mud and jumped.

But it was Zuri, not Sarth, who had Keraz rammed in the slop-corner behind her and the arch-slob on his face in front of her, her teeth bared, every muscle shouting, Come on, and I'll massacre you!

She was actually grinning. Zuri, who watched Amberlight die and never flicked a lash.

I have to reconstruct the rest; the bar-gate, open, jackals six-deep in the gap, my own folk making the other side of the crescent, shoved back by the monster's crash. Shoulders I parted with one desperate lunge, only to be yanked up in mid-leap.

Sarth's hands that grabbed me. Alkhes' voice, strained almost beyond recognition, that hissed in my ear, "No!"

No intervention from one without fighting skills. No intervention at all, because nothing and no-one would stop Zuri now.

She must have kicked again, somewhere over the kidneys: and then used the manacle-bight on his neck. I deduced this from where his hands went, over the wheeze of his breath.

Before he grumbled like a woken elephant and heaved, limb by limb, from the mud.

Zuri waited for him. Head cocked, teeth still bare, that grin, pure berserker, on her face.

He rubbed his back. He was a huge oaf, over six feet and broader than a warehouse door, and little enough was fat. We had had cause to fear his forays. It was he who half-killed Azo.

I make no doubt he could feel the quiet; the hungry silence behind him, a pack watching a challenged lead-wolf. He gave his kidneys one last rub; then he spat in the mud.

"All right, girlie," he said. "End of watch."

All the jackals shivered in their filthy boots, such a susurrus of bloody-minded joy I knew this was more than custom; it was a ritual. A familiar ritual, the one they had been longing for.

Zuri grinned harder. "Big boy," she said. "Keep it up."

I saw his cheekbones go dirty purple, but nobody, our side or theirs, dared a sound. They had cleared the doorway before he lumbered near enough to shove.

* * *

What point then in descanting upon imminent ruin, in curses or questions or lament? As little as in asking the cause. One more insult to Keraz, always their favorite butt, one verbal or physical obscenity more than Zuri would stand. I ought to have been paying attention. Now it was too late. Either we would lose my right arm, our Trouble-head, or we would call Wonsa's attention in a way he could not overlook.

Whether from intimidation or anticipation, the jackals did not meddle when we women got together in the council corner. Not that we said much. A few words of tactics between Zuri and Azo, lost on us. A few mumbles from Sunya and Deor about what the rest should do, a shattered silence from Esrafal; an attempt at apology from Keraz. What more to say? We had no weapons. We had no way of getting any. If Zuri won, we had one hope, and that was to break out immediately.

If Zuri lost?

I am not sure if that was worse than the prison in Amberlight. I do know I have never before been in council, and had no word, no scheme, however crazy, no goal, no subterfuge, to offer my House.

We sat so long the men came over. That the jackals made no protest said just how bad it was. We huddled in our dirty stinking cumbered ring under the torchlight, stunned; mute.

And then Ahio, next to me, sat up, and said, "What became of Dinda's statuette?"

Natural enough for the shaper to think of it; natural enough that all our jaws dropped. I must have looked sillier than Zuri. Ahio glanced around us, half diffident, half abashed.

"I only thought . . . *that* would be strong enough."

Strong enough to prove a weapon, strong enough, in the right hands, to knock a building over, to blow a city wall down, to blast a road clear out of Cataract.

Zuri looked at me. All of them looked at me, I who knew both the overall picture and the finer details, I the supposed House-head, I whose brain had finally recovered circulation. Sweet Work-mother! What a fool I felt!

"It would have gone dead; during the siege."

Of Amberlight. He had been negotiating the winter before, ahead of time; it must have faded by that summer's end.

Esrafal said, "What happens when they . . . die?"

"They just sit there. The great kingdoms, Dhasdein, Verrain, bury them. In a special, sacred ground."

Zuri, whose intelligencers knew every domestic palace detail for the River's length.

"And in Cataract?"

Ahio who breathed it; all our eyes that spoke the unbelieving, incredulous response, the more impossibly kindling hope.

"After he died," Azo tiptoed word to word, as if the very walls were holding their breath, "it wouldn't have been . . . put away."

"Nobody," Ahio, sitting straighter, holding her own breath, "here'd dare fiddle with it."

Not even Wonsa; the silence concluded that for us, as if it, too, had forgotten to breathe.

"So it's still—" "If we could just—" "It might—"

All their eyes returned to me. I could feel their hearts sink, as I dragged out the words.

"I've never heard of one revived."

Silence. Deepening, sinking like a holed ship. Before Sunya shifted feet with a jerk in the mud and spoke.

"And there's never been a seed before. Or men," how did she hold her voice straight? "that could touch it, or dreams that it sent. You said, It would get us out."

Again the eyes came back to me. How was I to say, This is less than a dream? Far less a valid, even a crazy hope?

Zuri read me fastest; she has construed my assent so often before, for so many lost, lunatic enterprises, it came as no surprise when she straightened her shoulders and said casually, "Then we'd best get going now."

She meant, before the fight.

"But how do we . . .?" Quiran will blurt a question more often than anyone else. Perhaps his medical work has given him some standing in his own mind.

Zuri grunted, already turning to study the bars; Azo had moved to her, Deor and Sunya shifting in step. If they were not troublecrew, they were Navy. They understood the tactics of assault.

"Wait."

Zuri did check. All the women did, taken by surprise.

"I think that one's mine."

He said it so quietly. So coolly. Except that if you knew him, you could read the jaw's rigidity, and if you had the right angle, see the sweat already beading his temples, under the night-black hair.

"No!"

That time I jumped myself. I have seen Sarth in wrath and outrage and deadly menace; I never heard him sound like that.

"I must! It'll be in the tyrant's quarters, the treasury, the personal shrine, it can't be anywhere else. None of you'll get that far. I'm the only one who might—!"

Sarth took him by the elbows and bore him back against the wall. Alkhes is a soldier and a street-fighter and trained troublecrew, and he might as well have fought an avalanche.

"I said, No."

Even I knew better than to interfere.

"Sarth—"

Sarth stared down at him; I do not know how that tower stillness can convey so much. Absolute blankness, total silence; a volcano ready to burst.

I would not have dared to speak. But Alkhes shook his hair back and all but threw it in that face.

"This time it's my turn."

Sarth's jaw muscle jumped. I heard Alkhes catch his breath. They glared at each other, and I read the past slashed like a pair of swords between those battling eyes.

You can't do it, Sarth was saying. You have only one way into the tyrant's palace, and it will give Wonsa a message he cannot mistake. I will not let you cold-bloodedly hazard yourself, all too possibly sell yourself into your worst nightmare, into what has too often become truth. Where you may all too possibly suffer more than violation, or torture, or death itself.

There is no choice, Alkhes' midnight stare retorted, for that very cause. Nobody else has my leverage. Not even you, who have done this for us once. Nor will I shirk a burden twice.

Without looking away, he said, "Tellurith?"

I could not reply. I could see how his throat had set; I could imagine what filled his memory, feel the speeding of his heart. If I was all but panicked at the thought, what must he feel?

"Tel?"

A soldier's voice. More than a soldier's voice. Once he had been Iskarda's Chosen, however crookedly Iskarda rolled the dice; once he had stood as a king, who dies to save his House. That place, that demand, was in his inflection now.

I swallowed twice, and managed a gulp. Before I got out, "Sarth."

He looked at me. May I never, whatever my perfidies, meet such a look again.

Very carefully, Alkhes put up his hands. Took Sarth by the wrists and, unresisted, drew his shoulders clear of that prisoning grasp.

I do not know what that look said. Forgive me, Be kind, Don't make it worse? Trust me? Let me die if I must; so long as I pay my debts?

Sarth's mouth crimped. I felt Zuri wince with me, as he freed his hands. Then he jerked Alkhes to him and gave him a hug that must have crushed his ribs, and added thickly, "Take your own advice."

I remember thinking, once Alkhes would have died, sooner than bear a man's embrace. Let alone hug him, openly, passionately in return.

* * *

It is difficult to remember now, but I must have been terrified. Looking back, it seems we were all amazingly calm. We agreed like sleepwalkers that it must start now, to give Alkhes all the time possible before the end of watch. As if he would unquestionably succeed. As if Zuri would as certainly win her fight. As if we would all meet again, simply as women in a marketplace. From start to finish a harebrained, rackety, lethal card-house of dovetailing impossibilities, and we set about it as if it were ordinary routine.

Easy as firing a light-gun up.

I don't know, Tanekhet; I can hear you ask, with the skinning-knife turn in your voice and the light sharp as Riversend winter in those forest-green eyes. I don't know how this was possible, I don't know if Ahio thought of it, any of it, by herself. How in the Mother's name am I to tell?

All I know is, Alkhes hugged me too, and kissed me, more than desperately. Before he walked across, almost steadily, and rattled the gate in the bars.

The jackals must have had a good gossip-net, for either they had heard the end of things in hall, or someone had been talking since. Because they leered and spread their usual smut; but when he said, "I want to see the Ruler," they spluttered and muttered; but they sent a messenger almost at once.

We had only to wait, then. With Alkhes in our midst, Sarth and I at his shoulders, the others pressing close, as if to armor him in thought, if nothing else . . . I know I could not bring myself, at the last, to share a physical touch. The line of his back said, too clearly, This is all that I can bear.

When the messenger returned, he did not look around at us; just walked forward steadily, oh, sweet Mother, how too, too steadily; a small, bedraggled figure with the bearing of a king, as they led him away.

* * *

Believe it or not, but the next part was easier. We had chosen to throw; now we had only to do our best with our own dice.

The Mother knows that was hard enough, not least for Zuri's part. Triple-seasoned troublecrew, going to meet a man twice her size and thrice her weight and guaranteed the dirtiest bully in Cataract, and she carried on like a maiden before festival night. I could not get the grin off her face. And I dared not shout at her, Zuri, this monster is going to kill you without the most impossible luck, he won't do it gently and we will have to stand and watch! All she would say was, "We'll take care of it."

She did have instructions for the rest of us. We were to stay absolutely clear of the fight, and we were to remain hair-triggered for the slightest chance at the main target; because whatever happened elsewhere, the keys were what mattered most.

"Miss those and the whole thing's a waste."

She told me that; with those spring-snow gray eyes alight, actually alight. I have never, ever seen Zuri animated. I cannot remember seeing her look happy, in the length of my life.

"Doesn't matter how you do it. Insult, tease, wave your boobs at 'em, bash 'em if they're inside, pick a pocket through the bars. Mark the key-carrier the minute they come down, and don't take your eyes off him. No matter what I do."

That last, she aimed at Sarth. Who stared back at her, topaz eyes smoldering, that tower aplomb straining at the edges, beginning to look a killer at last.

She choreographed us too; Navy and troublecrew nearest the door, Keraz and I farthest back. I have seldom felt so useless, but Zuri only shook her head. "Brains and boobs," she said, and grinned. Nor have I heard her be so crude. "You're the brains, Ruand. Keraz is the tender spot." Though in face and complexion a copy of Darthis, Keraz does actually have more bosom than most of us. "Keep 'em both out of reach."

I understand now why troublecrew wear those solid breastbands, and why they claim to fear hand-to-hand work less than a man. The Mother knows, I have seen Zuri fight before; yet when I let myself think of the ground, so unhelpful to the lighter combatant, the chains she wore, so easy for a stronger foe to grab, the dicta I had overheard troublecrew rehearse for years, that fighting a man you must never come to close quarters, never let yourself be grabbed. When I considered what must be her opponent's experience in such battery . . .

I will confess it, Tanekhet. I did not only fear; I cursed. I blasphemed the Mother, and most of all I damned the qherrique, that had got us into this viper-pit and would not get us out. If I live, I remember vowing, there will be such a reckoning as will make you long for the questions and indictments you have drawn from Sarth.

How long until watch-end? At most, a couple of hours from the original clash. As Zuri said, after Alkhes . . . left. Long enough. Bless the Mother, at least, that I had no time to wonder what might be happening up in the tyrant's palace, in some silken-sheeted bed, on some barbaric Heartland animal-skin rug. I had to focus my own wits on shucking off the stench of mud and mildew and human filth and death and excrement, and getting the best vantage point to watch the stairfoot; and the men who would emerge beyond the bars.

The pair left on watch had, again most unusually, withdrawn into the stairwell, so the sound was their one herald. Mutter, clatter, tramp. A great many, far too many booted feet. And the voices; a blood-hungry, brutal masculine crowd.

I think that is the one moment that I have truly, honestly regretted losing Amberlight.

Then they had debouched onto the patrol-way along the bars; five, ten, fifteen, twenty, near the entire jailcrew, grinning and jeering and pouring mouth-filth worse than ever before.

Zuri had choreographed the arrival too. She was lolling on the shelf, right opposite the door, with her feet on Deor's thigh and her head in Keraz' lap. When the uproar reached crescendo, she looked round and yawned. Then she patted Keraz' cheek, lifted herself on an elbow and drawled, "Oh. You're here."

If her opponent ever had battle-skills, they were not based in subtlety; I suspect, thinking back, that he had relied on brute force all his life. He sneered and shouted something about her girlie-sluts, but his cheekbones had darkened, even by the murky torch-glow. He yelled again, and gestured to the man beside him to open the bars.

Zuri swung herself languidly upright. Stretched, showing the line of her breasts through a once immaculate shirt. The mere sight of a woman moving like a woman was enough to set the jackals off; Zuri grinned and said, "Well, big boy. Coming in?"

He growled at her. She moved forward, and we shifted behind her, Keraz sliding down the shelf to me, Quiran and Herar close next to us, Deor and Sunya beyond, Sarth and Ahio on the other side, Azo right at Zuri's back. The cell was all of ten paces across, perhaps thirty long. Zuri took three steps forward and posed with shoulders back, breasts out, pelvis thrusting, one hand on a hip. I never saw anything less like troublecrew ready-stance in my life.

Whatever else he recognized he must have known that. His face congested and he shouted at the farthest minions to bring the torches up.

Zuri grinned at him again. The bars groaned open; he stepped inside. The key-bearer was right beside the door. He made to shut it, and Zuri looked past the monster and drawled, "Think he'll be safe?"

They both turned purple. Then the monster made one furious gesture behind him, the key-bearer flung the gate wide and stood straddle-legged in the gap.

And the monster charged.

He was damnably fast; Zuri had been looking past him and I nearly screamed at what I thought a fatal lapse. He was on her before I had my breath and he grabbed her, landing on her, hands slapping for her throat as they went full length in the mud.

I did not see what happened. I doubt anyone saw. A thrash of limbs and torsos and flying mud in a tangle of heavy cross-laced boots, leather trousers tough as armor, leather belly-support, huge heaving glistening back, Zuri completely out of sight. Sarth on tiptoe with murder unveiled in his face, Deor and Sunya focused like guns to fire.

Azo with a knee between the giant's shoulderblades and the manacle-bight brought down twisted and rigid as a bludgeon across his neck.

The monster's body sagged. Then it convulsed.

Zuri came uppermost on his lunges, tucked closer than a leopard in the disemboweling clutch. No face, no hands, a mere line of tucked-in head and arched straining back. He reared over face-up in the mud, and he was making noises I never heard come out a human mouth. Azo leapt aside and in again and the sound went up an octave. He thrashed like a crippled bull and for an instant the torchlight showed me his face.

She had gouged both his eyes out. Then I can only imagine that she must have . . . bitten off his nose. His hands had missed her throat and caught her manacles and he was trying to pull her off him but she had a loop round his bicep so that every heave dragged her closer.

And her head—her teeth—were in his throat.

I don't know what Azo did. Something to his privates, something involving another twist of chain, probably, I think now, just a distraction, or something to pin him so he could not roll Zuri back underneath and still crush her to death. His torso bucked, his legs beat like a monstrous toddler's, but Azo's grip was more than he could fight.

I did not think you could find a vital vein or artery in such a monstrous throat; not with human teeth. Really, they tell me, it is not the opening that matters, it is the pressure. On the brain-feeding arteries, which was where Zuri's hands were. Hands hard as iron from years of unarmed combat, far stronger than most men's, let alone most women's grip. She only used her teeth to be sure he could not throw her off.

The monstrous body fell back. Zuri came up off him on one elbow like a cobra, and smashed the other across the front of his unprotected throat.

She jerked the chains free, then. She still had a knee in his solar plexus. He was thrashing, spasming in near disabled agony, the great hands grabbed; she twisted clear and came upright on the lunge, and kicked him. Twisting to put the whole force of her body behind it, driving her foot edge-on right up under the chin.

The head flew back for all its size. There was a hideous clicking crunch.

The body thrashed again, but this time it was a purely muscular reflex. Zuri stood away. The great limbs trembled and quivered into subsidence, and the foul air suddenly brought me a new, sharper stench.

I remember my mouth was wide open, my throat dry, my heart pounding as if to burst me, every muscle aquake; I had not drawn breath when Sarth's arm plucked the key-bearer from the gateway and smashed his head into the bars while Ahio ripped the keys out of his hand, snap!

Something else snapped too. As Sarth dropped the suddenly limp body and dusted his hands together Ahio threw the keys clear across the cell.

I caught them; it is the marvel of my life, Tanekhet. I caught them, just like that. Slap of greasy revoltingly warm iron and rattle of thirty separate hafts stinging on my fingers, and not a moment to think.

Sarth was almost out the gate. Azo and Zuri understood, Herar understood too, for a sudden male hand wrenched me from the shelf and as Keraz landed beside me Zuri and Azo swept straight out the doorway, two mud and blood-stained furies bearing down on the jackals, who had not yet absorbed their champion's fall.

Sarth went with them; I had one glimpse of his shoulders, the thrust of a charging lion. Deor and Sunya pushed Ahio aside and threw themselves after. I heard the noise Sunya made. A leopard's coughing snarl. Herar was shoving us forward, Quiran and Chenath right behind, I twisted the keys underhand the way Zuri herself had once shown me and struck with the protruding wards at some belated jackal's face.

When the metal slashed his knuckles he squealed and fell back. Deft, solid Deor crossed before me, swinging chain like a broken cable, and the three men our side the gate broke and ran.

In the midst of literal murder, Zuri must have noticed that. She shouted something, and my husband, my gently bred Tower-man, flowed like running death up the steps.

Zuri and Azo had the others yarded behind a tumble of fallen shapes; all three troublecrew had struck to kill, and the Navy women had not been behind. Sliding round to the stair-side, Zuri waved her hands. She did it quite gently; but the grin on her bloodied lips would have terrified a war-god, and the jackals pissed themselves trying to get inside the bars.

She yanked the door to and pulled the keys away from me. I was there when she wanted them, I must have had the brains for that. The gate shut with a swing-bar, a latch and padlock. Azo thrust a loop of chain over the latch, lest any of them try to storm it while Zuri sorted the key out. But she had watched the process too often to mistake.

We were all gasping, wheezing, panting, eyes bulging from muddied, bloodied faces, the bloodlust staring in our eyes, whether we had killed or not. My House-folk. My Trouble-head, right beside me, stinking and shuddering and wheezing like a rowing-slave, but with the terrible grin, at last, fading off her face.

"Zuri . . .?"

I could just hear myself, but her eyes turned. Amid the muck, they recognized me. She grinned again; a different grin, the twisted, acknowledging survivor's grin that was, in its own way, an accolade.

I put my arms around her and she fell against me, and it was only Azo's clutch that kept us out of the mud.

Sarth was there when we straightened up. Breathing hard too, but without the look of a wakened sleeper like the rest of us. He nodded to Zuri; coolly, once.

Zuri nodded too. Took a long breath, and started moving us toward the steps.

Behind us, the jackals had also revived. Overtaken events. A solitary voice bawled, "You bloody, cheating *bitch!*"

A chorus overrode it. They slammed themselves against the bars and howled like very beasts.

Zuri wheeled and stalked back; instant hush. She grinned, showing them her bloodied teeth.

"What, did you think we'd fight *fair?*"

With the indescribable contempt of Amberlight troublecrew, who trained to fight women as dangerous as themselves and men much larger, their entire lives.

It came out hoarse; now I looked, I could see, under the mud, that there actually were marks on her throat. He must have got one hold at least, and how she ever got it off . . . Perhaps that was when she gouged his eyes.

She swept that stare past them, and her lip lifted again, savagely as Wonsa's own. Then she grinned once more, somewhere between a jeer and that berserker's smile, and lifted a hand to the supine corpse.

"You did," she said, "know how to fall."

* * *

The first thing we understood, after Zuri herded us up into stench-free, intoxicatingly open air, was the dark. I do not know why we had not expected night; I suppose watch-changes meant so little, down in the pit. So we were all gawping like off-work miners in the entryway when Zuri tweaked the keys from me and began trying the nearest doors.

Hunting smith's tools to get off our chains. She had noticed where they were taken; troublecrew cunning, troublecrew wits.

I was still staring into the starry dome that opened over us, still reading off the beloved reclaimed constellations and identifying a third quarter, before the late-rising moon, still savoring the scent of Cataract suppers that floated over the citadel wall, thoroughly dubious meats thick with fiery spice, still orienting myself to the citadel space. That light-riddled shape to the left was the back of the central hall, the garrison, and perhaps the honor-guard at dinner, was the rumor within. The shadow to our right, behind the jail-adit . . .

Was moving. Azo whipped in front of me, Sarth shoved me back and I felt his side vibrate to a silent growl. Zuri yanked the nearest non-combatant back. Stopped dead. Produced a thread of whisper.

"Alkhes?"

He came out of the dimness like a half-embodied ghost; drifting with the silence of troublecrew, slow and mindless as a sleepwalker, a white blur of face blotted by the chasm of eyes, the night-swallowing fall of hair. He had his hands up and out like the ancient statues of an offering-bearer, and for an instant all of us recoiled. It had come too pat, too eerily; for an instant I really did think he was the revenant of a man already dead.

Then Ahio made a grunt that Sunya strangled in her throat and Sarth hissed and snatched.

He stood meek as a sleepwalker in Sarth's grasp. A chink in the hall-back threw a renegade shaft of light that drowned in those black, blind, unblinking eyes. Sarth caught his breath and shook him and the light flicked what was in the outheld hands.

Ahio captured it, motion quick and involuntary as Sarth's; cupped it, as we held them in the shaper's shops. No mistaking the upright triangle of skirts lifting to the narrow waist, the inverted triangle of upper torso and lifted arms and atop that, the open triangle of the helical thunderbolts. Gray and glistening as solidified mist, a fore-arm, half an armslength high.

A nation-leader's statuette.

Zuri drew an audible breath and spun on her toes. Azo and Sunya and Deor revolved with her, it was no harder for me to guess her thoughts. Here we were havering atop a jail-break, still too hobbled to run, stuck in the citadel's heart, no idea of patrols, routines, guards. Or the state of the tyrant himself.

Beside me Sarth was touching, handling as gently as if he held another statuette. I heard him say, just under his breath, "Aglis?"

Alkhes did not reply. But I saw the shadow shift, as he took the half-step forward and buried his head against Sarth's chest.

Zuri said something as inaudible and wrenched at the keys.

Eventually she found the door. Bless the Mother, pincers make far less noise than hammers, and Chenath and Herar had muscles as well as wits, to give the troublecrew help. But I knew what, above all, Zuri would want. The minute she finished with me I groped over and slid my own hand up Alkhes' back.

"Caissyl?"

He moved a little; a soundless: I hear. By no means, It's all right. But we could not delay any longer. I said against his ear, "Wonsa . . . is he . . .?"

He lifted his head from Sarth's protection and spoke aloud at last, a voice as numb, as empty as those eyes.

"He'll be no problem to us."

I had no time. No, I did not dare ask any more. And Ahio was at my elbow, all but vibrating, prodding on breath's edge, "Ruand?"

Two lunacies had succeeded. Why not the third? I felt inside my shirt for the little, hoarded, still half-decent pouch.

The seed was warm in my palm. I cupped it, and reached for the statuette.

Then I spoke as I never addressed the qherrique in the length of my life, Tanekhet. Come on, I said, you treacherous whoring bastard, if you want me to go on with this . . . prove it now.

Nothing changed.

I had time to ease out the over-held breath. Time to re-draw it for obscenities that would have scalded a devil's ears; the true blow had not fallen when Esrafal on Ahio's other side jumped as if pinched and burst out, "Sing what?"

Before our mouths shut she spluttered again; then gulped and muttered, "Sing, Ruand. All of you, sing."

She hummed a note and tapped a chain against its links, and sang what was undoubtedly the first thing into her head, an ancient Amberlight plainsong used to invoke River-rise.

I could feel Zuri gaping too. To sing qherrique is the cutter's or shaper's avocation; private, utterly personal, never done except by a single woman, seeking that one specific assent. Esrafal flapped her hands at us, reached a line's end, and fairly spat out, "Sing!"

We sang; or muttered, trying to keep it under our breaths, half of us missing words and most of us off the tune, but even the men's deeper mumbles rumbled underneath.

The seed burned up, waking, rising, a miniature moon that dyed my fingers like candlelit wine. I jiggled it one-handed as the most arrant imbecile, wanting to howl, What next?

What except set it, like a coal to wood, against the statuette?

And it happened; I felt it happen, the way you used to feel it, working a block in the shaper's shop. The light's advent, the glow strengthening, the heatless, moonburn, holy fire.

The shadows came out around our feet as if we were standing stones with a moonrise inside. Far whiter, far purer, far steadier than any fire or candle, a beacon of the impossible raised in a scarecrow congregation's midst. I had time to see the eyes, the parted, worshipful lips. Before I gave Zuri a frantic glance, and she threw an eye at the hall, then down the hill, and jerked her chin. And I started to walk.

Crisis or not, trust Zuri to be devious. She had pointed me toward the citadel's northern wall, the quickest way across the city toward Upriver. The cataracts. The Jump-up Cliffs.

By some miracle, the palace had no outer patrols. The darkness parted round us like the bow-wave of a ship, and by some other uncovenanted miracle the citadel's internal traffic was quiet; I can only suppose they had all gone to eat. We marched along the blank palace wall, I was never so glad for Cataract's building style; the wall turned, the hill sloped down to lighter dark. A hand gripped my elbow and pulled me up.

"That." Alkhes said, his eyes blacker than ever as they caught the qherrique light, the hair a night-shroud over them, and the expression blank as its dark. "That first."

He was pointing at the palace. When I stared, he shook my arm as if I ought to understand. The eyes kindled then; a conflagration in some unfathomable inner space.

"Burn it," he said.

I thought I knew what he meant. I thought I understood, too well, the note on which he added, "He deserves that much."

The palace was timber above the plinth. A risk, yes, but as much of a diversion. Zuri's expression told me that.

I had never, will you credit, actually 'used', for want of a better word, a statuette. How do rulers apply them, I wonder? Do they look outward, or in? Do they ask assent, as at the mother-face, or commune as with the block, or point the things like guns and aim?

I was painfully prosaic; I turned its face to the palace, and concentrated on the thunderbolts.

Probably anything would have done. But the assent surged through me as it does with a big light-gun, and like a light-gun, the thunderbolts fired.

Crossed beams, thin and slicing as the deadliest of swords, converged at the point I had chosen, high in the timber wall. Biting deep, and deeper, until the smoke came, and then the blackening, and then the gout of crimson, stabbing flame.

Beside me Alkhes said, "Again."

Five blazes he had me kindle, and I still do not know why the guards did not pour out like prodded wasps. I do not ask you to believe it, Tanekhet, but believe this. We were half-down the slope, me with the statuette's beacon dragging our scarecrow comet-tail, before the wall ahead rang to the first appalled shout.

I think they took it for a demon, or a visiting god, or just a particularly venomous ghost. I do know I was never more glad for the superstition of most Heartland folk; for the four sentries ran like hares, just as we heard the hilltop buildings raise the alarm.

Zuri was at my elbow; the qherrique caught the beast's savagery in her eyes. She jerked her chin at the wall and bade me as she would her own troublecrew, "Get it down."

Solid cedar trunks, planted who knows how deep? The rest of us weaponless, murder woken behind. I aimed the statuette and gave it Zuri's order, with a waking savagery of my own. Break it, I said, and I remembered how the hill blew up at Amberlight. Blow it away.

And it did.

That time it was raw power, a blast that nearly kicked the statuette out of my hands. It lit the compound like a lightning flash, and it blew three full-grown cedar trunks to splinters the way a smith's hammer pulverizes a tooth.

There was, amazingly, almost no sound. So we could tramp quite calmly through the breach, for Zuri to slide away ahead of us, with an upward glance that told me she was going to blind-stab by the stars, while Azo and Sunya and Deor dropped back, each nursing a handful of shucked chains, to cover our backs.

I doubt any of us had time to reel at the portent we had wrought. We were too busy breaking our shins in the abominably rutted alleyways and straining to keep Zuri in sight, and in my case, worrying about Alkhes. The mere fact that Sarth had not gone with Zuri told me the condition he must be in.

And we were lucky, too, that the citadel folk entangled themselves in the fire, so it must have been some time till the routed sentinels even made themselves heard; long enough to take us half across the city, before the hounds marked our trail.

I heard Ahio grunt as she grabbed my arm to avoid the consequences of another rut; carrying the statuette I was all but blind. Then her arm stiffened, and above the nearby cursing and panting I too caught the clangor of beaten gongs and ululating Heartland wails that fountained from the citadel. Taken up ahead, as the city wall sounded the alarm.

Zuri stopped with a particularly pungent curse. Her eyes met mine; Trouble-head's consultation, brief as it was perfunctory. I nodded, and she dived back into the dark.

Our one best chance to get clear unhampered; make for the wall and hope, again, to blast our way out.

* * *

Whatever else he was, Wonsa had been an efficient as well as a new tyrant; he chose officers with both loyalty and wits. They could no sooner have found the citadel breach than they took our aim, and no sooner took it than they had detachments pelting down our trail and the wall ringing to cacophonies of alarm.

When the sound rose behind us, the bay of warriors on a hot trail, Zuri swung round to me; a mud-dark shadow like a stray leopard in an alley-mouth. Stop here, said the glitter in her eyes. Turn around and teach them, once and for all. Give them the fire.

Thought is faster than anything but qherrique. There was time to share that blood-lust, festered through so many indignities; and time to remember the audience hall, the spearmen writhing, limbs and livelihood seared away, eyes burnt out, dying.

I jerked my chin. Go on.

Her eyes blazed. There was time to wonder if it was Trouble-head tactics or killer's protest, before she slid around and ran.

We reached the wall unhindered, if not unmarked; I could hear it as we stumbled along, the qherrique lighting alley-walls like an endless lightning flash, to the bow-wave of slamming shutters above our heads. The city knew we were here, and whatever we were, they wanted nothing to do with us.

There is another glacis behind the wall. We emerged to find the sentry-walk alive with torches and reinforcements prancing like agitated cats, and the qherrique's appearance raised an uproar that would have signaled our position beyond doubt.

Zuri swung back on me, teeth baring now, a look that said, Can we run this time? The men on the wall danced and pointed and yowled all together, so like a convocation of cowardly dogs that I almost laughed. Then Sarth beside me said sharply, "Tellurith!"

In that escalading madness, the one sane voice. I could not touch him, I had both hands full of . . . light? Hope? Death? I did splutter, "Alkhes . . .?"

"He's all right. Tellurith?"

Are *you* all right? Or have you been sucked into this frenzy as well?

Someone pulled a veil off my brain. Of a sudden I was back in River Quarter, looking out a gutted warehouse wall onto great beams of light-gun fire sweeping the River, with Averion's voice an ice-slide in my memory: Be prepared to disengage.

I lifted my voice and said with only a few gasps, "Never mind the men. I'll cut down the wall."

Zuri heard me; it woke her, for I saw the berserker's grimace fade. She nodded and turned to settle what passed for our battle array.

I leveled the statuette, and started forward, and in my mind I pictured a light-gun beam, spread horizontally like a chisel of light, for a span of perhaps twenty feet, just above the ground.

The wall-wards hullooed with terror rather than bravado. If there had been slingers with any nerve we might well have died before we crossed, but if there were slingers, the sight of the qherrique was more than their aim could bear. We bore down on the wall unhindered until, less than twenty feet away, the light-beam bit.

This time the timber crumpled rather than disintegrated, as the beam cut through like a hot knife in cheese. The sentry-walk buckled, sagged and ripped apart and its occupants screamed and jumped or fell or ran for their lives as one, two, three solid cedars bowed majestically outward and the partitions between them collapsed in a great cloud of flying dust.

There was an almighty tangle of subsidiary timber and frantic humans everywhere, including the base of an overturned catapult, but the trace-hounds, who might have engaged us hand-to-hand, were just too far behind. We marched out as solemnly as a Dhasdeini engineering company behind its battering ram, through the entanglements of the breach and into the welcoming dark.

* * *

Almost instantly Zuri made me douse the statuette. I remember struggling to stow the seed while trying to decide how to carry the statuette itself, against a background of Zuri cursing our troop away to the right, stumbling and grunting in a maze of bean-trellises and potato furrows and the boulder-cumbersome exigencies of a well-fruited pumpkin patch. Cataract grows its greenstuffs close about the walls, on the rich River silt.

I understood vaguely that we had veered off our now predictable northern line and away from the River, the way we might be expected to break. I heard with equal vagueness the city tumult behind us, its military folk seething like outraged ants. I do recall, after I got the seed pouched, and Ahio commandeered the statuette to cradle in the remnants of her shirt, that I looked up into the infinity, the blessed largesse of open sky. And saw the Reaper, the great white summer star, rising eastward behind the Hunter in his jeweled belt, and identified the deeper darkness beneath him as trees; before the thick scratchy refuge of their foliage closed round us and Zuri panted, "Stop."

We dropped in our tracks; I remember that. And the feel of a trunk against my back, and the renewed awareness of jail-pit filth and stench and the passionate desire for a bath, the tally of bruises and scrapes and a raging thirst. With them came the sub-anxieties of flight; direction, transport, supplies, fresh clothes. Awareness that we might have escaped, but we were afoot and weaponless in Cataract's back yard, with neither provisions nor guidance for the obstacle that loomed so close ahead.

The cataracts. The Jump-up Cliffs.

I thought about that, when my mind insisted on seeing a larger view. I did not, I would not think about the questions that had opened behind us. The greatest one, least of all.

If it did not help us, was it because it could not or it would not, Tanekhet?

And was what happened with the statuette the work of the new qherrique, or a last shadow from the old?

Worst of all; if we could no longer trust it, or respect it, what was the point in going on?

* * *

Zuri, the Mother look upon her, still had the momentum of escape. In spaces of attention I heard her allotting this and tallying that, setting guards, planning all the necessities I could not face myself. Far more clearly I felt, at my other side, the silence, the entire absence that was Alkhes.

And with him, Sarth.

I will admit, Tanekhet, that what questions Sarth might raise made my very spirit quail. I was still cowering when Zuri slid down beside me to whisper hoarsely, "Ruand, we've spelled long as we can. We can head upRiver till daylight and then go to ground. Sunya and Deor are foraging; Ahio'll blot our trail. We can get clean later. Plenty of farmsteads close to Cataract, we can steal new clothes."

And weapons. To replace the irreplaceable we had left.

I tucked my legs under me. With the loss of action's drug, every muscle was solid lead. "All right," I mumbled. "I'm sorry, Zuri, I'm so slow . . . but you've done well."

Beside me, Alkhes said, "No."

He had stood up; I could tell from the voice's source. He was staring back the way we had come. Over the low blur of vegetable fields to that blot of darkness limned in patrol torches, under its lurid corona of flame.

Zuri said, "Huh?"

I thought I understood; and scourged myself, who had stopped thinking beyond the blood and fisticuffs, who had forgotten the very priorities I once enforced on him. Cataract. Whoever died, whatever turmoil ensued, the city would survive. And with it, a vendetta. And now as then, whether we escaped or not, that vendetta would recoil on those we left behind.

I think I heard Zuri groan. I did feel my own heart sink, as if someone had just weighted my back with one more impossible load.

"Oh, caissyl. Oh, Mother. Well, I suppose . . ."

He was still staring out at Cataract. As if I had not spoken, he said, "It was; it *is* his city. I won't let them throw it away."

I heard what he had said, then. And if I did not understand, I did realize as much.

Very carefully, very quietly, I said, "Caissyl . . . could you explain?"

More quietly, Sarth added, "Sit down, Aglis. Here. Now."

He obeyed that voice, as he must have obeyed it, sleepwalking out of the city, folding himself up, neatly as a child, in the crook of Sarth's arm. But his attention never shifted. Not even when I murmured to Zuri, "Move the others back," and then slid closer, so he was lapped in both our arms. Before I said, feeling as if I would waken some more terrible qherrique, "Go on, caissyl. We're listening."

* * *

It took him a minute or two to collect himself; I felt him breathe in the dark, three or four long, steadying inhalations. Before he started to speak.

They had struck off the chains in the citadel ward; mid-afternoon, full dazzling light. In the yard among their quarters, with a detachment of soldiers as surety, they had made him strip, given him a bucket of River water and a scrubbing brush and bade him clean up; for what cause, they were all too explicitly clear.

"I didn't—care—all that much." He meant the jail-crew's stares and taunts. His voice was breathy, broken, but now with a bone-deep, aftermath weariness. "I knew already . . . what it meant."

If the clean-up did not extend to a shave, they gave him some sort of short overrobe. Before they bound his arms behind him, at the elbows, Cataract style, and the soldiers marched him into the palace itself.

"I can't remember a thing about—where we went." I felt his ribs shift against my arm with the quicker, shakier breath. "I was just—trying to—trying not to—the thing I was most terrified of wasn't—it was that I'd—"

That he would fall out of the world. As he nearly did with you that day in Riversend, Tanekhet. As he would do when his mind could not bear any more reality, and involuntarily, uncontrollably, wiped it out.

And in Cataract, it was the one flight he could not make.

I have thought of that often, Tanekhet. I am not sure I can forgive the vice; the injustice, of whatever it was that sent us up the River, and deserted us in that prison, and left Alkhes, of all people, to bear that final, cruelest demand of all.

The march ended in some large inner room. "Living quarters. I think. There were rugs—I remember rugs, like they hang in the Heartland—on the wall. I can see that . . . clay-red, yellow and green patterns—zigzags, spearheads—" his voice wavered again, and we did not try to draw him from the refuge of detail to what waited beyond.

"There were people—quite a few people. . . I couldn't see them, I don't think I saw much at all. Voices . . . maybe ten." Trying now, with an intelligencer's deep-burnt reflex, to recall the details a spymaster would need. Fighting off, as he had fought off then, the knowledge of what those voices implied.

"Then I heard—him."

Sarth's arm tightened, for I felt it. But he did not speak.

Wonsa had sent the soldiers off, he remembered that. And before they left, one of them produced a rope from somewhere, and with the others' spears as deterrent, bound his feet.

"Wonsa was saying something about not so stupid—been at Amberlight." Doubtless word of Zuri's footwork, that first day in our cell, had filtered up. "I remember, falling over—was what worried me most."

As you use toothache to shade out an amputation's pain. He took another long, effortful breath.

"Then he must have walked over. He spoke to me, up close.

"'Welcome,' he said, 'General. It cools my heart to see you here. Trussed like a chicken for the pot. Let me tell you, we have quite a way with chickens in Cataract.'"

I felt every muscle shudder as he fought, hard as he must have in that moment, for control.

"I had my eyes shut. I thought, if I can't see I won't know if it, if it happens, if I can just think about something else . . . So I bit my lip, I kept thinking, if I can just concentrate on that, maybe I won't, won't—"

Sarth shifted closer. Under my arm, I could feel Alkhes' side and back, the light cloth dampening with sweat.

"H-he must have come up close . . ."

He broke off, drawing, catching, releasing another ragged, effortful breath.

"And I—And I—"

He could not have blacked out. I knew that already, but I had no idea of the rest; or of what I could do to salve it. Except hold him tighter, until he half-turned, groping, catching my hand.

"Then—it was like, like somebody else talking. Somebody entirely different.

"He said, 'Who did this?'"

He drew another huge, shivering breath.

"I didn't—I couldn't listen. The one thing in my head was, if I only bite hard enough, feeling that will keep me here, I won't notice the rest . . .

"But he must have—sent them away. I can remember the noise . . . A wooden floor. Because I heard the boots. And I heard him walk back.

"Then he said, 'Assandar.'"

His hand turned in mine, and the nails almost went through my palm.

"I can't tell—I can't explain—the way he said that. As if it was—as if my name was something he'd been keeping—like the loot they'll steal in a sack. Precious things—but not for the wealth. For what they mean in themselves—for the way they've been kept.

"Then he said, 'Look at me.'"

Beyond him, I felt Sarth twitch. And Alkhes shift to lay a hand on him, some understanding they alone could share.

"And I've always—whatever else I did, Tel, I've always—looked things in the face."

So he opened his eyes, and looked at Wonsa too.

"I don't—didn't know what had happened. But he looked—he even *looked* like somebody else.

"And something happened then. I could tell. Even though he—I—neither of us moved. I didn't—I had no idea what it meant."

He quivered a little, another long, faltering breath.

"But he put out his hand . . ."

Very slowly, as to the wildest of jungle creatures; touching, at last, with a single finger; to Alkhes' lower lip.

"It was the blood. I must have bitten right through, I never felt—He took his hand away, and looked at it. Just a little smear. I was—too gone to care. But he looked up at me, and he said—he said . . ."

He stopped again, filling his lungs, as for some giant leap.

"'You,' he said. 'Assandar. Witless as a deer in a trap. Because some man is going to come near you. Did That Woman do this?'"

His hand clenched on mine, silencing hurt along with wrath.

"I was so angry I said it straight out at him. I said, 'I was raped.'"

He turned his hand once more to contain mine, as if he remembered now whose it was, and I felt the shock's aftershock, and with it a double bewilderment.

"And he—Tel, it stopped him like That. Then he seemed to—get bigger all over. And then he said—so quiet, it was like drawing a knife. 'I will cut off their members and stake them out on an ant-bed. Just tell me which.'

"He must have thought it was down—that it happened here. I—the whole thing was so crazy, it was almost worse than—it was like some sort of spell. I was so—lost—I just answered, like he was a truth-seer. 'It was in Amberlight.'"

He swallowed and shook his head.

"He—It was like something threw his bearings too. He didn't say anything. But then . . .

"He got uncomfortable. Not moving. But I could tell. He looked at the ground, and then he braced himself. And then he said—he said—

"'That night in the parade-tent. It was a mistake.'"

This, I could tell, he had by heart from pure shock.

"'I did not understand,' he said, 'how it is between men in Dhasdein. In the Heartlands it would all have been by custom—right. I would have set down my sleeping skin and hung my spears at your gate. I would have gifted you my kill, and made songs in your praise. And you would have told me, clearly, properly. Yes. Or, No.'

"Tel, I couldn't say a word. The last thing I expected—that I ever dreamt of—was that.

"'But I had to stand, and be silent, and watch those others, those fat Dhasdeinis, those Verraini—*blacks*—speak to you, sit by you, *touching* you—I was a Cataract underling. I had no voice in council, not the right to speak your name . . . In the parade-tent, I got drunk, it made me silly as a little boy. I could not wait to find a mannerly way. So I grabbed you—spoke stupidly—And all I managed was demotion. Dinda wanted to appease the General; I could not come to council again. And you—'

"Will you believe, Tel—he didn't blame me. But I understood— I remembered—And I was so *ashamed*.

"He knew what I felt. He gave this shrug, and a little shake of his head, and it was like there'd been some mix-up with Catheor, someone I'd served with, known for years."

He stopped short. His head went down on his knee, and he said, muffled, half-strangled, "If it had happened some other way—if we'd met elsewhere—if I wasn't who I am—we could have been *friends*—"

It was Sarth who held him closer, and rubbed a hand up his back. But he still had hold of my hand, as if it were a lifeline. When he lifted his head again, it was to me he spoke.

"I was beyond . . . He came round beside me. Took my hand," I felt his own hand tremble. "Spread the fingers, ran his own across the palm . . . almost the way he first said, 'Assandar.' He said, 'I would watch you touch things—maps, the table edge, your sword, her coat—I longed to do this. So quick, so fine, so nervous. Like a Kawashi gazelle.'

"Then he let me go. And he said, 'I have had no dreams.'

"He's—he was—so quick, Tel. Like you. He'd worked out why I came. He knew what I—expected. He wanted to make it short. Maybe, by that time, even save me something . . .

"I c-couldn't answer. There'd been too many—shocks—and the plan was looking—I didn't know if I could do it at all." The anguish was raw in his voice.

"He must have seen that too. He touched me again. Just the back of his fingers, over the heart.

"'Semba,' he said."

I know the word now. In the Heartlands, it means, Lion. Young, small lion.

"He didn't really understand. He just thought he'd given me a knock-down and I wouldn't give up. I was—I was past thinking. But he walked round to face me. And I said, 'Neither have we.'

"That did surprise him. But he knew what it meant, Tel. For us—for me.

"'You still want me to listen,' he said.'"

He dropped his head back on his knee; now his voice was more than raw.

"And I—I had to say, 'Yes'—and *know* how he would take it— and know what was hidden under *that*—oh, Gods, I don't think I'll ever be clean again . . ."

Presently his breathing steadied; but he did not lift his head.

"He put his hands on my shoulders, and then he really looked at me. And after a while he said—he said—'You have found a man who does not make you scared.'

"I was past getting upset. I just said, 'Yes. I think I have.'"

Sarth leant across, drew his face up, and kissed him. Gently, lovingly, as for a sacrament.

"I—we both understood what that meant, too.

"So he gave me this funny little smile. And he said, 'Then I will ask no more than you came prepared to give. Lie with me, Semba. And then I will listen to you.'"

I felt Sarth, too, catch his breath as if he had been hit in the wind.

"No. I didn't pass out. We both knew it was—what I'd been ready to—But I couldn't—I just couldn't—*do* it so, so . . .

"When I didn't answer straight away, he put his hand on me. On my chest. Very gently. He said, 'I will not hurt you. I pledge it on my name. I will not hurt a hair of your head.'

"Oh, yes . . ." He sounded halfway between the laughter of distress and outright tears. "He misread that too. He patted me, and then he let me go. And stood back. And waited. And I—"

He took another huge, shaking breath. "I thought, This is what I expected. I thought it would be far worse than—I *will* have to do far worse—

"But Gods, the worst of it was that he wasn't vicious. That you could tell—I could tell—it meant—it meant so much to him. It was something he'd dreamt about—and if he had to take this way to get it—he would compromise himself too."

He straightened up between us, and put one arm around my neck, the other round Sarth's. And spoke with the deliberation of an officer to a firing squad.

"So I said, 'Yes.'"

I could feel what he expected of me; jealousy, anger, outright abuse. It was Sarth who turned him about first, and embraced him, saying in the body's language, You are absolved. But he did not relax, and release another huge sigh, until I hugged him too.

I could have left it there; but the tension of his arms told me there was more. And in a moment or two, he began again.

"After that . . . it was worse. He didn't show much, but . . . Gods, Tel, I have never felt such a *worm*. He put his hand on my elbow. Not pawing. It was . . . It was—more like—*respect*. And then he said, and he was almost smiling, you know, playing serious? 'I can untie these now, perhaps, without you trying to kill me again?'"

Sarth hugged him roughly. He sighed and dropped his head, as if mortally fatigued now, against that sanctuary.

"He rubbed my arms where they'd gone numb. I would rather he'd beaten in my head. Then he took me into the sleeping room—it must have been the ruler's personal suite, there were all these th-things . . ." His voice cracked. "Clothes; armor; little things . . .

"And he was gentle. He knew how to . . . He hardly hurt me at all."

* * *

He was silent then for so long I heard the others move behind us, the draw of Zuri's wary, edgy, watchful breath. I saw the light change, on the distant hill of fire. And still, his muscles told me it was not done.

At last he drew another great sigh and lifted his head.

"Afterwards . . . He took me in his arm, the way—the way . . ."

For a minute his voice failed completely. The silence finished it. The way you have, both of you. In the time of secrets that is closer than flesh's intimacy, the time when you are not merely lovers but sharers of the soul.

"And he s-said, 'Now, Semba. I am listening.'"

He knuckled at his eyes.

"I did my best, Tel. I told him about Iskarda. I told him why we had to leave. That we meant no harm to him or anything of his, we just wanted to pass. I know I'm not good with words—but I did my best.

"And he listened. He did listen, it wasn't just for show. He heard me right out. Then he rolled up on his arm, so he could see my face. And nodded, and touched my cheek. *You've done well.* And then he said . . .

"'Semba, you are a brave man and a loyal spearblade, and for you this is heart's truth. But you are not of Cataract.'

"Then he told me about the mess when he—they got back. He put the rags of their army back together, Tel. A junior—a demoted junior officer, with fifty Heartland rabble, and he got it all under control, and he brought them clean upRiver, and then he took on the factions in the city itself. Dinda's tag-ends. His own traitors. Every clan that had made its officer a war-lord. He cut or bashed or frightened the hearts out of them. And he made himself ruler, and he got the city on its feet."

He paused for breath. It was with shock that I identified the note in his voice. It was more pride than respect.

"'Now you come here and say, Let us pass, Semba. But what will happen, if you reach your Source?'

"I . . . Tel, I didn't know what to say. He smiled at me, just a little, and he patted my cheek. 'You will come back downriver. You and your women, and your women's weapons. And what will happen, when you rebuild Amberlight?'

"We won't, I started to say. Haven't you seen that? He just shook his head.

"'Semba, it is happening already. Or what did you do downstream?'

"What could I say?

"'Already you have restored Amberlight. A new government, a new age, fuh. They will be powerful, and they are women. And when you come back, what will they be to Iskarda?'

"I tried to say it wouldn't be like that . . . He put his finger across my mouth.

"'You gave us back the timber fief, and still you do not see. We have nothing but the River, Semba. And on the River, the gain of Amberlight is the loss of Cataract.'

"He let go then. He was watching me. As close as you are . . . With such a look . . .

"'I could make this city live, Semba,' he said. 'I was downriver. I understand what is wrong. We are a poor folk, we have no resources but the silver. And that is only good to buy from someone else. We must make others spend with us.' He lay back down beside me, then, and he was—he was talking the way we have, he was talking as if—as if he'd needed to speak like this forever, as if nobody around him could understand.

"And I don't suppose anybody could. Because he spoke to me like I—like I could to Antastes. To a leader you can trust. More than that—as if I was, as if I was his—hero—the one you more than admire. The one you expect to understand your ideas. Your greatest hopes. And I was there to hear him, finally. In the flesh.

"'It is no use,' he said 'to export cedar. We must work it here. We must make the chests and carvings and the expensive furniture, even the ships. We have the slips, we could turn out more than war-galleys. If we had the craftsmen, we could keep their profit. And then we could grow.'

"'And so with the Heartland trade. We should not sell, we must *work* the ebony, and the ivory, and all the rest. If we had people to do that, here . . .'

"He got up on his elbow again, and he looked at me as if—as if—I was some sort of oracle.

"'If we had people for that, Semba . . . we could forget the flesh-trade. We could forget war. We could be a true city. Whole. Strong. At peace.'

"Then he remembered who else I was."

He stopped, struggling to steady his voice.

"I could see his eyes change. And he said to me, and he knew what he was saying:

"'I did not spend my kin and folk and people's blood, Semba, to bring back the city. And then to have it taken away.'"

He put his head against Sarth's shoulder, as he had in the citadel, as if, in memory, vision was still unbearable.

"He . . . knew what I felt. He took my face in his hands. Then he kissed me, and he said, 'Stay with me a while, Semba. Later, we will think what to do.'

"And then he put his arm around me—and he went to sleep."

His voice broke. His breathing caught, for one terrible moment I thought it was a seizure and clutched him like my last hope of life.

"And I c-could see his side of it—and I unders-stood, I respected him—and I knew, whatever he felt about me—he w-wouldn't let us go . . ."

He put his hands over mine around his waist, and buried his forehead against Sarth. And even our refuge was not enough.

"I tried to think . . . I asked for a sign—a message—anything—"

I could see him in that inner room, left beside a sleeping enemy, with no sign, human or unhuman, to show him the lesser betrayal. I could imagine the torture of that denial, the despair. I tightened my arms about him, the last, futile refuge, and waited for the end.

"It wouldn't . . . answer. Nothing . . . answered. I had to decide . . ."

The words were dying in his throat.

"And in the end . . . this had come first."

I had to go back, he said to me, when we met outside Amberlight during the siege. When I thought he had betrayed the city as well as me. *I'd made contracts, I had obligations. I couldn't betray them without betraying myself.*

"I put . . . put . . . We were so close . . . I put my hands . . . on the big arteries. It only took a mo-oment. I took the p-pillow and I held . . . h-held . . ."

Sarth cupped a hand around his head and pushed it tight against his own chest and Alkhes broke into a spasm of sobbing that all but tore him apart.

* * *

Eternities afterwards, the tempest began to subside. Sarth still held him, and rocked him, very slightly, as you do a grievously grieving child. I hugged him in my turn; but then the light shifted, and Zuri was bending over me.

"Ruand?"

"No trouble." She stilled my jump. Troublecrew speech, no carrying whisper but a murmur in her throat. "But the moon's up, and there's half a watch gone. If you think we could be going . . .?"

Alkhes pulled his head up, drew back and turned about in Sarth's embrace. Came to his knees, his feet, the moonlight I only now noticed catching the sheet-white face, the death-dark of his eyes.

"I am not going anywhere," he said it so quietly, "until I have a reason. And a justification. For a—for a brave man's murder, and a city's crippling and the—the dirtiest breach of faith I ever made. I won't move, until we have an answer. And proof that we should go on at all."

Sarth said, "Neither will I."

CHAPTER VII

Assuana
7th Day, 2nd Summer Moon

May the River-lord's Nine-Armed Adversary fly away with all arrogant, ignorant, hot-headed, self-opinionated girls!

* * *

Yes, you see my direction, Tellurith—if you ever lay eyes on this. And yes, I picture you tearing hair by handfuls, too. And yes, credit me with some intelligence, this gem of inspiration is not my own. And yes, you may wonder that I curse so openly before you. I do so, my lady Tellurith, because the genius was your heir.

I will admit it was the last thing I expected. We had sent a message, yes, on the Verrain envoy's heels: full copy, a careful carrier, in code. It was as vital to warn Marbleport as to ensure a back-up for Iskarda. And we appraised them of the plan, they needed time to raise people too. But if I had known!

That Tez would take a patrol boat and sail straight up the River, reaching Amberlight the very next day . . .

Ridiculous. That a man of my age, my seasoning, should walk into that paltry warehouse and have the mere sound of a voice turn my heart over, scatter my wits like the greenest boy's. That the sight of her head bent toward Dhanissa across the table should reduce me to a stammering oaf.

If I fell into the door jamb and over the barrel-staves, I did manage to get decently into a seat. To incline my head at Juiza, posted at Dhanissa's elbow like one of your own Trouble-heads. To nod at the cobbler, to Ferrias, ousted beyond Tez and straining to the central dialogue—or monologue, that Tez was conducting, with the crispness of a senior officer. A House-head whose decision is already made.

After all, she is your heir, Tellurith. In your absence, she does bear the real weight of Iskarda.

So I was prepared to listen, and contribute, however counter-feit my aplomb. To make suggestions, and manage matters to the best advantage—

Except that the moment I sat down she looked around, nod-ded as to some Riversend messenger boy and announced, "Lord Tanekhet, we're sending you to Verrain."

I did contest it. I did that immediately, as coolly as I ever crossed Antastes. "Lady Tez, that might not be the best immedi-ate choice."

'Lady' Tez. And she did not so much as blink.

"You're Dhasdeini. A great lord. Antastes' right hand. A su-preme intelligencer. If anyone can talk Shuya out of this, it's you."

"Lady—Tez. Listen—please." Can you believe I had to spell it out? "I may be all those things. But if one thing is wholly certain, it is that nobody—not the River-lord himself—will talk Shuya out of this."

"How do you know?"

I found myself glaring as at a refractory emperor. "As you say," I could hear the ice-edge, "I was twenty years Dhasdein's head of intelligence."

I never thought—I never expected—I never remembered she is not yet thirty years old. I saw the color come up, and her eyes turn to brown glass marbles. I understood then, too late.

"I mean that I know Shuya better than her Viceroys. Lady Tez, I never meant—" May the River-lord pity me, when have I been so clumsy as this?

She turned her shoulder on me. "You can't fight," she told Dhanissa. "and neither can we. Our only hope is to bluff her out and wait for—the Ruand to come back."

Crazy child: she meant, for some divine stroke of assistance from the qherrique.

"Lady Tez, delegates, waiting is our only course, I do assure you, but—"

She looked straight at me then. "Are you challenging my choice?"

I stood up and said, "Lady Tez, may we discuss this informally, before the Assembly meet?"

You will appreciate the tactics. If I stood up I was halfway to walking out: I had the initiative, the onus of resistance was on her. And if there was one thing I gambled she would understand, it was the imbecility of open schism, before an Assembly only half-loyal either to her or Iskarda.

Whatever the reason, she did follow me. Round the barrels into the booth of the shipper's office, the old record-place. Dust and broken-down furniture, Lord above, I remember thinking, can we never quarrel somewhere fitted decently?

"I would never challenge you." I was trying, with all my heart, to make the inflection truth. "I only ask you to reflect, before the decision is fixed."

"I told Dhanissa—"

"Yes, you 'told' Dhanissa. And she will listen. Will you do as much for me?"

I was between her and the door, but this time I was not so foolish as to—press. All I had was the weapons I have always used. Face, eyes, body, the wordless languages whose skills I learnt with Antastes.

"Are you afraid?"

"Afraid?" But if that was indeed a gambit, there was no time to accept. "For myself?" I let the other languages answer that too, with the most delicate inflection. Pure contempt.

Her brows came down hard. The umbrage thawed minutely, into concentration. "What is it, then?"

"It's a tactical error that wastes an early vantage, Lady Tez. Shuya has begun with diplomacy. That won't last forever. Don't send your negotiator to close quarters, then. Take all the time that trading envoys will give."

I heard the street-criers: the familiar voices of delegates behind me, the creak of the dusty scriveners' desk under her hand.

She said, "You can refer everything back to us."

The Adversary seize her wits. For simple delay it would work just as well.

She is not mean-spirited enough to relish such a petty triumph. But her eyes did hold a glint.

"And who will show you tactics to follow? What ploys are available? How will you use my knowledge of the River from Verrain?"

"Write it down."

I did throw my hands up then. "Do you think Verrain has also lost its intelligencers?"

"They won't know—"

"Whatever they don't know they will crack in a fortnight. If I can, their cipher-crew can. Do you *want* to signal Shuya everything?"

Her lips tightened. She tapped a fingernail on the desk corner and growled, "Which is?"

I laid it out as carefully and far more completely than I ever did for Antastes. Everything I have told you: Shuya's options, her anomalies, their possible reasons, the alternatives facing Amberlight. The straitened choices facing Iskarda.

"With Verrain hostile, what markets have you left?" We both knew there was nothing upstream. She opened her mouth and I shook my head. "And what price is there for protection from Antastes? The only chance—for Iskarda as for Amberlight—is to keep from open warfare as long as we possibly can."

"You've demanded we do other things."

"My lady, one does not sit hoping to survive on an enemy's charity."

Her mouth corner quirked. I think, despite herself. "How does all this prevent your going to Verrain?"

I took a deep breath. "You know who I am, lady Tez."

Her eyes held mine. Steady, opaque as the River in flood.

"Antastes knows quite well I will become your adviser. And he understands what that means."

"That you'll use for—us—everything you used to know—about Dhasdein."

"Indeed. But it is one thing to know me a—a mover behind the scenes—and another to see me, present, accredited—operating as an Amberlight envoy. In Verrain."

I held her eyes.

"And if *you* think a great lord, a supreme intelligencer, Antastes' right hand, could talk Shuya into anything—how do you think it will seem to Antastes?"

She let her breath out at last.

"So in trying to baulk Shuya, we might really open the bilge-cocks. We might alienate Dhasdein."

I nearly said, You're thinking at last. Thank Dhe.

"More than that."

"They might think you've taken over Iskarda."

"And?"

She is Navy, after all. And before that, Amberlight.

"And in that case—they might pre-empt the threat."

"It's what I'd do."

"Especially," I went on over her intaken breath, "when you remember—the Quest."

For a second her eyes dilated as Dhanissa's had. I did not have to say, Now you recall what a knife-edge we dance along.

"It doesn't matter that I have renounced the Suzerainty. It would not matter if I swore on a templeful of statues that I was an Iskardan scullion. That I had neither interest in nor animosity toward Dhasdein."

"Antastes won't believe you."

"Antastes will never believe me. He cannot afford to believe me."

"Can we?"

It hurt so much it winded me. Dhe save me, only two others ever breached my armor, and one of them had thirty years imperial knowledge to do it with. But I lashed back the way I did at both of them, before I could help myself.

"If you can't, the worst place to learn it is Verrain."

Her breath was sharp as a whipcrack. "Should I send you back to Iskarda?"

The River-lord forgive me. I was too angry for sanity. But not for control.

"If," I said silkily, "you feel it would be safe."

"You said, 'I will do whatever the lady Tellurith asks of me.'"

I opened my mouth. I had the wits to stop at, "You—"

And not to finish, You are not Tellurith.

She glared at me. As angry as I was, and less careful of how it was fleshed.

"You *claimed* you were loyal to Iskarda."

"I *am* loyal to Iskarda. Why else dispute this?"

Her cheeks blazed. "You dare suggest that I'm—"

"I suggest nothing about you." Oh, Tellurith. I could have appeased. I could have been skillful. I could have offered submission. To anyone who mattered less.

"Then do as you're told, *lord* Tanekhet!"

"And will you or I write to say, 'Lady Tellurith, You left me a man who was Amberlight's, Iskarda's greatest weapon. We used him so well we have lost Amberlight and Iskarda both.'"

"You—!"

But after all, she is a Ruand too. And Sarth's daughter. I should have remembered that. The hand came down. The fist flattened. The lips set over the teeth.

"I've listened to you. Your advice is noted. Before we go to Assembly, I give you a choice—'lord' Tanekhet. You may go to Verrain. Or you can go back to Iskarda."

"Lady—Tez—Ruand." It shook me out of all address. "You know that is not—I *must* stay in Amberlight!"

She raised her eyebrows. Sarth's own stiletto, Why?

"I have told you why!"

The jaw clenched too. I read the pent-up answer in her eyes: not responsibility. Not duty. Nothing to do with the one we cannot mention. Nothing to do with Iskarda. It is because you are entirely besotted. Because you can't bear to be away from me.

Tez, I wanted to shout, for the gods' love, don't! Don't turn on me, the man wanted to beg, for one moment's mistake. Don't spurn honest counsel, the lord wanted to cry, just for the way it was made. Don't make your country pay the price, the ruler could have begged her, for the revenge of hurting me.

Maledictions on my training, Tellurith. That upheld *my* pride. And my hurt. And my anger, that at such a time she could impugn my loyalty.

Because I could not beg. Even then, I could not beg.

Not when she raised her brows, that look as stony, as adamant, as Sarth's very own, and drove her blade home. Enquiring, coldly as the stare, "Well?"

"Lady Tez." I bowed to her. Making grace the vessel of sheer insolence: making the title bite with all the false decorum I ever used on Antastes. "Your wish is my command."

As well I am so angry, Tellurith. Because at least it covers, it did cover the hurt. It let me return to the Assembly, and accept her—command—without more protest, verbal or otherwise, and thus not demean myself. If I have left my own—cause—in shards, I have saved my face.

A small compensation, it seems, for losing Tez as well, perhaps, as Amberlight.

And Iskarda.

* * *

I shall not send this to Tellurith. What could she do, wherever she is now, to counter such imbecility? Will it help if she too tears her hair out, if she worries and sweats and visions disasters she can avert less than I? And what if, unable to bear the load herself, she were to confide the inner secret to others?

To Sarth?

Gods. If he did not come back himself, he is capable of sending half Cataract after me.

~~So. I am in Verrain, lady Tellurith. And if I think the tactic is less than helpful, if not outright—~~

I am in Verrain, my lady Tellurith, and whatever I think of the tactic, I will do my heart and mind's best. For the sake of Amberlight. As of Iskarda.

I write from the palace in Assuana, which, as you will know—

How utterly bizarre to realize, Tellurith, that you do *not* know. That you have never been, in person, into Assuana. May not, for all I know, have ever met Shuya face to face.

I do presume your intelligencers. So you know *of* the city's size, the seam-bursting crowds and manic streets, the grass huts, mud-brick houses, marble Family palaces, the unbelievable medley of goods and breeds that swirls through the Assuana bazaars.

Not to mention the uproar when the smoke-signals whip out every merchant from the Houses to the nearest corner money-lender, to witness those vital events in Verrain's calendar. The arrival of Oasis caravans.

The streets are still as crowded, the air as acrid as in every summer, the inimitable Assuana bouquet of burning dung-cakes, dirty humanity, exotic goods and penned-up animals, with the underlying whiff of camel and desert heat. There are as many beggars and merchants and foreigners and spectacles. Oh, the spectacles, by which the Families vie for favor from the workers and rabble, and the lawless who underlie it all.

And the palace is just as I remember it: a damned great pile atop the capital's only excuse for a hill, with walls that make Antastes' look decorative, and a labyrinth inside. Stone, in a city where it is used only by the Families. Whitewashed, as everything is, around the desert, with the usual decorative arch-rims and ceiling-work, the geometric miracles of mosaic underfoot. Most of all, the austerely blank white outer walls that throw up their bare turquoise-green doors. Desert colors, green for cool and sanctuary in the white of the eternal sand.

That will interest you far less, no doubt, than my reception. And how it galls me, to admit your cursed girl put Shuya in a stick-fork after all.

Because of course Shuya could not push a Riversrun Suzer-ain, a great Dhasdeini lord, Antastes' right hand, off in some rat-ridden corner as she would a cobbler-delegate from Amberlight. Whatever message I am sending Antastes, what would that say for her?

I played her once at castles, when she too was just an envoy, settling the border after the Riversrun war. An excellent game. It lays out crystal clear the fundaments of character—of instinct— that dictate, for war as for intelligencing or diplomacy, what an opponent will do.

And Shuya playing castles is shrewd, and prudent, and pre-pared to spend for a victory, and never more deadly than in re-treat. But flamboyant?

No.

So my presence as envoy forces her to recall, not only what else might be in Iskarda, but that I am the face of Iskarda. Whose else face I might be, how can she tell? But because she is Shuya, she will not—yet—deny me an envoy's position outright.

And by that, she must acknowledge the status of Amberlight.

That I did enforce. When Tez wanted to send me downRiver as a representative of Marbleport, or a mediator from Iskarda, I sat back, folded my arms, and said, "I go as Amberlight's envoy or not at all."

You will understand: Marbleport could not set itself up as independent, or Iskarda become embroiled in a quarrel that ostensibly paid no heed to them. Far, far better to get full value from Shuya's own initiative.

So I disembarked from the patrol boat with a herald bearing my credentials, in a roll sealed with the double-wave sign that is the symbol of new Amberlight, with a trumpeter to clear the street, and an escort, of men and women severely equal, to walk behind and before. Luckily, the patrol-boat had crew who have been ashore in Assuana, so we did not have to ask the way.

How you would have enjoyed, Tellurith, the fuss at the palace gate.

They knew who I was, of course. That flew from intercepting sentry to guard officer and on up the command chain faster than lightning in reverse. I did not have to speak. It was the herald who intoned, with languid arrogance, my name, my patronymic, and my status. As envoy of Amberlight.

I picture you laughing at the image of me, donning my most insolent Riversend mask, disposing myself languidly with fan and walking stick, in the shadow of the gatehouse, for the bare three minutes—I will credit Shuya's people with communications as good as their intelligence—before the guard officer and a panting chamberlain bowed me through.

As you know, Shuya does not falter under pressure. They might have had the decision made, the suites cleared, weeks before—

I do not *think* that was the case. I left Amberlight that same evening. Nothing could have gone downstream first: Dhanissa saw to that. Unless there is some signal-chain unnoticed, they had no idea. And the to-do, however brief and unobtrusive, is most unlikely to have been feigned.

So I occupy an ambassador's suite in the diplomatic wing, a site no doubt already described to you. After changing Riversend for Iskarda, after the transformations in Amberlight, it is quite strange to reflect that this suite, with its huge slave-fans, its muslin-screened windows and the lofty cedar ceilings that resound worse than the cool bare marble-floors—

That this is all as it was before the fall of Amberlight. That in this city, at least, nothing has changed.

It is after midnight. My people—my entire threesome of herald, troublecrew and secretary—have retired. I have sat up by the great mahogany table in the ambassador's receiving room, the mosaics and gaudy tapestries ghostly in the light of my single lamp. The palace is so thickly walled as to be virtually sound-resistant. The city may or may not have retired to sleep.

Sitting here, my belly full of Shuya's exquisitely prepared desert banquet dishes, my back into the doorless corner and the quiet of contemplation round me—I have had time to think at last

The River-game has opened, Tellurith. You know, and I know, that the other states can no more eschew that game than Antastes can take wing and overfly the Archipelago.

I saw our new world as a matter of domestic alteration and leisurely experiment: a metamorphosis which, whatever its personal cost, would not go outside Iskarda. Foolish, so foolish of me, who could foresee that the qherrique's return would disturb the River's length, not to realize how far those transformations will go.

The first one overthrew Amberlight. Predictable enough, to be sure, the city was the merest shell. But the next?

Violent, almost certainly: nation-wide, it may be, and wholly unpredictable. In ten years time, nothing on the River may be as it was.

Even Dhasdein.

Nobody in Iskarda has thought that far. I very much doubt they have done so in Amberlight. There is a certain amount of worry about your fate, of course, and Cataract. But that Cataract itself should change . . .

That Verrain, in turn, might change—be changed—

Heart's truth, Tellurith. I was prepared to change myself. I was prepared to play the scullion, in a new world at Iskarda.

But if our new world overthrows Dhasdein as well?

Enough of such maunderings. The River-lord knows, I have as dour and delicate a day's work ahead as ever I looked to do. Let me exercise the wits of a scullion, if not an ambassador, and take myself to bed.

* * *

Reading that back, I have great difficulty in keeping straight my face.

I could—I should—have expected it. In a twisted way, it is almost a sort of flattery. That they should try it so quickly. That they should presume to know my habits so well.

Because I walked into the master bedroom last evening to meet not one honeytrap but two.

The girl was charming, however orthodox: Verrain looks, but desert blood, which alleviated the true Verraini skin, blue-black as overripe grapes, with the dramatic eyes and high-bridged

Quetzistani nose. A most expensive plaything, and my status more than granted, since her age says she can hardly have been used.

Snuggled under my exquisitely embroidered coverlet. Overlaying my fine linen sheets with a great cloud of silky-fine straight ebony hair.

Not at all Verraini, that. Reminiscent, in some fantasy's corner of my memory—

Of Alkhes.

Which would make her a subtle and damnably intentional echo, a deliberate signal of how much they know.

That would be even more than the other trap declared.

The man was not young at all. Beautiful enough, certainly. Quetzistani, assuredly a slave, possibly, just possibly, of the old royal house before the Jhuir. High blood, indubitably. There is a certain look, the length of the eyes, the level line of the brows, that is impossible to mistake.

And *he*, Tellurith, was chained to the inner doorway, with a jeweled collar of gazelle hide and a silken rope, another twisted round his wrists. And on his back, equally unmistakable, the half-healed marks of a whip.

An insult, that they should be so blatant? A warning, that they should know so much? Be so sure of my taste in victims, which was not only for the riff-raff, the criminal, but the—spoilt?

A compliment, that they should try so quickly to corrupt?

Would you credit, Tellurith, that what I wanted most of all was to laugh?

The River-lord look upon me. Writing it down, I feel once more how my lungs expand, my shoulders rise, the widening of a freedom beyond probity, a joy's exhilaration. Because—

Because I swear, Tellurith, that neither one left me more than a little vexed. Because whatever the cost in trial and harassment and heart's pain, Iskarda has taken me beyond such stuff. Erased the itch. Purged the demons. From that, at least, I am released.

So I had merely to rouse my troublecrew, summon palace folk, and command them, with the most perfect boredom, to remove their traps. Consummating their rout by the tone in which I added, "Someone has made a mistake."

Which some underling who only followed orders will doubtless expiate with the skin off his own back.

* * *

As you might expect, the rest of the day has been less enchanting. A predictable attempt to present my papers, predictably, failed. A morning spent kicking my heels in the reception hall, to a series of ever higher and more exquisitely worded, "No advance"—Dhe, I could have charted this in my sleep. Probably the banishment will last three days. I would bet on it with Kheizo, my very efficient troublecrew, were it not too open flippancy.

And the longer the delay, so long as it stops before open and irremediable umbrage, the better for us.

Which Shuya also knows. So I allowed myself a small, a very small sign of vexation before we withdrew at noon from the audience hall. A city excursion is naturally out of the question. My herald Dheya and I settled to play castles under the extremely elegant trees in the suite's inner court, and I sent my male secretary out to hire a singing girl.

My personnel caused almost as much trouble in Amberlight as the mission itself. In the end Juiza gave me women for herald and troublecrew, since no men are yet fit for the work: Hathris, the secretary, is a stevedore's tallyman, who can read and write and makes up the rest as he goes along. A match for the rest of this ramshackle mission, no doubt.

Little enough point in laboring that. But I judge the day's work has offered Shuya a clear message, with just enough provocation: I expected, I am very little troubled by your retaliation. Go further. Such tantrums play into my hands.

* * *

And it seems, into other most unexpected hands as well.

We knew they had come downstream. Dhanissa's intelligence in Verrain is sketchy, but they were unlikely to go beyond Assuana, especially if granted sanctuary. As we know they were. Yet to have reacted so quickly, so openly, so—brazenly—

She called on me in person, Tellurith. This very morning. With neither preamble nor warning. Your—former—House-head. Damas.

They are quartered here, Dheya has discovered—with Kheizo anchored inside as my security, it is she who gathers palace news—in one of the visiting dignitaries' suites: as in Riversend, they can accommodate high visitors, or high prisoners. It seems unlikely she chose this morning by chance, which would argue notable spy-links. And yet . . .

Somewhat unfortunate that with Kheizo busied over some internal hitch, the knock on the main door was answered by Hathris.

At any rate the first thing Damas said, when she forged through the work-room doorway with a presence that already had me on my feet, was, "What's a man doing here?"

I blinked. She recollected herself enough to offer a name. The color on her weathered cheeks signaled, Umbrage. And in truth, we had hardly proceeded beyond, Hathris is my secretary, appointed by the Commune of Amberlight, so sorry for this shabby reception, my troublecrew and herald are elsewhere, I do apologize, will you have tea? when she saved me the small-talk by demanding, "What are *you* doing here?"

I blinked in earnest. Your talk, your letter has given me a different picture of House-heads, Tellurith. Even of Damas.

But my arrival must have shaken her severely. For when I replied smoothly, "The Assembly appointed me ambassador," she gave a snort and snapped, "What about Antastes?"

I said, "I beg your pardon?" That look usually creates more pause.

"You were Antastes' Trouble-head. You were—" the gesture shaped it all. Everything Tez had said. "Mother defend us, the worst snag in Dhasdein, and they make *you* ambassador?"

I bowed. The elegance—and the wasp-sting—appeared wasted. She just glared at me, color still up. And then burst out, almost bitterly, "What do *you* care for Amberlight?"

I suppose I had conceived her as the street-players do, a tyrant, a blood-sucker wanting nothing but her own power. She broke out again before I collected myself.

"Was this your doing?"

That, I could answer with all the ease in the world. "Ma'am, you may believe that with the faith I hold to Amberlight, and to Iskarda beyond it, this would have been the last thing I chose. But I am pledged to them both. What they require of me, I do."

Her eyes slitted. "The girl, then? What's her name—Dhanissa? Did *she* concoct this? Just the half-baked sort of—"

"It was decided by the Assembly, ma'am." She would work through them name by name if I said, No.

"The Assembly!" That sneer was tyrant personified. "That pack of rabble-rousers and broken-down troublecrew! And you let them do it? You . . ."

"I told you, ma'am. The City has my pledge."

"Tellurith has your pledge!" Her eyes slitted again. "Did *she*—"

"If you have no word of Telluir House-head, ma'am, you can hardly expect to better that ignorance with me."

She did not answer immediately. But her eyes steadied, and her face composed itself. Then I was facing a House-head, with everything I have understood that means.

"You've attended Shuya. Your papers were not received."

"Ma'am."

A little pause. Was she thinking, This bodes badly for Amberlight? Or, This was my doing? Or, This was the best thing Shuya could do for Amberlight? I could no longer tell. But it was no time to lose the initiative. I said, "I presume Verrain has received you."

She inclined her head. A fellow Head of State, that gesture said, respecting old equals' status. What else would she do?

"I must ask, then, as Amberlight envoy. What is your position on the claim to Marbleport?"

I was asking an official declaration, a binding statement of position. She knew it. She answered with hardly a pause.

"The Houses in Exile have not yet decided how they regard your presence here. We can make no policy statement until that is clarified."

That gave me pause. I had expected flat rejection. Reinforcement of Shuya's snub. Not a qualified postponement: far less a sub-text that added, Unofficially, we may traffic with you.

I will confess this, Tellurith. It gave me more than pause. It gave me space for lunacy, for hope as crazy as leaving Riversend, for a gamble that, in retrospect, chills me to the heart. But in my mind was that unguarded way she had burst in, the more unguarded question: "What do *you* care for Amberlight?"

So I inclined my head to mark her statement. And said, "Ma'am, for the sake of the City—delay that statement as long as you can."

Her jaw snapped like a trap. The moment stretched like falling china, an eternity to breaking point. Before she shifted her weight, once.

And said, in an entirely different voice, "Why *did* you go to Iskarda?"

I could have shrugged and answered, What does it matter? But having dropped the shield, I had to leave it down.

I said, "Because Tellurith showed me something—I could not find anywhere else."

If eyes were surgeon's probes, she would have dug the backbone out of me. In truth, I did not expect her to understand. It would be enough, I thought, if she could be brought to believe.

"Tellurith," she said with a jerk. "The Mother's thanks I never fell into such—such—" The hunched shoulder said it all.

Deficiency, acknowledging itself, admitting its incomprehension, and reconciling itself. Like Darthis.

She straightened up.

"The Houses in Exile," she said, "heard the voice of the Mother. They chose to leave Amberlight. They honor the City in absence. They will," a very straight look indeed, "not advance its foes."

I freely admit myself schooled, Tellurith. From that one sentence, that one request, she had construed it all: that I misliked the strategy of my presence, and was kept to it by loyalty. That the loyalty was real. That I, too, understood Amberlight's only hope was in delay. That I had invoked her own loyalty, which I trusted to go beyond loss and exile, to the City that had cast her out. That I had asked her enlistment as my ally, overlooking my own abhorrence to her, for that City's sake.

She rose. I bowed, a ruler's courtesy, in the purest sincerity. "Madam," I said, "if I may in any way serve you, I beg you will not hesitate to ask."

I had straightened, to speak it with eyes as well as mouth. And I saw the spark in her own eye, the smothered spark of understanding, the vivid fleeting laugh that said she too understood the difference between, "not hesitate," and, "you have only" to ask.

She put out a hand, flicking something from my sleeve, ironic and quick and significant as the quirk of her mouth. You are a trifler, that gesture said: your parsimony is as clever as your patriotism, and I forgive you, because both are in service to Amberlight.

She said, "I'll keep it in mind, lord Tanekhet."

Oh, I know as well as you that she will back me only as far as it suits her own intentions. And the Amberlight she serves is not the one we—you, or I, or Dhanissa—would build. Nevertheless . . . I have been Antastes' head of intelligence. I have staked my life, and the empire with it, on my readings of such as she.

And I think that perhaps—just perhaps—I am not entirely alone here. After all.

* * *

I do not think I was too sanguine to say that. Nevertheless . . . With or without her hand in it, this has—

This has come alarmingly pat.

I must compose myself. You may never read this, Tellurith, but it must be clear. And I have to report that Shuya—Shuya . . .

The gap was two days, not three. I presented my credentials this morning. An everyday audience. You will know the procedure, the chamberlains who pass summons before breakfast, the ceremonial escort to the audience hall. Shuya leans more to the desert than does Riversend: no wallpaper, less furniture, more cushions, more tapestries, and a plethora of the long-tubed desert water-pipes in which they smoke the ubiquitous skau. Shuya herself is not above a pipe or two in audience. Whether to signify boredom, or to play ambuscades in the smoke.

Ten years have changed her very little. A little bigger—the Lord knows, she is built like his own River-horse, her lovers have my absolute respect—a little more ornately dressed, a fraction sharper to underlings. A few more lines on that broad, sheeny, black moon of a Verrain face. Disposed, as always, with a heap of embroidered cushions under her elbow on the President's dais, whither the favored advance, between the rows of cross-legged Family representatives, their retinues standing behind them, up to the focus of the six palace guards.

As you might expect, it began in pure ceremony. Papers accepted. Note delivered, request that the President honor it with her attention, inclination of the President's head, retreat. In theory, Tez's strategy remains masterly: denying Shuya the ruler's prerogative of rejection, excuses, delay, forcing her to deal with me as smartly as face-saving will allow.

In practice, Shuya has called her bluff.

I had reached the outer door, my retinue about me, was preparing the usual vail for the chamberlain. The hand that plucked my arm was both swift and discreet: someone from the inner court, high in the inner court, by the silk turban and emerald clasp on a brocaded vest. Murmuring, with power's deference, "If the ambassador would care to wait?"

They took me into the private anterooms. More cushions, refreshment, a pipe. Not, firmly if however decorously, my own folk. But Shuya herself would hardly dispose of an ambassador so early, so quickly, and so blatantly as that.

No, it was only till the closure of the public audience. When the inner curtains parted, I was ushered into Shuya's private meeting-place.

I will note that it is very desert-minded: a small court-yard, running-water channels as well as a fountain, potted dwarf orange-trees. The illusion of a desert distance in the city's heart. Shuya was already disposed upon a marble dais beside the pool, amid guards and retinue. I am almost certain one was the current favorite, but I had no time for soundings. The instant I entered she waved them all away.

Politic enough. As likely I would leap upon her with a dagger as that she would send one after me.

The onus of River manners, most handily, left her the opening: in castles, a very useful vantage. Especially to a skilful player. And she opened with Dhasdein.

So early, it should have nothing to do with the excursion to Quetzistan. Logic insisted that. Experience of Shuya, of the unexpected, made it hard to steady my breath. But after all, I have danced the sword-game with emperors.

It was not Quetzistan she aimed for. It was me.

She began with gossip. Therkon's latest lover, my nephew's changes as Suzerain. Hardly a painful probe, to me. Except that of itself would give her news.

So I changed the subject, just early enough to make her think me the tiniest touch sensitive, asking what word she had of the Empress. After all, she is in a sense my neophyte. It was I who raised her family: who set her on the throne.

So very like castles, diplomacy. It is your discards, as much as your choices, that build your opponent's map.

And I understand what you wrote about fencing with Damas, Tellurith. The feel of familiar counters, homely as strings to a musician, under your hand.

Shuya smiled and reached to puff on the kindled pipe. "Truly, a miracle. After, what is it—twenty years? An Empress in truth."

I murmured some banality. She did not offer the pipe. Its own kind of message, that she remembered that. As it was another message, that she did not ask which of us had performed the miracle, Tellurith.

What she said was, "Do you see many of her folk?"

Oh, she merits her position, twenty years atop the Families' turbulent pyramid. Right to that smallest point of leaving open the question, In Iskarda, or Amberlight?

While the implication spread to circle me: it must be a high vantage, that past knowledge which lets you foil your Dhasdeini foil. And the core of the probe demanded, Exactly how much do you still know?

I swept the fan before me and murmured, "Do you find many here?"

She smiled and took another puff. And drawled, "Less than in Amberlight."

Giving away the small change of her folk in Amberlight, adding the greater worth of admitted intelligence on matters there. Mentioning Amberlight, to force the main engagement, my mission in Verrain. Abandoning delay along with pride and all the ruler's other options, to announce, clear as Shirran battleflags: Speed is on my side.

I will admit, the heart sank in my belly, Tellurith.

Her bland moon face, her languidly hooded eyes, were veiled by the smoke. She was waiting, knowing my worth as well as I did, for the message of the riposte.

I bowed over the fan. She puffed again and smiled.

River-fiend. Knowing too that if she returned the silence I could not, from my lower rank as ambassador, let the conversation die: neither my credit nor my defense would sustain the slight.

Knowing quite well that to accept the topic of Amberlight was almost as bad as to turn the talk back upon Dhasdein. Or draw attention upon Quetzistan. Or worse, drag in the Quest by mentioning Cataract.

I swept the fan before me and murmured, "As Her Eminence says."

She coughed aloud, a great gout of smoke. I had just realized it was a laugh when she put down the pipe.

And smiled at me outright, that big face beaming as vividly and unexpectedly as a visiting moon, the lightning burst of praise and amusement that is Shuya's very best weapon. From the thundercloud, sweetness. From the tyrant, charm.

"Ah, lord Tanekhet," she said. "You're throwing yourself away."

It had been the worst of counters, assuredly: a feeble flat-stop, advancing no alternative, making no true riposte, leaving the way open to press the matter of Amberlight. The worst of counters, except all the rest.

Something of false modesty, yes. I had no need to counterfeit the flutter of the fan, the dropped eyes and meeker confusion of my, "Ma'am?"

She settled on an elbow and came straight back at me.

"Wasted, as an envoy for Amberlight."

What help is a fan, amid a pit of crocodiles?

Yes, you will see the jaws as well as I. Did she mean to provoke or suborn me? To excuses, indignation or defense of Amberlight, but in any case, to raise the issues I must above all suppress? Or was she bent on separating me from my role? Had the honeytraps been set in the better bad faith, not to expose but to woo?

At the very least, a fan can give you thinking time. For a charade of confusion, and the simulation of falser modesty, in which I murmured, "Ma'am—I don't understand."

"Do you not, lord Tanekhet?"

She did not allow me more trivialities. She puffed the pipe, and spoke like an oracle through the smoke.

"'Amberlight' is not a state. It's a pack of rabble jauntering in their betters' rags: ignorant, destitute, and too stupid to know what they've lost. Can the viceroy of Riversrun, the pacifier of Quetzistan—not see that?"

She knew the answer as well as you or I. Of course I knew what an empty hand I held. Of course neither she nor I would have sent me into the lion's jaws.

She settled back among her cushions. Her eyelids drooped, the one warning Shuya has never been able to conceal.

"What news," she said, "do you have from Cataract?"

I bowed over the fan to a degree as nicely calculated as ever I did: insolence, ire, affront. How dare you, it said, calumniate my loyalties, question my political competence, feel out my news-chains, and try to make that probe a threat?

Anything to stay the hurry in my pulse.

She gave me a master's minute to sweat before she spoke.

"Amberlight fell. What do you think will happen in Cataract?"

So she has had no privy news of triumph or catastrophe—if I could decide which was which. All she had was a parallel to my thoughts two nights before, that dried the breath in my throat.

"Your 'friends' up the hill there," she said, "have set a demon loose."

When I did not reply she flapped a hand, a glitter of rings that snapped, Don't shuffle with me.

"It doesn't matter if anybody has the thing. Or will ever have the thing. If Cataract oversets itself—what will the Heartlands do?"

Ah, Tellurith, my cretinous insularity. I had thought of the River I knew—and that stops at Cataract.

She nodded at me. Shaping my own nightmare before my eyes.

"How long then, before Mel'eth grows fidgety? Before there's trouble in Quetzistan? In the Archipelago?"

I did not quail or crumble or so much as hide my eyes. Even when the nightmare rose before me and I had to see that what I glimpsed that other night was real.

That after all, my loyalty is not whole.

That after all, I am tied—however backwardly, however fool-ishly—to Dhasdein.

To *my* image of Dhasdein.

But still, I was Tanekhet. I had the wits and the hardihood to strike before I fell.

I said, "And Verrain?"

"Of course."

That truly struck me dumb. She lay back on her elbow, the pipe discarded, pinning me with her own vision's stare.

"We are no solider than Amberlight. We rely on the Oases, and we hold the road—the trading posts—by force. If Cataract and Amberlight fall, how long will the flood respect us?"

Truly, she is a consummate diplomat. Especially when she has conviction to back her work.

Because she gave me time to construct the scenario, and the inevitable corollary. And about the time I saw civil demolition overflow the border into Quetzistan—about the time I saw my own hand lever out the avalanche's opening rock—she said, "The empire's true border is Verrain."

Dhasdein's satellite. Dhasdein's plunder-zone, assuredly. But also, Dhasdein's shield. We both know that, her stare said. We both know you have based your policy on that for years.

Otherwise the war would not have stopped with Riversrun. It was a shrewder policy to leave Verrain, clipped but not ruined, to cushion the thrusts of Amberlight.

"And if Verrain holds up," Shuya said deliberately, "how much trouble will reach Antastes?"

I opened my lips and shut them again. What use to speak of oaths and loyalty, even at a scullion's rank, to her?

"But if Verrain holds—why would we make more trouble upstream?"

Not enough for her to presume me an imperial agent, a traitor masquerading in Iskarda. Not enough to presume that loyalty as easily shucked as my ties to Amberlight: not enough to think I could be made a puppet for Verrain.

She wanted to bribe me as well.

You have no more imagined it than I did. She meant that, if I turned my coat, if I became her instrument, if I worked to defend Verrain, she would withdraw the claim to Marbleport.

With the old emperor, no doubt youth shielded me. He would not have expected, and so never saw the signs of homicide suppressed. If I did not speak in words to Shuya, I managed to keep my eyes down. Those, I could not have controlled.

Even so, she read the silence far too acutely: she waved a hand and heaved herself up on the cushions, sign to the rawest of courtiers that the audience was near its end.

"Enough for the moment," she said. "Take time, my lord ambassador, to consider what I propose."

The guards converged, the other underlings. I made the proper response and the correct obeisance—I must have, for I am here, in my rooms, intact—and they ushered me away.

O Tellurith. As the River-lord sees me, when I accepted what I thought would be the charge of our new world, I never dreamt it would reach such limits as this.

I thought I could pay the price. I thought I could renounce wealth, and luxury and—perversions—and power. And a lifetime's eminence. I thought I could bear to have my pride demolished, and my mind's city turned to rubble, from which I could, with pain and tribulation, build a new life. I thought I could bear the doubts, the imputations, the expectations of disloyalty, either to you or to Antastes.

I never expected to find the dream become my direst nightmare. To have such treacheries made real.

Maledictions on Shuya. Who has struck, whether or not she knew it, clear to this faulty diamond's core.

I could sit in this corner and hold myself together, like some fractured pot. I could—

I *ought* to run like a masterless cur all the way back to Amberlight.

I *ought* to concoct some artistically infectious disease, some elegant fit of the vapors, opt out of this mission, and flee clear to Iskarda.

And what would I say to Tez?

O, Tellurith. I need you now, as I only thought I did before. I need your flesh and blood and mind and wits, your shifts and counsel and lightning-bestowed extrications. But I need you most as a touchstone, a talisman. I need to see you and those men of yours to remind me, to assure me: that I did all this, that the reason for my ever dreaming I could do all this, is real.

There is no opening my heart to my own folk. For courage as for counsel, they, like Amberlight, rely on me.

Nor could I risk a message, however coded, to Amberlight. Shuya must not know what she has done. I ought to be triple-coding this.

As for Iskarda . . .

Or Marbleport . . .

O, Tellurith. Can neither you, nor the gods, nor your thrice-misbegotten qherrique, give me *some* inkling of what I should do?

* * *

G ods.
    If there are gods. If this is a god's humor, it is too black to call a jest. Even for me.

The news came today. Not the eye-witnesses themselves. This word has run ahead, leapt from craft to craft, faster than a storm-wind, faster than a running plague.

I have bidden Hathris lock the doors, put up a notice. Would I not have reason to be indisposed, put on sackcloth, slash my breast?

I foresaw this: I wrote of this. As Dhe sees me, I warned you. Did you not read at least so much?

I think my heart has died. I cannot bear to think that *you* have died—you, and your beloveds—O gods, never to meet, to talk, simply to watch Sarth again.

It cannot be otherwise. Despite Zuri and Azo and all the rest of them, despite the—

The damnable, treacherous, betraying, murdering qherrique.

It cannot be otherwise. Not once you were immured in those hellpits under Cataract.

It is over. The Quest is finished.

You are dead.

* * *

I think I am a coward after all. I left it there, last night, sent Hathris out for wine, locked the bedroom, and drank myself to sleep.

So this morning my head is split to the neckbone to compound the other woes. And I will have to go out, sometime today, and put a face on, and find words, and try—try—

Gods, or whatever remains to me, what am I to try?

Summon a ship, declare my mission over, and embark today? For Marbleport?

Send a message, requesting instructions, to Amberlight?

Send word, that will only be a double scourge of confirmation, to Iskarda?

How can I look one—a single one of them in the face?

I must have put my head down, splitting as it was, atop the page. And from grief, or sheer exhaustion, or the vile willowbark concoction Dheya forced on me, gone sound asleep.

Because the sun has come round. Even the hand-thick wall behind me transmits the weight of its western heat. I can feel, from the way Kheizo and Hathris and Dheya hover at the outer doorway, the pressure of the jackals gathered beyond.

So. Everything is so much simpler, at the end of everything. Why did I not remember that?

After all, the decision is really no decision. The doubts have been resolved. The pattern is clear. Am I, Tanekhet, who took up the world and hazarded it on a dice-throw, am I, if the gods outbid me, to squeal and cringe like some upcountry boy?

May you see me from beyond the other River, Tellurith. I will not disgrace you. If we are to go down, we will go down facing the enemy, fighting all the way.

There are shifts to pursue. There are tactics to try. There are many, many things yet that we can do before the end.

I shall get up now, and ask Dheya for another of those damnable possets of willowbark. And have Hathris order my clothes, and tell Kheizo to announce that in another hour the envoy will receive visitors.

Then I shall walk out there, as I did from the bedroom after Saarieq died, and I shall say, "This talk is sheer River-wind. I do not credit a single word."

CHAPTER VIII

Upriver
Summer

They have found more paper from somewhere. So I will go on with this, Tanekhet.

And confess, as I can to no-one else, the worst thing about that moment, in the Cataract vegetable gardens, under the indifferent moon; and it was not Alkhes' rebellion, or Sarth's backing, or a men's mutiny to threaten our entire enterprise.

It was that I wanted to agree.

I looked away over the blur of farmland toward the River, and up to the sliver of moon in the unresponsive sky, and saw in my mind's eye the waiting cliffs. Then I glanced back where Alkhes had never stopped looking, and all my eyes would hold was that corona of fire.

It may be that I am a House-head before all else; or it may be that my sight has shifted further yet, having born the weight of a community alone, myself, in Iskarda. Whatever it was, I understood then how our choices must fall.

So I put my arms around Alkhes' rigid back. And I said, "Yes. That was his city. Where should we look first?"

I heard Zuri draw her breath. But Alkhes' answer came directly from his body to mine; and before its end, Sarth rose too. Reached for my hand and set a kiss, solemn as a vow, on the inside of the wrist.

Which I understand now as double tribute; that I had averted our dilemma, perhaps the shattering of the company and the end of the Quest. But also that I had honored Wonsa; like Alkhes, for Alkhes, I had understood.

Then Zuri's breath exploded and she fairly spat at us, "Are you in your wits? Any of you? We've fired the palace, we killed the tyrant. They're gutting the city for us! If we don't get out of here now, we're going to be killed!" She was beyond manners as beyond propriety. "Blight and blast it, Tellurith!"

Behind her, Ahio said, invisible but solid as a dug-in mule, "I want my shaper back."

Over her Sunya added, softly but far more grimly, "I want Gearth."

"I will not leave him," she added into the hush, "to rot in prison mud. He shall keep his soul."

She meant, exhume the corpse. Have a proper Amberlight funeral, the body burned, ashes given to the River, setting the spirit free.

"Blight and *blast!*"

Troublecrew caution strangled Zuri there. In the bursting hush I felt the company vote; alignments conveyed less by shifting feet or body speech than a sense of will, borne on currents in the ambient air. Answering that silent demand, as silently. Yes. We are going back.

"Mother blast!"

Zuri strangled that as well; but the growl was choked so deep I felt her very stomach shake.

"Then would someone tell me exactly how?"

Which was when the adjacent trees rustled. And an invisible, total stranger said tentatively, "Missis Amberlight?"

Sarth grabbed Zuri before she flew like a startled leopard straight in the intruder's face. Through the whirl of hiss, spit and strike I heard Azo and Deor leap to shield the tangled bodies of the rest, muffled gasps and grunts and the jangle of snatched-up chains amid which the voice broke out rapidly, higher than before.

"Not trouble, no trouble, truce, Missis Amberlight, peace!"

I heard Sarth and then Zuri grunt. Winded, if not worse. I answered the only possible way; they could have killed us already, if that was their choice. I snapped, "Stand fast!"

Azo and the Navy women responded automatically. The rest calmed in response. Somewhere beyond them, I heard Sarth and Zuri quieten; short, harsh pants.

"Who are you?" I said. "What are you doing here?"

Silence again. Then, all but quavering, "Missis? We make truce?"

Did we have a choice?

"Truce." I took a step backward, then another, out on the open fields. What did we have to lose? "Show yourselves to us."

The others fell back with me; I caught the twinned shadow at their rear that said Zuri, and Sarth. We gathered ourselves on the margin of another pumpkin patch, and behind us the trees shivered. Rattled, and gave up their guests.

Azo caught her breath and I felt the others freeze as the foliage margin shifted. Stepped forward, twenty, thirty, forty yards of it, shadows upright and barely isolate, emerging, converging, ten, thirty, fifty, a hundred human shadows, sprung out of the uncommunicative earth.

"Stop!"

The advance froze.

"Don't you—do you have a herald, an envoy? Somebody who can speak for the rest?"

A pause, where I felt Azo bristle all over again. Then movement, far back in the shadows, who shifted, parted, gave room to a laboriously approaching shape.

There must have been doubts and terrors on their side too. I had a sense of contention, both verbal and physical, inside the shadows' verge; before the figure moved out, humped, effortful, into the half-light of the sinking moon.

It seemed only justice to come forward myself.

It was an old woman, dark to featurelessness in the moonlight, but not, I could tell, true black. Stooped with age, wearing some shapeless garment and a cloth or other headdress, not a proper hood, over her hair. I caught a fringing glint of white. Supporting her still solid body on a tall stick, craning up at me as we met.

Not the one who had spoken before. That voice, however high and strained, had been male.

She said, "I am Haturi. The Folk's Heart."

Hatura is a Heartland poison. Like me, you will know it all too well. Folk's Heart I deciphered instantly, a title, a leader's title. And she had authority with it, or she would not be hazarding herself like this. As for Haturi, some exiled clan, some Heartland tribe who had given the poison their name? Undoubtedly, a faction here in Cataract.

I said, "I am Tellurith. Ruand of Iskarda."

Do you know, Tanekhet, that is the first time I ever, unthinkingly, did not call myself Head of Telluir House?

She inclined her head. Four inches shorter than me, not much broader, but power swathed her like a cape. She gestured behind me and said, "You go back there?"

"There are things we need there. Things we have to do."

I let her retrace Zuri's response. The shrouded head bent a moment, and rose.

"Blood-men will butcher you."

"Perhaps."

A pause. Then, "You will wake Flesh of the Moon."

Qherrique. If they had not followed us from the city, they had communications inside.

"If we must."

A longer pause. Then, abruptly, "We are not blood-men. We work," a wave around; the fields. "We build," a wave past me. The City. "We live here. After blood-men. Before."

Not the warriors, but those who fed and housed and labored for them, perhaps of their blood, but never their kin, their fore-runners on the land, suffering their ascendancy, and stubbornly enduring in their wake. My heart climbed up, a great surge of hope in my throat.

I said, "We honor you."

She made a noise that translated as, Mmmph.

"You kill the Blood-man," she said.

The tone of that Mmmph warned me not to take it as unquali-fied praise.

"It was not," I said, "done willingly."

This time the dark behind her rippled too.

"My young men watch you break the wall. See Flesh of the Moon. Everybody knows about prison. Downriver folk, big fuss. Not expect this." She waved again. "My young men follow, hear you talk. Ready to shoot then—" She gestured once more, and my spine bristled as the dark sprouted shadows long and straight as spears that I knew were Heartland blowpipes; the weapon you use hatura with.

"But they listen first, to know Flesh of the Moon's will."

That time I waited for her.

"This Blood-man think more than war. He understand the . . ." she waved toward the River, up and down; trade. "Want to help city, to bring craft-folk. He might have been," for the first time a feeling surfaced; deep, long-suffering anger, born of hope as long-suffering, so briefly glimpsed, too soon destroyed, "some good."

Beside me, Alkhes buried his face in his hands.

She was looking past me, for her voice shifted at once. "That, too, my young men hear. They send somebody, run quick to me, say, Haturi, this more than we think, Hurry, Come here."

"So while you wait," delicately, her hand indicated Alkhes again; for him to overcome his grief, "I come. We decide . . . Ask for truce."

I put my arm, carefully, round Alkhes. More carefully, I sorted the options she had sketched. They could have killed us, and they had not. They could have let us go, to be killed, and they had not. Even when we had destroyed Wonsa, and all he meant to them.

I said, "What do you want from us?"

She let her breath out, hardly perceptible, but the ripple behind her was louder than a shout.

"You say, Go back. Want weapons, want . . ." A gesture to where, I had no doubt, Sunya stood, and with it a quick mimed beating of hands on breast; you want the dead, the source of grief. "We get weapons. We help." The gesture to Sunya again. "You come, bring Flesh of Moon."

I took a breath for myself. "And what then?"

"Then stop blood-men! You run away, get away, they still hunt your folk . . . Iss-karda. But you stop them. We help you stop them. No trouble, then. Then you help us."

"Help you in what?"

"Make city new."

I heard both Sarth and Zuri strangle a breath; I heard the others' puzzlement, resistance, distress. But Alkhes took his head out of his hands and shot at her, "How?"

She dipped her staff to him; a leader's gesture of respect.

"Give us a ruler," she said.

I heard Zuri's splutter clearly this time, and so did she. She spoke firmly over it. "Only one way to help city. Stop blood-men. Only one way to do that. Give them ruler who *make* them be still."

It made sense, inescapable good sense. Flee Cataract, and if another tyrant stilled the bloody internal strife, Iskarda would rue its very founding day. But if the warriors ripped the city to shreds, what help would it be to these?

There was only one remedy for us both; no hope of raising a people's rule here as there had been in Amberlight. The best the city could bear was another tyrant; but a tyrant who would carry on Wonsa's ascendancy, as well as his dream.

"Haturi," I heard myself say, "you know what we are doing here."

Her swathed head nodded. "You go on Quest. For Source. For Flesh of Moon."

"Then you understand we can't stop—"

"Not need all of you. Come back now, bring Flesh of Moon, stop blood-men, huh." A deep grunt of determination, success assured. "Get what you want. We help you then. Boats, gear, Jump-up cliffs. You go. But not all of you."

The Mother aid me; as the vision opened, the company diminished again, the impossible choice of one fit for the task but able to be spared for it, the inevitable, rending, hideously inescapable perfect choice, I all but cried aloud.

"Haturi, we can't!"

She stepped forward and laid one hand on my breast, as naturally as my mother would. "No, Tel-yurith . . ."

And over her Alkhes said as quietly, but with a tidal undercurrent of grief, "Not me."

"I killed him." He said it in my ear, but he was looking at her. "They would never suffer it. They'd never rest until somebody assassinated me."

She touched his wrist; agreement, deeper respect. And anticipated my next protest, the hand back to patting me. "Not you either, Tel-yurith. You Moon-speaker, must lead Quest."

"Then in the Mother's name," I was beyond all but a distracted roll-call, surely she could not imagine a ruler in Ahio or Esrafal, and how could we spare anyone else? "In the Mother's name, who?"

She took a deep breath. "War-hammer," she said.

"The . . . Flesh of the Moon? Haturi, if your folk could wake it at all, I don't know if it will work any more, not once we take away the seed—"

"Not Flesh of the Moon. War-hammer."

And when I still did not follow, she pointed across to them; Sarth and Zuri, poised like troublecrew but still locked like lovers, since he clearly did not trust her not to fly at another throat.

"Blood-men know about fight," she said. "Know what she is."

I should think all my bones turned to wood.

No! I wanted to scream. No! She's my Trouble-head, I couldn't run Iskarda without her, I gave her my husband to keep her there, this Quest has twice the danger and triple the importance and you want me to leave her behind? You expect me to get this pack of infants through the Heartland and back, with my right arm dangling in the slaughterhouse of Cataract?

They were looking at me. Alkhes and Haturi both. Invisible eyes, silent speech; two presences that wordlessly retorted, This is our city; will you abandon it to blood? And, Will you destroy my only chance to have my treachery redeemed?

I do not know what Zuri said. I do remember the noise Sarth made. A cataclysm, that he betrayed anything.

Then I thought what it might mean to Zuri herself.

Blood-lust. I had seen it in the prison; I understood now that I had seen a fundamental part of Zuri, something elsewhere perpetually smothered, which at last might be legitimately released. I remembered, crossing the city, the way she had wanted to turn on the hunters and blast them as we had the warriors in the hall; the way she had flown, instinctive as a killer-beast, for the truce-herald's invisible throat.

Sarth was beside me. He still had hold of her, I could hear her indignation and with it her fragile ignorance. But when he caught my wrist his fingers bit to the bone.

"Tellurith," he said.

Comprehension. Warning. Signal that he would not suffer it. The most dangerous of us all, warning me not to let his violence wake.

"Sarth?"

He froze. Then he shot the breath out his nostrils, one sharp concussive hiss.

I am the Ruand, I had said. This is the Quest. The House. Iskarda. You know the situation. Do we have a choice?

And he had answered, as starkly, as indignantly as I would myself: The Mother damn it!

Or whatever Sarth swears by, now.

Then he said, on a note I had not heard since the terrible old days, "At least let her know the choice."

Tender of her honor, her esteem, as he would be of mine. That was also the first time, Tanekhet, that I understood Zuri means as much to Sarth as I.

It is not something I can consider calmly, even yet.

* * *

Tibari has just brought me treasure-trove; another sheaf of paper, genuine, downRiver, properly rolled paper. Bizarre to see a man like that, tall as a house and slender as a spear, stalking among the couched warriors, armed and greaved, with a weapon in one hand and the other tendering, delicately as an honor baton, a Dhasdeini papyrus roll.

Yes. We are back; have been back, all this last section, in the citadel. Camping in the audience hall, about the only place that is truly safe, while we sort out Cataract.

After we gathered up the Haturas, there in the pumpkin field; scouts slipped off to call more from the surrounding dark, others slid forward to probe the city itself. And in a five minute conference that did not differ often enough to merit the name Discussion, Alkhes and Haturi and Zuri disposed of strategy, troops, assault and all.

We would approach the water gate. Openly, Haturas all around us, led by the kindled statuette.

Every move after that I doubted to my soul; but Haturi proposed it, and we had no choice but to trust her knowledge of her folk.

So when the reinforcements arrived, we woke the qherrique.

That is a little misleading; I *tried* to wake the qherrique. And I never raised a tingle until, feeling perfect idiots, our company joined hands and, as we had in the citadel, sang.

Then, behind its ensign, we marched on the Water Gate.

Halfway across the fields, Haturi asked, "You have a musician, Tel-yurith?" When I grunted, "Yes," as I stumbled over another field-corner, she enquired, "She want to sing?"

Given a song, Esrafal was more than ready. A Hatura started something, martial enough, by the beat of it. Gifted with an ear for words as well as musician's pitch, Esrafal heard him out a verse or two; a verse later she was harmonizing, beating time with a fistful of chains, and I had just understood she had made us an army to lead.

So it was in fine style, with pace quickened by the beat and the splendid Heartland voices to swell above us like a living banner, that we bore down on the water gate, with the cream of the City's defenders ranged along its flanks.

They knew we were coming; we had heard the panicked sentries' yammer and seen the squads of fireflies double toward our original breach. They could have sortied out to massacre us. They could have mown us down with the catapults. I only understood why Haturi had made such an entrance, and where, when she checked her 'troops' a hundred paces from the twitchy torchlit wall of metal and cedarwood, and called something in her high, old woman's voice.

The wall went quiet in a breath. I was looking at the leader of the right-hand detachment, splendid as a lion in his molded corselet and tall crimson plume, most likely the man in command; at that voice in the torch-glare I saw him all but flinch.

The torches sputtered, while on both sides the ranked troops shuffled and breathed. You could feel the shiver in the air. Beside me, Haturi spoke again, high and decisive for all the incomprehensible words, into that straining quiet.

Half the men on the wall-wards twitched. The leader made a quick, aborted movement. And answered Haturi, in a deep, resonant Heartland voice that included something like, "Ma-ma."

Around me, Haturas youths let out a breath, and stood quiet.

The leader shaded his brows with a hand. There was the strangest uncertainty in his tension now. He very nearly shuffled; before Haturi spoke again, quite shortly. The men on the wall quivered. But their leader, incongruously, half-relaxed, and Haturi turned to me, announcing complacently, "They talk truce."

* * *

After all, Tanekhet, it was less magic than shrewdly applied wits. Tibari was Wonsa's lieutenant. Haturi knew that his faction, however briefly, however beleaguered, was still in command; she knew he would race to meet the threat at its impact point.

And like Wonsa, Tibari and all his faction are Haturas too.

Upland Haturas, Tibari has been at pains to explain to me; not bred and born, like his Cataract blood-kin, into what the Heartlands call servitude. But blood-kin all the same; and like Alkhes, if for far longer, Tibari knew Wonsa's mind.

The Mother forgive us what we did here, Tanekhet; for Wonsa was far wiser, as well as less bloody, than any of us knew. Unlike the rest, he had been prepared to acknowledge the blood-link, had actually gone down into the city to propose his plans where they would matter most. Haturi's knowledge of those plans came from meetings with Wonsa himself.

So when the Folk's Heart told Tibari to put down his weapons and admit his leader's destroyers, and expect to find them and their magic on his people's side—Tibari did as she said.

* * *

Pass over the parley, the negotiations that got us and the still blazing qherrique and the assembled Haturas, with folk streaming into their train from all over the city, back to the citadel, to relieve Tibari's hard-pressed reserves from an incipient siege. Abbreviate, too, the skirmishes and haggling that have settled the other factions just short of mutiny: Tibari's folk are, for the moment, in control.

I do remember the meeting, there at the heart of moving crimson and torches' glow, when Tibari and Alkhes came face to face.

It is patronage to say it; but like his dead leader, Tibari is exceptionally civilized. Most Cataract officers would have ignored Alkhes; they are mercenaries. Most Heartlanders, blood or kinsworn, would have flown at his throat. Tibari did stiffen from heel to crown like a confronted lion; but only his eyes said, Murderer. Traitor. I will see you dead.

Alkhes stopped, with the first sign of life since he had settled the plans for the assault. The true sense was in his face, his bearing, as he said, so very softly, "I would rather have died myself."

That voice flawed Tibari's killer-gaze. As he blinked, Alkhes added, more quietly, "I was under oath."

Tibari blinked again. Then his eyes flickered to me, to the banner-glow of the qherrique. It was hardly appeasement; but I saw that he, like Alkhes, recognized honor-bindings. That he might grieve, but he understood.

He stared a moment longer, the helmet rim and torchlight turning his copper-mahogany eyes almost black. Before he grounded the long Heartland stabbing spear with a jab and a thump whose decision was itself a salute.

Watching Alkhes' face, I understood too; this was not merely an accommodation, not merely the protection such acknowledgement would prove among Wonsa's troops, not merely amnesty, however forced. This was absolution. Given by the only one who might command it; another fighting man; who, driven by the same necessity, might still see common ground across the shields.

* * *

Things have gone quickly since. We have reclaimed our weapons. We have . . . farewelled Gearth. Haturi has gathered supplies and gear and there will be, she says, folk for guides, at least to the top of the cliffs. Now only two obstacles remain.

Zuri, and the qherrique itself.

Which is why I am sitting here, in the alcove at the back of the hall that centers our encampment, on the shelf beside the statuette. With all the others, even Sarth and Alkhes, out of earshot by the hearth, and a perimeter made by Tibari's folk; waiting for the real battle to start.

* * *

Now I understand why my mother would say, Cross the enemy in arms before you tangle with a Trouble-head. But she ran down at last. Stopped pacing to and fro like a leopard caged. Came to stand beside me, one foot up on the seat. Said quietly, tiredly, "You know all that."

I said, "I know."

"And you still think Cataract . . ."

"Without you, we may lose the Quest. But if we don't settle the city before we leave . . ."

Alkhes would not go. And without him, neither would Sarth.

Like Sarth, she does not need words to follow our common thought. She growled in her throat, and stared into the wall.

"And what good will it be if we do succeed, without Iskarda?"

Of course she knew that too. Teach my Trouble-head strategy? Teach Haturi to suck eggs first.

She heaved a great sigh. Filed her nose. Tugged at the lapels of her fresh, second-best shirt. Miraculously, our gear aboard the patrol boat had been quite intact.

Then she said into the floor, "Have you thought that I may not be—the one for the job?"

"I've thought."

"But who else," she said it for me, "can do it at all?"

I put my hand on her knee. Once Zuri would have shied from that as Alkhes would at a touch from Sarth. Now she just gave me a look, and a wry twist of the mouth. And I understood all the things she could not say.

And I understood what Sarth had meant to her. Tower-trained, to unravel that knot of tangled, ingrown violence, to reason it through without words, and ease it into love; and to sustain the risks of doing it, from battery to very death.

"I can usually handle myself. With him . . . That night in Iskarda . . . that was a special case. Like here." The jerk of her thumb said, the prison cell. "Only—Tellurith, I've never been in *charge*—"

With no brake on what lay within her except what she could find for herself.

"It wouldn't be forever," I said.

"Eh?"

"A Regency. Just till they get the city together." I put it together as I spoke. For the irremediable choices you must offer some balance; some finite time of endurance, some visible hope. "You'd know—"

She looked at me, and the words died in my throat. How many years, said that look, how many tyrants' lifespans, will make a city of Cataract?

"Well, just till we come back . . ."

She did not have to look that time. I could not finish it myself.

She did have the charity not to retort, And without me, what hope is there of that? She did have the mercy, all but a divine mercy, not to mention Sarth.

But I thought of him. And it found me in that moment, with the clarity and completeness that is the Mother's own mark.

"What if," I said, "you had a fellow Head?"

"Eh?"

"Would you consider an outlander?"

"Hey?"

"One who knew the folk? And had their voice?"

"Ruand," said Zuri, with fragile patience, "what are you talking about?"

"What if I asked Haturi, to give you help?"

She drew in her breath. Her hand flexed over mine and closed. Then she said softly, "Yes."

*   *   *

Need I tell you that Haturi agreed? After a perhaps surprised pause, and a slitting of eyes, while she consulted her own oracle. In the light, her face speaks Wonsa's blood, a map of decades scribed deep on copper-mahogany over stark, age-refined bones, a crop of wiry gray short-trimmed hair, brass trade-rings in ears and nose. She considered a good minute. Before that thin-lipped mouth relaxed; then she reached along the bench and gave me one of her butterfly touches on the wrist.

"Yes," she said. "Clever, Tel-yurith."

"Harh," said Zuri. And sprang her ambush at last.

"If I agree to this, I want the qherrique."

That was my turn to say, "Huh?"

"Not the seed. The statuette."

"Oh, yes." She slitted her eyes at me, the gesture familiar as the closing of my own hand. Zuri's ultimatum point. "I know it may be past it, it mayn't work without the seed, it mayn't work for me at all. I want it, Tellurith."

"Zuri—"

"I need the back-up. I may need the firepower. I need them to know it's here."

"Zuri—"

The mouth slitted too.

"If you—and it—really want this . . . there'll be a way."

After all, what was it but another form of the ultimatum we would all soon pose? She nodded a little, dourly. As ready as me for blackmail to repay what we had already suffered in this enterprise, as ruinously costly to spirit as to flesh.

After all, I was asking her not merely to abandon her life's trust as my Trouble-head, not merely to accept exile and a role she was neither bred nor schooled for, but to risk her life.

Not to mention her very soul.

"And I want," she added evenly, "back-up for us both. My own folk."

I opened my mouth to squall like a cheated Verraini merchant, You can't have anyone else! She beckoned the others over and announced, "I've agreed to take on Cataract. I need help."

There was a short, hardly astounded pause. They had worked the possibilities out as well as Haturi did; I avoided Sarth's eye and wondered desperately how few I could persuade her to take. And blasphemed the qherrique again for driving me to such another obscene alternative; grudging folk to one of my folk, whom I had driven to needing them.

Then Ahio said, directing it somewhere between us both, "You keeping the statuette?"

Zuri nodded.

Ahio sighed and looked at me. "Ruand," she said, "whatever good I am on a cliff, I reckon I'll do more here."

A veteran shaper, with her Craft's resource as well as its scars. Who had spent her life, as Zuri had not, handling large blocks of qherrique.

What could I do but swallow and nod and say, "If we can make it work, Ahio . . . please."

As Zuri glanced around again Sunya said with her habitual quietness, "I've been troublecrew."

She met my glance and shook her head. "I'd just as soon stop at this."

Because it might be the city that had seen her husband die, but for all its memories, she had no more heart to go on. To persevere in the Quest.

Again, what could I say?

Especially at the way Zuri's body language spoke both gratitude and relief. One of her own folk in more than Ahio's sense. Someone who understood security, and danger, and war. A right arm to depend on. As she had been to me.

In the silence, it was Quiran who hazarded timidly, "But the statuette. How will you—"

Zuri gave me yet another dourly eloquent look. "We'll sort that out," she said, "too."

* * *

But first we had to install Zuri formally; have her acknowledged by the troops.

Haturi orchestrated that. In the hall, before the ruler's dais that now held two chairs, both draped with Heartland rugs, the palace's richest surviving ornamental table between them. And on it, the statuette.

Tibari's men answered their kin-leader's summons, and brought leaders from the rest. When they had settled to a sort of attention, Haturi stepped from among our group at the hearth-head, beckoned Zuri to one elbow and me to the other, and spoke.

They heard her out. Her status and kinship ensured that. But I could foresee the response in Tibari's eyes. The instant Haturi ended he fired a handful of missile-furious words.

Haturi answered in River-talk. "Tell us all."

His teeth clenched. Then he threw the words like a fistful of pebbles in Zuri's face.

"I am no toy for a Downstream whore."

It was all Zuri needed, of course. I saw her muscles drop into troublecrew's ready-slouch. She took three paces forward, into the open space.

"Come here," she said, "and tell me that."

Tibari's cheeks burned like red-hot bronze. He slammed the spear-butt down so hard the rafters rang. "I am a warrior."

"Feel safer," purred Zuri, "with an extra—spear?"

I thought he would throw himself at her. He threw the spear instead.

Zuri dodged; a slip of torso and twist of hip, the fluid reflex of a genuine Heartlander, trained from boyhood by dancing with the spears. Behind Tibari came a sharp, spontaneous, "Houh!" The Heartland sound of applause.

Unlike the jail-oaf, Tibari did not swear. He did tighten his sword-belt, with the utmost ostentation, before he started forward, deliberately as a father ready to put an obstreperous toddler to bed.

Zuri dropped into a hands-wide crouch. With ice in my belly I saw the grin, the too familiar grin, begin to invade her face.

Again, Tanekhet, I fear I am no fighters' connoisseur. Tibari was cunning, I will give him that. He must have heard about the jail-fight, for he did not charge. He circled. It was Zuri who rushed.

Into his hold and out again as he dodged, somersaulting over his arm and rolling off her shoulders, to slam his knee in passing with one lethal foot.

It landed as such a blow once did on Sarth; slap into the knee-joint, with such exquisitely judged force that she did not explode the kneecap itself, as such a blow can do, nor break the bone beneath. She just caught the nerve-point so paralyzingly he went down all but on his face.

Zuri flipped upright. Propped on a knee and a hand Tibari clawed for his sword, and she took two strides and kicked it high in the air.

The hearth-rim's cabled ornamental iron resounded to the clang. Tibari froze.

I thought there would never be an end to the pause. Before Zuri asked, coolly, quietly, "Enough?"

It was another endless moment before Tibari moved. Drawing the support hand laboriously under him, before he struggled to his feet. To stand swaying, until he brought his right hand up, a gesture of ancient ritual, and laid it open on his breast. And more slowly, bent his head.

As quickly, as naturally as opponents acknowledging a worthy bout, Zuri inclined her own. Moved sidelong, keeping her eyes on him, to the hearth. Retrieved the sword.

Asked, so quietly only he and we above the hearth-head could hear her, "Would their best have been enough?"

His head jerked. Their eyes met and held. And whatever that look said, I saw Tibari's shoulders loosen; then he lifted his chin.

Still watching him, Zuri murmured, "I have lost a city too."

That time the twitch was unmistakable.

She drew herself up a little. I saw her eyes, those snow-cold gray eyes that so rarely show anything, even in the thick of a brawl, and for that moment they looked open; almost warm.

Under her breath she said, "And I remember him."

This time Tibari did not move at all. But whatever his eyes or face or body-speech said, Zuri reversed the sword. Held it out, hilt first, and spoke this time full and clearly, "Will you take this from me?"

Their eyes gripped again. Before he managed the single, lurching step forward and his hand shut on the hilt.

Zuri backed toward the dais. On the lowest step, turned to the watching ranks. Waited, and had her answer: the lift of shields and slam of spears that is a Heartland, a Cataract ruler's salute.

* * *

Only when the troops had marched out, leaving Tibari perched on the hearthside for Zuri to instruct Quiran in application of a bruise poultice and ways to strap the joint, when Haturi had moved across to join them, did Sarth's hand close on me.

He turned me about. He was so white his eyes looked ebony and his expression went through me like an assassin's dagger-blade.

"She could," he spoke as precisely as he would sometimes in the tower, "have been killed."

"Sarth—"

His mouth went ugly. He let go and stepped back.

"Pray that the qherrique has answers," he said. "Because if it does not find some, I will."

* * *

So, Tanekhet, we cannot delay it any longer. The confrontation. The blackmail. The ultimatum. The recourse that is not supplication, to what has proved a truly faithless oracle. The passage that will decide the fate of our Quest.

And Iskarda's. And Amberlight's, and perhaps the entire River's.

And maybe, that of the qherrique itself.

We are all going. It is the company's right, from Zuri to Sarth, from Quiran to Alkhes; for Sunya, most of all. We have decided when and where. By consensus, the time is this coming night, the first of the full moon; the place was ordained by Keraz, donning her mother's authority at last.

"We can't do this in the citadel. Or the city either. We need a proper place. A holy place. Like in Iskarda."

I saw Alkhes shiver; of us all, perhaps only he and Keraz have seen that place firsthand, and for him "see" may not be the proper word. But Keraz was right enough.

There is a place, Haturi says. A Hatura initiation ground, I think, properly open to women alone. But since this is a matter for Flesh of the Moon, our men will be admitted too.

It has been another Cataract high-summer day, with the light flashing and glaring off every surface from spearblades to a wind-spun leaf, with dust flapping in the suddenly desiccated alley-ways and wind-whirls ploughing the River's breast. Summer here brings the desert suddenly, intimidatingly close. Not our summer, with harvest colors and ripe vegetation, brooding humidity and the building haze of storm. This is sere-dry, the nights bitter, the days hammer-hot, the sky high and bare as a temple vault, and that aridity hones the atmosphere, crackling from clothes, spark-ing from the brush as it meets your hair. As if all the world were qherrique.

The sunset colors are up now, bands of orange and washed scarlet above the long horizon sky. The holy place is an hour's walk away, up in the rougher country toward the cliffs. It may be a grove, or perhaps a bluff. That is what I, a daughter of the Mother, would expect. With Heartland folk, who can say?

But I must put the pen down and make ready. I know, Tanekhet, that you have felt so, and I half think it a futile gesture, myself; but I pray the news may be good, whatever it is, whenever I write again.

CHAPTER IX

Cataract
Mid-Summer's 2nd Day

Why is it, of late, I find myself writing in such states that I have no idea where to start?

The news is . . . Good is not a word for this. Or Bad; as always, Tanekhet, the qherrique makes every word in language come undone.

Let me begin in small things, as one does to cut a statuette. The Hatura holy place, then; which was not a bluff, but screened from eyes as from desert-wind in a valley's depth. And not a grove but a stamped, tamped, earth arena, on a flat apron in the bend of a vestigial desert watercourse, inside a perfect circle of trees.

Old trees. Big trees. Thick grown trees, and not our gentle helliens, but the double shield of desert thorn.

The guides showed us a gate, a barricade of interlaced thorn boughs, dragged by cunning holds amid their abattis, locked inside by a double pair of bars sliding into the nearest trunks. In truth, it is a Heartland stronghold, proof against men and animals both.

By the time they left the sunset had faded to gray, and a faint radiance announced the approaching moon. They had warned us to bring blankets and cloaks. They showed us the water-jars and privy place, and the fireplace at the arena's heart, with the thornwood piles, sole fuel for a sacred fire. As our officiant, Keraz enquired about kindling rituals; then they drew the Heartland scarves over their heads and vanished in the dusk, with Sunya and Deor following to shut the gate.

Silent and formidable as an Iskardan elder, Keraz lit the fire. But I did notice, as the company settled about the pit with its unadorned baked-brick rim, that she had offered no prayer.

There was no sound, then, but the kindling flames; no sight but the familiar, gravely closed faces, flicked and washed by firelight, and no sensation, but the waiting quiet.

I had thought, had hoped, that the company might begin for themselves; might pull together a procedure, a ceremony, some spontaneous outburst of the things we all had to ask. But as I looked around, I understood.

I will freely confess, Tanekhet, that how to proceed I had no idea. But at such moments, as with this letter, one starts at the obvious.

So I looked to Ahio, at Alkhes' left elbow, with the hump under her own heartside arm, and said, "Unwrap it now."

The fire dyed it to blood-tinged milk. With a shaper's caution, she did not lift or display but set it carefully to earth, on the cloth-of-gold brocade wrapping that had materialized from somewhere, before her crossed knees. Laid her hands either side, as you do in second-stage approaches to the block, and looked back to me.

I said, "In the Work-mother's name."

You may know it is the cutter's invocation. The shaper's as well. I don't know what I expected; I did not expect the statuette to glow.

And it did not.

I put a hand into my shirt for the silk-worked pouch.

The seed too caught fireglow like a crimson-tinged pearl. Deliberately, I handed it to Alkhes, nodding to Ahio; as deliberately, for all the tremor in his fingers, he passed it on. Just as deliberately, Ahio set it against the statuette.

When nothing happened, Esrafal sighed and thumped a palm against the fire-brick with a thud like a muted drum and commanded, "Sing."

We were more tuneful this time. Very soft, as becomes a holy place, but not a song for the qherrique; those you never record and never repeat. This was an evening hymn for the first quarter, to call the newborn moon.

The light welled up through the thorntrees as we sang, pooling in the arena, taking the deep recesses under the western trees and turning the thorn barriers laced behind them into eaves of mystery. It mingled with the firelight, it backlit some and caught other faces, until we were all daubed like ritual performers with silver and fire-rose. The moon cleared the treetops. The fire settled. The hymn reached its end, and reached it again.

And the statuette did not respond.

It was Keraz who made the sharp right-to-left sickle sweep by which the officiant signals, It is done. It was Esrafal's management that brought the voices to a reasonably melodic close. It was all our faces that spoke the denial, the frustration and disbelief and desperation, and then, rising like dammed floodwater, the rage.

It was Sarth, at my right elbow, who pronounced doom in that exquisitely expressionless tower voice, and a single monumentally banal word.

"So."

And I knew to my backbone that if nothing happened within a minute, he would stand up and walk out. That he would try to do so if I kneecapped him, that he would try if one of us drew a gun and burnt off his legs.

I clenched my own fists and felt tears and rage struggle redly at the back of my throat. Rot and gangrene you, I wanted to scream, Answer! Explain! Support us! Make this *work*!

The entire company was poised. I saw Sunya tighten an arm, Keraz shift a shoulder, Quiran tuck in a foot; I saw my own distress and bitter, furious disappointment on every face. I saw Esrafal staring across the flames, as at some tag-end not yet fully tied.

"Ruand," she said, "why did you tell me to sing?"

My face must have answered clearly, Huh?

"In the citadel. You yelled it right in my ear."

"But I didn't," I said.

Around her, the company's momentum checked.

Esrafal lifted her brows, and then settled her rump against the earth. "Well," she said, "*somebody* told me."

When I shook my head she went on, evenly, coolly, full into Sarth's barricaded stare. "So what I want to know, Ruand: who was it, if it wasn't you?"

Zuri sat forward sharply. Keraz turned about, Azo's lips parted. Sarth caught his breath; Esrafal stared back at him, copper high-lit plaits, bronze shadows on high-boned Amberlight cheeks.

They are both musicians. Perhaps, in that communion, he has shared questions he asks nowhere else. For clearly, she understood what else he is, beside the most lethal potential enemy of the Quest.

He glanced at Esrafal. Back to me. To the statuette. Then he stood up, and with the deadliest calm of that tower voice, said, "Answer us now. Or never look to be heard again."

I half-turned toward him instinctively; we were sitting close enough for my arm to touch Alkhes' knee. I felt him shift too, and across Sarth I glimpsed Zuri and Azo and Herar beyond her sway forward, craning across the flames.

And I felt the contact, like an internal qherrique strike, a slash across the backs of the eyes that seared its pattern on my eyelids as if burnt by qherrique flame.

A picture of you, Tanekhet.

In the Iskarda council-room. Full council, Darthis at Iatha's elbow and Iatha in the Ruand's chair. And you, Tanekhet, in your old modest merchant's coat and a new impeccable white shirt, ashen as if you were facing Antastes, those forest-light eyes dilated, the stare of a panther at bay. The look you flung from face to face as you cried, ". . . herself said, Men in their own right!"

Then I was spluttering, blinded, clutching Alkhes' elbow in red-starred dark.

* * *

We were a while sorting ourselves out; restoring eyesight, at the most prosaic point. Shaking, trying not to cry, with unbelief, with mad gratitude, with a frenzy of delight. With outrage and fury and a paroxysm of bewilderment.

"How did it do it?" shouted Ahio, always the most vehement, all but shaking the statuette. "What did *we* do? What was it? What does it mean?"

And Sarth, who had sat down in the blind-dark as if his legs had given under him, a hand clutching my shoulder so hard I wear the bruises still. Who clutched me as eyesight cleared to show the frenzied ring that shouted and gesticulated around the flames, clutched me so I felt his fingers tremble, though there was only tower impassivity clapped like a mask over his face.

Who at Ahio's bellow got out, at last, through lips stiff as desert-dried rawhide, "Wait. Think."

Ahio started to bawl. Esrafal jerked Chenath's sleeve, Chenath instinctively grabbed Deor, Deor's Navy reflexes caught Sunya and with training's instinct Sunya passed the signal on. Ahio stopped. Esrafal snapped fingers to take her eye and shook her head vehemently. Then looked pointedly away. Not to me, but to Sarth.

Very slowly, Sarth put a hand to his forehead. Drew his palm up it, a gesture I had never seen him make before; a mime of mental collection as much as of demolishing shock.

The hand came down; he looked at me, those eyes dark as unpolished bronze, and asked, "Do you remember who said that?"

I did remember then. Tanekhet had quoted words I said myself. To Sarth. In Riversend. About you, Tanekhet.

When you first asked to come with us. He had said, "Who's going to marry *him*?" And I answered, seeing the Mother's vision. "Maybe, it's time the House had men who are there in their own right."

Do you, Tanekhet, understand how my head reeled then? Can I imagine how yours is reeling now?

Sarth's hand closed on my wrist; I leant on his shoulder a moment. As I straightened, he took both my hands and spoke past me to the rest.

"Tellurith said that. About Tanekhet." And as they looked at him with hardly less blankness, he finished it off.

"Tanekhet wasn't there."

* * *

Fill in the babble, the hypotheses flying like maddened bees; through which I unpacked the sequence of impossibilities into Sarth's waiting eyes.

"Tanekhet wrote to me that he was—that somebody wanted to marry him." You will probably thank your River-lord, Tanekhet, that I had the wit, still, not to mention her name. "He was having a lot of trouble. Perhaps . . ."

"You think he got your letter. About Amberlight." His voice, deep, dark as the River, almost steady, took me up. "And you think he remembered Damas. And asked for a dream himself."

"And that was what he got."

Our eyes locked, a bridge across a widening chasm of impossibility. Then Sarth sat back. And repeated, with a shove of a hand into his hairline and a jagged shake of the head, "What did we *do*?"

Alkhes leant to the pair of us, his own hand on my arm. Zuri beyond Sarth said something sharp, and then caught his elbow, just as Ahio plucked at Alkhes' shirt. And the lightning struck.

Skull-splitting, blinding, a block of vision that clove my brain-core like an axe.

Darthis at that council table, looking at you, Tanekhet, the bulldog set of jaw that says she has made up her mind. Saying, with that flinty calm, "It will be in your own right."

When my eyes stopped running, I groped for Sarth's arm; just as his hand found mine and he said, openly desperate, "How? How?"

While I burst out, "Never mind, How! What?"

My distraction steadied him. I heard him draw a breath; invoking, I have no doubt, tower discipline. Almost coolly he said, "What will be in his own right?"

"In the House." It fell open like a puzzle turned right way up. "Even if he marries, he'll be there in his own right."

"Why?"

"Never mind, Why." Alkhes said it, shaky but still commanding as a general. "It isn't clear, we're not getting it, we need to fix the signal first. Not What, How?"

We stared at each other, children left with a Dhasdeini mirror-signal unit, live messages arriving and no way to decipher them. Sarth still had my arm; Alkhes caught my elbow as some idea struck, I saw it light like a torch in that torch-lit face just as Ahio jogged his back and Zuri tapped Sarth.

And the signal-bolt fired.

Dazzling this time, here and now and blasting with the vehemence of a—god's? frustration. Dark as bronze on mahogany and moving in firelight like an ornate Verrain hand-brooch come to life.

Sarth's hands and mine, clasped.

Shaking my head in a stupid attempt to knock the stars out I heard Sarth say frantically, "Don't touch!"

"That's it," he was saying when my eyes cleared. "We touched then, Tellurith, me, you, Zuri tapped my back. Ahio, did you . . .?"

Beyond Alkhes, Ahio's gravel voice was muted by awe, "I just tapped his shoulder?"

Sarth said past me, "Ahio, did you see?"

She had seen. Sunya, Deor and Chenath, and Keraz beyond him had shared the original sight; Zuri, like Ahio, had shared the second and third.

"It begins around here." Sarth again, almost composed. "It goes to whoever we touch. So . . ."

When he looked at me expectantly I wiped my eyes and vainly tried to be intelligent, before I gave in and retorted, "So?"

"So why don't we," he said calmly, "all link hands?"

We did it, of course. I prayed earnestly that with the entire circle linked the bolt would not rip my eyes clean away. But it was much less violent. Steadier, clearer, an extended scene.

One you will know, Tanekhet.

That council meeting, where you explained your dream. And what the council did with it.

It was Quiran, always the most intrepid if seldom the most knowledgeable, who finally pushed the word out like a raft into the mingled glow of moon and fire.

"Why?"

Sarth answered; chin on hand, staring into the flames, as motionless and beautiful and mind-shattering as an oracle.

"It went wrong."

I did manage, with great ado, not to be the one who shouted, "What?"

"He—Tanekhet—asked for a dream. You saw his face. He thought it would keep him safe. And it did not."

It was I who managed the next step. More quakily than Quiran's, I heard my voice venture into the quiet.

"So its message . . . went astray."

No doubt, Tanekhet, you will follow the rest; even if your own stake in this blinds you, for a while, to everything else. Yes. It sent you a dream. And the dream was misread.

And yes. You may use this, if the letter ever reaches you, as support incontrovertible, unassailable. Your reading was correct.

* * *

As for the other ramifications . . . You will hardly be surprised at who, in our time and place, was first to take them up.

"So it stopped sending dreams," Sarth almost whispered, "because the messages can go astray."

I recall Alkhes looking across me, brows lowered, catching, like me, the inflection of that voice.

Sarth never noticed. His eyes were locked on the fire.

"It left us to find a way out. To fix it all . . . ourselves."

Everything that had meant to him, to Alkhes, to Zuri and Keraz and above all to Sunya, was in that tone. I felt the company move, the surge of a crowd on the brink of riot.

Sarth raised his head. And with a motion peremptory as an oracle's, held out both his hands.

Zuri understood as quickly as I; his purpose was in her jaw's set as she grasped his right hand and reached hers to Azo beyond. Settling my own fingers, feeling Alkhes lock his hand on them as on a shield's grip, I saw the ring form, and the faces, clear around the fire.

Sarth said, "Do you know what that cost?"

Silence. Then an image, sharp as a knife's entry, clear as if caught in qherrique light. The trees outside Cataract, Alkhes in Sarth's own arms, weeping as if to tear apart his soul.

Sarth said, "Why?"

Sharper still this time. Alkhes' voice, breaking under the words like the back of a foundered ship.

"And I unders-stood, I respected him—and I knew, whatever he felt about me—he wou-ouldn't let us go . . ."

Alkhes tore his hand from mine. The ring and whatever the rest was shattered. Catching at him with the only solace I could give, I heard Sarth behind me, implacable as a judge.

"Why?"

Silence. Grimly, Sarth reached for my arm. Drew it from about Alkhes, grasped my wrist. Looked past me at Ahio.

Who, with the expression she had worn when she abandoned her shaper, put her hand on Alkhes' knee.

What came then was long familiar, deep-marked in all our memories. The picture of that upland lake with its opal-tinted waters under the flowering reeds, the dew-garlanded forest listening in the dawn, and the spring's whorl, where the waters come down from the snows.

And the haste, the frantic urgency. Go, go, go.

Half of us lurched up instantly; but Sarth yanked both my and Zuri's wrists and hurled the words at Esrafal. "Tell us why!"

Slowly, we sank back. The hands linked; the circle quieted, recentering itself on Sarth.

He repeated it, with precision that was more than the trance of an oracle. "Why?"

For what this image did, there are no proper words. It did not settle like a reflection in calming water, it had no finite edges, as does the glimpse caught by a lightning flash. It did not . . . coalesce, like cream rising, nor assemble from present elements as does a vision you discover in coiling smoke. It was . . . approximately, it was blurred, and for the first time there was something like a sense of strain.

Alkhes and I, on a road through the Sahandan. A glimpse of dried rice paddies, a motley line of carts and refugees ahead of us, the great gray pillar of a storm behind. Me in the clothes I took out of Amberlight, and my disreputable straw Korite hat. Alkhes a walking disaster-site, filthy, tattered, an arm in a sling, the other through a black horse's reins. Speaking slowly, shakily, an anguish of loss and remembrance that cut to my own heart.

"The night I touched it—I'll never forget . . ."

A long pause.

"And when it spoke. I know I never had much to do with it— but to feel that . . . to feel it there . . ."

That time it was I who pulled away.

When I looked at him, Sarth had two tiny upright lines between his brows; the first sign of perplexity I ever saw on that immaculate face.

Without looking he reached for my hand. Aloud he said, "That is our Why. But yours?"

Sharp and instant then as a very lightning flash. Me, Tanekhet, somewhere in Riversend, talking to your earth-scribes. Saying with the edge of exasperation, "Gentlemen, then or now, these questions are irrelevant. All they tell us is that your words do not work, do not work, do not work."

While Zuri and Herar blinked, Sarth sat back and let out a long, soundless sigh.

Then he said, "Tellurith, the messages. In Amberlight. Did they come in words?"

He read my expression as no-one else can. Glanced past me to Alkhes, to Ahio, and nodded; a philosopher whose hypothesis has been confirmed.

"It's never used words. It gave you a sense, a feeling; a Yes, when it was right. But a verbal—message, no."

Ahio opened her mouth and let it shut.

"Because," said Sarth deliberately, "it has no words. So it has to use ours. And it can't put them together for itself. It can only use something we've already said."

Around the circle ran a long, comprehending sigh. But Ahio grunted and looked at me.

You have heard it speak, said that stare, as I have, with the block, you have read the assent of the mother face. You have asked more complex questions, and had answers, as House-heads do. Why is it different now?

Sarth took my wrist. The image formed instantly; the hill of Amberlight, girdled with great pearl-glow slabs of qherrique. And then the seed, cupped in someone's muddy, trembling hand.

"It's different?"

The same image.

"It's too small?"

Exasperation, strong as the scent of sweat, and an image fairly exploding in my mind. Iskarda, me kneeling on the bedroom floorboards, giving thanks to heaven. "Because this time You have got it right."

Sarth began, "Got what," Zuri yanked his arm and snapped, "Don't ask, it can't tell us. Think!"

Sarth opened his mouth. Shut it again, and stared dourly into the fire. Across him Zuri demanded, "Got what right?"

"Got," I answered at length, "the balance. Women and men. Both hearing the, the dreams."

After a yet longer pause, it was Keraz who said evenly, "So where, exactly, did our words not work?"

"Could it not say what it wanted," she went on, when we all looked round, "or didn't we read it right?"

This time the pause was arrested; then Sarth sat up straight and stretched out his hands.

Words will not fit that time at all, Tanekhet. Struggle? Opacity? Inchoate shapes moving through smoke? A deep sea current, swirled in ways no leaf can read?

Or simply qherrique, trying once again to answer a question, and failing, for some cause beyond our comprehension. Or because there were no human words, no human referents at all?

Whatever it was, the invisible turbulence faded, and left only silence in its place.

"It's—"

Sarth stopped; I felt his hand clench, and read as easily the tiny sigh before he spoke again. We had reached that topic's limit. And he had other things, many other things, still to ask.

What he said was, "Did you know?"

No response. Sarth repeated, this time with an edge that rasped like emery dust, "Did you know?"

A fragment from the scene with the Dhasdeini scribes and my tone of exasperation. ". . . your words do not work, do not work, do not work."

Sarth's jaw set; imperceptible, that motion, as the moment that clouds curdle into rain. Very quietly, he said, "Did you know what would happen? In Cataract?"

This time it was the night the dispatches came, with me reading your letter, Tanekhet. The words I never spoke aloud, seen as they came up on the page.

. . . it concerns me most of all, Tellurith. Granted a patrol-boat, cutters, fifteen skilled and subtle folk bred in Amberlight, granted the—putative—assistance of the qherrique. What will that be, against the armed, habitual, roused malignance of a city like Cataract?

As the circle burst into talk Sarth rubbed his brow with the look of a baffled priest.

"Does it mean," Zuri said at last, "that it *couldn't* help?"

"Or that it worried too?" Azo, driven beyond her usual subordinate's reticence.

"Because it couldn't help—"

"Or because it couldn't see?"

Quiran tousled his hair in tufts and burst out, "But it did something at Amberlight!"

I said, "That was before a message went wrong."

Sarth had ignored us all. Now, imperatively, he held out his hands; when quiet came, he said in a voice that was all knife-blade, "How much did you know?"

The silence this time was absolute. Lengthening. Blank, with a blankness that shouted obduracy.

Sarth frowned, and looked a patent question at me. But it was Keraz who spoke, with the gesture of an Iskardan officiant, throwing the words as they do at the altar-side. She commanded, "Go on."

Go on, not with questions, but with interpretation. You are the one who does it best.

Sarth looked almost startled too. Then he rubbed his forehead, and sat a long moment staring into the fire.

Before he said abruptly, "Tellurith, what is qherrique?"

I opened my mouth to splutter; and managed to stop at, "Sarth?"

He smiled a little, bitterly. "'Your questions are irrelevant.' In the tower, they said, 'It is not yours to ask.'"

"The scribes," that tone jerked me into speech, "asked things like 'Is it an animal? Is it a plant? Is it like copper or diamond or rock?'"

Ahio spoke my answer, one rich, derisive snort.

"You told me once." He had been silent so long, I jumped when Alkhes spoke, "that words like talk, think, speak—didn't apply."

Sarth was looking at him too.

"But it did speak. And it must think. And it did—plan."

With a twist on that last word that must have cut open all our hearts.

Sarth's mouth corners curled. He reached for our hands, and flung the question into the fire.

"How much did you plan?"

There was no reply.

Sarth released us. After a moment, he said, "So is it sentient?"

More silence.

"Is it of this world?"

He swept his eyes around the circle. They stopped at Esrafal, who lifted her shoulders and replied. "Amanazar found a 'bed.' Just one."

It needed no more to invoke our common memory; that hill girdled in its bulwarks of qherrique. Thirteen of them, high as walls, broad as moats.

"So it has flesh. It lives. It grows."

He looked at my cupped hand, and I read the flicker in his eyes, the weight of blood on the unspoken words.

"Is it more than . . . of this world?"

He drew his gaze around us, deep and somber as the regard of living bronze. We looked into those eyes, that asked a question beyond the scope of any oracle, and found no way to reply.

"A demon?"

The answer was in the circle's body language, a response quicker, truer than any words; not with the rapport we have shared, the communion we have made. Not even with the demands that it has made on us.

"Then is it a god?"

It was Alkhes who said, "Eh?"

Sarth rested his head on a palm a long, poised moment; before he answered, in the voice of a man setting out to walk the rim of a precipice.

"What is a god, Aglis?"

"Uh," said Alkhes. My sweet soldier; a plain man, however devastating his soldier's wits. It was Ahio who answered, deep-throated, unhesitant.

"The Mother. That's the only god there is."

I heard Keraz murmur some ritual affirmation. Sarth's eyes dwelt on the fire.

"Can you tell me why?"

"Well—well—" Ahio's arms waved. "She knows all. She sees all. She gave the world birth and She will see its death. All things are in Her power. She never dies."

Sarth turned my hand over in his and looked at the seed that had somehow returned to my palm, and I alone knew how deep was the bitterness with which he murmured, "Never dies."

Before he lifted his head and said more clearly, if hardly less bitterly, "So all things fall by the Mother's will?"

Ahio opened her mouth and shut it again; like most of us, I doubt she had glimpsed the chasms qherrique has opened in my husband's mind.

If it shaped us all to its death in the fall of Amberlight, who could say what else it shaped? From a dead child's conception to the meeting on that River bank, from revolution in Amberlight to Ahio's own recollection of Dinda's statuette?

To the child's death?

To the deaths of Gearth, and Wonsa, and the worst cruelty of Alkhes' life? To every stain on the soul we have found in Cataract?

Sarth's mouth pinched. Aloud he said, "Do Her messages go astray?"

Silently, Keraz shook her head.

"But if they are Her word . . . How do you know?"

I felt Alkhes shudder against me, and I understood the tone in which he said, "You know. Believe me, you know."

He had been the Chosen. He had brought such a message, through whatever gate of drugs and ritual and the conscious mind's abeyance I could only guess.

Sarth leant an elbow on a knee. He sounded half-dreaming now, and I saw Esrafal's eyes fixed on him as on a very oracle.

"How else can She be known?"

The silence hung like a shelf imperfectly braced.

Keraz said, "She is in everything. The harvest. The year's return. The season. The—"

"Fall of good and bad," said Sarth, and there was vinegar in that voice as in the curl of his mouth. "And good seasons are the Mother's boon, as bad ones are her punishment."

Keraz opened her mouth and let it shut.

Sarth lifted his head and stared steadily into the fire and spoke almost as steadily, in the voice of a man pulling down his dearest dream, stone by stone.

"Those are all things they say about the River-lord. And Dhe, in Verrain. And all these godlets in Cataract. I daresay," with a twist of irony that knew what he would evoke, "the whores used to claim such power for their images in Amberlight."

Ahio's mouth opened on a roar of outrage. Sunya hit her in the ribs so hard it choked.

"I have been a god. Or at least, the image of a god," said Sarth.

He smiled a little, straight in Ahio's eyes. "A sculptor used me for a model of the River-lord. Will I hear, do you suppose, when Dhasdeinis pray for a good season, or a fair voyage, or a safe wedding day?"

Ahio gulped.

"What we call the Mother," he had looked back to the fire. The words came like more than prophecy. They were vision, but vision of the unthinkable. The geography of a country that has never known mortal foot. "What we call the Mother is whatever they call the River-lord. It's a name; a hope. A thing we must have. A way of pretending there is really—something—more in the world than chance."

Were we still in Amberlight, he might, had anyone let him get that far, have been burnt alive. But we had been through the city's death, and the Houses' fall, and the jail-pit of Cataract. We listened to our oracle, and found no way to answer, No.

Sarth sighed; and then spoke bleakly as the looks that dwelt on him, accepting the conclusion to which that premise had driven the philosopher himself.

"So the qherrique is not a god."

He took a deep breath.

"Or even the will of one."

I daresay the silence reverberated to our united soundless, *What?*

He glanced around. "Because it does die," he said. "Because its messages have already gone astray."

"So," he turned back to his own fiery oracle, leading him, that voice said, where no philosopher, no visionary, could ever wish to go. "The qherrique may not know everything. It may not be able to accomplish everything . . . It may make—it has made—mistakes."

We fell with him into the abyss he had conjured under our feet. Not a god. Not even the agent of a god. Not omniscient, then, not omnipotent, not the designer beyond whose goal evil itself emerges as the tool of providence. Mortal. Worldly. Fallible as ourselves.

Something that could not sustain the weight we load on gods, however capricious. The burden of unquestioned, undoubting trust.

There was an aching pause, during which I saw his own shoulders stiffen, and the eyes of the voyager confront the most terrible landfall yet.

"And perhaps," barely audible, "it may be wrong."

I knew what my own face said, because I read it on the rest. Before Sarth moved, with the ceremonial purpose of a priestess and a terrible determination that was more than sleepwalker or assassin or even an oracle's focus. Sitting back, straightening those rigid shoulders, before he spoke again, into the heart of the fire.

"You will not tell us what you want in this. What you knew. How much you planned."

I knew by the inflection that he was remembering, once more, that riverbank.

"But you want us to keep going."

He lifted his head and spoke with the weight of an ultimatum.

"Show us what you *can* do, then. Prove that this is not a mistake."

Then, softer, more inexorable than the fall of incense into the altar flame, "Give us some reason to go on."

* * *

Nothing replied.

As the silence drew out, grew unbearable, I felt the rage, the final wrath of disillusion building in my throat. The pause reached fracture point; and Keraz said with a snort, "Every Voice needs Ears," and held out her hands.

We felt it immediately. Down the neck, over the scalp, on the backs of the wrists; the brooding presence, the weight of purpose and some enormous intent that a cutter wakes, that talented shapers sometimes feel, in time to stop before the block rebels and fires.

Alkhes' body brought me Ahio's wrench at his wrist, and I understood. But it was Keraz who rapped, "Keep still!"

Ahio made something like a whimper, and clenched her lip in her teeth.

The sensation crescendoed, swift as building storm on a sultry summer day in Amberlight. An image blazed behind my eyes.

The statuette, with the seed against its base.

We passed it hand to hand. The storm waited. Ahio drew her hand back. The statuette began to glow.

To burn, to blaze, until it was incandescent, until every one of us had to shut eyes and avert heads and cower like cockroaches from a naked flame. The next image burned over that, inside our minds.

The statuette, braced between someone's hands.

Ahio caught her breath. Reached out.

Grunted as if punched and yanked her hands back before they were six inches away, wrung and then sucked fingers as if against a physical burn. The storm-brooding intensified. Another vision burned against my lids.

Here and now and present reality; Zuri's averted face.

I felt Sarth's hand clench in mine. I had no time to wonder, for the next picture was already in my brain.

The inner room at Amberlight, me in my House-head's gear with a train of worthies, and a dark, too familiar foreign face awaiting me, a greater train at his back. The place where Telluir House tuned and handed over ruler's statuettes.

* * *

You may not believe this, but it is seldom so very difficult, Tanekhet. I admit, I never before presided over a statuette that burnt like a moon about to melt, and never in such a ramshackle ceremony. In Amberlight, the preparation is stringent and rigorous, for everyone's sake. No more than a kinglet wants his eyes burnt out or his hands blown off does an Amberlight House want catastrophe to attend the transfer of its . . . merchandise. But however unprepared Zuri may have been, her resolution nobody could fault.

And when the moment came . . . when her hands closed on it, when the rapport's connection spoke, eloquently as it always does, in her dazzled, awestruck, for once unshielded eyes . . .

Give me a space for rancor, Tanekhet. Give me a time for envy, and a jealousy nobody can share; except a woman from old Amberlight.

And, perhaps, Alkhes.

She took it with her to her place. The light was ebbing, from molten incandescence to the pure moon glow that had led us out of Cataract, welling out, white and brilliant and unfaltering between her reverent hands. Ahio scrambled across to lay the brocade out, before she lowered it to earth.

The light waned until it was a mere a counterpoint to the fire. Zuri sighed like a sleeper waking, and looked at Sarth.

Who held out his hands, and when we took them, asked, "Will it wake again without the seed?"

Both Keraz and Ahio gave him a dirty look. Zuri smiled briefly, if incredibly, and inclined her head.

I really did have to fight myself then, Tanekhet. Because I knew what that meant. She had the true, the old, the House-head's rapport, where you could ask questions. And know the answers, not by hazard and others' words and interpretations of uncertainty, but with a bird's swift unspoken sense of north.

Sarth said, "Will it answer our questions now?"

Zuri looked startled. The statuette faded on the breath.

When we urged, Zuri tried to waken it; and it roused. When I asked, "Will it work for you in the city?" she nodded.

But as soon as Sarth asked that other question? Like a snuffed candle, phut.

We tried three times before we gave up. It was Sarth, then, who took the seed in his palm and said, very quietly, but with that knife-blade edge, "How does that prove you right?"

The seed burnt his palm so hard he hurled it clear away from him. As I picked it up, it stung mine.

Sarth grabbed my wrist before I could try again; I flinched away, but not in fear for myself.

"Give me one good reason," he spoke thickly, the nearest I ever heard Sarth to complete loss of control, "why we should not turn back now?"

I caught his wrist, the image caught us all. The road to Marbleport, a marching column in the distance; the scarlet of military kilts, the spark of swinging spears.

I yanked Sarth's shoulder before he could get up. "Wait! No! Sarth—!"

"If it thinks I will be forced—"

"Sarth!"

He sat. Literally grinding his teeth together, sweating like an over-goaded horse. But still, he trusted me that much. He sat.

Perhaps it was that he never handled the old qherrique, that he never knew the caprice, the violence, the many times inexplicable savagery with which it could react. Even then he expected the sanity, the decency, we look for in a god.

I gripped his wrist again and spoke aloud into the dark.

"Don't play tyrant with us. You owe these folk. You know you owe us more than explanations. If you can't offer surety, at the least, give us a pledge."

The silence held so long I almost gave up. I did have to squeeze Sarth's wrist. Then, very slowly, the statuette kindled to its pure qherrique fire.

The storm roused with it, but more quietly this time. There was something in it of resolution, something almost . . . human. A mind, if the word would only fit, drawing to a course of action, to a last, hazardous, all-important choice.

In my own mind a vision formed. My hand, taking up the seed.

I did feel my fingers tremble, and I had to jerk again at Sarth. But when it slid into my palm, despite everything, I recognized it.

Familiarity. A cherished presence, regained. Relief.

Ridiculous, ineradicable.

Trust.

The statuette blazed like a lightning flash, the fire flew up in a starburst of sparks and every coal went out. An image overrode the confusion in its wake; me in the pumpkin field with the Haturas, snapping, "Stand fast!"

After all, we trusted it so far. We sat.

* * *

And so we have our pledge, Tanekhet. We are assured of its . . . goodwill, if nothing else, and its powers, whatever they may be, however circumscribed by chance. And the company is resolved.

As soon as the gear is assembled, we are going on.

* * *

I will not write the rest for Tanekhet. This is for the company, for me and mine and no-one else. But for them I will try to capture it; that moment in the dark when the air changed, or the light did, or something shifted in my own bones and flesh.

I do not know what the others saw; something as close, as dear to them, to judge from what I did not so much hear or see as felt. Heart-shaking as that moment when whatever it was that came to us took me like a child to a mother's breast.

What I met *was* my mother. On a day in childhood, that thirty-two years' memory have cut to the clarity of some blue sunlit gem, smiling outside the tower door as she puts an arm around me. I am up to her shoulder, though only nine. She had meant to show me the mine, the very first time, and been deflected by a crisis in the shapers' shops. She smiles, holding me in that distant sunlight, as she says, "It will happen, sunbird. I promise. Next time, it will be all right."

I can hear it now, the familiar slightly burred slide of her voice, and under it the gravity that says she means every word.

That it is a pledge.

Which the intensity of a child's belief turned to living crystal, a bubble of never-fading time, of joy and expectation and sureness of the world's best safety. Knowing yourself loved.

That was what I felt, in the darkness of the thorn arena, last night.

* * *

Was it a god? Sarth argues, and his thoughts are irresistible as a Dhasdein phalanx, that it is not. If I had to approximate words, I would say it was whatever gods gift to a holy festival; when you are no longer a solitary consciousness, but aware, connected, a willing, knowing element in a greater . . . being? sentience?

Self?

I do remember we had all stood up; we were still holding hands, and we looked up at the moon that was now high and clear overhead, unsullied by the horizon's desert dust, and I recall quite well how Sarth's pulse jumped under my fingers, and the way he whispered, "Midsummer night."

That may have been what the message meant. I did not ask then. I am not asking now; but I am sure beyond doubting that we had what we demanded. We were given a pledge.

Tanekhet would not understand. Tanekhet, who has never shared a festival at Amberlight, let alone Iskarda, would certainly not understand what happened next; I could never make him see that it was not just flesh, nor simply custom, even some form of reverence. I could never convince him of what I know, sure as a qherrique's answer, within myself. That what we did might have used the rituals of a festival, or the simplest, yet the most complete of mortal avowals. But that it included more than us.

I do remember that nobody had to question; or explain. I recall we picked up blankets and cloaks and went off as calmly as in a familiar ritual, dividing as easily as if we had done it all our lives. Azo and Herar, Quiran and Keraz, Deor and Chenath—and Sunya. Ahio and Esrafal. Alkhes and I.

Zuri and Sarth.

There was darkness in the eastern thorn recesses. There was silence, that was the sacrament of the night. Throughout that entire interval we did not converse with any spoken word; and yet I have never known so entirely, so absolutely, another human mind.

I will remember that Alkhes wept; but with gladness, because love was surcease and forgetfulness, and its own sort of pledge; to move beyond memory's crippling, and yet not forget.

And I remember, too, that when the moon shifted halfway over, there was movement on the arena. And then they slid in beside us as if we were visible as day.

Zuri. And Sarth.

In that enchantment, I even understood the marks on his ribs that were not moon dapplings. The black eye, the other bruise on his face.

That also, whatever flowed with us showed me, was a lustration, a purgation, as making love had been to Alkhes. Whatever that jail-fight woke in her, this was its exorcism and its final release. And its own sort of farewell.

And whatever I make of that, it had been the same for Sarth.

But he did come to me, then; and with the three of us it was as it had been that other Midsummer night.

I can just bear to think of that. I can more easily remember the wonder that Alkhes coped with Zuri's presence, if it was two people away from himself. I can far more easily recall the, the joy; the enchantment; the moments beyond either death or life.

I do wonder, was the other presence with us on that night as well?

The next parallel I will not so much as think about. It gave us what we asked; if it could not give surety, it made us a pledge, it gifted us with solace, and release and joy in the surest refuge, among ourselves.

If it gave us one thing more . . .

I will not so much as pray. Who would hear it, after this? I will simply hold it, as I have held the memory, as I carry the seed, as I have held—something else—in the place under my heart.

Next time, it will be all right.]

CHAPTER X

Assuana
21st Day, 2nd Summer Moon

As the gods see me, Tellurith—!

I think I am laughing—I *know* I am laughing, I have the maddest urge to career around the suite as Kheizo and Dheya did, to flourish my arms, shout slogans and battlecries and vows of lunatic libations and, and—

Sit down and shake like a boat-brat with River fever. Because you are turning my dreams and nightmares both into reality. Right before my eyes.

* * *

Well. The good things, naturally the good things first, and if you were here I would kiss you myself—I would damned well *hug* you, my lady world-maker, as the gods see me I would try to take you to bed, and the Nine-armed Adversary fly away with *both* your men.

Alive. All three of you. O, Tellurith, I am a black-hearted reprobate, and I have been on my knees an hour before Dhe's little foreigner-shrine that is set ostentatiously in the main room corner. And when I find a votive that comes near this bounty, I will offer it. Whatever it is.

A god-provoking vow, no doubt of it. Today, what do I care?

Because you have done it again: reversed all expectations, defied all reasonable reality, found allies in the wind and resources out of empty air. And not only survived, the River-lord take you— you have done it. You have actually done it.

You have overturned Cataract.

I picture you raising eyebrows in astonishment. In some censure, at my lack of faith. Or at least, I would have pictured it, before that letter came.

With its first pages already all but indecipherable, the rat-scratch writing on that crumpled hunk of papyrus, the splattery, fading ink—not to mention the mildew, the mud-stains—

And the blood.

I will freely confess, Tellurith, that if I had to suffer this hell, I would sooner it prolonged till now, than have had that first half-letter by itself.

I am almost as thankful as for the news, to think that if I did try to summon some semblance, some shred of—sympathy—of condolence—it would be more egregious than silence, coming so late.

Far too late for that—massacre. Gods know, I never shared the siege of Amberlight. To have ordered, to see with your own eyes a light-gun's devastation, to have wreaked it yourself. Let be the prison.

Or—Alkhes.

It is my doing as much as any, that shadow on our joy. If I had never—tormented him—things might have been different, at Cataract, even at Amberlight. That it cost a man who might himself have transformed Cataract . . .

It is more than a votive. It is expiation I owe.

As for the rest . . . The escape, the resurrected qherrique, the Haturas, the siege undone—it is as mad and glorious a reversal as the end of a boat-town play. But to leave Zuri as Regent—I am as torn as you, Tellurith. I know what she means to you, let be to the Quest. And yet, to have secured, won over, to have *won* Cataract . . .

As the River-lord sees me, you are making my dreams come true.

All of them, Tellurith.

* * *

The qherrique? You will settle that soon enough. I feel, indeed I feel for you when you thought it had deserted you—have I not known that loss? I feel for Alkhes, left with that decision, as I try to feel, amid those speculations of his, for Sarth. But if it wants you to reach the River's Source, it will sort things out. And clearly, these events say it plainer than any intelligence report, you are meant to reach the Source.

On second thoughts, I had best strike that from the final draft. The qherrique—I know what I felt. I know what I hoped. Whatever else it may be, to Tellurith, to Alkhes, to Sarth, I do not pretend to understand. But clearly, to her at least, there is still a reckoning to make.

For the rest . . . I am flattered, my lady, to think that you would leave me the decision over Asaskian, the more so that you trust my experience, and my vanity—my vanity, forsooth, how much of that is left? to steer me clear of marriage, and most of all that your inclination runs with mine. And no doubt you will be delighted, when you hear that I have dodged so far as Amberlight, if not to Assuana. What you will think when—if—that letter reaches you, I will not pretend to guess.

* * *

Meanwhile, the news has ruptured Assuana too: after that nadir of desolation, it is—it is—Without your letters, I would not believe it myself. But they came downRiver together, on that same patrol boat, with my freighter in company. The first traffic dispatched, indubitably by Zuri's canny handling, out of Cataract. We had the word this morning—it flew through the city like lightgun fire, and the letters, bless my freighter-captain, right on its heels. I detect Dhanissa's hand in that.

I could wish to detect Tez's as well.

It may be that she, and Dhanissa through her, has taken that warning about uncoded dispatches to heart.

I did look for some word: some guidance might legitimately be offered, surely, to one who is their vanguard as well as their ambassador?

Well. Whatever their lapses, one dilemma is resolved. I am in expectation of a summons from Shuya hourly. But I can face her now, with the whole question of bribery blown away.

I ought to feel happier, Tellurith, about that.

I *am* happy, I swear it, for your deliverance, and as happy as you might be over the fate of Cataract. And I foresee with thankfulness a new outlet for Iskarda, a truly redoubtable ally for Amberlight. It may well be that Shuya will let the whole tactic of annexation quietly fade away.

And yet—

And yet—

"If Cataract fell—" In Shuya's terms, Cataract has fallen indeed. And if there is no telling yet what the Heartlands will do, is there more chance of quiet in Verrain?

In Dhasdein?

Mel'eth will falter, there is no slightest doubt of it. It has never been more than subdued, far less appeased, in the last two hundred years. How many insurrections did I, and the old Emperor before me, scotch in the egg?

Quetzistan . . . There is the Empress. It is possible Quetzistan may hold a little better. For the Archipelago, well, there is distance to serve as quarantine, if nothing else.

But Verrain?

There is still no surety that Shuya will abandon Marbleport. She may well consider it a valuable distraction, a strangling of Iskardan markets if things come to open breach: at the least, a thorn in the downRiver side of Amberlight. No, even now, I would not call those women back.

And the gods know, this, this—celestial benison—is only recompense for the last ten days. When I have danced the delayers' dance in bitter earnest, when I have been at worship, fasting, in mourning, simply indisposed: anything to avoid Shuya's audience, and having to commit myself, without a weapon in my hand or a hope of strength behind me, and to tell her outright, "No."

Probably she would have understood. And to what she did it would have made not a fiel's difference.

Assassins, poison, or simple expulsion, in my case? Breaking diplomatic relations, threats, outright invasion for Marbleport? I doubt only the last.

As it is, a budget of ploys remains. To begin with, her first Note still requires formal elucidation. That is, if she chooses to carry on as before.

What other shadows you have laid upon my future, what other misgivings wait in Shuya's nightmares, what other schisms may open my loyalties, I refuse to consider. For this once, you have given me hope, Tellurith.

* * *

I think I have done something . . .
    Something that you may not quite—like, Tellurith.

In effect, it is all your fault: if you had not wrought that miracle, if you had not transformed everything and left me delirious with resurrected dreams, and joy, and hope . . .

I would never have sworn Dhe the greatest votive possible. And in the drunkenness of my own liberation, would never have recalled less fortunate creatures of my acquaintance, and asked Dheya as she came for last orders after the palace servants cleared the dinner-table, "Do you remember those two who, ah, ended up in here the other night? I owe the gods a thanksgiving. I will buy them free."

A lesser woman, or one less intimately acquainted with Iskardan intelligence and hence with my finances, might have boggled at the cost. A lesser herald might have boggled at the project. Dheya is Uphill Amberlight. A Craft-Head's secretary, I believe, in Terraqa House.

So she did neither of those things: but I have learnt to read that pause, that slight motion, hardly a wrinkling, of her nose.

"There's a problem?"

Assent is a slighter shoulder hitch. "The young one—I don't think she'd care so much."

"Yes?" It no longer surprises, however it pleases me, to find how much Dheya knows.

"She's Palace bred. And once the fuss dies down," of my rejection, she meant, "she'll likely be let go to young Dinius—anyway."

Palace bred, so no folk or home to reclaim, let alone any knowledge of freedom itself. Half-promised to the second son of a high Family—Dheya took it for granted I too would know which—and once the slur of my rejection passed, he would still be ready to take her, as she had been, a virgin, intact.

And what girl bred to slavery would change a position as Family concubine for freedom to starve or whore in an Assuana street?

"Try the other," I said, "anyway."

Fool that I am, high noble that I was, a life's habit assumed that I had given the orders, I knew we had the funds, Dheya had not said it was impossible—indeed, if those scars told truth, the Palace would jump at the chance to offload an incorrigible hellion—so the thing would be done, and I need think no more of it.

Ha. I am schooled, Tellurith.

It was next evening the knock came, then a muted fuss at the outer door. Then a summons for Dheya, unheard of rescue-signal: and while I was debating whether to put down the wine and possibly shame them both by strolling out to investigate, Hathris shot into the dining room, unexcused as usual, with a most unusually agitated, "I think you better come, Tanekhet."

He says my simple name a good deal more easily than either woman: this time it might have popped out anyhow. So I did not ask explanations, let alone enquire after precautions, but followed him down the corridor.

Dheya met me at the reception room arch. Intercepted me, flustered as I have ever seen her, fairly spluttering, "I beg your pardon, Tanekhet—it's that slave."

"The one you freed," she answered my eyebrows. Dheya speaks body language fluently as any steward in Riversend. "He's here—now—he won't go away!"

"Won't go?" And in my nobly-bred stupidity, even after I understood why the girl would have refused, I still asked, "Why?"

"He wants to see you. He says he won't go till he sees you. He says—really, Hathris, disturbing the ambassador, what were you thinking of? Please go back, we can handle it—"

Of that I had no doubt. But something—new vision, or innate stupidity? made me say, "Of course, Dheya. But if he wants to see me, I might at least hear why."

For a moment I thought she would blockade me bodily. Then she came near as an Uphill woman can to throwing both hands in the air, and with a dirty look at Hathris, ushered me through the arch.

The slave was in the entrance-cage: like most Palace suites, ours has an inner and outer door, with the guard's post between. They were taking no chances. Dheya went in ahead of me, and Kheizo had his arms up his back, a hold on both little fingers, and his head against the wall. He was taller than I remembered: an inch or two over me. Mid-thirties, I estimate, desert-long and sinewy. And despite a poor Assuanan's throw shirt and floppy cotton trousers, the arrogance remained.

At sight of me Kheizo hissed through her teeth. Speaking the same code, Dheya shrugged: He would come, whatever the risk. The slave turned his head, a flare of lamplight on those inimitable brows and Quetzistani cheekbones, and I said, "You wanted to speak to me?"

He twitched his shoulders, Kheizo twitched back, and the silent snarl was a habitual lash at pain. I said, "Searched?" She nodded. I jerked my head. She turned him about, Dheya keeping between us, Kheizo a step behind him. At my nod, she let his arms down, keeping one precautionary finger grip.

He said, "You bought me out."

The accent was there. After—what? twenty years captivity? the highbred Quetzistani clip of the final consonant was unmistakable. Arrogant as the anger in the hardly delayed, "Why?"

I need not have answered: Kheizo's, Dheya's face said so. The old patterns of Amberlight endure, and he was far lower than River Quarter raff. But some complacency—some stupid hypocrisy—made me want my charity praised.

I said, "It was a votive gift."

He drew breath on an adder's hiss. The long-eyed, long-browed face, so like cast-bronze in the lantern-light, was warped by a pure, too familiar rage.

"And now your beneficence has pleasured the gods, my lord bountiful, what becomes of me?"

"You would know that," I let my eyes move over his face, "better than I."

"Hah!" It is the desert contempt-cough, explosive as spitting itself. "Your bandits stole our lands—destroyed our folk—murdered my family. You gave a usurper lord-right and drove our blood across your 'borderline.' *What*, O munificence, remains to know?"

The gods forgive me. With my charity so rudely repudiated, I was getting angry myself. "If your face bars what you think your blood-land, there is no doubt a living for a man—a whole man, a willing man—in Verrain."

"In Assuana? A Palace slave!"

The note of that insolence shot my mouth open. But in my eye-corner Dheya's lips pursed and she minutely shook her head.

At my glance the shake became blatant. "Not in Assuana," she said.

A Palace slave, his past written on his back, his descent written on his face. I ought to have known better. In the bazaars he would not last a week.

"Assuana is not Verrain."

"To be sure. I am trained to carry cushions, whore and wait at table. What camel-driver will hire *me*?"

I understood what earned the floggings: I was sorely tempted to expand them myself. "There are lands beyond Verrain."

"And how long would I last in Riversend?"

That was true too, for all his insolence. Twelve months ago I would have bade them heave him out and forgotten it. But I have had some schooling now in banishment.

"Amberlight," I said, "has just had a revolution. They may be poor, but they have room for strangers. They need workers. They will tolerate change."

"To be sure, O most munificent. And how shall I reach them, since you turned me loose without a fiel to my name?"

"I bought you freedom. Do you want a fortune as well?"

He spat with practice-honed precision, right between my feet. Kheizo yanked, he yelled and cursed: a spasm, a veritable convulsion of defiance, a reflex branded in by years of brutality, and a spirit that would neither suffer nor resign. I had time, as he struggled, to feel ashamed.

"Then you can come with me," I said.

I did not intend it, Tellurith. I swear it. It came out before I understood—

No. It came out because I understood. He might wear beggars' slops, and I silk and brocade, but I have known that rage. Above all, I think, it is the humiliation: that someone can do with you as he chooses. Can treat you as a pawn, a piece of baggage. And there is nothing you can do.

All my life, I have lashed out at it. As you saw with Antastes.

For the rest—we would go to Amberlight some time. Was that not span enough?

He had been struck speechless. Kheizo and Dheya's faces said more than enough. I turned on my heel and ordered, "Bring him in."

In the main room I turned. They had him by a wrist each, as if they feared, unsecured, he would leap on me. His own face was a study in stupefaction. I should have enjoyed it while I could.

"I will not ask how you came here," I said. "But that is the Palace outside. If you go out again, you know your chances of returning better than I. You are hired as house servant. Don't vex my people, don't spoil my possessions, and don't make idle talk. Hathris will pay your wages. Dheya will tell you what to do."

* * *

Then I stalked off, a grand exit toward my bedroom, drawing my coat-tails clear, I thought, of the entire thing.

Ha. Heap no coals upon my head, Tellurith. I have added more than sufficient myself.

First of all, being Quetzistani to his unregenerate backbone, he was outraged to encounter women in positions of command. Thus when he defied Kheizo's first order, she bent the wall with his shoulder and sprang his left-hand thumb, after which, when he abused her parentage, Dheya broke the nearest plant-pot on his head.

To follow, he utterly spurned the Palace charity slops, so we had to find better or have him march around nude. And his "better" is Dheya's version of blasphemy: I had to import an entire market tailor's shop, and issue a decree to veto the silver-threaded silk, the velvet vest, and the brocade indoor trousers which he felt were the only quality equal to his worth.

Next was the bedroom rebellion, when he threatened suicide before sharing with Hathris. And the uproar over thrice-daily prayers, to be accompanied with full-scale lustrations, which I never heard of in Quetzistan, and whose effect on her polished reception room floor has brought Dheya near apoplexy. The siege of the pork-dishes, which, as a thrifty house-steward in Assuana, Dheya serves the household frequently. As ambassador, I gather, I am above this, but he—

Having gone unfed four nights in a row, he has exacted a special exemption: when the rest eat pork, he shares from my own dish.

None of this has taught him his place. Hathris he scorns as laborer-scum. Kheizo he calls a "shrew-whore" whenever possible, but when she gives an order he moves. With Dheya he has conducted a running battle, from obstruction to argument, misunderstanding, or simple mischief. Which culminated, today, in an outright confrontation with me.

Dheya arrived in the midst of my sixth attempt at some kind of pre-emptive letter, should Shuya call the bluff of the Amberlight note. She interrupted me—unheard of from Dheya—with a demand of, "Ambassador?" And when I raised my brows she announced, "He's done it again."

No need to wonder, Which he? I asked, for what seemed the fiftieth time, "What is it now?"

Her spine was a pine-trunk and there was a livid spot on either cheek. If she answered with her customary aplomb, it came through gritted teeth.

"I would wish you to see this for yourself."

We went right down to the kitchen: a place I will admit I have rarely visited. The cook, who is Palace hire and proud of it, was still foaming behind the pastry table. Before it, in a far too familiar tableau, Kheizo had my hellcat on his knees with both arms twisted up his back.

The cook exploded on sight of me. The hellcat started shouting, until Kheizo's jerk made it a howl of wrath.

I unraveled it eventually; having botched his fifth day's mopping of the suite corridor, he had been transferred to scullion work. Summoned to curb instant rebellion, Kheizo had applied a couple of troublecrew persuasions, and when he got himself unkinked, relayed the cook's order to pluck and season a fine fat river duck. "My spice-rack! The best bird in the market! And the whorespawn lizard-eater dropped the whole thing in the fire!"

The cook's rage soared to obscenity. Kheizo glowered. Dheya turned her back and sighed. And demanded, "Ambassador?"

It was an ultimatum. It was appeal to the emperor. It was the court of final decree.

"Let him up," I said.

Disentangled, that coal-bronze mane disheveled, those cast-bronze cheekbones bruised, he gave me another mad-dog glare: Quetzistani. High blood. Enslaved, and maddened, with a spirit abraded by humiliation, driven now beyond all compromise.

"Twenty years," I said. "How have you survived?"

That haughty mouth snapped shut. He had expected abuse. Not a demand to think.

"Well?"

The elongated eyes slitted. Too infuriating, being required to explain why, when he must have practiced submission to live, he should now raise insurrection that would squander the freedom he had won.

I let the silence go until we both knew another moment would irremediably humiliate him. Then I said, "You are not a slave."

Letting the innuendo finish: If your work here displeases you, the remedy is in your hands.

Though not in malice, Dheya's face, said, Yes. Go. Kheizo, troublecrew, as astute but less obvious, seconded her with blankness. The cook, far out of the sense of things, merely gaped.

He read it all in a glance. Scowled at Kheizo, glared at Dheya. Hurled those eyes, with the rage and pride of a cornered falcon, back to me.

I said, "You have ruined my dinner and destroyed my cook's most valuable possession. Cook, make a list and the house will recompense you. Dheya, give him the price and send him to buy another duck. If it's not here in an hour, dock that from his pay."

Why am I such an idiot, Tellurith?

Because I could have forced the issue. Could have demanded, Do you want to leave? That pride would never have let him retort, No. Or I could have threatened, Mend your ways, or I'll have you flogged. Could simply have done it. Both of which, in the long term, would have the same result.

What is it, in that madman's look, that wholly insane defiance, that lengthens my patience and makes me exert every skill learnt in handling an emperor, just to keep the fool in my household, alive, unbroken—free to loose more scorpions on me?

* * *

Well. Shuya has moved, Tellurith.

I had the summons this morning. Public audience. A day that announces from every arch and marble-fretted window that summer's zenith nears by the hour, a sultry, sweaty, sullen heat of desert-fenced dirt and steaming River that made a fine backdrop for her mood.

That it would be bad I knew at a glance: her eyes were narrowed, through the pipe-smoke, like an angry mule's. I was third in the line, too low for honor, but too high for privacy. She meant the rest of the audience to hear what she said.

"So, my lord ambassador," she opened, the moment I ended my bow, "can no-one read in Amberlight?"

"I beg Her Eminence's pardon?" I said.

She flapped the Amberlight note at me. "Your—Assembly—fear my Note has been miscopied. Or my scribe mistook my meaning. They do not understand me. Have the scribes all fled as well?"

"Your Eminence." I bowed again. "I am the Assembly's ambassador. I am not privy to their deliberations. No doubt, if they say so, what they say is true."

Her eyes slitted in earnest and I braced myself for, at the least, abuse. But she spoke with a forbearance that was almost worse.

"Hear my words, ambassador. Verrain has been greatly patient with its neighbors. In especial, with the one-time sovereign city of Amberlight. For thirty years Verrain has borne the annexation—the utterly illegal annexation!—of the district, and the harbor, of the town called Marbleport. Convey to your—Assembly—ambassador—that their President would fail the Families if I allowed Verrain to suffer this slight another day."

"One time sovereign." Blatant signal that she would question the government's legitimacy if denied. "Another day." Clearer signal that she did not intend to be delayed.

I bowed once more. "Your Eminence, I will compose a Note. And as soon as there is suitable transport, I will have your words conveyed to the Assembly of Amberlight."

Time enough to waste in composition: in conveyancing, both to find and dispatch a suitable ship. More time, as I can direct them, to mull over the answer, which may open the legal obfuscations, if only of Marbleport's legal deeding to Amberlight, and hence a requirement for my personal advice. If insufficient time for news from Quetzistan. Oh, yes. Shuya knows some of that as well as I. It is a measure of your work upRiver, Tellurith, that she is not—yet—ready to call my bluff.

And the depth of my concluding bow was calculated to convey awareness of that as well.

* * *

I was hardly through our door, with grateful thoughts of iced sherbet, doffing that furnace of a coat, and respite under at least one decent fan, when Dheya swooped again.

"Don't tell me who," I sighed, doffing the coat regardless, for Hathris to bear away. "What's he done this time?"

It was week's end, all the wages were due. They needed a name, to credit with the new servant's hire. "And he's flatly refusing to give me one!"

He was in Hathris' cubbyhole, which pretends to the name of office. Some advance, I suppose, that if Kheizo was present she had not yet attacked him. But I took one look at the faces and waved Hathris out.

Then I thought again, and nodded to Kheizo as well.

She made the shoulder-hunch that signals, No, and shot her eyes sideways. My safety is her priority. That look said quite plainly, Alone with him is not wise.

"No," I agreed. "But this time, it's the only way."

An ex-tallyman, Hathris' record-keeping is meticulous. The papyrus ledger sheets were immaculate as the cut of my hellcat's heavy silk indoor trousers, his long black brocade vest, the cloud-fine, billowing muslin shirt. As smooth as the fresh shave that had put a gloss on those cheekbones and glints in the obsidian-dark eyes.

He lowered at me under the sheaf of forelock, hair as thick if not as fine as Sarth's, and very near the same bronze-mahogany. In another mood, I might call his looks breathtaking. Certainly, it was a stunning glower.

I said, "They need a name for the records. Without it, you cannot claim your pay."

The lower lip jutted: full and deep against the finely modeled upper lip and nostrils. Sensual, at any other time.

"I know," I said, "that Quetzistani—"

"I am not Quetzistani!"

"What?"

"Outland insults—Outland pig-wits—Quetzistan is *your* name—we are The People! And I am Ku*o clan of the Nairan line!"

As if his face said anything else: had any creature in any other of my households thus affronted me, I would have taken three words and scythed him off at the knees.

If I did not have his head off in good truth.

"You will not want," I used the coolest patience, "to keep whatever the Palace called you. I know your folk's true names are sacrosanct, but they take a common-name. You can use that instead."

There was the minutest hesitation. He has driven himself so far into resistance, into reflexive defiance, he can barely imagine compromise.

I said nothing: I have used the same tactics with the long-winged desert hawks, which are so near crazy after capture the only way to tame them is through passivity.

He swallowed so hard it was a physical jerk.

"I will be—I am—Keshaq."

It means, The Thirsty. Or, The Unappeased.

Involuntary, the note of contention, defiance. The omen was not a matter of comment from me.

I nodded and said, "Hathris can record it." Then I half-turned for the door. And as he began, instinctively, to relax, I added quietly, "You know this will not do."

Every hackle flew up. Were he a hawk he would have bated himself upside down.

"You are a free man. You can leave my service whenever you choose. But things must alter, if you stay."

The upswept nostrils flared. A silent obscenity.

"No more mischief. No more defiance. No more flouting Kheizo. Above all, no more brangling with Dheya. She is my herald and my steward. The house depends on her."

I said it with as little contention as I could manage, and with the chill I have used to Antastes. Believe me patient, that voice said, believe me forbearing. But do not think me weak. And believe, if it came to a choice between you and a valued superior, that indulgence would not prevail.

Apparently he is not an utter idiot. The tirade died stillborn. Then, with the spring of an enraged cheetah, he drew himself up.

"I am Ku*o. I am a man! It is not fit that these hussies—these bare-faced abominations! should rule the household, hold the doors, give *me* orders—it is monstrous! Unthinkable! The house is defiled!"

"The house is my house." My voice came out chill as a Delta winter-wind. "The orders are my orders. And if you go to Amberlight, you will find this is the City's way as well. In your land, women are disdained for being women. In Amberlight, women and men alike can claim their proper worth."

I see now that I unintentionally falsified. That I spoke to the vision of Iskarda, rather than Amberlight, and the vision rather than the arduous, muddled reality. But his mouth flew open as if he would explode.

"In Amberlight! Man-eaters, eunuch-makers, devil's abominations! They ought to be—!"

"That will do."

I have been a great lord, an army's Viceroy. It pleases me indecently that not all of it was a waste.

"They are," I said, "your one hope of a place where you may earn your bread, and live out your days in liberty. Would you rather what you had before?"

That mouth snapped shut, bang! The eyes fulminated. Long and black and burning as a fanatic's. Not least because I had left him no riposte but, No.

It was only temporary. "Then if I must shame myself by women's orders, give me honorable work. I am Ku*o! I am true-blood! Not a kitchen-drudge!"

Whatever my face said, he all but took a pace back. I had no time to marvel. I was too busy trying to control myself.

"*I*," I said after a moment, "am the highest blood in Riversend. And I have given my fealty to a woman. And I have added tallies and done kitchen-work, and been honored to count myself among her folk."

For an instant his very jaw sagged. "You?"

I smiled at him. With everything of Lord Tanekhet, knowledge, world-weariness, unbearable rank, total cynicism. And turned away.

He let me all but through the door before it came.

"Wait!"

I turned back. It took two or three breaths, and a teeth-gritting, before he could manage to speak.

"You will go—to Amberlight?"

Still half-knotted in the business with Shuya, I answered before I thought. "Perhaps."

And saw the raging consternation. The terror's abyss beneath. Before I understood what "perhaps" meant to him.

"I mean, perhaps not immediately. But I shall certainly go there at some time. I am their ambassador."

That doubtless went straight over his head. All he heard was, Yes.

He swallowed again. The next question would not come near words. Only the eyes asked it, that near-black intensity that demanded, as unguardedly and desperately as a child pleads, Does the going include me?

I could have said, In a month's time you can take your wages and pay your own way anywhere. I should have said, Amberlight is not my final destination, and you may find no welcome there. I might have said, The freedom to choose is what you fought for, all these years.

The River-lord shield me, Tellurith. If He Himself can combat such insanity as this.

Because what I did was to walk back to the table, and tap the clear black lines on the ledger-sheet, and say, "Every name here is part of my household. Where I go, they go."

I saw the flicker of disbelief. Perhaps of surprise. Relief, unmistakably. And something that might, just might have been a shaken gratitude, before he ducked his head with the swing of an abashed schoolboy, and made a business of turning away.

* * *

Something does appear to have got through: this morning Dheya and I sat down to a game of castles, to pass the extreme heat of the day. Disposed under the courtyard trees, with a Palace slave to pull the waterfan, she opened with one of her wickedly thorny gambits and said on top of it, "He looks like a Sahandan thunderstorm. But when Cook told him to peel vegetables, he did it. Properly."

I rescued a front-rank piece and murmured, "Ah."

She flicked a glance up under her brows. Did I not know better, I might have thought it smothered a laugh.

"He must be thirty-five at least. And he's been throwing tantrums like some half-grown boy."

I left the other imperiled piece suspended as it dawned on me. "He was probably no more than fifteen—fourteen—when he was— enslaved. Slaves learn too much of some things. Of others . . . In the free world, he *is* a half-grown boy."

She made the noncommittal noise that means, I need more.

"A boy," I said after a moment, "who has had his whole trust in life destroyed. Who has tried our patience to the limit, not because he wants to break it, but because he fears so terribly that it will break. Who needs, as desperately, to be sure he will not be betrayed."

They—you never, I remember, had slaves in Amberlight. She listened almost intensely: a quiet, slightly graying woman, all but nondescript, a superb house-steward, a consummate intelligencer, with women's fighting skills that, outside Amberlight, do not exist. I have played her at castles ten, fifteen times: and I know her inner self no better than I know yours, Tellurith.

Down to the exact nuance of the tone in which, taking my neglected rank-piece, she said, "Ah," herself.

* * *

Evidently the treaty holds: back from audience this morning, I was offered sherbet by a vision girded in the full hauteur of a Palace server, its every silent, perfect ministration redolent of disdain. Lingering to check the vessel's contents, as there is real need now, Kheizo had to wrestle with her face.

Yes. Shuya has raised the stakes.

With some chagrin I admit I knew nothing about it till too late. One would imagine this suite impregnable: foot-thick stone walls, no external windows, a single outer door—that, of course, is only if one does not consider the Palace "outside." But from the inner courtyard it is child's play to force one of the light, latticed internal doors into the suite itself.

Except that Kheizo, Amberlight troublecrew, alone and hence doubly suspicious of everything, had booby-trapped the lot.

So when a fouled string dropped half a dozen iron ballast weights on her pillow, she was moving before she had time to think. Which is something of a pity, since when they collided face-on in the passageway she did not pull her strike. And now anything the intruder tells us will not be in words.

She actually apologized for that, when I blundered onto the scene with a half-lit candle and sheet for garment, my heart still climbing out both ears. After she shoved me clear into the passage niche, over which Dheya mounted guard in her night-robe. Unlike Kheizo, she evidently does not sleep in her clothes.

The intruder lay between us, face down on the polished boards. Quite still. A twist to his head that needed no further explanation. Kheizo's backhand as he tried to charge past her had broken his neck.

"I'm sorry, ambassador."

I yanked the sheet up and the candle down and said, "Better him than us. Now . . ."

He was wearing market gear and worker's sandals, but as Dheya noted, those hands had never swung a pick. He carried no money, no burglar's tools or weapons, no personal effects. But my study door was ajar, marking where Kheizo caught up with him; and there was a key in the lock.

"So he knew what he wanted. And he knew where to go."

And with Palace help, beyond question. Palace aims as well as Palace intelligence.

He was after my papers: I would give the River-lord odds that what he actually wanted was your letters, Tellurith.

Because Shuya will not jump without testing the water, and the latest stream in the River is Cataract. And the one sure, inside word on that upheaval, and on your intentions, is mine.

No doubt it was also a signal to upset, to daunt: You may be a diplomat. Do not consider yourself immune.

Kheizo's eyes said all this back to me, as we stared at each other across the half-open study door. Adding the question neither of us had to ask aloud.

How did he reach the inner court?

Before she turned on her heel and told Dheya, "Floorboards. Walls. Tomorrow." Dheya's eyebrows asked, And now? and Kheizo glanced back at me. Amberlight troublecrew, taking midnight mayhem with an aplomb I could not match.

"Ambassador, with your leave, we'll get the fan-slaves up."

There was the pretext of increased heat: and if our raider did have back-up, or a further sortie arrived, half-a-dozen slaves would make an outcry to wake Shuya herself.

At which point an unguarded footfall and a fuddled, "What—why—" announced my hellcat, draped in a quilt, his mane on end, a yawn dislocating his jaw. Sight of the body snapped it shut with an audible, "Uh!"

"Yes," I said. "Visitors. Oblige our troublecrew by clearing the corridor. And staying inside till dawn."

His eyes went from the body to me and back. To Kheizo, so deceptively quiet, with the hilt of the wholly illicit light-gun peeping from under her black and green shirt. Twenty years of slavery, who knows how many Palace intrigues and perils, spoke in that look. Not the queries and outcries of an innocent, but observation, deduction: and instant retreat.

* * *

It was unnecessary to sound every wall and floorboard: at first light Kheizo found a buckled guttering and a rope round the rooftop finial. A perfect reason to deny Palace collusion, naturally.

So I have played the next step in the game, as naturally, and taken my complaint to public audience.

Where Shuya's riposte was to demand word from Amberlight. To which I, as naturally, responded that I had not yet found transport that appeared trustworthy. And she promptly volunteered a Verrain courier service, whose fees would be paid to Amberlight.

Not an offer that I can refuse.

Nor a better chance to salt the enemy's intelligence. I have concocted a letter that appears at once wary of illegal readers, yet not wary enough, while concealing what I do want to convey. Which is mostly a demand for assistance. Damn Tez. The better part of this chance will be wasted, for want of previous word. I need secure information on Quetzistan, I need proper briefing for my next move and a choice of scenarios, I need to know their position on Cataract. If she cannot write from ambush, let her find a woman who does.

* * *

Well. I have the word, at least, from Quetzistan. Straight from the plaintiff's mouth.

The Palace lamentations were literally audible. As for the city—I was edified, at morning audience, by the sound of every Family representative howling for Shuya's blood.

The palpable evidence must be strewn across fifty sandhills. The word flew in by smoke-signal, faster than any camel could run: a Quetzistani raid halfway to Hamadryah has completely destroyed the mid-summer caravan.

One must congratulate Juiza's folk, for their dispatch as much as their thoroughness. I would certainly do so, had the backwash, thanks to Tez's damnable machinations, not recoiled straight on me.

You will know, as I said, that Shuya is never more perilous than in retreat. There was a summons for public audience, my request for a private meeting was flatly refused, and before the Family representatives had time to bridle at a foreigner given precedence, she was pouring the vials of her wrath on me.

Shuya's private rages are legendary. Raging she was, and never a doubt of it, but it showed only in those eyes' glitter and the baring of those river-horse teeth. She saved the impetus for her words.

Which accused me, as the credited envoy of Amberlight, of being that city's intelligence agent, sent to distract Verrain with diplomatic nonsense while planning to hamstring them: in a word, of inciting Quetzistani to destroy the caravan.

For the Families that was more than enough. I had ado not to be expelled bodily. I have sent requests for a private audience, which I do not doubt will be denied.

In the meantime, I keep a chain of messengers in play, repudiating the accusations with diplomatic indignation, and requesting audience. If Shuya is bent on this course, she shall carry the full scandal's weight. I have composed a Note in which every hint of my own or of Amberlight's involvement in this "unfortunate calamity" is stringently denied. I have demanded, in the strongest terms, one shred of concrete proof that implicates either of us.

A stroke of genius, thus to link our status, and use it to condemn us both. If it could be carried with the Families, she would have all the backing needed to expel me and proceed straight to open war.

I could arrange a counter-stroke: if I had the faintest idea what those idiots upstream are doing about Cataract. If I knew the raid's back-trail was clean. If I could be sure—

In the meantime, I have told Kheizo to hire market bravos for a back-up, and Hathris to admit no-one without my word, and Dheya to consider us under siege. We order in supplies through the hired-men. We have let go all the Palace workers, except the cook, who refuses to leave.

And my hellcat has done the extra housework, from cleaning to kitchen-duties, without demur. He has run messages and carried washing, with a mien so utterly unlike himself that Dheya has twice consulted me.

Perhaps it is the siege-threat. Perhaps he has realized his own stake in this. Perhaps he is simply stunned. This kind of political uproar cannot be something he has seen firsthand.

I refuse, with every atom of my body, to believe that he is afraid.

* * *

This time—this time, Tellurith, I *know* you will not like what I have done.

I do assure you, it was none of my intent—

Cowardice. It was not my intent: but it was my choice.

Going to bed late, after yet another evening's exasperation over the undelivered Note, the meager intelligence Dheya can glean for me, restricted to market gossip from the bravos, the edifices of pure supposition I am reduced to building on what Tez, Dhanissa, Amberlight, Iskarda wants. So it was near midnight when I stamped in sheer frustration to my bedroom door.

And stopped on the threshold. Caught by Kheizo's absence, the anomalous single lamp. And across the bed in that dimness, the upright, motionless shape.

My arm clenched to jerk back the door: my other hand dropped to the occasional table with its guilelessly positioned bronze statuette. The River-lord, offering water, offers a weapon of at least some sort. My mouth opened for the alarm, and the absence of Kheizo, ubiquitous every other night in the passageway, clamped it shut.

For one instant—for one instant, Tellurith, I really did contemplate Amberlight—Iskardan treachery.

Shall I confess it was worse than a real knife to the heart?

Then the shape moved. A voice I knew said, "Ambassador?"

For another instant I knew undiluted relief. But my home ground is the Imperial court: I sucked betrayal with my nurse's milk.

I shall confess that the second stab was almost worse.

I left my hands where they were. Shifted weight for a backward spring. And answered, "What is it, Keshaq?"

It was even: quiet, controlled. But the shape twitched as if I had shouted, Have you decided to revenge Quetzistan after all?

And the constraint, the—strangeness—was less familiar in his reply.

"I have come to pay my debts."

That time I twitched myself.

There was room, while my mind raced as it has in the mouth of a dozen other traps, to note the house's complete, unnatural quiet. No sign of Kheizo. No sign, no sound of Dheya either. The hair was climbing on my neck. Debts. To be sure, in his mind, Quetzistan, loss of home and folk and country and a life's enslavement might well count as debt. A great enough debt to massacre my household, before dealing with the true enemy?

The shape moved: vague, in that alarming half-light, yet the jerkiness of tension, the indecision, was clear enough.

Not the movement of an avenger ready to strike. Still less that of a fanatic with his mind sealed from anything else.

Quite quietly, I said, "What debts?"

For a very long minute he did not reply. I only saw his hands move, another signal of uncertainty, their edges touched copper-gold by the lamp.

Then he said, with more difficulty, "They know I am here."

For an instant my every muscle relaxed. Not wholesale murder then, not fanatic revenge, not a trap. Whatever it might be, it was not the worst.

Then I understood what it did mean.

He too can read body talk with the ease of a great lord. Or a slave. Before I had got past tensing he spoke again.

"Will it please you—come inside?"

Will it surprise you, that on the chance of those minutiae—a movement, an inflection—and the no-chance of what Dheya's, Kheizo's complicity told me—I did what he asked?

The ambassadorial bed is standard for a Palace notable: carven cedar bedstead, draped with curtains and mosquito-wards ten-feet high, embroidered coverlet. Wide as a cow-pasture, partitioning the room. He managed half the distance round its foot before he stuck.

By then I had recovered enough to take the initiative. I said, "Is there cause to do this now?"

I all but heard him gulp. When he spoke, it was low: more than uncertain. The voice of a man hazarding his very life.

"I have only three skills. To carry cushions and wait at table—is not enough."

Then I understood, Tellurith.

No doubt you will blame me—no doubt but you will revile me, and not just for the consequences. Have I not vowed in these letters, over and over, that I am bound heart and soul, that I have eaten that heart out, in fidelity to Tez? Have I not rejected others and gone through fire with it, for her sake?

I hear you snorting, with that winter-look of yours: Having sworn yourself to one unattainable woman, what are you doing in bed with a man, "lord" Tanekhet?

I admit it all. Now let me admit something else.

That I have been tempted as well as tormented, by a beautiful woman as well as an unattainable one, and through all that I have been eight months celibate—I, who in Riversend would not have denied my body two nights in a week. Who had for years before that bedded nothing but men—and the last a man whose memory would turn the River-lord's Adversary monk. As you ought to know, Tellurith.

And he looks—he moves—at times, the very way he talks is an echo, however faulty, however remote, of Sarth.

And yes, I do remember, and yes, I was heartsore, and yes, I was isolated, and tired and torn in myself. And certainly, I was afraid. So to be offered consolation—however temporary, however illegal, however it arrived—

And he did attract me, and he is beautiful and he—

If Tez will not look at me, why should I look only at Tez?

So I took a deep breath, and a forward step of my own, and said, "Come here."

Mutely, he came. Bare, the lamp showed as he finally moved out of silhouette, to the waist. Oiled, as Palace custom is, gilding those muscles whose contours I had already admired, with a waft of vanilla, the poor man's special-night scent, from his still-damp hair. The long mouth was folded tight. The long eyes were cast upward, ovals of shadow deepening to ebony, under those lowered bars of brow. Only experience would divine he was less sullen than scared.

At arm's length, he stopped. The lamp, beside us on the larger table, limned the curves of shoulder and chest, the spectacular profile, the sharp line of jaw: a sculpture in half-cooled bronze.

With a heart beating, fast as a bird's, a pulsating shadow against the column of his throat.

I said, "Between thee and me, there can be no talk of debt."

And left time to see his eyes change, and be sure that change was not relief. Before I added, "But there might be . . . an exchange of gifts."

He drew an audible breath. And took another step, so I put my hand up easily to lay against his chest.

The heart kicked under my touch. I ran my hand up the hard warmth of muscle, across the bar of collarbone, round the back of his neck, into that thick, clinging weight of bronze-black hair, and drew his mouth down to mine.

And he pulled back with a gasp and a strangled, "Huh?"

I said, "What?" myself. He was staring, that old frightened-hawk stare, one hand up as if to rub his mouth. "What's wrong?"

He did rub his mouth then. Shaking his head to and fro, rolling his eyes. "Why did you—what was that for?"

Then I understood something else, Tellurith.

I am trained to whore, he had said. And he meant just that. For sex, for coupling, for men's use of his body, as briefly and indifferently as they would a street-corner moll. To whore, and nothing else.

"They call it a kiss," I said.

He took his hand down and looked at it. Looked back at me. Muttered, in blank bewilderment, "I never learnt—"

I kept the anger out of my voice. After all, it was not at him.

"That's because you were taught to whore. What we are making here is love."

He took his hand right down, his body coming to painful attention, and stared.

"Kisses are—when you make love, it's customary to exchange them. Between people who want each other. People who care."

The blankness disappeared: if he did not understand it all, he had read more than I intended. More, then, than I meant. The wary stance became open: became willing.

Became—I am shamed to say it—eagerness.

Not passion, not yet.

This was only—*only*—hope.

* * *

So I had time to know what I was gambling, and the full weight of its fragility, before he took the final step forward. And my arms slid round him. And I said, "Now, let's try again."

* * *

The first time I gave him pleasure it startled him into a quick, low gasp: a smothered jerk. I remember holding him close as our breaths slowed and our sweat dried, with a cold anger in my heart. Imagining the Palace eunuchs, the trainers, teaching him, with who knows what brutality, that he was a slave, a vessel. That if he did experience pleasure—however unlikely—it was not to be shown. It was not to distract the clients.

Despite all my perversions, how a man can want to ease himself with a block of living wood is beyond me, Tellurith.

The second time, when he tried to master himself I said in his ear, "It is permitted to feel, when you make love."

He forgot his training, that had kept him still almost every time I touched him, except when I drew him out of all control. He rolled over and stared at me, inches away, his breath, still fast and ragged, all over my face. And that look—

If I could lay hands on his trainers, Tellurith, I would make good Wonsa's threat. I would cut off their members and stake them out for the ants.

I drew his head on my shoulder and wiped the sweat from his back. Combed fingers through his hair. Curbed my desire to say, You can touch me too. You can respond, when I touch you. You are not a pleasure-doll. You are a man.

The third time, he did cry out: sharply, briefly, muffling it against my arm as if it were a skill he had not mastered, and was ashamed to ask how. That time I had taken my own pleasure. As it faded, I felt him understand that we had finished for the night. I lay back on the lavender-scented pillows our voyage had rumpled so charmingly, with his head in the crook of my arm and my fingers tangled in that thicket of sweaty hair. And as his breathing eased, I recalled the apostates who had admitted him.

I hooked a lock about my finger, thick and springy as the mane of a fine desert colt. "How did Kheizo," I murmured, "know you were here?"

He did not tense. That sweet lassitude, or perhaps the novelty of its sweetness, had left him incapable of wariness.

"She stopped me," he murmured, "at the door."

"How did you—ah—persuade her it was all right?"

A long pause this time. A hint of defiance.

"I told her. What I wanted," he said.

I curled the lock again. "And what did she say?"

He turned his head then, the eyes slowly returning to the everyday. To the passage of time, and the besetments and dangers of what we call life. I could hear the resurrected wariness.

"She called Dheya. They talked. I—I nearly walked away. Then Kheizo started nodding. And Dheya waved to me. And I heard her tell Kheizo, 'It might be the best thing, after all'."

He was watching me. Assessing, with the slave's intuition, the import of my muscles' reclaimed tension, the line of my mouth.

"What did she mean?" he said.

It was no innocent's question, however naive. It said he had caught my understanding, the nuances of my response: that he knew there was something to understand, and he dared—or felt he had the right—at any rate, he expected I would have the integrity to explain.

I did not say, Probably she meant that it might be a way to subdue you, once and for all. We both knew that whatever they had considered, the priority would not lie with him.

"I daresay," I could not quite master the irony, "they feel you may provide an extra alarm. Or they may be concerned for my health. It's likely," the irony did escape me, "they worry over my broken heart."

There was another of those very long silences he handles so well. Then he said, almost casually, "Do you have a broken heart?"

"Dozens of them. My heart has broken once a week, regularly, since I was eight years old."

Against my arm he stopped a laugh, a tiny catch of breath. His body said the rest: its aftermath relaxation chilling, under that flippancy, withdrawing, at that deflection, into self-possession, closing the walls against pleasure, and love, and however momentarily, trust.

I shook him lightly by the nape and said, "It's nothing important. Not to you."

His eyes closed. A slave's docility, on which can rest his life. A incipient lover's acceptance of a closing door, that he may have entered once and will never find open again.

And I lacked the—the courage—the integrity—to tell him, Yes. I have a broken heart. And that pair out there have even better intelligence than I thought. Because despite it all, in soul I am still faithful. You are a consolation, a substitute. Whatever I might have meant to you, to me you can be nothing but an interlude, a lapse: second-best.

I yawned and shifted as you do in readiness for sleep. He took his head off my arm and began to lever himself up.

"Where are you going?"

He stopped in mid-push. The long eyes opened down on me, ebony and ivory, washed golden in the sideglow of the lamp.

"You want to sleep . . ."

"So?"

A duck of the head. The eyes disappeared. "We always leave—"

I lay there with the understanding, and the anger, and the shame burning up in me. *We always leave.* The pleasure-toys, the whores, who were good enough to satisfy their clients' needs, but not to be rewarded with tenderness. Not to share their beds.

I reached up and gave his hair one good yank. He fell down on me with a gasp of mingled pain and shock.

"You have not been whoring," I said. "You have been making love. Another way to say it is, To sleep together. And my lovers do sleep with me. All night."

For a moment he went so still I thought he had collapsed, or fainted, or died of shock. Then the rigor melted on a huge indrawn breath. Before I felt him shudder, and jerk, but not in pleasure this time: and the damp, through the sheet tangled between us, of the sudden, uncontrollably escaping tears.

When the spasm ebbed he rolled over, driving his head in my armpit and all but hurling the arm across my chest. His fingers clamped a fistful of sheet, and held it fast: held on even when he fell asleep. So I lay till morning, dozing, drowsing, waking to trace the lamp shadows on the ceiling, feeling that arm across me. As if I were some precious possession he would hold as long as he had breath in him, and never, ever let it slip away again. Even in death.

CHAPTER XI

Beyond Cataract
First Autumn Moon

Y ou consummate *idiot*, Tanekhet!
No. No. Not the way to change it, if change were possible. The Mother knows, it is not entirely his fault. The women have been as stupid, as wrong-headed, as, as—ah, *bah*!

* * *

M y lord Tanekhet,
I have received your letters from Iskarda, Assuana and Amberlight. And there is very little use in my repeating what you understand too well yourself.

I will admit I am astonished. That a man of your past, your skills, your address, should fumble so disastrously, not with one woman but with two . . .

No. No. Again, what use to beat the dog for what already has his tail between his legs?

* * *

M y lord Tanekhet,
I have received your letters from downRiver. I will admit that the news is at times, shall we say, astonishing? But at this stage I can only comment on matters past. Such as your encounter with Tez, at Iskarda. I will admit I do find that astonishing. A man of your skills, your past, your address, to so drop his guard, and then make such a shambles of retrieving the mistake—

Mother's Love. I will have to re-draft that too.

Enough to say, at this point, that Tez might well have inclined to you, in the time before we left Iskarda; at least, it seemed so to Sarth. But she is ferociously proud, and grudging in forgiveness of wounds, and above all, she will not suffer triflers.

All of which you have already learnt.

As for the long-term of this, this, enamourment . . . If she had to choose a man, I would almost she chose anyone else; and not solely for her own sake, as you very well understand, but for the trouble there will be with Sarth.

Blast and blind it, Tanekhet, if you *had* to tangle your cock between two women, must it be these two at once?

I very much doubt it is mere infatuation with Asaskian. She has had her choice of Iskarda these last two years. Seventeen she may be, and reactionary, but she knows her mind; and however unwitting it is, you are disastrously appealing to a woman like that.

I will credit you with trying to avoid it. I will say, as I said before, that if anyone could, it would be you. But what Sarth will make of *that*, we may both conceive.

Probably you had better marry her. As soon as possible; if you are in her house, established, accepted as her husband, Sarth will have to consider twice.

Tez?

It sounds as if this is real. The Mother knows, I cannot conceive why else you should blunder so horrendously, in a dance you must have played out scores of times.

You know quite well what I will make of it. I suppose, if I am honest, I pity you.

But I have no idea how we are to undo this tangle, except to offer the hardest, most ideal advice. Marry Asaskian as soon as possible.

And put Tez out of your mind. Out of your life.

* * *

For the dream; no, I never saw you as a simple stallion, although we both know we will need new blood soon enough. As I said, I had wanted you not to marry at all. And if you missed my last letter, then, once more, That dream was a true message, and you read it right.

A great pity that its advice is no longer feasible.

As for your doings in Amberlight; in Assuana, for the Mother's sweet unending love!

Tez must be worse bitten than you can imagine. I can conceive nothing but a gross misvision, a warping of personal judgment, an absolute miscarriage of responsibility, that would bring her to such a step.

If that is the case, if you have spoilt the judgment of my Heir, the House's viceroy, as well as Iskarda's marble factor, then you deserve more than you have suffered, Tanekhet.

Enough of that as well. The thing is done, and you are already reaping the consequence. As you say, it is not only the most arrant waste of vantage with Shuya, it will send Antastes messages . . . the Mother spare me, if I thought I could get downRiver fast enough I would leave this moment.

But that is already beyond my choice.

I will admit, if there is anything in your letters that touched me, it was that last avowal. A fine thing, a noble thing, to know that faith was true, and you were prepared to stand to it beyond the River, for yourself as well as us. For that I can forgive you much, Tanekhet.

But you do realize? I fear by now you have more than realized that those damn letters will upset Shuya, just as the news will shake Assuana, if not Verrain itself. The Families will panic; especially since the lost caravan. Oh, I am quite aware of why you did it, and your reasoning was good. Then.

If it were the slightest use I would shout at you, Watch out, Tanekhet! Because Shuya will try to get those letters, and failing that, she will try to get at you, and if Verrain totters as I can see happening, she will try to kill you. Either as a sop to the Families, or because she wants a pledge to win Antastes.

You see the danger, no doubt. Except with these blighted women, I have never known you less than brilliantly astute. You hardly need me to tell you that Amberlight will doubt your loyalty, and Shuya will try to turn you, and if that game with fire you tried in Amberlight miscarries, you will be in her hands, Tanekhet. You are already in Antastes' danger-zone, just by going to Amberlight. And playing an accredited ambassador?

Tez must have lost her wits, outright.

But if Shuya throws in with Antastes, as she is considering, if I read that conversation well, then Amberlight is in dire peril. As you understand clearly enough.

The other possibility is deadlier; you seem to have foreseen that as well. Verrain itself may collapse. Shuya may fall. There may be Family insurrection, possibly a Palace coup. If that happens . . . oh, Mother, if *that* happens I only hope your troublecrew gets you out of Assuana before the thunder breaks.

Because if Verrain goes down, nothing separates Antastes from Amberlight. And nothing would be a better pretext for action than a renegade Dhasdeini involved in a neighbor and ally's collapse.

I pray the Mother . . . I know Sarth has cut off Her existence, but I need Her now; I need to think, to feel, to imagine, that something will take care for my City, for my House, beyond the flawed schemes of humankind. Blight and blast it, why did I go on this damnable Quest!

* * *

Enough. What use to plague him with terrors he will see as well as I do, and that neither of us, at this time and distance, can avert? Or to squander a whole leaf of papyrus on words I cannot send?

* * *

As you see from the heading, if you ever receive this letter, we have done it, Tanekhet. We have surmounted the most fearsome of the journey's obstacles. We are past Cataract; we have climbed the Jump-up cliffs.

Undoubtedly, this place has a Heartland name, but I cannot fathom which is the main one, and it would mean as little to you if I did. Suffice it that the Haturas made good their word. They gave us provisions and gear, and they guided us through what the River has long called impossible. They took us up the Jump-up. Without so much as a rope.

From below there, in what Heartlanders call The Sink, the cliffs are imposing enough; no more than two hundred feet tall, as experiment has told me, but mostly sheer, or else thick with outcrops as crocodile hide. Sullen twilight gray, daubed with black streaks of lichen and water-path, veiled, sometimes, in somber green niches full of trees. A wall, an escarpment, uncompromising as a siege vallation, splitting the world to the edge of mortal sight.

The Heartlanders themselves do not know how far it goes; the folk up here shrug and say, "To the sun's feet." They call it the Girdle of the World.

That it is pregnable was our greatest surprise since that night with the qherrique; although, as the Mother sees us, we ought to have known, or at least deduced. If the River is impassable with falls, rapids, thorns and rock-walls, how else would Heartland traffic reach Cataract?

It comes down the secret paths, of course. Ancient as the cliffs, ours smelt, and hidden closer than a nation's sacred place. There are a good many, I gather. Each belongs to a tribe or clan or faction. Each is guarded as jealously as a shrine. They blindfolded us for the passage, so I still have no idea just where the way is, although it felt like three or four miles from the city walls, and it was vilely steep and equally rough. I stubbed at least five toes. I think part was a tunnel; at least, it was phenomenally dank.

But at the end, they undid our eyes, and turned us about. And there, over the cliff rim and past the spread of delicately stippled savannah, penciled by the moon, already blurred with distance, lay the dark snake of the River, and the tiny lights of Cataract.

Already remote. A world divided, lost.

I have no idea why I persist in thinking that; ordinary enough, no doubt, when earth itself underlines what your heart feels. A new place, yes, a further stage in the journey, yes, an attainment in itself, the end of the known lands, surely. But divided? Lost?

Such nonsense. As if there are not vexations enough.

Let me postpone them with the country, which is new to us both. Savannah, yes, fine-boned, rolling savannah, thin-grassed, tawny as lion-hide by summer's end, with the sparsest of tall, thorny trees, solitary or in isolated clumps, foliage showing almost black. A country that looks deserted, and is anything else.

The folk are cattle-people, which chiefly explains the scanty grass. Enormous herds, red and tawny and piebald-spatched, drift over the land like clouds, tended by their tall, sinewy, pure-bronze folk. At home, they wear little but work-belts and unshaped cotton drapes, mud or strawberry roan or almost blood-color; and being nomads, they wander their pasture circuits with a new village of thorn-boughs and mud erected at each long-fixed season camp. No wonder they see the acme of civilization in Cataract.

As you might also guess, for all the land's apparent emptiness, they are as march-jealous as neighboring dogs. The slaving, and the continuous clan warfare, no doubt; numerous ruins second that. But until now we have had Haturas guides to negotiate our passage. Calling on old alliances and obligations, and sometimes, I suspect, the reputation of the qherrique, for a good deal of those interminable harangues have been devoted to gesturing at us.

We are traveling as close to the River as we may. There does not seem to be a horse above the cliffs, but the going is reasonably fast, even for folk on foot; although the Mother knows it has been blighted uncomfortable. I have toughened up now, but I swear I am burnt coffee-black and have shrunk three inches everywhere, besides walking out of a second set of shoes.

The food? Heartlanders sometimes eat cattle-meat. More often it is porridge from the ragged corn they grow in summer camp. We carry our own salt with the rest; and trade-tokens as well, for when the courtesy ties run out.

The good side is that with safe-conducts we can camp as we please, and we have not yet seen any of the notorious wild beasts. The Haturas say this is because Heartlanders blood their young men on the lions, and they are so heroic lions run at the sight. The old man at the last village told me the great wild herds have migrated upRiver for summer's end, drawing the predators in their wake. Whatever the truth, it may be a while yet before we must ring ourselves in thorn boughs every night.

And as you might imagine, the true vexations will be inside the fence.

Sarth, yes. The qherrique, yes. Because Sarth will not let it alone; he has questions, and he wants answers, and there has hardly been a night when, with that cool, unobtrusive, irresistible tower manipulation, he has not got us in a circle, with hands clasped about the coals.

Because it will not speak, except to the group of us, gathered, handfasted, as we did that night near Cataract.

The Haturas will have no part of it; they roll their eyes and edge away. When we do camp near villages, the mere sight of the seed's waking clears them off as well; which is no doubt reason to give thanks.

As I probably should for the rest, since it does gag the questions I know are truly burning on his tongue: How did the seed come to us, was it indeed carried with the child, who put it there and how, and above all, why?

It is still capricious, for want of a better word; and impatient, and there is as much trouble over what it can say, I suspect, as what it will. And the Mother knows, it makes us pay for what we get. As I remember all too clearly, from that night; was it the second, or the third? when Sarth, frowning down into the coals after yet another abortive tangle, asked suddenly, "Do you understand, Yes?"

There was a pause; the usual pause, we are growing used to the timing now. Not an incipient refusal; process, perhaps. Then an image, sharp as they come sometimes, cut like crystal. Cut, I am beginning to suspect, not by its memory, but by ours.

My head, tilted back against a sheaf of moonlight and moon-dappled grass, Alkhes' head, midnight silk, bowed against my throat. My eyes open to the moonlight, my face lost in desire's consummating moment, and I am whispering, "Yes, yes, *yes* . . ."

The company had the grace to look away. I felt my own face burn, felt Alkhes' hand clamp painfully on mine. Felt Sarth bite back, physically, the exasperation, dismissal, rage.

"Do you," with the cut of a whiplash, "understand, No?"

A good deal faster this time; the speed of mischief, if not malice outright. Alkhes whipping on his heel in a palace doorway, all eyes and white-faced frenzy, bawling, "NO!"

"The Mother blast it," growled Esrafal, nursing her wrist in the circle's disintegration, Sarth all but spitting, the rest of us clutching ears or foreheads in the wake of the shattered rapport. And Alkhes on his feet, breathing, pure killer-general, "That, will be, enough."

Sarth glowered. But at his most infuriated I have never had to doubt Sarth's judgment of a situation. Or of Alkhes.

He got up too; handed the seed stiffly back to me; answered, the undervoice of an equally outraged lion, "For tonight."

And yes, it makes bad blood between them, or more tension, at the very least. I am not sure that it, the qherrique, does not know that. Or feel it, or however it reasons? feels? thinks? Over and over we have come to that blocked doorway: where our words do not work, do not work, do not work.

But Sarth has persevered, and give him credit, with imagination. For that next night, when the seed began to glow, the first thing he said was, "Can you see me? I am saying, Yes."

He said it again. And again. Before he asked, only the tension of his fingers to show what he was staking, "Do you understand, Yes?"

This time it came almost immediately; one might nearly think it chastened. Sarth's face against the firelight, the cooled-bronze plane of cheekbones, the midnight-topaz eyes confronting us, the exact same intonation. "Yes."

I felt Sarth's hand relax. "And," he said, "I am saying, No."

* * *

Do you realize it has never had words before, Tanekhet? Looking back, I see how truly he guessed, that night near Cataract. Because it gave us understandings; it gave us, feelings; as Alkhes once said, a wordless conviction, like recognizing a landmark or knowing north; but speech, words, a true conversation, No.

We have established, though, that this time it is "different." We have not fully fathomed how; the answer keeps showing the seed, then the City hillside, and it is one of the points that drive Sarth crazy. Because he burns to know, Is it because you were carried away from Amberlight in a human body or seed or blood? Is it because, this time, you have shared a human birth?

And before the company, he will not ask.

But we do know it has the old qherrique's memory. And whether it was not there before, or not accessible, or we never thought to ask, that memory reaches to the foundation of Amberlight.

An image I will keep to the end of my own life; when Sarth asked, "What is the very first thing you remember?" And the picture came up in our minds, remote, silent, yet clear as a child's first memory. Pale blue sky, a familiar, unfamiliar skyline; the hill of Amberlight, without a building to be seen. Grass, boulders, winter sunlight. And a woman's face.

We have been blessed beyond all others, Tanekhet. If her foundation is gone, we know the story was no fiction. With our own eyes, we have seen Amanazar.

I think very likely it remembers everything; at least, it remembers every specific incident we have tried. And they are quite clear, and alarmingly . . . comprehended, I think I need to say. As if recalled by some immortal, omniscient Head of every House.

I think that may be the truth.

I think I begin to understand how it functioned; that it was a, a, consciousness. Linked, not just to one House-head, but to us all; that it took its, its sense of happenings from the council's, from the, perhaps the collective rulers' vision; of Amberlight.

Seven hundred years. We thought our City gone forever. And it is all here; every moment of its lifetime, perfect, preserved.

Amber in a wholly different sense, Tanekhet.

That is the bright, the miraculous side; the dark is the tantrums and the silences and when all else fails, the old familiar retort. Blast, sting, dazzled eyes, burnt fingers, at least twice, one of us knocked clean out.

Because if it has seven hundred years of memory, it has a seven-year-old child's patience, and a seven-year-old's manners, and, I think, sometimes, a seven-year-old's comprehension as well.

So it will not; cannot? answer so many of Sarth's other questions. It will not speak about the City's fall. Or the—our—child. Or the future, or whether it sees the future.

Or why we must go to the Source.

The first couple of times Sarth asked that, the answer was yours, Tanekhet; your speech to the House in Iskarda, full-length, word for word. The third time, we got my "do not work" speech.

The fourth time it knocked Quiran out.

Sarth and Alkhes all but came to blows over that. I had physically, literally, to push them apart, and recite that this is how the qherrique has always been, and finally, grab Sarth by the elbows and bawl, "That's *enough!*"

It is a good part of the trouble, I think. Because he truly is a philosopher, as I came to understand it in Riversend; because he builds the world with his mind, not in visions or imagination, but with questions' excavation, and the rigorous, triple-tempered scaffolding of reason, and the absolute, categorical adherence to and demand for and unslakeable *need* for facts.

And that building is as much a compulsion for him as the qherrique's rapport was for us in Amberlight.

* * *

So you can imagine his reaction, when we assembled last night, and Sarth asked, "How shall we begin?" And Keraz answered, in her officiant's voice, "With the Mother's Ear."

They must have discussed it on the march; for how long, who can guess? The faces mustered factions at a glance. Keraz, so Quiran, of course, and with him Herar and even diffident Chenath; a matter that advances men. Deor, half-won, Esrafal, no doubt at all. Only Azo, dour, doughty troublecrew, with a new load of worry on her shoulders, was waiting wholeheartedly for my lead.

It would have given Darthis apoplexy; it should have given me unalloyed delight. There was one second, as I saw Alkhes understand, the shock, the dawning comprehension; they wanted a man for the Mother's intermediary. An Ear, to ask the House's questions. They wanted Sarth.

He too had understood at a glance. His eyes shot wide. Then he wrenched back and said violently, "No!"

Alkhes' grasp gave me the men's puzzlement. Keraz' incomprehension was on her face.

"The qherrique hears you," she said. "And you can find, you know, the things we ought to ask. The House—"

"No!"

He yanked his hand from mine. His face had pinched. Firelight turns his eyes tarnished amber. Now they were all black.

"But, Sarth?" Alkhes, wits assembled; ready to burst out, It's an honor unimaginable, it's what you, I, Tellurith have worked for. It's everything we could want!

Sarth ripped his other hand from Azo's; came to his feet in a lunge and charged off into the dark.

I must have stemmed the incipient insult, offered some adequate reason, quieted them all. Alkhes too. Because I knew not even he could go with me then.

If I am not troublecrew I can stalk well enough, across a fire's outer perimeter, through the chancy shadows that give on moonless night. I knew enough to keep low, and soon enough, the night sky gave me the silhouette I was hoping for. An isolate thorntree, with the shape of a human back, a man's shoulders, breaking the mast-smooth descent of its trunk.

I straightened and walked without concealment, making my footfalls herald, knowing, as surely as you know the sound of your own breathing, that he would not run away.

He raised his head. Turned about. Squared his shoulders, a gesture I read so clearly it cancelled the lift of that half-seen chin; cool, determined, stubborn as only Sarth can be. Whatever I said, he meant to hold his ground. And by his standards, he had committed a breach of manners close to obscenity; however unconsciously, he expected to pay for it.

But however I punished him, he did not expect me to understand.

I walked right up and laid a hand on his chest. The jerk of his heart carried through dampness, that would become sodden sweat, over the front of his shirt.

I said, "It's Iskarda. Given that, and what happened at Cataract; it's inevitable."

His muscles conveyed everything he did not say. It was all true; it was just what he had expected. Well-meaning, and demanding, and utterly blind.

I said, "So is what you said."

His arm jerked outright. Then he caught my hands, not a graceful tower gesture but a snatch that hurt my knuckles and said desperately, "Tellurith, I can't."

I said, "I know."

"Are they blind? Are they imbeciles? Didn't they hear what I *said* that night? I don't believe any more! I don't—what?"

I put both hands on his chest and said, "I know, beloved. I know what you are."

"What—?"

"Sssh." The shock, the absolute bewilderment clove my own heart. "It's not easy, but it is simple. You're a philosopher, Sarth."

Unlike me, he has not spent time with Antastes' scholars in Riversend; so unlike me, he has never recognized the sort of mind they share, the processes of thought that have drawn him inexorably as iron to the lodestone, out of our comfortable world, into the bitter immensities he had shown us that night. He has never had a companion, far less a teacher. An eagle, raised among ducks, baffled and terrified because neither they nor he understood his necessity to fly.

"That means," I said softly, "that you don't need to believe things, you need to know. And whatever knowing brings, you can't turn back."

He went entirely still. Then he trembled from head to foot. Understanding? Recognition? Joy?

"T-Tellurith . . ."

An eagle, told the sky is his rightful province; shown the function of his wings.

Then, carefully, he took my hands again. In understanding, the philosopher had to trace his construction's path.

"I stopped believing in Iskarda. After Midwinter night. Because I thought, what god—what Mother—could behave like that?"

I made a Go-on noise and concealed my own shock.

"In Riversend—I had to recant. Because of the child."

As the Mother sees me, I have been blinder than you, Tanekhet. I let my expectations, my vision of him as a tower man, a fine body, a pretty face, a superb bed-partner, perhaps troublecrew, a more and more redoubtable mind and independence, I let all that be enough. I never knew my husband had lost his faith and forced it back again, I never knew he had been bargaining and wrestling with gods. And he slept beside me, every night.

"Sssh. Sssh." He said it back to me, cutting off the remorse he could foresee as clearly as I had his stubbornness. "You had—more important things to think about."

There was nothing more important; I did manage to tell him that.

"And then—the child. I thought—I could not stop myself thinking—if the qherrique destroyed Amberlight, was that the Mother's will, the way you told Darthis? Then if it was, where does qherrique begin and the Mother stop? How much of what happened to us—was *meant*? How much of anything is meant? Do we have a choice? Do we ever have any choice?"

The questions Alkhes once asked me, the questions I have avoided for myself, the questions I never thought, until I watched him interrogate the qherrique, would cross Sarth's mind.

I said, "I don't know, beloved. Nobody knows. And not everybody wants, not everybody can bear the thought of finding out."

He was quiet a moment. Before he said, almost resignedly, "No."

I turned his hands over in mine and said, "You can try; you are a philosopher. Keraz will follow you. So, then, will the rest. They took what you showed them, at Cataract. But they need to do it on their terms."

"And that means, being the Mother's Ear."

"Sarth . . . to them you *are* the Mother's Ear. In the very truest sense."

"But the qherrique—! Tellurith!"

"Hush, beloved, I know. You know. You've told them. It's not a god. There may not ever be a god. You can bear it. They can't."

"Can you, Tellurith?"

What would you have said, Tanekhet? I wonder what you will say, if; or when; you read this? How many of us have reached the altitudes of such vertiginous austerity? How many of us could live there, if we did?

And how many of them could bear with the shifts of those below?

I said, "To me, it doesn't matter as it does to you. I think I could live with it; either way."

I felt his shoulders abruptly relax; he said almost jerkily, "I haven't lost you the Mother? I haven't left you without—something to trust?"

"For me," I said, and felt it happening as I spoke, "I think there's a way of having both at once."

His hands jumped. Then he caught me to him, half-laughing, half something else, spluttering into my hair. "I should have thought, I could have expected—Tellurith!"

We hugged each other then, in a familiar sanctuary relief; that if there was not absolute unity of will and understanding, there was room for other understanding. For compromise, in the best sense, and still, the familiar mutual sustainment. The trust.

Eventually I let him go. Then I said, "I know that for you, to be what they want would be rank hypocrisy. I know there's no way to explain that without mortally insulting them . . ."

"Oh, Tellurith." It was half sigh, half laugh. "And I know what you'll say next. '*But*'—"

I had to laugh. Oh, he knows me far too well.

"*But*, now you know somebody understands . . . couldn't you do it anyway?"

He had my very intonation. I had to laugh again, amid the shock, and the other things that stopped my throat.

"Tellurith; what if I said, it isn't just the hypocrisy on my own account? What if I said, I can't countenance letting them deceive themselves. Even if it is what they want?"

I heard us both breathe, once, twice. I felt him waiting, beside me in the dark; and I saw my own nature, that he had mapped in those two sentences. Leader, House-head, who could share the philosopher's vision, but lacked its pitiless integrity. Whose world was the compromises, the shifts and manipulations that would maintain a company, and get it to its goal, and who could subordinate even a philosopher's soul to survival. Of the company. Of the Quest. Of my House.

But who could, perhaps, this once, allow herself the luxury of naked truth.

I said, "You know the answer to that."

It was another eternity before he shifted his weight. Straightened up. For one terrible moment I thought he meant to cleave to my integrity, and my heart went to water, I nearly cried, No, hold your principles, we have to stay together, us if not the company, I give in!

He found my hand. Lifted, kissed it. Solemnly, with more than tower's grace; then he sighed and said, "How can I deny what you are? And still be what you say I am?"

My mouth was dry. My ears rang, as from a thunderclap. I saw his nature then as never before, and had time for grief and honor both; that I am something else, and that I cannot let him be what he ought, and have us all survive.

I took his face in my hands and kissed him, full on the mouth. I said, "I will try to respect what you are. Beloved. For that, you have my word."

He understood what that means too. The faith of a House-head, of Iskarda, of Amberlight. The pledge we give all too rarely, because it is almost impossible to keep. I felt his hands tremble against my ribs. Then he kissed me in response; accepting the vow. And let go, muscles shifting to say he was ready to go back.

* * *

I did manage to cancel the session, so he had at least a day's thinking time; before he mustered us around this hearthstone, and looked across the flames to Keraz. And began, on something like a gulp.

"S'hurre."

Craft-folk. Women. The Mother's favored, far more than Her Chosen men. The schooling he has had to overcome, time and again, ever since we left Amberlight.

"Your suggestion honors me far above my worth."

Tower composure; serene, elegant, impregnable. As distant as his profile, graven, perfect as a very statue's face.

"And what you ask would please, would more than please our Head."

Appeasement, diplomacy, yes, on all sides. I could feel Alkhes let his hackles down.

"Could I do so, I would accept your offer with the deepest gratitude."

Keraz waited; she knows the use of silence as fully as her dam.

"But do you remember what I said? The night outside Cataract?"

He waited then, until Keraz realized what he wanted. A brow rose a fraction. She answered in something near a growl.

"That the Mother was no more than any other river-god, and the qherrique was not Her voice, or any god at all."

I felt Alkhes' hand clench on mine. Oh, I should have recalled, Tanekhet, that whatever the words, what we hear of them is our own choice.

I drew breath to intervene, and Sarth's fingers shut, gently, inexorably, over mine.

"And I said, that for me, gods were something we invent. A way to believe there is more in the world than chance."

Keraz' jaw clenched too, her eyes shot to mine, I knew perfectly well that in Iskarda she would have bawled, Heresy, Blasphemy, there would have been tumult, outrage, trial; perhaps, still, a burning alive. I gave her back a searing scowl that retorted, Quiet.

She bit down on something, hard. Then she said, quietly formidable, "Ruand, is this your choice?"

And it was there, Tanekhet; one of those moments when a matter of trivial precedence blows without warning into a crossroad for your life.

I bit my own lip to steady my voice. But the words came as they do sometimes, unpondered, unhesitating; as they used to come, once, from the qherrique.

I said, "The qherrique told us, Men and women together; this time, we have that right. But the change I see goes beyond that. I see a House that lives together, but whose folk, men or women— can be different."

"Even," Keraz rapped at me, "if they think there are no gods at all?"

"Even that," I said. "If they are loyal to the House."

Eyes flicked, once, and flicked back. Not a woman of them doubted that. Then the rest sank in. As the eyes bulged, the mouths fell open, I went on; to Sarth.

"With the qherrique, will you still be our voice?"

He knew what I meant. Loyal to the House; that is, work for and be used by the House, as I had used him, as grandmother Zhee and Zuri and every one of us had used him, from the day of his birth. The use I would make, now, both proof and cause of his right to stay among us, whatever his beliefs.

He bowed to me as only Sarth could. "I will do," he said, "whatever the Ruand asks."

Keraz' eyes told me she had understood. Told me she was weighing the rest with the speed and shrewdness of a Head's heir; as she has been, in fact if not in name, most of her life.

"Different beliefs," she said, to me. And when I nodded, she looked past me. "If we honor your beliefs, will you honor ours?"

I saw the understanding, the rebellion, that flashed over his face. Before he tilted his chin up, and answered with tower calm as well as tower intelligence "If you make me an Ear for the qherrique, and nothing more."

Keraz gave him one quick, half-chagrined, then briefly amused, more briefly respectful stare. Glanced back to me and said, "A bargain, Ruand? If we, and he, believe as we choose, then for us, he is the Mother's Ear. With the qherrique, and nothing more."

My heart was too far up my throat with relief to think very far past this crisis so swiftly met, managed, passed. I did have the wits to say, "For the length of the Quest," and see relief in Sarth's posture, before Keraz shot me one last readable glance, a hard bargainer admitting herself matched. And spat on her palm, as you do to honor a price-pledge, and held out her hand.

So, if or when we come back, this Quest will bring something I never expected, Tanekhet; though how it will shift things, or how it will benefit anyone but Sarth, from here, I cannot tell.

* * *

Not, at least, for the other trial. Zuri, yes. The loss that is more than vexation. That is outright pain.

I can imagine what Sarth feels; not a day I have not missed her, cruelly as an amputated arm. Not a day I have not thought, "Zuri will . . ." and had to make adjustments, and substitutes, and bear the stress of wondering, will the makeshifts hold? Where once there was certainty, a shield you never had to doubt.

I did face it out with Sarth, the first week upCliff; we had rolled out our blankets in one of those open camps, its shelter the pretence of a thorntree clump and the fading coals. We had all finished grumbling and groaning and rubbing borrowed salve into our unaccustomed legs; the rest were settling, while the first, exploratory patrol had taken Azo and Alkhes out round the camp. As he let my foot off his knee, and began to tie up the salve-phial, I said, "What is it, Sarth?"

Seven days in a thundercloud palpable as it was explicable. How could I not ask?

His face was turned away, a shadow statue blurred by the dwindling coals. His voice was straight from the tower.

He said, "You know."

In the heat of the Haturas' proposal I had gagged him with a supposition, a demand for loyalty. For all the flinching round my ribs, he merited better now.

I said, "I miss her too."

He turned right round. Almost clumsily, startling as the raw anger in that stare.

"You know how she is, Tellurith. You *know* what could happen. How could you do this to her?"

I did not repeat all the arguments he knew as well as I. If what I did say was dangerous, I remembered too well those past nights of chasing an opponent elegantly impregnable in malice and irony, who checked only to pierce my own defenses, before he slid from my grasp.

I said, "You know."

He glared at me. Not the face of the oracle at Cataract; nor of that enemy in the tower.

"The House. The perdured, thrice-damned House. Do you ever see the people, Tellurith? Do you ever think about the ones who do the job and carry the load and pay the price? Do you ever consider that they, that *we* might have feelings, want things, just occasionally matter as much—more! than your damnable *House*?"

Truly, he has changed, Tanekhet; the man in the tower might have attacked me, yes. He would never have shown me the rage, the festering loss behind his shield.

So if he left me winded as so often, this time I had some way to answer, some substance to grasp.

"Sarth, you know. The people *are* the House."

"Oh," he said, "yes."

Pure tower. Edged as a dagger, straight into the heart.

I said, "And without it, where would you be?"

He jerked as if I had hit him across the face.

"It was the House," I said, "that began rebuilding Iskarda. That's making a place for you. Would you have preferred to stay in Amberlight?"

His breath came out on something like a grunt.

"Shall I turn my back now, go off downRiver, tell Zuri to forget Cataract? Drop the whole project? Just walk out?"

He did grunt then. He half put out a hand to me, and I cut it off.

"Yes, other people do the job and carry the load and pay the price. I just make the decisions. But tell me this, Sarth. Where are they? Where are we? Where are any of them, without me?"

He opened his mouth and I jammed the words down his throat.

"If it upsets you so much, why don't *you* walk away?"

He was half a face against the firelight, the shadowed side barred and shuttered as a judge; the other half was alive and eloquent, the sensations, the injury of living flesh.

"Did you grudge me," he said, "that much?"

I hit him. Straight across the mouth.

And no, I am not proud of it. And yes, like his anger, it was uncontrollable. And yes, it said far too much.

Because I did grudge him, Tanekhet. Not the sharing, that I have always had. But knowing that to him, she mattered as much; that she had come into that place I always thought, had always had the surety, was mine alone.

He took his hand down. Opened his mouth. A shadow moved between us, and Alkhes whispered, "*What* is this?"

Whispered? Purred it, the silken undervoice of a big, deadly cat.

I whipped round, and his stance spoke danger it has never held before. He had read beyond the surface of my blow; he knew where the real wound had been dealt. He was a hairsbreadth, the merest hairsbreadth, from flying at Sarth's throat.

I jumped up like a lunatic to throw myself between them and yelled, "It's nothing! It's all right!"

I knew better than to grab Alkhes; least of all at his dagger arm. I felt Sarth rise, the air shake, the violence teetering as it has of late between them, but never so close to breaking out.

"Stop it," I said. It cracked, but it was a replica of a Head's voice. "We were arguing. I lost my temper. I'm overtired, that's all, I'm—sorry, Sarth."

His face measured the enormity. Both enormities. I felt Alkhes read it, the way he always does. He looked at me; not question, but demand.

Is this truth? Are you satisfied? Or shall I put things right?

"Zuri. We're both missing Zuri. We're upset. It's nothing anybody can help."

Both of them read the intonation; all the arguments, all the exculpations had been made long since. If wounds remained, they were the scars of necessity. Who can dispute that?

Alkhes just looked at me, a soldier, awaiting orders, the strategy and its need taken as read.

Sarth had himself in hand, but the tower carapace could not hide the turmoil of pain and rage beneath. So deep, so cruel . . . I put out my hands and then I went to him, not waiting to see if he would welcome me, saying, "Oh, Sarth."

His arms came round me. But I felt his eyes meet Alkhes' and hold, a long, long stare over my head.

A stare, a measuring that was almost enemies'. Before his muscles suddenly undid and he embraced me and said, almost hoarsely, "I beg your pardon. I'm sorry, Tellurith. I ought not—I should not have said that."

We went to bed then, and in a better language sorted the rest of it. The first breach in our marriage since before Riversend. And not mended yet. Oh, yes, that terrible fracture between them has reknit; or at least, healed over. But the root of the anger remains. And the journey, the continuing stress, the gall of her absence, will not let it die.

Least of all tomorrow, when we move beyond the last of the Haturas clan-ties and must negotiate passage for ourselves.

* * *

Upriver
8th Day, 2nd Autumn Moon

As the Mother sees me, I expected marvels and upheavals, but this—

Let me begin with the most obvious. The easiest.

There is another cataract.

Not a waterfall, but a rapid, certainly; three or four miles of them, to be accurate, with a blasted hard passage through the thorn-thickets at the Riverside. And then another village, a true march-ward. And then, Mother be praised, then there are boats again.

River boats in the truest sense; the River now is slow-flowing and wide as a minor ocean, so they are shallow-drafted, wide-bottomed lateen rigs, or polecraft-craft, canoes, punts. But we can sail again, bliss and glory, and if it is no faster it is blessedly easier on the feet.

And the herds are here; oh, Tanekhet! The herds are here at last, the wild herds, who turn the Heartlanders' cattle to a fistful of ants. They stretch from horizon to horizon, the shaggy, hump-necked wild-cattle and the spotted cow-tailed plains horses, the deadly dangerous great-beasts, with their flat, broad, scythes of horn. The land has flattened into hardly rolling vistas of open grass, and they blot its tawny expanses with their legions, their myriads, chains, skeins, streams of them, dark to the pure horizon line, perfect to the tiniest silhouettes.

And the hunters are here too.

We have seen the lions, sleeping at midday, or perched on the occasional rock-wigged knoll. We have seen coveys of tigercats who run down their prey, and the spotted leopard, which hunts by night. And sailing past, we have seen at the water edge the logs of somnolent crocodiles.

And river-horses. Tanekhet, if your similes for Shuya are accurate . . . gods!

They loll in the shallows, and our boat-folk treat them far more gingerly than crocodiles. Small wonder, when you see the opening of that mouth, that can halve canoes at a munch.

The village is not the usual clutter of wattle and thatch, but a permanent site; palisade, mud-brick houses, sometimes with six or seven rooms, a market space. We came there at evening, after struggling round the thorn-thickets, scratched and dusty and leg-weary, and more than apprehensive over where we would sleep the night.

The Haturas had left us greeting words, encounter protocols; as the gate-dust settled round the cluster of women, children, don-keys, it was Azo who advanced into the first pauses, pointings, an uproar of startled dogs. Another nomad rarity. Thank the Mother they did not loose them, for Azo would have used her light gun, sure as life.

She held her hand out, palm up, the usual signal of peace. The crowd swirled and disintegrated; we stopped at the usual hailing distance, and presently the envoys emerged.

Two women, two men. Which is not usual among nomads either. Darker than downRiver, less new-cast than slightly tar-nished bronze. Wearing headcloths, again unusual, above the ter-racotta robes. There is a blood-border here, if nothing else.

Studying us, not to gauge the unknown, but to identify rumors, foreword's truth. All but checking us off against the story's list.

The older man held his right hand up; the response to Azo, the opening assurance of peace. The younger touched his palms together on his breast. Welcome, goodwill. The older woman, the oldest of the four, said, "The folk of the Quest."

Electrifying, to hear our nonce-term taken in earnest by some-one else.

Azo inclined her own head. Keraz and Deor side-stepped, her-alding the leader, I made the palm-sign back. But as we performed the maneuvers, yes, we were welcome, yes, we might stay the night, yes, there was food we might, this time, buy for ourselves, as it all unrolled exactly as it should, I could feel their attention sliding; not to the company in general, but to my men.

They ushered us toward the gate. Azo and Deor moved lei-surely to the fore; Alkhes, with my cutter, fell back to the rear, positions long since habitual. We passed under the timber lintel, onto the ragged dirt-space that suggests a street.

Folk had gathered inside; for the first time since Cataract, women were visible, and ancients, and children, with a thickening mix of men. My eye slid over the usual bare feet, occasional bead necklet, bizarrely pierced nose. Nothing speaks the Heartland poverty clearer than their ornaments; one had a harp tuner's key, of all things, thrust through an ear. They were nearly silent, in the usual Heartland reserve; but with a simmer of attention, of muted excitement, beneath.

There was a scuffle behind. I whipped about in time to see Keraz and Esrafal finish their about-face and reach Alkhes.

Who had stopped dead, staring at someone in the crowd. Every muscle locked. Blood draining from his face. Who, as I looked, let the cutter slide through his hands and folded gently after it into the dirt.

All too familiar, that motion, Tanekhet. Sarth and I flew to him, there was the predictable fuss, I hardly noticed in the panic that choked my lungs; a dim sense of Sarth talking, someone pushing people off, widening a circle of unshod feet. Quiran, making the quick physician's check of eyes, mouth, wrist; looking up with bewilderment that became appalled comprehension, so I knew he too remembered Midwinter night.

Before Alkhes shuddered and opened his eyes.

I have given the Mother incense because he was not . . . because it was sanity, however shattered, in that stare. Even when it went past Quiran, and the eyes re-dilated, their whites no paler than his face.

She stood facing me at his feet. A tall girl; a woman, in the usual terracotta robe, if girdled with an unusual knife. Well-muscled legs, arms bare to the shoulder. Short-cropped head. Well opened eyes and carven mouth, and an eagle's beak of nose.

Even in a woman's face.

I had time to feel my own limbs melt. Before she gave him one last stare, blank as desert sand; and turned on her heel amid the crowd and went silently, unhindered, out of sight.

* * *

The rest were kind enough; they offered to carry him, cleared us a hut, showed us the meat and flour-sellers and the well. Volunteered a pillow and their own cow-healer, accepted that we wanted nothing else. After the strained, silent supper, Sarth and I took Alkhes outside, into the illusory privacy of the hut wall, a vista of empty dust and palisade stakes cutting patterns in the moon-dark's stars.

In all that time, he had not said a word. Nor had we asked, though I knew Sarth had recognized her too; and we both knew the wreckage, the never-healed wounds that he had left behind.

Her kinsman. Dead in Cataract.

We were both sitting almost on top of him, Sarth with a hand on his shoulder, me clutching Alkhes' other hand in my lap. He was still staring straight ahead, glassy-eyed as a man in fever. But as I changed my hold, a great shudder went through him; and he whispered, "I can't leave."

Not till we had found her. Not till the encounter; till the reckoning, the final resolution, was made.

* * *

"It's his sister." Azo squatted complacently over the breakfast cakes. I had meant to enquire that morning, never doubting this request too had been anticipated, would be fulfilled; Azo, exemplary troublecrew, had got there first.

"And her father. Family moved north after a Haturas feud. Mother was killed. Older brother too. There's a new wife, more children. He was a herd-Ruand. They live up near the gate."

A man with repute as well as a past. A man who might exact a high toll for his last, perhaps his most grievous loss.

"They ask him for judgments. A hard man, but fair."

No doubt that Azo had surpassed herself. History, geography, biography complete. I patted her shoulder; looked across the fire into unfocused, depthless black, and said, "Ask the village Ruand when we could meet."

Best to make it formal; a matter for the community. It would be a public spectacle in any case. And best to make it soon, for everyone's sake.

Their Ruand must have agreed, for the word came back almost at once. All this morning, Jirba would be at his hut.

Alkhes received that as he had all the rest, in that sleep-walker's trance of the night in Cataract. Even when he stood up; looked from me to Sarth as we rose with intent clear on our faces; shrugged, and made for the door.

We set him in the middle, as we had slept that night, to make it plain we were only his support. The village was seemly enough; no calls, no crowding, hardly a ripple in the traffic. Most actually veiled their stares.

Jirba was in his doorway, doing nothing with an old man's dignity. He had aged as they do in the Heartlands, flesh tightening onto the aquiline bones, but a big yellow-dun turban covered his hair. As masked as the impassive face, as those too familiar dark-bronze eyes. At the correct distance he rose; inclined his head; and gestured us inside.

The house was large in village terms, and anomalously quiet. There was no sign of the girl. Nor did Jirba offer us Heartland hospitality of sour milk drink or imported tea, or the coffee women brew in brass pots by the hearth. In the centre of what was clearly the main room stood a batch of cowhide stools. Jirba nodded toward them. As Sarth and I stepped aside, he and Alkhes came face to face.

Like Tibari before him, Jirba went absolutely still. But Alkhes stopped in his stride, and in that moment the trance broke: I saw his face shift as a rain-loosened hill does, and like Sarth, looked away.

Jirba did not. Perhaps he knew that this, too, was part of his price.

The pause seemed endless; then Alkhes drew himself up in that military posture, as Dhasdeini soldiers do to encounter a high officer or a great event; of honor or disgrace.

And said, as he had to Tibari, "I would sooner have died myself."

That pause drew out until it cut like very fine, tightly-twisted wire. Before Jirba moved a hand; the slight, economical palm-turn that Heartland folk use thirty times a day; that says anything from, I accept your apology, to, It's finished, to, It doesn't matter, now.

And the tears began running down Alkhes' face.

Jirba must have been startled then, I think. He shifted weight abruptly and for the first time I saw Alkhes through his eyes. Outlander, emissary of downRiver, the fabulous, hated and desired world that had taken his son. Soldier, officer, general. And younger, slighter, weaponless. Guards down in this extremity, vulnerable as the boy he looked.

He made one half-gesture that could almost have begun an embrace. Then, in a voice deeper than Sarth's, he said, "Come, enough."

It might have been scorn; an open rebuke. But if it was not gentle, it was quiet. Alkhes bent his head and wiped a hand across his face. A soldier, given leave to recollect himself.

When he looked up, Jirba said, "How they say; is it true?"

What have the tales made of it, running upRiver? All too clearly they have come this far, in what detail, remembering the Haturas' eavesdropping, I can only conceive, and my heart shrank at the thought. It could have been tragedy noble as gods'. It could have been squalid beyond redemption. And which way did Jirba think?

Meeting that stare, Alkhes drew himself up.

"Sir," he said. "I do not know how they—what they say. But I killed your son. It was not in battle. It was not by choice. It was something I can never forgive myself. I—" The words roughened and caught. He took in his breath. "For you, that means nothing. For you . . . What do you ask from me?"

For all his command, I think Jirba was surprised again. There was a pause that said more than consideration, before he spoke.

"What would you give?"

Alkhes turned both hands out, answering clearer than words. Whatever you ask.

After another aeon, Jirba turned on his heel and walked, smoothly but swiftly, toward the inner room.

Sarth and I breathed, shifted, would have spoken. Alkhes stared straight past us. He was very white, and his eyes were huge; but his face had set, grown almost impassive. Shut away, as if every fiber of him was locked in some all-consuming ritual.

When Jirba reappeared he was carrying a battered leather scabbard. Above the sheath stood a brass-headed ivory hilt.

If the chief Heartland weapon is the spear, you will know their hand-to-hand choice, Tanekhet. The slashing knife they sometimes trade in blood for, that shears as easily through trees as armor and flesh. Broad as a man's hand, long as his arm, its upper edge ending in that wicked, disemboweling hook.

Still watching Alkhes, Jirba came back to us. Halted, and drew the knife.

I felt Sarth's muscles tense. My fists were clenched so tight they ached. Reparation I had been prepared for; blood I had known might well be sought. I had never let myself imagine it might be such blood as this.

Like Alkhes, Jirba ignored us. They were locked in together now, in some secret, wordless rite. Jirba set the sheath down, grasped the knife two-handed. Took the last closing step, and laid the edge against Alkhes' throat.

He understood what it meant, yes. And he knew it was no more than he had offered. And yet . . .

What I am not sure I can bear, Tanekhet, is that I think he welcomed it.

Needless to say, the blade was assassin-sharp. Jirba drew down the merest fraction, and I saw the first blood start, a dark, dark red beading, above the line of Alkhes' shirt.

Jirba said, "This?"

Alkhes never hesitated. After all, he was bred a soldier; the first stake he ever gambled was his life.

He said, "Yes."

Jirba's arm tensed. The rose-black beads swelled and began to run. Alkhes put his hands behind him, one clasping the other wrist, and braced himself.

Jirba gave him a sketch of a strange, difficult smile. Lifted the blade clear, and said softly, "Not enough."

Whatever he wanted, he had a good part of his repayment then.

That was when I said, To the River-bottom with their ritual along with recompense, and put my arm around my husband, and let honor judge falling on his face worse than my holding him up.

His face was buried in his hands; he did sag against me. Sarth caught him from the other side. Jirba wiped the blade on his own shirt-sleeve, and as meticulously, set it in the sheath. Laid the whole thing on the waist-high grain jar at his back. Then he watched, but without the reaction I might have expected. Without contempt.

Until Alkhes took his hands down. Set his shoulders. Put my arm away, gently but absently as a hampering bough, and raised his head.

Jirba said, "It was not by choice?"

Alkhes' jaw clenched. "No."

Jirba pondered again. At last he turned away, and paced, this time with an old man's stride, to the inner door. Before he came, once more, to look in Alkhes' face.

"You took my son's death upon you," he said. "Would you take his life as well?"

Alkhes did blink.

"Our folk believe," Jirba went on at last, hauling up words as if out of a desert well, "that a man killed untimely, carries his misdeeds across the River. That he must meet the Judge with an uncleansed soul."

He looked down at his own hands.

"And among our folk are some will lift the burden. Will carry the stains for him until they are cleansed, or die themselves. Holy folk, for a penance; others, who make it their calling. For a price. And sometimes—it is done for love."

He looked up at Alkhes. And Alkhes answered with no more hesitation than before. "Yes."

For the first time Jirba's eyes narrowed. "Yes, which?"

"Yes," Alkhes answered evenly, staring him full in the face. "I will do it. And yes. It will be for love."

Jirba looked away then. I think I saw fractures in that face's granite, before he said, to the outer doorway, "That will be well."

* * *

So after a day's fasting we all went down at sunset to the River side; where, as the last colors faded, Alkhes knelt at the water's edge, and Jirba cut a lock of his hair with a knife so old handle and blade were one sliver of black, razor-sharp glass. And set the lock in a carefully turned and polished little wooden bowl, and then reached for Alkhes' wrist.

So there was blood after all, let neatly as by any temple offici- ant, enough to cover the hair. Before the village-Ruand brought an ancient pair of pewter tongs, holding a single coal, that Jirba used to kindle the edge of the bowl. When it was aglow, he lowered it with infinite care to the water and pushed it out. And we all watched the tiny flame recede, the soul-light, as the River bore it away.

Only when the flame-bud vanished and the villagers shifted and sighed, did Alkhes draw a long breath, and look around him, as if waking at last. And Jirba stood up, offering him a hand to rise.

The sin-bearer has honor for his deed, for pay or not. That this was far more I read in Alkhes' expression, in the way his hand jumped, all but imperceptibly, before he accepted the grasp.

Once inside the gate the informal procession melted away; but as we came up Jirba paused, impassive as ever, saying, "There is a place at my hearth."

Sarth stepped back. I would have followed, but Jirba's gesture said, You, too.

If the house was as deserted, this time the hearth held fire; and coffee waited, freshly brewed, in its polished brass pot at the hearthstone's edge. I could smell its after-flavor, lingering in the shadowed spaces of the room.

Jirba poured for us all. Sat a long time, staring into his cup. Before he lifted his head, and said, "Have you ever thought, that my son also had no choice?"

Alkhes put his own cup down. So carefully, only a spoonful spilt.

"When he said, In the Heartlands, it would have been custom. Did you know what he meant?"

Mutely, Alkhes shook his head.

"Among our folk, it is well-known. The proper name is thalan. It is when a young, untried warrior sets his heart on an older, proven blade. The young one, the laf, he takes his sleeping skins and sets his spears at the other, the sharfir's gate. He gifts his kills to the sharfir's house, he makes songs in the sharfir's praise. And if the sharfir's answer is, Yes, he takes the spears inside. Then the laf joins his household. He fights and hunts at the sharfir's side, he learns what skills the sharfir may teach. And if the sharfir deems him worthy, he may share his bed."

Alkhes might have forgotten how to breathe.

"It is a mark of honor," said Jirba gently. "However they think Downstream."

Alkhes moved then. Finding his hand half-extended, drawing it back. And his wits roused as well, for he said softly, "So he thought it came right; after all."

That time it was Jirba who blinked.

Then he nodded slowly, and gave Alkhes a different kind of look. "At first, yes, it went astray. He was too impatient, you did not understand. But when you did say, Yes . . ."

Alkhes shut his eyes. The firelight turned him suddenly haggard as his own ghost.

"Wait," Jirba said almost inaudibly. "Semba, wait."

Alkhes' eyes shot open. Very nearly, Jirba smiled.

"That traveled too," he said, "yes."

I think—I am fairly sure that Alkhes blushed. Jirba nodded very slightly. Before he said, "Can you see the rest?"

Alkhes stared; then he began to stiffen, muscle by muscle, as he sat. I almost moved closer, at what was happening in his face.

"I asked him the impossible." It was a whisper, no more. "And then I gave him—honor. So he couldn't—"

He could not finish. Instead, with terrifying slowness, he curled up on himself, and buried his head, deeper and deeper, in his hands.

With a look that was oddly compassionate, Jirba went on.

"So he could not say, No, for your sake. And he could not, for his city's sake, say, Yes. He could only keep faith with the bond. Leave his sharfir the choice."

To dispose of his City, his folk, his own life.

Alkhes ground his face into his hands. "Oh," I heard him whisper, as if his very soul was breaking. "Oh, gods . . ."

Something did move in Jirba's face then; he leant forward and grasped that bowed, spasmed shoulder in his own gnarled hand.

"Semba," he said. "This is not part of the price."

When Alkhes did not move, Jirba gave him a quick, brusque shake. "It was meant to free you," he said. "As you freed my son."

Coals rattled, falling in the hearth. Somewhere invisible, I heard muted voices, the sound of a cradle's click. And at last, Alkhes lifted his head.

The marks of tears shone on that drained, ravaged face, but there was something near starvation beneath. Jirba looked into that silent question, and understood what it asked. He answered solemnly, "That is truth."

* * *

It is not an all-salve; perhaps the wound will never wholly heal. But I think, I think, it has been the first real balm that he has known, since the night it happened, Tanekhet.

* * *

And that old fiend waited, till Alkhes had wiped his face, and his muscles relaxed, and he had even begun to look round, with that dazed, dazzled air of a man just reprieved from death. Before Jirba said, "But there *is* more."

I nearly did shout at him then; only having to kick Sarth under the stool shut my mouth. But Alkhes had already mastered the flinch. And lifted his chin, and asked, almost steadily, "Now?"

Jirba did smile then, a gleam briefer than a desert shower. Before he turned half-away and shouted, "Varris!"

A quick tread, a flash at the inner doorway of steel or iron. A tall shadow on the edge of the firelight, girt in a strawberry-roan blanket, with a shield at one shoulder, and a Heartland warrior's spears in the other hand.

Alkhes was up in a bound that Sarth very nearly matched. Both of them were braced in front of me, yet again prepared to shield me with their naked flesh.

With sublime disdain she ignored them, grounded the spears and halted, poised at the light's brink. Jirba said, "This is my daughter. My son's sister. Whose own price is that she become laf in his place."

I took Sarth by a wrist and pulled. He sank down beside me, both of us blind to everything but Alkhes, spluttering in the firelight, literally out of breath.

"But—You said, warriors, you said—she can't!"

"I," she said, "am a warrior too."

The accent, the bronze-bell intonation. I did not wonder Alkhes choked; it was Wonsa, an octave higher, to the life.

Alkhes looked at Jirba as at his last hope of help, and Jirba said, "Our women can be warriors. Yes."

"And I want," she picked it up, clear and cool as adamant, "what my brother should have had. You accepted him. You owe what he lost to me."

Alkhes sat down as if his knees had gone, and wiped both hands over his face.

"I can't—I don't—"

She did not dignify that with a reply. He took one look at her stance and turned to her sire.

"Sir—sir—you know where we're going. You know what I am. I've lost you one child. Will you throw away the other as well?"

She thumped the spear butt on the earthen floor. Not hard, but peremptory enough. "The choice is mine."

Alkhes turned from one to the other. When Jirba's face seconded it, he looked helplessly back to her.

"But I'm married—"

Jirba raised both his brows. "So are most sharfir."

"You mean the wives—!"

"This is thalan, Semba. Is there nothing such Downstream?"

Alkhes opened his mouth and shut it on the words. Amberlight. Iskarda.

"Yes, sir, but, but I—*this* marriage is—"

"And do none of you have other ties?"

That reduced Alkhes to total rout; I stood up, crooked a finger, and led the girl outside.

It was still twilight, just light enough, by the distant fireglow and river-shine, to read another's face. She is a hand taller than I, but well shorter than Sarth. I took her gaze quite easily as I said, "Do you want this to make him pay? Or to repay?"

For an instant she bridled, withdrawing into that Heartland reserve. Then she let her chin down and answered, warily, "Repayment, yes. But not—not—"

Not for malice. For the sake of his pain. For revenge.

"And nothing more?"

Another stiffening. Then all of a piece the wall yielded, and something near a glow softened those copper-russet eyes.

"Payment, yes. But he is a high one, a great champion. He has a Name. And he is great in heart. For the asking, he gave my father his life. For the asking, he freed my brother's soul. Who would not seek thalan, with a sharfir like that?"

For all the breached reserve, all the overlay of past loss and grief, it was unmistakable; hero-worship; adulation, for a warrior who is more than a skill with death.

"My brother wrote to me." With utmost naturalness she grounded a spear and leant on it. It is the way they sculpt Dhasdeini soldiers' memorials; the very pose. "When we were young we would talk about thalan. He knew I knew he had been looking; seeking a fit sharfir. The letter said, 'I have found a man worth the last blood in a laf's heart. He is white as a Sealander, with eyes black as the bitumen pits, little as a half-grown boy. And as beautiful and impossible as a Kawashi gazelle.'"

Reading my expression, she almost smiled. "You know the name? The Kawash live far," a gesture west, "out to the desert's edge. Rock-seas and sand-dunes, and the Kawashi gazelle. They breed nowhere else. They are white and honey, the color of sand and rock, except their muzzles, and the insides of their ears, are black."

This time, it was a smile.

"They are cunning as crocodiles and faster than a running tigercat. So when a hunter has achieved everything else, if he dares, he goes to the Kawash. And asks to hunt gazelle."

The smile died. "They are so few and precious, you may only take them alive. From ambush, with a net. To kill one, to break a leg in the catch, will wipe your honor from the earth. And if you do succeed, you may just clip some hairs. A few hairs, from inside an ear. And show them to the Kawash who hunts with you, before you let them blow away."

So quick, so fine, so nervous. I heard Alkhes repeating a dead man's words, a lifetime away. *Like a Kawashi gazelle.*

"Do you also understand," I said, "that we are not Heartlanders?"

For an instant she looked genuinely blank.

"We are going to the Source, yes. But . . . afterwards, we will go back Downstream. Into the Sink. To our own place. Does thalan hold so far as that?"

She put her chin up. Of course.

"To a strange folk. Another country. For the rest of your life?"

"Did he do less for you?"

"He is my husband. Do you not want marriage; children? For your own?"

She brought her chin down in earnest then, the eyes fixing their target. "Are there no other strangers in your House?"

Blown by my own mother-face, Tanekhet.

I said, "Who or what the House accepts is a matter for the House's choice."

Then I stalked back indoors; Alkhes swung about on his stool, looking drained and shadowed past disintegration, and I said, "Honored sir, you will excuse us. Your daughter shall have her answer by the next sun's rise. My husband needs time to think, and the company must consult."

* * *

Alkhes was mute all through the trek back to our hut. But when we were in bed, private as might be in our hut corner, when Sarth drew his head onto a shoulder and I put an arm across him and settled close at his back, he drew a long, tremulous sigh. And at long last I felt his body, clenched all day as if battling mortal pain, loosen and relax.

Sarth tightened his arm a fraction and said his first words in hours. "It's all right, Aglis."

When Alkhes sighed again it was the speech of comfort, solace, sanctuary realized. Bone-deep relief.

So in a while I could shift my own arm over his waist, my hand on the arch of Sarth's ribs beyond, and murmur, "What do you want to do?"

His voice was ragged; but for all the devastation, he was Alkhes. He had been thinking too.

"I don't want to take her. Gods, this part's bad enough. But back downRiver . . . anything could happen. We might—"

Might never, ourselves, get back to, let alone past Cataract. If we did, we might find Iskarda gone, and ourselves embroiled in a war that would erase the River's world.

"I couldn't stand it if I—if I—lost her as well."

I hugged him. Feeble talisman against the memory that was bleeding yet. "It's her choice."

"Her choice! Gods, I never wanted—what am I supposed to *do* for her? I'm married already, Tel! I don't want," he found my hand, as his arm had already tightened over Sarth, "anybody else. And if I'm never going to—to—favor her, how can I say, Yes?"

After a moment Sarth said, "There was more to it than bed."

Alkhes answered for me. "Hey?"

"The lafq," said Sarth precisely, "fight with the sharfir. And learn from him. The rest is if the sharfir calls them worthy. You don't have to do it. You could just teach her war."

We both understood. Not simply war, but the skills of a street-fighter, intelligencer. Troublecrew. The road he had opened for Sarth himself.

Alkhes said, "Gods," on an entirely different note.

We waited then, feeling the weight and shape of him in our arms, the beloved physical reality. Feeling the revolutions of the mind, the intangible beyond touching, and yet his being's core.

Until he climbed slowly on an elbow, and sat looking down at us. The glow of the brazier caught his expression, washing back off the wall.

He took a handful of hair and wound it, for a moment, on Sarth's breast. Touched the other index finger, lighter than a moth-wing, to my face.

"I don't think I can say, Yes, I will take you, but not—not for everything. It would be . . . it would dishonor us both."

His eyes held mine, then. It was my prerogatives, after all, this touched nearest of all.

"And I know I couldn't say, I'll take you, meaning, but not for everything; and keep that unsaid."

I sketched the last doorway, although I already knew the response.

"You could say, No."

The answer was in his muscles' shift, quick as reflex, before he spoke.

"I said, Anything. I can't renege on that."

It was Sarth who said, "And somewhere, somehow . . . you do want to say, Yes."

Alkhes glanced round, startled, and then not startled at all. I saw the rueful little smile, before he touched Sarth's cheek.

"Yes," he said at last. "Yes, after all the, the problems and the worries, and the, the things I just don't know how in a River-lord's hell will work. It's the one thing I can do for him. The one thing that builds something and isn't just—" the look in his eyes then cut me to the heart. "The one thing he might have asked."

The one thing Wonsa had asked, I thought, and in the moment of its granting, cruel necessity, a crueler taskmaster, had made Alkhes himself take it away.

He looked between us again, took breath, and stopped. Gave himself a sudden little shake. "Ah, Gods, you know everything else!" He met my eyes then with something like defiance. "And yes. I do want it because she's like him."

It was defiance then, open, almost scared. But Sarth reached out and tweaked him down on his own chest, and with an arm locked over his neck scruffed his hair and said mildly, "This isn't Dhasdein, Aglis."

I do not know what underlay that. All too clearly, something from their mutual past, for Alkhes' shoulders relaxed; he gave Sarth a quick, equally rough hug, and then, with a brave note of briskness, he said, "We better get some sleep. We still have to tell the rest."

* * *

We did that over breakfast; when I discovered my ignorance of thalan, and other things as well.

"They say it's very old." Azo again, determined to prove Zuri's omniscient mantle had not fallen awry. "There's no set tests, but the laf is expected to be a hunter as well as a warrior. Before you're worthy to seek thalan anywhere, you have to snare a great-beast, and meet either a tigercat or a lion. And kill a man." Delicately, she turned a cake. "Apparently, that's the easiest of the lot."

And, startling me, "There are stories," put in Deor.

"You hear 'em on the cedar rafts," she answered my stare. "Not many women ever did it, and a lot seem to have followed blood-kin. Brothers, fathers, even husbands." She did not add, Like this. "There aren't so many nowadays. And it's commoner," already she had changed 'upRiver' for the Heartland version, "Upstream."

"Mmmph," I said. "What happens if there's a child?"

Deor gave me a one-shouldered shrug.

"There's a ballad," Esrafal spoke in the dreamy voice of re-called lore. "About great sharfir and famous lafq. It's nearly as old as Amanazar. There are two, no, three verses about children that a laf gave her sharfir, after his wife—failed."

There was a pause that teetered like a foot on brittle ice, when nobody looked at me. Esrafal, sublimely unaware, went calmly on.

"And four verses where they're women, laf and sharfir both; and another two or three about women whose laf was a man."

Quitting the memory-spell, she added wryly, "That doesn't happen now." When she went on her voice was deliberately blank.

"The ballad says, it started with the People of the Source."

Typical Esrafal, to drop a lore-blast unheralded and shake us all. Amid the burst of exclamations I read Azo's chagrin, even as I felt the charge run down my own back.

"I never remembered it," Esrafal was saying calmly, to Deor's badgering, "until I heard the word again. Last night."

In the pause, Alkhes said with what would have been my own restraint, "Is there anything—else—you remember about the Source?"

Esrafal shook her head. "There are so many songs. I can't call them to mind. Just . . . sometimes, they come back."

Into the eloquent pause Keraz added with some dryness, "There are other things we might consider."

She had talked to women at the River, after the ceremony. About Varris herself.

"She was the only girl from the first marriage." Something in Keraz' voice said this had meaning to her too. "The new wife isn't much older. And she has three sons."

We are learning, Tanekhet; that even in the Heartland, where women may take thalan or rule like Haturi, the heart of a house-hold is the man's treasure. Sons. Boys.

Keraz let us work it out; the last child of a past marriage, a daughter, now superfluous. What sort of life would the family give her? What dowry could she expect, to get her out?

"Jirba," said Keraz coolly, "doesn't mislike her. Doesn't favor the rest overmuch. But—"

She sat back then, and let the assembly take up for themselves the full weight of that, "But."

Whatever his calling, Quiran is Iskardan; he would vote with Keraz as a matter of course. Chenath would follow Deor, as Herar would Azo. Who would bear the true load of a new presence in the company, one whose loyalty we could not take as sure.

I looked at Azo, and she looked at me. Then she looked past me and said, "Alkhes, what do *you* want?"

After that, you can guess the House's choice.

* * *

So we have done something you will certainly censure, Tanekhet, something almost as foolish, and certainly more equivocal, than leaving Zuri in Cataract.

The actual pledge was simple enough. When we finished breakfast, they were already outside; Jirba and his daughter, standing patiently in the early sun, with a cluster of villagers behind them, anomalously silent. And Varris' spears propped beside the door.

Alkhes took one look and almost baulked after all. Before he turned, swallowing visibly, to the waiting girl.

"I don't know the, the . . . what do I do?"

Not the most formal, most polite of ways to announce, the answer is, Yes. But the way her shoulders let go, her chin came up, told me how desperately she had wanted, how much she had feared he would say, No.

It was Jirba who replied, clearly not by form, but impassively enough. "If the sharfir accepts the laf, he takes the spears inside his gate."

Alkhes looked at the spears. Back to her. Then his shoulders straightened. With a bearing that spoke army, Dhasdein, a past reaching from Imperial guard to coalition general, he reached out; took the spears up, two-handed, parade-style, and with a gait as formal, carried them through the door.

* * *

That may not be the root of it, but things have gone amazingly since. We did not have to hire a boat, we were offered passage, on one of the bigger sail-craft, with a lower deck and a hold and its own crew, its own provisions, for as far as we like. And though it was supposed to be going upRiver, I am almost sure they timed the voyage for us.

As for Varris; I will give her this, she has fitted in far better than you might think. She has played herald when we need provisions or anchorage. She has hunted, as you might expect, and she hunts accursedly well; we have eaten wild-beast, or some breed of plains-deer, almost every night. Moreover, she has fitted better into the company than I could have hoped. Heartland reserve, perhaps; but she is quiet, polite, attentive, without becoming a sycophant, and to all of us, her manners speak only respect.

At least she has made no attempt to importune Alkhes, as I, and I think he, feared she might. The hunting is a display, no doubt of it. But with him too she is perfectly respectful, and she has never pressed for any favor at all.

It is Alkhes who has accepted his responsibilities. We were barely a day upRiver, anchored for the evening, with the boat-crew busy over the clay-bedded cooking brazier, when Alkhes cast an eye round the deck and said to Azo, "Big enough to work out?"

Walking, we have all been far too tired. But after a day's relative idleness? Azo never took the time to be surprised.

Until Alkhes beckoned his laf; I have written it quite easily; who was perched modestly by the mast, and said, "I can't teach hand-to-hand. But we'll show you a bout, and then, maybe, Azo will work with you."

The one war-skill the Heartlands do lack. Astonishing, since there is such a famous school in Cataract. But obviously its repute is known. Watching her face lighten, the eagerness under the warrior's focused gravity as she faced up to Azo, I confess, I felt the singe of jealousy.

She works out with them now as a matter of course. He has begun to teach her other troublecrew work himself. I daresay he will want me to try her with the cutter, or a light-gun, soon enough.

After all, it is eminently reasonable; we have gained a warrior, we have lost our supreme troublecrew. We would be stupid as well as wasteful, not to put at least a novice in her place.

And the fourth or the fifth night, when Sarth began his imperceptible shepherding to muster the company on the foredeck, it was Alkhes who glanced astern and asked, "Varris, too?"

He is no fool, my sweet soldier. He had spoken loud enough to reach the entire company. Varris as well.

Sarth checked. Very nearly blinked. Looked at me.

That too was logical, if not reasonable. If she was truly part of the company, how could I say, No? If she was not, the qherrique might well say it for us all.

And I will admit, one small scurvy part of me wanted to see what it would do.

Alkhes settled her: at his own side, Ahio's old place. Esrafal beyond gave her a quick, small smile, said, "Do as we do," as she reached for a twitched, half-withheld hand, then took a musician's breath, and began the evening's song.

Unlike the Haturas and the Downstream folk, the crew did not retreat. So it was inside a double ring of dusk-blurred silent attention that the seed began to glow.

Yes. With a stranger in the circle, still it answered us.

Alkhes, of course, would not be content with that. In the split second between when Sarth drew breath and when he spoke, Alkhes said, "Say we have another in the company."

Sarth let my hand down and stared at him. Supremely unaware of the double risk of double innovation, Alkhes merely frowned. "Go on," he said.

Concerned, with that ingenuous soldier's gallantry, not with the risk of the qherrique or the interests of the company, but that there should be no slighting of his recruit.

Sarth raised one exquisite, exquisitely scathing brow, and spoke.

There was the usual pause. Then an image of Jirba at his hearth, a woman's shape at the shadow-rim, Jirba saying, "This is my daughter. My son's sister. Who asks her own price."

None of us noticed what I remember now. That Jirba had actually said, "Whose own price is that she become laf in his place."

Even when, to my knowledge, it is the first time the qherrique has altered, abridged someone's words.

Alkhes just nodded and went on, "Varris, yes." I felt his hand relax, I saw the landmark noted in Keraz' face, in Azo's glance. She was accepted. She was, in more than our terms, part of the House.

Sarth lifted his shoulders in a just perceptible shrug. For a tower man, an hour's descant on impetuous ignorant Outlanders, risk, phenomenon, irrelevance.

"How far," he said, "is there to go?"

His own audacity, that had spoken what was rooted in all our minds, impossible to voice, lest the answer shatter all our hopes.

A longer pause than usual. I thought it was a refusal, I had already begun to frame a second choice; then Alkhes' arm jerked against me as Varris leapt half to her feet with a huge, startled gasp.

With a soldier's reflex Alkhes yanked her down. "It's all right!" With a laf's reflex she took his word as law. As she fell back in her place, eye-whites showing, the images reached us all.

Jirba's hearth-room in the firelight, Jirba on his stool, a woman beyond him with a child at breast. In the place where we had sat, a grizzled Heartlander with a turban to match Jirba's, chased brass coffee-pot in hand, on his face the Heartland equivalent of an indulgent smile.

"From Home-cove to the Crocodile pool, with a fair Dry season wind, a month's sail. From Crocodile pool to the Forest-landing, a fortnight, with luck. Load the beans, if the Hazi's in good humor and the tokens suit, in two or three days. And back before the Wet-winds change, and next time I'll bring a Reedfolk basket, shall I, to please the house daughter's pretty eyes?"

"It uses our words." Alkhes was snapping, shaking Varris' shoulder to and fro. "It uses our words!"

"It . . . it—" With a hero's effort she got control of herself. Slowed her breathing, got her hand down from her mouth; with a mighty gulp, straightened up. "That was—"

"A friend of your father's," said Sarth coolly. "Who sails Upstream. And once, you asked where he went."

"It uses our memories," he said, across Alkhes and me. "When it has none of its own."

No need to meet Azo's eyes. I kept my tone easy as I said, "Is Forest-landing near the Source?"

She rolled her eyes. Met Alkhes' look and deciphered it far too easily, before she answered me.

"Forest-landing is as far as we . . . as these boats go."

She stopped and stiffened, and went on with a note of defiance that the crew's faces explained all too well.

"It's where the coffee grows."

* * *

Possibly I will not send this to Tanekhet at all. I am not sure I will not burn the entire sheet. All too surely, he would understand the value of this news far better than I.

Coffee. The daily staple of Amberlight. In Riversend, unknown. Paid for, even in Amberlight, weight for weight in gold. Not the most expensive trickle in that scanty stream from the Heartlands, but the heart of its mystery. As the Mother sees me, if downRiver knew its source, it could be the foundation of an economy. For Cataract, it could fulfill Wonsa's dream.

Or it could, in other hands, be the remaking of Amberlight.

If we knew the source, if we ourselves could manage a share in the trade, it could be the saving of Iskarda.

* * *

Varris knew what she had done with those words. The rending, the re-alignment of loyalties was clear in her eyes; and clearer still the cause, as they hung on Alkhes.

Who, soldier that he is, read the import in our expressions, crew or company, all too well, and with a soldier's speed deflected us all.

"Who are the Reed-folk?"

Varris' back relaxed, and the crew's with it. She answered quite readily, "The Reedlands border on Forest-landing. Upstream."

Enigma and menace enough, and still more information than we had managed in a month below the cataract. Amid the company's daunted faces, Azo dourly followed up.

"How far then to the Source?"

At which Varris too lifted her shoulders in the universal River sign. I don't know.

Azo looked at me; I looked back at her, marking the existence of the pit-trap, the goldmine, as I would with Zuri herself. Deor was thinking more immediately. Already her face had corrugated in a frown.

"How do you get through the reeds?" she said.

She had her hand on Chenath's knee. His hand was on Esrafal's, Esrafal still had a hold of Varris, and Varris, you may be quite sure, had not let go of Alkhes; any more than Alkhes had released me. The image hit with the white blast of a lightning strike, a span of River-breast blue and silver between forest curtains of leaves and sunlight and rampant greenery. Ahead, a wall. Looming as solid and looking as tall as the Jump-up cliffs, green and yellow-dappled and thick-woven and impregnable, a living palisade.

"Well, yes," Deor broke out before the rest of us, "but how do you get through?"

Silence. Not the blankness of refusal, nor the resistance of irritation or malice. We have come to read those sensations, as a shaper could read the moods of a half-cut block. This might have been consternation. Then the image of the lake at dawn, the spring, the frantic urgency, Go, go, go.

Alkhes yanked Varris down again. "It's the Source," he said. "The original dream. It's all right." But the set of his brows said it was not right at all.

Deliberately, Sarth tightened his fingers on my hand, shifted his grasp on Azo's. And repeated, "How do we get through?"

Silence. The Source's image. When Sarth repeated it, no answer at all.

Sarth looked past me at Varris and said, "Your people don't know."

She stared back at him, her Heartland aplomb shaken at last. Before she blurted, "We don't go through."

"But the, the Reed-folk do?"

"The Reed-folk trade at Forest-landing, but they—"She cast a hunted glance around her, into the crew-folk's unblinking stare.

"They don't have boats." A deep breath. Eyes desperately on Alkhes. "Barah said, 'That's where the River ends.'"

The company's silent consternation ricocheted from the crew's stare. All too clearly, whatever other story had come upRiver, it had not included our vision of the Source.

It was Alkhes who looked first; Keraz who followed, led by her own vision, Esrafal, fellow musician, who did it on her own account. The rest fell in, the crew copied them; every eye, every mind, resorting to our own oracle.

Sarth took a deep breath, and again flexed his fingers on mine. Before he said with the careful enunciation of danger, "Who are the People of the Source?"

The seed shot one sheet of white-hot fire. We recovered minds' and eyes' vision to find it gray and empty as death. And Sarth on his face between us; knocked out cold.

* * *

What does it mean, Tanekhet? How in the Mother's name am I to know?

Because we have not managed a contact for the last three days.

So what are we to do? What *can* we do? Except sail on up this perdurable River, making the best time we can to the end of everything, and hope as wildly as religious Kasterian lunatics that when we reach Forest-landing, *some* guidance, some road will appear.

We cannot go back; not with the Riverworld's foundations dissolving behind us and new governments springing like mushrooms in our wake. There has to be a discovery, and a reality, and an explanation, however lunatic. We cannot merely sail up against a reed-bed and abandon the Quest.

Iskarda would never survive it. No more might Amberlight and Cataract. As for the coffee-growers, who are another, almost a more precious source . . .

Gods of the entire River pantheon. Is *that* what we are supposed to see?

* * *

All too clearly, it is not.

Because we did get a response that time. And an answer, as vehemently delivered as by Alkhes in Riversend, a categoric, unequivocal, NO.

So there must be some way through. Some secret path, some mysterious doorway, some thread to follow across the Reed-folk's land, and who knows how far beyond it, to the mountains of the Source itself.

I would burn more than incense to the Mother, Tanekhet, if She could give me the slightest inkling what.

* * *

Gods above. Oh, sweet Work-mother, oh, every god of the Riversrun, how do I deal with *this*?

Burn the papyrus. I would burn it, if I could. But I am like the Head's tiring maid in the old story, who had to tell the River-reeds before she burst of it, that her Head had grown ass's ears. If I can just acquaint this innocuous paper, squander this lesser resource, if I can void the thought, the knowledge, the, the, what am I to call it, the unthinkable, unimaginable, the, the *calamity* that has fallen into my mind like a qherrique strike.

Calamity?

Miracle. Uncovenanted impossibility, shattering, incredible, oh, Mother, too, too improbable hope.

I cannot pray. I cannot beseech anyone, anything, to intervene in this. I cannot, I cannot bear to imagine its failing—

The very idea is an ill-wish I dare not bring to conscious thought. The fates or luck or whatever manages time would strike it, at the possibility's barest entertainment, like glass-blower's treasure from my hand.

Oh, Mother, sweet Work-mother, I *have* to speak. I will write the fact, the bare fact, and nothing else.

I have not cycled, it dawned on me this morning, for the last three months.

CHAPTER XII

Amberlight
5th Day, Third Summer Moon

This time I have well and truly done it, Tellurith.

To be honest, I—and others—have done a great number of things since my last letter, of which this, the personal, is probably the least significant.

So it makes a good place to begin.

* * *

On the first morning after that—no, I cannot, I will not call it damnable—that lapse of mine: when I roused fully, to the familiar sound of Dheya's orders, the rattle of distant water-pots, Kheizo's soft, familiar tread outside my bedroom door.

The man beside me heard them too. I had felt those unguarded moments of shortened breath, shifted limbs, that signal returned consciousness. And I had felt the very conscious stillness that succeeded them.

I rolled over under his arm, and took his face between my hands and kissed him on the mouth. "Two things," I said, "this morning, I must tell to you."

His eyes were open. So close, I could finally distinguish pupils and irises. They are not unbroken darkness after all: their mahogany is speckled with tiny golden flecks. Quite visible as, so steadily, so unblinkingly, he looked at me.

"Keshaq, I cannot make you a Favorite. I cannot so much as acknowledge this has happened. My diplomatic standing is our one protection here. We have been raided once already. And I do not put it past Shuya to try something rougher: poison, assassins. I have too many hostages. I cannot afford another. Especially one like that."

I meant—the Gods know, I should have said: One like you.

That, at least, he had been trained for. Favorites, and prestige, and the way it could be turned into a lever, he understood.

"And if I cannot acknowledge you, then nothing else can change. It is too late to let you go. Outside, you would not last a day clear of Shuya's intelligencers."

That too, he understood. I saw the flare of comprehension, of simple terror, then the way the mouth locked tight.

"And inside—you must still be a house-servant." I put a hand up to push away the tangled hair. "So if that means mopping floors and carrying my breakfast —that is what you must do."

When justice, not to mention my inclinations, I could not say, would have you sit and eat with me.

"And if I could acknowledge you—" I took a deep breath. "You would still not outrank Dheya and Kheizo."

The eyes flashed, the nostrils flared. He started to sit up and I pushed him down.

"You must get used to this, because when we go to Amberlight, you will find it everywhere. Everywhere. And—" I took another deep breath— "I have accepted it. This is the way I have chosen to live."

Silence. The gold flecks were very bright in those long, smoldering eyes. I kept my face quiet, and my hands still, and stared back, thinking, Now. The choice is yours.

His lips parted: a short, sharp breath. He shut his eyes a moment. Then averted his head and muttered, "If that's what you want."

Not the most gracious of responses. Not the kindest of requests, either. I said, "It's not what I want. But it's what we must."

I kissed him again, and felt his mouth as well as his muscles relax, before I let go, and we both began climbing out of bed.

* * *

Only now, writing it down, do I realize how many assumptions of a future, how many implicit expectations lay in what I said to him. But then, I spent the entire day refusing to see the slightest implication of my words.

Right down to the moment, late into first night watch, the rest of the household presumably settled, when Dheya tapped on my study door.

Came inside. Closed it behind her. Said, "Ambassador, everything's secure. Kheizo has the patrol. And that boy is standing out there, waiting to hear if you want him, and eating his heart out over it. Shall I tell him, Yes, or, No?"

I put the pen down. Curiously, I did not resent her presumption—if that is what it was. With Amberlight people, things are so different. I did want to swear at her. I wanted to baulk, and prevaricate, and deny everything.

What I said was, "What might be the best thing here, Dheya?"

A muscle moved at her mouth corner. The sole time, I think, that she has acknowledged one of my hits.

Then she said, "Most simply—*Yes* would settle the pair of you. You've gone round and round for days, you thinking bedroom and playing lord ambassador, him pretending he's an outlaw, and looking your clothes off every time you walk away."

"And less simply?"

She studied me a while: that steady, unwavering regard of a woman who has never had to let sex shade her intelligence.

"Less simply," she said "this has been a hard time. And you need—you deserve—some peace. Ambassador."

The River-lord knows if she reads my papers. The Iskardan intelligencers do not need to tell her how this mission has tested me. And an Amberlight woman might well guess, from that day the first news came, just how nearly I have failed.

Our eyes locked, across the muted lamplight, in the quiet of the silenced house.

"We would both wish you that," she said.

No mention of Hathris, naturally. Iskardan, Amberlight women, who take it for granted that they can protect, decide for, discount men. Who are retainers, but never servants as I have understood the word. Who are "my people" in a sense no others ever had. Who will not simply back and support but make decisions for me. Taking me, in a wider sense than I ever imagined, as their responsibility.

I said, "Thank you, Dheya."

She inclined her head. In the pause of amicable understanding, I said, "And least simply?"

She took a little breath.

"Least simply," she said, "it might sort out things with the Iskardan marble factor."

I looked down at the pen, catching light like a tiny balance beam as I turned it in my fingers. Presently I said, "Does the whole River know?"

"Of course not." She spoke quite sharply. "Here, it's our job. In Amberlight or Iskarda—you could say better than I."

I must have blinked. She produced a minimal shoulder twitch.

"Everybody heard you had a—difference—before you left Amberlight. It's only the way your voice changes when you talk about her that says more." A more minimal smile. "And we only notice that because we've come to know you—quite well."

I put the pen right down and straightened up. "I am grateful for your concern," I said. Honestly. "But it's nothing to worry over now."

She stood quiet so long I nearly spoke again: before she sighed and murmured, "This Outsider love."

I did blink. She sighed again.

"Why is it you all think love can only be one-to-one, and man and woman at that? As the Mother sees me, women in Amberlight have taken partners and then married husbands, or married men and then taken partners, time out of mind. There's hardly a man but was tied to four or five women, in the Towers. And as for men and men . . . it doesn't have partners' status, and marriage overrides it, naturally—but plenty of men have made each other happy, with a wife or without. Why are Outlanders so—unimaginative?"

Credit me this far, Tellurith. That despite the pain of memory, of betrayal, of my so-called broken heart laid bare—I was near laughing, before the end.

"Gods above, Dheya!" I think is what I said. "Do you mean— Have I—even if I—if we—would she—"

I must have waved my hand toward the door: Keshaq. She nodded matter-of-factly back.

"What she feels about you—who am I to say? But she's born and bred Amberlight. If you did stay with this boy—and never patch it up with her—still that's the better case. If she *were* to patch it up . . . she'd think the less of you for leaving him. And he won't stand in *her* way."

Was there a hint of admiration in that last? At the time I hardly heeded, I was so torn between competing hopes.

The Gods know, Tellurith, I *ought* to have thought of it. I *ought* to have expected it: have I not had your own example before my eyes, have I not made it my own dream's keystone? And have I not recited back to you, in these very letters, the customs of Amberlight? The love-band, the communal husbands, the Outland slurs upon women who loved each other too much to love men . . . how did I imagine the City continued, if they did not accept both?

Why did I assume that, because I expected to love only one woman, she should do the same? Perhaps I have gained some scrap of wisdom. Or perhaps it was pure jealousy. But I had to ask the next thing. Even if it drew the heart out of my mouth.

"Dheya—does she have a—a partner—now?"

I could bear it, I was thinking, in the dazzle of that shifted vision. If they—she—can accept what I might have, I could accept the same for her.

Dheya all but killed me, waiting, before she spoke.

"One or two people who mattered. Maybe someone in the Navy, before." Before the fall of Amberlight. "But to the best of my knowledge, for the moment—no."

My body must have spoken, clearer than words. She gave me a small, Dheyan nod.

"But she will marry someday," she said. "She knows that. It's an obligation. Because now—she's the Heir."

She came up to the desk. And she actually patted my shoulder: before her own face sobered, and she looked me full in the eye.

"As for the lad out there . . . It's your choice, Tanekhet. But you've taken him up. You spoke to me once about trust. You'll kill him, if you break that now."

I put my hands flat on the desk, looking up at her. Before I said, "Very well, Dheya."

* * *

Ridiculous, so ridiculous, that my mouth was dry, my heart playing butterflies, when I walked out that door. For a man who was the fancy of a moment, an unknown, a servant, or a slave. For someone who was nothing but a substitute—

Who is a commitment. A pledge, Tellurith.

A pledge that will hold not merely in Assuana, but to Amberlight. And beyond.

I have no idea what you will say to this—what Tez will say—what we will do with him—in Iskarda. I only know—

That I walked out into the dimness of the big reception room, and had to clear my throat before I said softly, "Keshaq?"

Instantly the shadow moved. Over by the wall: the passage to my bedroom door. Acknowledgement. Hesitation. Even now, he could not be sure.

I walked across the reception room, the sleek mosaic gritting slightly under my feet.

"I'm sorry I kept you waiting." My voice sounded quite normal: almost cool. "Shall we go to bed?"

I heard his indrawn breath. But he did not, as I half-expected, throw his arms around me.

What he did was go on his knees and catch both my hands, and press them to his forehead. The Quetzistani gesture of fealty, of irrevocable allegiance. That made it literal truth when he added huskily, "My lord."

* * *

When things quieted down that night, we did talk. Shiftingly, fitfully, but almost clear to dawn, with the deepening ease, the dawning confidence that, far more than bodies' conflagration, is the bedrock for what we both knew we had begun.

And almost the first thing I said was, "I have something more to tell you, Keshaq."

He lay still as an ambushed crocodile in my arm, and let that redoubtable silence, rejoin, Yes?

"I do have—a broken heart."

His breath did not catch. His pulse did not jump. He turned his head a little, an oval of shadow on the pillow-white, letting those eyes tell me, Go on.

"It was a woman."

His body answered, still now in a different way.

"I haven't forgotten her, no."

It was harder, far harder than I ever imagined: not that he understood, not even that he had misunderstood the corollary. But that he should take its import without protest, without question, let alone a curse.

I turned his face further toward me. A lover's gesture. I tried not to make it an owner's as well.

"That does not," I said, "exclude you."

The eyes opened then, so wide their obsidian swam in a crescent of shadowy white. I laid my hand along his cheekbone and let the touch affirm it, as I said, "In Amberlight, such things are understood."

The sculpted shadows of lip and upper lip slid, and slid again. I saw his throat move. Before he shut his eyes, and drew my hand, another almost ritual gesture, down to hold against his breast.

And given a little more time, a little more silent conversation, given a pledge of tomorrow, and just enough history together, I could ask what I had wondered from the moment I set eyes on him. "How did a son of Ku*o clan ever finish here?"

We both understood: how did a scion of Quetzistan's highest family, who should have died in the Dhasdeini bloodbath, end as a Verrain President's whore?

He was lying on his back, his head on my arm, my hand drawn over his other shoulder, still clasped on his breast. So I had every physical earnest, from breathing to heartbeat, that what I heard, at the end of that well-deep silence, was truth.

"The Ku*o matriarch . . . was my aunt."

In the—old days—as you know, my lady Tellurith, rule in Quetzistan belonged to the oldest woman in the royal line.

His mother had died in childbed. His father fell, as royal males should, buying a moment's more life for his leader, the night Dhasdein came.

"My cousins—Hesh was twelve, Weive thirteen. They went to the gelders . . ."

To end in a brothel, in Mel'eth, in Shirran, perhaps actually in Cataract. The male line had to be stamped out, policy decreed it. Not by martyrdom, which is only an inflammation to Quetzistan: but there has always been a small but choice trade, up and down the River, in beautiful boys.

He drew a breath that hurt us both and finished the sentence at last.

"They said I was too old."

But not too old to catch the eye of a lord among the Dhasdeini vultures who flocked after the army into Quetzistan. A little travel, a little sightseeing, a little profit, again with tacit permission from the throne. Hardly a wonder that a Ku*o stripling caught that connoisseur's eye on the block, and never mind the price, or his purpose afterwards. Let him stand in the corner like a statuette. The beauty was reason in itself.

"He had me trained—to carry wine. He said—my looks—were treasure enough."

The eyes swung round to me, dark, so dark, with shadows deeper than night. With all the past, and all the knowledge of a slave.

So I knew without asking that then, at least, he had not been brutalized. Trained as a house-slave perhaps, but not flogged. And perhaps not seduced.

I turned on my side to let him feel my body against him, and climbed on an elbow. Saying, as silently, I am listening. Go on.

He held my look a moment. Then, very slowly, his eyes slid closed.

"When it happened . . . I was—" he swallowed. "I'd just started—to train."

He meant, crossed the official threshold to manhood, and begun his warrior's schooling. So he had not been at the royal tents, the night the climactic ambush was sprung.

"It was so—fast. I had no time—"

I understood what I was hearing then. Not merely the chronicle of slavery's events, but the inner story, the one that slavery stamps out of existence. His own story: of a royal male, a nascent warrior, who ought to have died with his father in what was a full scale, triple-pronged army attack, the central assault on the royal tents, subsidiaries to massacre the royal guard and storm the training school. So a fifteen year old boy, probably roused from sleep to the assault's reality, did not have time.

To die fighting. Or just to fall on his sword.

I took breath before I spoke. In that aching quiet, the words sounded as distant, as carefully balanced above disintegration, as his own.

"I let my father die."

The eyes flew open. Deep, deep, without any scintilla of gold at all.

"I knew that—something was planned. I heard it—round the emperor. But I could not tell him. So I left for the summer visit—and—"

My own throat shut. I could only make a little hand movement, and grit my teeth at the dreadfully returning advent of those adolescent, those last, terrible tears.

After that I never wept again. I cauterized weeping, Tellurith, as I cauterized love.

I felt him roll over, faster and far less guardedly than I had done. I felt the eyes gripping my face, palpable as a hand.

Before he lay down again, releasing his body limb by limb, muscle by muscle, leaving me to regain command of myself. Honoring my distress, with the silence in which I had honored his.

Until I opened my eyes.

Then he said, still more carefully, "Afterwards . . . I couldn't do anything. I couldn't—understand."

Greater trust. Deeper truth. Because to what he had been, such torpor was ignominy. And who knows what misguided guilt, how many hours self-loathing it had woken, as well as simple loss?

Because it was not cowardice: it was aftershock. One sees it so often, the apathy, the spell-locked inability to think, let alone to function, far less to fight or kill in return. The aftermath of losing, by surprise and violence, an entire life.

I said, "The man who killed my father—died in his bed."

The eyes that met mine understood that. Understood its absolution far better than any sympathy could have conveyed. He took his lip delicately in his teeth. I said, "What happened then?"

He understood that too: sympathy's exchange completed. Neither of us could bear any more.

What had happened then was five years—hibernation, one might say. While he played wine-bearer and charmed his owner's eye, and could not find it in him to do anything else. Until his owner died.

On a Verraini estate. Whence his wine-bearer, sold by an un-sympathetic heir he could not be bothered to charm, had ended on the Assuana slave-market block.

"And I caught a Family eye."

The minute flinch of eyelids had told me the kind of catching already. Gelded or not, beautiful young men are a commodity too. And the captive, being Family, would have expected a fine return for what, no doubt, had been a noble price.

I reached out and put back his forelock. I did not let my hand linger. It was understanding I wanted to convey, not a dilution of the same lechery.

"The first time he just swore. The second time—I remembered who I was."

I said, "Oh."

The tone, if I say it myself, was a masterpiece. The eyebrows capped it, in a gesture perfected before my mirror, long ago. Neither patronage nor sympathy, but a certain wry imagination of the calamities that had undoubtedly occurred. Right up to his punching a Verrain Family debaucher's teeth down his throat.

He made a small snort, half agreement, half savage laughter, and went on with hardly a jolt.

"He kept me a month. It was the first time I was flogged."

I sighed and re-deployed my eyebrows, and he must have startled himself with the ghost of a laugh that said, Yes. I was as obdurate as I have been with you.

"Then someone from the Court called. To inspect a concubine."

Closing the chain, from slave pen to Dhasdeini lord, on to Verrain noble, and then, by a piece of horse trading the seller had doubtless rejoiced in, to the altitudes of the Court itself. To what, the tension of his shoulders told me, had been the worst captivity at all.

* * *

He did not tell me this all at once. What I record next is a digest: a mosaic, assembled across three weeks' night and lovers' intimacy and the plant-slow growth of trust.

Put briefly, his place in the Court had been intended from the start. And when he fought it with all the pride and fury that had slept for those six years, they would been justified to geld or hamstring him or simply cut his throat. But the one was too risky, at his age, the next would have destroyed his looks, the last would have wasted a more than royal price. And thrift is drummed into Shuya's folk. So they kept him. And determined to make him what they wanted. Whether he fought it or not.

I am not sure how much you understand of slavery, Tellurith. Intrigue, and violence, and treachery, I know were everyday within as without Amberlight. And with them a truly murderous ruthlessness. But slavery . . .

It is a matter of the will as much as anything. Not muscle, not physical endurance, but the ability to deny the inevitable, to sustain the spirit, to refuse assent. A great deal depends on the individual. On both sides of the chain.

And his buyer was a high slave-quarters chamberlain: with his own pride, his judgment, at stake, and the resources of Shuya's slave quarters at his back.

They broke him eventually. There is no-one, given sufficient time and skill and determination, that you cannot break. In his case, it was also so very simple. Usual, with prisoners of fiery rather than craven spirit, the first gambit I would have used myself.

Not the beatings, or the bindings, the abandonments to darkness and starvation, nor yet the repeated, prolonged, exquisitely expert rapes. All that he would have suffered, and still spat in their faces. Even after they drove him beyond battery and attempted murder to try suicide.

No, what they found him was a friend.

A younger boy: Palace bred, being schooled himself. Who turned to him, once, in the hell of the training rooms, and leant on his shoulder, and took his comfort as he wept. Who made him feel stronger. Needed. Who came, inevitably, to matter to him.

Who they threatened, then, and blackmailed him into sacrificing himself?

Far too simple, Tellurith.

Who told him, one night when they had been left five minutes alone together, and my hellcat really was at breaking point: and when he spoke of suicide, that—friend—answered, "However you live, it's their defeat."

I gather it took him a few days to work through that. But it gave him just sufficient pause, that night, to tip the scales.

Then it became a creed, a rationale, for going on. For suffering whatever they did to him. With the bitterest determination, that to survive was the only possible victory.

Which suited the Palace perfectly. Let him fight and brawl and bear every punishment imaginable. They would never finish him off.

Because it was exactly what his trade required. Not simply to whore, but to whore with cruelty. To be used, by one whose pleasure is in pain.

I suppose I—he—we—should thank the River-lord, Tellurith, that such trade is rarer than you might think. So he had time to recover, between bouts of—use—or simple rebellion. And however they warped his will, they never entirely sapped his endurance. So he was still there—scarred, and violent, and rage-marked to his soul's core—the night I arrived.

"Did you know who I was?"

It was the first thing I had asked. I could not help myself.

He nodded. The eyes were as somber as the set of that mouth.

"They told me," he said.

I knew what they had told him. His very presence had made it inevitable.

"They jeered at me. Taunted me. Told me I was past it, whatever happened, it would be my last. And they said—I was a dead man walking." The long mouth quivered and set rigid. He added it softly, into the dark.

"They said I wouldn't come out alive."

* * *

Once, that would have been sober truth.

* * *

Did you know that part also, Tellurith? That it would go beyond cruelty, and maiming, and—simple—torture? That more and more often, my only surcease was to watch them die?

* * *

I am not proud of it. Even now, when you and Tez and Iskarda have bent and beaten and hammered it out of me, I am not proud. But I owe it to you to write this. As I owed it to say what I did to him.

Without pleas, or exoneration, or the bare solace of touching. As quietly as he, into the empty dark.

"Did you know that it was all—all of it—thanks to me?"

That time the silence lasted longer than eternity: I counted it, second after second, on the beats of my own heart.

Until he drew a breath that lifted his chest strongly as a sob. And let it drift away. Before he said, "I knew."

I did not touch him. Some crimes are too heinous to absolve through the flesh. I let the silence answer, So if you knew that I, to found my life, ruined yours along with Quetzistan, that your destruction was my master-work, that it was I in the most literal and solitary truth who was responsible—why did you not, in good truth, pay your debts?

He rolled on an elbow and drew another huge breath. It caught as it ebbed, a little jerk and sob that spoke rage and stress and murder's purest, revenge's most violent temptation. And their defeat.

"What would have been the use?" he said.

With a world of pride and blood and breeding relinquished, with the grief of abjured courage and abandoned determination, the fall of everything that had made him what he was, with a sadness, a resignation, that all but broke my heart.

He put out a hand. A finger touched my cheek, lighter than a passing moth. I felt, in its tiny falter, the shock and wonder at my tears.

The second time he ever touched me, of his own free will.

I knew better than to return it. With a creature whose fear is not wildness but distrust and terror that has been burned into him, any response is too much. The very hesitance was pain enough. So truly, so deeply they had taught him, to be nothing but a use.

But his muscles softened suddenly, and he lay down beside me, settling his head on the pillow as if it finally belonged there, stretching himself on his side as you do to keep sight of a lover as you fall asleep, and I felt the motion to lay an arm across me, checked in mid-flex.

He did not dare that yet. He spoke instead, his breath soft as the inflection, on my cheek.

"I tried to do it. I told myself I was supposed to, you deserved it, I owed it. To them. To myself."

He lifted a wrist, twisted and let it drop.

"But every time I tried—it would come apart." Mystification, faint, fading, become something else.

"It wasn't even—that you let me go. That night. Or that you bought me out."

He climbed up on an elbow. The words came faster, their very rhythms an easing, a more than physical release.

"Or that you took me in after I came and besieged the house, and accused and insulted you—Dhe, if you'd known how I was scared . . ."

Of abandonment, and destitution, and a freedom that would cost no less than his life. How could I have blamed him for that? I took breath to say, I was in all truth to blame. I did not understand the consequences of my act. He put a finger—unthinkable, urgent, miraculous insolence—across my lips.

"It was because even after that, when I was here, all the time, all those crazy things I did, you kept—getting around them. Seeing how to—handling it so I never had to—so I could never—"

Drive us both beyond recovery. Never allow him, as he had tried so hard and so thoroughly, to destroy what he had won.

I put a hand on the back of his neck and left it there, as he checked. Veered and finished, with as much wonder as disbelief.

"All along—you *understood*."

Banal, threadbare word to convey all that he intended. Insight, empathy, comprehension, incredible from a master as from an enemy. A comrade, a fellow-sufferer's understanding. Tolerance.

He slid back down beside me and finished all but under his breath.

"In the end I still—had to pay my debts."

Can you understand that to have good returned for my good, in such a case, is the worst revenge he could have had on me, Tellurith?

I tried not to show him that. I kissed him, and tried to let kindness, and affection, and gratitude and—yes, love, what other word is there for it? pass in the touch of my lips.

* * *

The gods retain a sense of humor, Tellurith. Or how could they heap my head with such more than sufficient coals of contrition, and compunction, and unworthy recompense?

I outrun myself. Let me get out of the bedroom and these least—Dhe, am I still to mock myself? these least significant happenings, for the political stuff.

Such as the assassination.

Even yet, it is the victim that leaves me angriest. Kheizo, yes, a high risk, troublecrew, knowing the odds, Dheya, who, if less shielded, knew them just as well, Hathris who accepted a phalanx-front post. Myself, the undoubted target, but far, far worthier. In both senses. Anyone else—

Dhe knows, we were already careful enough. We ate nothing not bought by our own cook, checked in the door by our own troublecrew, prepared in our own kitchen, we had no-one in dining-room or kitchen not vouched for. And still . . .

She—the cook—

Her *name* was Rihasso.

Is it not curious, that I have never before taken time to learn one of my cooks' names?

It was my fault, Tellurith: had I not been fair enough to catch her loyalty, so she stayed when others left, had I not given her the fraction of attention great lords use to flatter their servants, to make her proud of her skills, to make her want my praise. Had she not been ambitious, as I heard Kheizo say tersely to Dheya later, of some dish that would, "cheer me up."

Apparently it is famous in the Assuana bazaars, less for the flavor than the extravagance. Sucking lamb, seethed with wild riverside mushrooms, only available through a rare, perfect combination of rain and early heat, and so many spices that its bazaar name is, The Steward Died.

A few hints to Dheya had mustered us all to do it justice: a formal-informal dinner, at the ambassadorial dining table, which made Hathris nervous and Kheizo grimly amused, before Rihasso entered, a veritable parade, bringing the dish herself.

All of us there except my hellcat, who should have been playing server, but had flitted off to primp and prink instead. And since Rihasso's face made delay unthinkable, I had filled the plates. Everyone was waiting, from Dheya at the table end to Rihasso, balancing her goblet of a belly on those delicate feet beside me, for the first connoisseur's taste.

The meat is eaten straight off skewers, the juice mopped with flat pieces of desert bread. I was maneuvering for a mouthful of equal enthusiasm and elegance, Kheizo herself was intent. So there was no warning. Not the merest thud of feet. Just an air-born body in the back that hurled the skewer flying and crumpled the chair under me and swept the dish off the table in a spout of shattering plates.

"Don't touch it! Don't eat!"

That came through a faceful of bread and carpet as Kheizo's intervention spoke from the yell and ferocious jerk away of his weight. One learns some reflexes, even at court. I rolled under the table and grabbed the nearest bread-knife and he bawled at me, on his knees amid the gravy with both wrists up his back.

"Wipe your face!"

With such terror that my hand flew up of itself.

Kheizo is troublecrew. No, Are you crazy, What's wrong, What do you mean, there can't be poison, How do you know? Just, "What is it?" and a jerk to bring answer on his wrists.

"Haturas! You can smell it! In the dish!"

Kheizo's eyes slitted. She jerked her head at Dheya, already near enough to help me up. To pass a napkin, while Kheizo let her prisoner rise, and stared at the debris, at Rihasso, eyes bulging, cheeks just purpling at the imputation that she would have missed, let alone condoned such a thing.

Kheizo said sharply, "It's for darts."

"They cook it." He was beyond squabbling too. Only the reflex remained, not to struggle, not to fly to me, because that would trigger her own alarms. "Put it with the spice. In—Quetzistan."

Kheizo shook him. Briefly, for attention, not retribution. "How could you tell?"

"The smell." He was starting to shake now. The words slid away down his throat. "I knew . . . the smell."

Kheizo's eyes whipped round us, once. "You didn't swallow any, Tanekhet?" Flicked to Dheya, back to him. "You?" He had been kitchen-worker all afternoon. Her eyes went past him and stopped.

Rihasso had both hands over her mouth. The blood was draining, like the bleaching of a grape from her broad, pendulous Verrain-black face. Superfluous when she whispered, in answer to Kheizo's furious shake.

"Tasted it before I served. To be sure it was tender. Just a taste."

She did tell us there was a slightly different scent to the cumin she bought that day, and the spice-seller had sworn it was a new type. Just imported, he claimed, at great expense, from the Heartlands, brought downriver in one of the first ships from Cataract.

I think that he made her—us—pay extra is the worst cut of all.

We did what we could. A physician—not for cure, to ease the end. And for witness. I made sure of that. I summoned every high chamberlain I could find as well as Shuya's own potion-broker, I raised the roof with my accusations and lamentations and rage. I can assure you none was feigned.

* * *

We pointed them at the spice-seller, of course, and of course, he was long gone. We stayed with her—I stayed with her—until the convulsions became impossible, and the physician told us it was use aspnor root or worse. A poison to ease poison, Tellurith. I held her hand so long as she could know of it. Then I went out, to pen Shuya a Note.

Naturally, a pre-emptive strike: accusing Verrain of, at the worst, culpable negligence, that had killed one of their own people in an attempt on an ambassador's life, invoking diplomatic immunity and reprisal from my government, the River's scorn and repudiation for such a national disgrace. Had they declined to take it, I would have stood in the audience hall and read it out.

Except that Shuya read hers first.

It was pronounced by the presiding chamberlain, while I was still bogged in entrance protocols. Before the Families' assembled representatives, its very readiness a flagrant admission of guilt. Accusing *me* of murder and conspiracy that had killed a Verrain national who trusted herself in my hands. Threatening reprisals against the, "so-called nation state," who had dared to foist me on Verrain, and promising to turn every stone that would show Amberlight was behind both me and the death.

I had to leave, then, before the Families took matters into their own hands.

I did my best, Tellurith. Dheya found criers who proclaimed our innocence and our outrage through the bazaars. I took my entire fighting train to the funeral, out in that shabby suburb where I gifted her husband and her family two hundred gold pieces, publicly, beside the pyre. I spent another fifty on a Note passed, through channels only Dheya knows, into the President's chambers, to Shuya herself.

Saying that to harass and intimidate any ambassador, but especially Amberlight's ambassador, was, at the moment, the height of fatuity. Offering to explain that. By word of mouth.

Yes, I should have consulted, yes, I should have waited for instructions, yes, the whole thing was a deadly gamble, the most arrant bluff. But without word from Tez, or Dhanissa, or Iskarda, let alone from you—was I to sit meekly and let Shuya pitchfork me out of Verrain?

And open a legitimized war with Amberlight?

You will understand the reasoning, whether you agree or not. Shuya is skilled in advance and redoubtable in retreat, splendidly skilled with seduction and immune to all but the most outrageous of bribes. The one thing she cannot bear is the hint of a menace unknown.

So she gave me my audience. Private, if not in the orange-court. A boudoir, perhaps, reached past a Palace guard detachment, body search, and two of her deaf but monstrous chamberlains. It was a steaming high summer day, the air limp as dead lettuce: I merited no fan slave, no sherbet, far less the offer of a pipe. Just an insultingly distant hassock, and a slitted, river-horse glare.

Oh, she knows the worth of silence as well as ruler's insolence. I made my obeisance an equal insult. The glare became a glower.

"What," she chopped off each word between her teeth, "is this threat?"

"Your Eminence," I let the contrasting courtesy balance along the fine edge of contempt, "some troublemaker has murdered a Verrain citizen inside your own palace. Inside a diplomatic suite. The attack was undoubtedly aimed at me. Through various—misunderstandings—my Note of protest has not been received. Now I am told that Her Eminence, that Verrain itself accuses me, an accredited envoy, of the death—"

"Why should I not?"

Baring those river-horse teeth. Beheading the diplomatic fanplay. Yet still unwise to think she had been stampeded into open threat. Far less simple fear.

"Ma'am." I bowed again. And continued the screed. "Beyond the obligations of an envoy to his City and her assembly, I was raised a nobleman of Dhasdein. My personal—integrity," with one of my most delicate sneers, "would forbid such a deed. I wish to convey my own and my City's deepest grief at the death. I have already offered the family compensation, on my own and my City's behalf. Finally, I wish to convey the strongest protests, on my own and my City's behalf, against what is rank slander, and hardly befitting such a nation as Verrain. I can only assume this accusation has escaped the—notice—of the President."

You will understand that three quarters of this was for the walls. Which, even round a President's boudoir, are guaranteed ears.

She must have known that also. I saw her fist clamp, and wondered if she would throw things as the stories say. But she sounded perfectly cool.

"Does your Assembly sanction this—threat?"

Stampeded, no. Knowing as well as I that no word had come: calling my bluff, asking what backing I had for such a claim. Demanding, that is, the proof her burglar had died to find.

I elevated my eyebrows. "I am Amberlight's ambassador."

"I should expect to see the directive. Personally."

I raised my eyebrows still higher. She threw herself back on the cushions with a snort.

"Not a word from your assembly since you arrived and you offer threats—threats! against Verrain!"

"Oh," I said, and heard my intonation, cooler than Iskan ice, "letters have come to me."

She understood. Even Shuya could not hide the tiny flicker, no more than a pupils' dilation, as she remembered those letters, the only letters I had indubitably received, letters whose arrival the whole city witnessed, letters a man had died trying to bring to her.

I doubt I could have managed it with anyone whose own wits would not have made those leaps, and then sprung beyond them, from firsthand news of Cataract to advice of future direction, to directives, for me, for Iskarda, for Amberlight. From you, Tellurith. The House-head of Iskarda, catalyst for the fall of Amberlight, presiding genius of the upheaval in Cataract.

What doubt that such advice, such directives, would include alliance between the three?

And how, then, to doubt that Amberlight now had a truly redoubtable ally, whose hand would cover not only a threatened city but a contested border, even an insolent, isolate ambassador?

I thought I was so clever, Tellurith.

No. I did not congratulate myself, any more than an over-pressed swordsman glories in an averted thrust. Some pride I may have felt. Was it not what I am here for, after all? But mostly, as the glare altered in those eyes, what I felt was relief.

I bowed a third time. She all but ignored me. Not quiescence, not surrender: that absence was calculation, I knew perfectly well. But I thought I knew its direction. So I moderated the insolence with which I said, "If Her Eminence will excuse me, I will be honored, in the next public assembly, to supply Verrain with a full, written Note."

She did not snarl. As she might have, seeing herself baulked in earnest. Her lids had dropped. But it was not anger, any more than it was fear, with which she waved me away.

* * *

At home, they were all waiting, when the guard relinquished me, and the bravos finished at the door. Lined up like a beleaguered garrison, Kheizo, and Dheya, and Hathris. And my hellcat too.

The women, of course, can read my body-talk and were easing before I cleared the entry. It was Hathris who scuttled at me with cries of, "What happened?" and, "Did you see her?" and, "What did she say?" and, "Is it all right?"

So I spelt it out for all of them, there in the reception room. A more unmannerly ambassadorial consultation I cannot imagine.

Or a kinder one.

Dheya and Kheizo let Hathris splutter out the further questions, what had I said, what had she said, what did this mean, what did that suggest? He had never asked such things before. I had never divulged such things before. Not in thirty years Court-life, twenty as a head of Dhasdein intelligence.

He sat down with us too. Keshaq. Strange, that I still find the name hard to write. He did not speak, who might have glossed my words with palace knowledge. Or contested Dheya and Kheizo's occasional comments, deductions, suggestions. But I felt, intensely as a grip on my shoulder, that black, burning stare.

But he never said a word, until we were in bed that night. When he rolled over, and laid an arm over me, fiercely as the first night, and said into the pillow, "Burn the letters, my lord."

I dug my fingers into his nape and answered, "We have no spy they trust."

It had been a clever thought, yes, but unless they had proof, it would only open the greater threat of searches, possibly torture, if they did not believe our claims.

Against my side his fist clenched. I shut my own fingers on a handful of hair and said, "Not your trade."

His fist relaxed: mercifully, he had taken it aright. Not, You were trained as a whore, you lack the wits for this, but, You were trained in something else. You are not to blame.

Nor would a palace whore know the currents of influence and information among the higher circles, where Shuya's policy might be a matter of debate. He knew that too. His fist clenched again. I shook him briefly and said, "If there's something you can do, you'll know."

How did I dare, Tellurith? Not merely to presume I understood, but to presume that I could hazard him—that I would ask it, and he accept, if either of us recognized such a thing? And to say it, so complacently, as if no gods could overhear?

Or anything else?

I know there will be no answer to that, Tellurith. I have only the question, the hypothesis, the irony that the gods have yet again returned on me, the postulation, the doubt . . .

The results.

* * *

The first of those appeared a bare two days afterward.

Kheizo whose first morning patrol found the allotted door-guard had become a pair of Palace guards, their official reticence yielding only that they were there, "by orders," and that, "by orders," none of us, from the ambassador downward, might leave. The proclamation came at guard change: read out by another wood-faced veteran. "For public safety," the Republic of Verrain had ordained a state guard and seclusion for Amberlight's ambassador.

Which meant house arrest, on the pretext of public danger, with the message that there was indeed public threat. A greater pressure than burglary or assassination, as well as greater vulnerability to threats within. Of our bravos' whereabouts, or our provisioning, among other things, no word at all.

When the messenger left we gathered in the court, rather than the reception room. I thought it some strange consensus, some instinctive search for open air. Until I looked past my hellcat's face, frozen in the best palace impassivity, into Kheizo and Dheya's stares.

Dheya answered Kheizo's eyebrows with, "Three or four days." Kheizo glanced at Keshaq, allowing the slightest wryness to show. Dheya sighed, and said, "When we finish here."

Whereupon Kheizo turned to me. Calm, contained, hand tucked against the front of her shirt. Where the light-gun is stowed. And said quietly, "We can leave."

When I opened my eyes she nodded the barest fraction upward. I frowned. She nodded again. "One or two." Meaning, there were guards on the roof. Naturally. And moved her hand against her shirt, and added, "We can still leave."

The aplomb of Amberlight troublecrew: calmly proposing an exit over the roofs, sheets roped about the finial, no doubt, the way the burglar came. Guards disposed of in silence, by that illicit light-gun, no doubt at all. An escape hatch, a safety-net: calming knowledge of a last resort.

Dheya too was looking at me. And Hathris, but he was farther out of his depth than Keshaq, who had some grasp at least of palace factors in the decision they had offered me.

Amberlight's ambassador. Amberlight's outpost, whose withdrawal would open all sorts of ploys to Verrain. Whose flight would signal weakness the River's length. Closing a vital channel into Assuana, losing a vital proximity to Shuya, a vital potential to alter matters at their source.

Whose death, in some ignominiously orchestrated riot or assassination, would lose Amberlight far more than an ambassador.

Who was in Verrain at the direct orders of—Iskarda. His last directive to hold his position: nothing more. Whose own brief had been to keep matters at the level of diplomacy, while disrupting them behind the scenes, and who now found himself unpleasantly close to disruption's target, rather than drawing the bow.

I said to Dheya, "'Three or four days'?"

"Bread," she said. "Milk. Eggs."

Supplies, then. The time we could hold out if the Palace made it a genuine siege. I glanced to Kheizo.

Who nodded again. And repeated, quieter than ever, "We can leave."

"Would we make the River?"

No doubt about that at all.

"The border?"

Her eyebrows added the slightest touch of affront. Do you doubt my means?

"No," I said, and felt myself smile. And straighten my shoulders, with something nearer bravado than was ever proper for a Dhasdeini nobleman, let alone an ambassador.

"We are," I said, "the representatives of Amberlight. It ill behoves us to slink out of a nation that impugns our City, until we are forced to go."

Which grandiloquence Dheya promptly deflated with a little sigh and, "I think I remember how to pan-cook eggs."

Whereupon Keshaq astounded all of us by announcing, "I can make breakfast bread."

* * *

You may be relieved to know they sent in food, three times a day. So my hellcat's first kitchen duty was to join Kheizo as poison-tester, which he promptly expanded into the office of food-taster. Quite blatantly, doing it for me.

"I doubt they would be *that* foolish," was the most comfort Kheizo would spare me. With a quirk of the eyebrow that added, Not yet.

No consolation to follow her reasoning: that they could as easily expand seclusion into house arrest and that into full imprisonment, and once that convention was stripped away, we could be as simply executed. If not murdered in our beds.

I will admit to a certain—anxiety, Tellurith. I have known danger before, yes. Have lived with the peril, the constantly strained nerves that is the Court's native air. But that, however similar the ending of a noble execution, is a little different. A little more—elegant.

I really think we were meant to flee: information is understandably scanty, but I strongly suspect that an interception, rabble, thugs, outright darkworlders, was already primed. So the lull occurred because, when we baulked, Shuya had to find other, more powerful weapons. Had to spring the main attack, at last.

Or had to shape it, fabricate its means, from the start.

If that is so, I have been a catalyst, as you were, in a way that we may all rue, Tellurith.

* * *

Well. From here, there is no telling. What I can tell is the wait-ing time. Two days. Three. Four. Before the thunder broke.

I am unsure how much this will surprise you, Tellurith. But I will say outright, my lady, that it surprised *me* mightily, the night the knock came on the door.

Our response, I am honored to say, had all the aplomb you might ask. A couple of lifted eyebrows, a smooth marshalling of non-combatants, while Kheizo, our spearhead, went with that un-obtrusively swift step to the gate.

I had time to notice that Dheya had the light gun, and was in front of me. Shouldering Keshaq. No surprise there. And more time to decide if I would go with dignity or fight to the last nail, before Kheizo was coming back. Far more quickly, with tension open in her face, and a jerk of the chin to Dheya, Stand easy, now. For me, a proffered hand and, "Sent for you, Ambassador."

How they got it past a palace guard—how they got it *to* the palace guard, I could not imagine. Then.

It was a tiny billet of papyrus, rolled tight as a physician's bolus, probably meant at need to go the selfsame way. Its tight springs were marked, end to end, in code.

Amberlight code.

I do not know if she knew that much about Iskarda, or pre-sumed from Riversend, or expected schooling in the City itself: or if she had no other choice. I do know I had ado, unrolling it over the courtyard table in the unsteady lamplight, not to laugh.

Dheya needed no telling. Wax and stylus were at my elbow before I said for the men's benefit, "I can crack this. Yes."

It was quite explicit. And Amberlight succinct.

Expulsion tonight. The Families know. Lynching in the street. People's vote. Pledge to the emperor.

* * *

Did I not say, Shuya is never more perilous than in retreat? I could have applauded the brilliance, were it not my head at threat. Truly a master-stroke. Expel me from the palace, keeping the President's hands clean, no doubt with a claim that I had fled in fear of reprisal for Rihasso's death—or outright guilt. Incite the Families, already itching to dismember me. A couple of mislaid orders, the Families' intelligencers would do the rest. And their bravos. The vengeance of the people, Verrain's own verdict, deliv-ered, far from official protestation, in the street.

And with such public affirmation, Shuya would comfortably re-move a gadfly, open the way to Amberlight—and woo the emperor.

Thrifty, you may well say. No doubt that Antastes would have been grateful, too.

I send you this word, then: that we know, now, which way Shuya would have jumped.

I picture your eyebrows lifting. *Would*, I hear you say. *Would*, lord Tanekhet?

Would, my lady Tellurith.

* * *

They finished reading it over my shoulder. I could feel Dheya and Kheizo trading preparations. Keshaq's face was still bronze-cast, Hathris had just begun to gape. I wiped the wax clear, Dheya reached over the lamp. The papyrus went up in a quickening coil of flame, a brief black smoke, and over it I met Dheya's eyes.

She meant to give me the decision: the silence told me that. I was less grateful than you might think. They have done unmendable damage to a Dhasdeini man's arrogance.

I raised a brow to Kheizo. She looked at the smoke, I nodded. She nodded. "They were Heads," she said, "but they were Amberlight."

So the message was fit to trust. I raised my brows again, and she nodded once more, cooler than ever. "Yes," she said. "Now."

Dheya vanished, with a yank on the sleeve to Hathris. Keshaq gave me one unfathomable glance and vanished too. Kheizo slid the light-gun into her belt and said, "Wear some decent boots."

So we were in full preparation, funds and weapons gathered, Kheizo swinging a sheet loop to rope the finial, when the guards opened the door.

As usual, I saw most of it from behind Kheizo's back. And she would have gone at them barehanded, I quite clearly saw the light-gun at Dheya's side as they made, with the solid purpose of a phalanx, for the reception-room arch.

Except for what came inside.

A green flag: Verrain truce signal. In this case, some sort of official stave topped with an emerald scarf. My first inkling of the true shock was in my hellcat's gasp.

The guards had withdrawn, Kheizo and Dheya had fanned for cover across the reception room. He stood alone, framed in the archway lamplight, makeshift standard held delicately, the very gesture a self-parody, in one superbly manicured hand.

Shuya's notoriety, favorites. When I left Dhasdein it was a jumped-up slaveboy, eighteen at most, Heartland bred, supposedly Dalqu sept. Very little of such detail survives the slave-bazaar, but Dalqu have a reputation for looks to match their insolence.

Certainly, his rise from the sale-coffle to Shuya's chamberlain was meteoric. So he is as likely to have matched it in his fall.

Because the man in my doorway, though he could have been more than twenty, although he is dazzling enough to have drawn an emperor, and had dressed like one, was pure Verraini blood.

Six feet and a half, if not more. Muscled to match, ostentatiously, through the sheer muslin trousers and the long emerald-worked vest under the pearl and emerald-crusted, glistening, midnight-black brocade robe. Black as his own gleaming skin, blue-black, rippling, sculpted to a Verraini River-god's statue, with living pearl teeth and great, somber, superbly set pearl and ebony eyes.

He dismissed our doings as he had the guards: a favorite's unconcern, impregnable. The light-gun did not merit a second glance. His eyes came past them, and he said with perfect projection and immaculate Palace accent, "Ambassador?"

Keshaq had wits to let me pass: I inclined my head, the exact degree that signals honor, but not official honor, and walked half across the floor before I said, "The gods grace my house."

He inclined his own head. The great pearls in his earlobes glistened. Unlike a favorite, he did not smile.

I said, "If we lack fitting welcome, no doubt it is understood."

He did smile then. The slightest movement of a mouth corner. Not a favorite's grace, malice, frivolity. The irony, the weight of power, behind the understanding of a judge.

Perhaps an immortal Judge.

Before he looked past me, and said, "Come here."

Dheya, Kheizo, took my intent at a glance. I sensed Dheya easing down the light-gun as Keshaq walked past me, into the light.

They stood face to face, all but eye to eye. Beside that height and muscle my hellcat looked slender as a boy, but there was a matching knowledge, a matching dark of memory and experience, in that enlinked stare.

The stranger said, "It is time."

My hellcat's body answered, quick as the blow of a knife: every muscle crying welcome, every line shouting, Now?

"It's ready." A slight backward inclination of that splendid head. Out there. The voice, the stance, every breath defined it, terrible as a River inundation. And as sure. I saw it, clear as eyesight, even as the hair stood upright on my nape.

Yes, said those eyes, as he looked back to me: the regard of sentient night. Verrain's lifeblood, Verrain's foundation, Verrain's staple and Verrain's curse: all of us who hewed and carried and labored, who tended and worked and whored. All of us who were bought and sold for money, whether to die in a mill or share a President's bed.

It had been some time on the rise. There must have been word of it, dreams of it, it had run through their veins like a fever, the River-god knows it probably did come like a fever, from Amber-light, from Cataract. Nothing is so infectious as liberty.

I ought to have been afraid, Tellurith. It was what Shuya feared, when she gave my nightmares force. Properly, I ought, for my breed, for my—heritage—have tried to resist.

Or feared in an entirely different way.

Because Verrain was going to fall from inside. From right inside. From a Palace coup, a Palace massacre. And to them, I was with Shuya, no less than all the other owners, tormentors, exploiters, from the Families down to slave-runners in the streets.

He had the Verraini voice along with the Verraini looks. Deep, all but rumbling, the River in a human throat. But it was not to me he spoke.

"Which way?"

I felt Dheya's hand clench on the light-gun and made one furious suppressed gesture. A single light-gun would no more turn this than a River-flood heeds a mooring post.

Keshaq understood too: those long eyes had opened wide. The cast-bronze face, suddenly immobile, wore a sheen of sweat.

The Judge waited. All through the palace I saw them waiting, at bedroom doors and banquet entry ways, with the cleaver, the nail scissors, the knife. Poised for the first, the decisive blow. Whose focus was here, because it was this last scheme, this final injustice—perhaps to liberty's ambassador? that had tipped the scales.

Because here alone, perhaps, there might be fellowship across the death-line. An exception might be made. And who but the rebels' emissary, the Judge's viceroy, fellow slave and companion whore, could make the choice?

Keshaq's fingers opened sharply. Shut. He drew himself up, and spoke.

"He freed me. Then he hired me. That first time—he sent me away."

A favorite, privy to all a ruler's intrigues, would have known from what. Could have deciphered the backward sequence and understood its cause.

My hellcat lifted his chin, Quetzistani and defiant to the world's end, and said clearly, "I went to his bed. Myself."

In silence, the Judge demanded, Then?

Keshaq straightened fiercely, hand outthrust, palm forward, fingers up, the unmistakable gesture of refusal, and it came out harsh and sharp as a very blow.

"All of them."

* * *

So. This is your own privy report, my lady Tellurith, from the very furthest inside and first beginning of the Palace rising, the massacre, and the revolution in Verrain.

Other news may have gone up the River. I know it will have flown on the very wind. You may know, by now, that they achieved it perfectly: a classic Palace coup. Those least noticed, least visible, turning on their masters, to finish them in their beds.

As Shuya finished, I can assume. At whose hand, I do not know.

And from there the flames raced outward, division and bloody resolution among the palace guard, right through the palace from the rebels' core, and out across the city, into a night of wreck and murder and destruction such as Assuana—as Verrain—has never known.

The Families went too. Or nearly all of them, no doubt stragglers slid through the net. It was an infection, and once taken hold, it ran its inevitable course.

Revolution, after all, is the fever that incubates liberty.

So, bloodier than in Cataract, certainly far bloodier than in Amberlight. River traffic is blockaded, the borders are shut, by whose order no-one knows, but clearly, Verrain is convulsed.

Who rules—if there is rule—in Assuana, I have no idea. I would wish—would like to imagine—that it is the Judge. I would wish he survived that cataclysm, scathed or not. The memory of those eyes is terrible, but strangely comforting. If we spawn vengeance, and nations' downfall, and bloody retribution, they choose no petty agents, Tellurith.

* * *

Our story? Vouched for by his viceroy, freed by the Judge to our intended flight, up Kheizo's rope and across the roofs, down into the streets, and by Kheizo's skill and Dheya's painstaking scout-work, safe to the Riverside. Just before the deluge broke.

We had reached the deck of the fishing-tramp whose crew took us aboard without a glance, and without question, pushed us out, I was at the rail, with Damas at my shoulder, when we saw the floodhead burst. Raging outward from the Palace gate in a visible, audible ripple of torches, uproar, running figures. Growing, spreading fire.

I can hear you yelling this time. To the pits with Assuana, what do you mean, *with Damas*?

My hellcat's verdict. The Judge's work. Because his folk knew about the message: that was probably how we survived, certainly how it reached us at all. And when my hellcat had—voted—when Dheya finally let the gun down, when Kheizo released her breath and looked to me, Which way? It was the Judge who told me, "And the rest of Amberlight."

If it distresses you, I am sorry, Tellurith. But they did warn us. And they were Amberlight—although if Damas ever understands she was ransomed by the tie to her draggle-tail successors, she may well die of the disgrace.

And they had organized the boat.

So I have tiptoed across an Assuana roof with your redoubtable Damas, and sailed upRiver with Amberlight's other exiles. And I must admit, unrepentantly, that I negotiated their homecoming as well.

* * *

Give her grace, I think Damas was amused by that. They have quarters in some Downhill business house: for their diminished train, room enough. Damas may go into trade herself, I think. Eutharie may join her. Ciruil is all but an invalid. Most of their folk have been absorbed back into Amberlight.

I have reason then, to think you may not be best pleased, and not least at my personal—idiosyncrasies. Although, may the River-lord bless her, Dhanissa saw us come ashore together at what passed for the state welcome, and must have guessed our connection, if to an Amberlight woman our body-talk did not shout it aloud. And she still threw her arms around me like a—a farmgirl—a—daughter—and cried, "Welcome home, Tanekhet!"

With the same bubbling warmth she gave Keshaq.

How I wish I could legitimately babble to you about the delights of watching him encounter Amberlight. Not merely the Assembly's dogfight, the ramshackle markets and the more ramshackle men and women's arrangements for City life, from who leases pavement barrow stands to who washes up. Above all, the women themselves.

Only now, returning from Verrain, do I fully appreciate those faces, that carriage, the way they look every passer in the eye, the way they stride as if the world belonged to them, the inexpressible, unmistakable, inimitable air of absolute adequacy, complete self-confidence.

Whatever their past, they are the faces of my new world, Tellurith.

If you ever had my last letter, you will know how I have faltered at the full vision of that world. Now, with Verrain gone, I wonder I am not more—distressed. Concerned. Fearful, I suppose.

Because with Verrain gone, this new world that we are making, whose margins are already far beyond Iskarda, is face to face with Dhasdein.

And which way my heart will turn if *that* becomes a confrontation . . .

I will say this here, that I can admit nowhere else, to no-one else, Tellurith. I am sworn, I am committed, I have chosen Iskarda and—all it stands for—time and again.

But if it came to a choice with Dhasdein?

Even now, I do not know.

* * *

I have done it again. Circled and prevaricated, bypassed and dodged—

Tez, then, at last.

Our first landing was naturally Marbleport. Naturally with no more warning than a hail to the inshore patrol, naturally tumbling ashore dirty and disheveled from flight and nights aboard in quarters where I would not settle a pig, the news bursting with us on their unsuspecting heads.

I had to talk fast there too: too tired and fraught for lover's idiocies, under a frigid stare rapidly solidifying, with the all too likely chance she would kick our saviors straight back downstream. But Damas sorted that herself. A step past me, a cool, "One moment, if you please, ambassador," a grip on Tez's arm—she did not protest *that* hand—and fifty paces down the quay.

To return with understanding, if not welcome, clearly achieved. Nodding to me again, saying loud enough to reach most of the swelling audience, "The ambassador can tell you the full tale. We owe him greatly. As greatly as does Marbleport. And Amberlight. And Iskarda itself."

How wholly embarrassing, you cannot imagine. But it did appease Marbleport, and it warned Tez to whisk us all off-quay, to that same inn where we—stayed before. And to let us recruit ourselves before the full interrogation began.

But first, there was Keshaq.

He had followed me ashore. When we began to move he stepped forward. To my right hand, as a Quetzistani warrior would. Stopping Tez in her tracks. As her eyes slitted I said, "Lady Tez, this is Keshaq."

She too must have known Quetzistani custom, have deciphered the name. And though he committed no lover's blunders, simpering or giggling or trying to hang on me, his stance, or his simple stare, told her the rest.

She was surprised, Tellurith. Wooden Amberlight faces may be, and Tez as good as the best, but I saw the flicker of shock. And I think—I think—that whatever crossed her face behind it might even—even—have been relief.

I do *not* know how I should receive that.

But her manners, thankfully, were perfect. When I said, "Keshaq is from Assuana. But he was born K*uo clan," she must have fathomed the rest in a jump. But she gave him a guest's greeting, full respect if not warmth. And she said, "You are welcome in Marbleport."

With enough feeling to show she understood what that border meant to a freed palace slave. If not with the pause, the look between us, the sudden radiant smile and the great flourish of arms with which Dhanissa cried, "And now you're here! Oh, welcome, Keshaq!"

I suppose, considering what was between us, the way we parted, the—exhaustion and, and unexpectedness with which we re-encountered, what he clearly meant to me, it was enough.

I hear you snorting, loud as a signal-drum, Tellurith: *What, you go away swearing her eternal thwarted devotion and come back trailing a beautiful man, then expect effusions, Tanekhet?*

Very well, then, in good truth, I was—relieved. It was a good basis for a mannerly—transit—with surety of no appalling tantrums or other embarrassments. To her or to Keshaq. Had she wounded him, I am not sure—

No. Even now, I am sure.

* * *

I had my chance to moon at her uninterrupted in the full report-session that afternoon. When the first thing she said was, "Why in the Mother's name didn't you keep in touch?" And I could burst out with something near the entire depth of rancor, "Why didn't you keep in touch with *me*?"

A yet greater wonder, Tellurith, when after mutual self-recrimination, we realized that of course, Shuya would block letters going either way. Be sure, there will be a witch-hunt in Marbleport and Amberlight: but if the agent was in Assuana, we will never know—though *I* know, too well. Had Tez and I not parted brass-rags, as they say in Marbleport, one of us would have found the silence unnatural, long since.

Yet Tez did not berate—did not so much as criticize me. Just pillowed her chin a moment on that sharp-muscled hand. Then declared, with that special decisiveness, "Not your fault—Tanekhet."

I must be improving, too. For I managed an hour—a whole, deliciously anguished hour of private interview, and kept my mind to the politics, and my words to business, and at the end—

I managed to rise and walk out and not so much as sue for a glance, a word, any slightest sign that I meant more to her than Amberlight's ambassador.

I think it would kill me, to do it again.

Enough. The venture is over. We are safe back, Amberlight is—relatively—safe, and the wider repercussions I cannot yet think about. Enough to be here, in the City's warmth, with Keshaq to—be Keshaq. The gods know when or if this letter will come to you, but I will dispatch it regardless. And may the same gods look upon your journey, my lady Tellurith. Wherever you are now.

CHAPTER XIII

Below the Source
Second Winter Moon

O, Tanekhet.
    You were right. Grief is a vase, yes; a precious Shirran vase, one of those wraith-curves of all but transparent alabaster, purer than a dream, less tangible than breath. Lodged under the lungs. Cracking, fragmenting, with every beat of the deaf, persistent heart.

* * *

I had to go away there, as far into the bows as sketches privacy, and cry. The wind dried the tears as fast as they ran; even coming from astern, with its swelling winter boisterousness, with the River's rising pace to hurry us, and a ship bent, from ruddertip to bowstay and every mind between them, on the most furious haste.

At least we did reclaim Chenath. And Keraz, and Esrafal. And they are whole again. Safe.

* * *

I will not send this to Tanekhet. I will write, since there is nothing else to do, I will write it down and purge away the grief, and the rebellion and the—the—

The hate.

Almost worse than the loss, the parting, the death; almost worse is confessing that.

Hate.

For my kinsfolk. For my lovers. My husbands.

My House.

For the River that I, we, *it*, whoever we are, have been building, for whatever I was supposed to believe in when I began.

When I embarked upon this . . . Quest.

Beware, the old adage says, of petitioning the Mother too earnestly for your desires. Because She may give you what you ask.

I will record that upRiver, from the Heartlands' Home-cove to Forest-landing, with an unusually brisk wind, was five weeks' sail. As the crows fly over the langorously somnolent River, probably less than four hundred miles, to that mile-wide expanse of water lying almost motionless, a sudden benison of space and sunshine after you have sailed, and tacked, and towed, and rowed, and poled, twenty miles and more into the forest-depths.

A stilt-legged quay thrusts from a brown frill of trodden shoreline, where the eddies pull upRiver shipping left; behind that spread the blurred shapes of forest timber, posts, lathes, thatcheries of arm-broad leaves. The huts melt into the forest shade. What you see, over the heads of the gaudy gathering crowd, are the woven walls of compounds, and the roofs of the long, low, shaggy, open-sided sheds.

And upstream, the truth of Varris', of Barah's memories; the River's portcullis, solid-woven reeds.

Since Tanekhet will never see this, I can write freely about the coffee-plantations that wind into the forest aisles as haphazardly as patches of chance-spread shrubs. They grow it thus for the sun-spaces, and the rain, and because, they say, their gods forbid them to mutilate the forest that is their mother and sister, their life and sustenance. One must admit, it would be a most convenient camouflage, did an enemy ever come this way.

The harvest comes in daily, portered in thick reed baskets to the compound, spread on long rattan tables for the beans to air and dry, then parceled in those now familiar little packages, a double handful of beans, a twist of fluff-tree silk to keep them dry, and, I think, a palm-frond leaf knotted deftly round it all; before it is carted to the package-sheds at the water's edge, ready to trade.

Why, you may ask, do they trade at all?

No. Not *you*, not this time. If I ask, it can only be myself.

* * *

First, then, they trade with the Reed-folk, openly, on the shore-edge, for ducks and fish and above all, the baskets and mats and plates and every other form of reed-ware imaginable. Forest-landing's indispensables. Traded for coffee that the Reed-folk swear keeps them wakeful in the hunter's watch, deflects mosquitoes, fights the fever off.

It seems a genuine partnership, that, ironically, has limited both sides. The Forest-folk can thatch, but make a basket? Unthinkable. The Reed-folk can fish and hunt, but do it without coffee? Impossible.

The downstream trade? I did fence over that with the Hazi, if not that first morning, perched cross-legged on her scented, split-reed mats. The forest-mist heating and thickening to the usual midday showerbath, and the mosquito-burners smoking away behind us, pungent as the fresh-brewed pot beside the rolled-up rattan blinds.

She is halfway through her first term. They hold office for a year; men or women, young or old. Chosen by the community, with less corruption, I do believe, than any government I have ever known. There are no great merchant houses, no Families, no inherited rule, no jockeying for or coercing of votes. Everyone past puberty can go to the year's first new moon assembly, and propose themselves as Hazi. And the one who draws the most approval, wins.

Truly, astonishing.

The downstream trade? I know it passed, once, as far as Amberlight. I know it goes still to Cataract. For all her reticence, that proof is everywhere; not merely the ornaments of fur and horn and hide, obviously traded from what we thought the Heartlands' core, or the furniture of ebony and mahogany, the ivory combs, the rings or necklets of gold, but the brass coffee-pots, cast as indubitably in Dhasdein, the sarongs and body wraps of gaudy Dhasdeini cloth, the expensive Verrain or Shirran pottery. Whether the coffee itself goes that far, something is coming back.

"*Beyond* the reeds?" She is about mid-twenties, comely in a Forest way; which means almost as dark as a Verraini, thicker lips and wildly corkscrewing hair. Hers was threaded with strings of gold and lapis beads. Office, or personal wealth? "Beyond the reeds, nobody knows."

"But there would be word . . . stories . . . rumors? Surely?"

She frowned at me. Perplexity, not distaste. Again, our reputation had preceded us, and again, it elicited less excitement than silent wonder. Almost, it seems, awe.

"Stories?" Another wave of an uncertain, perhaps frustrated hand. "We tell stories about Downstream. About the Plainsfolk. The Reed-folk tell stories. About the water-snake. The crocodile. The River-horse."

I said, "No-one tells about the People of the Source?"

For one instant she flashed her eyes at me, Forest-folk signal of fear as much as shock. But if her government seems straight from paradise, her folk are sophisticate enough.

"Forest-landing is your harbor," she said. "Ask wherever, whoever, you wish." The tone courteous as ever. No sign, except in its perfect tranquility, of any mask at all. "The Reed-folk will speak for themselves. You could talk at market." She moved her cup aside, a signal clear anywhere on earth. "May the wind favor your sail."

* * *

"**A**nd nobody makes up stories," Esrafal said, "at all." Azo shot a glance at her across the cooking brazier, through the redolent coils of mosquito-blockade smoke.

"We know stories about Amanazar. Dhasdein has stories about what happens past the Archipelago. Verrainis will tell you there's a country beyond the Oases where people walk on their heads." Her little, sardonic drum-riff echoed Azo's snort. "Nobody stops making stories, just for lack of truth."

Azo sat up straight. Moved her eyes from Deor to me.

After a while I said, "Do the Reed-folk drink?"

Sarth lifted one eyebrow. Alkhes grunted, Varris twitched. Azo parted her lips; gave one brusque nod.

"Music," she said, "it'll loosen up anyone." Her eyes came back to Alkhes. She added, with resignation, "You probably have the strongest head."

* * *

The Reed-folk drink with gusto, especially on somebody else's stake. If Esrafal was all but voiceless, despite a hangover, Alkhes was coherent enough.

And bringing sufficient evidence of secrecy, yes. A people's ruler might keep silence, or claim ignorance supported by her folk. Only intent, and some fierce compulsion, and near to outright conspiracy, would gag the neighbors as well.

After a while, Keraz straightened her back; moved her eyes carefully from Alkhes, still squinting into the mild early sun, to Esrafal, nursing her head over the drum-edge, to Sarth. When he gave her a glance blank as a waiting crocodile's, she sighed and spoke.

"If neither music nor liquor nor the Mother's own Ear can give an answer, and we know there is a question . . . do we need to wait?"

Quiran blurted, "But there's nowhere to go!"

"Others might say so." Keraz shivered suddenly, in what I thought then was merely nerves. "For us; is there a choice?"

* * *

The Landing folk thought not. They went from polite disbelief to outright opposition in the space of a day. When we ignored their tales of drowning in pathless reed-beds, and took their cries of, "But there is no way!" with a determination to make one, it became stony dislike. A trial of my cutter and Azo's light-gun very nearly got us lynched.

"Your harbor, yes." We had agitated the Hazi herself; but not to threat. "You have the Lady's favor. But if the reeds burn, the Reed-folk will punish us!"

With nothing more than withheld trade. That was true enough.

"I feel," I answered, "for your folk. For my own folk, alas, I fear we have no choice. But perhaps an envoy?"

So the Landing would have interceded with the Reed-folk for us. Except the market was empty, from that morning on.

"It's quite clear you haven't helped us." Alkhes told the Hazi for me, brisk as a soldier in adversity. "So whatever we do, your folk won't get the blame."

We found the Reed-folk's main water-gate for ourselves. We charged the guns, we took what stores we had left, since they would trade or gift us none. We had bound reeds in bundles and tied the bundles together as Alkhes said they do in the Delta, and for all the rolled eyes and cries that Reed-folk would spear us for sacrilege, the rafts would be chopped in two by a River-horse, we would be poisoned by water-snakes or snatched overboard by crocodiles, the things did float.

And the day before we planned to leave, when Keraz' fever finally surfaced, the Hazi did agree to keep her safe.

"They'll look after you," I said, changing the wet cloth, thick with some forest herb, over her head. "The Hazi says everyone in the Landing gets it, on and off, most of their lives. Their healers are good."

As they were, familiar with the symptoms, but not inured to the point of casualness, with remedies in which they had calm confidence.

She shook her head to and fro and jerked back the cloth. The glazed eyes and sunken cheeks brought out the jut of her jaw, pure Darthis.

"It isn't me—"

She bit the rest off, but for all she could do, her eyes went past me; toward Quiran. That stare said it all. We might leave her behind and continue none the worse for it, for all we could tell. He was our healer, however little that meant. Before he was her man.

And the outcome was as obvious, in the way her teeth set, in the tears that had already left their tracks on Quiran's rigid face.

I said, "We'll wait till you're ready," and left them to say whatever they needed.

Yet another parting, another rending of ties dearer than blood. How many more will be asked of us, before the end?

* * *

We had another next morning; when we came out to untie the rafts, under a fog-gray sunrise whose clouds threw up shafts of rose-mist light like outspread spears, Chenath was shivering.

And Deor was still growling, "It's nothing, he's damp, it's just the damn mist," when Quiran, nearly as grim as she was, took the back of his wrist from Chenath's forehead and turned to me, saying flatly, "Ruand, look at Esrafal's eyes."

What point in forcing them to double hazard, just to encourage ourselves? What point in taking them into the unknown, to indeterminate labor and peril with no chance of another safe shelter when, as it was already doing with Keraz, the fever grew worse?

We might have waited till the fever passed. We might almost, the most prudent course, have waited till it took us all. The Mother, or the gods, or perhaps it was something else, shut that final door.

Because that very day, that selfsame morning, the ship arrived. With your next letter, Tanekhet.

* * *

Rot and gangrene it. Well, if I burn this when it is finished, what matter? Let me pretend it is for your ear.

And there was no more waiting, after what you poured in mine.

"Done something I will not like," forsooth. You knew quite well I would not give a Delta bailiff's blessing if you took a hundred lovers and threw in a goat. So long as you excluded Tez.

It may be she understood that too. If, at least, I read that meeting right. Relief, indeed. Why should you have been surprised? I can only hope the madness is over. For you both.

But for the rest . . . Shuya gone, the Families decimated, Verrain overthrown. And you thought yourself safe, Tanekhet!

I cannot believe—well, I can believe that the aftermath of long strain, and menace, and heart's grief, and your own nightmare's birth, could numb feelings as well as wits. That you could think it enough that the pair of you . . . and Damas, rot her cutting ear! were out of Verrain.

Did you think to notice you had left the River trade cut in two like a rammed ship? Did you never consider what you have done to your own revenues? Or that both Iskarda and Amberlight's markets are gone, at a blow?

Could you not see what has happened to Dhasdein?

The provinces will crack, there is no shadow of doubt. And chaos will bear down on Riversend, unless Antastes acts first.

Not to requite you; not to punish Amberlight, not to grab more of the River. Not even to exploit Verrain's ruin. But because he must distract his kinglets, turn their attention outward, harness them to some project, some attack, some threat. Or go down himself.

The Mother shield my folk, I remember praying, as I sat by the Hazi's coffee-pot and watched the sun vanish in the first midday rain. All my folk; Cataract, Amberlight, Iskarda.

And there was only one way I could help.

The Landing folk did give us water-shedders, I will concede that; cloaks sewn from over-lapping, flexible, giant leaves. And their physicians taught Quiran the fever's phases and duration, offered packets of their herbs and word of where, in the forest, he might find more. I tried to tell myself it would help. I tried to tell myself that knowing our lost ones were together would comfort us. I tried not to think about who might be next, and what might already be happening downstream. It was a fresh, almost clear sunrise, the merest patches of cloud to turn golden as false hope overhead, when we finally untied the rafts and paddled away.

* * *

Do you ever have one of those recurring nightmares, Tanekhet? The one where your heart's heart and your gods' dream and your world's salvation is in threat of final ruin, just round the corner, just on the brink of sight? And there is nobody else to save it, and you must do it this moment, and you run, and run, and run until you know your heart will burst, and there is something, mud, bonds, sheer damnable paralysis that will not let your legs go faster, and it is all going to destruction right there in front of you, and nothing, *nothing* will get you there in time?

That was the reed-beds, Tanekhet.

There are passageways; at least, there are waterways, meandering and labyrinthine as the channels of any river delta, narrow, tenuous, crossing and parting and most often ending in some new barricade. At times an islet, far more often a beast-wallow, or just another wall, impenetrable, obdurate; the reeds.

They are well over head-high, even on Sarth. They shut out the wind and pen in the mosquitoes, they trap the sun to increase your miseries of sweat. They build islets and shallows, they knot themselves, fallen and entangled, beyond the strength of any Dhasdeini battering ram. Their barricades, no current can pierce.

They do not channel, they clog and sieve the River, water seeping through, ubiquitous, untraceable, amid every mile of their floating, earthless, treacherous roots. There is no way to travel there, except afloat.

And without a current's power, channels are beasts or men's or haphazard events' work. A wind-storm, a reed-sickness, can lay open whole tracts. Far riskier are the plats of Reed-folk canoes. Worst of all are the treads of beasts.

Beasts do live there, yes, in multitudes. Birds above all, clouds of them, reed-runners, mud and waterbirds of every conceivable color and shape. Great beasts, the crocodile and River-horse, yes, but far more swamp-pigs and water-deer who trench up the shallows; strange reed-running scavengers in packs like savannah-dogs, and others we knew only by their tracks, for like so many, they feed at night. So we had, after a fashion, paths.

And we were lucky to begin with the Reed-folk's market-track, for the reeds a regular high-road, and running near our bearing as we could ask. With neither map nor chart, we had decided to take the River's downstream direction by the sun, and heed nothing else. Deor and Azo plotted that for us, with esoteric mutters about the time of year, and the way the sun would shift. So we followed paths that suited us; and cut the way, with light-gun and cutter-blade, when they did not.

We had just one brush with the Reed-folk, three days in. Alkhes who winded that ambush, by the luck of a wind-change and a whiff of oily, Reed-folk sweat. He and Varris who reconnoitered it, against my protesting hisses and Sarth's fury, creeping over the quaky reed-mats on foot. Azo and Alkhes who, when we paddled with seeming blitheness into the midst of them, taught them the peril of the Quest.

With the guns. With qherrique. With the Mother's fire.

It cost them, at most, five men's lives. It won us free passage from then on, and the scent of doused fires and abandoned camps to tell us how they fled our path.

At the price of an arrow-slice across Alkhes' shoulder point, and a stone-chipped arrowhead in Herar's arm.

How those did not go bad I have no idea; Quiran swabbed them out, of course, with Deor's hoarded Heartland barley-spirit, but the pair were drenched to the shoulder every single day, if not with fetid swamp-water, then with mud-splatters and running sweat; and the Mother knows, the food was nothing to help injured men.

Alkhes has the mark still, a red welt far darker than his other scars. Herar has a sunken, pocked pit. Otherwise, they are unharmed.

Of course, that denied us any chance of help; of proper guides, of learning the swamp-ways, of resting, ever, in some friendly camp. From the beginning, we had to fend for ourselves.

Sometimes we struck an islet where we might bivouac, instead of sleeping, blanket muffled, hungry and miserable, aboard the rafts. Eating? We cooked wherever it could safely be done, and ate cold porridge or meal-cakes or marsh-flavored meat for the rest.

For guides? We had Deor, again, our only water-Crafter.

Not the qherrique?

No.

And no, I do not have an explanation. I only know that, when we formed our circle the fourth night, after we had met a snarl in the labyrinth that needed more than human guidance, we sang, and we sang, until our throats were sore.

And nothing replied.

It never did reply. If there were answers, they came from our own deductions. Beyond that, for scouting and reconnaissance, for risk and toil and hazard-work, we had Azo. And Alkhes. And Sarth.

And Varris.

Give her the due she deserves. She was as bold as they, as indefatigable to wade, to plumb and pole and risk herself in some strait, damnable, possible crocodile path, to prod shaky reed-mats or prospect island-hopes. She was better at hunting, with the Reed-folk throwing sticks she copied at Forest-landing, than anyone else. And she had the Heartland hunter's skill with unknown countryside. To pick up peril by the one wrong footprint, the prickle down the backbone, the elusive momentary scent of disturbed mud, soiled water; rank, musky beast. Or rotten flesh.

There was peril, then, yes, palpable, eternally imminent, to string the nerves and mar any sort of rest. Discomfort, certainly, if not outright hardship, and hard labor atop it. But worst of all was the nightmare. Even with a clear waterway, scouted, safe, there was always that effortful, arduous, infuriating, most tiring of all, inability to make any sort of *haste*.

The Mother knows how far it is as the crow flies. I swear the Mother herself could not calculate how many waterborne miles we made of it. But I can tell you how long it took; because we calculated that, at every spent, drenched and infuriated evening halt.

Five weeks. As long as it took to sail four hundred miles of River, longer than it took to walk from first to second cataract;

and you may call me Cretin, if it is more than two hundred miles from Forest-landing.

To the other side.

* * *

We did take damage beyond the bruises and scratches and small wear of each day's war. The worst was the fever that Herar, and Sarth, and Alkhes, and Quiran himself began running before the end of the second week; Azo and Deor took it sometime in the third, and Varris by the beginning of the fourth.

Whatever it was, it was different to Keraz' and Esrafal's. No ferocious heat and decisive disablement, no delirium, no crisis, which the Landing healers assured us Keraz had almost reached. Just a slight, unshakeable fever, a nagging headache; a sense of debilitation to worsen the load, and a daily cycle from lull, and the weakness of past crisis, to evening's resurgence; dulled appetite, glazed eyes, and the toll of chill, misery, shivering.

There cannot be men anywhere like ours; I saw what they could do, in the fall of Amberlight. I have seen what they are capable of in Iskarda. But for sheer unremitting physical effort, and will, and grim endurance, I have never seen anything like what our men did, the four of them, among the reeds.

It was they who bore the physical brunt. While Deor played pilot and Azo and Varris scouted or stood sentinel, after whatever help the light-blades could give us, it was the men who took on the backbreaking effort of poling, pushing, and literally dragging the swathes of reeds from our path. Herar, and even Quiran, atop his other work, did it. And they would not share with us.

"Take the gun," Sarth would grunt at Azo, shouldering her aside. And, "Drop another duck," Alkhes would order Varris. And once-dandy Herar, a filthy mendicant staring Deor straight in the eye, would growl, "You can steer. I can't."

While I was allowed to oversee, and sweat, and try to shape a plan or issue orders, nothing more.

That was Sarth's fault. All Sarth. The Mother's bane on philosophers who are too blasted alert, and precise, and number-wary. Especially when they happen to be husbands, who have both the knowledge and propinquity to tally numbers that can matter to no-one else.

No. Not malediction. I cannot say that. Even now.

Any more than that evening, ten days in, when we struck our first islet, and had a fire, blessed exception, and room to stretch out at last; so we were all sprawled flat around the coal-bed, digesting the last of Varris' superb forest-ducks. Azo had just cut the day's notch on the tally stick, and Deor had glanced, water-Crafter's, Amberlight habit, at the moon rising; a slender crescent, opening the first winter month. Quiran said something. An attempt, I could feel, to fill the gulf Keraz had left. Answering, I felt Sarth's eyes.

Nothing so unusual, to have your husband look at you. They checked for me, my presence, my safety, as troublecrew as well as lovers, how many times each day? They looked at me, Sarth perhaps more often than Alkhes, for comfort, for reassurance, as a substitute for anything more, how many times a night? But not as Sarth was looking then.

With danger at every elbow, we were all over-sensitive. I glanced around; and had time to catch his expression, flat and impersonal as philosopher's addition, with a steely concentration that made me raise an eyebrow and return a glance that coded, What is it, love?

At which he gave me a quick, brusque headshake and turned away.

Little enough to stew over, after all. It did nag me, sleeping between them, in our travelers' chastity. I was still taken unawares when he came up behind me at the islet edge where I was trying to fresh-comb my plaits next morning, and said under his breath, "How many months, Tellurith?"

I dropped Varris' monstrous Heartland comb in the water and cursed. "How many months *what*? You've seen the tally-stick—"

"Not that."

The camp was a bustle partitioned off by ten feet of reeds; the comb had floated; the world vanished, not into reeds and mist, but behind two steady topaz eyes.

"You haven't cycled," he said, softly, precisely, "since we left Cataract."

My face must have answered, beyond prevarication. How do *you* know that?

"For the— Do you think I would not notice?" An undertone that went beyond impatience, a stress on the "I" that said as unconsciously, I'm your husband. And beyond that; for you, how could I not know?

I confess it, Tanekhet. I stood there, I, Telluir's House-head, gulping like the greenest girl.

For one second his face answered; all the love, the River's depth of love that I know he has for me, that goes beyond mere passion as it does beyond sex, beyond years of shared past and mutual knowledge, into whatever profundities he, I am sure, would no longer call a soul.

Then he said as quietly, as precisely as ever, "Have you lost your wits?"

I knew what he meant; why had I not told them, why were we going on, was I completely out of my mind to put a child, this child, at such raving risk? Did I know that if he did not love me to delusion he would, for such lunacy, have beaten in my head?

I looked him back in the eye, that topaz eye that could be as cold as jeweled armor, and answered, as softly, "No."

Sarth, whose wits are more redoubtable than Alkhes'. Who read in that word everything I had replied. How can I not risk the child? What will there be for it, if we cannot complete the Quest?

His shoulders flexed, and the stare fairly made me cower. The sole protest he could afford; compiling every argument, recrimination, reminder of his stake in this and the way I had overridden it. Only Sarth could say all that in a look; and only Sarth would have had the courage, the inburnt discipline; above all, the diamond-edge of philosopher's vision, to suppress the cries of his emotions, the insistence of his intellect.

To admit that I was right.

He was almost within arm's length. I could reach his hand. I did reach for it, and he let me take it, with another look that conveyed worlds of outraged comprehension, and the resignation that would stifle both. I spread his fingers and laid them firmly across the breadth of my belly, just below the waist.

And I read what his face could not, this time, hide. He shut his eyes. His hand moved, so slightly, flattening, curving, more eloquent than any words.

In the endless pause the world came back; the creak of a loaded raft, the last muted clatter of a stowed pot, a snatch of Azo's voice. The scent of mud, and reeds, and stagnant water, and unwashed human sweat. A familiar step.

Alkhes came round the reed-wall, silent as a soldier outside friendly lines, wariness tightening his stride as well as his face. He saw us, read our hands' pose; and I saw the understanding explode on him like a catapult bolt.

Sarth grabbed him just before he could speak. He gasped and swallowed, then let himself out of a striking coil and blindly pushed Sarth's hands down. His lips moved. It was by instinct too, perhaps, that I read it; if not direct from those eyes, black and huger than a Heartland night.

Is it true?

I nodded. Suddenly, seeing their expressions, I could not do anything more. Suddenly the reeds, the risk, the whole stupid enterprise meant nothing. Nothing mattered; except this.

How do I know which one reached me first? How long were we lost in the union of minds' and bodies' joy? Nor can I recall what any of us said. Until Sarth pushed me back to arm's length, both hands gripping my shoulders, and said, "Quiran. Now."

I said, "It's three months on. It's been all right. I never show much at first. There'll be such a fuss. And what does Quiran know? What could anyone do?"

He just gave me that look, and repeated "Quiran, Tellurith."

* * *

Pass over the predictable uproar amid the rest. They were no stupider than Sarth; it was in Azo's face, as she said brusquely, "You go on the second raft today, Ruand. You," this to Alkhes, "are her watch. Charge that damn cutter. Quiran?" And stalked away.

Beyond embarrassment, and natural trepidation, Quiran was the most collected of all. He did say at once, "Ruand, Caitha never showed me much . . ." But when I gestured at Sarth and Alkhes, looming like twin thunderclouds behind me, and said, "Do your best," his face broke into a quick, understanding grin, that became simple physician's eagerness.

Not that he could do much. Palpate my belly, through the clothes, since more than modesty made stripping impossible; ask the ritual questions, When did I think it had been conceived, when was my last cycle, had I had morning sickness, did anything seem amiss? And then lay his ear against me, the physician's final test, to check the heart whose beat might just, now, be audible.

He knelt there so long my men had already taken alarm. I had to scowl at Sarth to keep him quiet. Until Quiran clambered to his feet, with that careful lack of expression that is a physician's alarm signal, and murmured, "I'll just try this."

"Picked it up at the Landing." From somewhere he had acquired half a roll of grubby, partly buckled papyrus. He rolled it tighter and then tighter, murmuring, "They use it for a difficult pulse." Then, with careful apology, he settled one end against my belly, the other against his ear, and shut his eyes.

Again it seemed the world ebbed away. I was looking at Alkhes, I remember; reading, all too clearly, a kin or lover's dread in the stiffening of his face. I tried to make my eyes say, It's all right. It was Sarth who put a hand on his shoulder, and left it there, until Quiran lifted his head.

"Mmm." Already he had picked it up from Caitha. A true physician's signal; expressing nothing but a baffled interest. "I can hear it—them—quite clearly . . ."

Had he not stopped there it would still have been lost in the chorus, whose inflections you can fill in for yourself.

When the uproar died down, I repeated, I hoped politely, "*Them?*"

Quiran's gaze came back to me, professional still.

"Yes, Ruand. I think so. There's always a good deal of noise, of course, with a pregnancy." The sounds of stomach and gut, the rumbling and bubbling of life itself. "But I'm almost certain it's not an echo. Or some distortion. No. There are," at last, he permitted himself some human emotion. The smile spread from ear to ear. "Two."

I wonder what you would make of that, Tanekhet. You would be a good deal more reserved, I know, than my folk, certainly than my men, who kissed and hugged me to stranglepoint. Amid the mounting anxiety, you might almost have been amused. But you know what that last child meant to us; I am quite certain you would have shared our delight.

Which lasted till I thought to re-examine Quiran's face. After which I seized the nearest lull to fix him with a House-head's eye and enquire, "What's the rest?"

He squirmed and wriggled and did his best to dissimulate. But he was only an apprentice after all. "Quiran," I said, in warning, and he gave in.

"Ruand, I've only ever listened to one other baby, and Caitha never had time to tell me all the signals. I don't know . . . It could be nothing, it might be—I just don't know—"

"What is it, Quiran?"

Sarth, at my shoulder. On a note that took Quiran's color, as it would have taken mine.

"Ruand, the other one was about the same age, and there—" he stuck; caught Sarth's eye, and let it out with a gasp.

"There, the pulse was twice as fast."

"It mayn't matter, it may vary with two." He started spluttering into the pause. "I don't know if it's normal or abnormal, it may be totally irrelevant, Ruand—?"

Why did you make me tell you? he meant. When I have no answers, and if I did, there was nothing I could do?

Our eyes held. Then I looked at the reeds and said what he needed; the only thing that either of us could say. "Whatever it means, we should be breaking camp."

* * *

I have no idea what it means either. I do know an embryo's, even a baby's heart beats faster than the mother's, I have heard that for myself. I was three and a half months on, and Quiran agreed, when pressed, that very little showed, but with me, very little shows until the six or seventh. If it is twins, why should this be different?

I do know that, however it happened, whatever it means, I was the only one who never took a fever in the reeds.

How in the Mother's name do *I* know what it means? Was it the pregnancy, or from the Mother? Or something else?

Next time, it will be all right.

* * *

W ould you credit, Tanekhet, that now. That now . . . I cannot make it matter anymore?

* * *

I f I am to catalogue all the pangs and tribulations from my heart's bane onward, should that include it all?

The petty, the paltry, the mean and ignominious? Damages to my self-esteem, rather than my heart?

Very well. Let me admit, here and now, that if I never took a fever, the reeds left me other galls. The worse, perhaps, because they were not physical. What medicine is there for the slow, slight, irrevocable loss of heart's wellbeing, the drift and warp of what you thought unshakeable? The grief of foreseen, irresistible loss?

The Mother knows, Alkhes had seen me pregnant before, and in as great a peril, and been as passionate in care for me as he had previously in desire. And had as little idea of the father, and cared as little as Sarth.

But that time he did not have another woman at his elbow; young, well-favored, available. Bound to him by warrior's honor, and worshipping him, if not yet in body, then with her whole ardent soul.

I am not sure, when I try to be cool, and just, and impersonal, that he ever realized what was happening to him. It was so slow, so imperceptible; the traffic of living, conveyed by something as small as who you address without thinking, whose eyes you seek out first. Fostered by circumstance, a matter of personality and propinquity. Never a deliberate choice. I am quite sure of that. If it had ever become that clear, he would have thrown himself back to me in horror and revulsion and desperate avowal, and broken everything.

But they were perpetually drawn together, not merely by the journey, the rafts, the company, but because they were troublec-rew. And that ties the bonds of trust and comradeship, in the forging of shared risks, the welding of death's encounter; and perhaps, the debt of life itself.

Not to mention that they were already laf and sharfir. And to Alkhes, that was a sacred trust.

More than propinquity, then; their natures, on both sides. On hers, a young, honorable warrior, already toiled in hero-worship, who began the journey within a tie whose most intimate consummation was an acknowledged possibility. On his, both soldier and troublecrew, with a heart to which honor and gallantry are irresistible.

So how could he deny a fellow fighter whose courage and skill and daring matched his own? A peer, in the flesh-and-blood knowledge of his life-work, yet his junior in experience; so to understanding, she added the intoxicating taste of a fine young warrior's honor and respect?

All the things he could not get; that he never had, from me.

Perhaps that has lanced the core of it. The lack I have. The things I cannot do. The mean, petty gnawing of inadequacy that underlies the resentment, the rage . . . The worse, because I had no slightest cause for venting them.

And because I had felt them all before.

Was it any worse, the slight, almost intangible cooling between us, the shift in focus as he turned more and more readily to his fighting-mate, the shared jokes, the catchwords, the kindling gloss I recognized all too well if they did not, that comes when more than friendship bonds a pair? Was that worse than what I suffered, keeping spleen and malice from my dealings with Khira and her daughters, from the knowledge of their mere existence, that I carried like a tumor all those years in Amberlight?

Was it any worse than what Sarth felt, when I first bedded Alkhes?

* * *

Naturally, Sarth understood. Sarth, great-hearted enough not only to see but to pardon what was happening, and loving enough not to enjoy the requital; instead, with his tower-bred subtlety, to manage the near impossible. To let me know he knew, without a word, and without the slightest extra injury, to comfort me.

Nothing so blatant as quarrels or excessive compliments; just his presence, whenever it was needed, for anything from conveying a decision to stepping off a raft. His attention, the most fundamental human compliment, given with a depth and alacrity that is the most devastating courtship of all. If he could not kill Alkhes on the spot—and he would have done it at a look, whatever was between them, he would have done it as instantly as Alkhes would have destroyed him, that night we quarreled upCliff—nevertheless, he was determined that I should not suffer, not in credit, or esteem, or in any other way.

The Mother knows how I have deserved such love as that.

* * *

The Mother knows, too, I had reason to be grateful for that buffer before the end. When the food was running low, and the over-patched rafts beginning to disintegrate, and the fever's toll sapping the most determined of us. And still we could go no faster, there was no foreseeable, imaginable end to it, and courage, and determination, and naturally, tempers, began to fray under the leeching of despair.

Nobody had to say it. It was in the lengthening silences, the fade of the last humor, dregs of a spirit that had upheld us four solid weeks. In the lethargy with which they eyed the day-counter, when Azo stuck it up beside a fire; and we all tallied the notches, and felt the despair settle, rank as swamp-mist, smothering us.

Five unbroken weeks.

There is no measuring distance, inside the reeds. The vista never shifts. When you do get a long horizon, it is all of a bowshot, at best, and there is never anything at the end. Except more reeds. Sky overhead, turning through the upper-air patterns, from light to dark, cloud to fine, to the chilling shade of winter's harbinger. Horizons? Landmarks? A sense of changing distance? No.

So if we were off our guard that day, it was understandable. If we had no idea of where we were, of what it meant, that the channel-tracks had multiplied, maddening us with yet more possible wrong choices, and the worst peril of all had announced its increase, with the frequent spoor, the prevalent stink of River-horse, there was cause.

We were tired. It was late afternoon. No islets had appeared, which meant a miserable night on board. Varris had missed a shot at the only visible birds. The reed barricades had been thicker than ever, so the men were near exhausted, whatever they claimed. All of us, indeed, were near the end of our strength.

We were stravaging down a reasonably broad water-plat; Sarth and Azo were advance-guard, wading, floundering, on the water-margins, Alkhes and Quiran wrestling the flotsam that perpetually clotted round the raft-bows, Deor and Herar poling the first raft, the second towing, and Varris as rear-guard. Balanced lightly, for all the sunken rings under her eyes and the pallor in those bronze cheeks, at the rear of the dunnage, one hand on a spear haft, the other on the unused tiller; where she could watch the whole entourage; and me as well.

I was sitting in the middle of the second raft, at the vantage point of comfort, I was informed, as well as safety. What use to say it felt like banishment? I was as dejected as the rest, half-stupefied with fatigue, and paying as little attention, beyond the now routine anxiety, as anyone else.

So when Deor's pole rebounded backward from her thrust, when the reed-margin bellowed like a fleshly volcano and the tow-rope snapped and Deor and Herar and Alkhes and Quiran flew like spilled pegs from a basket and the River-horse erupted from the mud between us, chopped the first raft in two with a thunderclap munch and spun like a sentient submarine boulder, all I saw was monstrous mud-brown streaming flanks and that pink hell-pit maw of teeth.

I know instinct made me try to leap and run. I heard the thin human cries beyond its uproar and did have the brains to claw backward over the dunnage even as my thinking mind shrieked that it was coming our way and everyone who could have defended me was cut off behind its back. More than time to understand the fragility of untrained human flesh.

Something grabbed my shoulder and momentum spun me with it, off the side with the raft's predictable yaw, into a bank of reeds. Vile slippery stems and tangled plats crashed into me, vile water grabbed me by the hips, sheer terror boosted me up on reed mats that swayed and wobbled under me and the last of the shove propelled me headlong into the thicket's depths.

I did scream then and fought like a maniac, only too sure I would be trapped there for the thing's follow-up and with a Head's birth-reflex suspecting treachery. I crashed around in the reed depths, blundering and staggering as my feet broke the rotten mat beneath, and the half-screen of thrashing stems showed me what was behind.

It was River-horse country, we should have known that. They can smash a canoe at a bite. They are bigger than a draft-horse and far deadlier than a crocodile. They are somnolent as vipers, until roused. And breeding season, how could we know? Females tetchy, males territory-crazed, we had glimpsed that, but not understood. It was a male we had stumbled over, ambushed, as they do, all but submerged in the channel-side, somnolence or malice keeping it quiet as Sarth and Azo passed. Until Deor's pole took it full in the eye.

Which probably saved all our lives, for though it was destructive as a hurricane it mis-sighted worse than usual. So when Varris hurled me into the channel-side I was in its blind-spot, and it raged straight on at her.

The Mother knows, she is truly a warrior. I still see her upright over the tiller bar, riding the convulsed raft like a gull on a tempest-front, the coiled cable of arm and wrist as she hurled the shield full at the thing, the back-swing and drive, savage and elegant as a striking serpent, with which, as the monstrous upper jaw reared high above her, she did not throw but drove her Heartland spear clean into the roof of its throat.

Half-blind in that one eye, unsighted by the shield, it did not foresee the blow. It had no time to swerve. It brayed like a giant's war-trumpet and lunged into the raft debris and Varris sprang as only a warrior could, clear from foundering reeds into the channel-margin as the hideous maw slammed shut. And the spear, driven by the beast's own monstrous jaw, too far back to spit out, too well lodged to slide downward, slammed up through the palate clear into the brain.

It is the only shot with which a spearman—spear-fighter—can hope to take a River-horse and live. And she got it perfectly. Off-guard, with a split moment to think and both our lives depending on it. All our lives.

The fate of nations. The outcome of the Quest.

All owed to a Heartland spear-fighter's single thrust.

* * *

It was not like a human ambush, Tanekhet. That may be quick, yes, over in an eye-blink. But human ambushes, I remember all too clearly; there is always the hideous, protracted aftermath. Rally. Extrication. Roll-call. Examination. Of your casualties, and theirs. And then the cleaning up.

Here were all the physical symptoms, yes, heart and blood frantic with the fright, breath tearing an arid throat, bruises and rips and scathes reaching consciousness, limbs shaking like broken sticks. But beyond that . . .

Churned mud and double-filthy water, floating, sinking, ubiquitous reeds. A solitary surviving pack. A perimeter of milk-white and coffee-mud faces. The totally unprecedented stench. And the great, streaming, suddenly inanimate hulk beached, hardly bleeding. Just dead. Emptied. Dropped there, like a god's rubbish, in our midst.

Then time snaps forward and starts to run again, and the next memory is being squashed like an overripe pumpkin in Sarth's grasp. Before the cascade of yells and cries, curses, prayers, thanksgiving and lamentation washed over me, along with their crowding bodies, their desperately thankful hands.

And the other vignette, as Sarth releases me. Just before Quiran grabs me, physicianly panic overriding even an Iskardan man's diffidence. The other tableau beyond me. Varris.

And Alkhes.

He must already have made sure she was unhurt. Streaming mud, panting like a race-rower, yes, but intact. They had met, but they had not touched. There was no need.

I did it, her stare said, those hazel eyes for once without any mask at all. *I have proved myself worthy of you. In the most honorable way. I saved not only you, and your Quest, but your own core and cynosure. Your woman's life.*

And his answered, as frankly, with all the honor, all the pride and . . . affection? love? she could have asked. *You did it, yes. You are my protégé and now, you are my heart's, my warrior heart's delight.*

Did I imagine, for a moment, behind her, the shadow of another warrior, with that glory on the masculine version of her face?

* * *

Having assured themselves that their Head and her treasures, within and without, were safe; having recovered equilibrium, and grown accustomed to the idea that they had not lost their lives, the rest began to count the actual loss.

Rafts beyond salvage. Food spoilt, packs lost, gear damaged, if not irretrievably ruined. The light-guns, by something's final benison, intact. But how would light-guns get us out of this trackless, now roadless, unprovisioned waste?

I do not know what *they* were doing. The faces around me were enough. Azo, Herar, Quiran, Deor, Sarth. Relief and reprieve fading, the imprint of calamity, perhaps of final calamity, taking their place. And my soul cringed at what I knew was imminent; the moment when some one of them would say it. Ubiquitous, utterly predictable.

Ruand, what do we do now?

I looked away. Let me not see *them*, I thought. Let me not see the others' expectation, or the moment when they realize I have nothing to answer it. Let me imagine none of it exists. Let me be entirely somewhere else.

I looked across the fouled waterway, into the everlasting barricade of the farther side. Expunge the reeds, I told myself. Conceive some far country where none of this exists. Where you do not have to think about tomorrow, tonight, now, this moment, where you can just open your mind and float away.

It was the reeds that opened. There was not another bank beyond them. Nor water, or even the promise of a halfway solid aisle.

Over the back of the collapsed River-horse shone a ragged portal, full of pure, late evening horizon sky.

I know it was horizon, not only from the delicate eggshell blue, so different from the zenith shade; but because there were treetops caught on it. Rounded, foliage-patterned treetops, not straight lines, neither horizontal nor oblique nor vertical, but the clumps and masses of silhouetted leaves.

And rising over them, the shoulder of a mountain. Tree-clothed. Caped in snow.

* * *

Was it all chance? Right up to the collision, the actual River-horse? If it had not been there, if we had not roused it, it would not have torn the reed-walls down.

And we would have gone on paddling, floundering, struggling, parallel with what now revealed itself as the swamp's margin; probably until we died.

Was it the Mother's own intervention? Or . . .

Next time, it will be all right.

I do not know. I do not know, do not know, do not know, Tanekhet.

* * *

At the time we did not ask. By silent consensus we just picked up whatever flotsam was retrievable; waded out, knee, thigh-deep in silt and liquid mud and whatever other unspeakable filled the waterway, clambered back up on the reed-bases, and started to walk.

It was not very far. A bowshot? Half a mile? I do remember clearly how whatever water there was shallowed, and the footing under us firmed. The reeds dwindled. The swamp stink, so vilely all-pervading, began to fade, as incredibly as the miasma of the Cataract jail cell, and the air took on movement.

Then we came up a hoof-trampled margin through a fringe of water-lilies and a last rim of coffee-crystal water, onto solid ground.

* * *

We lit a fire with the light-gun, while Varris and Alkhes went hunting with the cutter and her last throwing stick; and we had managed, with near hysterical hilarity, to shed some clothes to dry, while we reposed about the flames on blessedly dry grass and dust, before they brought some margin-dwelling creature back. It was only with our bellies full that we could detach our eyes from that glorious skyline, turning to platinum and frozen moonlight under the last sun-sheets, and contemplate the rest.

Way-wandered, provisionless, with no idea how far or which way to go. Or even where, from our position, the River met the swamp.

When that came up, Sarth settled on his haunches and without looking at any of us, held out both his hands.

We made a sad job of the singing without Esrafal. But it was quite unmistakable, when the seed began to glow.

The first thing Sarth said was, "Can you hear us now?"

And that image of him from the distant Heartland answered, clear, unhesitating, "Yes."

Sarth folded his lips. Thank the Mother yet again for a tower man's control, that wasted no time on pointless protestations or equally pointless demands of, Then why not before? Or, Why *not* before? He said, "Where is the River now?"

Silence. Then the familiar, the everlasting image of the lakeside, the spring bubbling up in the dawn. But not, this time, with the frantic urgency. This was no stop-gap, Tanekhet, we all felt it. This was a reply.

The image faded. Our eyes reclaimed each other. Bitter disappointment had just begun to grow in Azo's stare when Varris, shivering slightly, as they all were, shifted her hand, locked on Alkhes' farther knee, and said in that soft bell-voice, "The mountain is the same."

She had seen what we were too silly with exasperation to notice. When we stared up into the still faintly-lit horizon, the shoulder of snow was, just recognizably, the same as the farthest visible peak to the right of the imaged lake.

* * *

So we owed her that as well, Tanekhet. Why is gratitude sometimes such a bitter pill to swallow, that you would rather ruin your own enterprise and die?

But we had an aim. We had a destination. More than slightly off our line according to the old River; indeed, the shoulder was a good thirty degrees to the left, driving Azo and Deor near panic before Alkhes snapped, "You were sour enough when it *wouldn't* answer! What's the problem now?"

As for why it would not answer; who could say?

Sarth, of course. Tramping along next day, with the light-guns, and the clothes we stood in, and Quiran's instruments; praise the Mother, he never took off that pouch, even to wade. And half a pack of gear, including Deor's spare shoes, already gifted to Azo, who had left hers in the mud. Carefully not thinking that the rest of us would be barefoot in one decent day's travel, that we were marching into unknown country, without so much as knowledge of water ahead.

The great shawls of snow that had turned diamond and ethereal sapphire in the sunrise were sunlit silver again, when Sarth came up beside me; matched five strides; and murmured, "It remembers Amanazar. Do you suppose, in her day . . . the reeds weren't there?"

Something in that made my heart leap, wildly as a startled frog; some half-glimpsed revelation that could not be taken in words but that would explain everything. Reeds, my wits shouted, struggling in the rear, reeds, time, seven hundred years, Amanazar?

Beside me, Sarth sighed and shrugged. Code for, You are right, it was a foolish speculation. And I recall quite clearly the sense of that intuition fading, unrealized; that even as I said, "The Landing knows *something* is here," I knew it was not where our thoughts should point.

Mother knows, the country was pleasing enough; savannah like the lower Heartlands, but rising steadily over each long ridge-line, and the air was quite different. This air moves, with upland tang and resilience, with a springtime purity over miles of lemon-green and bronze-striped grass, over the flat-topped green-bronze acacias, under the huge silvered conglomerations of cloud.

Heartland clouds. High country Heartland clouds, that can turn to anvil-headed storms of pewter and smoke and majestic freestanding columns of rain; or that simply striped us with their shadows as if we had passed under some flying divinity's wing.

There was no sign of habitation, not the ruins of a bough-shelter, the hint of a boundary-marker, a single taint of distant smoke. No predators either, a sign we ought to have read better than we did. Especially when there were beasts in plenty; not the mighty herds, but groups of wildly leaping little cream and russet antelope, clans of taller buck with wide crescent horns

For all his fever, the second evening Alkhes managed to bring down a young doe. So we dined on tender roasted meat, fit to offset the loss of our staple food-supply with our swamp-drowned flour. Not enough to make me forget the sight of Varris helping Alkhes skin. No jests now, no laughter; the understanding of comrades whose fellowship is beyond speech.

Deor and Azo still worried about the bearing; but on the third afternoon Sarth was working up another ridge-side as scout when he suddenly stood upright on what passed for a horizon, joyous amazement in every line.

Because the wide, shallow hollow beyond him cradled the River in its folds.

What we found was not our River; just a sizeable upland stream, a mere hundred yards across, deep enough, to be sure, an earthily red-tinged current sliding smoothly past the clots of acacias, and the occasional rock knob, and riverine shrubs pruned neat as gardens by the deer. But the mountain was there, its shoulder rising directly upStream. And when all guides except the unworldly have been reft from you, whose directions can you take?

* * *

I am delaying. Squandering time. Describing the trivial, if not the irrelevant.

Because it was two nights after, encamped in a charming little bay of cropped grass between a convenient watering cove and margins of tall, sheltering shrubs, that Alkhes came to me.

"Tel," he said, "can I speak to you?"

I ought to have expected it. I did expect it. I had stubbornly denied expecting it, when I watched it coming closer every day. And still the reality stabbed, cruel as any blow Sarth ever struck.

I said, "Up here?" And walked out of the bay, up the Riverside.

He knew what he was doing. It was in the gratitude with which he followed me; in that stance, half wound-down troublecrew, half belligerently scared waif. In those eyes, whose dark was the tearing of pledges, honor's desperation; the expectation of grief.

I stopped under a tall feathery River willow and turned to get his face into the fading light. He set his teeth, and drew himself up.

"Tel . . . you know what I pledged to—Varris."

The pause was not what you might think. I knew it was that, to him, now, the name was something for outsiders. To him she was already the one and only "her."

I managed to keep my voice cool. "I know."

"She saved us. All of us. Everything."

He stopped again, and it did not need the last sunset light to tell me those eyes held a plea. You knew, they said, when you let me enter this bond, what might be the result. You know that if ever a laf deserved honor of a sharfir, this is the one. You know what we owe her. You know that to deny it will hurt my honor, that is the heart of me, as much as to fulfill it.

Because that will dishonor my pledge to you.

He did not protest, It will change nothing between us, you know I love you, he did not dig himself a deeper pit by arguing, You agreed to this, back at the start; any more than he offered the pathetic extenuations, She means nothing but the sex, I never intended this, It's just for tonight. He has been in Amberlight, in Iskarda, with Sarth and me, too long. He said only the single word.

"Tel?"

He was trembling ever so slightly, his jaw faintly, unconsciously clenched. Fatigue and fever chill; I had seen it every evening. And perhaps, the undervoice of what those eyes said. I have to do it. To refuse would dishonor us all.

I should have been able to do it too, Tanekhet. The Mother knows, I had shared Sarth, in Iskarda as in Amberlight, and in Iskarda, I knew it was a tie, however convoluted, of love. I had expected *them* to share. Had demanded that Alkhes break his whole life's custom for me. Was I so small-hearted, so unsure, that I could not give him grace for this?

Yes.

Because Sarth did not go to Zuri of his own choice. Whatever it meant to him afterwards, it was I who made the decision, who had let him go.

And with Alkhes too, it had been my choice; I had forced Sarth on him, forced him to accept a part rather than all of me. There had never been a division in *his* love.

Grant me this, it makes a bitter sort of triumph. Because I did not rage at him. I did not scour his treachery, or malign her; I did not let out my spleen and jealousy on anyone else. I just took a breath as deep as his had been, and said, "I know."

After it all, he was Alkhes; in wits, as in the heart's tongue, formidably skilled as Sarth. Every lineament of that face said, You understand. The Mother be thanked.

How much *he* understood . . .

He had seen how I felt about Khira, even in Iskarda. When she and all but one of her daughters were dead. Perhaps, he understood just what future he gambled, as well as the past. If Varris gave him a girl . . . But he knew I understood *him*, the compulsion of his honor, the weight of the bond; the division, to make either choice.

He reached a hand out, tentative, as he had never, ever been with me. Laid the palm against my cheek; it was shaking a little, and rough as stone from the swamps, and the fever made it just too slightly, disquietingly hot; but there was understanding, and pain, as well as gratitude when he said huskily, "Tel . . . thanks."

It was what he had said to me, the first morning after he came to my bed.

I bit my tongue until the blood came. But I did not close my eyes. I actually managed not to flinch. I could not hug him, not so much as push that falling wing of hair back; that was a lover's touch. It was beyond me to say, Go well, or, Be happy, or to make some gesture of forgiveness, let alone love. I did say, "I will see you in the morning."

And however I looked, there was resolution, but no eagerness, in the way he walked away.

* * *

I do not know how they settled the rest. When I reached camp, both were gone. And the look on various faces told me Alkhes had not done it secretly.

To be expected, yes. If he would not slink from me, far less would he shame me by furtiveness before the rest. It was no hole-and-corner bribe, for either of them. It was a mark of honor; a just, more than just reward.

I had no time to consider my own reaction; I was not out of the trees before Sarth intercepted me. "Intercepted," in good truth; setting himself between me and the camp fire as if he were a rampart to be stormed, rather than my oldest bastion.

"Tellurith," he said.

Only the note to tell me this was as private as Alkhes' request; that he would take no gainsaying; and that he meant to sort it out in bed.

I said, "Did you find somewhere to sleep?"

The next blessing of dry land, not to mention vegetation, was night-time privacy. He had made us a place behind the shrubs, with lopped branches under the linen of our spread overshirts; the only extra thing we had been wearing that last day on the rafts.

I sat down on the boughs' edge. He moved behind me, and began to take down my hair.

I was too stupefied to think it more than another of his attentions, those determinedly tender efforts to shore my wounded esteem. A distraction, I thought, and blessed him, with what care I had to spare from myself, and his tower heritage as well.

Then he took me by the shoulders and turned me about and said, evenly as ever, "Tellurith? Make love to me."

The moon was late; he was a star shadow who denied me his very eyes. I was too astounded to do more than stare.

"My bedmate," he said, in that quiet, that cool tower voice, "has slighted me. Without so much as a goodbye. My last wife is who knows how far downRiver; by now she may be worse than dead. My first wife has been with child four months and never thought to let me know. I don't even know if it is my child. I have no answers to any of my questions. I have worked myself blind clearing your way, playing your troublecrew, being your Mother's Ear. Looking after you . . . I have fever; I am so tired I want to die. This once, Tellurith, show me I matter. *You* make love to *me*."

What would it take, Tanekhet, to wring something like that from Sarth?

No point in asking. You will never read this. I have too much care for his pride; I know his mind. Have you share such a confession? He would sooner die.

I thought I would die too, from sheer, simple shame.

To have used him so completely, so carelessly, so thanklessly, so obliviously, to have been so wrapped in my own petty smarts and stings, to have eaten up his kindness as I had his strength. His pride. Sweet Mother, had earth opened in front of me, I would have thrown myself in.

It took a minute to get my breath; then I turned about, and took him round the neck and whispered, "I'm sorry. I'm so sorry, beloved." Before I gave him my first kiss.

You cannot imagine how thankful I am, at the last, to have given him that.

* * *

So did she split us, Tanekhet, as the jeweler's point and hammer will split a diamond, tapped into the only fault? Has our marriage, the keystone of your world's vision, fallen apart?

Not from that.

Alkhes did have the wits; or the grace, not to come near us next night. Nor to paper over the rift with too normal commerce on the march, and not to shame Varris by too obviously yearning toward the community he had lost. It was the third night before Sarth said, "I have questions to ask," and settled at the fireside, holding out both hands; but then Alkhes, without so much as a falter, came immediately to my side, and in his turn held out both hands; one to Varris, the other to me.

What point to make a tragedy of it, to upset what fragile equilibrium we could manage, for the sake of my petty pride? I took the hand he offered; and saw the relief, deep as night itself, in the turn of those black eyes.

Whatever he does, blast him, Alkhes can reach halfway to forgiveness just from how he looks. How does a soldier, Telluir troublecrew, a high-flying mercenary, the Mother's Chosen, a godforsaken *general*, manage to seem a half-scared boy?

At any rate, it was in relative peace, if not comfort, that we continued the march.

* * *

Or the trek, perhaps. Softer going by the River, and rawhide moccasins from the hide of kills when shoes fell apart. Food, plant or animal, from the land. Other hides, vilely stinking or not, as shelter from the storms that would occasionally plough over us, and from the increasingly cold nights. Because the land was rising fast.

We were among foothills now, short-pitched little hills with an underlay of meat-red soil and trees suddenly thickening about us, forest growth lofty as temples, leaves of viridian or chartreuse or emerald, soughing like the sea in what had been eternally empty sky. A last vista of savannah, and the ridges shut us in. But there were little upland meadows amid the trees, gilded with sunshine. Full of low-growing, pink and saffron flowers.

The River takes the shortest way, as it does over the Jump-up cliffs; we had to swerve from defiles and miniature cataracts. Not that we complained, winding to and fro over the cool, shadowed slopes, in the freshening air; especially when we could use the qherrique, like an Archipelago mariner's lodestone, to find direction on the march.

Deor who discovered that, at the first complication after the savannah vanished, and the mountain was invisible behind nearer crests. As we havered in a valley fork she said irritably, "Mother blast it, can't it tell the way yet?"

At which Azo's mouth fell open; before she rounded on me, saying urgently, "Ruand, ask!"

I could feel it before I had the seed out. Warmth, response, clear through the silk into the palm of my hand, the way you could feel the answer in the mother-face at Amberlight. As our hands linked the image sprang on us, the left-hand valley-head, the mountain peering over it, peak streaming a great tail of snow-foam cloud.

We started off again, stringing out automatically. Climbing, descending, steadily, doggedly, our pitiful possessions no burden now. As light as our knowledge of where we were going. We had no plan or precautions any longer.

We were in the hands of . . . Whatever you call the qherrique.

We were climbing that noonday, near the top of a tall ascent, pushing past boulders every so often, scrambling over outstanding roots, sweating despite the shade of timber that had become lofty mountain pine. From their gloom a sunlit, emerald and fallow-gold rug of earth tumbled behind us, hills and lesser hills and a suggestion of reeds on the horizon sky.

Sarth and Azo had the lead. Alkhes was behind me; Varris had detoured, in her silent unannounced way, doubtless after some hint of game. We were grateful, as we had been more and more frequently, for a sort of animal tread; I had just squeezed between two house-huge boulders and taken breath for the next climb, thinking that pregnancy was cutting my wind at last, when I heard Azo cough.

Not fever. Not a catch in the throat. Troublecrew signal, clear from Amberlight. Watch out!

The lot of us froze. Except Alkhes, who was beside me in a blur of strides, cutter up and charged.

The first time we had used that sound. The first trouble that was not wholly unforeseen, or else well foreseen.

And human, rather than beast.

The cutter beam struck up into the branches' gloom, a clear white bar. Azo and Sarth were invisible. So was whatever they had met. But down the hillside came a brief, human sound.

Not any voice of ours.

Herar was looking desperately but stealthily behind, lest Varris come unwarned. Quiran and Alkhes knew their priorities; they were close enough to stand on my toes, rigid, senses strained uphill.

A bird called, clear unfamiliar mountain song. Something else called, a chatter like falling tiles. Wind pulsed in the pine-tops. Then above me, Azo spoke.

"Ruand," she said. "Advance."

Not duress. Not peril, deadly or otherwise. She would never have called me in either of those. Nor summoned me, so formally, for any other human kind.

Because it was the signal of troublecrew in Amberlight, encountering, and making truce, with the skirmishers of another House.

Alkhes and Quiran looked at me. Alkhes' eyes were flared, outland soldier's hair-trigger stare. I shook my head, and gestured to the cutter. Put it out.

He frowned ferociously. When I did not yield, he let the beam die. Disappeared it, and as we started forward, settled a hand near his knife.

The tread went up again, round a knot of pines. Into woven shadow and sunshine and brisk mountain wind, and out, in a ripple of silky grass, onto the crest.

They stood waist deep in it, confronting each other, as gangs would encounter in Amberlight streets. A little crouched, tensely balanced, perfectly motionless.

Sarth and Azo, absolute monoliths. And the five women beyond.

And they—Tanekhet, they were *us*.

* * *

Our hair. Our eyes. Our faces. Our clothes, our coloring, our height. From the earth-brown leggings above the cross-gaitered hunting boots, to the dappled fawn and brown working shirts, to the slitted amber and topaz eyes staring from the high-boned, aquiline faces, to the spare fletching feathers stuck through brandy-brown and copper plaits.

We must all have stood as if struck to living stone. I do remember the eyes though, of the woman in the centre. Narrowed eyes, slitted tight, the color in the mirror of mine. Widening slowly, so the pupils flexed, in the sunshine; as I have seen Averion's pupils flex when someone irritated her. The stare of a great, rousing cat.

Then, very carefully, she lifted a hand.

Not the palm-outward, fingers-upward veto of the River, but the hand with fingers splayed and pointing downward, that says, Stop. You dare the thunderbolt.

The oldest hand-sign known in Amberlight. Made, they say, over the first qherrique-bed, to ward off her importunate lover. By Amanazar.

I made the Ruand's greeting, House-head to House-head, that is almost as old as Amanazar. Fingers pressed to the breast, then to the lips, head inclined.

They had read the recognition on our faces. They knew that too. The looks spoke open amazement, but they had our discipline. Not one moved.

So I knew their leader, before, knowing what that recognition meant as well as I do, she inclined her head.

She is my height, to a hair; with something of my cheekbones, and indubitably, my nose. And my "recklessness" as Zuri has so often called it. For she shifted stance, and like our own troublecrews the women either side of her read the signal and eased the pressure on their bows.

I forgot to mention the bows, Tanekhet. Four of them, all drawn to the fletching, ready to let fly.

The leader gathered herself to action's tension. And spoke.

"Strangers; what is your land?"

"We come from Downstream." I said it quite easily. I did not gesture, knowing the unease that would evoke among us. "Once, we lived in Amberlight."

The lips parted imperceptibly; the eyes, less controllable, flared. If we were looking in a mirror, they were looking at legends too. I saw the young woman on the outer right swallow, Amberlight!

"Now," I said, "I am the Ruand of Iskarda. My name is Tellurith."

When I waited, she understood. The long, mobile lips tensed; the slightest fraction, I would watch it in the mirror and work to suppress it when I was just sixteen years old.

The decision came. Solidified. She put up her head.

"We," she said, "are the People of the Source."

CHAPTER XIV

Iskarda
25th Day, Second Winter Moon

No doubt you have long since said, *You gods-forsaken imbecile,* Tellurith.

And yes, that last letter was written from a fool's paradise. And yes, I have my reward.

* * *

Midsummer, I know you were in Cataract. If nothing else, I know you did reach an understanding with the qherrique, and Zuri was—is—confirmed as Regent. And you went on. Up-River. Of your leaving I have surety enough. But no direct word from you, my lady Tellurith, for near five months.

If you fail—if you vanish, into whatever legend—if we simply never hear your fates, what is the worth of anything we attempt?

I should still lay out the sum of that. If it never reaches you, if I never have an answer, the obligation remains. You are my—ruler. My—liege-lady. I owe you a report.

* * *

Will it amuse or infuriate you, I wonder, to begin, yet again, with my own experience? Or have you foreseen that too? But, yes. Threat, intrigue, slander, mortal peril, subtle or unsubtle violence, all the terrors of great power and high altitude I have known lifelong.

Poverty, no.

In Iskarda, still I had resources. Independence. And elsewhere, I was the accredited Iskardan adviser, or Amberlight's own ambassador.

When we came back to Amberlight . . . a day in those ramshackle streets, an afternoon in that tattered assembly lacking so much as a decent set of chairs, half an hour of those faces where the stamp of hunger stood clearer by the hour—How could I say,

Feed and house me? Recall I am a government official? Support me in the manner to which I am used?

Kheizo found us lodgings: Downhill, just above River quarter, two rooms in a rambling establishment once an inn and now half workshops and half lodging house, with a glance at outlawry and a touch of brothel opposite. A great many people in Amberlight, now, are doing whatever they can to survive.

Which made me box Keshaq's ears, when he suggested doing the same.

"They think I am 'exotic.' Don't you see them looking, in the street?" Preening, just a tint of it, along with the mockery, the irony no slave can ever lose. "There's not much money here, but they'll pay." A certain amount of vanity, before the irony came uppermost. "And it's one thing I can do."

"I'll take your hide off first!"

I had not meant to shout. Any more than to strike. My palm was tingling. Wringing. That was the least of it.

"Keshaq, I beg your pardon. I—" With shame I admit it: I had shaken myself out of all composure along with sense. Blame my own concern, my own uncertainties: my own fear of being, for the first time in my life, cast on my flesh and blood's resources. Perhaps, out in the street.

"Keshaq, I never meant . . ."

He had been knocked past argument along with that newborn initiative. Or impudence. For an instant I saw him back in Assuana. Before Assuana. A just-taken, terrified, ignorant young—

Slave.

I took two strides and caught him, gently, I had that much wit left, by the waist.

For an instant that past's reflex kept him rigid. But then he sighed and relaxed, however cautiously, into my grasp.

"I would sooner," I said, when I could speak, "stand on a street-corner myself."

I felt him physically brace himself. Before he took my face in both hands and turned it upward, a license he had never dared before, and said flatly, "No."

"For me, it would be nothing." That stare added, Be quiet. "After the other—nothing at all. But you, my lord . . ."

His hands tightened. When he went on it was almost brusque. "I will not see anyone—anyone! put shame on *you*."

So I had my warning, Tellurith. The River-lord knows, I heard it clear enough.

But I had no foresight with it. So I simply shook him a little, and hugged him to off-set it, and announced, with my best dignity, "I do not intend to shame either of us."

When he still demanded to help, I sent him down to the wharves. Hard physical labor, and poorly paid, and the most menial in Amberlight, surely, but a work-out for those muscles, and always available. And better than the street-corner, a thousand times, yes.

Nor, as I had to point out with some asperity, is it any kind of shame to set up as a public scribe in the marketplace of Amberlight.

Indeed, you may laugh, my lady Tellurith.

As they undoubtedly laughed in Dhasdein, if—when—the word reached them. But it was an honest trade, it took my burden off the state, it could have supported us both. And it was the first time in my life that I have earned my bread with my own two hands.

Oh, Dheya helped, with a thin but steady stream of recommendations, before I built a reputation for fine calligraphy out-shone by a most finicky regard for grammar. And Damas, if you will credit it, hired me for a steady afternoon a week. But if Keshaq still protested, claimed his charms would have supported us both in the manner my rank warranted, to Dhanissa and the Assembly an independent adviser was a clear and uncovenanted relief.

So I went to assemblies, and shared their inner councils: and my stratagems, not to mention ruses, were needed to keep the peace.

The men trouble, yes. It died down at the height of threat from Verrain. The moment they absorbed that thunderclap, it broke out worse than before.

Explicable enough with winter in sight, and with it the full impact of Verrain's fall: it had been a fair market for the Sahandan rice, but worse was the severance of River trade itself. No through traffic, so no supplies needed or tolls paid. No trade not merely with Verrain, but with Dhasdein. And no passing on the trickle of exotics from Cataract.

And no outlets for Iskarda.

You will know all this, my lady Tellurith. You will have thought or cursed it all out when my letter came. Once the paralysis of escape wore off, I saw it far too clearly for myself.

We—they—are lucky the population was reduced so drastically. With Verrain gone, the old Amberlight could not have fed its citizens a month. But the new Amberlight lacks its bulkheads of rule and order. When it became too clear we would be living the winter, and perhaps the next year, on our own resources, things got very ugly indeed.

Hoarding, and racketeers, surely, and a bad black-market run by a cluster of troublecrew, I regret to tell you, who had moved into the River quarter and were making a lively living from a crowd of—shall we say, commandeered whores? Another reason I did not want Keshaq anywhere near the corner of a street.

Give your reformers this: they coped, once braced to it, well enough. A hasty series of statutes pushed through assembly, a force of troublecrew volunteers commissioned, with hearty assistance from the women of River quarter, a more hastily appointed roster of magistrates. Some very rough skirmishes, a couple of pitched minor battles, and most of it was under control. I am—I find myself somewhat proud to recall that Kheizo, given patrol command on my recommendation, covered herself with honor throughout.

And yes, I advised most of it. It is not easy to think in state or municipal terms for a city where the Houses kept order for five hundred years. But it brought law, or the apparatus for it, before second autumn moon. Shift made to redirect and store the Sahandan grain and to install rationing before it reached famine point. A few harsh lessons for men who thought they could now have their wishes by brute force.

I wonder, my lady Tellurith, how that battle will go, once all the light-guns are dead?

For the moment, there are more than enough left to prevail. Enough to let me sit alone in the marketplace, and walk home safe with the day's earnings in my belt, and enter the other, newer territory in my life.

Would you credit, that was also the first time I have lived— actually lived, in unbroken domestic intimacy, with someone I—

Loved.

With Saari herself, there were servants. Relations. Always some sort of audience. A great noble's least summer residence is a perpetual traffic way. Before those shabby little rooms in Amberlight, I never knew what it meant, to live together. To share your innermost dwelling space with someone else.

The River-lord knows, it was small enough: an inner room crowded by the ramshackle bed, both furnished with past tenants' jetsam, a rickety table, the shelf above the brazier with a pottery statuette of Dhe, clumsy, unpainted, unmistakable reminder of Verrain. Of my own youth. The catchless chest that easily fitted all our clothes. The dingily painted walls, the scent . . .

Of frust and slum-mud and rarely-washed winter gear, and too many poor man's dinners: but also the lingering overlay of incense, that Keshaq would buy on the flimsiest excuse. Deeper, subtler, the slight musk of his body odor, the aftermath of my shaving soap, the under-tang of sex. The smell that said, a step inside the doorway, This is our place.

The River-lord knows, we fought enough at first to mark it for all time. Neither of us used to dealing for ourselves in anything from buying tomorrow's breakfast to remembering to make the bed. Sweep and wash up? For the first month, it was pure chaos. But then . . .

Most often he would find me in the market-place. Buy something for dinner as we passed the food-stalls, putting up their wares under the first flaring torch. Through the streets, the pair of us enough to repel scavengers, up the unlit stairs into the deeper dusk that spoke of home. To find, in the dusk at the lamp's edge, the true home of his embrace.

Away from Assuana, assured of his welcome, able to discard the past, he was as ardent a lover as he was superlatively trained. No. Skilled. It is a world of difference. But ardent, yes, with the whole flood of gratitude behind it. And behind that, a famine's need to feel and show affection, a starvation hunger for love. Not to mention a healthy, mature, free man's urge for sex.

To share, to exchange love with mind and body, unstintingly, without concern or calculation. I do not think I have done that in my life's length.

And in a slum, poverty, lost rank and resources, overhanging jeopardy. A sanctuary grounded on the fragility of flesh and blood, with no guarantee that tomorrow would not find it all destroyed.

It is almost shocking, in such a sketch, to recognize happiness.

* * *

So, I hear you say. After such an urban idyll, what are you doing, back in Iskarda?

It began, as you might have expected, with Verrain.

And with my own besotment, because when he had no work Keshaq would, by nature, go with me. Even into assembly. And usually he would settle at my back, not disdaining the floor if necessary, and keep silence, because that is what pledged Quetzistani warriors do. So he was there, the day the first communiqué arrived.

It will hardly surprise you that we were a month into autumn before any sign of order appeared in Verrain. You will know how the country lies—lay: the President, fixed by those damnable statuettes atop the pyramid in Assuana, balanced on the Families, whose wealth and blood engrossed almost all the prime River land in their entrenched estates. All fertile, all productive as only Verrain can be. All powered, and run, and ruled, by slaves.

Fading into the arid desert margins, where unfortunate free farmers eked out their lives on the leavings of water, brought, at scurrilous prices, down the Family canals. Every bad season, every hint of famine, leaves their subsistence villages devastated. And their children the grim choice of starvation or sale.

After that the desert proper carries nomadic clanfolk, whose goats and camel-breeding slide imperceptibly into the looks and speech and customs of Quetzistan. Excepting, you recall, the post-stations and imported service-folk and soldiers who keep open the way to the fragile, exotic city of Hamadryah, stronghold of the caravans.

One road to the Oases. One road that has pinned down the Dhasdein border, and curbed the nomads, and upheld all Verrain.

In Assuana the fall was over in a week. Tyrant dead, Families wiped out, fugitives sprayed like spurting blood, upRiver, down-River, and you can predict the directions. Family fugitives into the sanctuary of empire, small folk, caught in the teeth of murder and faction, to the chancy refuge of Amberlight.

The ensuing reports convinced me they had lost the Judge with the rest. It was a charnel house, first anarchy, then faction war, the remnant of Family guards or house-folk, Palace survivors, gang-lords from the urban rabble, seeing a way to rise at last. No true leader could have allowed it. Not if he had retained his leverage, his authority, his very life.

The first autumn month brought most of the refugees, inflaming our problems with pressure on our food and living space. By then we—Amberlight—had the border closed. With the Iskans to barricade the River, that is easy enough. It must have been very different for Dhasdein.

A great many slaves are pure Verraini, like the Judge. Most were Heartlanders, but many, like Keshaq, were Dhasdein's overflow. Mel'ethi, Shirranese, convicted as criminals, deported as political threats, sold for debt. And Quetzistani as well.

So where Heartlanders and Verraini stayed, settled, or went for bandits, the rest made for the borderlands. Merged with the nomads, oozed over the line that has never been more than marks on an imperial map, into the Dhasdeini provinces, a slow, invisible, irresistible flood.

While upRiver, the free farmers moved in on the released Riverland, and the nomads who had starved at their backs moved in on them.

What happened in Assuana, no-one, I think, will ever wholly know. Too many of the players were momentary, and far too many are dead. I do know that the first official message arrived five days into the second autumn moon.

"Nathyx son of Issandua." Juiza held it at arm's length. The month's assembly-Head, Uphill troublecrew, nostrils already curled. "Claiming, by blood and heritage, the sovereignty of Verrain."

"Heritage!" shouted the cobbler. "Sovereignty!" snorted someone else.

And Keshaq rose at my back and said, "You speak of the land's spearhead. The people's liberator."

I was—most of us were too startled to reply. You might sooner have looked for refutation from the wall. Certainly, not refutation with a hand on its belt-knife and a glare like that.

The cobbler, rash and rabid as any terrier, was the first to add the evidence. Make the calculation. And retort.

"You mean, Shuya's whore."

Keshaq's eyes slitted and I grabbed his wrist. The knife he had acquired on the wharf was also made to throw.

He had kept his wits. Under my grasp his forearm stilled. But the high-bred Quetizstani accent was clear as a slap.

"Keep your tongue to what you understand."

More than time to intervene. "Might we hear," I enquired, in my weariest lord's voice, "what the message from Verrain says?"

Oh, Tellurith. Given the sender, and his precarious eminence, and the stewpot over which he was teetering, I could have written it myself.

By blood and blade Nathyx had made himself Assuana's warlord. The details he spared us, but one could read between the boasts. Not a great deal of the city remained intact, folk were pouring out of it like rats. He claimed that the better part of Verrain would rally to him, but given the chaos in the countryside it was a hollow claim. If he could hold Assuana and somehow secure the district-commands, still the borders were beyond his control.

And with the borders went the Oasis road.

So he wanted an alliance, yes. Recognition of his regime from Amberlight.

Help.

Naturally he did not say that outright. The message ended with an urgent request that Amberlight receive a Verraini ambassador. Even the cobbler needed no help to decipher that.

"He—they—want us to recognize them. If we do that, so far as the River sees, they're an independent state."

I nodded back into Dhanissa's stare.

"And," Ferrias added resignedly, farsighted now as any statesman, "they'll want troops. And food."

The cobbler started to shout. Juiza slapped the table and glared.

"Lord Tanekhet," she said, "what do you advise?"

I gave myself a moment, as I would with Antastes. And offered a different gamble first.

When I turned and beckoned, the glower defied me, but he rose with a Quetzistani warrior's obedience. I gestured to the chair beyond me, asked, "Ruand, your permission?" And went on, "What can you tell us about Nathyx?"

The cobbler started to yap again. I gave him a straight stare and said, "Do *you* know? Personally?"

Conveniently, it also gave Keshaq thinking space.

"He is a born Verraini. A free farmer's son. Sold in a drought, when he was eight years old. To a Family estate. Passed on to the Palace when he—" he looked to me for the equivalent of the Quetzistani term for youth, neither child nor man. I said, "At training time?"

He nodded, relieved. "By twenty-two—last winter—he was the Ruler's favorite."

She liked them young. You will remember that.

"So," Keshaq drew himself up, fully aware of what I had really asked. "Verrainis will follow him, yes. The farm-folk, because he was one of them. The slaves, because he was one of them. The foreign slaves too. As for the city rabble . . ." The curl of the lip said it all. What would a man who survived the Palace maelstrom have to fear from them? "He could rule the country—if he can keep his place. If he can only get some support to tide him—over the worst."

Their eyes were on me: Ferrias and Dhanissa, visionaries' ardor already overlaid with politicians' weariness. Juiza, dour and cynic as Zuri herself. The cobbler, far behind the hunt. And Keshaq.

Long eyes, dark as memory, the gold all extinguished, silent in the silent, bronze-cast face.

* * *

"Ruand," I said, formally directing it to Juiza. "On the one hand, Verrain has overthrown its tyrants. Given recognition, it would be a people's state. The sister realm of Amberlight."

I let that lie a moment. Remember, it told them, you won your liberty the exact same way.

"More to the point," I said, when Dhanissa's eyes demanded, What else? "Verrain has been your best and nearest market. If we—you—are to keep this City afloat, we need its trade. And beyond that, we need the River trade. All of us—from Cataract to Riversend—need that."

Dhanissa stirred. "And," she said, too softly, "Iskarda."

I could see every woman round that table adding it up: Iskarda is Tellurith's power base. The only hope of sustaining order—here, as in the River-world at large—is that Tellurith will bring a solution back downRiver.

And to implement it, there must still be an Iskarda.

"Citizens, you know the most already. We—you—are by no means established. Let alone defensible. You need a neighbor. If not an ally, then a buffer zone." I took a little breath and said it at last. "Between us and Dhasdein."

Nobody spoke. The full import was clear enough, in the whitening of Juiza's nostrils, the set of Dhanissa's face.

"Under all that, there remains the Oasis road. The Oasis gold."

The greatest prize in the new Riverworld. It was Qualla, the stevedore from the far enclave of River Quarter, who said it out.

"Verrain must have the gold to survive. And if Verrain isn't strong enough to hold it—Dhasdein will."

I inclined my head. "Lastly, there is the matter of—Shuya's statuette."

Amid the general, "Huh?" Juiza said sharply, "It waned at summer's end!"

I took a good long breath, before I said, "That may no longer be—permanent."

So then I had to explain the news that they had never heard. The full story of how you prevailed in Cataract.

As I feared, it distracted them into unreasonable hope. They had you back downRiver, Verrain re-founded, Amberlight secured, Dhasdein a puppet-state, and were dividing the Oasis gold between us, before I could bring myself to interrupt.

"Citizens—that is all *if* we get back Tellurith."

In Dhanissa's face the elation died so swiftly. Truly, she has gone from adolescent nymph to House-head in five short months.

Ferrias said, "What about Cataract?"

"We do not," I rehearsed what we all knew, "have any form of diplomatic communication with Cataract. We can hardly send an unprefaced appeal for help upRiver—"

"We might," snapped Tesra, the male stevedores' delegate, "send an ambassador."

"So we might." He had urged it before. "Again, then, consider that Zuri is a consort Ruler. Foreign. A woman. The epitome of downRiver, of what they see as their eternal enemy. Amberlight. The mere fact she has made no official move suggests to me, at least, that she considers it too unsafe. So how long will her rule last if they see us courting her? And if Zuri fell, what use would Cataract be to us?"

It has been the bane of our councils, my lady Tellurith. Would that the thrice-damned qherrique *could* communicate between us, so I might know, even now, if what happened had your frank, or Zuri's alone.

All I know is, after that first message, everything had stopped until, at the end of second summer month, all the foreign ships were released downRiver, with an official invitation to trade. No freight, and no news but wild rumor and speculation about events ashore. There was talk of blood-baths, executions and expulsions, of which I would heed about half. It was crystal clear that Zuri had control of the city, and possibly maintained that hold with an iron hand.

Some traders, mostly the old hands, did return. They brought back scanty cargoes of ebony and ivory, some cinnamon and coffee, a couple of tigercats, all of which, after Verrain's fall, had to be sold at knock-down prices in Amberlight. A good number of Verraini and Dhasdeini ships are—were—stuck at the Amberlight border, or moored in Marbleport, since no sane skipper would risk his vessel downstream, unless he was running refugees.

None brought first-hand news of Cataract. The goods were boated off-shore like the meager stores, and the boat-folk would not talk. Not a word.

Nor was there any official communication. Not a proclamation of sovereignty, an offer to open diplomatic relations, an outright declaration of war. I could have managed those.

Dhanissa knew all that. She sighed and pushed the Verrain parchment across the table. Glanced round the delegates. Then squared her shoulders. "And the other side, Lord Tanekhet?"

I laid my own hands flat on the table, examining their rough-nailed, ink-marked fingers, before I spoke.

"If we recognize Verrain—we will have, at least for the rest of this year, to support Nathyx. That means food, at the very least.

With no certain, let be immediate payment. We will have to accept their refugees, which will divide our remaining supplies.

"Beyond that, we will have to enter the faction wars: we will be committed to backing Nathyx. And almost certainly, he will need military support.

"Which means risking some of our most precious resources—the cutters, the light guns—along with our most precious folk."

Dhanissa drew an audible breath. And waved me on, knowing too well it was not over yet.

"It's very likely, we—you—will have to garrison the Oasis road."

Because without the Oases, the rest was pointless. Juiza, at least, understood that.

"And at that point, citizens—if not long before it—we will confront Dhasdein."

The cobbler opened his mouth and let it shut.

"Antastes will move: he has to move, whether he wants Verrain or not. Refugees will unsettle Quetzistan and Mel'eth, whatever we or anyone in Verrain does. Antastes must hold them, to keep his empire whole. The only way to do that is to start a foreign war. For that, he needs a target: the logical one is the Oasis gold."

No-one seemed to be breathing. The very rumble of Amberlight, usually an unremitting background, cart wheels, cocks and cattle and human voices, seemed to have died away.

"Citizens, it's a choice of children." The old River tale, of the mother the gods asked for one child's life as price for all the rest. "We—you—can back Nathyx. Honor, decency, demands it. But if you—we—do—can we meet the price?"

It was Juiza who shifted at last. Rubbed her bottom lip, and spoke with the quiver that marks a sapping wound, "Where are we if we don't?"

"Verrain is still between us. Even Antastes will take some time to absorb the entire country. Let alone bring it under control."

It will make no difference, their faces answered, except in conscience, to us.

"And we can—help with that."

Qualla straightened up. "You don't want us to back 'em outright," she said, too evenly. "But you'd be prepared to spend a little bit of silver—and blood—to keep 'em kicking, after they're in the bog. With no hope of getting out."

"It is," I said, letting her understand both senses, "an intelligencer's choice."

Somebody from a Far Quay quarter said tartly, "What'll happen to you?"

"Your income," she amplified, at my raised eyebrow. "If we back Verrain, get the River trade moving, your ships'll run, anyway, won't they? If we don't . . ."

Do you imagine, I wanted to say, that if Antastes takes Verrain I will give a copper fiel for my life? What I said was, "If Antastes takes Verrain, I will long since have departed Amberlight."

"Come, citizens," I said as their jaws dropped. The vexation was more than I could hide. "His old Trouble-head, his renegade Suzerain, a proven agitator, your Assuana figurehead? Sitting just across his tottery new border? Can you dream a better pretext to take you as well?"

Something in their looks changed. It was Dhanissa, this time, who grabbed words back on the tip of the tongue. "Tanekhet—lord Tanekhet—"

She stopped. Then went on, almost gently, "Where would you go? What—would you do?"

I managed to lift a shoulder with delicate negligence. What need to answer what she saw too clearly? That far from worrying about a few revenues, I would have to throw away a second—a new life?

"Counselor, that is not the question here."

I made it gentle. Your women read nuance far too easily. She bit the rest off. It was Juiza who picked the conversation up.

"So, lord Tanekhet." One of the rare times she gave me the full title. "You counsel us—now, this moment—not to recognize Nathyx. Not to help his faction. Not to—back Verrain."

I bent my head. She recognized it was more than her own acknowledgement. "Whatever my—your—our feelings, ma'am. At this time, that is the best counsel I can give."

* * *

When the meeting ended Keshaq had not spoken. He was silent in the street, across the market, the long, long walk home. Inside at last, the rooms blurry in the lengthened reach of twilight, I turned to him before I groped for the lamp.

"You want to back them," I said.

He came slowly round the table: put down the string-container of vegetables, the last apples, unbuckled and laid by his belt. Slowly, if without uncertainty, put both arms around me, the way he would do now of his own volition. His eyes looked past me, out the cramped window, where evening fires had begun to dye the alley-walls, shadow-gray, murky red.

With a finger he traced my jaw line. At last he said, "I owe him—everything."

"Oh, caissyl." He is just tall enough for me to hide my eyes against his shoulder. Warmth and solidity still, but coarse home-spun rather than brocaded silk, and no perfume but an honest day's sweat. "If I thought we could do it and survive . . ."

"You would say so." A faint note of surprise. He had so much trust in my integrity.

"I know Dhasdein. I know Antastes. If we throw Verrain to him, there is a chance—just a chance—we can save Amberlight."

"And Iskarda."

He said it, still, with the care of unfamiliarity. Amberlight he was learning, slowly as a child, who had been all but a child in so many things when he was thrust back into the free world. Iskarda remained a mirage, of which he knew only that it was my ultimate dream, my highest guardship, my last and wildest hope.

"And Iskarda."

At the last, he was charitable. I know very well he realized—

What lay—what lies on the equation's other side.

I can silence it for the most part. In Amberlight, with a City's survival on my shoulders, it was far easier. The odds were clearer, the weight of my new world more palpable, it was far truer to know myself part of Amberlight, an envoy, an ambassador, your liege-man. With the trust, however qualified, of Iskarda as well.

And in pitting our frail hopes against what I knew as the might of Dhasdein's armory, it was far easier to dismiss the counter-query: You have seen the fall of Amberlight, of Verrain, of Cataract. Against the—weapons—that this fragile interloper has proved able to mobilize—

Can Dhasdein itself prevail?

The River-lord remember him forever. At least, whatever he heard, whatever he felt in me, Keshaq said none of that.

He did straighten, with infinite gentleness, the perpetually tangled queue against my neck. Slid his hand under it, feeling out the strained muscles with that expert, loving touch. I read far too much understanding, too much of loss and grief and his own denied integrity, and a companion's, a shared rather than a lover's consolation, in that caress.

* * *

And the next step you foresee all too clearly, Tellurith. The assembly delayed for Marbleport's, Iskarda's response? Surely. So four days later, back upRiver came Tez herself.

Doubly vexed, be sure, that she must return in person to quell renewed Amberlight foolishness. Sending an advance message so she stamped into a full assembly, sparks in her very hair. Unlike her father, she does not barricade rages behind stone.

"Citizens," was her opening salvo, "have you all lost your heads?"

"Or do I understand," she glared like an outraged tigercat, "you will refuse alliance with Verrain?"

Juiza still had the chair: Uphill troublecrew, she had seen Headly tantrums before. She settled back against the rickety seat and returned, "Why should we accept?"

"Why . . .!" She bit her lips tight. Her eyes flashed, one scythe slash, to me. This, it said, is all your doing.

"Citizens, have you noticed that Verrain is your downRiver border? That it is, at the very least, a buffer state against Dhasdein? Why in the Mother's name do you imagine four hundred years of House-heads left Verrain between us, for all the trouble and trials and plotting and intriguing, for all the risk they would ally with Dhasdein against us—as they *did*, over and over—if there was not something in it for us?

"And now!" Had there been a table handy it would have taken a solid thump. "They've overthrown a tyrant, just as we—you did! They are at the riskiest point of the aftermath. If we—you—desert them now, you had as well call the House-heads back Uphill and cede the sovereignty of Amberlight!"

Juiza folded her hands one over the other. "What," she said, "would be the price?"

Tez glared at her. "Food—money—troops, possibly. What of it? Back Nathyx, you've rebuilt your buffer-state. If you want to think like an—intelligencer—" flare of the nostrils, "it comes cheap at the price."

"It puts us," said Juiza evenly, "in Verrain's camp."

"So?"

"So when Antastes moves against Verrain, we will have to back our ally. That means *we* will have to fight Dhasdein."

"Mother blast it, if you back Verrain fast and hard enough Antastes will stop in his tracks!"

"We have," said Juiza, very precisely, "some fifty light-guns. Some hundred and fifty trained troublecrew. No warships. No treasury. No arsenal. No troops. Verrain will already be leaning on us. And with that, you want us to say, No, to Antastes?"

"Oh, may the Mother succor me!" Tez literally tore her hair. "You crew of ninnyhammers, send to Cataract!"

Juiza opened her mouth: looked at me, let it shut. Tez gave me one glance that burned to the marrow and slammed a palm with the other fist.

"Cataract has the cedar: Cataract has built its war-galleys time out of mind. Cataract has trained fighting men bursting its peace at the seams. Cataract has Zuri in charge!"

She lashed her eyes around us. Whatever our faces said, it made her literally grind her teeth.

"Zuri," the voice of barely breathing rage, "is troublecrew. She *expects* to fight. She knows the River. She knows what's happened—or did you blockade upRiver too? Of *course* she won't sit on her backside bleating, *Let Antastes have the Oases*, the Mother blast it, what other resources do we have? And how else can we keep them but with one united front? Send a message! If you don't have a dozen galleys off-shore and a brigade on the road by moon's end, I'll jump off Arcis myself!"

Juiza's eyes came round to me. Dhanissa's, Ferrias'. From behind me, I felt, pressing as the point of a nail, Keshaq's midnight stare.

It was not pique: I swear to you, on my mother's name, it was not pique. I swear it stuck like drying glue in my throat. For the gods' love, I wanted to say, Can you see—can you believe—this is not against *you*? That it is for Amberlight?

I said, "But can Zuri move Cataract?"

That look said all I had feared and more. She ripped in a breath. But she had her wits and Amberlight training still. The faces around the table cut off the rest.

Juiza re-folded her hands. She said, too evenly, "Ruand, have you anything—firm—about the situation in Cataract?"

After a too, too long moment, Tez set her jaw. "I know Zuri. *You* know Zuri. She'll have been building galleys since the day she took the throne!"

Juiza sighed. "I know our resources," she said evenly. "Our situation. And I am troublecrew. If I were Zuri and I had such a message, the first answer I would send—whatever the situation up there, the first answer I know I would have to send—would be, What can you offer *us*?"

Dhanissa and Ferrias understood: the iron of ten months rulership was in them already. It was Tez who opened her lips, and closed them, and that expression—

What lunacy is it, that for a woman who had, who would have spurned me for a coward and an intriguer as quick as glance at me, I would still turn my wits inside out?

I said, "The gold."

They all stared. I spoke it as a priest relays an oracle, charting the vision as it opened to my own eyes.

"We send to Zuri, requesting military support. Troops, if not war galleys. We offer a triple alliance: Verrain, Cataract, Amberlight. Its purpose is to protect the Oasis gold. Which the alliance will share."

* * *

Do I hear you say, For once you justified your existence, Tanekhet?

* * *

The motion naturally passed immediately. The letters went almost as fast, written to my dictation, sent by the fastest pinnaces we could spare. Of Nathyx's response I had no doubt. For Zuri, I could only hope we had not upset some still unknown fulcrum. It was a huge prize to gamble, on one woman's knowledge of another, on past sureties, and inner knowledge of Amberlight.

Do I hear you saying, And into your own gold, Tanekhet?

That was sure before the messages left, Tellurith.

In Tez's eyes.

In Keshaq's.

I could feel them amid the congratulatory babble, palpable as a handful of velvet on my neck. I could image the moment he would turn to me in our shabby little refuge, his expression, his touch. His honor, his integrity, his old allegiance, all redeemed.

Tez . . .

She never said anything outright. It was all in that first look. For the moment of that unguarded—amazed—unconditionally grateful expression, I could believe she truly cared for me.

Traitor that I am: because it was that look I locked into memory in the darkness. In Keshaq's embrace.

* * *

As you may imagine, Nathyx's answer came a deal the faster, with a quartet of gold bars, doubtless the last bullion in Assuana, ostensibly "ship funding," to seal the pledge. No fool, Nathyx.

His ambassador came with them, laden with official proclamations and a treaty for the Assembly's signature: a woman, ex-Palace slave, black as Nathyx, pure Verraini if twice his age, and a bargainer to match Juiza. Word of the alliance, she told us nonchalantly, was already trumpeted far and wide through Assuana, and into the countryside beyond. Her Land-leader had begun to organize a garrison for the Oasis road.

That was over in a fortnight. Zuri's answer took long enough to stretch all our nerves.

It did not come in words, or gold either. It came by six sea-soned war-galleys, loaded with marines to the gunwales, moored at Main Quay by the third week of third autumn moon. And word of troops marching downRiver, to arrive before second winter moon.

No, they did not come for free, and yes, she did take care for Cataract. Did you have a hand in that, Tellurith? And naturally, as troublecrew, she made it both fulfillment of her pledge and surety for ours. A request delivered by her ambassador, a Hatura warrior and his suite.

Gold, yes, gold was acceptable: but she wanted grain, and ar-tisans as well.

For the grain she offered trade, and with Verrain's market gone, we could manage some response. The artisans were for ship-commission: wood-workers, carvers, gold and silversmiths, and she would take them from Verrain as well. She and her City guaranteed a house and half a year's support to as many as cared to go.

I know now, Tellurith, whose vision she carried on.

In that third moon, with the alliance confirmed, with security burgeoning like some street-magician's flower, with trade's hope restored if not its actuality, a River at least half-open, the bustle of deploying galleys and preparing troop-quarters and mustering emigrants, with communications running by smoke and mirror-signal so we were in contact almost daily with Cataract, with Assuana, with Iskarda, with Marbleport—

And with some real hope that we might make Antastes pause, actually negotiate . . . with that euphoria lifting my own heart, there were times, as that autumn moon dwindled, when I saw my new world, Tellurith: clear, present, palpable as flesh and blood under my hand.

Before Antastes' message came.

* * *

You will know that chaos and upheaval works for intelligencers both ways, and that permeable borders run both ways, and you know as well as I that if we sowed a harvest of exiled parti-sans, we also sowed a solid crop of loyalists when we made a Jhuir Quetzistani empress of Dhasdein. And you know Quetzistani desert-skills. If the River was impregnable, Antastes still had his intelligence, his conduit for messages. And he has never been one to move too late.

It was an official decree. Signed, stamped, sealed with the serpent and lightning-bolt across the heavy parchment, its silk envelope, slit now, stained with bearer's sweat. They must have taken it across untracked desert, clear around Verrain, over the Iskans, into the very heart of Amberlight. Tez dropped it on the Assembly table as if it were an unscotched snake.

"An ultimatum," she said, "for Iskarda."

Antastes has seen our weak hinge as clearly as Shuya did. What would you expect?

"Iskarda is reminded that we are imperial allies. Signed and sworn: a copy included to refresh our minds. I sent that to Darthis. As imperial allies, we are requested and required to renounce all dealings with and support for the renegade government of Amberlight. And all its so-called allies, including the equally illegitimate usurper of Verrain. Dhasdein will mobilize troops for the empire's defense. It requires all allies' and subject states' support."

She lifted her eyes at last.

"Dhasdein has imposed a levy. Thirty qherrique weapons and their handlers, to prove the faith of Iskarda."

In that bubble of silence I heard Dhanissa breathe: Ferrias' knuckles crack. I swear, in the utter abeyance of every outer sound, I heard Keshaq's muscles stiffening at my back.

Antastes, arch-politicker, had outdone Shuya's wits. Forget Verrain, too messy for easy conquest, populous, divided, borders leaky as a sieve, a potential hemorrhage of resources, a perfect battle-zone for Amberlight. Forget Amberlight itself, shielded behind that zone, and dismiss outright any chance of touching Cataract. Take a small target, manageable. Doubly vulnerable. On one side, the opponent's true head, on the other, a community already, perhaps fatally, pledged to Dhasdein.

And lean on that pledge, in a way that could only split the alliance forever. However Iskarda jumped.

Tez looked around again, and this time I saw the Navy officer I had never known. The corkscrewed curls twined loose by Riverwind, the working shirt and the tattered straw hat she had flung down behind her, all dissolved into armor and light-gun and aplomb equal to every battle-turn: peril, onslaught, ambush, that measuring, golden-spatched stare would find resources for them all.

Dhanissa pulled herself up a little in her seat and spoke with matching quiet.

"What does Iskarda mean to do?"

Just visibly, Tez drew herself up. But she spoke quite calmly. As if this were all routine: as for an Amberlight Navy officer, last stands and lost causes and stone-cool calmness in disaster may have been, for all I know.

"We delay. We send no answer for a month. That will get us Zuri's troops. Then a prevarication. Our House-head is absent. We have to consult. Then outright protests. With the greatest respect, Dhasdein has no business in this matter. Verrain and Amberlight and Cataract are independent states."

Well may you laugh, or splutter in delighted indignation, as I would have with a fiel's less command. The vixen had taken my strategies clean out of my mouth.

Her eye turned to me. For one instant that knowledge spoke in the glance, with a comrade's awareness, a comrade's glint of mirth. Before Dhanissa clapped her hands and burst out, "Of course! Just like Tanekhet!"

The Assembly revived around her, clatter of glee, agreement, shaken hope. Only I, perhaps, saw the spark go out in Tez's look.

Only I, of a surety, felt the lead fall on my heart, ingot after ingot, as I understood what I must say next.

Because no-one else could, would see it: half the delegates were out of their seats already, mobbing Tez, slapping her back, Dhanissa had grabbed papyrus and a pen and was urging her to write the answer, there and then.

At the last my courage failed. I got out of the chair and worked my way to the door. Only when the assembly came streaming past me, when Tez and Dhanissa were in armslength, did I step into their path and ask, "My ladies, if I might have a word?"

Dhanissa waved her usual exuberant, Yes. Tez looked straight up in my face, and in those eyes was everything I had feared to say.

She too had a sense of situation. She gathered me up in passing with a hand above the elbow, no lady's mannered dependence but the grip of a pentarch manhandling strays. Swept me down the street with them, the turn and alleyway into Dhanissa's house, past the workshop's bustle, the kitchen-door, into the chilly perfect parlor, River quarter gentility, where, with Dhanissa and Ferrias beside her, she turned at bay.

"Was I right?" she said.

Momentum had left us standing far too close. In the chill room I felt her body warmth, smelt her essence, that tangy mix of common soap and woman's sweat: the very flecks of golden brown in her eyes were visible, clear as their expression, bare inches from mine.

"Antastes has decided. He's going to fight us. This isn't a loyalty-test, it's meant to split the alliance. And it's just the start."

Ah, Tellurith. The imbecility of flesh and blood and manhood: it was not what she said that dried my mouth, that had the heart hammering up under my jaw and words scattering like scared pigeons in my throat.

"Isn't it?"

The headiest sensation of all. She had not only learnt from me, was not merely using my tactics. Her judgment, her actions, had leant, in ways that question told too clearly, on my affirmation. It was more than kindness. It was respect.

"Yes," I said, shock overridden by necessity so it jerked out of me. "Yes."

Her shoulders relaxed: her chin came up a little. We were still all but touching. She is my height, you know as well as I do. For that moment our eyes looked into each other as closely, as completely, as that exchange of selves you feel between a mother and a child.

My head swam. I think my vision spun. I might have stood there forever, paralyzed. But she put out a hand, a single finger. And touched me, a moth-wing brush, at the point of my jaw. And briefly, so briefly, smiled.

Give me a moment. It is not so easy, to find the doors of paradise, and have them close in your face.

* * *

Well. You may believe that in true male imbecility I spent the next week walking on air. That my delirium left me blind as the rest of the City as we strutted about taking delay for a valid counter, mere understanding of our case as power to resist what was building downRiver. As if our puny defiance were enough to thwart the onslaught of Dhasdein.

Oh, Tellurith, I should, I ought to have, I did know better. Give me some margin if I wanted to stretch that moment in her sunshine, if I wanted to keep her—her—kindness—so badly, I was prepared to deny the future, along with everyone else.

And like every other fool who baulks at destiny, I was haled kicking and howling to its will, a bare five days later, when the next message flew upRiver. From Nathyx.

Not parchment but a mirror signal, passed upRiver faster than a horse can gallop, let alone a pinnace sail. No flowery fencing and no compliments this time. No pleas either. He knew what he asked.

"Dhasdein has taken Deyiko. Five thousand troops across the border. All possible assistance required now."

You could hardly scourge me harder than I scourge myself. I knew Antastes. I should have known he would not stop at diplomatic pressure or opening maneuvers, not once he knew about the alliance. The message to Iskarda showed how the wind had set. I ought to have known—I *did* know—it would not wait our convenience to become a storm.

* * *

I did not say all that, in the hush of the assembly room, their foolish buoyancy lost, their callow hopes in shreds. What I said, with careful coolness, was, "Ruand, I suggest we call for volunteers."

Dhanissa had the chair again: she opened her mouth and let it shut. Ferrias beside her shot upright with a real spark in her eye. Juiza, with the dour glint I have come to read as approval, did not have to nod.

It was Tez, at Dhanissa's right-hand, who said with calm more dangerous than any outburst, "What are you talking about?"

Why in the River-lord's mercy could Antastes not have waited a day more, could the mirror units not have had a breakdown, could the wind not turn so she sailed as she intended, the previous day?

No doubt you will answer, if you have the composure, *Because fate is fate, or else it could be changed.*

I looked down at my hands on the table. I did not want to see her face when I said what must be said.

"Dhasdein has marched in force. That means an invasion. More troops will follow. Antastes has called our bluff."

Tesra has learnt some political skills. Enough not to explode with patriotic bellowings, but to ask, "Then why not send them everything we've got?"

The upRiver wind rattled in the crooked window. With it came a surge of hubbub from the marketplace. Not uproar but the everyday life of Amberlight.

"Because," I said, too evenly, "none of it will help."

The Assembly rustled. Dhanissa stiffened. At my back, I felt Keshaq stir.

I did not look at Tez: I only felt the bubble of that contact, that previous gratitude, that fragile, fragile accord, and then comrades' union in the face of destiny, all shatter. All cascade down in tiny silent shards amid the ruins of her respect.

I have no doubt you will not honor me either, but perhaps you will understand. Perhaps you may come to believe my loyalty, Tellurith, as it is no longer credited here. You may even pity me. Because it was no comfort, to know I had broken my heart's hopes for the half-chance of saving my new world.

Her voice was cool as that first question. And it was not aimed at me.

"Delegates. Fellows in the Alliance. We should back our comrades now with every resource we have. Our honor demands it. As much as our City's hopes."

"Delegates," I said as quietly, "we have fifty light-guns and a hundred and fifty troublecrew, eight Customs pinnaces, and three hundred heavy-armed troops. What will that do, against an advance-guard of five thousand men?"

She came in almost atop me. "And we have six seasoned war-galleys. With the River blocked and threat of a sortie behind them, how far will five thousand Dhasdeinis go?"

The Assembly breathed and moved. Old Amberlight reflex, to think first of war by water. Good sense, that Dhasdein would not leave a naval force in their wake. Pure bravado for the rest.

"Six war-galleys are Antastes' annual levy from Wave Island," I said. "It does not even cover the whole Archipelago."

Their eyes went back to her: a swing of attention, as a duel-audience flicks its eyes to opposing thrusts. I lifted my head and addressed them, with the skills of working an assembly that I have learnt so well.

"Delegates, our signed word compels us to back Verrain. I am not faithless: I do not council this from cowardice, or just because I know the odds. I tell you, plain and outright, we cannot back Verrain without reservation. Not if the City is to survive."

I used every skill of voice and tone and presence, and I spoke, as you must at such a pass, with all the conviction in my soul. The rank of faces down the table swayed to me. I saw Dhanissa's eyes change. I saw Juiza set her jaw.

I saw Tez lean forward a little in her seat, and her face was as blank, as perilous, as I ever saw her sire's.

"You want to save our lives with our allies' blood."

"I want," I kept it quiet, "to save our lives."

"By giving Antastes Verrain without a casualty—without a fight?"

"Antastes will not get Verrain without a fight."

Her nostrils flared. It came like a dagger-flick.

"And Amberlight gets a—cheap—defense."

I did manage, despite the metaphorical blood on my ribs, not to flinch.

"We can send troops. Send volunteers. I do not council we ignore our allies. I only urge us to remember the odds. To keep reserves for—the City's own need."

"So you see Antastes taking Amberlight?"

At that pounce I had to lift my head. Their eyes all spoke it: the uncertainty, the disillusion that she was waking with every word. And now the doubt. Of me. Of the City itself.

"Not," I said, "if we are careful now."

"Ah. So we let Antastes blood his troops on whatever Nathyx can muster. We let Verrain take the invasion's brunt. We sit on our behinds and watch Nathyx either killed or executed, and hope that Verrain will give Antastes a gutful. Of loss—or loot. Or we hope Cataract will bleed for us as well. Or that someone starts a revolt in the Islands, or the bountiful Mother reaches down and tweaks off his generals' heads. Anything—anything—" still she did not raise her voice—"but do as honor bids us. Dare to act for ourselves."

"Honor does not come into this. Do you want the City to survive?"

Her pupils dilated, one black fire of contempt. Then she whipped a glance like a scourge around the delegates.

"Choose now, citizens: do we wait on others to die for us, or do we keep our honor as well as our City—and fight?"

Guess, then, which way they would vote.

When the uproar subsided I tried the last, the final throw.

"If the City is determined, I beg the Assembly to hear me on this one thing. Don't send the Cataract galleys to Deyiko."

Belatedly reclaiming her role, Dhanissa waved for quiet: and asked almost temperately, "Why?"

"Because," it was time to be brutal, "you will need them for the City's last defense."

That one did bite. They remember Amberlight's fall, the siege-wall, the River-chains, far too well.

Tez shifted her hand on the table. One small, decisive twist.

"If we stop Antastes it must be in south Verrain. Deyiko's not two hundred miles from the Iskans. The galleys are our best—our only hope."

Of a sudden I was too weary to go on. I sat back and turned my hands up on the table. "We have a conflict of strategies," I said. "If you know Zuri, my lady, *I* know Antastes. He will not stop. He *cannot* stop. What is more, I know his resources. I say, Wait, aim to survive. But you want to throw once and hazard everything. Very well. Throw, then. And be the dice-fall on your own heads."

There is power in genuine despair. For a moment, the Assembly was almost cowed.

Tez's eyes dilated. Her back went stiff. She spoke as she would have fired a light-gun. Precise. Lethal. Merciless.

"Is it *Amberlight's* survival that worries you?"

And doubtless you will say, That too you should have expected, Tanekhet. I knew her experience, in war, in detention. I knew her nature: Sarth's nature, with whatever impetuosity and probable harshness she added from her dam. I ought to have known, once I pushed her to the limit, that she would not quibble over the riposte.

It struck me, though. Harder than a blow over the heart. I sat silent an instant too long.

"You accuse my lord of treachery?"

The slashing knife made a bar across Tez's throat, a bright, gleaming bar. Without a quiver, that light-beam. Not even from his indrawn breath.

"Keshaq!"

I was just fast enough. Juiza's light-gun was up, but she did not fire.

"Keshaq!"

He did not look around. He was behind her, the knife slipped round across her throat. He said softly, "If they shoot me, she goes too."

"Keshaq—my lady, wait!"

The terror in that must have been more than clear. And it bared the depth of Juiza's trust: for even then, veteran troublec-rew, treachery and violence and threat to the House's heir right before her, still she gave me a chance.

She let me get, awkwardly as if snow-numb, out of my seat. Walk round behind Dhanissa, rigid in outrage as much as shock. Touch, so carefully, his left, not his weapon-arm.

"Keshaq—please."

I never put so much into a pair of words. I never spoke two words on which so much depended. And that, at least, he heard.

His eyes moved slowly from side to side. Juiza, light-gun aimed. Other delegates, danger's paralysis thawing to the readi-ness of trained if not violent folk. Seeing a menace in their midst. Ready, too ready, if the moment came, to strike.

"Citizens," I heard my voice shake and I did not care. "This is my liege-vassal. Quetzistani. You know their loyalty. I vouch—I will vouch—for the lady Tez's safety. With my life."

Melodramatic? Surely. But it was not for them I spoke. It was for Keshaq.

Infinitesimally, I saw his shoulders ease. I took his elbow. Let the touch second the question. "Keshaq?"

His knife-wrist relaxed. I drew him backward, making my own body, my proximity, his shield.

One step, two. Three. Then I could back him up against the wall and annex the knife and turn, keeping him behind me, to meet the outrage of Amberlight.

It was Tez who gagged the outcry, with one peremptorily flapped hand. She had swung her chair about. She had not broken into sweat: she was not so much as breathing faster. Only my stomach rolled at the look in her eyes.

"Sit," she said, "down."

To me. With an inflection that made me jam Keshaq's stomach with an elbow and hiss through my teeth as if he were a balky mule.

"My lady," I managed, and her brows rose.

"You vouched for my safety. With your life."

You understand. I—he understood. And what could I do, but draw him down the wall to stand again behind me, and give him a look of my own meant to nail him where he stood?

She waited till the small noises of my movement died away, in the unbreathing hush. Then she gathered eyes around the table and spoke as a Navy officer, an Amberlight leader, the Head of a House.

"This is my council, as Telluir's Heir, as delegate for Iskarda. We—all of us—should back Verrain now with every resource we have. Send the Cataract galleys downRiver. With the Cataract troops. With every fighter we judge we can spare from the chance of an overland counter-attack."

Can you vision how the faces changed? If they had forgotten how that message reached Marbleport, she had not.

"Going downRiver, we should co-ordinate with Nathyx. He holds the land. We use the galleys to control the River, ferry troops to relieve him, and harass Dhasdein's rear."

Her eyes met mine, and I could not read that look.

"And we send an official message to Antastes. Asking if Dhasdein is proof against what befell Amberlight, and Verrain, and Cataract. Telling him," the pause was so gentle, "if he attacks us, to beware the qherrique."

Among the lot of them, only Dhanissa managed a gulp.

Tez's glance came back to her. Too armored for exultation, let alone a smile.

"Then we signal Nathyx. Right now. Telling him to find—wherever, however—Shuya's statuette."

Juiza's mouth fell open. Tez silenced her with a look.

"Telling him to meet us with it on our way downRiver. And then *we* will raise the qherrique."

It was Qualla who got her breath back first.

"You mean—you think—"

Tez's eyes pinned her. Cold and steady as a sharpened lance. "Tellurith did it. Why shouldn't we?"

"That," spluttered Eizo, a veteran Shaper, "was with the seed!"

Tez's stare actually grew colder. "If this is the qherrique's battle . . . there will be a way."

She had left them all literally gasping. Incoherencies of reprieve, of all but delirious shock. And I—what could I say to that?

"Every resource," she said, and gathered a breath. "When we meet Nathyx, we arrange to send guerrillas into Shirran and Mel'eth.

"They can blend with the Verrain renegades. We can exploit the trouble they've already made. Antastes is supposed to be moving in case his provinces rise. Let's give him something to move about."

Oh, Tellurith, in the gods' honest truth, it was masterly. It was worthy of her—of you—it was the mobilization of *every* resource, the all-out blow to the jugular that I had never dreamt. If we were indeed to hazard everything, that was the line to take.

I was too graveled for the barest gesture of assent. Let be praise, let be what would seem a sycophant's rhapsody, when it was truly less than she deserved. I had not so much as got my wind when her look came back to me and a knife touched my heart.

"And," she said, "into Quetzistan."

I understood then, and my belly came up my throat. I said, "No."

Her eyes swept me. The traverse of a light-gun, for the last, demolishing salvo of the fight.

"In the case of Quetzistan, we have a unique resource."

All I could manage was, "No."

The eyes swung away. "A prince," she said to the assembly, "of the old K*uo blood."

"No!" I heard it come out, too loudly, I could imagine what my face said and did not care. "The K*uo were stamped out. They won't know—he was exiled at fifteen!"

How could I say, He was a slave, he knows only Palace intrigue, he's not a warrior, far less desert-skilled—how could I beg for him so meanly, before his very face?

"The K*uo were proscribed. A Verraini guerrilla they'll just—execute. A proscribed exile—"

They would execute him too. Hang, draw and quarter him, a royal traitor's death.

If she had done it in private, I could have explained it all. I could have pleaded. I could—I would have begged. But before the full assembly? Before his very face?

"The alliance," she said, "needs every resource."

"No."

"It's a chance to raise all Quetzistan."

"No."

"You will not support the alliance?"

Treachery. Proven, this time, undeniable.

"*I* will support the alliance."

He came to my shoulder, that soft-footed, desert stride. So lithe, so imposing, so counterfeit. Out there amid factions whose folk he had never met, with no core of partisans, no military skills, he would not last a day.

Sheer terror got it from my throat. "Are you my vassal or not?"

It spun him clean around, staring. A look that became something else.

"Well?"

I tried not to see what was happening in his face. "Well?"

His eyes dropped. When he made the Quetzistani sign of submission, this time, it was almost grief.

I motioned him back to the wall. As he moved, I looked past him at Tez.

"Your plans may succeed," I said, "or not. But win or lose, they will carry a fearsome butcher's bill. And you may waste the blood of Verrain, and Cataract, and Amberlight. But you shall not squander this."

She held my stare: there was nothing in her own. Not sympathy. Not hate. Not so much as disgust.

"With a good chance to raise Quetzistan . . . we could keep the galleys in Amberlight."

I think my heart stopped. I know my lungs would not fill. Could the Nine-armed Adversary have offered you such a choice?

I felt Keshaq—my entire skin was ears, I felt him coil up behind me and fairly hurled it into the gap. "No!"

Her eyes narrowed then. Oh, she has fought in war, yes. She is brutal beyond any intelligencer.

"Lord Tanekhet, you are no longer in accord with the alliance. Your allegiance is in doubt. Will you let your vassal go as he has offered?"

I have been in straits before, with Antastes' father as with Antastes, and thought myself at wits' and sufferance's end, and seen death as a tenable means of escape. But never such a strait as that.

I took a breath. It seemed to sear all the way down my throat. "No."

She looked around the assembly. White-faced, some, stunned, all of them. As precisely, as coolly as ever, she said, "Then you will return to Iskarda tomorrow. Telluir House ends your term as Adviser to Amberlight."

* * *

And *that*, my lady Tellurith, is why I am here in Iskarda. Bruised in soul, disgraced, discredited. No doubt I should be grateful to have house-room at all.

I *am* grateful, to the gods alone, to have kept Keshaq.

How I have changed, Tellurith. That what bit deepest in the entire wreck was not—

Not Tez herself, and a breach that is undoubtedly mortal—

But the way I had dishonored a minor player: a mere piece, I would have said once, on the castles-board, one of the multitude I have used, abused, disposed of, lifelong. Without a second thought.

That what terrified me most, walking out those dingy warehouse doors for the last time, was not the repercussions for the River, for Amberlight, for Tez herself, let be the revived trials of Iskarda looming ahead of me.

It was the thought of losing Keshaq.

I had wits to keep silent till we were home. Late afternoon, the rooms, usually seen by lamp-light, more than usually tawdry, the backlight of disaster harshening everyday trivia. Mended clothes, yesterday's fruit, battered plates. I put a hand among them, and turned to meet my fate.

His eyes told me as little as his face. If not a warrior's, it was a slave's again: absolutely blank.

After all, I told myself, I am Tanekhet. I have faced down emperors.

He said, "When will you leave?"

'You.' I had to pause, as I have seen felled wrestlers do, before they can get up.

"When—they decide . . ." Can you credit, that I was shattered beyond bitterness?

The eyes flared. Anger, outrage, a lightning slash across the cooled-bronze face.

What point in trying to explain, in begging, Forgive me, in confessing, I marred your honor out of sheer cowardice? Because I could not bear to lose you, and then to see you lose your life? He had made his decision. It was a courtesy that he had come home once more, that he had not stalked away, repudiating me in the street.

I looked around the flotsam of our habitance, trying to pull threads together. Speech, plans, direction. Life.

"You can take the clothes. I—earnestly apologize . . . I have no resources—no—funds—you might use to—to—"

The eyes flared wide open, blaze of darkness, flame of whites. I almost cringed. I knew the quality of his wrath.

"I do not want *funds*." It came out throttled, as if he too had something in his throat.

"No, I—I beg your pardon—I beg your pardon, Keshaq."

It came at the last with neither intent nor governance. It was not recompense, no explanation, no sort of decent—closure—it was never intended to cover everything. But it was all I could manage to say.

His face altered as if he had been struck. He took a step closer. His lips parted. The words quivered, for I heard it, in his throat.

"My lord—"

I shut my eyes. It was the only way to make it bearable.

I did not hear the step. I did feel his hands as he pressed mine to his forehead, that gesture of allegiance. I heard the way his voice shook as he spoke.

"Even if you leave me, you are my lord. Even in Iskarda."

It took me time to get so far as, "What?"

He looked up. That face was open now. Grief, loss, resignation. Understanding, and relinquishment, of what had become the centre of his life.

"You are going . . ."

I yanked him up to me. Gripped his shoulders, I saw the bruises later, and he never flinched.

"I thought *you* were going. That *you* despised *me*, you meant to—separate, you—"

His mouth fell open. "I thought you despised me. I shamed you. A mannerless slave, a—not fit for Iskarda."

"Not *fit!*"

It took me a while to command myself. Then I took his face between my hands and stared full in those long, those profound, those suddenly readable eyes.

"*You* are fit to company the River-lord. *I* shamed you before the assembly. I crossed your honor. I could not—could not let you be a—soldier—warrior—I—"

He touched my face in turn. So very gently. And said, "You were losing her."

To understand, and yet not to grudge all she meant. To realize where he stood against that, to know I had shamed him, to keep even a less-loved one, in a scramble of pure selfishness. And then to forgive me. To convict himself in my place, and take desertion as a fitting punishment . . .

What have I done, to earn a love like that?

I will be honest, Tellurith. Shaken I may have been, and guilty, and moved beyond speech, but that is the first time, since my father died, that anyone has seen me weep.

"You are not leaving," I said at last. Fingers knotted in his collar, as if I could not get them out. "You are not going anywhere. Except with me. To Iskarda."

I still could not say it outright: *It was my fault, my shame, my guilt.* But he, who had read to the core of my heart's maze, took that false arrogance at its proper worth.

* * *

It surprised me that they let me take him without the slightest demur. Dheya and Kheizo doubtless had a hand in that. They came to see me leave, that bleak clouded morning, aboard the message-pinnace for Marbleport. As did Juiza, and Dhanissa, and Ferrias, and a good many others more surprising. No demonstration of loss, no flouting of Tez's command, of course. Nevertheless, in the personal farewells, the quiet, repeated, Thanks and Good lucks, I read an esteem, an affection, that amazes me still.

And Iskarda?

It was all the *same*, Tellurith. When we had labored round the last bend, with the mules sweating and blowing despite that frigid air where Keshaq's very lips were turning blue, when the immaculate snow-folds, gleaming pearl-like under heavy clouds, had opened on the faded walls, the slate roofs, the brown swathes of trampled mud—when we got down in the market square, huddled in our coats while the train disbanded and someone led the mules away—

There was Iatha, scrubbing mittens and puffing in the trenchant midday air, and Desis behind her, rugged-up and ruddy, to be sure, but no more different than the foot-traffic, the threads of women with tools or hunter's gear, the men heaving loads of wood, the talk of blocks and cutters and even—even! the thrice-damned water-pipes, all fraying past around me, as if—

As if I had turned away for a moment, a night's sleep, and the season changed, and nothing else. As if it would last forever, a House in amber, its every foible and smallest increment preserved.

They greeted us—me—as if it were everyday to find the Steward of Telluir House out to meet some man in the snow. And they knew, I could tell by their faces, about Keshaq.

To them, apparently, it is all of a piece. I left, I caused dissent and confusion as well as fulfilling my purpose—or how, as Desis openly said, did Verrain fall? I came back. But I am a man. It was expected of me.

Including, it seems, Keshaq.

They had made space for him. A room to himself, right next to mine.

Back in Zariah's house, yes.

Asaskian?

We met that evening, over the dining table. Keshaq was at my heel, Quetzistani fashion, but perfect in making him minimally conspicuous. She came in late as House-stewards do, a covey of leaders about her, including Zariah herself. Talk was of the quarry, some concern about a fault. She helped herself from the communal dish: took a bread-round. Swept her eyes over me, and said with the most absolute, most distant, most impregnably neutral courtesy, "Greetings, lord Tanekhet."

She has never addressed me without the title since. Not even while Keshaq is out hauling water and hewing wood and making his own way amid the underlings with the skill a slave learns, while I—

I have been returned to that cubbyhole at her own office's back.

They do not admit me to the councils any more. So what I know about the River, Tellurith, is bare common knowledge. The double-chewed pap that the powerful see fit to pass along.

I do know there is fighting on the Dhasdeini border and who knows how far up the Riverside. I know there was alliance with Nathyx, I know the Cataract troops reached Amberlight, but not how many went on downRiver. But the Cataract galleys did. So I presume the message to Antastes went, and the guerrillas as well.

And along with the galleys, Tez.

I had to bite my tongue to blood when I heard that, Tellurith. In Zariah's kitchen, amid a crowd of men. No place to burst out in high-ranking oaths and fulminations about the risk, the lunacy, the military disaster of risking such a hostage in the heart of affairs. In the River-lord's name, *what* does she imagine she can do?

I devoutly pray that in truth you have no word of it, Tellurith. I would not wish anyone more nightmares than the thought—purely as adviser, partisan, strategist, before we come to—lover's fears—than the thought of it gives me.

So where is she now? At Deyiko? In the battle-front? Commanding the galley-squadron? Collaborating with Nathyx? That, in itself, is more than enough to get her executed—

If we lose.

May the River-lord pity me, Tellurith. I can no longer tell what I mean by "we."

As well, perhaps, that I have no news, that I am not trusted to shape policy. That I am washed up here, a piece of, of, jetsam, with nothing to do but tramp up to the quarry for tallies when they call on me, and seek other work to keep me occupied.

Which I shall be forced to in earnest later today. When I have finished the report, here in this dank, increasingly chilly cubby-hole. With no alternative but the remnant of those cyphers I left behind.

Out-dated, irrelevant. Ancient history. Impotent, futile, forlorn, weary beyond grieving.

As I am myself.

* * *

Oh, gods. Oh *gods*.
    Oh, may the River-lord . . . No, not the River-lord. If I knew that damned stuff had power, could hear me . . . I swear, I would turn to *it* and pray.

'Out-dated. Irrelevant.' Will They never cease to mock me? Will They never cease to turn my words back, quick as a Delta fowling stick, on my fool blabbering head?

Out-dated. Ancient history. *Irrelevant!*

Tellurith. I will write it here. Before I burn this. All of it.

Your cyphers. Your cursed House-head's cyphers, your double-damned troublecrew archives . . .

I have to stop and wipe the sweat.

Your archives. They have a—a—I have just found—just unearthed—

Gods, Tellurith, hear me. Answer me. Bid your infuriating familiar pass the message, tell me what I should—how I should—

Because I have found a thing, amid your pestilential trivia, that could end the war at a stroke. That could bring Dhasdein to ruin around me.

That could, at a word, take Antastes' head.

CHAPTER XV

Below the Source
Third Winter Moon

Do you know the truly confounding thing about doubles, Tanekhet?

Not that they are you, or ought to be you, or give every sign of being your perfect replica. But that, despite everything that tells you otherwise, they are not you at all.

* * *

The very first moments taught us that; when they read our eyes, stance, every muscle of our faces, as perfectly as we had read theirs, and their own faces answered: How do you know about us?

With such an obvious, inevitable corollary, shouted so superfluously by the rising arrowheads, that I spoke as quickly as with Damas.

"We had a musician who knew very old stories. Out of Amberlight."

It did partially work; the arrowheads dipped again. And they had a human vanity. That shouted from the ensuing expressions. The heart of legends remembered *us*?

"And there were signs upRiver. Once we knew where to look.

"Nobody at Forest Landing would talk about what was past the reeds." I responded to the leader's cocked brow as she would have to mine. "It wasn't what they said, it was what they didn't say. Reed and Landing-folk both." I knew, too, I must provide extenuation. Are not the strategies of the pre-emptive strike mine and my City's both? "It was the same with the qherrique."

Did I say that by my own intent?

Whatever the wellspring, the stream's course was beyond doubt. The slitted eyes shot wide. Her answer came with the speed of simple shock.

"You *have* qherrique?"

"Don't you?"

I freely admit, I was unbalanced myself. Stress on the "you" or the "qherrique" would have been predictable, Have to Have-not, Uphill to River Quarter, whether with condescension or not. Stress on the "have" . . .

At that moment, Tanekhet, it was truly unthinkable.

We both caught ourselves back; too much had been revealed, too soon, too unsuitably, the knowledge was as plain between us as with Zhee and I. I took a half-step back. She raised a hand in the forbidding signal, eyes shuttering, just as mine would. When she said, "This is a matter for the Eharyn," I knew we had gone beyond reconnaissance probes on an open hillside; this was a case for the House.

So I was quite ready when she said, "You will come with us," on the exact border between command and question that Zuri would have used to a visiting dignitary of unknown affiliations; I inclined my head in acceptance that replied, Of course. And read the flash of irony before she began hand-signals to dispose her folk; that retorted as clearly. You, not resist effectively? With qherrique?

I am not sure how much Varis or Alkhes or Quiran read. Azo, naturally, and Deor understood. And undoubtedly, Sarth. I nodded in reply to the glances that asked, Obey? And my answer retorted, Do we want a choice?

We traversed the hill's crest, finding another game track that we read now at its true worth; in the valley before us the River waited, as it should have been. But the valley was our first mountain land.

Its plunging depths held taller, much taller timber, with the lush, lofty canopy of high wetlands, clotted and yet softer than the forest below. Open grassplots sequined at ridiculous angles over the suddenly precipitous further slope, their shimmering seed-drifts and floral embroideries highlit in the vivid noon sun. The light of rainlands, too pellucid and pure to last; and that rain was in the air, its upland bite sharpened now by damp. Up here, we knew without asking, it would rain as at Forest-landing, once a day or better, and with the extra altitude, it would hardly ever dry.

How am I to say the rest?

Beyond all that, was the sense of another country; a place set apart, as palpably as by walls and border guards, from the mundane world. Its distance, its difference, was not merely in every unknown tree, plant, sunbeam, each tiny, new-found detail. It was in the very air.

The others felt it too. Deor checked at the hillbrow. Quiran stopped on one foot and half-drew back; an instant later Alkhes swung round and I read his expression, born of the same reflex as Quiran's. *Tellurith, this is a holy place.*

And Iskarda had taught them holy places were not for men.

The rest had baulked too. Azo turned, her look asking us both, Is it right for strangers to enter here?

The leader read it all. With some approval, it was evident. She nodded to Azo. Go on.

Silent, as behoves those admitted to a sanctuary, we started down the mountainside.

Between the slots of tree-root the path was just short of outright mud. Dampness breathed from the shadowed, all but frigid air. Birds called, undisturbed by the passage of human beings; in an occasional vista I caught, above the shining shields of grass, twists of distant smoke.

We had moved into single file. As we emerged into the grateful sun, the shimmer and suddenly brilliant plants of the lowest clearing, a true water-meadow, the leader lifted a hand, and as the line checked, she said, "Ihar, conduct the men."

They were so like us; I had forgotten the mirror was Amberlight. Not Iskarda.

She read my stance. Clearer, she read the startlement in Quiran and Herar's faces; the shock, the disbelief, the dawning outrage, then the sudden, appalled incredulity in Alkhes' stare.

He had never doubted I would speak out for them, as I had done with Darthis in Iskarda. He read my hesitation as clearly as Sarth. Before it had gone more than a heartbeat too long, he understood.

I looked away, because I could not bear to meet his eyes. I looked at Sarth instead.

Whose look cut the deeper because it lacked everything in Alkhes'. Tower inscrutability, that said he had been wounded, been betrayed too often. To him, it was no surprise at all.

I ought to have explained, Tanekhet. It was circumstance, it was policy, the situation was the reverse of Iskarda. These were our hosts, and not our vassals. We were destitute, without vantage except the light-guns, and that was a threat impossible to risk. And we had no right to change their customs. We were not there to stay.

Such a small choice, Tanekhet. Did I not write to you before, about tiny crossroads never expected, that turn the pattern of your life?

She had read their eyes as clearly as I. Her brows rose a fraction. She answered my look as to a visiting peer.

"This is Thilliansar. The Mother's cradle. Our men and women live apart."

As you did, the tone said clearly. As every legend tells you did, in Amberlight.

I could have said it, still; Amberlight is gone. Our ways are different now. I could have made it an issue, could have enforced it, appealed to guest-right.

Made trouble and uproar, and who knows how it might have ended. They might have resisted. They might have expelled us. It might have come to bloodshed and worse. It might have destroyed, at its moment of fruition, not only us, but the Quest.

And none of that could be said; I could only give Azo the troublecrew Stand-down, the tiny upward jerk of the chin that says most flatly, No. I did hope to my heart's core that my men, at least, would understand all it implied, and later, tell the other two. But I could not bring myself to look at them before I glanced back at—her—and said, quietly, calmly, "As your customs bid."

* * *

They went with Ihar, quietly. Mannerly, as Sarth would, not to shame us, were they leading him to execution on the spot. It was only Alkhes' eyes I had to evade; but as they moved away, I felt that one glance clear to the heart.

She must have picked up most of it. When we approached the Riverside, as we stepped up onto the little stone bridge across its narrow, crystal, foam-garlanded depths; as the riverine foliage released us on a span of cultivation whose tall corn and unknown mountain plants reached toward a feathery brown suggestion of high-roofed thatch. As we climbed again, the meadows opening above us, she offered a placation. She began, carefully as ever, to explain the ways of her folk.

It is like, but not quite like Amberlight. There is no Uphill and Downhill; all men and women live apart, and the trades are not restricted but shared. The men take the valleys, where they plough and cultivate for everyone, the women live on the heights and hunt. Women are the weapon-smiths, men make the ploughs and hoes. Women shepherd and shear, men spin and weave. Women work in wood, men make the pots. Children are conceived at the twice-yearly festivals. They live with their mothers until they are five, then the boys come downhill to the men. A mother is one and known; a father is every man among the folk.

But women are the harpists and song-makers, the lore-keepers, the Mother's servers; at the heights of power, Amberlight was no different.

So I had some idea what to expect, when the game-track thickened to a fair graveled path, and with one last heave over a spur-back, brought us into the women's place.

Small, was my first thought; smaller than Iskarda before we came. A palms-width of level valley between two sheltering spurs, with a little waterfall cascading behind into a natural pool, and out under another small but shapely stone bridge. The houses fanned around the spur-feet, leaving the centre open, with a cluster of trees about the bridge, and a stone paving that spoke of market and assembly in their shade. Most of the ground was paved, or graveled, and there were gutter channels everywhere.

The houses spoke wet highlands too. Wooden houses, unpainted but stained with some sort of varnish to mahogany, chestnut, shining, gold-streaked browns, on walls of simple but beautifully mortised planks, with high-peaked shingle roofs, with austere decoration; finials at the roof peaks, faces on the gutter ends. Chairs, fine but not ornately decorated, on the wide-eaved porches above shapely stone steps. Worn steps. Old steps, speaking a place long established, with the grace, the patina of age. The whole settlement was eloquent of that; long planning, careful but not rigid organization, the beauty distilled from undisturbed, elegant and harmonious thought.

The folk were restrained and beautiful as their place. I cannot count the variations their clothes make on ochre, fawn, dappled, clotted, striped and patterned browns that play so subtly against the colors of their wood. A little after noon, the craft-folk were leaving work, the hunters coming home. The central space was alive with streams of meeting, greeting, arrangement, lightly exchanged talk. Laughter too. And children, flying like loom-shuttles amid squeals and higher laughter, threading the traffic everywhere.

No. Not traffic. The dance of life's contentment, of folk who, dwelling in a land enchanted, know the price and the value of their felicity, and are quietly, unshakably gay.

Even our advent could not destroy that. They looked, yes, from all sides; they broke off conversations, or stood still, and more than one Crafter dropped a hand easily to the hilt of the broad knife at every belt. Some traded glances or signs with our escort-leader, and the consequences ran out through the crowd. But however swiftly the signals traveled, those who bore them moved with unruffled grace.

They took us to the bridge-grove, as you might expect. The Eharyn were close behind, as you also might expect, materializing from clumps of conversation, from work-place and forest-edge, trickling in across every path that netted the centre-ground. Older women, as you might again expect, with the aura of decision and authority in every quiet, composed stare. The Ruands, yes. The Heads.

And again, it was like, yet unlike Amberlight. Because they were Heads, yes; but not House-heads. There was none of that fraught, waiting sense of rival powers, leashed for a greater need, but perpetually charged and trembling to explode. Thilliansar is neither a City nor a House. It is a folk. They were the Eharyn, the folk's Council. Nothing more.

The other thing was entirely different. Heads, yes, Craftheads, certainly; smith and hunter, physician and wood-carver, harpist and priestess. But not cutters and shapers and engravers and polishers, not the folk of Shaping and Powershops. Not Crafts as it was meant in Amberlight.

Can I make you understand how that felt, Tanekhet? The steadily creeping, strengthening chill in the belly, as they came in, one by one, all with the mirror-true Amberlight faces, bones, eyes hair, their trades written in gear or hands or stance. And not one with a cutter or shaper. Not one with the telltale, unmistakable gray dust upon her clothes, ingrained in her fingers, let be the scars that the youngest Crafter's prentice wears.

Almost as in Amberlight, the council headship cycles from Craft to Craft. By the moon, as we did. I realized that as the priestess, identifiable only by the small but exquisite silver crescent in her ear, fished an ivory rod from her sleeve and nodded to the hunter. Who set her bow against a tree, slid onto the polished boulder that made the Head's seat, and as the rest eased down on copings and wooden benches, as our escort settled us with a host's courtesy, touched the tree beside her thrice with the rod. Inclined her head to us, and said, "Errissal?"

Which was how I learnt our escort's name.

An opening succinct and wary as ours might have been. No welcome, or otherwise, until she heard from her out-guard what we might portend.

Errissal's account was troublecrew succinct too. Including where we met, what we said we were, our full numbers. But nothing about the qherrique.

I caught Azo's eye. Its glance, iron-faced as Zuri's, agreed, Evidently, Amberlight tells them enough.

The hunter turned back to us. Began, with Amberlight's courtesy, by asking all our names.

Yes, you will see it already. Azo, Deor, simplicity itself. Varris?

It eases me to remember that still, I was magnanimous. "This is Varris," I said, "from the Heartlands. Who is pledged among our company. By thalan."

No doubt that they understood the word; from the minute rise of the hunter's brow, it was a matter for some respect. She gave Varris a special inclination, before she opened the main advance.

"Tellurith. We are honored by your company." But not welcome. Not yet. "May we know what brings you here?"

Straight to the point, as you would with a stranger, a possibly kin, perhaps allied stranger, in Amberlight. No perilous flowery promises. No threats either; for us both, the message of those bows would be enough.

I opened my lips. And as if we were truly back in Amberlight, something ordered, Wait.

"Ruand," I said. "I would willingly tell you all we know. But first, as is the custom of our company, we must consult."

Her eyes narrowed a fraction. I said, "As we did in Amberlight."

She knew what *that* meant. If a hope remained that we would find what we expected, it died then. At the tiny flicker of hope in her own eyes.

"What will you need of us?"

"We would need a quiet place. Not necessarily holy, but apart. And," I managed not to pause, "it needs all of us."

She started to wave me on, graciously, of course, the four of you are nothing—she understood, checked.

"Yes," I said. "A place where we could take the men."

I saw the shock, that time. A thread of scandal, rigorously suppressed. Then she said softly, pronouncing the word with the care of unfamiliarity, "Iskarda."

Whatever else they missed, they had heard the stories. They knew of the fall, and the successor to Amberlight.

It was no time to ask, What else? I stood up, bowing deeply to show my gratitude, my respect. And Azo, rising at my elbow, shivered as she moved. Involuntary, inevitable. We had climbed high, but we had not shed the fever, and its fresh onset always began around noon.

The Ruand's eyes focused. She said abruptly, "You have traveled far, through peril and hardship we never met." The Mother knows, that was clear enough. "Your folk are out of health, perhaps." She read my expression and gave its gratitude a courteous acknowledgement. "Need this meeting be at once? Thilliansar has supplies enough. And," a slight smile at the wiry woman who had settled at her own elbow, "physicians as well."

"Ruand." I could not help the sigh. If they pitched us out this evening, so long as they gave us supplies, and some advice if not physic itself, we could survive. Then I remembered. "Ruand . . . for all of us?"

Her own nature glinted through the quirk of a brow, the flitting grin. "Everybody knows the men hide the best shirts under the loom-frames. And their healers are almost the match of ours."

* * *

They gave us gear, yes, all we could have asked for; once the Eharyn ruled us welcome, it came without stint. They took us willingly into their houses. At least, into Atha the hunter's house, since they knew, as we would, how separation would seem a threat.

And again, there was an uncanny echo, only this time, of Iskarda. In the cellar, storerooms, fireplaces and heating vents, the kitchen's nerve-centre, knotted in a nest of suites, inhabited by a cluster of kin; grandmothers, sister-mothers, aunts, nieces, daughters, cousins to the third degree. All the women who will one day overflow an Iskardan house like Zariah or Charras's.

Or mine.

But always, that gaping divergence. The emptiness that should have held the men.

It ached, Tanekhet. All that afternoon, settling into the room they cleared for us, with the blessed solace of cleanliness and whole garments and knowing ourselves welcomed somewhere at last, there was a gap beside me, a waiting silence, a bond calling to be rejoined.

Their physician Teah had never dealt with the reed fever, but she knew its repute, and the mountains offer a plenitude of herbs. She dosed my three on the spot and promised me that downhill, one Xhias would be doing the same for our men. They fed us bread ground from the dried fruit of some upland plant, sheep cheese, hairy green-hearted fruit, sweeter than joyful astonishment, that I never saw before.

* * *

We are making good time; a week, and Forest-landing is so far behind us, they are already saying ten days should see us to second cataract. There have been no storms, no adverse gales. No mishaps. Our very path seems charmed.

But can we make it fast enough?

I do assure you, Tanekhet, with every fiber of our conscious minds and wills, every one of us is trying.

And it is so good to have them back. Safe. Keraz, and Esrafal and Chenath. To see bonds re-made, and couples whole again. . .

I had to go away and cry there. What matter to admit it, here, where no-one will ever read? Just as I can admit I am squandering papyrus as well as time. How the smallest, most irrelevant thing can rip the just-formed intimation of a scab from the wound.

* * *

But again, Thilliansar; our meeting-place was halfway down the mountain, reached by a tiny side-trail, nestled into a boulder-knob above the stream. Exquisitely framed in portals of jewel-bright mountain-orchids, zenith-sapphire, sun-gold, amethyst. Floored in dry rock, roofed in mammoth boulders, civilized with thick felt rugs and a couple of passable sheep-skins. Just big enough for the eight of us, since it was usually meant for two.

In that too Thilliansar is like and unlike Amberlight; the women take partners, as we do, but unlike us, it is only among your nearer cohorts. Not over ten years apart. Unlike Amberlight again, partnerships are also recognized among the men. Except they have no age-bars; the younger partner must simply be over puberty.

And for those on both sides for whom partnerships are not enough, there is freedom to meet, to make love and be together. But not in the settlements.

And not to make a child, unless it be at festival.

There have been exceptions? Naturally. You know there are always exceptions. The foothills are free to those who must join their lives completely, or die in the attempt. There is no penalty, except loss of home and folk. For most, a few years of that have been enough.

There are no stories of star-crossed couples, of misbegotten children and endemic blood-feuds and vengeance from kin or folk. Perhaps they never happen, perhaps they have been obliterated. Somehow, I doubt it. Perhaps the lack of fuss about it is their very strength. Or perhaps they know, perhaps they always know, down to their marrow-bones, that what they have may be enchanted, but it is also precarious. Rare, precious, fragile. Something that, when it asks the ultimate loyalty, has always invoked that knowledge.

And when the ultimate choice came, its folk have always answered, Yes.

* * *

I think I can write this. If I am very careful, I can write it without spewing a heart-load of bile and gall and protestation. If I cannot excise protest, I can manage the way it is given vent.

* * *

They gave us directions to the cave and added, at last with a touch of levity, that we would evict nobody that night. They passed the message, by a pair of ear-rattlingly loud hand-drums. By moonrise, our escort—she—*Errissal* said, the men would be on their way up.

It was one of those freakish nights when the moon is clear before the sun ever sets; when we met at the track-mouth, in ruddy gloaming where the moon sailed like a curved qherrique boat, it was light enough to read a face.

How shall I write, now, with composure, that it filled me with jealous joy because Alkhes' eyes sought me first?

The men too were clean, properly if oddly dressed, the same browns and dappled fawns we wore, with trousers instead of leggings, just as in Amberlight. And like Azo and Deor, they wore that air of relief that comes in constant pain's aftermath.

We moved inside, worked out where to set the pair of candle-lamps, in something less like relief than adolescent awkwardness. Almost, it might have been a youthful lovers' tryst. But in those days, only one partner had filled my thoughts.

He settled beside me as he always did; and as always when we re-encountered, the sense of him there was a bulwark regained, a home-coming, a sweet relief.

I must stop this, before I wash the papyrus clear away.

We talked a little; reassurance, comparing notes. Then before the tension could build I slipped the seed into my palm, and held it out to Sarth.

The slanting lamplight showed me his eyes, darkened to ovals of old bronze, and what their expression meant. He said, "Are you sure, Tellurith?"

He had said nothing at the division on the bridge. Nothing when we met. He always had a general's timing. But I knew it was not malice now.

I said, "You are our Ear. I have one question for you. How much should we say?"

He understood that too. All of it. It was in the poise of his shoulders, as he laid the seed amidst us and held out his hands.

The glow came immediately. Impatience, one might almost think. Sarth gazed into it as into that fire outside Cataract.

Then he said, "Should we tell everything?"

I do not think it was the oracle. I think it was only Sarth. Only his philosopher's mind and his troublecrew sense of risk, and his tower training in sheer effrontery; and the rest, that is pure Sarth. That reasoned, to ask, How much, will only cause difficulty. Begin with the most unlikely, and reason back.

Not even he could have expected that reply. So unhesitating, so fast.

And not the usual image. This one was vivid, searingly vivid, riding on a sense of pent breath and heart blocking the throat. A moment of complete, terrifying commitment. A wall of Heartland tapestries and weapon trophies, framing Wonsa's face.

The reactions you can predict; all of them, from Alkhes down. But it was Sarth, finally, who held his hands out, whose look told me as clearly as words had explained his question, We must be sure. And who once again overthrew my expectations.

Because he asked, not, Are you sure? But, "Why?"

That brought pause enough. A long, gathering pause.

What came next was not a coherent snatch of image, however oracular. This was a mosaic, a badly-sewn tapestry; a jerking train of fragmented pictures, each one bearing its own word.

"They know . . ." Zuri. Somewhere, the light said, in Cataract. "The Source," Esrafal, remote in my Iskardan kitchen, off-hand as only Esrafal could be at such a moment. A pause. "We," Alkhes' face, under a net of sunset river boughs, "have to," Keraz, against a Forest-landing wall, "trust."

Zuri again. A long time ago, back in Iskarda. By the clench of Sarth's hand about my fingers, I had a good idea what trust she had meant.

The last words came with a jerk atop that. My face, in the Iskarda council-room, seen through a blur of anger, furious shock. "If not for them, do it for me!"

I can remember how carefully Sarth released my fingers. The strained note, so startlingly clear in his voice, the quotation marked with conscious irony, as he said, "Do we have a choice?"

* * *

So next morning, we, *I*, told Thilliansar everything.

Alkhes would have disputed the men's omission. I read it in every line of him as I put the seed away, as we prepared to rise. I saw his mouth open, the all too visible glower. Before Sarth reached behind me to take his wrist and say, so softly, "Let it go, Aglis."

I tried not to remember that as I spoke to Thilliansar. I concentrated on the words; on the effort, so against the grain of everything driven into me lifelong; never, never tell everything. Not to your closest friend.

But after a while, it was their faces that, for all their stillness, spoke.

When the tale was complete, I waited a moment. Before I said, "How much did you know?"

Atha looked at the priestess. Who answered, quietly as I. "We had a seer."

Kythara. A dream-seer, the truest sight they know. Dead now, ancient then; four years ago, when she wakened weeping, screaming, from the dream of a city crumpled like paper under a lightning-shot pall of dust. Crying, "Amberlight!"

After a while I asked, "Did you know what she meant?"

The priestess, Pryax, gave me a question in answer. "Do you know who we are?"

At my expression, ever so slightly, she smiled. "Yes. You are the children of Amanazar. We are those she left behind."

Kin, Tanekhet, yes. All the stories Esrafal remembers say it. Amberlight folk came downRiver, to find the qherrique and settle on the hillside, forsaking their nomad life. We had always assumed, in our arrogance, that all of them came.

For a hundred years or so they still traveled downRiver; at the first, the oldest market, outside what was once Dead Dyke canal, the sundered folk still met. But then the wars began. And we learnt to use the qherrique.

The first sack came from upRiver, cutting us off. The link broke forever when Amberlight built the first city wall, a hundred and ten years beyond. After that, as Amberlight strengthened, they had to look to saving themselves.

They told us the story I know from the other side, the assaults and invasions and the one and only sack. The River coalitions, Dhasdein's predecessor, Cataract's ancestors, Verrain's foundation, four hundred years ago. And probes into the Heartlands, that drove them back along what was once our common five-year grazing road, clear to the River's Head.

Until they withdrew to the mountains permanently; until four hundred years ago, their ancestors planted the reeds.

That barrier took a long time to rise; to become part of the landscape, to evolve its inhabitants, and finally, to drop the bar of silence that protected Forest-landing and the Heartlands, as much as our kin.

Because if word had traveled downRiver, the Sink-folk, as they say, like the Heartlanders, would have scorched them all.

Just to learn if our other selves had qherrique too.

When Pryax finished there was a long silence in the brightly dappled morning shade. People talked or called in the settlement, birds whistled, the wind soughed, as it does perpetually, in the boughs over my head. I looked down the mountain the way you can at Iskarda, out over the great rug of sun-dappled lowlands to the green horizon smudge. I remember thinking, irrelevantly, that it explained the lack of trade-goods. That in all we saw, from knives to plait bands, there was nothing from downRiver. If there were imports, we did not recognize them.

"You saw us coming," Azo said.

Pryax lifted her shoulders. "We were . . . concerned."

Four years had quieted the consternation, the uprooted shock of a world without Amberlight, wakening caution instead. They had sent outliers, not to contact the Reed-folk, but to listen near their camps. So they knew the fall was truth.

And like the rest of the Heartlands, they had heard about the Quest.

But still they waited, as we would in Amberlight. However divided, however guilty of their exile, we were their blood. They did not judge; they waited, to see what the Mother would say.

And She spoke to them. From Amberlight. From Cataract. From the Heartlands itself.

"So we said, 'If the Mother leads them through, we will not send them away'."

They had watched the reed-margins, sent out continual patrols. They have kept the warriors' nature, honed by occasional raiders over the ranges, by the River's never-dispelled threat. And in time, their patience was repaid.

Silence came again, then. A silence in which I felt the heart beat up, harder and harder, into my throat.

I looked at Deor, tense as a steerswoman with a rapid in sight. At Azo, who was watching me, mouth set like a trap. At Varris, even Varris, wearing her warrior's mask.

I looked back to Pryax and said, "Do you know the Source?"

They must have known what their complete lack of any Crafter, any light-tool meant, for us, for the Quest. Their faces showed only comprehension, and perhaps, an all too eloquent tinge of regret. Pryax turned both hands out, the ancient gesture of resignation to the Mother's will.

"We can take you there," she said.

Azo caught my eye. I too spoke quietly, but Pryax knew what it meant, when I said, "All of us."

* * *

It was a two-day trek, up into the high ranges, the deep mountain forests, through perpetual chill, all but unbroken rain. They gave us warm gear, and some of their oiled goat's-wool cloaks. We carried provisions, because the high valleys are sacred to the Mother; one does not hunt. And they gave us guides. Pryax, the Mother's Voice. Atha, who knew the country.

And Errissal.

A priestess' daughter, she had been a novice herself; a trained hunter, for reinforcement, and with us, she had a vested interest.

It was long, straining trip. I thought my thigh muscles would snap before Atha halted that second evening, halfway up yet another horrendous ascent; wiped away sweat and raindrops; and gestured along the hillside, murmuring, "We always go up at dawn."

We were buried in a valley so deep the timber shut out all but leaking drops, an occasional draft, the roar of great boughs overhead. The forests are a wonderful place; plants grow there three times downhill size, the aisles wind through veils of lichen, yellower than saffron flower, or are floored in miles of crimson moss, like pools of undying blood. And there are animals I never saw or heard before. But we were past admiring all that. We trooped after Atha into yet another stone-built shelter, too weary so much as to think about what tomorrow would bring.

That it was all about to reach its climax. That in one way or another, we had reached the end of the Quest.

* * *

I woke with a jump in ember-studded darkness, to a hand shaking my arm. To Errissal's now familiar voice murmuring, "It's time."

The others were afoot already. Someone had shaken up the coals, but only for light. We would not break our fast, they told us, until we came back.

Until we had reached the Source.

How shall I describe that, Tanekhet? Groping in the dark, the bleak, pre-dawn hush, up that last stretch of path? With the sky paling over our left shoulders and the quarter moon hung, as we had seen it so often, over the ridge-top, silver-cut amid the velvet hems of dark. But with flesh and blood around me, real muscles bearing me forward, real rock and mud under my feet. The light strengthening, the stillness yielding, the first animal sounds. And then the rise's crest.

They were there; as I had seen them so often, they were there as my head came up, snow-dust and opal-mist, hovering in the murky zone between moon and dawn. Teeth, spearheads, cusps of distilled ice. Mountains, snow mountains, whiter than white's imagining, under the curve of sinking moon.

Beside me I heard Sarth straighten and sigh. I heard his voice as it described what my eyes had seen, that very first time.

The lake was bowered deep in forest, small, but broad enough to catch the dawn; that counter-flush was already over our right shoulders, pale apricot, morning gold. And as in the dream, I knew we were both going to turn around.

The plains were there, past Alkhes', Azo's, Varris' heads. Enormously distant, wide as infinity, and as happens in some high places, the foothills, the swamp, were out of sight. What I saw was Heartland savannah, far downRiver, flat and tawny, dense-textured as a wet lion's hide.

The trees were there too. Packed on the hillside, serried ranks of canopy dropping into the depths. We could hear the crackle of boughs, the distant animal whoops. And the dewdrops sparkled on their leaf-rims, huge as diamonds, above the orchids, midnight purple, nested under the outer leaves.

And the scent was there.

It was quiet, quieter than any dream, as if we had entered a place untrodden since the making of the world. But the dawn-waft drew across us and I caught it, deep forest loam, and mushrooms, and a world of growing plants; and the tang of cinnamon, that grows in no forest Riverfolk know.

We turned again, all of us, as if still in the dream, and began to walk toward the lake.

There was a path under the forest eaves. Tinier than a tree-climber's plat, probably not human at all. It took us round the lake-rim, just above the luxuriant growth that hid the edge.

The light had widened, its gold and apricot deepening smoothly across an all but cloudless sky. The lake breathed to the dawn wind, the faintest of ruffles in its ice-pale jade whose verges, under the tree-mirrors, became jagged malachite. And there was the little turbulence, the bubble of water among the reed stems, the great clump rising, high, high sweet Mother, ten, twelve feet to the globe of spikes at their rustling tips. With the flowers among them, pale cream and daffodil. And the spring at their feet.

* * *

The water flowed, the light spread. The snows went from ghost pale to silver to sapphire and amethyst and back to daylit white. Downhill the tree-climbers called as they forged away. And still none of us had moved.

It was Alkhes who did it at the last. Soldier and fighter, bred to decisiveness. Who went forward to the water-rim; stared among the reeds, pushed a toe into the grass; patrolled with the lithe, lethal movements of danger past the spring-head, along the further shoreline. Sortied into the timber. Came, still with that poised, perilous motion, back to us.

Before he said, so very quietly, "There's nothing here."

I heard myself answer, infinitely remote. "No."

He looked at Pryax then. Who bent her head, and gave him the faintest, saddest of smiles.

He said, "You knew."

She said, "We hoped."

His eyes dilated. In that shadowless morning they were blacker than breathing dark. His nostrils dilated too. For a moment I thought he would burst out, fly at her. But he was Alkhes.

"Hoped what? It would jump out of the ground for us and you'd have what you never turned a hand to get? What were you going to do with *us*?"

Even Pryax half recoiled. Azo's mouth snapped open, Atha and Errissal shot to danger stance. I took three quick steps and got my hands against his chest. "Caissyl, no!"

I felt every muscle leap with killer's reflex, and block. I had done the stupidest thing you can with trained troublecrew, and it was only because we were both what we are that I survived.

"No what, Tellurith?" His eyes blazed into mine, his breath was hot as a leopard's on my cheek. "How many thousand miles did we travel here? How much did we go through, how many people did we lose, how many people did we *kill*?" The memory caught him, a slashed muscle whose scar will always pinch. He choked and grabbed my shoulders. "What did we have to—and you tell me, *No?*"

I caught him round the ribs. Restraint, support. For us both. "Not them, caissyl, it's not them. Wait!"

"Wait?" A killer's purr in earnest now, dropping into the lethal, focused trance; I shook him and shouted, "No!" Tore the seed from under cloak and shirt and thrust wide both my arms.

Sarth grabbed my right hand; I snatched Alkhes with the left, and praise the Mother, he came. As Varris seized his own left hand I saw Azo beyond Sarth catch at Errissal, and Deor snatch Atha, and Quiran, one hand in Varris's, pull at Pryax herself.

Herar, isolated between them, reached, perforce, for both strangers' hands. On the narrow band of greensward the deformed circle shut.

Sarth's eyes were burning too. But when I opened my hand on the seed, he spoke quite quietly, with that edge only Sarth can achieve.

"Can you hear us now?"

No song, no. None of us could have managed it. Strangers in the circle, yes; none of us cared. Perhaps it knew that. For instantly, the seed began to glow.

Sarth composed himself. Effort palpable as a dam's building. Settled his grasp on our hands, and said one word.

"Why?"

The picture came as instantly. I felt Atha and Pryax jerk, but we needed only the first glimpse.

You in the Iskardan council-chamber, Tanekhet. Rehearsing, yet again, the reasons we must find the Source.

I heard Sarth breathe through his teeth. The edge had become ice.

"You brought us here. You made us . . . what we are. You owe us an explanation. *Why?*"

No answer. Sarth's jaw went rigid and I grabbed his hand as if he meant physical threat.

"If you baulk now—"

An all too familiar searing flash.

Picking myself from the grass, wiping stars away, praying, despite my own rage and abandonment, that he would not try again, I felt a strange hand snatch at me. Errissal shouted, "Wait!"

"That was a message?" She caught my other arm, holding me face to face, as agitated as us. "It spoke?" I managed to nod. "Then why was it not an answer?"

"It's an old message. It's something we've all seen. Most of us were there—"

"Then what does it say!" She gripped my arms and shook me. "Why does it keep telling you? Think!"

And I heard Keraz in that ring of trees outside Cataract: Which of its words have we not understood?

I grabbed Sarth for myself and shouted in his face, "Why's it telling us? Think!"

Silence then, the hush of an arrested storm, the ten of us propped like scarecrows on a stick. While Sarth slowly, slowly, rubbed both hands up his cheeks, over his forehead. Palming off sweat. Wiping clear that dispassionate, philosopher's vision, once again doing what I asked of him. Trying, amid his own demolition, to transform the ruin of our world.

The wind breathed. I let my lungs work. Saw Varris change stance, and re-stop her breath. Felt the tremor in my own muscles, that I could see in Alkhes'.

Sarth shifted. His eyes came back to me. Dispassionate still, but focused now, the edge of intellect, that slices hairs no sword will touch.

"Tellurith," he said, "if there had been qherrique here . . . what would we have done?"

Weapons. Communication. Surety. Defense. It must have shouted from my very flesh.

"We would have used it. Yes. We would have saved, protected Iskarda."

I let my eyes say, Go on.

"But to save Iskarda . . . what would we have to do?"

I opened my mouth and it hit me, more blinding than any qherrique bolt.

Alkhes was not a breath behind; I heard him gasp, heard him strangle the yell. Without looking Sarth put a hand out, gripped him by the neck and shook him, as if to silence a beloved child.

I licked my stiffened lips. The words came shakily, staggering under vision's weight.

"We would have had to reach, an, an understanding; with Amberlight."

Sarth looked back at me. Silent as judgment, beautiful as a gods' messenger, the color of the distant plains and morning, with his bronze-mahogany hair, unplaited, streaming over the shoulder of the dun-colored cloak.

Very quietly, I said, "And we have."

He did not have to nod.

"We would have had to fight. Or make truce, but probably fight, Cataract."

Those eyes, tawny as a lion's, answered mine: *And we have.*

"And deal, somehow, with Verrain."

Azo gasped and twitched. I put my hand on her shoulder too, and kept my eyes on Sarth's.

"And," he said softly, "someone has."

The others were catching up. I heard the rustle run, the stifled gasps.

"We would have," I said, "to re-arrange the Riverworld."

Sarth shifted his shoulders; looked at the seed that was somehow back in the palm of my hand, and murmured, into the ringing hush, "And that is already done."

It was Alkhes who went on at last. A little thickly, as if he could not catch his breath.

"We didn't have to find anything. We just had to have the Quest."

Azo said the next part; quaky as my legs felt.

"They did it themselves. Because they *thought* . . . just like Shuya. With Tanekhet."

My legs gave. I sat down on the grass, thump. Staring out, as our kin must have, on a re-ordered world.

There was nothing here; there never had been. There had only been the desperate necessity that you understood, Tanekhet. To get us and the qherrique out of capture-distance, to shield our absolute vulnerability, and make the great ones of our world imagine we were a power. And let them, in that imagination, destroy themselves.

It was Quiran who went on. Sounding as dazed as the rest of us.

"It's over. We've done it. We've finished the Quest."

* * *

There was sun on my face, palpable sunlight, the next time I remember someone spoke.

"And . . . now. What do we do now?"

I had not assembled a reply. I, the House-head, the ever-resourceful, the ultimate organizer, had not brought my mind from the past that had dropped round us like a collapsed door. It was Atha who responded, a tone struggling for calm and achieving a half-hysteric cheerfulness.

"Breakfast. That's what *I'm* doing now."

* * *

Blessed mundanity, savior of all cataclysms. Only, as we trooped down the trackway, as the talk began, if just of the moment's trivia, my brain did start to work.

One earthquake you can assimilate. Though it fells, at a stroke, everything that has comprised your earth. Two, possibly. But three, and four?

I spoke, I know, and possibly arbitrated little things, one cup of tea or two, rest now or later for the fever, put the fire out? Not yet, I must have replied. Because I am sitting on the edge of the broad stone platform, with its welcome subterranean warmth, staring vacantly out where Errissal and Atha debate the distance of the rain that announces itself with every thickening of the down-valley light. When Sarth sits down beside me and says, Sarth-quietly, "What is it, Tellurith?"

One pebble, to release an avalanche.

It all fell on me together. The aftermath of ending, the weight of disappointment, the emptiness of closing such a chapter in a life. All the burden of the past. And the future with it; now I could not evade the vision, the unthinkable vision that was dawning beyond.

I buried my face in his jacket-sleeve like the stupidest Downhill boy-child gagged by his distress.

I felt his muscles leap, I all but felt the jerk of his heart. He threw his arm around me. In the dark of his warmth and alarm I heard the other quick, too-familiar step, felt the second arm at my back, Alkhes' equally panicked, "Tel?"

Only conceive how intensely they must have been aware of me. How absolutely and continuously sensitive they must have been to my every look, movement, breath. Guardians? Lovers? Nearer a second self.

"Tel, it isn't—are you all right?"

I knew what he meant then. I managed to shake my head and get out, into Sarth's sleeve, "The child's safe."

Why I did not say 'children,' who can say? The Mother knows, beyond the usual concerns of carrying, I had hardly thought about them since we reached the hills. I still had my balance, there was no morning sickness, after the journey my clothes still fitted. And there had been too much else.

I sat up. My eyes were dry. I looked between them into the graylit doorway, just as Errissal came with her long, elastic hunter's step round the jamb. Met my eyes, and with my own intuition for a sensitive moment, glanced away to Pryax, and jerked a head. Outside.

So we were left among our own folk.

It was Alkhes who said it for me. Rising to his feet, all warrior, all Outland general and too-shrewd strategist.

"Tel," too quietly, "what do we do now?"

I blinked up at him. Sarth also knew too much. He left me to answer; to spell out what he already saw for himself.

"I suppose, we go home," I said.

Alkhes took two paces to my left. Four paces back. Swung round, those black eyes pinning me like an obsidian lance.

"Home. Iskarda. With—that." His gesture meant the seed, for all it was directed at my breast.

"How long, Tel, before it's any use?"

My lips shaped the wholly superfluous, What?

His eyes hardened, black now as adamant. "We have to plant it, or something; don't we? At Iskarda? How long then, before it grows? Before it's big enough to use?"

This time I did not say anything at all.

The eyes, already searing as black embers, opened wide. "I know what you said to Antastes. No enslavement. Ever again. But Tel, if we don't use it—how do we survive?"

I could not reply; he stared into my eyes and spoke it all out for me, the vision waiting across the ashen threshold of that future world.

"You know as well as I do what that little turd said. 'Just wait till the cutters are gone. Just wait till we'—Tel, if we don't have qherrique, what can you—what can women do?"

'You.' Have you seen a mansion fall, Tanekhet, from one tiny breach in the wall? One little, little, inconsequential split?

When I stared he threw his hands in the air and it burst from him in a distress equal to mine.

"We'll have no tools, no weapons, let alone anything to ask a message from. Tel, we can change the River without qherrique. But we can't keep Iskarda!"

Not as I had dreamt. Not as I had wanted. What we all wanted, Tanekhet. You as well.

"Without qherrique . . . the Outlanders won't need to conquer us. Inside ten years, we'll be just like Dhasdein."

He did not shout this time; he whispered. My deadly little Outlander, who woke the blast that threw down a matriarchal tyranny. And was looking, all but in tears, at its reversal. At an Iskarda reduced to the slavery of women that went on in his renounced world.

I felt Sarth's body flinch. Not merely the muscles, but gut-deep, inside. I stared back into my seer's vision, and I could find no reply.

Alkhes went down on his knees in front of me and caught me by both hands. "Tel, for the Gods' sake, talk to me! Answer me! What are we going to do?"

There was a ringing in my ears, as after you are hit by qherrique, or the roof comes down, in the mine. After all, some reflex, some scrap of House-head remained. I heard myself answer, blurrily, "I have to think, Alkhes."

* * *

In Amberlight I could have found some House corner. In Iskarda I would have taken to the hills. Going back to Thilliansar I could only mask myself in the journey's single file, and pretend fatigue.

But by evening I could bear it no longer; I slid out of the shelter, with a look to Sarth that said, Latrine, and clambered amid the tangle of vines and fallen timber up the hill.

As usual, the shelter was halfway down, stone-built, with a central sunken fireplace to warm the floor, solid amid the chill, dripping entanglement outside. I found a rock though, thrusting through crimson moss like the carpet of a battlefield. I sat down, hunched my back into the wind, and waited for something, the qherrique, the Mother, anything, to answer me.

Nothing did.

I do not mean I could not think rationally, Tanekhet. How often have I encountered that? True thoughts never begin there in any case. I mean that when I threw my mind open, dropped the conscious questions, reached out into nothing as I would once with the qherrique, waited for the inspiration . . .

I could not reach my other mind, the Mother's lightning, whatever you like to say. Could not let the patterns melt and wait for the new shape to assemble. My mind would not be still.

I might have sat there all night, in desperation, in panic, in blank despair. Except for that rustle down the hillside; and the casual, "Tellurith?"

She came out of the vines at the precise moment that was neither encroachment nor coercing delay. Slid onto the rock next to me. We are of a height. Her shoulder was a couple of inches below mine. She settled, staring out with me into the closing night.

Presently she said, "During my initiate, I used to come up here. Because my third aunt said, When it rains, you can hear the frogs at choir."

The best I could do was, "Eh?"

"They sing. She said." The undercurrent of amusement agreed, Yes, ludicrous. Nursery-talk. Bear with me. It has a point.

I took a breath clear to my lungs' depth. Frigid air, dripping vegetation; the forest's body-scent, cleaner than living ice. Surgery. Cautery. Escape.

I said "Sing what?"

"In a choir, just like we do. Sopranos up top." She lifted her voice an octave and shrilled into the night with the monotony of a repeated phrase on a flute. "*More rain, more rain, more rain . . .*" Came back to normal as she spoke. "The altos are next. *Up to your neck, up to your neck, up to your neck . . .* The men do the lower parts. Baritones.." Down the range again, and in a light male voice she sang, "*Can't swim, can't swim, can't swim . . .*" A pause. "Deepest is the bass." She sank another whole octave, puffed her chest and boomed into the dark, a rhythm fit to anchor a whole choir. *"Too deep, too deep, too deep . . ."*

I could hear them, frog throats distended, frog eyes bugging, ranged on their leaves and chanting like some great festival chorus, the strands of harmony plaiting, running over, night and rain and water given voice.

It was better than a poultice, quicker than poppy-juice. I said, "In the Mother's name. How many kinds *are* there up here?"

"I should think a couple of hundred. Doing my forest-work, I found three new ones myself."

"Forest-work?"

"During the initiate. We spend six moons in the tree-land; learning its folk, living on its fruit. It's expected that you bring back something; new, not known before."

Three kinds of frogs. I thought of my initiate, in House-affairs, in the mine. Intrigue, and peril, even at its greatest moment, when I first sang the mother-face. Oh, I thought, to have been born where knowledge is so innocent.

She must have felt my distress; with that reticence so grateful, so much of our folk, she did not ask. I might have been sitting with Iatha, my own childhood mate.

In a moment or two, I said, "I'd best go back."

She did not ask why. Just rose lithely off the rock and let me go ahead.

* * *

The men did know better than to ask that night; and next day we were on the trail again, so I could withdraw into half-solitude. Drug myself with motion and fatigue and the present moment, pretend everything was all right.

But every time I tried to think, my mind would flinch from the very exertion, and clearer and clearer I felt the grayness, the lethargy, worse than any inability to focus or any failure to find a solution. The growing awareness that I did not *want* to think.

Not because I could not. Tanekhet . . . it was because I no longer cared.

And I fled that as you do the symptoms of a mortal illness that you cannot, will not admit might be true. When Errissal fell into step with me on a wider valley-stretch, I turned to her as to my sole hope of help.

She must have understood; we talked about tree-lichens, the nature of the crimson moss, what animals whooped through the branches overhead. The trades of Thilliansar. The trades, after a while, of Amberlight. The River, the presences she knew only by name. Cataract. Verrain. The Heartlands. The Oases. Dhasdein.

When we moved off again at midday, she rejoined me. Slogging into the afternoon, with the last ridge-crest like a mirage across the valley before us, we talked about closer things. Our folk's customs. Friends. Kinfolk. Her family. Mine.

She had taken one partner, but they separated, though peacefully, a couple of years since. "I think we knew each other too well." I had never taken one at all. She shrugged. "There are plenty like that among our folk." She had borne two children. The boy was eight now, living downhill. The girl had taken a birth-fever, and died.

"Oh, yes," she said quietly, staring up the trail. "It was—sad."

She was unsure she would try again. She was thirty-eight now; four years younger than I. Mirror-images, surely. Talking to her had all the comfort, all the ease, all the ability to leave things unspoken, of conversing with myself.

* * *

We are past the Crocodile-pool. The steersman says we should reach the cataract village in no more than three days.

After that, we may have to walk.

The Mother defend us, Tanekhet. I am not sure which is the more unbearable. To look back, or to look ahead.

* * *

Errissal and I talked all the way up the last ridge-side; falling to the rear as I had to catch my wind, and complained, with what once would have seemed rashness, about its shortness with the child. She nodded. Gave me a hand over a boulder, and said, "May this one be good for you, Tellurith."

With such honest hope, such kindness, such lack of strain or rancor for her own losses, that I took her hand in mine as we walked and said, "I pray for it, most of all."

And then I could tell her the rest.

She listened without a word. Only, when I got to the last, her hand spasmed on mine. When I finished, and we thought to let go, I could see the finger marks. Driven into my palm-edge, red as scars. As if she had born it herself.

We were halfway down to the settlement when she asked, as easy on the current of our talk as if enquiring what we fancied to eat tonight. "What will you do now, Tellurith?"

I had not thought; had not begun to face the truth within me, or to build a House-head's shield. But unlike the others, she was not dependent on me.

After a while I said, "Go back. I suppose."

She looked sideways, brief and painlessly as a friend. She must have heard the undertone; weariness, reluctance. More than the confrontation of a hard future. The reluctance to face it at all.

I write it first here; as I thought it first there, Tanekhet.

The settlement emerged below us, austere, and well-made, and reticent, and beautiful, in its remote, unhomely and yet utterly familiar way, as she was herself. Frogs, I thought, and wondered, What would it be like, to have lived here, in this fastness, all your life?

She said, "Watch these roots." Went over, held a hand to me. Kept it, as we took the next few paces, as easily as a friend will help a pregnant friend. Said, "Second festival is this full moon. Another," she glanced skyward, "four days."

When I looked around, she said, "They all need time to rest. To get over the fever. To get used to it. You'll travel faster, in the end."

All true enough. All put in that non-committal voice that said, this is a friend's opinion. Not advice, let alone importunings.

"And you need time to think," she said.

The track made its final turn, the settlement core opened ahead. Late afternoon, it was crisscrossed with long shadows and mellow golden sunlight, in which house fronts and passersby shone as if dipped in fairytale. A couple of people paused at sight of us; someone saw Atha and waved. Sarth and Alkhes had paused too, at the track-gate, looking back. Waiting for me.

Errissal let go my hand and touched me lightly on the shoulder. "I'll see you at supper," she said.

Because, did I tell you, Tanekhet? She is Atha's cousin-kin through her mother. They live in the same house.

* * *

I saw her at supper; we sat together, in the long room that is both informal eating-place and kitchen, where table-mates change by the meal. After I had seen the men off, down the mountainside.

The Mother knows, I felt their reluctance. They needed to have the company's comfort, if nothing else. My heart ached that I could find nothing to answer Sarth's one questioning glance. But what was the point of breaking custom, of making a furor, even for their sake, then?

Errissal, gratefully, did not make me talk about it. We spoke of the festival, the ceremony, the preparations, both settlements cooking and fettling madly for the next three days; the days of preparation, just as we have at Iskarda.

And eventually, with the cleaning-up done and the Kitchen-head departed, over extra coffee, alone at the long table, we did speak of men. How they were in Amberlight. How they are, at Iskarda. What I had hoped, wanted for them. Dreamed of. And at last, of my own.

It was easy to speak about them. Fondly, proudly, at length about their virtues and their achievements.

How much they meant to me.

The coals were fading. She took the cups to wash, stirred the fire. Put down the poker, stretched her back and gave me a sleepy, comrade's smile. "There's a lot to do tomorrow. I suppose," she said, "we should go to bed."

* * *

I have never been one to find the lightning; which is what they say in Amberlight about those who fall, as off a mountainside, into love.

With me it is never a lightning bolt. Just a gradual, almost unconscious series of questions, a long succession whose answers are all, Yes.

As it was with Alkhes; and with Sarth before him. Married, yes, that was the work of a moment. It was two years and more, long past the physical consummation, before I understood that I did more than find him easy company, good in bed, a friend and companion. That, in good truth, I loved.

* * *

We are in the cataract village; we tied up this evening. I thought we would have to walk, I pictured eternities by the River-verge.

But as the Mother sees me, they are going to run a rowing galley downRiver for us. Risk the rocks, the strangers downStream, take us clear, they swear, to the Jump-up itself. Give us one day, they are saying, to gather provisions and oarsmen. We will have to camp at night, but it will still be fast.

So I have another day where there is nothing to do but write.

* * *

Perhaps it was the separation, Tanekhet. However we resisted it, however often we arranged to meet, the men were downhill, we were up. They slid, however unintentionally, from the mind's forefront. I still loved them. I still cared.

But they were not there. They were the future, and the River, and everything that spoke despair and failure. They were the visible symbols of fruit that had become ashes in my mouth.

And up the mountain was Now; women, and the buzz of festival preparations, and the freedom, however briefly, of being unburdened with dependents and authority, in another world. A world like the oldest one we had known, but a world where the wrong, the oppression, almost did not exist.

And there was Errissal.

Fellow-worker. Listener. Sharer of time and the little events that twine the strands of custom, the rope of proximity, the bonds of acceptance, and comfort, and liking; she *was* my fellow. She *was* my peer.

Oh, yes, I knew it, Tanekhet; and yes, it was a pay-back of sorts. Let Alkhes feel, I thought, what I did with Varris. Let Sarth understand what it is to be less than the one and only first. If neither of them had an inkling, in my mind they knew, and this was my revenge.

* * *

I ought to have remembered that whatever my idyll, whatever their fears and frets, neither of them would cease to think. I ought to have anticipated the message that third noonday. A request, "from the Iskardan men," for a meeting of the company, at the rock-shelter, that night.

When we arrived they had already lit the lamps. The moon was still behind the mountain, but near the morrow's full, so the track brimmed with its ghost-shadow light. Blinking into the lamp-glow, I found Sarth across the shelter-width, tall and indistinct and somber as some beautiful Amberlight ghost. But I saw all too clearly the way he drew himself up.

"Tellurith," he said, "what are we going to do?"

With just the degree of neutrality that said, I do not ask from fear or as coercion. In this restrained tower way, I am just advising you. An answer is only what we expect.

When I said nothing he visibly, palpably braced himself.

"Then shall we settle this, once and for all? Shall we ask the qherrique?"

What could it tell me, that I did not know in my own heart, if I could have borne to look? What it *might* tell me . . . But there was no earthly pretext to refuse.

We linked hands; hummed a little, almost perfunctory, as you would once with your own cutter, that hardly needed the rapport. When the seed glowed, overriding lamps with that white, pure light, Sarth closed his hand on mine in a way that should have warned me, and spoke, so emptily it was a bellow of alarm.

"How did you leave Amberlight?"

The pause felt almost startled. The image was certainly so; Sarth, spinning in his tracks in your guest-room, Tanekhet, shooting at us, "What?"

Sarth's grip said, Bear with me. It told me also how much this cost. And then I understood what, despite the audience, he was finally going to ask.

"How did you come," so evenly, "from Amberlight to the River? Where—we met?"

Two words this time. Separate, jarring images, drawn from our speech, mine, Alkhes', somewhere too fast to catch.

[Not] [understand.]

Sarth's fingers clenched. Too evenly he said, "Did you come with the child?"

A long silence this time; then the image of Sarth, looking upward into Zuri's face, a glimpse of pillows, a quiet, so quiet, "Yes."

Beside me Alkhes winced. Sarth said, "Aglis."

Quiet, yes, and absolute command. I felt Alkhes clench his muscles as for a surgeon's knife.

Sarth said, deliberately, "In the blood; or not?"

The answer this time was fast and unhesitating. The words from this letter that will never be sent: I do not know, do not know, do not know.

I let my own fingers warn, Let it be.

Sarth paused; shifted his hand on mine, a touch of warning, of reassurance. His arm told me he was bracing to a knife himself.

He said, "With the child? Or instead?"

It did not knock us over, but we were all half blinded from the flash. The word rang in our heads, Zuri's voice, an outraged shout.

[With!]

Sarth let me go. Wiping my eyes, I felt the ease in my own soul, as if something had released a sinew too long strained. I put a hand on his back and caught, against the flash-stars, the way he had buried his face in both his hands, the heave of his smothered breaths.

No-one else moved. No-one spoke. The lamps fluttered. Clear through their dusky shadows, the seed's brilliance glowed; all but incandescent, as it had been that night in Cataract.

Sarth wiped both eyes with the heels of his hands and straightened up. When he had our hands again, he said, more easily, "Was it what you intended? The Quest?"

This time it was a perfectly normal, Yes.

"Why?"

Silence. Then the scene on that road through the Sahandan, Alkhes and I, mourning, remembering, the rapport we would never have again.

As I gripped my hand against Alkhes' jerk Sarth said sharply, "Wait, Aglis. Think."

In the hesitation he added more forcefully, "What didn't we understand? We missed the message last time. It told us this before. Think!"

Silence. Breathing. The pulse-beat of the lamps. The seed, its light unchanged. Why did I have the sensation that something held its breath?

It was Azo who spoke. "Last time. You," she meant Sarth, "said, That is our Why. But yours? And it said, Your words don't work." She hesitated. "So, like Keraz said. Why not?"

Sarth let my hand go; he was so still, for that unending moment, that he might have turned, vein by vein, to sentient stone.

Then he lifted his head and said, just audibly, "Did you mean . . . that was your Why as well?"

The seed flamed up, a great gout of incandescence. We did not have to link hands, it was in all our heads, a triumphal shout.

[*Yes!*]

* * *

How I wish I could picture you reading this, in the warehouse council-room or those rackety lodgings at Amberlight. Even at Iskarda. How I wish I could imagine the roll of those forest-green eyes skyward and the exquisitely annihilating politeness of your expression as you respond.

I see, you say. *You carried it upRiver for a year: you communed with it, and used it, and built a city and ruled the River with it, for seven hundred years. You lived by and for it and suicided when you lost the Craft of doing so. You know—you knew then, if you had allowed yourselves to know—that it was both living and sentient. And it only now dawns on you that for a sentient—entity—powerful enough to level your City and three armies in the blast, for such a being to have endured seven hundred years of human use, abuse, and importunity, nay, to let you cut off and trade pieces of its living flesh—there must have been some profit for the qherrique as well?*

Oh, I hear you say. *Truly remarkable, my lady Tellurith.*

Laughing, at the thought of your so perfect, so princely exasperation, has lifted my spirits after all.

* * *

Even if, even now, I could beat my temples as no few of us did then, rather than merely sit thunderstruck at our rank, absolute, all-but-eternal stupidity.

Of course it took something from us. Of course it did not bear all that suffering, and the Mother knows, from the blasts we met from the slabs or at the mother-face, it was no senseless rock we cut; of course it did not endure that for seven hundred years without some recompense.

There were times we actually wondered what. I know Damas and I did. As Alkhes did, on that road. Were we puppets, or servants?

Or friends?

We have our answer. We were dark to the light, sun to the shadow, words to the music, ears for the speaker, voice to the speaker's ear. Not puppets, not servants. The necessary sharers of the song.

What must it have thought, if the word pertains; have felt, have endured, when it decided, for whatever its reasons, to blast all that away?

How much must it desire that communion, that harmony, that it would return, having destroyed Amberlight and its old self along with us, to place itself within the reach and purpose of humans again?

I think we wept, Tanekhet. As we understood all that, I am very sure that all of us, Varris too; we wept.

* * *

So we have the greatest Why at last. Why it came back. Why it suffered, still suffers us. Why it led us up the River and let us suffer on our own account, why it took up your vision and engineered the Quest.

Why it has—helped us? reshape the Riverworld.

When we had absorbed it; when we had taken it all in, and each made our own penance, and, finally, composed ourselves; it was Sarth who wiped his eyes, and held out his hands, and hardly waiting for our touch, spoke as simply as a child.

"I am so sorry," he said.

The seed answered for itself. A darkening, a rising flicker, a pulse and steadying. The awareness was in our minds, as it would be once in Amberlight.

Understood. Accepted. All right.

Sarth wiped his eyes again; it takes time, after all, to accept forgiveness. Even if it is not from a god.

And finally, we could clasp hands again, while he drew a long, long breath, announcing a new start, a chapter finally closed; and said, "Advise us. What should we do now?"

Another flash of me with the earth-scribes, this time with a sort of tired patience: words do not work, do not work.

"Wait!" Alkhes jerked my hand in his vehemence. "It will answer, it did. The problem's in *our* words. Ask it some other way!"

Sarth stopped short; turned around and stared at him a moment, and suddenly relaxed. "Oracles," he said. "Of course."

"Oracles," Quiran enquired, clearly goaded, "what?"

Sarth gave him a small, unpatronizing philosopher's smile. The mind's triumph in a problem resolved.

"With oracles there are two ways to ask. A question general enough to cover all the possibilities; or a question specific enough to get exactly what you want. I've been doing it wrongly. I've tried to leave all the pathways clear. What it needs is to know, which path?"

He gripped my hand again and said, "Should we go or stay?"

The answer came as quickly, as unexpectedly upon my unsuspecting heart, his own word returned from that same question, his own voice and face.

"Go."

I felt the whole circle's individual, physical response. I tried desperately not to pass on mine.

Sarth said, "And if we stay?"

He knew my mind, Tanekhet. He has always known it, closer than anyone, even Alkhes. Perhaps, even than the qherrique.

The answer came almost as immediately. Alkhes in that travel-shelter, staring, with vision's anguish, into my face. "Inside ten years, we'll be just like Dhasdein."

It was Alkhes who spoke, bursting the bounds of custom and ceremony and caution as well. "You can't stop it, if we go!"

The light fluxed, a flare and steadying that was palpable as a question asked aloud.

"Even if we could bear to—there's not enough of you! The cutters will wear out! The light-guns will die. If we, if troublecrew *could* keep control, we can't work the quarry without them!"

The flare this time was brilliant. The sense was imageless and clear as crystal, and something I never ever felt before, a great gust of sheer joyous mirth. And the image after it, our cluster on the hill at Cataract, with the light rising over us, blazing, majestically illuminant, from Dinda's statuette.

"You mean you can restore the cutters *as well*?"

Alkhes who got there first, with his soldier's concern for weaponry and his utter disregard for protocol, bursting out in something between delight and utter disbelief. But the answer was quick as birdsong. A clear, orthodox, Yes.

"Oh," Alkhes managed, and sagged back against me, this time, somewhere between delight and shock. "Oh, Gods."

* * *

How long did we take, Tanekhet, to assimilate *that*?
It was Sarth who finally concluded the transports; amid our babble I had felt him grow quieter and quieter, but I had absolutely no expectation that, when he finally held out his hands and the circle hushed, he would ask, "How long?"

"What?"

Sarth's own face, this time, no more than mildly startled, somewhere in Iskarda.

"Even a cutter," Sarth said, "will wear out, eventually."

Silence. Extended, but not obdurate. The fluxing of the light, faint and slow as the flutter of the candleflame, told us this was thought.

When the image came, we all recognized it. We had seen it before, that night in Cataract. The inner room of Telluir House, where we handed over the statuettes.

This time it was I who spoke before I thought. "You mean you would *do it again*?"

The reply was Sarth again. Firm beyond dispute. "Yes."

I opened my mouth and Sarth himself cut over me. "Why?"

Once again the image of that road in the Sahandan. "That night I touched it . . . I'll never forget . . ."

Sarth's grip said, Wait. I felt his arduous collection, of feeling and thought. Before, yet more carefully, he spoke.

"What we did was enslavement. We enslaved you. We enslaved ourselves. And the River as well."

The image came firmly, confidently. Myself in the Riversend throne-room, eye to eye with Antastes. "There are no mother-lodes. And if there were . . . I would never see it enslaved again."

Sarth sat back with a jolt. "You mean," he spoke unevenly, "you will trust us—not to follow that temptation? You are prepared to suffer, what you suffered; and take the chance as well, that next year, fifty years, a hundred years away . . . we will not forget?"

The image had a distinct flavor of irony, a picture none of us ever would forget; the death of Amberlight, the spears of qherrique driving home, the hill crumbling, under its sepulcher of dust.

I felt Sarth's shoulder twitch. I knew his mouth corners would have twitched too, when he answered with equal irony, "There is that."

It was Alkhes, not so much insensitive as ever pragmatic, who shifted at last, with a huge gusty sigh, and the awe, the . . . I do not know what word will do, not joy, not gratitude, not thankfulness; what word covers the knowledge of being, beyond imagination, blessed?

But it was Alkhes whose voice conveyed it, as he said, "It's agreed, then. We go back. You help us keep the quarry going. And the rest. And in the end . . ."

The image overrode him, familiar from so many former times. The hill at Amberlight, cinctured in its great bulwarks of qherrique.

Alkhes sighed. "And in the end," he finished, more softly, "Iskarda will be like that."

How does one offer thanksgiving, palpable gratitude, to a benefactor not divine, not human, that offers, on the bridge of its own—flesh? to preserve your dream? your future? your world?

It was Quiran who asked, impulsive as ever. "How do we, what *can* we do, for you?"

Amusement, then; indubitably amusement, bearing the image with it, as wind bears a butterfly. Alkhes, one hand on the wall of Telluir House-head's apartments, revelation, an initiate's wonder, almost ecstasy, in his face.

Echoed by the faces around me; understanding, at last, that whatever we had drawn from the conjunction, however we had shamed it with human abuse, we had after all, given recompense.

* * *

So you will imagine, Tanekhet, that when the festival came, an evening later, Thilliansar's guests did, indeed, have something to celebrate.

Midwinter festival, but nothing like it is in Iskarda; I thank the Mother to my heart's depths for that. In Thilliansar there is ceremony, yes, and a mark of the year's turn, but it is a celebration; and there is no sacrifice.

Or snow either. So much farther north, under the snowline, winter is merely intenser chill and wet, a cause for mulled wine and enormous meals and bigger fires in those shapely stone chimneys, and for gathering close, by the fireside or anywhere else.

Midsummer, Errissal told me, is celebrated in the open, on the heights. For Midwinter both settlements go down to the River. On the bridge, the month's priestess and the men's month-Head encounter, each with the tall silver ceremonial cup, each abrim with the potent mountain spirit they make from fermented breadfruit flesh, that makes our Korite barley-drink seem like children's pap. They speak together a thanksgiving for the year past, a gratitude for warmth and life, a petition for the year to come. Then they cross their arms and drink, as deeply as they can manage, from each other's cup. It is the best of all omens if both get to the dregs before they have to take a breath.

And they managed it that night.

* * *

We embarked two days ago. The rowers are all but killing themselves. If everything holds, and the wind is still behind us, unseasonable, says the steerswoman, and makes the sign of placation to her gods; we should be at the last halt before the Jump-up in ten days or so.

* * *

The ceremony is held on the bridge, but because it is so often wet, the celebration is held in the men's great-house. Where the women have a bridge-grove, the men have roofed their settlement's core. It is an immense round-ended rectangle built around two ancient fig trees that reach clear through the roof. Pillars the size of tree-trunks run its length, supporting the hewn rafters and the smaller timbers that extend the overhanging thatch into an ample colonnade. It shelters most life in the settlement, but the inner part is walled, for warmth in wind and rain, and seclusion too.

Except at festival. Then they throw the whole thing open, men and women lay out the feast tables and do the last cooking, and then drink and dance together, the crowds surging clear through the house, while musicians play upon the central dais, the core of the festival.

I do not remember what I drank. Or ate. I do recall the music, from a men's and women's consort, the jests and taunts that flew as they worked into harmony, the electric tension that sang consort of another kind. The music was wholly strange; rattling hand-drums supplemented by a monster three feet across, along with a sistrum, a stringed instrument whose like I never saw, and a pair of honey-tongued wooden flutes. The dances were strange too; but at a festival, it is more than familiarity that wings your feet.

I recall I danced with Alkhes, the first mixed dance. By then, Sarth and his flute were among the musicians, thoroughly absorbed. I recall, the next dance, sharing partners with Azo. I recall clearly the charge, galvanic and yet earthier than any sense of rousing qherrique, that tingled through the crowd, honed by firelight and the flare of alcohol and a feast's abundance, borne on the weight of sweat and cooking and best perfumes and most simply, many humans, strenuously, joyously, vividly alive, the odor that was powerful as the merriment and rising excitement; and, yes, the knowledge of loosed desire.

In that, too, it was like and unlike Iskarda; because we knew, we all knew, how so many of these dances would conclude, and all of us were willing to see our pleasures shared. There are no reservations, on a Thilliansar festival night.

Which was why, after Varris pulled Alkhes away from me only to lose him to a pair of determined mountain women, when I saw Quiran whirled off by Atha's second niece and Deor enveloped by a long-limbed, mahogany-haired ploughman, and Sarth, between bouts of music, besieged by four girls at once, and Azo and Herar parted by a rambunctious sortie of both men and women, I was glad to lean back on a pillar where my last partner had deposited me, to shake my head at another dauntless spirit, and laugh, and wipe off sweat, and pant.

As on the mountain, she was there before I knew. A feather-touch on my shoulder, a tendered cup; a casual, "Would you like some water, Tellurith?"

Like so many utensils in Thilliansar, the cup was exquisitely turned, austerely modeled wood. High mountain cedar, rarest of timber trees, with a frieze around its foot. Barb-fringed vine leaves, and frogs.

"It's mine, yes." She smiled too as I began laughing. "Ephara made it for me. My initiation cup."

Ephara was her aunt, a notable wood-carver. I lifted it to her in toast, and gratitude, before I took a sip.

The water was colder and more pure than night. River water, taken direct from the stream, so close to its source. Straight from the snows. As I pledged her, our eyes met across the cup.

Did I say I never drew the lightning, Tanekhet?

There was a moment amid the jovial uproar as silent as at the Source. I felt myself still; I felt everything still, the universe finding its fulcrum, as if between us we could balance the world.

Then she shut a hand over mine and tilted the cup to her own mouth.

* * *

After that we danced. We danced with men and women, with men and men and women and women, we changed partners in the rounds and never elsewhere. And the cord held between us, intangible as a strand of sunlight, unbreakable as a chain of silk, sure as a mountain's founding rock. We did not glue ourselves together like so many, side to side, lip to lip; the understanding was enough.

And as with the rest, there was perfect harmony at the moment a dance closed, and we set aside a leaf-plate. Drained the cup. Threaded our way to the thatch-edge, in another musicians' break, exchanging words with those about. Feeling hands slip into each other, as we turned toward the night.

We were anything but alone by then; there was a steady seepage of people, couples and otherwise, all around the house. I am not sure precisely what it was that made me, on the moonlight's proper threshold, glance suddenly back.

He stood caught in the eave-glow, flute in one hand, the other half-outstretched. I knew the words in his mouth, the very timbre of that voice, the note on which he would have said, I've almost finished here. Will you wait for me, Tellurith?

For an instant the night's fortress of light and warmth and gaiety fell into one black gulf. There was nothing but the blood in my ears, rushing in my head; my eyes, burning. My hand burning, where it held Errissal's. My breath stuck, on a word aborted in my throat.

He made a tiny gesture, as if to raise, and then let fall the flute. Then he turned on his heel and disappeared into the surging heat and light without a backward glance.

* * *

I do not remember what I felt about that; I know I did not think about it. I shut it from my mind as if they, as if he had never been anything to me. Nothing but the merest duty. As if I were the silliest girl throwing away a House, squandering half a City, for the sake of some man's pretty face.

Nor do I recall where we went. Some niche on the mountainside, arranged and prepared by custom, never seen in day's full light. I do remember everything we said, every kiss, every touch. I am not going to write any of it down. Flesh and blood are flesh and blood. They can only bear so much.

Except that, at the end, we are lying on some anonymous furry hide with a chance-found blanket over us, amid the scents of flesh and festival, and the cold outer perimeter of the dark; outside our shelter the moon is going down, cold at last in a paling sky. And we both know the night, and so much else with it, is nearly done.

My shoulder pillowed her head. She slid her free hand down my side; slowly, langorously, but no longer the deliberate ignition of desire. Instead she cupped my belly, with a delicacy, a breath-held sense of wonder and fragility, loving, cherishing, that all but broke my heart.

I set my own hand over hers. Long fingers, palm broader than it was long, the pattern of my own. She breathed in against my throat.

"Will you send word? UpRiver? I'd like to know that you're— all right."

She said it so softly; so humbly, as if she had no right to ask. With perfect resignation to the loss of everything we had just found together, with perfect acceptance that she would only hear about the birth, remoter than a stranger, that she would never see my child. Let alone be there to know and raise her, grafted into her life. That we would part, in the coming morning, and our lives never join again.

Some decisions need no debate at all. That one arrived complete, absolute as the way our eyes had met above the cup.

I said, "I'm not going."

Her pulse jumped under my hand. Her lashes twitched against my skin. I tightened my fingers, clasping the two of them, the community I had never imagined and now could not imagine being without.

"The River is settled. The qherrique will look after Iskarda. If they need to talk to it, there's Sarth. They don't need me any longer. For anything at all."

Silence. Even her hand was frozen, cupped under mine.

"I shall stay here anyway." I put my whole arm around her. "But I would wish you as my partner. Our lives' length. And for five years at least, it will be our child."

Downhill, a river-bird called. Uphill, a tree-dwelling monkey troop whooped along their road of boughs. Somewhere on the hillside, hushed human voices spoke another festival's end.

Her hand moved. Her lips moved against my neck. Her body trembled. One brief upheaval of shock.

Then she kissed me through both our tears, and whispered as if it were the Mother's own blessing, "Oh, Tellurith."

What you would think of this, Tanekhet? You who were so sure I would disapprove your liaison with Keshaq? You who married three women, and only one of them for love? Who have known the conflicts of duty and desire, and had your way in both? Has Tez taught you compassion for such a victory's reverse?

Would it matter to you that we were women, rather than men? That I was Head of Telluir House, rather than Suzerain of Riversend? Would you side with me? Or with them?

Perhaps I wrong you; perhaps you would look at me with those forest-green eyes stripped of mockery, as you did once in Riversend, and say, Everyone is due a little selfishness. Everyone has the right to happiness. No matter what it costs.

More likely you would turn on me in that way you do, that high-bred voice never raised as you cut the flesh from my bones.

Do not let me stand in your way, my lady Tellurith. Passion conquers all. Everyone knows that. What right has anyone to dispute? Permit me to absolve you. Desert your House. Desert the community you founded, in every sense. The community that depends on you, as you know they can depend on no-one else. Desert the men—as well as the women—for whom you were building a new world. Hand the River nations on into the grasp of the fools, squabblers, bunglers, who infest every new enterprise. Consider the account ruled off, the ledger closed. Your politicking over. You have done, you say, enough.

Quite so, my lady Tellurith. Desert your company too, that you have led clear from Riversend to the River's Source. What do the good opinions, the trust, the future of women like Azo and Deor matter? They are just subordinates.

As for your men . . .

Why should you consider the feelings of men, you who were born and raised in old Amberlight? What should it matter, when a woman takes your fancy, that you will desert two men who have given you more than heart and soul? Who have given you desire and devotion, blood and tears, body and spirit both? Who would, who so often nearly have died for you: let be the smaller, the far harder sacrifices of unremitting care and attention and support? Why should they matter now? Least of all when you will gift your—lover—with their only begotten child?

Let be, Tanekhet. Enough, enough.

* * *

They did not say that; none of them said it. When I called the meeting that next dripping noon, and we settled into some briefly vacated hut, heavy with the scent of men and unwashed wool and the labor that had been expended over the tall, silent loom. When I told them. All.

Azo and Deor . . . They all knew about the night, the festival's conjunction. Naturally. To those two the tie was commonplace enough; unusual for me, perhaps, but a night's passage. It was the rest they had never dreamed.

But they are old Amberlight; if our songs remember Thilliansar, are they not also rife with tales of women's love? Not simply the star-crossed but the great partnerships, the legendary pairings; and is the understanding not implicit in them all? However you would deride it. The world is well lost, the world is always to be lost, for one perfect woman's love.

So their faces, however startled, however desolate, already spoke a kind of acceptance. When I had no more than got it out.

Varris? I will tell the truth to myself if to no-one else. I had not one shred of concern for what Varris thought or felt. Whether or not it was contempt.

Quiran and Herar? They, too, were Amberlight. Or Iskarda. In the abeyance of all else, they looked to their women; and Azo's face told them more than enough. Shock, yes, perhaps desolation. But it was not for them to protest.

I looked back to Azo. Who read my eye as a Trouble-head could, gathered her cohort with a glance, and jerked her head.

I listened to the shuffling navigation of loom-lumber, the door. There was a worn place in the felted floor-rug just by my toe. In its well-fettled, goats'-hide, Thilliansar boot.

Eventually even I found the courage to look up.

Alkhes would have said it all; the reproaches, the indictments, the justified, more than justified pleas and too-truly deserved recriminations. He might have wept. He surely would have cursed. He would, beyond doubt, have cut me to the heart, where you could only reach the bone. I took one look at that face, with the glaze of shock and the numbness of mortal hurt just beginning to thaw, and proved myself a coward forever. I looked at Sarth instead.

He was not white. It was that graven, marmoreal look of moments when he goes away behind the tower's armor, and leaves nothing more vulnerable than a breathing block of flesh. But his eyes . . . Those tawny, lion's eyes; the soul, yes, it is true, however strange to say it, the soul of Amberlight.

Of generations, centuries of men and women who had broken their hearts and ruined their lives and kept their honor whole. Who had put the City first.

But he was not going to say that; I understood then that he did not mean to say anything. Not because he was enraged beyond speech, not because he was too hurt to muster words. Not because I had finally overtried his love. And not because he still loved me; or understood what I was doing, or accepted it. Or because it would do no heavenly good.

But because he had expected this.

Because he had not expected me to honor my House and my folk any more than to respect the debts I owed to him and Alkhes. Despite everything they had given me, everything they had done for me.

He had not even expected me to respect their rights in the unborn child.

My vision went red. I screamed at him; I did not choose words, I only wanted to strike him to the soul as I had been struck myself.

"I have a right to it! I've done what I was supposed to! I got you out of Amberlight! I built a House for you! I ruined my life! I lost my City! I gave up my *children* for you! I gave you back the qherrique!"

I tore the silken packet out of my shirt and hurled it at him. "I gave you what you wanted, rot and gangrene you, both of you! You've got your new world. You can take it home and live with it, you don't need me anymore!"

The qherrique landed on the floor between us, a barely audible thump. Alkhes lunged, Sarth grabbed him and jerked. The sheer force struck him mute.

"You said it to me! Don't you remember? You asked me, all the way back there at Clifftop. 'Do you ever see the people, Tellurith? Do you ever think that we might have feelings, want things, just occasionally matter as much as your damnable *House*?"

Alkhes made a sound in his throat. Sweet Mother. I can hear it now.

Sarth never said a word; those eyes just watched me, impersonally, inhumanly, as an indifferent lion's. The man was locked away, deeper than any blow, any wound could ever touch.

"Well I *am* considering the people, Sarth! For the first time in my life, I'm considering myself!"

The tears were coming; they filmed his features, as if they were washing him away from me. Out of vision, out of memory, out of my life.

"I'm grateful," it had to be managed, a long-schooled control of breath, of voice, over the earthquake building in my throat, "for everything you've done for me. Everything you've given me" I had both hands over my belly. Holding, protecting it. Shielding it. Owning it. Repulsing, driving any other out. "I know what the child—both the children—meant to you."

Alkhes tore free then. He cried out to me as a drowning man might. "Tellurith!"

Sarth grabbed him again; I could imagine the steel of those hands that snatched and shook him, struck him dumb with one brutal jerk.

"It's not as if," it was an uncovenanted blessing to concentrate on the words, the steadiness of my voice, "it need be the only one. You both have," how gratefully the long-pent rage and jealousy surfaced, a fire to cauterize everything else, "you both have other people. Varris. Zuri. If Zuri won't bear you a child then Asaskian would break a leg to do it. And as for Varris . . .!"

I heard myself laugh. The sound of it splintered, vicious as broken glass. Sarth's face said nothing. Even then.

Alkhes' eyes spoke for them both. Not the shame of admission or acceptance, or hurt for his own loss; this was grief, a burning, unbearable pain for what *I* was losing; my honor, my loyalty, for the destruction of everything in me he had ever admired. That had meant more to him, my Outland soldier, than my love, my flesh itself.

A soldier, wounded mortally, he drew himself up. Took a huge, shuddering breath.

Then he turned his back.

Sarth caught him again; gently this time. Those lion's eyes never left my face. But he pulled Alkhes against him as he had that night in Cataract, and over his—my—our lover's head his eyes said, implacably, We are alone now. It is finished. You are not wanted here any longer. Go.

* * *

I must have gone back uphill; met people; given orders, made arrangements. I must have sounded at least fractionally sane. I have no memory of my own folk, though I could reconstruct their words; their faces. The hush, the disaster and tragedy's hush, that must have overhung all Thilliansar.

When I remember again, I am on a rock atop the ridge behind the settlement; my shirt is sodden, my eyes wring, my swollen nose aches in the eternal wind. My entire body is a shell; feeling, thought, everything wept away.

Except there are arms around me.

Errissal.

She took me up the mountain, to a women's retreat. A cave, how perfectly apt for rebirth; at the valley head, a V-mouthed slot, a twilit chamber, fettled for human use with fireplace, rock shelves, bedding. Some food as well. I recall she coaxed something down me, as darkness fell, and she lit the lamp.

And as grief circles back to surround you, I remembered again.

She must have been as sure, as accomplished in consolation as she was in courtship; the Mother knows, her own heart must have been warm with jubilation, one would think any comfort pure hypocrisy. But it was not.

I remember that. As I remember waking, thick-headed, heartsore, in the most physical sense; when you come back to life after sleep has taken you in the sheer exhaustion of being all wept out, in earnest truth. The pallid V of dawn beyond my feet, and a great cloud taking the morning, in a rose and carmine tower of light. The quiet of exhaustion becoming, at last, blessed numbness. Resignation. The torn edges of the wound at least ceasing to bleed.

Her hand under my head, her warmth beside me. The comfort I had only taken, before, from other flesh and blood.

* * *

We stayed there the next few days. I can fill in events at the settlement, of which Errissal never spoke. My shattered company's salvage; settling a new leader. The decision she had to take.

I did not ask; most of all, I never asked about what I could never so much as contemplate. The trust I had broken. The burden I had flung down so carelessly, the responsibility I had thrown, heavier than grief, on others' shoulders.

Of leaving. The homeward journey. Iskarda.

Instead I tucked my head under my figurative wing and told myself, in some inner mind's chamber I would not so much as admit existed, that once they were gone, I would no longer hurt. Then life, the life for which I had paid so much, could begin again.

And I had Errissal.

Moonlight to the sunset of memory's death. Promise amid disaster; the faintest green shoots, on a fire-blasted plain, of hope. Night's undemanding presence, that does not require struggle and protestations. Because it knows that in the end, it will prevail.

It was the fifth night that I dreamed.

* * *

And yes, one of those dreams, Tanekhet. It catapulted me upright into the first dead light of morning with a scream that all but ripped the heart out of my throat.

Errissal cleared the bedclothes but did not, typically, wrestle or snatch or prison me in a would-be helpful hug. I regained self-mastery half-upright on the bed foot, choking and sobbing and trying not to run clear down the mountain-side. When I could wipe the sweat and catch the tears back, still she did not say, "What is it, my dear?"

What it was—is—was Iskarda.

Mid-morning on a bitter, ice-clear winter day. The mud and morning frost of the market-place, folk everywhere. But not walking, talking, chaffering, bearing weapons and tools with the casual Iskardan pride.

Herded together at the market centre; some with packs, some with hands bound behind their backs. All with the desperately frozen stances of catastrophe.

And up and down the street, holding the fence of spearheads tight, marshalling, penning the prisoners, soldiers with crimson kilts and helmet plumes and big round shields emblazoned with thunderbolts.

The insignia of Dhasdein.

A series of vignettes then. Iatha hauled from a doorway, carried bodily, fighting like a tigercat, hurled down like a sack, winded, among the rest.

You, Tanekhet. Led out into the street, your sober merchant coat torn, your shirt half off your back, hair loose over a face that speaks main force all too well. The great bruise rising on your cheek-bone, and the way those panther eyes burn in a bleached-white face.

And your wrists, locked in chains.

But what woke me was the image of an officer, coming with troops behind him from the house at the square-head that I know as well as my own. His soldiers prodding Darthis in their midst.

Weaponless, bare-headed. With some sort of pack over her shoulder, above her winter coat. An old woman, dispossessed and powerless, turned out in the road.

* * *

I sat a long time; such a long time, on the bed-end, before I could bear to turn.

She had gone to the fireplace; with her usual resource and composure, woken the coals, and the moment I moved, she brought me a cup. Not water this time. Hot, fresh coffee. The drink of the River's Source.

The light had broadened; below us on the ridge-face, the sun would be striking jewels in the dew, the forest would be pristine under the movements of first light. Birds. Monkeys. Frogs.

My eyes refilled. It might have been memory; the Mother knows, I had wept Her heavenly cistern full. But I knew, already, that it was not.

I never paused to think it was out of my hands; that I had renounced the Quest, cast myself out of the company, if anyone should have had that dream, it was not I. I set the cup away, focused my eyes on that triangle of green-edged, leaf-laced turquoise beyond the doorway, and hurled it like a spear-shaft, straight into space.

Do I have to go?

The image came back at me like a Heartland throwing stick. Sarth's face by lamplight, tears still wet on his cheeks, those eyes, depths of bronze-lit amber, full of comprehension, penitence, grief.

I am so sorry, he said.

* * *

It was full fresh morning then, a rare fine winter's morning, with the sparkle of the air like Your own wine. I felt its every breath run through my veins as keenly as if I were a man at the foot of the scaffold. Yearning, paining for the earth from which he was about to die.

I set the cup down. Took a breath and braced my shoulders as I have seen Alkhes do for the weight of a shield. An arm came round me. A weight settled, warm, solid, familiar, the promise of a future never imagined, sweeter than any imaginable, at my back.

She slid the other arm around my neck; already we had our lovers' rituals, our particular places and touch. Her fingers traced, delicately as over jewelry, the angle of my collarbone under the shirt. Her breath was warm among the loose tendrils of plait against my neck.

In another moment she said, so very quietly, "You have to go."

I put my head in my hands. Such a banal gesture, Tanekhet. But then, banality is founded on the realities we find, over and over. The eternal, unchanging actions. Love. Birth. Joy. Trouble. Distress. Death.

"I think," I heard myself say, so distant, "I must."

Then the rest of that sentence caught up.

She nodded, minutely, when I had freed myself and turned about and stared, disbelieving, unable to disbelieve, into those golden-tawny eyes.

"I saw it. Yes."

How do I know why, Tanekhet? How did I speak to it bare-minded, if not from the extremity of need and desperation? For us both? How did she hear, if not from our minds' and bodies' joining, from the twin mirror that was no mirror, no double, at all?

She cradled me as if I was a very child while I wept. Again, yes. All I seem to have done, these last months, is weep.

When the tears finally stemmed, I put my own hand, once again, yet again, on her nape. And made the last futile gesture of all.

"Come with me," I said.

She tapped my lower lip, the barest touch of her middle finger, and from somewhere, faintly, ironic as any oracle, with understanding and acceptance, but still no malice, she smiled.

"We could do it. It is possible. What would anyone notice? Just another woman from Iskarda, from Amberlight. You *know* how alike we . . ."

She pressed my lip this time, so gently. And shook her head.

"Clythx—caissyl—beloved—"

She took my face in her hands and kissed me, gentler than a mother's valediction, on the brow. Held me back and gazed into my eyes.

"You know," she said, "why."

Oh, I knew, Tanekhet. All too well.

Because as much as I was bound to go for my folk's sake, as much as I could not put down the burden of the House at the last, she was bound to stay, for her folk's sake. Because downRiver, someone would find out. Someone, one day, would work out what she was.

A stranger. No kin to anyone, yet welcomed in the House, and so close a resemblance that she must be kin. How long then, to trace our journey backward, to pin her appearance at its source?

No matter if Amberlight and Iskarda ruled the River, if Cataract were our devoted vassal and the Heartland all our eyes and ears. *Somebody*, sometime, would realize. Somebody would find Thilliansar.

I shut my eyes; give me time, I wanted to say. To have found a world, two worlds, and to lose the one that was my heart's home. It is not something one does in a breath.

She put her arms around me. We sat amid the tangled blankets, the noises of advancing morning, and held each other as if we could turn back time, as if, if we only believed in it for long enough, this moment would never end.

* * *

It was well past nightfall when I reached the men's settlement. After all, we *had* to linger most of the day. Then there was the first meeting, Thilliansar to confront, to share in the decision, to plan, to offer advice. All the myriad preparations to start.

For once, I acted the autocrat. For once I resurrected old Amberlight, where men did not consult but were told. So it was only later that I had to face the worst encounter of all.

Like us, they had stayed together, but the men make smaller houses; they all slept in a single, separate hut. I pushed aside the curtain of fringed, swinging palm fronds, and groped into the dusk beyond.

Quiran was asleep already, a solid immobile lump. Herar glanced up, then sat open-mouthed with a lapful of half untangled wool-skeins against the central bed of coals. I put a finger to my lips.

They were against the back wall; sharing blankets as the three of us used to do. Sarth's hair was a dimmer darkness laid over the pillow of cloaks, framing the dark ovals of open eye, the pale oval of his face. And Alkhes had curled up against him, head in Sarth's armpit, arm over his chest, as if he clung, like a sailor overboard, against some sea that would sweep him quite away.

I came past the brazier. Sarth's face never moved; but quite deliberately, he cupped a hand around that fall of black silky hair; covering Alkhes' ears.

The light was at my back. I looked down at him and read, clearer than a qherrique's vision, what lay behind that stare. Not hope. Not hatred. A passionless, all too sure expectation that whatever I intended, he was going to suffer again.

What words could obliterate my other words? What future could be assured by any pledge?

I sat on my heels beside him and pitched my voice to match. "Something's happened," I said, "to Iskarda."

CHAPTER XVI

Deyiko. Dhasdein Border
14th Day, Second Spring Moon

My lady Tellurith . . .
 You will remain my lady, whatever falls. However you regard me. Do you recall what I vowed that day in Riversend? *To the death.*

Even if that death is by your will.

* * *

In truth, I am uncertain if this is a letter, or a journal, or a— memoir—or a—written defense. I do know I am quite, quite sure, that this time, you will not merely dislike—this time you will rue, you will weep, you may all too justifiably requite what I have done in blood.

My scribe asserts, with pithy additions, that I am a fool: adds that if I always wrote like this it is a miracle you ever troubled to read the result, and adjures me, more than pithily, to get on with it.

So. Let me begin, then, in Iskarda.

Second winter moon, after my—expulsion from Amberlight. After the discovery of those thrice-damned cyphers. Gods, if I had known what waited in that demure scrap-heap—

I am directed to be less maudlin. And again, to get on with it.

So. I return to the violence of my agitation those last days in Iskarda, when I sat gagged on the sidelines of a battle that would decide my world's future, with the fates of my—

With the fates of my country, still my native country, and that of my sworn homeland, my new world, nestled, like a twinned fire-arrow, in my two hands.

* * *

If this means I am a traitor, so. If you can say that, considering what my—treachery—has wrought. If you can *not* say that, considering its cost. If I had known—if I had only taken sufficient moments' imagination—

My scribe says, Enough. And, I am not the River-lord, to take the governance of the world upon my sole human back. But I know, and you know, Tellurith: there is no exculpation, for those who accept the burden of leadership.

My scribe adds hard soldier's counsel about the price of all great enterprises, whose worth is, too often, paid in blood.

This is not exculpation, then: but it may explain why I did not have my wits about me in that heel-end of winter, why I let my inner agitation muffle even the scraps of rumor from downRiver, that were only another barb of uneasable worry about Tez.

If I had only spared a fraction more time from my fatuous personal afflictions, if I had taken one *thought*—

It might have been different, that biting bright morning when I brought Iatha up a message from Zariah's house. Crossed the street, with ears scythed by the through-wind above mud heaps furred gray with frost: glanced up to the hilltops, knife-edge white against a pristine blue sky. Skirted a pair of wood-boys, a work-bound bullock team. And came short upon Desis and Iatha herself, peering out under their hands from the courtyard gate.

"Broken gear?" Desis was frowning hard. Iatha, scowling fit to turn a hurricane, returned an unintelligible, "Mmmph." But I have learnt some of that body language. Enough to make me break stride and courtesy both and demand, "What's wrong?"

Iatha, naturally, scowled harder. Desis—

Still my partisan: she answered, brusquely enough. But not on my account.

"Lost signal. Stopped mid-word, five minutes gone." And then, anticipating me, "Marbleport road."

May the gods forgive me. If you cannot. I stood there, muscles seized, my very brain turned to water, as it all came clear, Tellurith. All in that one searing moment. In that month too late.

I did at last get my hands to move. To grab Desis. Not to shout as I ordered, "Get the light-guns—call troublecrew. Sound the alarm." To shove Iatha and keep some coolness in my frantic, "Call Darthis, tell everyone grab a weapon and scatter—go, Iatha, *go*—!"

Desis was troublecrew: she spun on a heel and fled. Iatha gawped one second before she grabbed my arm and whipped me into the courtyard, snarling, "What in the fiery pits—?"

I tore away. It was no time for manners, there was no time at all. I spun for the market-square where Keshaq would be among the water-carriers, and hurled over my shoulder, "Dhasdein!"

Foolish, so foolish, Tellurith. I was thinking like a Dhasdeini too. Like a Trouble-head, a Viceroy, a great noble, whose intelligencers can drop cover in a moment, whose troops can up-stakes on a command, whose household are trained to scatter, anonymous fugitives, on the instant of disgrace.

I flew at Keshaq amid a knot of boys and buckets and his face told me how it looked but there was no time even for that. I shoved two boys aside, yanked the yoke off his shoulder. By the gods' mercy, he wore his knife. I shoved him at the uphill slope and hissed in his ear, "Keep off the snow, get high, don't come down till after dark. Don't look back!"

No time to explain. No time . . .

Since my scribe presses me, I will say it. No time for his due. Of heart's pain, and a perhaps eternal parting, for one who was dear as my heart.

Thank the gods at least that he was Quetzistani and Verrain palace trained and had his outdoor coat. He gave me one white-eyed look before he jumped the buckets and ran.

I had time to scourge home the rest. Time to scurry up the market-square, and by what seemed gods' felicity, run slap athwart Darthis: who read my face and met me with a slash of "What is it?" So I had time, before Iatha's tempest overtook me, to pant, "Dhasdein!"

Iatha grabbed. Darthis interposed a shoulder of solid stone. "Where? How?"

"The mirror signal—stopped. They'll have the tower. They'll have the road. They'll be closing in—"

Iatha's bellow died in her throat. Darthis snapped, "And?"

"Scatter—take weapons—break for the hills—run!"

Iatha's jaw snapped tight. "And the children?" Darthis rapped.

I must have gaped as stupidly as those boys. She snorted. "The old folk? Grandmothers? My grandsire, ten years in his bed?"

"They'll be moving up—they may have us surrounded now! Dhe's eyes, woman, do you want to save *anything*?"

Their eyes flashed, crossing, once. Then Darthis shouted into troublecrew sprinting across the square's slant. "Assembly! Sound the alarm!"

Would it have been any use, if they had done what I said?

Because I myself was not thinking far enough, Tellurith. Was it not I who perfected the tactic, in Riversrun, in Quetzistan? If you want captives rather than casualties, if you intend to net not merely the infirm but the fighting heart of a hostile community, give them what seems an accidental warning, yes. But only when your cordons are already spread.

Darthis and Iatha were still planted like rocks amid the first influx of shouting civilians, the entanglement of frenzied troublecrew, the village had hardly realized it was an alarm—

When the slopes above us, the byres below us, the quarry road's turn, grew a dark, glittery, binding rope of armored heads.

* * *

They knotted the snare-ties first. Coolly, steadily, over the uproar in the square, the quarry-workers' stampede, the troublecrews' vain search for assault posts, the hurly-burly of—civilians—running from every passageway. Over it all, I heard the signals. The command cries. The smooth, flawless shift and deployment, until, with most of Iskarda crammed under their spears in the market square, at last, the trumpets called.

"The decree," I said, when Darthis and Iatha turned with the stare of captives, in their own place already strangers, falling back on their one interpreter. "The official—orders."

Antastes honored us, Tellurith. Indeed, he honored us. Those human blockades were fleet-marines, the cream of Dhasdein's fighting force. I knew the thick, oiled shimmer of spearheads, the sheen of cast corselets, the thunderbolt and serpent-blazoned shields. As familiar as the shapes among them, the fish-scale sarks and wide-mouthed quivers of Archipelago archers. The best archers the empire fields.

So there was no point in charging the spearfront. Even when our vantage showed us, quite clearly, red officers' crests moving up the quarry road.

They opened the shields: six men, four guards, an aide. A herald. I knew the leopard-hide draped over his breast. He drew out the white curl of parchment. The official scroll.

"Antastes, son of Thearkos . . ." But you know the rigmarole as well as I. As Darthis and Iatha did. They waited, jaws clenched, for the meat.

" . . . default upon the obligations of an ally. Summoned at the time of the empire's need. Nevertheless, the emperor will have mercy. The levy cancelled . . . Iskarda—all Iskardans—to be their own pledge. Taken into protective detainment . . . at the emperor's direction . . . under the empire's shield."

Not mere imprisonment, no. Not executions, not massacre. That would not have been sure enough.

Deportation: uproot the entire community and drag it into the lands of strangers. Into Dhasdein's foreign heart. Not a partial loss of combatants, but excision of an entire community. Their world's foundations, gone.

And you know what went with them, Tellurith.

* * *

Ionly realized what I had done when Iatha, Darthis' eyes, said,
Yes. Go. I did feel the cobbles under my steps. How I navigated
the crowd, I have no idea. I do recall my own voice, ringing in my
ears.

"Halt!"

The passage behind the herald had closed. The spears wavered, at my voice.

"Send your commander here!"

If ever I thanked the River-lord for the haughtiest of outraged
noble Dhasdeini accents, it was then.

There was a long pause. Then the spears parted, and he came
out to me, his bodyguard fanning round him, his aides at heel. Not
a young man, as you might expect for taking a village, a field skir-
mish. The decorations, the sagging jawline said seniority, before I
read the gold rings on his official baton. A regimental commander.
Probably in charge of the entire expedition: maybe with viceregal
authority.

And no hope of confusion and delay and some plan concocted
during an appeal to his superior.

I said, "Your credentials, sir?"

His hand twitched. An aborted salute. He said, "Your authority?"

It was no time for rules. For consultation. "I am," I said, "the
Voice of Iskarda."

Whatever his experience of protocol, his knowledge of Iskardan custom, my tone must have been enough. His briefing, or his
own experience, told him who I really was. His eye went past me.
Whatever they thought, their faces must have been clear too.

"Tarriz, son of Fiol," he said. "Field commander." Infinitesimally, his eyes narrowed. "Brother of Quizir."

Brother to Dhasdein's brigadier, lost in the siege of Amberlight. Yes, a family with feud—private, personal—against Alkhes.
Yes, therefore, more than a mere military appointment. And yes,
no hope of negotiation, for understanding, for mercy. No way to
evade the emperor's blow.

Indeed, it was a masterstroke, from the choice of a man with
personal malice to propel his work, to a move that would pre-empt
our delaying bluff. That would make it pretext for a root-and-
branch attack, beheading our alliance at a stroke. Bypass Verrain, ignore Cataract, forget Amberlight. Smash not only present
defense but future resistance. Obliterate Iskarda.

The muddy snow, the fulminating press behind me, the tensed muscles of war and power in front, all blurred under the vision's weight. I spread both arms, in a gesture more seer than noble, and spoke for the audience. All of them.

"Do you have the emperor's ear?"

He knew I had changed the battleground, but not how. His body talk spoke menace and uncertainty. He answered, accepting my ground, equally loud.

"I am the emperor's man."

"Then serve the emperor now. Take his troops back to Riversend. Tell him, in his wisdom, to play the wise man. To choose a battle he might win."

His brows snapped down under the helmet rim. He lost the ceremonial nuance. "What?"

"Iskarda." I pitched my voice as I have done in great council chambers, so it ricocheted off the opposing house-fronts like a gong. "Iskarda is under the protection of the qherrique."

I might have expected him to pause: to think, if not to be cowed. The one thing I ought to have expected, had I been thinking at all clearly—

Was the momentary flinch, then the widened eyes, the body-speech of revived, burgeoning confidence, the over-compensating burst of disbelief. Comprehension. The outright guffaw.

"Qherrique, is it?"

He grinned then. The brief, contemptuous grin of a triumphant fighting man.

"I suppose your 'qherrique' let us bring up the Archipelago fleet without a word leaked? And knock your galleys to smithereens? And get this task force upRiver in three days flat? It was your 'qherrique' that put our troops ashore," a scornful wave down-River, "got 'em through the hills overnight, gave us Quasharn to send a dummy signal—that your clever sluts up here swallowed point and butt—and put us up your arses this morning before you'd woken up?"

He stepped back, then, and really grinned at me. "If that's your qherrique, *Voice*, it can protect you any time."

I suppose my belly rolled, my eyes swam. What showed behind me was mirrored on his face. It was that, perhaps as much as my own past, the bitter, bitter lessons of composure held in the face of heart's ruin, that forced me to stem my own rout.

I heard it in my voice: cold and lethal as no other, the voice of Riversrun's Suzerain. The right-arm, the brain of the emperor.

"That is what they thought in Verrain. In Cataract."

Soldiers who are iron to the brain's core can still feel a superstitious chill. It was in his blink. I gestured, an oracle, a priest.
Magnanimous. Never knowing what the god will say through you
next.

"Take my warning." And the truth was in my voice, when I
had not, even then, understood that it was in my heart.

"Tell the emperor there is a threat he does not know of yet: a
threat he never conceived of. But the qherrique will use it—if he
touches Iskarda."

I saw his eyes change. Superstition, the impact of my certainty that went beyond omens—oh, Dhe, it did indeed go beyond
omens—the remembrance of Amberlight, Verrain, Cataract. Victory, beyond imagination, torn by unimaginable intervention from
the jaws of sure defeat. The loss of the empire. Antastes' fall.

Or, if Antastes did not fall, his own punishment.

I saw the beam swing back, drawn by the hair-weight of a
family's rancor. Truly, the gods set the strangest plumb-weights
in their scales.

He twitched the baton: the bodyguard began closing in. He
spoke as I had, for the entire audience.

"Iskarda broke alliance. Iskarda is Dhasdein's defaulter. I am
the hand of the emperor."

Then he gestured to his nearest pentarchy, and said, "Take
this man. Close arrest."

They shifted ranks. Iatha bellowed, "This is the Voice of Iskarda! He has diplomatic rights! He—"

"He is the exiled Dhasdeini traitor, Tanekhet. He knows some
secret that threatens the empire." He turned his back on her and
said the rest to the pentarch. "Headquarters. Chains."

How small, indeed, are the gods' scale-weights. If he had not
said that then: if he had not told me what was coming. If he had
not confronted me with the final ignominy, my most private—

My most private nightmare, Tellurith.

My scribe says, Go on. My scribe says, What the gods have
written, no human silence can undo.

I fought then, Tellurith: I fought as madly and indiscriminate-
ly as an arrested whore in the streets of Amberlight, I kicked and
tried to punch and must have screamed aloud.

There was time, later, to total the damage. Torn clothes. A
closed eye, a tooth-slashed lip. Ribs that were, if not broken,
cracked fit to stab at every breath. Bruises everywhere. One that
missed a kidney by the merest—

Not the real damage, Tellurith.

* * *

The rest must have been already primed: shock and terror and their own realized nightmare, all my knowledge of Iskarda's import in the scheme of things, all the burden of military disaster already atop their minds, the last weight to tip anyone from, Wait and see, and, Make a chance, to, It's over. There's nothing to wait for: make it tell.

That threw the whole market square, screaming, armed or weaponless, on the enemy's spears.

Did I write, once, of my thankfulness at missing the massacre in Cataract?

Perhaps I should thank some—god—that the moment Desis whipped her light gun out and cut half a dozen spearmen off at the knees I threw myself as madly against my own captors' hands. So half of it was just a knee-high shambles of flying feet and slumped corpses and screaming fallen and running blood. And half I never saw at all, after the pentarch hit me, with his spear-butt, behind the ear.

My scribe says this is evasion. That I am your liegeman, and your Iskardan adviser, and I owe it to you—to myself—to give you a clear accounting—

Whether you already know or not.

* * *

Desis, then. Heartshot by an archer, in the forefront of the first rush.

Quetho. Shapers-head, true to the past of Amberlight, overcome by main force: hacked to pieces, when her cutter finally ran out.

Pheroka. Cutter, clan-Head, house-leader, beheaded in the brawl when they broke the front rank of spears.

Huis, Kressis, Uether. Men of Iskarda, village or House. Killed, fighting with staves, marble-slabs, a carving-knife, when they cleaned out the houses.

Zariah. Killed in defense of her House. And her house.

Asaskian.

You will slay *me*, Tellurith. I know quite clearly you will execute me. If you can reach me before Sarth.

Dead? No. Not dead. Felled over her mother's body, in the realization of that nightmare she had lived with, and was too great-hearted to destroy me for its exorcism, felled . . .

Her right arm struck off.

* * *

Caitha saved her. Other women who have some leech-craft tourniqueted the arm, bandaged it, somehow kept her warm through the shock until Caitha reached her. Along with the thirty-seven others wounded lightly, severely, or mortally, the six who died.

After they gathered up the prisoners. Cleared the houses with the drag-net, the very device I perfected in Riversrun, brought out every living soul. Loaded the incapable onto Iskarda's own mule-carts and herded them all, men, women, children, babes in arms, down that fifty miles of good road to Marbleport.

They took me too, I am told, in the same cart with Darthis and Iatha: chained, a blade against their throats and their lives hostage for their folks' submission.

The same way they stopped the resistance in Iskarda.

They did not burn the village. I know that tactic too. It is not a mercy: it was designed to make people go quietly, to think that they do still have something to lose, so they refrain from a last suicidal resistance. So they save their captors more casualties.

So they can make an example that is not a martyr's. So they are no longer heroes, because they hold something back.

Oh, in all truth I . . . I *ought* to execute myself. Gods above and below, how *could* I have been so crass, so blind, so mind-stoppingly stupid not to have seen, not to have imagined—When he knew they had my counsel, when he *knew* what I would say, when I knew already it was war to the knife-hilt, and I had *seen* which way he was going—

As my scribe says, I must compose myself. This tells you nothing. And what use is it, to spew recrimination for a past already settled and—

Dead.

Buried.

No.

They would not let us—they would not let us so much as burn our dead. They had already set their cordons: they brought in people wood-cutting, a couple of hunters checking snares. He could never have escaped.

But in the village, he could never have evaded them. He would have been caught . . .

I have no way to tell if he was caught, if he was not simply stabbed, shot, left in his blood and the death never reported, oh, Dhe, the corpse never tallied at all—

My scribe says, more kindly this time, after the cordial and ammonia salts and an actual visit and profane reproof from Caitha, that such a blank is also the only hope. That perhaps, in some yet unknown miracle, he was saved. That he is still somewhere: mislaid, lost, displaced . . .

I am quite aware of my weakness. If I cannot command composure, telling, remembering such—things—why should I refrain from tears?

* * *

Icame round by the signal tower on the road to Marbleport. Evening halt: the prisoners' first conscious experience of captivity. I remember a truly vile headache, and the rigors of a late winter bivouac: people bedding down in their meager store of blankets, their winter coats. Somebody coaxing foul army mess-soup down me, and half a cup of snow-melt water. Because there was nothing else.

And Caitha, as the guards crossed spear-hafts in front of her when she wanted to tend my hurts.

Dhe, the River-lord, all the gods be praised, Tellurith, for your women's wits.

Because she let Iatha and Darthis swear and protest and shout, "Mother blast you! He's one of us!" Because she did not try to break the barrier: just stood back and nodded, hands on her hips. And said, "If you lose him, won't worry me."

It must have taken ten minutes for orders to traverse the command chain, to be endorsed with what I guess was vitriol by Tarriz himself. Caitha finished salving Iatha's slashed, now stitched shoulder, gathered her gear. Moved over to me.

The firelight was dancing with pain-stars, my vision blurred not merely the sentinels but her downbent face. I had so little time. I had so little resources for judgment, consideration: let alone anguish. Before I had to make the choice.

But I knew then that there never is a single choosing. That by fractions and increments, all the way from that first meeting we had in Riversend, the choice was already—had already been made.

Now the act was all that remained.

I had sense enough to whisper, when the surges of camp-noise reached their height. And she had wits enough to decipher it— Dhe's eyes! To decipher that, Tellurith—a true physician, without so much as a twitch.

As she wiped salve on my eye, as she washed the blood off my lip, I added the last, the most important part.

"Tell everyone. But only our folk . . . until Deyiko."

That it was our first destination, I had not the slightest doubt. When they uproot a hostile people, is not Dhasdeini policy to resettle them, by force if necessary, deep in Dhasdein's lands? They would go downRiver. And in this case twice over, for the spectacle: the final, morale-breaking spectacle to cripple our fighters. The heart of the alliance, the hope of the future, captured. Exhibited. In enemy hands.

Even then, Caitha never gave a twitch. But I knew she understood, when she murmured, as she probed the contusion along my jawline, "Ah."

And I knew, with all my faith in the training of Amberlight, that when the moment came, my plan would be used.

* * *

It was as well I chose that moment, that chance. They let me bed down, huddled with Darthis and Iatha in the hostage-group: they shared cloaks with me, who had only a torn indoor coat. And when the troops came to haul me off as a dangerous, segregated prisoner, they fought and argued and repeated that cry, "He's one of ours!"

It was nothing I had not foreseen. It was, in truth, an absolute necessity if I—was to do anything. But I understood what the separation meant. They gifted me a small, warm candle of memory to bear into that deepening dark.

By next afternoon we reached Marbleport: a Marbleport already secured by advance guards, ships captured, communications cut. They commandeered every freighter in the roads, above half of them out of Dhasdein. There were—five and a half hundred of us, at most. They crammed them in, tighter than any slum prisoners: it was a brief run, after all, through the Narrows on the winter's dwindling flood and on to Quasharn's wharf-side, under the loaded catapults of the strike force itself.

I saw that, Tellurith: I do not think it was kindness that let me breathe in my manacles atop the gangplank, and glance across the River's steel-gray breadth. A bleak late-winter evening: below the Iskans, snow had already crumpled into mud. Dulled lights, shadowy roofs. And the ships lying to in the roads, the entire ten-strong squadron. When I saw them properly, the heart died in my breast.

Because the size and oar-pattern told me they were the new Archipelago galleys, whose single banks and five-man sweeps had swept our old triple-bankers off the outer sea. And I knew then that Tarriz had spoken simple truth. Our River galleys would have been crushed beyond recovery. They had brought up the Archipelago fleet.

* * *

Tarriz received me on his flagship: in the Admiral's quarters, cramped if lordly in comparison to a triple-banker's. Guards hauled me in, roughly enough, if they did not throw me on the floor. Tarriz waved them out: and stared a good while, ensconced in the ivory-embossed official chair, before he jerked his head at the wall. And said, "Lean."

No seat, for a political prisoner, a dangerous agitator, a declared traitor. A noble renegade. An extra turn of the foreshadowed thumb-screws for a man who, after a bad head-blow and manhandling, not to mention three days' starvation, could barely keep his feet.

I do not mention this for sympathy, but to clarify my situation, my weapons and my strategy, Tellurith.

Doubtless he considered me beyond personal threat, and he had some idea what I might betray. Hence the guards' departure. I leant more than gratefully. I let myself sway a little too. He had me stand another, he doubtless thought, endless couple of minutes, before he said, "Talk."

Doubtless, too, it was intended to be threateningly cryptic. I had no difficulty in retorting, "About what?"

He got out of the chair. Took three strides, and backhanded me into the wall.

I came round, I am not sure how long after. Needless to say, on the floor. The blow had struck my previous head-bruise against the timber. I could not speak. I could hardly see.

He threw some water on me: all his actions had a barely concealed viciousness. I had been his overlord, his impregnable superior, his enemy's shield. He must have dreamed, planned these moments, when he could take his own pleasure with the emperor's.

When he thought I could focus, he kicked me, sighting carefully, in the bandaged ribs. I should imagine, at the least, I grunted. Possibly I screamed.

"Tell me the secret," he said.

"It's there. I could hear it." He had come close enough to stare straight down in my face. Through the starbursts, his narrowed, agate-brown eyes swam. A commander now, faced with a prisoner who had information he meant to have. At whatever price.

"You can tell me." He nudged his boot in my ribs again. "Or I can call the intelligencers."

Meaning, the fleet's intelligence officers: and their torturers.

I managed to roll off the manacle chain, and eventually, to sit up. I knew he would be gloating, luxuriating in my weakness, my humiliation. I wiped my mouth, which had begun bleeding again. My head was still swimming. My belly—

Let me confess it, Tellurith. I was terrified.

Oh, not just at the threat of physical torture, the thing I had ordered, enjoyed, and never, ever experienced for myself. Nor at disaster's shadow, or the terrors that loomed beyond. Prison, trial, execution? No. Oh no. But that I was not just dancing with an interrogator over perhaps priceless information. That I had to spin that dance into a maneuver more protracted, more delicate, more difficult than the taking of Iskarda.

And all to reach a hazard infinitely worse.

So I took the time to ease my head, to steady my breathing, to try and quiet my belly. Before the real initiative was launched.

Then I squinted up at Tarriz, and with the most delicately modulated blend of terror and defiance, said, "Call them, then."

O, Tellurith. Do you know what it is, to hazard your worlds, all your worlds, on your sole, shaken judgment, your assessment of the wits, rather than the stupidity, of an unknown man?

His eyes slitted. I felt the blood ooze at my mouth-corner. I heard the sentries shift outside the door.

He walked back to his chair.

Leaning on its top, he said, sounding quite casual, "Think you'll handle the rack all right? Some hot coals? A little carving? I suppose you'd know."

I bit my lip. Hard enough, I could not have controlled the wince. And let him see me swallow, before I lifted my chin.

It is a known, indeed, Tellurith, it is a famous gesture. It became my signature, in thirty years of Court intrigue. Tanekhet—the lord Tanekhet—the Suzerain, Viceroy Tanekhet's last answer. Silent, unequivocal. *No.*

With the heart in my throat, because we were already past the greatest gamble: and he had told me, with that last question, that he knew enough about me to recognize what it meant.

He growled in his chest. "Oh, so tough, are you?"

I tilted my chin a little further. Looked him in the eye, and smiled.

Thank Dhe for all those years I spent before the mirror, perfecting each gesture, till the slightest twitch, the smallest half-smile or lifted brow or head's inclination was precise as a poet's simile. Thank Dhe further for the years of learning to gauge a man's wit by his gear, the look in his eyes, a handful of words.

I saw the anger rouse: challenge recognized. The instinct to requite it in good earnest. And then—I swear my heart stopped—the check.

He stared at me, for that moment inscrutable as a courtier, and I knotted my other hand on the floor-boards behind me, and kept my chin up, the disdain in my eyes. Let it deepen just that fraction that said it was an involuntary revelation of triumph: You have played into my hands.

His brows snapped to as they had under the helmet, and he stiffened sharply. As he understood.

He left the chair and patrolled round me: a soldier, a more than usually clever soldier, who had unmasked a snake in the guise of a wounded scorpion, and was inclined to laud his wits even as he rubbed it in.

"They said you were a damned—water-fox." They are Delta demons. If I ever wondered about his parentage, it was settled then. "A damned . . ." He shook his head. Not admiration. Savage relief.

"So you think you'll find a bunch of bunglers and die before they get it out of you?" He came round to face me, and now he smiled. "Oh, no, *my lord* Tanekhet. You really do have a secret that could wreck the empire. And you thought you could keep it. Still."

He smiled again. "But I have the fastest galley on the River, and downcurrent, Deyiko's less than two days' sail. And at Deyiko is the High Commander. With the empire's best intelligence. You can try your secret, *my lord*, against them."

A stupider man might have needed more office: some spluttering, some denials, a crumble into plea. But by then, I had the strongest faith in Tarriz' wits.

I gave him one look where cornered rage became chagrin, and chagrin veiled too thinly over deepening, desperate fear. Oh, Dhe, Tellurith: that part I did not have to feign. Then I thrust my chin up, and, every inch an affronted, haughty, consummately arrogant nobleman, averted my head.

* * *

Imperial fives do not have a dungeon: they shackled me below, between the oar-banks, so I never saw the Riverside where our broken galleys lay like human carrion, I never actually saw the last corpses that rose amid startled, appalled profanity to disintegrate against our oarblades, or the sniping with ragged guerrilla outposts above and below the battle-site. The water way was clear, clear enough for Tarriz to hazard his fastest galley alone. If Nathyx and whatever land forces we had left were still fighting, I did not have to be told their resistance would be all but impotent.

The Archipelago folk were brusque but not brutal. I had water and a cess-bucket. Like all prisoners, I learned to shut my mind along with my eyes and ears. On the second evening they made good Tarriz' boast and marched me ashore in Deyiko.

You will remember the town: Verrain's imperial borderpost, barricaded with customs offices and toll-booms, an outgrowth of officialdom grafted on another Riverside hamlet. Its shanty straggle remained visible beneath the walls of tents and crowded anchorage and picketed auxiliaries, everything that announced an army's centre of command.

Logical enough, if not only for the military: a long way behind the action by that stage, but there was other reason to keep this command-centre safe.

As I found after the marine detachment dragged me through the rudimentary main street, past the sole grandeur of the River-lord's temple, into what had been the mayor's mansion. And after the rattle of challenge and counter-challenge, atop a most exigent flight of marble-paved stairs, I confronted the commander himself.

He had just finished supper: a most frugal meal, in his case, a quail or two in aspic, white bread from an imported Dhasdeini baker—his stomach is as delicate as it is fastidious—ice freighted downRiver to cool an equally delicate Shirran white. The cup was half-empty, an autumn gleam above a heap of paper that said, Unread dispatch. He looked up at the aide's re-entry, saying, in a voice of goaded courtesy, "Well, bring him in."

The marines opened out. He looked across the lamp and froze.

After a space so long I heard the marine corporal breathe, he set down the cup. Sat back in his chair. Said, " . . . Tanekhet."

My lord, as clearly repressed as the rest: the days when he would run to me, as a toddler, a child, a worshipful boy. A gawky adolescent, to whom a smile, my barest look, would be a day length's joy.

I said, "Your Highness."

His eyes spoke for him. Long and dark as his mother's, and despite all his Court schooling, far, far too eloquent. Affirming what his presence blazoned clear as a comet: that Antastes would—that he must—show the empire, willy-nilly, the situation's peril along with the threat's stature. That he must send his Commander-in-Chief clear to the empire's edge.

And make that commander his heir.

You will forgive me, Tellurith, if I spared a moment to savor the protests, the wrath and outrage that must have convulsed the Imperial troublecrew. To say nothing of the army, saddled with a rank cypher atop such an enterprise, and the contortions of subordinates trying to lead from behind while keeping imperial feathers smooth. Dhe love me. Given the time, I could have laughed.

Were I not wondering, with a still splitting headache and a belly so empty its cramps were more like labor pangs, and a most lamentable tendency to need holding up, not to mention the embarrassment of clothes worse than a ragman's and a six day beard, just what was left of the cypher I had known: the carefully invisible Crown Prince.

He took the topmost paper up. I wronged him, Tellurith: he had read them after all. He looked at me across the table, the lamplight, the gulf between us, and said, "Tarriz writes that you have something to say to me."

I let my face answer, as I had done for so many years. I saw him read it, and recognize his own reflex. The long mouth tightened in a way I had not seen before.

Then he told the corporal, "The guard commander will relieve you," and laid the dispatch down. I knew how well he read that look of mine, because to me, he said nothing at all.

* * *

The intelligencers' work-room was in the wine-cellar—no doubt the general staff drank it clear for them, and it was eminently in character: dark, damp, underground, with plenty of earth to muffle untoward noise. I daresay Queziar and his minions were also about their supper, and cursed me heartily.

Oh, yes. I knew the intelligencers—the torturers. How not, when I had chosen, made, promoted all of them?

Queziar was uncertain what to do with my acknowledging nod: a pitiful stratagem, but pride matters, Tellurith. Especially to endurance, which is always from the spirit. And especially when time comes into it.

They went through the preliminaries: searched, secured me face outward against the wall. They did not yet strip me, or, indeed, batter me at all. And presently came the sound for which we were all waiting: the footsteps of Therkon and his suite.

As Crown Prince he was elegant, however invisible. As Commander-in-Chief the elegance remained. I admired his shave, and savored his perfume. And the perfection of his manicure, as he touched his ivory baton under my chin.

Quietly, so quietly, he said, "Tanekhet."

"Your Highness," I replied.

He was a courtier. He did not sigh and roll his eyes, though he was facing away from the room. But I saw him set his teeth.

"Is this truly necessary?"

I lifted my chin.

He looked over his shoulder. They had, also routine, lit the brazier: the small pokers were heating. The fire brought out the room's residual odors, sweat, blood, excrement, urine. Fear, agony. Death.

"The upRiver ships are gone," he said. "We sank nine of twelve and wrecked three ashore. The casualties—you know how men in armor swim."

I inclined my head.

A gesture he had seen a thousand times. The dart of memory vibrated in the target. Eloquent in his eyes.

"The land-forces are rag-tag," he said. "Our vanguard is twenty miles from Assuana. We have the Oasis road."

I inclined my head again: I felicitate you.

"Tanekhet . . ."

Be sane. Be kind to us both. You will turn yourself to screaming rags, and there is nothing left to justify it.

He shifted the baton against my jaw, turning my face in profile.

"Even as a child," he said, "I knew no-one else could be so beautiful."

Indeed, a blow worthy of my teaching. Subtle, and to the core of what he understood as me.

He used the baton to move my face back. To make me meet his eyes.

"You know," he said softly, "Queziar."

How not, when I had chosen, trained, so often overseen and directed him?

"Can you really—really—put us both through this?"

I let him hold my eyes, and show me the distress in his, and understand his grief and horror at the wreckage that my obduracy would make of a man he had loved, a beauty he had idolized, a leader, a model he had made his own, and his yearning certainty that none of it had to happen, that we just had to be civilized, reach an accommodation. What is the point, said those long, tender eyes, in wrecking, in torturing yourself for this?

Truly, the keenest weapons never touch the flesh.

I moved my jaw a little, to tell him he had me gagged. When he dropped the baton I said, "I am honored, Your Highness. And desolated. That I cannot oblige."

He let the baton down. We looked at each other a moment longer. Then he said, the distress patent, "Tanekhet—why?"

Any man would do it, nailing his colors to the wall along with his flesh. It was also the moment to drive in my own first wedge.

"Because," I said, "I have taken another service. And vowed my loyalty."

He stared at me: his confusion was as carefully orchestrated as my bravado.

"Service?" Puzzled. Forbearing. Ready, even now, to absolve, to release, to forgive. "You mean—to Iskarda?"

"I mean," I answered, "to the qherrique."

His brows contracted. Like his mother's, they are a keystone of his looks. His beauty, let me be honest. Quetzistani high blood. Too, too like another face—I saw it form over his in the lamplight, and had ado not to turn away.

"You think it will save you?" he said.

I looked him in the eye and let the words come with all the clarity I could give them.

"I think, that if you force it, it will bring the emperor down."

Raised at Court, schooled by me, Therkon has little superstition left. He has seen too many omens made. He frowned harder. Then he sighed, the note of a just master thwarted, and nodded to Queziar.

And said, as they moved forward, "Remember, I want him kept alive."

* * *

It was still no more than preliminaries: a taste of the future, a carefully judged legacy of bodily pain to deepen through the dark. No whips yet, and, despite the brazier's threat, no irons: no bludgeons, either, let alone the crudeness of boots. Nothing splashy, that is not how I taught Queziar. Just the judicious, barely visible, precisely aimed blows, delivered not for damage but for maximum painfulness, with the naked hand.

They took me back very early next morning. They had fed me, and let me relieve myself, attentions designed to make the contrast bite. Queziar's way is mine: leisure, for care and discrimination, to let the threat have maximum effect, and the sufferer work on himself. The morning session told me how much this answer mattered, how little Therkon himself believed the military threat was all they faced. Queziar would never have gone from working pressure points to coarse assault on major body areas, in one session, without extreme urgency.

Despite everything, I find, we keep so much foolish pride. I tried not to cry out, Tellurith. When I had breath, I actually attempted not to scream. They worked on my kidneys, my ribs, my belly, for the most part: even with another subject, Queziar would not, yet, have moved to the face. I was still coherent and certainly aware when Therkon arrived at noon.

Queziar held the lamp as he approached, and he did not try to conceal his indrawn breath. "Oh," he said, "Tanekhet."

Without the bonds I could not have stood upright. I was not breathing well, but there was no blood yet, except where I had bitten my own tongue.

"Gods—" He had taken in the contusions now. The horror was genuine. "This is lunacy . . ."

I took a breath of my own. If I was careful, despite the ribs' damage, I could do it without a scream. Queziar had used the older injuries, with thrift he also learnt from me.

"Remember," I managed, without much of a wheeze, "the qherrique."

He gave me one look. Then he set his jaw, and gestured to Queziar to drag up the recorder's chair: sat down, facing me, the baton across his knees, and ordered, "Go on."

Oh, indeed, the keenest edges are in the mind. He knew that I would suffer twice for every sound they wrung from me before him: and conversely, that I would suffer, for every sound he made for me.

* * *

They reached the groin before that session's end. If I did not scream, it was because they left no breath for it. When Queziar decreed a break, they unbound and let me fall on the floor, to feel the damage from another angle, before Therkon had them give me water. And bread, though not his Dhasdeini poppy roll.

When I could think again, lying there on the paving as I have seen so many prisoners, I counted days in my head. This was only the first. The prison-ships would move slowly, for display. They could be no less than three or four days behind me. If Queziar could not give me time, I had to make it for myself.

So when they hauled me up again, I screamed and fainted. It was not so hard, with my ribs given the right cant over a muscular shoulder, and it was thoroughly genuine. I came round on the paving, my face wet, and a quite distraught Therkon kneeling over me.

"Tanekhet, Tanekhet, this isn't, this can't be necessary. Oh, gods . . ."

I groaned a deal more and tried to turn my head away. He took me by the chin and made me meet his eyes.

"We can rescind your exile. We can give you back Dhasdeini citizenship. We can give you the Suzerainty. Or if you must live in that—that—we can restore your revenues. The estates. For the Lord's sake, Tanekhet."

I rolled my eyes up and let the arm pinned under me impact on the ribs. When I came round again he was almost in tears.

"Tanekhet, please . . ."

I spent a minute or two breathing hoarsely before I whispered, "Would the emperor—pardon Iskarda?"

I saw the answer in his eyes: in the way his mouth settled, the curve of a mask for tragedy. I wheezed again and he put a hand against Queziar's chest. "It's not going to save you, Tanekhet!"

Surely, in that moment, Dhe had already looked on me. If he had not mentioned it, I must have done so myself.

"It will save me," I whispered. I rolled my eyes around to the three assistants at Queziar's back. Mel'ethi, two of them, and therefore rife with more gods than the rest of the empire combined. I let my eyes give it all a tortured man's impact as I whispered, "And it will remember you."

* * *

An attempt to suborn his people earnestly irritated Queziar. He took to the whip almost immediately, the long-lashed, thin-tipped whip, which allows a maximum number of cuts for each inch of skin. They started on my back, and had worked down to my loins by the onset of evening. I fainted a good number of times to draw it out, since even Queziar in haste and temper would not waste cuts on a man beyond feeling them. He would have gone into the night, though, had not Therkon, for his sake or mine, forbidden it.

"Let him absorb this lot," he decreed. And, less knowledgeably, "He's taking too much damage too soon."

I saw Queziar roll an eye. Like me, he knows how much damage a torture subject can take, and remain capable of coherent speech.

But Therkon had other means in mind. After they had stowed me for the evening, after a time that, doubtless, covered his supper and another bath or so, he came to the cell. This time with nothing but an oil-lamp and a stool. And a guard, out of lowspoken earshot, in the corridor outside.

His opening salvo was, "This is pointless, Tanekhet."

I managed to open an eye. Queziar still had not touched my face, but the weeping and the smoke belowstairs made it hard to see.

"He's going to massacre you. He's going to cut you up, inch by inch . . ."

His voice failed him. There were real tears on his cheeks as he got down on his knees and took my face in his hands.

"For the Lord's love, Tanekhet, I used to admire you—I used to—you were so beautiful—so elegant—so absolutely—perfect . . . I tried to dress like you. To walk like you. I thought, if I could get that right, I might—"

Become more than a cypher, more than a discounted, bewildered boy. Learn the armor, the impregnable, inimitable courtier's menace, and be puissance and presence too.

The tears fell on my face. "It's all destroyed. What there *was* went upRiver with Tellurith and it's gone, you know it has. They're dead in the Heartlands. Nobody ever gets back. They'll never find the Source, and what good would it be if they did? There's no hope, Tanekhet."

Spoken without vehemence: without an attempt at suasion, let alone coercion. With grief, and despair, and a sense of bereavement poignant as my own. Truly, the great torturers work on a man's spirit, and they need no iron for their tools.

"If it *could* act, why has it let us take Verrain? Beat the galleys off the River, raid Iskarda, roll up the land-troops like a market-woman's carpet? It's not fighting for you. It isn't listening. It's all a lie. And you're going to give it your life—more than your life, Tanekhet."

I whispered, "A lie—in Amberlight? In Cataract?"

"Amberlight was ready to fall. Cataract never got back on its feet. You delude yourself."

"And Verrain?"

The lamp caught his eye whites, the curve of the beautifully enameled earring, the traitorously reminiscent modeling of his upper lip. Then he lowered my head carefully back on the floor and got up. And said, "I hope you've thought this over by morning, Tanekhet."

* * *

Next day Queziar dislocated my shoulder—or was it the morning after? And that day the first of the irons? The sequence becomes confused around that time. I know he still had not touched my face that night. When I had the strength, lying on the cell floor, I groped in the straw—so very typical of them—and drew out three stalks to secrete in the further corner. If all else blurred, I knew I must keep account of the time. I do remember that in the next noonbreak Therkon told me they had secured Hamadryah, and the nomads on the Quetzistani border had offered to treat.

"It won't save you, Tanekhet." He was sitting by my head, heedless of the floor's effect on his immaculate scarlet officer's kilt. He did look well in battledress. "Verrain's gone. It's all over but the sweeping up. And once we have Verrain, nothing will save Amberlight." He stroked the hair back, matted, filthy, over my forehead, that was cold with pain-sweat. I knew it because his fingers felt so warm. "Save yourself."

I opened my eyes carefully. Queziar remained an artist: if I hurt badly enough to black out, I was nowhere near the end of my body's strength. I tried my voice, which, after the water, was audible, however hoarse. When I guessed the assistants were in earshot I whispered, "You put me in an impossible position, prince."

"How is that?"

Eagerness. Desperate eagerness. Not all by intent.

"You tell me—to betray the qherrique. And ask me—to betray the empire instead."

He leapt up on his knees and grabbed my closer hand. "You won't betray the empire? You still follow Dhasdein? This was all a cover? Gods, Tanekhet—!"

I cut him off with a small shake of the head. Opened the other eye, and saw Queziar's face. He, if no-one else, knew my apostasy was genuine.

"Not a cover." I let his hope, his ardor die just far enough. Before I added, "But not wish—to see the emperor ruined."

He opened his mouth to burst out with a boy's naivety, It need not happen, just tell me, we can work it out, it's not so bad as you think. I literally saw the courtier, the prince, the commander regain control.

Quite carefully, he said, "Let me be the judge of that."

I shook my head, and did not try to stifle the consequent groan. It lent force to the way I said aloud, "Let me go. Save the empire, prince. Because if I speak, it will—it *will* bring the empire down."

* * *

Queziar spent the afternoon working on my chest with the irons. Or was that the day before? I think it was the fourth day, because I recall the way the straw stuck as I worked free the counting stalk. I had fainted so often that Therkon hardly had to argue him into a night's respite, though I was beginning to prove a challenge to him. I do remember that, next morning—I am fairly sure it was the fifth morning—he took to hanging me by the dislocated shoulder and re-opening my back with the whip. By that session's end, I was almost too hoarse to scream, and Therkon was in literal tears.

I recall counting as I lay on the work-room paving, which if painful on my burned belly was blessedly cool: three days, four, five. The usual time for a freighter from Quasharn to Deyiko is a week. But that includes a market stop in Assuana, not to mention watering.

On the other hand, my mind objected, would they want to display the prisoners at every village quay? Who would be so foolhardy? If the enemy did not crumple, they might well, over a protracted voyage, try a rescue attempt. If the prisoners did not anticipate them. They were women of Iskarda, of Amberlight: even in chains, disarmed, they were dangerous.

The thought must have encouraged me to something like bravado, because next morning—I do know it was next morning—Queziar began using a vice on my joints.

No doubt I should be grateful that he started with my wrists. And more grateful, however ironically, that Therkon would not let him crush them outright. By evening I had screamed myself voiceless, but my wrists, my elbows, my ankles were, if excruciatingly painful, relatively intact.

Therkon stopped them at sunset. But instead of the cell, he ordered me taken upstairs.

They sat me at the table, in one of his own chairs. He brought me water, and then wine, with his own hands. I was so thirsty, I had drunk deeply before I thought.

He let me sit a little, so far as I could sit, between the touches of the chair-leather on my screaming shoulder, my burned chest, my whipped back. He had his servant move the lamp so it shone full on my face. Then he beckoned Queziar beside him, the best face-reader I know, and asked, "What do you know that would bring the empire down?"

When I just looked at him, he reached out and took up my right hand. He turned the wrist over, and when I finished gasping, laid his fingers across my pulse. Waited till it settled, relatively, and then, looking full in my face, he said, "Did you know this secret in Riversend?"

I moved my hand and gasped to hide the pulse's jerk.

"Or did you learn it in this—Iskarda?"

Truly, he had heard all I could teach him. And he was fighting for his life and his inheritance, and his way was far deadlier than any torment of Queziar's.

"A secret that could bring down the empire—a name? An object? Visible? Portable?"

I was spent, and in considerable pain. And that traitor pulse was out of my control.

"Not something you saw. Something you heard, then? Something you were told?"

His eyes dwelt on my face. "Something you read?"

He did not need Queziar's nod. His mouth had hardened. For the first time, I saw his father in him, and his grandsire as well. "Reading, yes. In Iskarda."

I pulled against the chair back, rolled my eyes up as the whip-weals opened, and let myself fall into the faint.

It was Queziar who picked me up: put me back in the chair, and held my shoulders, while Therkon sat sidelong on the table, fingers on my pulse, eyes, so calm, so inexorable, fixed on my face.

"Maybe—it was something someone wrote?"

Queziar held my shoulders tight.

"About Dhasdein." Meditatively. "Now, would something like that be known in a hill village?" He let the moment slide. "Or would it have come from Amberlight?"

I got my voice back by swallowing the blood in my mouth. I turned my own wrist to grasp his fingers and said through my teeth, "Do you *want* to destroy your life?"

"Not the empire, then," he answered softly, "so much as the emperor."

It was the sixth evening. Had they hurried, had they made no displays, the convoy could still not be in Deyiko. I jerked my arm and put myself out again.

The walls, the table, Therkon's scarlet-kilted thigh revolved madly in the streaming light. Distantly, his voice said, "The royal line?"

I put my other hand on his wrist. He let me breathe, and gather my voice. I made it perfectly clear, with as much of my old, arsenic drawl as I could manage.

"What would the son of a Quetzistani slut, brokered for a couple of Riverside gewgaws, know about royal lines?"

He backhanded me harder than Tarriz ever achieved. The chair went over with me. A while later, Queziar, I think, took me back to the cell.

* * *

I knew, when I woke, that it was the seventh morning. Conscious knowledge? Rational calculation? Counting grass stems? The moon, at last, in my blood? I do know that I heard the prince's aide tell a departing officer, " . . . moor them offshore," and then, "parade tomorrow." And then something about, " . . . too dangerous," before they started heaving me down the steps.

The minute I saw Therkon's face, I knew that, whatever happened elsewhere, my own crisis had come.

He watched them tie me up against the wall, facing into the room. When Queziar leant a heavy arm in the centre of my chest, pressing fingers into the burns and the whip-weals into the wall, his eyes never changed. When Queziar set up the hand-vice he walked over and looked on as the biggest assistant fastened the grips, screwed down the locking nut, and stood back, giving place to Queziar himself.

With the fingernail pincers in his hands.

I struggled then in earnest. It was not artifice, though I saw Therkon's eyes fix on the change. It sounds ridiculous, does it not? Have my elbows crushed, my back flogged raw, my belly flayed, my genitals kicked black, and endure: and then fold up, at the thought of losing a fingernail.

But I have watched it before. And felt every hideous twinge, down to my own nails' roots. And if there is one thing of which I truly am vain, Tellurith—

It is—was—my hands.

* * *

This time it is I who have kept composure. And my scribe who has had to save the papyrus, by running away in tears.

* * *

So. Let us finish this.

Therkon did not try to persuade me, that time. He only watched, with all the pain and pity gone.

Queziar began with the index finger. I screamed in earnest too. Oh, Dhe, it was worse than I had imagined, and I had imagined horrors, Tellurith. I had not been able to reach a whisper for two days, and I nearly raised the roof.

Queziar shook the nail away. I cursed him then, the way prisoners do when their defenses finally go down, with all the knowledge and all the invective and all the agony at my disposal, hoping, as so many prisoners have hoped in vain, to madden him so much he would overstrike and finish it.

He looked at Therkon. Who, whatever his inexperience, knew what he was hearing. And nodded at him: go on.

The middle finger was worse. As terrible as the bloody wreck he left behind, as terrible, through the drowning pain, as the knowledge that my hands would never be a court noble's, would never be Tanekhet's again.

The blood in my mouth must somehow have got into my eyes: I recall quite clearly the stink of the irons and burnt flesh, Queziar's sweat. The red haze through which I saw, blurring in and out of focus, Therkon's impassive face. The clarity with which something said in my head, One more. This is the seventh morning. The third finger. No-one could possibly expect Tanekhet to bear any more. One more and you can break.

And when Queziar tore out the third nail I screamed it at the top of my lungs at last, "No, no, no, no more! Gods, please, no more!"

Queziar knows surrender when he hears it. He put the pincers by. I cannot decide if it was triumph or regret that shifted momentarily across his face.

Therkon came past him: he held my head up, and studied my eyes. And nodded, deciding it was truth.

And then, uncovenanted divine boon, he beckoned the recorder up as well.

Quietly, but without kindness now, he said, "What is it, Tanekhet?"

I looked up into his face. He is taller than I, and I was hanging in the restraints. I coughed my throat clear. I could see the assistants beyond him. And a last gift of the gods, the heads of at least three staff-officers showed outside the half-open door.

Very clearly, at the top of what voice I had, I said, "I found a cypher between House-heads in old Amberlight. An agreement to keep silence. To let the Crown Prince Antastes claim his statuette. Even after the qherrique said: this is not the emperor's son."

* * *

A nd all it took, to overthrow an empire, was a handful of words? Must I cipher Dhasdein for you, Tellurith? An empire, yes, meaning a conglomerate of states, tribes, provinces, conquered and retained by force, weakness, fear.

And religion: for Dhasdein, that above all. They are—were—reconciled to bondage, because it is divinely ordained. The emperor rules by the gods' mandate. He is the living form of the River-lord. Every year the emperor offers himself as the empire's sacrifice, and every year the River-lord declines: affirms him in his role, convinces the empire of its rightful subordination, its submission to royal lineage, whose succession signals the divinity's will.

What will befall the empire, if the emperor's succession fails?

Especially when that empire is already fighting a supernatural opponent, when its supporters' superstitions have been woken, and the story is vouched for in a tortured noble's blood?

Give the boy his due, Therkon did his best. It took him less than a minute to get his jaw up, after what must have been his own heart-blow. To say loudly, "This is nonsense. An outright lie. Recorder, strike that message. You—"

Before he saw the way Queziar was looking at him. The assistants' faces. Before he heard, as I had, the creak of receding footsteps on the stairs.

It must have run through the headquarters before noon: a couple of assistant intelligencers, a gaggle of eavesdropping staff officers, a mere bagatelle, yes. It might still have been stifled, denied, a purge made of the witnesses, had the Iskardans not been there. Had they not acted prompt to their time.

They did not force the tale on the enemy. They did nothing to vouch for it at all: they just told each other, loudly, all over the convoy, in the sailors' earshot. And whatever their own beliefs, the sailors spread it into the Deyiko boat traffic that was still swarming round and through and in between everything.

Including the galleys of the fleet.

The Archipelago is the backbone of the imperial navy, yes. But the Archipelago has an even longer score of wrongs and injustices than Verrain, and its folk remember them all.

Do you know the rest already, Tellurith?

By evening the fleet marines had reputedly turned sullen. The sailors were flouting orders by next dawn. The freighter crews turned on their guards, you will surely know this part, over a man unfairly struck at breakfast, and by mid-morning the convoy had tossed its military presence overboard, up-anchored, and set sail for Assuana.

With the Iskardans, freed, topside, acting as marines.

From there it ran like dry rot through old timber, like fever through a siege-camp, like green-death up a poisoned limb. Through the troops, into the countryside, back over the border, into Quetzistan, Riversrun, Mel'eth, Shirran, the Delta, Riversend. Over sea into the Archipelago. Nothing travels like word of a disaster, and this was not only disaster but a resounding scandal, the seed of a calamity none of us ever dreamed.

So it went, like the master thread drawn through a tapestry, and the empire unraveled behind it, dissolved, faded away, like a castle children build from spring-eve snow.

* * *

How much of this is superfluous? My—scribe informed me, this morning, on pain of suppressing any agitation, that the mirror signals had you landing, four days back, in Assuana. Welcomed. In triumph. Leaving a River in equilibrium from the Heartlands to Amberlight, with your folk—almost all your folk—safe. And Zuri with you: an alliance confirmed, a city's kingposts set behind her, her Regency relinquished for other, dearer bonds.

All three of you safe. Whatever you found upRiver. Whatever it may mean to me.

* * *

I suppose Therkon might have murdered me anyway: I am unsure why he did not. None of this comes from my own memory, which decays entirely somewhere on the way out of the torture room. I presume, because it seems most likely, that they took me back to the cell. I presume, for want of other knowledge, they left me there when the army pulled out: leaving its advance guard to Nathyx' tender mercies in a roused and riotous countryside, watching its galleys sail off downstream, with the Archipelago flag hoisted, in place of the serpent and thunderbolt.

Of course there were loyalists: there are always loyalists, among those too deeply involved in their lords' crimes to escape. I am told most of the Quetzistani troops went with Therkon, for instance. The Mel'ethis, on the other hand, deserted like leaves in autumn. Before Therkon could decide what counters to make, two thirds of his army had melted away.

And I? When they left me, I must already have been deep in the throes of what appears to have been jail fever. Given beating, torture, galley bilges, the dank cellar, whatever infection hung around the fleet or round Deyiko, fever is hardly a surprise. Nor is the fragmenting of my memory.

There are images of blotted darkness, of blinding light, of unknown rafters, snatches of a strange door-frame. A vista, from knee-level, up some foreign street. There is visceral record of a fever patient's burning thirst and hallucinations and general if fractured sense of bodily misery. I have no idea who found me. Still less who brought me to Caitha, filthy, skeletal, all but unrecognizable, raving for days before I sank in a coma that might, that should have been the end of me.

Ask Caitha how she saved me: better still, ask the River-lord. Or Dhe's own self, who franks a physician's mysteries. Merely thank either of Them, that Caitha was among the Verrain vanguard, sweeping back downRiver to bring up at Deyiko.

I have no memory of that, either. My first clear—my first new memory is of waking, slowly, so slowly, with the languor of a fever patient whose crisis is past, in an ebbed, remote lucidity as unfamiliar as the feel of sheets. Of a clean body, and most miraculous, a mattress under me. Of lying there, poured out like standing water, luxuriating in no more than the sense of bodily harmony renewed. In knowledge that the fever was gone.

When I opened my eyes, Tez was sitting beside the bed.

* * *

Now I come to ponder it, I have the sense—of myself, not of others' telling—that I had surfaced to find her there before. Perhaps many times. Splintered moments, before the fever pulled me back and down.

At the time, the best that my vaunted aplomb, my courtier's composure, the lauded address of Lord Tanekhet could manage, was to ask, in a thread of a voice, "What are you doing here?"

In retrospect, that really was the hint of a flush. I can decode the momentary sense of a flinch. Before she answered, cool as on that last day in Amberlight, "You asked for me."

She was clean. Bronzed. Whole. Dressed in a Verraini officer's under-tunic, its shoulders wealed with the indelible armor-marks. Off-duty, temporarily. Her head was bare, her hair . . .

Her hair was long enough to plait at last: not a Crafter's tail, but the double braids that signal a mature woman of Iskarda.

I was still too weak for wits, let be control. I was beyond reasoning at all. How could I have asked for her when the one thing printed on my soul beyond erasure was that she never wanted to see me again? Why had I done it, what had I said? I was torn, Tellurith, between complete bewilderment and uncontrollable embarrassment, and an infant weakness that wanted only to burst into tears and grab, there and then, its heart's desire.

I did hear my voice crack on the, "Ask . . .?"

"You kept saying it. 'Get Tez. I must tell Tez. There's something Tez must know.'"

"Kept saying . . ."

"I should think," level as her stare, "you said it for at least five days."

She looked down at her hands, folded on her knee. She still sat like an officer, lightly, collectedly.

"Eventually they thought it must be so important, they got a message through."

She looked up, eyes level as her voice.

"But by the time I got here, you were in coma. Caitha didn't know if you would come out."

I knew what I felt then: mortification, to the quick of my very soul. To have bawled like a veritable infant for the unattainable, to pull a serving officer from her duty and keep her idle who knew how long—and this officer above all . . . There was only the most ignominious escape route left.

I felt my cheeks burn, and turned my face desperately into the blank, windowless wall.

There was no sound of movement. No breath intaken, no shift of feet. Only, at last, her words, more impassive than ever.

"What did you want to say to me?"

Did I say my soul was mortified before?

Not because of my—infatuation. Not because of the way we had parted—over and over, the way we parted, with so much I had been forced to leave unsaid. Not for all the things I might have said, for Keshaq's sake if not my own.

But because, when I searched, there was nothing in my memory. Therkon, Queziar, day-counts, tactics. They were what should have obsessed me, surely, in any delirium. If not the fall of Iskarda. But what could I have wanted to say to Tez?

Except for things that could never be said at all?

Given the strength, I would have got up and walked away. Or, more like a baby than ever, pulled the covers over my head. Given the slightest mental resource, I would have tried to lie. The effort itself was too much. I did what neither Queziar nor Therkon could have compelled me to, not if they had torn me limb from limb.

I shut my eyes, and whispered, "I don't know."

She did not reply.

In the silence I pictured her understanding, her contempt. Her wrath, renewed, justified, for this blundering fool who had not merely let the enemy uproot Iskarda but could find nothing better, in his decrepitude, than to drag her from her business on some delirious pretext: and now could not so much as invent a reason that he wanted her.

I could have sunk clean through the bed. Through the floor as well.

And she executed a perfect, immaculate Tez. She did not revile me. She did not offer possibilities or embark on questions, kind or cruel. She did not get up and stamp away. She sat there, silent as a very gate-spirit, and used her presence to compel me as surely as Queziar would with a rack.

I recall quite clearly that I screwed my eyes shut. That I scrabbled for pretexts, water, a fainting fit, a bed-pan, anything short of pure hysterics to get her out of there. I would have sat up, to buttress myself that far. My damnable body could not even turn over in the bed.

In the end, there was only one choice: I kept my eyes shut, took a deep breath, and tried, with all the fortitude that was left to me, to steady, if not to arm my voice.

And I said, "You need not stay anymore."

If it sounded husky, I had torture and fever as an excuse. I tried—how I tried—not to make it hostile: merely cool, and remote, as a great lord ought to speak, with courtesy to one for whom he feels nothing, not even compunction for the trouble he has caused.

She moved then. I heard her shift, and rearrange her feet. Then she said, "My watch lasts another glass."

So she had not merely visited, she had downed weapons to share nursing me. Gods, what humiliation did she intend? To cap it all, I had to lie there. With her in reach, in earshot. And suffer whatever indignities the illness wrought, with her to watch it all.

I did—at the least, Tellurith, I did have sufficient composure not to protest. Not to beg. To keep my eyes shut, my face still, upturned on the pillow, and pretend that I was not so much an invalid as the effigy on a noble's tomb.

The room was very quiet Wherever it was, the environs were silent too: I could hear no movement in the building. No voices rose, no doors slammed, no feet clattered on stairs, nothing sounded outside, except a vague rumor that might have been people or vehicles a long way away. Or perhaps it was only the wind.

The silence went on widening until I could hear my breath. The shift of sheets against some kind of very fine linen shift, over the burns on my chest. The rhythm of blood in my ears. The silence was the eye of a maelstrom, that was going to suck me down, down, down, and I would never come up.

Tez spoke into that silence, quieter, more inevitably, than the fall of an autumn leaf.

"I would have stayed in any case."

* * *

For a time longer than eternity, I simply did not believe my ears. And when I did—

Need I tell you how it was when I did, Tellurith?

She waited through it all. The belated comprehension, the more belated decipherment. The—

Until I could manage to move. Open my eyes. Look at her. Oh, Dhe, to meet those golden-flecked eyes, so steady, so unwavering, so quiet, now the battle was joined. The fate declared.

"Lady—" I said, and this time my voice did crack. "Tez—my lady—I don't—I don't know how to—"

Gods, how could I say to her, I understand what you just said. Everything you said. Everything most impossible, incredible, unbelievable, all, more than all I ever desired, and renounced, with tears and anguish, as being forever beyond me, everything I would have died for—And I have no idea how to respond to such a declaration from a woman of my new world, and I dare not answer as I would have outside Iskarda. And I cannot say any of this, and if I do not speak my heart will surely burst.

At the last, flesh at least came to my aid. I struggled with the sheet, heavy as a galley cable, until I could drag out one hand. My right hand, the fingers bandaged, I discovered, as I stretched it out, the muscles trembling, the whole arm wavering, trying to make the gesture say it all.

I thought she would not move. Then, just before my body and spirit collapsed together, she reached out too.

I pulled her onto the bed. Half of it was her volition, half the weight of a limb I could no longer uphold. She landed beside me with the resilience of a fighter, her free hand propped the far side of my chest.

"Tez," I said. "Oh, Tez."

* * *

She left me however long it took to compose myself: but when I opened my eyes she bent at last, shifting the hand that had still tendered my injuries, protecting my burned chest. The golden-flecked eyes were unwontedly somber, her jaw set rigid. Almost as in distress.

"I lost the ships," she said.

Brusquely. Harshly. The note construed for me: the galleys. The Cataract galleys that I had begged them not to send down-River. That the Archipelago fives had wiped out.

"We couldn't find Shuya's statuette."

Who else could turn a lovers' declaration to a council meeting? But those eyes were bleak now. Desolation, memory's grief. It had been her strategy: she had enforced it. She had not only failed her own folk, she had failed Verrain, and with Verrain, Cataract. It was guilt that stained her hands, as well as squandered blood.

"The Dhasdeinis—got the Oasis road. Hamadryah. They'd have knocked us off the River. There was nothing left. If I had listened to you—"

"I lost Iskarda," I said.

She stopped on a gulp.

"I should have known what he would do." I had to shut my eyes. Even with her. "I was the only one who could have known. And I sat on my backside, dithering—"

She put her hand over my mouth. I felt her draw breath, and guessed a swallow as well.

"But you still—brought down the emperor."

I opened my eyes. All the unlikely accolades that may ever come to me, Tellurith—if any do—all the honor anyone could ever ask, all the knowledge of my role in the final phase, the endurance and the skill, however reprehensible, that let me cozen Tarriz and best Therkon and bring on the last, impossible victory—all the honor I will ever need was there, in that moment. In Tez's eyes.

She held my look: kept holding it, as she reached out for my bandaged hand. Took it in both her own. Very softly, still watching me, she said, "Even the manicurist."

A lump closed my throat. She meant the taunts she—Antastes—everyone—had hurled at me before we left Riversend. That I would have to do without my tailors, my cooks, my perfumier. Even my manicurist.

She smiled suddenly, brilliantly, a smile I never saw from Tez before, and touched my cheek. A lover's touch at last, delicate, cherishing, drawing her fingers to the mouth corner, to the angle of my jaw. The rasp of stubble against her hand suddenly deciphered the chill at my temples, the foreign airiness, hitherto disregarded, at my neck, and I all but groaned aloud.

"What is it? Tanekhet?"

"Oh, gods," I was trying not to weep from sheer weakness atop happiness, unable to control the laugh that was getting hysterical. "They've cropped my hair, I haven't shaved since Iskarda . . . I must look . . ."

I felt her breath catch and strain, before she started laughing in earnest. "The Mother aid me." Her hands caught my face. The only part of me that it was, after all, safe to touch. "Worry about your looks? Now I *know* you're better, Tanekhet."

I did laugh—we laughed, sharing the moment's wealth as lovers do. I was still laughing when she sobered: leant forward again, and drew her hands, slowly as a sculptor gauging his subject, down the line of my brows, my cheekbones, my lips, my jaw.

Still holding me, she said softly, "If you knew how long I've wanted to do this . . ."

People remain, Tellurith, who can make my heart hurry like the greenest boy's. I said, trying for nonchalance, "Since this watch began?"

She shook her head. Her eyes were soft as I have never seen them before.

"Since the day you made your case to Antastes. Or to the House. Or the day you walked onto that boat-dock. So arrogant. So exquisite. Such a lord."

I looked at my bandaged hand: touched it to my jaw, could not help sliding it over my cropped head. I know the value of my hair. At my expression she laughed out loud, clear and freely, and love-tapped me on the cheek. "And you are still so blighted *vain*."

I started laughing too. Heart's ease, heart's desire reached at last, love's haven made. What else would I do?

Then I remembered other things.

She held my stare. I swallowed hard. Then I said, "Asaskian."

I felt rather than saw the frown begin. I tried to catch her hand and said, "This time, will you let me explain?"

She sighed. Then she worked my other hand free of the sheet, and resigned herself.

"She courted me. She—wanted me. The—everyone in Iskarda thought it would be a good match. That it must be what Tellurith meant me for. Darthis actually said it: 'She can't have brought you to sit making tally-marks'."

It was understanding now. Both offense and laughter were gone.

"And I—"

I took a long breath and stripped the last armor off. "What I wanted was you."

We let our eyes speak then. Until she looked down, laced my fingers with hers and murmured, "Only me?"

"I—to begin with, yes. With Asaskian . . . that day. I was tired. And she was—is—beautiful. And you would not look at me. And I thought, just that moment, what can one moment matter. But—"

"But it did."

I sighed. "I have never made so many false judgments—mistakes—never had luck fall so badly, as in Iskarda."

"Poor love." She did laugh a little. "The master plotter, and all your plots kept coming undone."

"Especially when they involved you."

This time she did not smile. After a moment, she said, "And Asaskian?"

"Now?"

She nodded.

"Tez . . ." Not for the first time, I wished she would take the offensive and show me what her priorities were. But she sat still.

"I—admire her. I know she wants—wanted me. If I—Dheiya said: in Amberlight, people expected to share. If I—if she—if Iskarda demanded it—could you?"

She sighed then, a long, easing sigh, and leant down and kissed me at last, a butterfly brush over my mouth. "Oh, my dear, my trouble has never been sharing you."

"What then?" I must have sounded as eager as Therkon.

"She's so beautiful. I thought, given Asaskian, why would you ever look at me?"

I was too weak to exact the penalty that deserved. I could not even get her to lie down and embrace me, let alone rest her head on my chest. I held her hand as she propped herself on the bed, and did my best to make that serve as eloquence. It seemed to work. Until presently she met my eyes, and said, "And Keshaq?"

"Keshaq." I shut my eyes in earnest, feeling the dart pierce me through and through. "About Keshaq—I don't know."

* * *

Since my scribe deserted me when I began this section of the—narrative—I have had to write that last myself. Since she now decrees I have outrun my strength, the pen is back with her.

I told her the truth about Keshaq too: that it began as distraction, a substitution, that it grew to a bond, to a pledge I could not break.

That perhaps, I still cannot say it without anguish, there may be no need to dissolve it, because it has already been broken for me.

My scribe repeats that silence and absence is not firm news of death. And repeats too what she said then, taking my hand again, looking into my eyes with that unflinching honesty, informed now by warmth that melts my heart every time I look at her.

My scribe retorts, with more than asperity, that I have no need to let it also melt my brain. That I must not give up hope: that if Keshaq did survive, she would think the less of me, should I turn my back on him. Far less than if I repudiated a bond with Asaskian.

Tellurith . . . Whatever you think of my part in Verrain, in Amberlight, in Iskarda, of my culpable negligence in the fall of Iskarda, and my hands now stained with your House-folk's blood—

I *know* you will not sanction this.

Love her, yes. Reach an understanding with her, perhaps. But however it may be joined with others', to make a formal bond—

To marry her?

My scribe interjects with extreme indignation that she has no intention of marrying anyone, and certainly not me. I return Dheya's warning: she is House heir. She must marry. The line must go on, through a legitimate child.

And I have no doubt at all, Tellurith, that you—and far more, Sarth—will not at all appreciate this understanding we have made. This . . . this joy that I have tasted, this last few days, you will not wish to see continue. Perhaps you will put an end to it.

My scribe speaks yet more vehemently of her say in this. I answer that you are House-head. That I have never known you put the House below personal—happiness.

The mirror signals say you are sailing downRiver: there is to be a general, a final resolution of River affairs, here at Deyiko. Amberlight, Cataract, Verrain, and whoever becomes Voice for what remains of the empire will meet, to settle everything.

My scribe tells me now, to my more than astonishment, that although the Archipelago has seceded and Mel'eth and Shirran may follow, Quetzistan and Riversrun have chosen to keep the title, empire. And the name, Dhasdein.

And that after the tidal wave of scandal swept through the Imperial quarter in Riversend, Antastes relinquished the seat of emperor.

That Antastes walked out into the River waters off the Delta mouth, and kept walking. And has never been seen again.

I repent the things I have, at times, said of my one-time master. At the last, he knew what is asked of an emperor. Whatever his blood-claim, he gave the assent. He offered the sacrifice.

Far more wonderful, my scribe says Quetzistan and Riversrun have chosen a joint ruler: they will take as leader, they proclaim, the Empress, whose claim to the imperial throne may be on the distaff side, but is known to be pure, and who may be succeeded, in the fullness of time, by her son.

Shades of the past. Shades of old Quetzistan—

That is our name. Shades of the People, the desert folk, whose customs we—I—so brutally overthrew.

Will you overthrow my happiness in the same way, Tellurith?

* * *

You have embarked. You should be here in another two or three days. And this report is finished: I have given you the truth of my heart, as I have given you the heart of my loyalty. Of my lapses, my blunders, my failures, you are all too aware. I asked you once, in what I thought was gravest distress, what I ought to do. For all my scribe's protests, I, at least, will be content to accept your decision now.

It has been a long journey from the boat-dock in Riversend. I thought I would change myself: I did not know, Tellurith, that we would metamorphose the River as well.

But I could be content now, whatever you decree for my fate. If only . . .

My scribe has gone to the door. I find we are still in the Deyiko mayor's mansion, in an attic back-room commandeered by the inexorable Caitha, because only there could I be tended in sufficient quiet. Would you credit that she had the alley outside blocked, and demanded—from an advancing army! that they pave the rear street for the length of this house in wool?

My scribe has just come back. She has put the pen into my hand. It is my part then, to write it: to describe the shine in her eyes, the glow breaking, irresistible as dawn, as she said, "There's someone to see you." And when I asked, in some astonishment, "Who, then?" She answered, the smile breaking free completely.

"He calls himself Keshaq."

CHAPTER XVII

Deyiko. Spring
Tellurith's Diary

How strange, to write for no-one but myself; to surrender that silent listener, that other eye before which you ponder your concerns, evolve your plans, record and construct your past. After so long in that imagined dialogue, to write a diary feels almost like going deaf.

But the journey is over. There are no more letters; or at least, not to Tanekhet.

And we are here, at Deyiko, the River's potentates assembled for the final settlement; the fixing of boundaries, the establishment of states and nations. The end of the war.

If one can call it a war, whose principal opponents never so much as met.

For myself, I do call it so. If I never crossed a formal battlefield, I, like so many others, have borne casualties enough.

I should thank the Mother, no doubt, that if the worst remains irreparable, some losses that seemed as final have, after all, been redeemed.

Such as my marriage.

Because if they, if Sarth, above all, has begun forgiving me . . . I, too, can turn to them, now, and take genuine comfort. Feel genuine desire. Genuine love.

I should thank the Mother fasting for that.

* * *

And no doubt I should offer votives for the qherrique saved, the River stabilized, Amberlight and Verrain and Cataract preserved, and confusion, but not massacre, in the settling of Dhasdein. If there were deaths and losses and bloody destruction, and mourning up and down the River, the deaths have not been in vain. They were not cancelled by defeat or squandering. They were not waste.

And Amberlight has a people's government, and Haturi is confirmed as ruler of Cataract. A process we completed when we arrived, the first blazing annunciation of return, survival, victory, at Cataract's water gate.

Although the news that greeted us was parlous, with downRiver at its nadir; Verrain all but conquered, the Cataract galleys lost, the imperial juggernaut poised to turn on Amberlight. Worst of all, Iskarda's folk slain or deported, a spectacle trumpeted the River's length, Tanekhet vanished into who could imagine what surreptitious torture, imprisonment, illegal death?

And no hope of our arriving in time to make a difference, if we ever could have made a difference, without even the dubious aid of Shuya's statuette.

In the first half-glass of meeting Zuri told us all of that; a Zuri torn between black gloom and delirious joy that we had returned at all, that we had achieved the Quest. And the rest. All the time she was detailing calamities with that iron-jawed impassivity, her eyes kept sliding sideways. Even Zuri could not keep those eyes completely cold when they lingered upon Sarth.

And when the desperate counsel was agreed, that we should take galleys from Cataract's last reserve and hurry on downRiver, in the lunatic hope that the qherrique could somehow do something, some last-ditch miracle; still I could feel the seep in her attention, the constant struggle to stay official, when all she wanted—

Is it any wonder that when they vanished that night into her rooms, I hid myself and wept?

But I watched them go, and I did not relieve my spleen upon Sarth. Or upon Zuri, when in a flurry of decrees and accommodations she and Haturi agreed to end her Regency; agreed to turn Cataract over to its own, truly its own folk.

Perhaps, too, Wonsa's vision will prevail; Zuri has summoned artisans and craft-workers and established them with land and houses, and the graft has begun to take. For that at least, the upheavals downRiver were a blessing, for they sent floods of folk after a haven that promised stability, however threatening its repute.

Cataract is beginning to look a city, a real city, at last.

I wish Wonsa could have seen it; I know Alkhes was thinking that, as we stood at the galley-rail, with Zuri pointing out new houses, the half-built craft-shops, the signs, everywhere, of a city building for more than war.

Not least of her achievements that she could leave at a moment's notice, with little sign of affection, perhaps, but without uproar, and with the honest respect, as well as gratitude, of so many she left behind.

They have changed, all three of them. How could it be otherwise? Yet it remains disconcerting; to see Sunya stride about, enlarged, panoplied in unconscious, almost Head's authority, and the garb of a Haturas officer, and men spring to obey her words. To find Ahio speaking, sitting, standing, with that same enlargement, who was a Shaper, with all that implies, but a leader, a Head, a commander, no.

But Ahio has come back with us. For her the first allegiance will always be, not Cataract, or Amberlight, or Iskarda, but the qherrique. It was Sunya who, when the time came, chose to stay.

I cannot find it in me to blame her. I can find much to feel for her. Would I want to leave whatever solace I had found, in a stranger's land, with my beloved forever gone?

From the most pragmatic view, it is a safeguard to be thankful for. Someone to second Haturi. To keep watch on the statuette, as well as our own interests. She will do it, and now, she will do it surpassingly well.

I am not sure if Zuri has expelled her demons altogether; I do know she has met them alone in open battle, and prevailed. The signals of that victory are unmistakable. I do not know how she can ever contract into an Iskardan Trouble-head, circumscribed in a single village's scope.

I am not sure Cataract will let her shrink. They have made her their envoy for the peace-talks. They have trusted her to do it with no detailed mandate. Will they not want her, later, for other grand initiatives?

Will she not want to go?

Enough of that. Enough to remember, for now, that Cataract is settled and expanding. And Zuri is back at my side.

At Sarth's.

Where she went again that first night downRiver; and who could blame her, and who could deny her, who had suffered the worst of the separation, and who could possibly justify the torments of jealousy?

I tried not to. I tried to do no more than creep away to the bows and weep.

Which was where Alkhes found me. Captured me? Coming soldier-silent to fold me in his arms with that grip that is both extreme tenderness and indisputable strength, and say into my ear, "Oh, Tel. Tel, you're killing me. Don't. Don't do this to yourself."

I forgot Varris. I forgot that all the way to the Jump-up we had hardly spoken, beyond courtesy or necessity, and less from his wish than mine. I could not bear to be with them; with either of them; lest even that veneer burst.

And if that happened, I was mortally terrified that I would in truth, begin to hate.

But to hear him say that, with so much pain . . .

I turned about in his arms and buried my face against his neck, and let him hold me as he had not for so long, and at long last, took some easing from his presence as I wept.

When I quieted he let go; took my hand, turned me to the scaling-plank; the galley was moored broadside, not beached. I thought I understood, and began hanging back; but he turned me about, with the last of the firelight on his face to show its truth, and said, "No, Tel. Just come to bed with me. Just let me hold you and—at least you don't have to be alone."

He still had my hand. I wiped my nose like a brat with the free one and said, hearing it thick and husky as a mourner's voice, "Where did you mean to sleep?"

* * *

After that he came to me, with scrupulous fairness, every second night. And he had enough of Sarth's empathy to leave it at bed-company; simply to be there, the warmth of loving kindness and physical presence beside me, a tangible, a still beloved bulwark against the dark of memory. The emptiness of night.

We made Amberlight in three days. That night, after the now more familiar thunderclap of strain and jubilation, after the ragged River Quarter folk and threadbare merchants had cheered us through their streets, after we had told our tale, not to the Assembly in its heroically shabby warehouse, but to the entire City, out on the breadth of the Main Quay, when they finished the stinted celebration, war-rations, Sahandan rice wine, we were ushered up to what passed for honored guest quarters; back, inevitable irony, in the Engravers' Hall.

It was then that Sarth came to me.

I was half-ready for bed; hair down, leggings off. The tap on the door made me grab with what was now reflex for the pouch under my shirt; and change the gesture to cover my belly, that had swollen toward a reasonable dimension at last. Before I asked, less coolly than I wanted, "Who is it?"

And that deep, unmistakable voice answered, "Tellurith?"

If he is less volatile than Alkhes and far less ingenuous, and far more tolerant of ruler's dishonor, when Sarth's forgiveness fails, he is implacable as flint. Once that judgment has been made, you could reverse the River's flow before he turns it back.

At Thilliansar he had judged me; when Alkhes let me alone from pity, I knew Sarth had felt no such tenderness.

The silence pulled like wet leather. My heart thumped, words dried in my mouth. I knew his cruelty, none better. I could not conceive why he should unleash it now, but neither could I conceive what else would bring him back.

Outside the door, he said again, "Tellurith?"

The perfect quiet and impenetrable courtesy of a tower man. Only one way I would find out.

I said, "Yes."

The door opened. He filled its interval, so tall and splendid, with the single candle-flame sculpting that perfect, statue's face.

As expressive as a statue's. In that light, even his eyes were dark.

I waited. Whatever it said to him, I could not find words to take the lead. We looked at each other across the bed, across my increased belly and those betrayingly positioned hands.

I saw his eyes fall; I saw, too, the change, so tiny, so unreadable, in the set of his mouth.

Before he looked up and said, as evenly as ever, "Alkhes said you ought not be alone."

I could have been insulted; I could have repudiated the suggestion of weakness, I might have read it as compulsion rather than his own choice. But I know—oh, Mother, do I not know Sarth, down to his last breath and heartbeat, the tiniest channel of choices in his brain? Whether he was here willingly or not, whether it was choice or pretext, this was the nearest to a reconciliation that he would ever come.

And I wanted him; was I not entitled to want him, after such loss and sacrifice, after such a renouncement as I had made? Was I not entitled to whatever comfort I could find?

To say nothing of whatever he deserved.

I said, "Close the door when you come in."

* * *

And when we had settled at last, in that mosaic of past happiness retrieved and other happiness so achingly recalled, when we had adjusted ourselves, with the ease of long custom, to the rigors of the lumpy, if ample bed . . . Sarth put a hand on my belly, as simply as if he had done it everyday coming downRiver, and murmured, "May I?"

He was no physician. But did he not have the right?

He laid his ear against me. When he shifted at last, it was easy to draw him higher, before I laid that head down against my breast.

He did not speak. He did not move either. But I can read the nuances of that body in my sleep.

"What is it?" I said.

He did not answer at first. When he did, it was with the coolness of the philosopher, a form of the physician's mask.

"This is the eighth month."

I had not the slightest doubt it was accurate.

"I come to term at the most inconvenient times."

He moved his arm a little over my waist. "At eight months, though, before . . ."

I had been bigger, no doubt of it, approaching the full, unconcealable extension of a terminating pregnancy.

"They aren't all the same size."

I almost burst out with the rest, What is it, what's worrying you, what do you think is wrong? At the very last second, he broke the quiet.

"But for twins?"

"Perhaps *they* are smaller." It was too direful, too threatening, that something should go wrong, this time, above all this time. "Perhaps we mistook the conception, they may just be little, they may—"

He laid his palm so gently over my mouth. Then he took it away and kissed me, with all the tenderness that Sarth is capable of, and after that he spoke, so close my mouth took the breath as well as the sound.

"Tellurith, we'll have physicians this time. It will be all right."

* * *

We might have had physicians, but it appeared they would be upRiver; for we could not get past Amberlight. The border was lawless, Dhasdeini troops were only miles from Assuana, the conquest of Verrain looked a matter of days. The Assembly, the entire City vetoed it. "No!" cried Dhanissa. "Risk the qherrique, the one thing they absolutely want? Get you massacred by some bandit on the River-edge, or the ship rammed or—are you out of your wits! When—if Dhasdein gets here you can do something. But until they reach the Iskans, no!"

Seconded by Alkhes, and Sarth, and the rest of Amberlight. And Zuri; when she gave me that look, I knew better than to try again.

* * *

So it was to Amberlight that the incredible, impossible story finally came. When Tanekhet's last stratagem, his best and most deadly intelligence-trap was sprung; and the army, the emperor, Dhasdein, the war, the whole huge appalling edifice of defeat and ruination dissolved away.

The first word upRiver was mere battle rumor, too garbled to convey anything but surety of a cataclysm; then, more slowly, came the first, unbelievable trickle of wonder, of hope. The full story only arrived this last week, the birth of the second spring moon. With the clearing of the River, and the establishment of Nathyx's government, as leaders of the Free People of Verrain.

And word that the Iskardans had safely joined Nathyx' troops; and the request that Amberlight and Cataract send envoys down-River, to a congress of River states.

Amberlight sent Dhanissa and Juiza and Ferrias. Zuri speaks for Cataract. Verrain has Nathyx himself. Mel'eth and Shirran are still settling leaders, and the Archipelago has sent observers only. Iskarda is present as a body; all the survivors, who have refused to go home until the treaties are made.

Dhasdein has sent its empress, and her Viceroy. The empress's son.

So there have been no few awkwardnesses, as former enemies encounter across what will be a conference table. And no few delirious reunions, especially for those of Iskarda.

To see Iatha again.

And Darthis, and Hayras, and Charras, and all those loved, lost, remembered faces, to have the House around me, if the houses are still far behind.

To see Caitha, and have one delivery with a physician I can trust with more than my life.

And she may be needed; because we are into the tenth month this morning, and the anomalies proliferate. I am hardly larger than I was at Amberlight.

And there are two heartbeats. Caitha hears them too. Yet Caitha herself cannot find two heads.

I tell myself it is mere chance positioning. I tell myself they are alive, that is all that matters, forget the length of the pregnancy, forget that Caitha acridly refuses to induce labor, with sharp if cryptic comments about, "not this time." I tell my men to calm themselves, and keep busy thinking about anything else.

Such as the duty I have been requested, or is that ordered? Very clearly, very specifically, to perform.

It was the first time we could bring ourselves to congregate; the whole company of the Quest, with all its strayed and its acquired members; except the dead. When we could not wait on human counsel any longer, we made our circle in the centre of the choir-ground, the nearest to a holy place that remains in Amberlight, and asked, What shall we do about the war?

And for all our efforts, for all our specific and our more and more infuriated questions, only one answer came.

Next time, it will be all right.

It gave me that when I asked about the children for myself. What it told me, at the moment we were ready to break the circle, was something else.

The first unsolicited message we have ever had; a flare from the seed, cradled at our centre, a ripple around our linked hands, of sensation, of pure lightning, that said, Pay heed.

And then the picture of a table in some room with Nathyx at one corner and the Crown Prince at the other, with Darthis and Iatha and Dhanissa and Zuri ranged between. And Tanekhet, unmistakably Tanekhet, at the table's head.

With me beside him; or was he beside me?

Whichever way you take it, it was Tanekhet and I, he with his hair brutally cropped and a bandage on three fingers, in a Verrain version of his merchant clothes, I in a shirt and leggings that said, workaday Amberlight.

And between us, the qherrique, cupped in our joined hands.

So I am going to the peace-talks, but not as the envoy of any human state. I can only hope that the crises of talks and labor can be managed not to coincide.

And I have another meeting to attend first.

* * *

For such a patient, snatched from death's own gullet, Caitha is a very lioness. When we did escape the thicket of promises not to tire, let alone stress him, it hardly surprised me to find she had left partisans as well.

Tanekhet has not long been permitted out of bed. He was ensconced in a chair in his sick-room's foyer, lying back as fragile convalescents do. The marks of fever, not to mention the rest, are very clear; if he was shaved, and the rough shirt was clean, his cropped hair makes him look ridiculously like a first year military cadet.

And his face, so wan, and gaunt, so gaunt, all brows and pain lines and cheekbones, with those eyes; forest-green, instantly recognizable, but far too big for their frame.

And the change in their expression. All the hauteur, the invincible composure, the lordling's confidence, gone. He looked subdued. Uuncertain. As tentative as those hands, with the palmless glove concealing the three fingers that are not yet completely healed.

I knew his partisans instantly; the tall man at his left shoulder, with the flamboyant Quetzistani looks and scars bristling through every muscle's pose and the attitude of defiant protectiveness; if he did not have a hand on Tanekhet's shoulder, it hovered inches away.

And at his right?

Equally defiant, and far more protective; corkscrew curls plaited at last, golden-brown eyes narrowed, a lover's threat and ardor finally looking at me. Out of Khira's face.

I felt Sarth stiffen at my own shoulder and doubted the wisdom of bringing backing myself. But they had a right to be there; both of them.

Tanekhet made a little movement of his head; acknowledgement of a superior, courtesy, apology that he could not rise. He said, "My lady Tellurith."

His voice has changed too. Weakness, yes, and that untoward hesitation, one might almost say submissiveness. But above all, the hoarseness; what was a panther's purr, so beautiful, so flexible, was now a roughened echo of itself.

I said, "My lord Tanekhet."

He frowned a little. Then, with a faint gesture, he said, "My lady, may I make known my liege-vassal? He is of K*uo clan in the Nairan line. His name is Keshaq."

I answered with genuine feeling, "It is a pleasure to see you here."

Both their faces warmed, Tanekhet almost to animation. "I thought he was lost." He actually sat up a little. "He is, he was, a proscribed traitor. I tried to get him out, at Iskarda." It wavered and Tez put a hand on him; warning as well as protectiveness. With equal naturalness he covered it with his own; but he went on, the forest-light eyes alive now, almost their old light.

"When he found the cordon closed he hid in the fountain-culvert. Afterward, he went into Verrain."

The glance they exchanged was transparent as if it had been among our own trio. Joy, relief, gratitude. And beyond that, pride. That Keshaq had born his part in the battle; that he was a victor, not merely a survivor who safely crawled away.

Then Tanekhet looked back to me, the light fading. And I said, "Hello, Tez."

We have been here three days without a sight of her. Oh, I had the reports, that she survived her galley because her officers got her ashore, to go outlaw in the countryside, joining the guerrillas and eventually Nathyx; that it was as his skirmishers' commander she reached Deyiko, and secured the town. I had received a formal, dutiful greeting note. Excusing herself, under pressure of work, from a meeting. When she was not on duty, I knew where she had been.

Equally formal, she gave me a Navy salute, somewhat cumbered by her other hand on Tanekhet's shoulder, and replied, "Ruand."

Tanekhet's eyes flicked between us. Not the lord's assessment, the intriguer's readiness for stratagem. It was pure anxiety; the look of a man stripped of resources, with a struggle pending and no way to influence it; and his heart's core in the scales.

Again with that convalescent's effort, he said, "My lady. Will you sit down?"

There was a motley sick-room grouping of chairs. I chose the straightest, and through his own pre-occupations, saw him notice my belly, and the sudden lightening, the waking if diffident smile.

"May I . . . I am so happy for you."

And he meant it. As I wrote to him once, although he never saw it, he, of all people, knew just what it meant to us.

I said, "Thank you; I only hope good wishes aren't premature."

He read that too, clear as the tiny ripple that ran, this time, through my partisans. His acuteness he has never lost. He said, "Caitha is here; and this time—you are home."

I could only nod.

He might have stolen the vantage; but he waited for me to take it, to say, "There is a good deal we have to discuss."

He straightened then, as I had seen him do at his resources' end, to a last onslaught from Antastes. I saw the cost in Keshaq's midnight stare, with its still-banked threat. I did not want to imagine Sarth's equally unblinking, equally menacing response.

"Did you have—my letter, Tellurith?"

I nodded.

And you have made your decision, his eyes said. And it is not favorable.

The old Tanekhet would have resisted, argued, manipulated, managed a dozen shifts of equal skill and impudence. The new one just let his head back against the chair and murmured, "I see."

"You never had the last letters from me."

Because I burnt them, before we reached Cataract. Because no-one ought ever to have seen them, except me, and the Mother, and the ambient air. But if he had not gone with us, he too had been a Quester; he too had given, he might give the cause as much as I had, and he had a right to know the story. All of it.

He was answering, with labored courtesy. "I never had a letter after you left Cataract."

I said, "Then you should hear the rest."

I saw him brace himself, expecting a long account, gauging his strength, as convalescents do. As torture victims might, with a span of suffering still to pass. I drew the silken pouch from my shirt and hauled my chair in armslength, and said, "Hold out your hands."

What told me it was feasible, to pass images between two people only, and one of them never in the circle before? But he had touched the qherrique, and it had spoken to him. And he had been the Voice, in a sense the Chosen, of Iskarda.

His eyes went wide; then, with an effort that spoke his weakness clearer than words, he lifted both hands from his lap, and, shakily, reached them out to mine.

I laced our fingers together, and with my free hand slid the seed into the cup.

Then I thought back to the cliffs above Cataract, and let the images flow through me; everything that all of us had seen, and what we had felt as well.

When the last vision receded, new houses and half a market suburb dwindling over the galley rail, I could rediscover the world; the room around us; Tanekhet's eyes.

He made a move to untangle his hands. I lowered them carefully onto his knees. I knew, by the trembling, he had not the strength to do it for himself.

He acknowledged it with an absent nod. Then he whispered, "Oh, Tellurith."

I know now he would not have scathed me for that first choice I made in Thilliansar. That whatever happened to him since we left Iskarda, now he, at least, would have understood.

I slid the seed back into the pouch. Not looking up, I said, "You had a right to know it all."

He lay back in the chair. And then he said earnestly, "I am so sorry, Tellurith."

I nodded. I could not have spoken aloud. When I did get my head up, he was looking past me, beginning to frown.

Then he said, "Second winter moon?"

"Your dream," he answered my look. The frown deepened. When I asked silently, What, he swallowed. Then he said harshly, "I was never chained before Marbleport. And Iatha: she was not manhandled. She was already in the square. With a knife to her throat."

He stopped again. And added abruptly, "And what you dreamt was not fleet marines. Those were imperial guards."

We gaped at each other. Resolution came, inevitably, in Sarth's deep, velvet voice.

"It was a foresight," he said.

We both turned, but he did not notice. His eyes were living topaz, their regard drawn inward to his philosopher's world.

"I don't think it sees time like we do," he went on at last. "I'm not sure if it has a Was and Will-be. It may be more like sequences. Things that *could* happen, but until Is, there's no knowing which. Once Is happens, there is only Was."

He roused. "But until it comes, Is could be any of them. Perhaps, what you dreamt was one of the possibilities. But not the Is we know."

It was another of those visions that remake our world. Not time as a sure succession, from what Will Be, foreseen, fixed, ordained, to Is, the ever-here and never-tangible, transforming incessantly into the equally ordained Was; rather a plait of river-channels, a delta of choices running forever until we reach them, and they thin to the single line of Is, pouring past you, into that equally unattainable but forever ordained unity. Was.

In a moment I said, "Yes."

The glance warmed. A vision transmitted, philosopher's vision shared. Moved to Tanekhet, and grew implacably cold.

Tanekhet met that look, the first time they had exchanged glances, I realized, and I felt him tense like a man immersed in icy water, trying to catch his breath. But after all, he was Tanekhet. It was I who had to make him look away.

"You know my thoughts now," I said.

His eyes came back. The interest had gone. Now even the resistance died.

"Tez is the House heir. It is her obligation to marry, yes, to preserve the line. The House. It may be her obligation to take a husband who is, at least, acceptable; to all of Iskarda."

Tez said flatly, "I have made my choice."

"And if Iskarda says, No?"

She snapped her fingers. Navy hand-talk. To the pits with them.

"You offered," I said, "to be my daughter. Knowing what that meant."

Her face clenched. I knew I was hitting foul, but not how deep.

"I offered to be your daughter, yes. I am—" she looked beyond me, and bit her lip—"his daughter too."

"But your own choice comes before the House?"

I could not suppress everything. I felt Alkhes wince and Sarth twitch again, and Tanekhet winced as well.

Tez tightened her hand on his shoulder, and looked me in the eye.

"I offered to be your daughter. I *am* my father's daughter," what that meant, all that meant, was in the look. "But—I lost my mother. My sisters. My ship. My City. I very nearly lost it twice. I lost the Cataract galleys. I have—" she stopped and clenched her teeth. "I have a right to something. Why should I be House-head, and give it an heir, and give up my life for it, and get nothing back?"

Because I had to, the words boiled up in my throat like molten lead. *Because I lost my mother, and my City, and Iskarda, and my children, and the dearest love of my life, for the sake of the House. I came back, because the qherrique asked it and my beloved was too honorable to hold me back. What do you know about loss?*

She misread my expression. Her jaw came out, her head went back.

"I know what you think of Tanekhet: bad blood, worse past. Iskarda will never accept his child. But you let him into the House. You let him give up everything he had for us. And we doubted him, and we mistreated him, I mistreated him—and he still fought for us. He was tortured for us! And he did the most important thing. Without him, there wouldn't be an Amberlight, let alone Iskarda!"

Tanekhet twisted under her hand, his discomfort palpable. She only tightened her fingers. Her eyes sparked, and sharpened with the shine of tears.

"But *you* have the House, and your husbands as well. What right have you to tell me, No?"

It was Alkhes who grabbed my arm. "No, Tel!" It was Sarth who stepped past me, silent and terrible as a lion roused.

"What Tellurith has given for the House, you have no idea." It was his tower voice, soft, implacable, armed to wound mortally. "But you are my blood-daughter, and I tell you this. Make this man the House-head's consort, and I am no longer your sire."

Tez's breath caught, one sharp, mortal jerk. Then her eyes slitted and I hauled Sarth backward with a force beyond fear and shouted, "No! No!"

It broke the bond; the tightening bond of violence in which their common blood would have knotted them till they fought to the death. Sarth just stopped himself backhanding me. Tanekhet caught Tez's wrist in one hand and Keshaq's in the other and cried, "Stop!"

The room heaved to the swells of breathing, perilous as a nest of lions in a Dhasdeini arena, wanting one small trigger to fight to the death.

Then Tanekhet's grip failed; he fell back wheezing like a lung-fever patient, Tez whipped about, Keshaq hurled himself between us, Alkhes put me behind him and got before Sarth, a hand against his chest, and repeated desperately, "No."

He is as lethal a fighter; it was a clash I had seen before, and been frightened out of my wits. But I saw in those black eyes the knowledge, the certainty, that if Sarth chose to contest it this time, Alkhes would lose.

I opened my mouth. And let it shut. Alkhes did not move. Did not blink. And at last, Sarth's shoulders relaxed. He lifted his own hand. Pulled Alkhes' down. Held it a moment, then let go and turned his back.

Alkhes went after him; Keshaq and Tez were bent over Tanekhet. And Tanekhet looked at me past Tez's shoulder, a look that said silently, Help us. Get us out of this.

I let go the chair, and, carefully, straightened up. My back jabbed, as it does in the last months. I cleared my throat.

Tez straightened too, cautious as a prisoner at the light-gun's point. Keshaq crouched and glared and Tanekhet, with what looked his last strength, laid a hand on the hair clubbed at his vassal's neck and left it there. I felt Alkhes turn; and draw with him, silently resistant, Sarth.

I said, "I know your feelings. Both your feelings. You guessed mine. Now you know your father's. And you can imagine the rest of the House."

Tanekhet's hope faded, slowly as the ebb of life itself. Tez had gone rigid, every muscle clenched.

I looked at Sarth and said, "This is your blood-daughter. Will you deny her happiness?"

For an instant, imperceptibly, his face moved. Then he looked back at Tanekhet, and it hardened into very adamant. He said in the softest of whispers, "Before I see that man a House consort, I will see him dead."

Tez spat something and I snapped at her, "Be quiet!"

It was a Head's voice. For the vital moment, she obeyed.

"Sarth?"

He looked at me then. His face twisted. I was asking him the impossible, as I had asked it so often, and so often, he had responded.

But not that he accept his daughter in Tanekhet's bed.

He lifted a hand, and let it drop. And silently, shook his head.

Tez was glaring, biting down hard to still her trembling lip. I said, "And you? Will you go on?"

She just stared.

"If this is what you will do to your father, what will it do to the House? Are you prepared for that?" I took a breath. "Are you prepared to split Iskarda?"

Tez drew herself up; a muscle worked in her jaw. She was very pale, now, under the campaign bronze, as I remembered her, fresh from prison in Riversend.

Tanekhet reached out. She took him by the wrist without looking, a gesture that said, clear as its custom, Be quiet.

"I am not prepared," she said, "to give him up."

Atop her, Tanekhet said in a thread of a voice, "No."

We both looked at him. His eyes were closed, but his mouth was set, and I knew suddenly how he would look in the torture room. Not composed, perhaps; certainly not strong. But yielding, no.

Tez jerked toward him, beginning to speak. He shook his head and spoke past her, with the pain and the effort no clearer than the obduracy of the choice.

"I gave up a world for Iskarda. I will not lose it again."

Tez made one sound; the deepest unbelief, the wildest grief. He opened his eyes and answered her with pain and yearning that went deeper still. And then, so slowly, shook his head.

The room was deathly still, as if we had stretched the moment of a lightning flash. Until, moving slowly, so slowly, as if she were wounded far worse than he, Tez began to undo her fingers from his wrist.

And in that instant, endless as the fall of a heart-shot man who has not yet struck the ground, Alkhes grabbed my arm and jerked me about and hissed in my face, "Do something, Tel!"

I gasped. He shook me, one quick frantic jerk.

"Think of something. Fix it! Gods, Tel!" There was sweat on his lip. "Don't let them do this—Tel!"

With such passion and such desperation and such absolute world-shifting certainty that I could do it, that I would do it, that for all the cruelty I had shown him, for all the times I had put the House before him or me or either of us, I would still respond, demanding it still with such utter trust that I would show humanity, and the greater, lunatic belief that if anything could be done, I could do it. That if I wanted, I could overturn time and fate and reverse the will of the gods themselves.

"You can't let this happen, Tel! Not now!"

And as I looked in those eyes I understood what he meant. Not now, when the war was over. Not when Tanekhet had suffered so much. Not even when it might destroy Iskarda.

Not when I had made such a sacrifice myself.

I looked back to Sarth; he was staring at me, and for once his eyes were naked too. I looked at Tanekhet and Tanekhet had forgotten Tez, but Tez had turned and was staring for herself. I was the focus of their opposing need, their hope, the pivot on which all things turned, the Mother's own lightning rod.

I will write this here, though I never tell it to Tanekhet; who was so sure, so long ago, that the lightning comes to me, not from the qherrique, but from my own self.

Because that was what happened; when I looked within, and said to that silent inner world, Show me now. Change the moment. Make this not to be.

And it did.

I gathered my muscles; I was aware, in passing, of the sudden leap of light in Alkhes' face, of Sarth coming to tension like a subtly drawn bow. Of Tez taking a half-step forward. And most of all the hope, the wild, imploring hope that lit in Tanekhet's face.

I heard myself speak, as if from a world away.

"If you will not give up Tanekhet," I said, "and your father will not have him as Heir's consort—then you can have him. But not as Heir."

Tez's eyes dilated. I felt the dint of it, as she put a hand to her breast; then she looked down, and her face changed. She drew breath as round an arrow and said, "Oh. Of course."

"*Not* an heir to replace you." My hands curved about my belly instinctively, No, they were saying, no other, especially this one, shall have to suffer as we have. "No Heir at all."

I think they must all have stopped breathing. Everything stood still around me; thought, motion, life, the very air. It was Alkhes, at last, who took two steps back. Subsided on a chair. And said faintly, "What?"

"Thilliansar." It came clearly now as one of Sarth's visions, as that moment in Riversend, an insight that took me into another world. "They have a House, yes. But a House without a Head. And so a House that needs no Heir."

Tez seemed stricken to stone; Keshaq was equally dumbstruck. But as my vision assembled reality, it caught on Alkhes' face; and all the requital I could have wanted was in that luminous, radiant, night-in-starlight stare.

Then Sarth sat down plump next to him and buried his head in his hands and began to laugh, huge hiccupping gasps that broke into a strangled, "Oh . . . Tellurith!"

I turned about. Tanekhet was watching me too. Eyes alight, the forest-glow of a deep pool filled with sun, the face of a visionary who has preached the millennium, and within his own days' span, seen it arrive.

He bent his head, and then he kissed his hand to me. When he looked up again, he was smiling as he said, just audible, "My lady world-maker. Yes."

* * *

"We can have a council," I said, when Sarth finally collected himself. "Just like they do in Thilliansar. Just like the Heads did in Amberlight." Suddenly my own chest seemed enlarging, my own breath came light as intoxication, my own eyes looked into a new, larger world. "No more Heads, just the House itself."

And I, too, I realized, can be free.

Sarth's eyes were fixed on me; if he was not reading my mind, in that instant, then minds do not exist. I saw the understanding, and I saw its corollary too.

I said with a jerk, "If your daughter does not have to marry the House-consort? Then, will you give the marriage your assent?"

I know what you were truly thinking, those lion-eyes answered, unappeased. Before their consciousness veiled. He stood up too; watching me, rather than Tanekhet or Tez herself, as, very deliberately, he spoke.

"I would not wish my daughter married to this man, as House-Heir or not."

But there is more; carefully, he inclined his head to me.

"But, my lady world-maker, if we can lose the House-head, why should we not lose marriage as well?"

I said, "Eh?"

"Marriage," he answered evenly. "It was needed in Amberlight. To tie Houses, to keep alliances. To give us children who were heirs. But if we don't need heirs?"

There was a sharp silence. Tanekhet, I saw, was staring at Sarth as if he had never seen him before.

"Children," he said abruptly, with an echo of his old self.

"Children," Sarth answered, meeting his eyes, "need to be legitimate. But they can be so; if the parents acknowledge them. If the mother alone acknowledges them."

Tanekhet's brows climbed; Sarth raised one of his own. "Marriage was for alliance, protection of Houses, wealth. What did it ever have to do with 'love'?"

A faint, but not wholly ironic emphasis. Tanekhet's own brows flexed.

"Suppose people wanted a, a formal contract? An acknowledged, a legal relationship?"

"Then let them make it," Sarth answered, "the way women always have in Amberlight. Let them plight a troth."

Tez twitched. Both their eyes shifted, but it was Keshaq who spoke.

"Yes. Yes!"

When we all stared, he turned, spectacularly with those looks, bronze-burnt red.

"They would do that," he said, "in the slave-quarters. They—we—no matter where you went, or who bought you. For us, the troth was all that would count."

He looked around at Tanekhet, and his soul was in his eyes; and Tanekhet's answered, before he stretched out a hand and pulled Keshaq to him and said, smiling, "Yes."

Sarth watched this and raised a brow. Tez watched them too. Before she said, to me directly, "So we could have a troth? The three of us. Just like you?"

I was catching up for myself; and learning a fellow-feeling as well. "Yes," I said, thinking it out. "You don't have to get married. And it needn't be one-to-one, like the Outlands, and it would have nothing to do with the children's legitimacy. And it could be, like us."

Between man and man as well as woman and man. And woman and woman too.

"But not, Marriage." Alkhes came to stand beside me, and suddenly, abruptly, thrust his arm through mine. "We need a new name. Maybe not even, Troth." I looked the question, and he grinned at me, all the frost of pain and tension gone.

"Because it's not just troth between you and me and me and Varris, and you and Sarth and Sarth and Zuri." He looked around. "And Tez and—Tanekhet. And Tanekhet and Keshaq."

"And perhaps," said Tez, "Asaskian."

"She would like it," she answered my startlement, glancing past me to Tanekhet, with Keshaq's head against his shoulder as he knelt beside the chair. "It would be all right with me."

"So." Alkhes had passed serenity, he was buoyant; all but bouncing on his toes. "Not a knot, that sounds bad. Not a tie, that does too. Or a chain. Not a contract either—"

The first cramp hit me, like a spear-butt in the belly's foot.

I must have yelled; in a moment everyone but Tanekhet had hold of me, amid a babble that vividly recalled panics on the Quest. I got a hand free to press my belly myself, and tried not to shout in anyone's face.

"Someone get Caitha. We can discuss names afterwards. I think . . . I'm going into labor now."

* * *

There had been a strange absence of false starts, I will admit that. Right to the ninth month, when my balance was going and my bladder shrunk, when my back ached perpetually and the purported embryos were careening about my womb like monkeys in a tree, there were none of those false labor pangs you sometimes get weeks in advance. When it began, it was for once and for all.

* * *

I find this writing difficult; not for the subject, nor, this time, for any pain. Rather for the tranquility, the ease . . . can one call a victory's aftermath lethargy? The sense that almost everything I ever wanted has come at last, with toil and struggle and bloody determination, yes, but also with triumphant perfection, into my hands.

That the labor was easy, I still find difficult to believe. That it was not too fast, like the—like the one before, but that it was not protracted, as two of mine were, was more astonishing. Especially when Caitha never had to give me drugs, either to speed or to slow it down. The contractions came up, regular as a moon's passing, and swept over me, steady, majestic as the rhythm of mid-ocean waves. And this time, too, I had my men to help, to sustain and steady me, but this time we were warm and dry and safe indoors.

If it was in Tanekhet's bed.

Because it did come fast; so fast my waters broke before Caitha arrived, and she took one look and said, "She's going nowhere." To Tez she added, "Get him another room." Then to me, gripping my arm, "Inside there."

Somebody brought the hot water, the clean sheets, Caitha's instruments. Caitha gave orders, demanded supplies, and never, from the first moment until the hour-later delivery, ever left my side.

And when the baby slid out at last, she held it up by the heels, adjusting for the birth cord. Wiped the face. Slapped the bottom. I heard the first faint breath and then.

Oh, gracious Mother.

Then I heard my first whole, healthy, girl-child cry.

Things quieted eventually. The afterbirth came, we cleaned up everything; Caitha dismissed her underlings. Iatha arrived. I managed, finally, to make Alkhes and Sarth stop crying. I managed, with some difficulty, since the baby was fastened in the crook of my arm, to kiss Tez. I managed, at last, to lay her at the breast, and look at her properly, clean now, sleeping, safe.

Despite anyone's claims, no day-old baby resembles anyone. They have smoky-brown or puddle-blue eyes and most have black birth-hair and many are covered in birth-wax and a great many are wrinkled like well-cured prunes. But despite being a big child, her skin was almost smooth. It is clear, already, that she will have Amberlight coloring, a tawny milk-coffee shade like mine. Whose eyes she has, it is still impossible to tell.

But her features—

When they finally had me downstairs, in my own room; after what seemed like all Iskarda had filed through the presence chamber, as Alkhes insisted on calling it, and the other envoys had visited too. Not least, magnificent as I remember her, the Empress. After we got through the more than awkward moments as her Heir stepped into the room after her, and looked around. And from the corner whence he had refused to shift, Tanekhet gazed back at his former enemy. His torturer. His erstwhile Crown Prince.

But at the last, there was just me and Alkhes and Sarth, and Tez and Tanekhet and Keshaq, lingering in the final twilight, when someone came to light the tall oil-lamp.

The bed was in a corner. I was sitting up, the baby at my breast. They set the lamp on the closest table. I held her up, idly, supporting her head, to catch her shadow on the whitewashed wall.

And nearly dropped her as my own heart spasmed and Alkhes gasped as if shot.

"Gods above!"

Her profile was on the whitewash, clear as on a silhouette maker's screen. Newborn baby's profile, a fuzz of hair, double chins, the skull clear, just faintly lopsided. One baby. One head.

Two shadows. Two profiles, two profiles I have watched so often, I could recognize them in a newborn baby's face.

Sharp-nosed, high-cheekboned, winged razor-brows, sharp-cut if sensitive lips. Darker, slightly behind the other. Whose outer, slightly more nebulous outline was still perfectly legible, with its classic sweep of nose and eye-socket, its high forehead and elegant mouth and perfect statue's jaw.

My hands were trembling. I eased her back against me, trying to be sure my own heart beat; trying to be sure my lungs would work at all.

Tez was speechless. Alkhes was no better. It was Tanekhet, urbanity finally reviving, who at last stepped into the pause.

"I imagine, that any questions of paternity are now resolved."

* * *

She is back in the cradle. For the moment an ideal child, she has fed again, and hardly cried yet. Now she is deep asleep. Tomorrow, it may be another matter.

Tomorrow. What will her tomorrows be like?

With a double shadow, and what was once a double heartbeat; what shared this child's womb?

It took Caitha some time to accept that there never were two of them, more to abandon her bafflement about the heart-beat, with irate mutters of, "Never made a mistake before." As for the slowness of that beat; I will ask about all that tomorrow, when I am allowed up; although I hardly feel a doubt.

Next time, it will be all right.

And what will our tomorrows be, in a world that houses such a child?

Will she hear the qherrique? Will she speak for the qherrique? What future will she shape, in a world where she need not put her House before her love, or her marriage above her children, when she can open all the doors I barely perceive?

Iskarda. Amberlight. Cataract. Verrain.

Dhasdein.

The Heartlands.

To all humans, then? And to the more than human. Or is she that already? Is she ours in more than human sense? Can even that Other shape what her future will be?

So quiet here, for the moment, breathing, sleeping, warm, alive. We are all watching the shape of her, as I sit here, with their hands linked behind my back. In a moment I will put the pen down . . .

* * *

Kind Mother. Sweet Mother. Forgive me for ever doubting You. Or if You never existed, forgive me for doubting you, mystery, our other seed, the future of our god on earth.

I was indeed ready to put the pen down when a tap came on the door; a Verraini officer, commander of the night watch, who offered his pretext for entry, with clear embarrassment, into Alkhes' watchful hands.

"I beg pardon for disturbing you, sir. But Tanekhet said the lady Tellurith would want this straight away. The packet boat's just arrived."

Alkhes brought it to me, and picked up the lamp. Illuminated, it became papyrus, reed papyrus. Mud-stained, crumpled, with my name on the outer envelope: "Tellurith of Iskarda." As I turned it over, a scent of the Heartlands caught me, endless savannah, sun-bleached grass.

And something beyond that, fainter, to anything but memory all but unintelligible; the reedy, watery tang and aroma of a swamp.

As my heart panged, my eyes deciphered the drawing at the corner's edge.

A twist of vine-leaves, a tendril, that I last saw round the foot of a wooden cup; framing a small, couched, blandly impudent mountain frog.

www.ingramcontent.com/pod-product-compliance
Lightning Source LLC
Chambersburg PA
CBHW022203030726
47494CB00019B/158